11/3/11

HER EVERY FEAR

ALSO BY PETER SWANSON

THE KIND WORTH KILLING

THE GIRL WITH A CLOCK FOR A HEART

HER
EVERY
FEAR

PETER
SWANSON

FABER & FABER

First published in the UK in 2017
by Faber & Faber Limited
Bloomsbury House, 74–77 Great Russell Street,
London WC1B 3DA

First published in the United States in 2017
by HarperCollins Publishers,
195 Broadway, New York, NY 10007

Printed and bound by CPI Group (UK) Ltd, Croydon, CR0 4YY

Excerpt from "A Staffordshire Murderer" from *Children in Exile: Poems 1968–1984*
by James Fenton. Copyright © 1985 by James Fenton. Reprinted by permission of
Farrar, Straus and Giroux, LLC.

ISBN 978-0-571-32710-2

FSC
www.fsc.org
MIX
Paper from
responsible sources
FSC® C020471

Northamptonshire Libraries & Information Services NC	
Askews & Holts	

10 9 8 7 6 5 4 3 2

For Susan, Jim, David, and Jeremy

Every fear is a desire. Every desire is fear.

The cigarettes are burning under the trees

Where the Staffordshire murderers wait for their accomplices

And victims. Every victim is an accomplice.

—James Fenton, "A Staffordshire Murderer"

HER EVERY FEAR

PART I

•

LONG-LEGGEDY BEASTIES

CHAPTER 1

THE FASTEST ROUTE FROM LOGAN Airport to downtown
Boston is a mile-long tunnel called the Sumner. Dark, damp, and
low ceilinged, the Sumner feels as though it were built a hundred
years ago, which it very nearly was. And on Friday, April 24, a
warm spring evening, a Boston University freshman ran out of
gas halfway through the tunnel, reducing rush-hour traffic to just
one slow-moving lane, instead of the usual two. Kate Priddy, who
had never been to Boston and had no idea she would wind up in a
tunnel under Boston Harbor, sat in the back of a stopped taxicab
and began to panic.

It was not her first panic attack, not even of that particular day.
She'd had one earlier that morning when she'd stepped outside of
her flat in Belsize Park in London into a cold, gray dawn and suddenly felt like the whole idea of the apartment swap had been the
worst idea she'd ever agreed to. But she'd done her breathing exercises, and repeated her mantra, and told herself that it was too late
to back out now. Her second cousin, whom she'd never met, was
on an overnight flight from Boston to London at this very instant.
He was taking her flat for six months while she was going to live in
his apartment in Beacon Hill.

But this attack, with the taxicab stalled in the dark tunnel, was
far worse than anything she'd had for a long while. The glisten-
ing walls of the endless tunnel curved at the top. It was like being
inside a massive constricting snake, and Kate felt her stomach fold
within her, her mouth turn dry.

The taxicab crept forward. The backseat smelled of body odor
and the flowery perfume of some car deodorant. Kate wanted to
roll down the window, but didn't know what taxicab customs

were like in the United States. Her stomach folded again, starting to cramp. *When did I last go to the toilet,* she thought, and her panic ratcheted up a notch. It was such a familiar feeling: heart speeding up, limbs turning cold, the world sharpening before her eyes. But she knew what to do. Her therapist's voice was in her head. *It's just a panic attack, an accidental surge of adrenaline. It can't hurt you, or kill you, and no one will notice it. Just let it happen. Float with it. Ride it out.*

But this one's different, Kate told herself. The danger felt real. And suddenly she was back at the cottage in Windermere, crouched and cowering in the locked closet, her nightgown wet with urine, George Daniels on the other side of the door. She felt almost like she'd felt then, cold hands inside of her, twisting her stomach like it was a damp dish towel. There'd been the shotgun blast, then the terrible silence that lasted for hours and hours. When she'd finally been pulled from the closet, her joints stiff and her vocal cords raw from screaming, she didn't know how she was still alive, how the fear hadn't killed her.

The sound of an echoing horn brought her back inside the cab. She pushed the thoughts of Windermere, of George, away, and breathed in as deeply as she could, even though it felt like something heavy was sitting on her chest.

Face it. Accept it. Float with it. Let time pass.

The words weren't working, and Kate could feel her throat closing, becoming a pinhole, her lungs frantically trying to pull in oxygen. The back of the cab now smelled like that closet had, mustiness and rot, as though something had died many summers ago in the walls. She thought of running, and that thought filled her with even more panic. She thought of her pills, her prescription benzodiazepines, that she rarely took anymore but that she'd brought anyway, the way a child who doesn't need his blankie anymore still keeps it close at hand. But the pills were in her suitcase, which was in the bloody boot of the cab. She opened her dry mouth to say something to the cabdriver, to ask him to pop the boot, but the words didn't come out. And that was the moment—one she'd had many times—when she became convinced that she really was dying. *Panic attacks can't kill you. Of course they can't,* she thought, and squeezed her eyes shut anyway, as though a train were barreling down on her. It was the worst thing to do. The world dissolved into a closet full of blackness, death choking her. Her insides began to liquefy.

Face it. Accept it. Float with it. Let time pass.

The cab jolted forward a whole car length, then stopped again, and that small movement made her feel slightly better, as though saying the mantra had caused the car to move in the first place. She repeated it again, while doing her breathing exercises.

The driver shook a hand, his fingers spread, and muttered something at the dirty windshield in a language Kate didn't understand. For some reason, she'd thought that cabdrivers in America would be stereotypically American—short men with caps and cigar stubs and loud American voices. But this cabdriver was turbaned and heavily bearded; except for the fact that he was sitting on the left side of the car, she might as well have been in London.

"How long is this tunnel?" Kate managed to ask through the partition. Her voice sounded cracked and timid in her own ears.

"There's something up ahead."

"Is it always like this?"

"Sometimes," the driver said, then shrugged.

Kate gave up and moved back from the partition. She rubbed her hands along her thighs. The cab kept jerking forward, a few feet at a time, but after it passed the stalled Chevy, two lanes opened up and the cab was moving again. Kate breathed in through her nose and out through her mouth. She unclenched a hand and one of her knuckles cracked. She began to tap her thumb against her fingertips in ordered succession. The pinhole that was her throat opened up a little.

They cleared the tunnel, and Kate caught a glimpse of swollen clouds dominating the sky just before the cab dipped and swayed into another tunnel, but one in which the traffic was barreling along. The cabdriver made up for lost time before emerging onto another fast-moving road that wound along the Charles River. There was enough light left in the sky for Kate to make out the backsides of brick houses whipping past on her left. On the river, a rower on a scull skimmed along its placid surface.

The driver took a sudden, lurching left, doubling back to get onto a narrow road, square, brick houses on either side, blossoming trees along the sidewalk.

"Bury Street," announced the driver.

"It's 101."

"Got it." The driver sped up, then slowed down and halted suddenly, one wheel riding up onto the sidewalk, in front of a brick archway surmounted by a small stone on which the number 101 was carved. Kate could see into a courtyard with a low fountain. The apartment building, three stories high, ran along three sides of the courtyard. Kate's stomach ached a little, a leftover from her earlier panic attack, and she thought guiltily of her second cousin, Corbin Dell, arriving at her unexceptional flat in North London earlier in the day. But he'd known what he was getting. They'd sent several e-mails back and forth. Her one-bedroom was cozy and conveniently located near a tube station, but Corbin's place— she'd seen the pictures—was like something out of a Henry James novel. Still, she hadn't been prepared for the courtyard entrance, very Italian, that seemed out of place with the small amount of Boston she'd already seen.

She waited on the curb while the driver removed her two bags—a large rollie and an even larger duffel bag. She'd gotten dollars at her bank in London the previous week and she paid the driver with the thin, papery notes, not quite knowing what to tip, so probably giving him too much. After he drove off, she balanced the duffel bag onto the rollie and made her way through the archway.

She was midway across the courtyard, paved half in flagstone and half in brick, when the central door swung open and a doorman shaped like a pear darted out waving his hand.

"Hello, hello," he said. He wore a long brown raincoat over a suit, and a peaked cap. Under the cap he wore dark-framed glasses with thick lenses. He had dark black skin and a very white mustache, one side slightly thicker than the other.

"Hi," Kate said. "I'm Katherine Priddy. I'm here to stay in Corbin Dell's apartment."

"Right. I know all about it. Mr. Dell's moving to London for half a year and you're moving here. London's loss and Boston's gain, I suspect." He winked at her, and some of the tension that was still gripping her chest dissipated.

"I don't know about that," Kate said.

"I'm rarely wrong," he said. Kate had read somewhere that Bostonians were notorious for their lack of warmth, but the doorman was proving otherwise.

"I see you brought everything you own," he said, surveying the two bags. Kate sensed, more than saw, a woman pass by her and into the building. The doorman didn't seem to notice.

"If you can get the suitcase, I can get the duffel," Kate said, and the two of them managed to navigate the three worn marble steps that led to the building's lobby. He left the suitcase on the tiled floor and moved swiftly to the other side of the front desk. He was light on his feet for a heavy man.

"I promised Mrs. Valentine I'd call when you got here. She's the president of the building association, and wanted to give you the tour of your new apartment."

"Oh okay," Kate said, looking around. The lobby was narrow but beautiful. A glass-encased four-lamp chandelier hung from the high ceiling. The walls were painted in a lustrous shade of cream.

"Miss Priddy is down here in the lobby," he said into the telephone, then replaced the receiver. "She'll be right down. Let's get your luggage onto the elevator. You're on the third floor of the north wing. You have a nice view of the Charles. Have you been to Boston before?"

While Kate told him that she had actually never been to the States before, a tall, painfully thin woman somewhere in her seventies came down one of the side stairs, her shoes clacking percussively on the tiled steps. She wore a long black dress and a floral scarf around her neck. Her hair was silver and pinned up into an elaborate bun. Kate wondered if she always dressed like this or if she was going out later. The woman introduced herself as Carol and shook Kate's hand. Her hand was like a bundle of chopsticks covered in a layer of tissue paper.

"I'm sure you could have figured out Corbin's apartment all by yourself, Kate, but I thought it wouldn't hurt to have a welcoming committee." After the doorman had loaded Kate's luggage into the elevator, Carol got the key from him, then took Kate up the winding stairway. "Do you mind walking? It's my daily exercise."

Kate told her she was happy to walk, relieved that she didn't have to ride the elevator.

At the third floor, Carol turned left and Kate followed her down a dark, carpeted hall, with a doorway on the left, one on the right, and one at the end. A woman about Kate's age was rapping on the door on the left. Kate thought she was the woman who had flitted by earlier in the courtyard.

"Can I help you?" Carol asked loudly.

The woman turned. She wore jeans and a scoop-neck sweater. Her dark hair was cut in a bob, and she was almost pretty, except for the lack of a chin. It was so noticeable that Kate wondered, for a moment, if she'd been in some kind of terrible chin-obliterating accident.

"Do you work here? Could I get a key for this door? I'm worried about my friend." Her voice was nasal, pitched high with anxiety.

"Why are you worried?" Carol asked. "Is everything okay?"

"I can't get in touch with her. We were supposed to have lunch, and I called her work and she didn't show up there, either. And now I'm worried."

"Did you talk with our doorman?"

"No, I just came straight up here. It's not like her, you know. I've texted her, like, a thousand times."

"I'm sorry," Carol said. "I don't have a key, myself, but maybe you should speak with our doorman Bob. He'll know something. What's the name of your friend?" Carol had started to walk again, and so did Kate.

"Audrey Marshall. Do you know her?"

"I've met her, dear, but don't know much about her. Go talk with Bob. He'll help you. He *should* have helped you when you first arrived."

Kate found herself walking along the edge of the hall, her shoulder almost rubbing against the paneled wall. The upset friend, with her shrill, panicked voice, had caused Kate's chest to seize up again, the panic inside of her like an expanding balloon. She thought of her pills, in the toiletry bag in the rollie, unreachable for now.

"It's so unusual," Carol was saying, as she slid a key into the lock of the door at the end, "for someone to be in here without having gone through the doorman first. I'm sure there's actually nothing wrong with anybody." She said this as though nothing bad had ever happened to anyone anywhere. It was the type of ridiculous but well-meaning proclamation that Kate's father might make. Kate, herself, from the moment she saw the worried woman knocking frantically on her new neighbor's door, knew that someone was dead. It was how her mind worked. And knowing that her mind worked that way—constantly stretching logic all the way to its worst possible conclusion—did not lessen her certainty. Already that day, Kate had *known* that the youth with the sweaty forehead and the fuzzy mustache in the departures lounge was carrying a homemade explosive device in his backpack. And she had *known* that the stretch of turbulence over the Atlantic Ocean would grow in ferocity until it ripped one of the jet's wings off as easily as a sadistic child shredding a butterfly. These hadn't happened, but that didn't mean that behind the door down the hall, there wasn't a dead or dying girl. Of course there was.

Kate turned her attention to Carol, who was still fiddling with the key. She wondered if the tumblers of the lock were too much for Carol's birdlike bones to handle, then heard, with immense relief, the oily snap of the door unlocking. Even though she'd never been in Corbin's apartment, she'd already taken possession of it in her mind. She badly wanted to get inside and feel the safety of a home. It felt like years since she'd stepped out of the comfort of her London flat, double-checking the lock of the outside door, a minicab idling at the curb. Carol swung the door inward just as Kate heard voices again in the hall. She turned to see the doorman, Bob, lugging the duffel bag, the chinless woman at his side protesting her case. "Let me take care of this young lady first, then we'll see to your friend," he was saying.

Carol ushered Kate into her new home, and Kate immediately asked for the toilet. "Of course, dear, there's one attached to the bedroom," Carol said, pointing, and Kate walked rapidly, barely taking in the extravagance of her surroundings before shutting herself into an enormous bathroom, tiled in black and white. She sat on the toilet lid, and even though she knew the pills weren't there, she opened her purse anyway. Inside, tucked into the side pocket, was her plastic bottle of benzodiazepines. As soon as she saw them, she remembered moving the bottle from her suitcase to her bag early that morning. How had she forgotten that so soon? With trembling hands she unscrewed the lid and dry-swallowed a pill. A feeling of dread—almost worse than the panic—spread over her.

She should never have come to America.

CHAPTER 2

EVEN THOUGH THE APARTMENT WAS enormous, it shouldn't have taken Carol Valentine thirty minutes to deliver the tour, but she clearly relished the role. She pointed out the walnut-stained oak floors, the coffered ceilings, the working fireplace, and what she called the Juliet balcony, which was really just a hip-high railing one foot out from the floor-to-ceiling French doors that Kate knew she would never open. The apartment wasn't particularly high up, but it was high enough.

"You like it?" Carol asked, after the tour was complete, even though Kate had expressed her admiration about thirty times already.

"I do. I love it. Cozy."

"It's beautifully furnished, don't you think? You'd think a young man like Corbin . . ." Carol left the thought unfinished and smiled with just her mouth, the papery skin that covered her face shifting in such a way that Kate felt like she could see the exact contours of the woman's skull. "What's your apartment—your flat—like in London?"

"All of it would fit in this living room," Kate said. "I'm feeling a little guilty. I got the better bargain."

"Yes, but London . . ."

Kate yawned, quickly covering her mouth.

"My dear, you must be exhausted. I forgot all about the time change."

"I am tired," Kate said. "It's my bedtime if I were home."

"Well, try to stay up a little later than you usually do so you get used to it here. And as soon as you get settled in, you'll have to come and have a drink. I'm on the other side, exactly opposite.

Our place has the same layout as yours. These end apartments are the absolute best in the building. Especially yours, since you have a view toward the city *and* a view toward the river." She lowered her voice, as though the other apartments might hear what she was saying.

"It's beautiful," Kate said.

"The building was modeled after a Venetian palazzo, you know."

"I thought it looked Italian. The courtyard."

"The architect was from Boston, but he visited Italy and came back here. This was *years* ago, of course. My husband would love to tell you all about it when you come for that drink."

Carol left, and Kate shut the door behind her. She stood for a moment, still rattled by what had happened in the bathroom, finding her pills in her purse after forgetting that she'd moved them there. But since then, she'd talked herself through it a little, and she'd calmed down. Or maybe the pill was simply doing its job, spreading its calming fingers over her skin.

She retoured the apartment herself this time, taking in all the details, the built-in bookshelves, the paintings on the wall. Every room was beautifully furnished but somehow impersonal, as though all the items had been picked out by a decorator, which they probably had. In the bedroom, across from a king-sized bed with a cushioned headboard, there was a low bureau, the top of which was covered with about fifteen framed photographs. Family pictures, most in black and white, most taken on holiday. Boats and beaches. Kate studied them. She recognized Corbin's father, her mother's cousin, but only from other photographs she'd seen. He was in most of the pictures, usually with Corbin and Kate's other second cousin, Philip. Kate wondered why Corbin had no pictures of his mother on the bureau, but then it occurred to her that this apartment had been owned by Corbin's divorced father before he died, and these must be the father's pictures, not the son's.

Kate wondered how much of the rest of the apartment was in the style of the father. She guessed most of it. From what she'd gathered from her mother, Richard Dell had moved to Boston sometime in the 1970s to be with his American wife. His work had something to do with finance ("moving lots and lots of money around," Lucy Priddy told her daughter), and during the 1980s, he made a fortune. Richard and Amanda, his wife, had lived on the North Shore, in a seaside mansion in the town of New Essex. When their children were teenagers, they got divorced, Amanda keeping the seaside house and Richard buying the apartment at 101 Bury Street in Boston. The apartment had been left to Corbin after Richard died in a swimming accident while on holiday in Bermuda.

Kate had learned all this information two months earlier, during Sunday dinner with her parents.

"Your second cousin Corbin got in touch with me," Lucy had said. They were in the conservatory, done with dinner, but still drinking wine. Kate's father, Patrick, was taking Alice, their border terrier, for her walk.

"Oh," Kate said.

"I don't think you've ever met him. Have you met him?"

"He's your cousin Richard's son, right? The one who died a few years ago?"

"He drowned, yes. You met Richard, actually, at Charlotte's wedding. I don't know if you remember. I met Corbin for the first time at his father's funeral." Kate's parents had traveled all the way to Massachusetts for the funeral, although they'd tied the trip in with a driving tour up the Maine coast, something they'd both always wanted to do.

"He seemed very sweet. And so handsome. Almost looked like—who's that actor you like from *Spooks*? Rupert something."

"Rupert Penry-Jones. Why are you telling me this? I feel like you're on the verge of telling me you've arranged my marriage to a second cousin. Have we gone back in time?"

Lucy laughed; the spontaneous version, not the contrived ringing bells that sometimes came out in social situations. "Yes, darling. It's all arranged. No, but I'm telling you this for a reason. I haven't slipped into full senility. Corbin Dell is moving to London—a company transfer, or something—for six months, and he sent me an e-mail because he knows you live in London."

"He didn't ask to stay with me, did he?"

"No, no. Of course not. But he did say he wanted to check and see if you were potentially interested in a home swap. He said he'd love to have someone staying at his place in Boston, and then he could stay at your place, and that way he'd save some money, and you'd have the opportunity to spend half a year in America."

Kate took a sip of her wine. It was white, and far too sweet. "What would I do in Boston?"

"I thought that maybe you could take classes, like you've been talking about. They must have graphic design schools. And you'd keep drawing, of course."

"What about my job?" Kate had just gone from part-time to full-time at an art-supply store in Hampstead.

"Well, that's not a career, exactly, is it?"

Kate, who agreed with her mother on that point, was annoyed nonetheless and said nothing. A part of her knew that this was the type of situation she'd be foolish to turn down. Six months in another country. She'd never been to America, and Boston was supposed to be nice. A manageable city, she'd heard, not like New York or Chicago, or London, for that matter. She'd have a place to live. Probably a beautiful place to live. And the more that these reasons popped into her head, the more anxious she got, realizing that she would probably turn it down. It was too soon. She was better, but she wasn't completely well yet.

"I feel like I'm just getting settled in London, and everything is going smoothly, and I just don't know if I should rock the boat."

"Absolutely, Kate. He asked, so I thought I'd ask. I totally understand." As her mother spoke, Kate realized that her mother had never believed that Kate would actually take the opportunity to move to Boston for half a year. It was this thought that pestered Kate for the remainder of the afternoon. Her father returned from walking Alice, and the three decided to go to the White Swan in Braintree center for one more before Kate had to catch a train back to London. Kate was tipsy on the ride home, her mind picturing all the things that could go right in Boston, then all the things that could go wrong. And she kept thinking about the tone of her mother's voice, the way she'd clearly known that Kate was going to say no. It was that, more than anything, that caused Kate to ring up her parents when she got back to her flat in London and tell them that she'd changed her mind.

"Oh," her mother said.

"I think I'd be foolish to not do it. There's nothing keeping me here, right now. Except you and Dad, of course."

"We'd come visit."

"Tell Corbin I'd like to do it. Or better yet, send me his e-mail and I'll tell him myself."

She'd written Corbin that night, before she lost her nerve. He'd been thrilled. They arranged the swap from late April to early October. Kate had given notice at her job, then had found a graphic design school were she could take courses in InDesign and Illustrator. And now she was here, her first class scheduled for Monday afternoon. Kate walked back down the hallway that led to the living room, where Bob the doorman had deposited her bags. She knew she should unpack, but a wave of tiredness spread through her. Also, hunger. She went to the kitchen, with its limestone counters and stainless steel appliances. It looked like it had never been used. She opened the fridge. All alone on the middle shelf was a bottle of champagne, a yellow sticky note attached to it. *Welcome, Kate— Enjoy!* was written in cramped handwriting. A pang of guilt went through Kate that she hadn't left anything for Corbin in her flat, although she'd left him a much longer note, welcoming him and describing the neighborhood.

Except for the champagne and an assortment of condiments, the refrigerator was practically bare. She opened the freezer and found a stack of frozen dinners from someplace called Trader Joe's. She read the directions on the back of a frozen boeuf bourguignon and decided she could handle it. The box was familiar and yet different, the nutritional information using ounces instead of grams and calories instead of energy. She figured out the microwave and began to heat up the dinner, then filled and emptied a water glass from the tap before wondering if the water was okay to drink. It tasted okay, but different than the water she was used to drinking. More minerals. After pouring herself a glass of champagne, she walked to the front door and pressed her eye to the peephole, wondering what had happened with the missing girl down the hall. Would Bob have let the friend in? Probably not, she thought, and wondered what the friend would do next. The police would probably not be helpful. Kate had watched enough American police procedurals to know that you couldn't file a missing persons report if the person had been missing for less than a day. The hallway was empty. Maybe Kate had overreacted and nothing was really wrong. Maybe the girl had grown tired of her pushy, chinless friend.

Kate ate the dinner, surprisingly good, sitting on one of the stools around the L-shaped granite island in the kitchen. She poured a second glass of champagne, took one sip, and was overcome again with exhaustion. Her head was heavy on her neck, her stomach slightly queasy. She had planned on unpacking and setting up her laptop so that she could send e-mails, and she'd hoped to watch some American television, but instead she rolled her suitcase into the bedroom, dug around in it to find her toiletry kit, plus the boxers and T-shirt she liked to sleep in, then managed to brush her teeth and wash her face before climbing between the cool, crisp sheets. Despite being exhausted, she lay awake for a time, listening to the barely discernible sounds of the apartment: the far-off rumble of traffic, the muffled click of a heating system, something else—a soft hissing—she couldn't identify. The bed, she thought, before falling asleep, was the most comfortable bed she had ever lain on. She sank into its grip.

KATE WOKE ONCE. INTERMITTENT BLUE lights were flashing along a diagonal stretch of the high ceilings. *Where are the sirens?* Kate thought. Then: *Where am I?* And, finally, after a confused two seconds, she remembered. Her mouth was dry and she was desperately thirsty. She heard what sounded like a distant train. She rolled to either side, looking for the illuminated numbers of a clock to tell her what time it was, but, except for the police lights streaking through the curtained windows, the room was black.

Kate sat up, then lay back down. She was far too tired to even find the bathroom and get a drink of water. What was the name of that neighbor again? The girl who was missing? Audrey Marshall, Kate remembered. She was good with names. It was her superpower, George had said. He'd dubbed her Never-Forgets-a-Name-Girl. Kate closed her eyes, heard someone whispering to her in a dream, and jolted awake again. The voices disappeared, and the room was dark again. Had she dreamed the police lights? *I'll find out about it tomorrow,* she thought, and let herself fall back into a black pool of sleep.

CHAPTER 3

SHE DID FIND OUT ABOUT it, but not until late the following day.

She woke early, the room still dark. She knew she should try to sleep in a little later, to adjust herself to Boston time, but she was wide awake and desperate for coffee.

It took a while, but she found the coffeemaker and some coffee and figured out how it all worked. While the coffee brewed, she walked around the enormous apartment again. The thin light of morning was beginning to suffuse the windows. The largest room of the apartment, the central living room, had the view of the Charles River, quiet in the gray dawn, traces of mist above its unruffled surface. There was a footbridge that spanned both the river and the road next to it.

The living room looked ready for a cocktail party. There were scattered chairs, plus two large couches facing one another, and in between them a glass-topped coffee table. Kate hated glass tables. Putting anything on one made her think it would instantly shatter, or at least crack. She always lived in the next moment, the tragic moment. For this reason, she'd always loathed low railings, crossing busy streets, waiters carrying multiple plates. These had always been prickly, annoying phobias, but then, five years earlier, the incident with George had happened and her life had changed forever. She couldn't leave her house for over a year. No, worse than that. She couldn't even imagine leaving her house; fear and grief had immobilized her. Her parents and her therapist had slowly pulled her out of that hole, and life had gotten better. It was inconceivable to her that she had made it all the way to the States, to this enormous apartment with its glass table. She didn't like the glass table, but she could live with it.

There was no television in the living room, and she wondered, with a sense of horror, if the apartment was television free. Then she remembered what Carol Valentine had called "the den," a dark-wood-paneled room with a soft leather couch. For a brief moment, she couldn't remember where the den was located, but it was off the hallway that led toward the two guest bedrooms. She was right; the television was there—a monstrous screen hidden behind wooden doors built into a bookshelf. On the table (thankfully not glass) in front of the couch, there was a universal remote on top of a laminated card listing at least a hundred channels.

There was also a large wooden desk in the den, and Kate noticed a sticky note on its surface. It listed the name of a wireless account ("Angel Face") and a password. It made her realize that she ought to check in with her parents, and also with Corbin, to make sure he'd made it safely to her own flat.

Kate retrieved her laptop and adapter from her suitcase, stopped back in the kitchen for a mug of black coffee, and returned to the den. She marveled once again at the expanse of the apartment. She sat at the desk, the leather chair creaking authentically. She had many e-mails, mostly junk, but one from her mother and one from Corbin. She opened Corbin's first:

Kate,

It only took the driver a few false turns but we finally found your beautiful flat, and I read your incredibly thoughtful note. I'm ashamed I didn't write a similar thing for you, and I have no excuse, but once I'm used to the jet lag I will send you an exhaustive list of good bars and restaurants near my apartment. I promise.

Quick question: I see you have a washer but don't see a dryer. Am I missing something?

More later. I'm looking forward to the next six months.

Corbin

Kate wrote back:

I am too. When I walked into your place, I thought that I must have
come to the wrong apartment. How gorgeous. I'm truly ashamed
of my measly flat with a washing machine that also thinks it's a
dryer. It *is* a dryer, as well, that's why you're so confused. There are
instructions in the drawer on the left of the sink, I think. My advice,
however, is that if you start a clothes wash don't expect dry clothes
for at least a day. Please don't hesitate to write with any more
questions. I really am in love with your apartment. Best, Kate

P.S. Thanks for the lovely champagne, which is gone, of course.

Next, Kate read her mother's e-mail—"so proud of you,
darling"—and responded to that as well. She sipped at her coffee,
so much better than the instant coffee she was used to drinking.
She could hear a police siren in the distance and suddenly remembered the night before, falling asleep, and how she could see police
lights on her ceiling. Had that been real, or part of a dream? For a
moment she didn't know, and she was filled with a sense of dread
again, the same feeling she'd had when she found her pills in her
purse after being sure they weren't there. *Am I losing my mind?* she
thought. Then told herself: *No, it wasn't a dream.* It had definitely
been real. Maybe something actually had happened with the girl
from down the hall.

Kate unpacked her toiletries, then showered in the en suite
bathroom. The shower was enormous, the head coming straight
out of the ceiling, dumping a deluge of water. Again, Kate thought
of her own flat in London, the bathtub that had been converted

to a shower with its rubber tube that was always flopping out of its holder. After showering, Kate dressed in dark tights and her favorite Boden dress, and decided that she would brave the outside world. Before coming to Boston, she'd studied Google Maps images of her neighborhood and located the nearest pharmacy and the nearest market. Her plan was to go out and get the basic essentials to get her through the next few days. On Monday, she was starting at the Graphics Institute in Cambridge, about five subway stops away. She was not looking forward to that particular ride, but she knew she could do it—her therapist in London had had her take the tube several times as practice.

"The tube's a choice," Kate had said to Theodora. "I can take taxis everywhere."

"It's all a choice, isn't it," her therapist had said back to her. That placid northern accent had irritated Kate to no end when she had first met Theodora, but she had grown used to it, just as she'd grown used to the halo of curly hair and the purple jumpers.

"Well, I don't choose to skydive, either. You're not going to make me do that, are you?"

"No, I won't make you skydive, but riding the Underground, and taking elevators, and flying I will make you do. That's all part of a life you want, isn't it, Kate?"

She'd been right, of course. Life was full of tight places and sealed exits. She'd learn to deal with them.

Kate left the apartment, locking the door behind her. She slowed as she passed the missing girl's door, listening for any sounds, but there weren't any. She took the stairs down to the lobby, passed the doorman, and walked straight out into the courtyard. The sky was gray and scalloped, the light so much like dusk that Kate had an alarmed moment when she wondered if she'd slept through the entire day. A waft of cigarette smoke reached her nostrils. Kate had quit smoking after university, but she still loved the smell. She looked for the source and saw a man perched on the edge of the courtyard's central fountain. He was rubbing the cigarette out on a flagstone. Kate was walking past him as he began to stand.

"Sorry," he said, indicating the snuffed-out cigarette in his fingers.

"I don't mind," Kate said, stopping and looking at him. He was thin, verging on gaunt, but with wide shoulders. His narrow face was dominated by a large, crooked nose. His eyes were grayish-green and deeply sunken, and his skin was lightly pocked with ancient acne. He should have been ugly, but he wasn't. All his outsized features combined into a sad and handsome face.

"I actually don't smoke. I've quit. But then I found this one cigarette in my drawer and figured I'd smoke it, just to remind myself how awful it is."

His voice was deep and friendly, and Kate, jet-lagged and still confused about the time of day, felt a ruffle of weakness in her legs. "Was it awful?" she asked.

"No, of course not. It was great."

"Smoking's great," Kate said. Why were they speaking like old friends? Was this how people spoke with strangers in America?

"You smoke?"

"I did. I quit. It wasn't easy."

"How'd you do it?"

"By not smoking."

The man laughed. His teeth were alarmingly white, the top ones straight and the bottom ones slightly overlapping. "I'm Alan Cherney."

"I'm Kate. I'm living here, temporarily." She was shy suddenly, and didn't provide her last name.

"You're English?" he asked.

"I am. I'm staying at my cousin's apartment, here, and he's staying at my flat in London."

"Which apartment is it?" Alan Cherney's eyes scanned the building.

Kate bobbed her head in the direction of her wing. "Uh, Corbin Dell's place. Up there."

"Ah, north wing. I'm on the other side, third floor. I know Corbin. A little."

"You know him better than I know him. We've never met."

"That's funny," Alan said. "How'd that come about?"

Kate told him the story, omitting the fact that the trip for Kate was at least partly inspired by her need to overcome the past traumas of her life.

"Well, you got a good deal," Alan said. "These are pretty nice apartments."

"How long have you lived here?"

"Just over a year. I moved in with a girlfriend—a rich girlfriend—and she moved out, and I can't really afford it anymore, so I need to start thinking about finding a new place."

"Sorry about that."

"Sorry about what?" he said. "Sorry I lost my girlfriend, or sorry I'm going to have to move out?"

Kate laughed. "I don't know. Sorry about both."

He smirked and said: "Sorry you used to have a rich girlfriend and a beautiful apartment, and next month you'll be alone in some hovel."

"Something like that."

A gust of wind peeled a sodden yellow leaf off the brick courtyard and plastered it on Kate's boot. She bent over to pick it off. When she stood, there was a moment of silence, and Kate realized she'd been talking with this stranger for close to fifteen minutes.

"Well," she said, but didn't continue. Her eyes skidded off his, and she felt the prickle of a blush suffusing her cheeks. For one brief, terrifying moment she knew that if he'd asked, she'd have followed him straight up to his apartment and into his bed. He was handsome, yes, even with the large, crooked nose, but she'd have followed him because it felt as though they had known each other for years.

"You need to go," he said, speaking her thought out loud.

"Yes." And then they both laughed.

"I'm in apartment 3L," he said. "I'm not leaving anytime soon. We'll see each other."

"Okay," Kate said.

She started to move away, then stopped. "Do you know a woman named Audrey Marshall? She lives here."

Alan's brow creased. "I do know Audrey. Well, I know *who* she is. I don't actually know her."

"When I got in last night, a friend of hers was at her door, looking for her, saying she'd gone missing."

Kate expected him to dismiss it, but instead he said: "That doesn't sound good. She's not the type to go missing."

"What do you mean?"

"Oh, I don't know. I guess I mean she's always around. I see her around. A lot. I'm sure she'll turn up."

KATE HAD BROUGHT A PRINTED map of her neighborhood, but she'd studied it so many times in the previous weeks that she didn't need to remove it from her bag. She navigated down Bury to Charles Street, where she got a breakfast sandwich and another coffee from a packed Starbucks. The second coffee was a mistake. She was jittery and wired while shopping at an upscale grocery store with tight, congested aisles. She had been planning on getting ingredients for a pasta she liked to make with smoked salmon, but a mild panic had set in, and she bought only a loaf of sourdough bread, some cheddar cheese, milk, and two bottles of red wine. Back out on the street, warm, mild rain had mixed in with the gusty air. It felt good against her skin after the overheated store, and she walked slowly back along Charles, noting, for future reference, a bar that looked well lit and friendly, plus a coffeehouse much less crowded than Starbucks had been.

She deliberately walked past the gaslit side street that would take her back up the hill to Bury Street, and continued to the outskirts of the Public Garden. Her groceries were heavy, but she wanted to at least see the famous park. The rain was picking up, and several parents were ushering their kids away from a line of bronze ducks. Willow trees shimmered by the pond. She almost entered the park, but decided against it. She was here for six months and there would be time.

Kate swung through the doors into the lobby. She introduced herself to the doorman, Sanibel, a thin man with high cheekbones and ink-black hair. He offered to help her with her bags. She said, "No, thanks," just as a white cat that had been perched on the lobby desk jumped to the floor and rubbed against Kate's shin.

"That's Sanders," the doorman said.

"Does Sanders belong to you?"

"No, no. He belongs to Mrs. Halperin. Upstairs." He indicated with a fractional move of his head the direction of Kate's own apartment. "He likes to go everywhere, though. All over. Unlike Mrs. Halperin."

Kate walked up the stairs, Sanders following her. Carol Valentine had mentioned Florence Halperin; she had the other apartment on Kate's wing. Passing the door, Kate noticed it was cracked open, presumably for Sanders, but the cat followed Kate down to her own door and managed to slide into the apartment, even with Kate trying to block the way with her foot.

She put away her groceries, then went and found Sanders. He had leapt onto one of the windowsills and was looking out at the rainy day. Kate scooped him up, expecting resistance, but he arranged his back paws on Kate's forearm and his front paws on her shoulder, and purred quietly into her neck. Kate, usually ambivalent toward cats, felt a surge of affection. She carried him to the hallway, saying, "Wrong apartment, Sanders," and dropped him back onto the hall carpet. She quickly shut the door as he padded away.

Kate went to the bedroom and got the sketchbook that she'd brought with her from London. It was brand-new, a way to commemorate the beginning of her time in a new country. She removed a charcoal pencil from a fresh pack, then sat down on the lushly carpeted floor and thought about trying to draw Sanders. Instead, she drew Alan Cherney's face, getting it just about perfect. Something was a little off, the eyes spaced too close together, the hairline a little too low, so she pulled out a kneaded eraser and fixed it. It took her longer to fix the sketch than it had to draw it, but then it was him. She wrote his name, and the date under it, then added BOSTON, MASSACHUSETTS. She almost exclusively drew portraits, and her sketchbooks were comprised of the faces of people she had recently met. She had stacks of these notebooks, the earliest ones from grade school. Flipping through them—something she often did, especially when she'd been housebound—was like reading a diary. She'd find faces of close friends that she'd sketched hours after she'd met them for the first time, and she'd find faces of people she'd forgotten all about. Looking at Alan's likeness, she wondered if, ten years from now, she'd even recognize who he was. Or maybe it would turn out to be the drawing she'd done right after meeting her future husband. Probably the former.

She flipped to a blank page, closed her eyes, and tried to picture Carol Valentine, the older woman who had given her the tour of the apartment. She could remember her eyes, her forehead, her hair, and her neck, but couldn't quite picture her nose and mouth. Instead of drawing her, she drew herself; she could remember the way she'd looked that morning in the mirror of the bathroom. Her hair, recently cut, tucked behind one ear. Her eyes a little puffier than usual from the long, dehydrating flight. But she gave herself a slight smile, a smile that ended up looking like the frightened smile of a nervous bridesmaid about to deliver a speech. It didn't quite capture her mood, but she left it as it was. She almost never erased her self-portraits.

On the next page, she drew Sanibel, the doorman she'd just met. Instead of drawing just his face, she drew him standing next to his desk, and she added Sanders down by his legs. She was not used to drawing cats, and Sanders looked wrong, menacing when he was anything but.

She slid the sketchbook under the bed and stood. She was hungry again, went to the kitchen, and ate some bread and cheese, thought about opening some wine, then decided against it. The rain outside was now slashing against the windows, and she thought, randomly, of a painter whipping a spray of paint across a canvas. She stared at the kitchen windows for a while, deciding that she loved her new apartment, not for its obvious luxury, but for its high ceilings and oversized windows. She could breathe in this place. She decided to make tea, realized she hadn't bought any, but then found a box of Red Rose in one of the high cupboards. She filled a kettle with water, put it on the gas stove, then went into the living room. One wall had built-in bookshelves, and she looked at some of the selections. Hardcover nonfiction, mostly, although there was one complete shelf of John D. MacDonald paperbacks. She plucked one out. *Darker Than Amber*. A Travis McGee adventure. The cover had a pulpy image of a sexy girl in a crop top. The pages were yellowed with age. These had to have belonged to Corbin's father, Kate thought. Where were Corbin's books? Did he have any? Below the Travis McGee books was a shelf of other paperback mysteries. She pulled out a Dick Francis—*Bonecrack*—that she didn't think she'd read yet, and brought it with her to the long beige sofa under the largest window in the room. She lay down and read the first few paragraphs, then closed her eyes and fell immediately to sleep.

She dreamed of the park, the pond now whipping and rippling in the ferocious rain. She stood under one of the willow trees, its branches yellow. George Daniels was on the other side of the pond. Kate wasn't surprised that he was in Boston—and she wasn't surprised that he was still alive—because in her dreams he was always alive, and he was always coming after her. He spotted her hiding under her willow tree and began to swim across the pond. Kate had a rifle with her, and when George came out of the pond, dripping and smiling, she shot him several times, the bullets pocking his shirt but not doing much else. One of the bullets struck him on the chin, and he brushed it away like it was a horsefly. He kept coming.

She woke, neck and chest filmed in sweat, then smelled something bitter and acrid in the air. She remembered the kettle, leapt from the couch, the Dick Francis falling to the floor, and ran to the kitchen to shut the gas off. The kettle had boiled dry and was beginning to smoke. She opened one of the windows as far as she could and, using a hand towel, put the smoldering kettle on the windowsill. The rain striking it made sharp hissing sounds. Something about the near-disaster made tears spring to her eyes. Then she remembered her dream. George in the park, the bullets barely penetrating his shirt. It almost made her smile that he'd followed her to America in her dreams. Of course he had. If her dreams were a realm, George was king for life.

After the kettle cooled down she took it from the windowsill. Its bottom was completely black; she'd have to buy a replacement. The metal was still warm, so she put it in the deep stainless steel sink and returned to the couch. This time she read half of the book before falling back to sleep.

SHE WAS WOKEN BY A knock on the door. She blinked herself awake, momentarily confused by what time it was. It was daylight outside still, but the inside of the apartment was dark and dusky. There was another knock, louder and longer. She stood, her knees popping. How long had she been asleep?

She went to the door and peered through its peephole. She almost expected to see Alan, but it was a woman's face through the fish-eye lens, a woman with close-cropped hair, coffee-colored skin, and dark brown eyes. The calm disinterest in those eyes made Kate say *policewoman* to herself. *Audrey Marshall's dead,* came a voice. It was George Daniels, whispering in her head. Kate swung the door open.

CHAPTER 4

THE WOMAN INTRODUCED HERSELF AS Detective James, unclipping a badge from her belt and holding it up for Kate to see. Kate invited her in, noticing before she shut the door that two uniformed officers stood a little ways down the hall, one of their radios crackling.

"Is Audrey Marshall dead?" Kate asked automatically.

"Why do you ask that?" the detective asked, a touch of surprise in her eyes.

"I, uh, heard that she was missing."

"When did you hear she was missing?"

Kate explained about her arrival the evening before, the friend in the hallway who was pounding on the door.

"When was that exactly?" the detective asked, pulling out a small notebook from the inside of her dark gray suit jacket.

Kate gave her best guess at the approximate time and the detective wrote it down. Kate studied her while she wrote. She had a long face, with high cheekbones, and Kate didn't think she was wearing any makeup. The detective raised her eyes from her notebook, and Kate watched her nostrils minutely flare.

"I left the kettle on," Kate said.

"I'm sorry. I don't—"

"I left the kettle on the stove earlier and I burnt it. That's the smell."

"Oh. I did notice that."

"Do you want to sit down?"

The detective's eyes scanned the room briefly before she said,

"No, thanks. I'm just collecting statements right now. And I'd like to get a little more information from you regarding timelines."

"She is dead, right?" Kate asked.

"We are investigating a suspicious death in the apartment next to yours. We don't have a proper identification yet on the body."

"Okay."

"You said you just came over here from London, right? You didn't know her?"

"No, I don't know anyone here. It was a murder, then?"

"We're treating it as a suspicious death, yes. What can you tell me about the owner of this apartment?"

"He's a second cousin. Corbin Dell. I don't actually know him, either. We've never met, but we arranged this house swap because he's been transferred to London for his work."

The detective wrote something else down on her pad, while asking: "I don't suppose you know whether Corbin Dell had any kind of relationship with Audrey Marshall?"

"No, I have no idea."

"Can you give me the phone number for your apartment in London?"

"It doesn't have one, actually. I just use my mobile. But I have Corbin's e-mail. I can get it for you, if you'd like?"

"That'd be great," the detective said.

Kate went to the computer in the study and brought up her e-mail page. There were several unread messages, in bold, at the top, including a response from Corbin. She opened it:

Thanks for recommending the Beef and Pudding. Can't say I'd have
tried that one if left to my own devices. It reminded me a little
of a place called St. Stephen's Tavern near where you are. Check
it out. Also, met a neighbor of yours named Martha something.
She seemed to recognize me, or else she heard my loud American
accent and just guessed. Hope all's well. C

Kate found a piece of scrap paper and jotted down Corbin's e-mail address. She'd worry about the Martha situation later.

She brought the scrap of paper to Detective James, who was now looking at the screen of her cell phone. "Thanks. I'll write him," she said, folding the piece of paper and sliding it into her jacket pocket.

"Should I let him know before you do? He just e-mailed me, and if I wrote him back . . ."

"You can tell him the police were here and that we'll be in touch. I don't want to make any pronouncements about Audrey Marshall till we have an identification, okay?"

"Yes, of course."

"You've been very helpful." She was turning back toward the door. Kate went around her and opened it. There was now a small crowd in the hall, including an older man in a suit who immediately spotted Detective James and said, "Jesus. There you are."

Before leaving, Detective James said: "We might need to search your apartment. Would you agree to that?"

"Why?" Kate asked.

The detective pressed her lips together before saying, "If we find anything that might connect the death next door with your cousin, then we'll need to take a look around. That's all."

"It's okay with me, I guess," Kate said.

"Thank you very much. We'll be in touch." The detective handed Kate her card before leaving. Kate studied it after shutting the door. ROBERTA JAMES, DETECTIVE. Under the name were the Boston Police Department shield, a phone number, and an e-mail.

Kate pressed her ear to the door to see if she could hear anything from the hallway. There were noises—the squawk of radios and the muddy tones of indiscernible voices. She looked through the peephole and saw the same detective knocking on the door of the third apartment on her hall. The door swung open, and the detective held up her badge to its resident; Kate couldn't see into the apartment. While the other neighbor was being questioned, two more plainclothes officers entered the hall from the stairwell, both heavyset men in dark suits. One was clean-shaven and the other sported a gray goatee.

A ripple of panic swept over Kate, not so much because of the murdered neighbor, but because her exit was blocked by all those police officers. Something about walking down a hallway filled with police and crime scene investigators seemed impossible. Kate backed her way into the apartment, breathing through her nostrils and blowing out through her mouth. She calmed herself and picked over the brief conversation with the detective. Was it standard practice after a murder to search the nearby residences? Kate didn't think so. There must be a reason. She went to the computer and searched for Audrey Marshall. It was a common name, bringing up many genealogy sites and several Facebook profiles. She added Boston to the search and found a blocked LinkedIn profile but with an image attached. She clicked on it. It wasn't a large image, and it was in black and white, but showed a woman with intensely large eyes and a boy's short haircut, almost like Jean Seberg's hair in that movie *Breathless*. She worked for a publishing house in Boston, and all her previous employment had been in New York City. Kate knew she'd found the right Audrey Marshall. She stared into the pixelated eyes on the computer screen and they stared back at her. *I'm dead now,* those eyes said, *but this is what I looked like when I was alive.* Audrey Marshall had been pretty, and Kate wondered if Corbin Dell and she had been involved in any way. They must have known each other, or seen each other frequently when they were coming and going.

Kate stood, knowing what she needed to do. Well, knowing what she *wanted* to do. She'd search the apartment herself. If the police were going to look around, maybe she'd look around first, and be able to find what they were looking for. It would give her something to do, a purpose. She started her search in the bedroom, going through every drawer, looking for hiding places, lifting the mattress. She was struck, as she had been when she first looked around the place, by the lack of personal items. She did find an old battered bureau in the corner of the walk-in closet that was filled with photographs, most still in their envelopes from the developing place. She quickly flipped through several of them; they were obviously photographs that had belonged to Corbin's father. Old family vacations. Christmas Day celebrations. A whole roll dedicated to what looked like a vintage Porsche speedster. Where were Corbin's photographs? On his computer, and his phone, of course, like Kate's own pictures.

She searched the bathroom, then the main living area, and then the kitchen. It was in the kitchen that she found something that might be relevant. In one of the drawers, behind the cutlery tray, there were several loose keys. Some were unmarked, but a few were affixed with a white circular tag, block letters saying what they were for. One said STORAGE, and one said N.E. HOUSE, and one had the initials AM. Did Corbin have a key to Audrey Marshall's apartment? If so, why? It could mean so many things. Maybe they had been in a romantic relationship, close enough that they'd exchanged keys. Or it could simply be a key he kept so that he could water her plants when she was away.

She continued to search the rest of the apartment. She found more remnants from Corbin's father's life than she found from Corbin's. In the den, in a closet, she found a cardboard box of videotapes with labels like CLARISSA'S WEDDING and CHATHAM RENTAL, AUGUST '95. There was an old leather football in the box as well. Kate ran her finger over its dusty surface. This box with the videotapes and football was sitting on a larger plastic container that looked like a recent addition to the closet. Kate moved the box of videotapes and pulled out the container. Inside was a stack of college textbooks, economics related. There were two framed degrees, one for an M.B.A. from Andrus College in New York

City and one for a B.A. from Mather College in Connecticut. Both were made out to Corbin Harriman Dell. She pulled the whole container out into the better light of the den. Was it odd that Corbin would bury his own things underneath the boxes that had belonged to his father? She went through the container's contents. In the midst of the textbooks, there were a bundle of papers, a few photographs, and a small notebook all tied up with a piece of kitchen twine. She ruffled the edges of the papers and the photographs to see what they were. Several seemed to be grade sheets from college or business school, but she was able to dislodge one of the photographs, a glossy image of a dark-haired woman, about college age, sitting on a cold, windy-looking beach. She was in jeans and an oversized turtleneck sweater. She was looking away from the camera, her mouth open as though she was speaking. She flipped the photograph over and read the writing on the back: RACHAEL AT ANNISQUAM BEACH. There was no date. Kate thought: *Where is Rachael now?* And her mind imagined tragedies and murdered girls. She shivered, tapped her fingertips together. *Just because I think something doesn't make it true,* she told herself. Another one of her internal mantras.

Kate was about to slide the photograph back into its bundle, then decided, on impulse, to also look at the notebook. She unpicked the knotted string and pulled the notebook out. It was leather bound, embossed with the seal from Andrus College. She flipped it open, feeling guilty, but it was just a regular engagement diary, segmented into days. It was from six years ago, and was filled with a spiky, minuscule handwriting. She read a few entries—mostly class times and due dates, but sprinkled throughout were social engagements, such as "drinks with H," or "dinner party at the Esterhouses." She closed the diary, rebundled it, and returned it to its container.

She was walking back across the apartment, wondering whether she should write Corbin back in London, when there was another knock on the door. It was Detective Roberta James again, this time accompanied by two uniformed officers.

"We'd like to look around your place, if you'd give us permission to do so." The detective's jaw seemed tight, her voice controlled.

"Sure, I guess," Kate said. She wondered if she was making a mistake letting them just march into Corbin's apartment. Should she have asked for a warrant?

"It won't take long," the detective said, as the two officers, each wearing light blue latex gloves, made their way into the apartment. Kate watched them turn left toward the bedroom. As was always the case with American police, she found herself fixated on the guns on their belts. She wondered what would happen if she reached out and touched one of them. Would she be thrown to the ground and handcuffed immediately? "I have a couple more questions," Detective James continued. "We could sit."

Kate led the detective to the two couches that faced one another and they both sat. "This is a beautiful apartment," Detective James said.

"I know, isn't it? My place in London isn't like this at all. Just an ordinary flat."

"So, in your conversations leading up to this apartment swap, did you two talk about neighbors at all? Did Corbin ever mention Audrey Marshall?"

"No, nothing. He didn't talk about anyone. Can I ask you what you're hoping to find by looking in here?"

The detective pressed her lips together, then said: "I'm not *hoping* to find anything, but we need to look. We have no reason to suspect that Corbin was involved in anything, if that's what you're wondering."

"No, no, I know."

"What can you tell me about your cousin's flight from here to London?"

"All I know is that he took a night flight that got into London on Friday morning, so he would have left on Thursday night."

Detective James wrote in her notebook, while one of the police officers came through the living room heading to the other side of the apartment. They seemed to be searching quickly.

"And you didn't meet up with him in London before you left to come here?"

"No. Like I said, I've never actually met him."

"Okay." The detective slid her notebook back into the inside pocket of her jacket. She pressed the palms of her hands against her knees and stood. "I'm going to see how the search is going. Should be almost done. Have you found any locked doors here, or were there any rooms or closets that you were told were off-limits?"

"No."

Kate stayed seated as Detective James slowly walked toward the west side of the apartment, pausing to look out a window. It had stopped raining, and the clouds were breaking up. The detective moved a curtain with a finger, stared outside, then moved on. She was tall, with perfect posture, and Kate automatically hitched back her own shoulders. One of the police officers with the latex gloves came back into the living room. The detective looked questioningly at him, and he said, "Nothing." It sounded as though he had a cold. The other policeman emerged from the kitchen. Kate hadn't heard the sound of drawers being opened. Should she mention the key she'd seen with the initials on it? Was that the type of thing they were looking for?

Before she could decide, all three were headed toward the exit, the detective thanking Kate and asking her to call if anything came up. Kate stood, but they were through the door before she could even respond. She was alone again in the apartment.

CHAPTER 5

KATE MADE BREAD AND CHEESE again for dinner, and opened a bottle of wine. She ate in the den, flipping through cable channels, then settling on an American reality show about crab fishermen in Alaska. When that was through, she found a channel that was showing a thriller called *Midnight Lace,* with Doris Day and Rex Harrison. She started watching; it wasn't very good, but it had just enough of a plot to distract her from thinking exclusively about what was happening down the hallway.

Halfway through the film, Kate discovered a lever on the leather sofa that caused the end seat to recline separately from the rest of the sofa. She maneuvered it all the way back so that she was practically prone and continued to watch the film. She was suddenly exhausted, her limbs like dead appendages. And then, almost instantly, the film was different, something in black and white, although it also starred Rex Harrison. He was bearded and in a black turtleneck. The movie was familiar, and Kate thought she'd seen it before. She'd fallen asleep—she must have—without even knowing it. She felt disoriented and alarmed. The clock on the cable box said it was 5:45 in the morning. Kate's mouth was gluey, and she had a sliver of a headache from the wine she'd drunk. She felt that the past day had been many days, punctuated by naps as deep and troubling as full nights of sleep. It was only Sunday, but it felt like she'd been in Boston for a week.

She flipped the television off, returned the reclining sofa to its normal position, and stood. Her nose was running and she slid a hand in her dress pocket to look for tissues. She didn't find any, but her fingers touched a single key. She pulled it out of her pocket. It was the key she'd seen earlier, in the cutlery drawer, the one with AM written on its label in block letters. Kate didn't re-member putting it in her pocket. When had she done it? Earlier, when she first looked in the drawer, or since then? She rapidly shook her head, trying to wake herself, trying to force herself to remember.

She walked to the kitchen, the air around her seeming to part at a slower rate than it normally did. God, she was knackered. It had been years since she'd traveled to a different time zone and ex-perienced jet lag. She placed the key on the counter and began to make coffee. When it started to brew, she picked up the key again, and knew, suddenly, that she needed to find out if this key opened Audrey Marshall's apartment. *I'll just turn it, and find out, and then I can let the police know,* she told herself. It probably wasn't the right key. *AM* could mean many things.

Not even putting shoes on, Kate left her apartment and went to Audrey Marshall's door. Crime scene tape had been plastered in an X pattern from side to side. She slid the key into the lock, turned it, and pushed. The room yawned open before her. Knowing she shouldn't do it, but knowing that she had to, Kate ducked under the tape and entered the apartment. The tiredness and the fear made her feel as though she was watching herself, observing, not doing. She shut the door behind her, using her elbow, then stood still, her arms down by her sides, allowing her eyes to adjust. She was looking from a short foyer into a living room, much smaller than the living room in her end apartment, but just as elegant. Kate scanned the floor for any sign of where the body of Audrey Mar-shall had been found, but saw nothing. Was she in the right place? She took three careful steps into the interior of the apartment. There was an almost chemical smell in the air. It was dark, but the curtains were open, and the faint glow from the dawn sky allowed her to see the outlines of furniture, a coffee table cluttered with books and wine bottles.

There hasn't been a murder here, she thought. *Where's the blood, the overturned chair, the smell of death?* Was she dreaming now, or had she been dreaming before?

Even with these thoughts, she was strangely calm. One of the paradoxes of her anxious life was that in the midst of doing something slightly reckless, Kate often felt the most normal. It was as though her anxiety, always with her, was given a reason for existing. Standing in a murdered woman's apartment the morning after the body had been found, she thought the quickness of her heart and the coldness of her limbs made sense. She was about to turn back, but instead took a few more steps forward so that she could get a better look out of the large picture window. The window faced the courtyard, and Kate could make out pale orange light over the flat roof of the opposite wing. The windows on the other wing of the building were all dark, but Kate sensed motion in the window directly across from where she was looking. She instinctively took a step backward into the deeper shadows of the apartment.

She watched as a light came on and a figure passed in front of the window, then stopped and looked across. There was just enough light for Kate to know for sure that the figure was Alan Cherney, the man she'd met in the courtyard. The hair was right, and the angularity of the features, the slope of the shoulders. Kate stopped breathing, worried that any movement would mean that he could see her. They stood like that for a long, terrible moment, Kate unable to move. He kept staring across the way. At one point, he raised a hand and rubbed at one of his eyes. Then the dawn light that had been building in the western sky edged over the roof, and Kate suddenly realized that Alan might be able to see her. She moved backward, tracing her steps, like someone trying not to make tracks in the snow.

He kept watching, and Kate pressed her back to the door, frightened of being seen and frightened to take her eyes off him.

CHAPTER 6

ALAN STARED THROUGH HIS WINDOW into Audrey Marshall's dark apartment. For one moment, he could have sworn there was someone there, staring back at him. He'd barely slept in twenty-four hours, though, and the gray shadows across the way blurred and shimmered in his vision. Still, he watched—legs trembling with exhaustion, queasy with hunger—like a cat that watches the crack between the molding and the floor for the mouse that appeared there once upon a time.

Police cars had clogged the street all afternoon. An ambulance had arrived, and uniformed officers were in and out of the building.

Why was he still watching Audrey's apartment? Out of habit, he supposed. He'd known her intimately, having watched her in the privacy of her home for so long. He knew how she walked across a room, what she wore to bed, how long she brushed her teeth. Everything—almost everything—he'd known about Audrey he learned by watching out his window.

It had begun over a year ago, a few months after Alan and Quinn had moved in together. It had been a Saturday in December, a typical Saturday with Quinn. They'd had brunch with friends, then been shopping, then gone to the gym, then bought a Christmas tree that was almost too big to get up into the apartment and that had shed pine needles along the stairs and down the hall. The plan that night had been to stay in, decorate the tree (their first as a couple), drink eggnog, and watch a movie. But Quinn's best friend Viv had texted that everyone was going over to some new hotel bar that had just opened.

"Let's go," Quinn said, finishing off the eggnog that she'd been sipping at for over half an hour.

"Really?"

"It'll be fun. The bartender there is the same guy who used to bartend over at Beehive. You remember that drink he used to make, with the sherry in it, that you used to go on about . . ."

"The Aston Martin."

"That's right. The Aston Martin. Let's go drink one."

Alan was all set to agree, drank down his own eggnog, then surprised himself by saying, "Maybe I'll just stay here tonight."

"Seriously?" Quinn said. She was standing now, stripping off the Lululemon yoga pants she'd been wearing since they returned home.

"I'm tired," Alan said. It was a lie. He wanted to stay home in order to spend some time alone. His head was pleasantly fuzzy from the brandy in the eggnog, and the idea of a Saturday night alone suddenly felt heavenly. He could keep drinking, find a horror film to watch, something gory that Quinn would never agree to.

"We don't have to go if you don't want to," Quinn said.

"You go. I don't have a problem with it. It's a relationship milestone. You going out and me staying in, and neither of us minding."

"Oh, you're just assuming I don't mind," she said, but she was smiling. In the end, after changing, and having another drink, and putting on makeup, Quinn went out.

Alan had been alone in the apartment before, of course, but it felt different on a Saturday night with Quinn off with friends. Before looking for a film to watch, he put *Chet Baker Sings* on the old record player he had been dragging from apartment to apartment his whole life, made himself another drink, then wandered from lamp to lamp, adjusting the lighting to the way he liked it. It had just begun to snow earlier that evening, when he and Quinn had returned with the tree, so Alan went to the large picture window in the living room, parted the curtains, and looked out to see what the weather was doing. It had stopped coming down, but everything was covered with a thin scrim of pure white snow. He studied the footsteps in the courtyard, trying to identify Quinn's, but there were too many.

There was a light on in the apartment on the other side of the courtyard. Alan looked, his eyes taking a moment to adjust. The woman who lived there—Alan couldn't remember her name, if he'd ever known it—had left her own curtains half parted. She was seated on her couch, her back against one of the arms, a book open in her lap. There was a single tall lamp above her that produced a cone of warm yellow light. On the coffee table in front of the couch was a glass of red wine, an open bottle next to it. It was such an idealized image, almost cliché, that Alan laughed out loud to himself. He took a step to the left so that she was framed more perfectly in the space between the parted curtains.

The woman startled a little and looked up from her book, and Alan took an instinctive step back, sure that he'd somehow been spotted. She stood, though, without looking toward the window at all. She disappeared out of sight, then returned to the couch, that white cat called Sanders walking with her. The cat leapt onto the coffee table. The woman returned to the sofa and the book, idly scratching Sanders under its chin. He belonged to a woman on the other side of the building, but was allowed to roam the place at free will. Alan had seen him frequently in the lobby, sometimes sleeping on top of the reception desk.

Alan snapped the nearest lamp off, so that his own living room was plunged into near darkness, and continued to watch the woman. She looked so at peace, so content within the small sphere of her existence, that Alan felt an almost physical pain in his chest, a sharp desire to be with her. He imagined himself stretched out on the other side of the couch, their bare feet touching. In this fantasy, he only knew that they were completely at ease with one another.

The track on the record was "My Buddy," and Alan realized just how long he had been staring out the window. He pushed the curtains closed and sat back down on the couch. His phone vibrated: a text from Quinn that she was at the bar. He wrote back, telling her to say Hi to everyone. She wrote back a half second later: Mike said to say you are a losah!

The record ended, and Alan sat in the quiet apartment. He thought of playing something else, or looking for a movie to watch, but all he could think about was continuing to watch the woman. He got up, returned to the window, and peered through again. She was still reading on the couch, but Sanders the cat was gone, and she'd pulled her legs up so that her book was propped against her knees. Alan remembered that he had binoculars, a small pair that he'd bought that year he'd split a Celtics season ticket in the nosebleeds with some of his college friends. He couldn't remember exactly where they were, but guessed they were still in the canvas messenger bag he'd been using back then. He went and checked, and he'd guessed right. With the binoculars in his hand, he hesitated, knowing somehow that there was a genuine difference between simply watching your neighbor through a window and watching her with a pair of binoculars. It will be just for a moment, he told himself. A way to get a really good look at her, maybe even see what book she's reading.

He returned to the window, and peered through the binoculars. It made her look as though she was about eight feet away. He could see her features clearly, the texture of her clothes, the way she was absentmindedly touching one of her earlobes with a finger. The book was called *Wolf Hall,* large black-and-white font on a red cover. She licked the tip of a finger with her tongue before turning a page.

Alan felt his breathing slow down and get heavier. Looking at her up close he felt dirtier, aware that what he was doing was wrong, but unable to stop himself. She wore old jeans, the denim splitting at the knees, and a tight crewneck sweater with black and brown stripes. She yawned, arching her back, and he could see a sliver of her pink stomach. Alan felt himself stiffen in his pants, and that reaction caused him to lower the binoculars, pull the curtains shut, and step away. Feverish shame swept over him, as though he had suddenly become ill.

He put the binoculars in his underwear drawer, then undressed, pulled on a pair of boxers and a T-shirt, brushed his teeth, and got into bed. He read for a while. John Le Carré's *Tinker, Tailor, Soldier, Spy*. He'd read it before, but not since middle school. His eyes scanned the words while he thought of the girl in the window. He wondered what her life was like, if she had a boyfriend. Maybe he was out for the night the way Quinn was. He didn't think so, though. There was something about the way she looked in her apartment that made Alan think she lived there alone.

He tried to read some more, then shut the book, turned out the light, and lay awake, listening to the baseboard heating click on and off. There was no way he was going to be able to fall asleep, he told himself, and then he did.

Quinn slid next to him under the covers. She smelled like red wine and Marlboro Lights. "You smoked?" Alan asked. They'd quit together recently.

"Shhh," she said. She was naked, and she slid one of his hands between her legs, then climbed on top of him. Quinn was gray and featureless in the darkness of the room, and Alan, half awake, imagined it was his neighbor, the girl whose name he didn't even know, moving back and forth on top of him.

IT DIDN'T TAKE HIM LONG to learn her name. The following Monday, after Quinn had left for work, Alan walked through the building's lobby and to the other wing. It was easy to figure out which was her door; she was in apartment 3C. Back down in the lobby, Alan asked the doorman if he could look through the bundle of mail that had just arrived. And there she was on a credit card solicitation: Audrey Marshall, Apartment 3C.

Over the course of that winter he got to know her schedule, when she got out of bed in the morning and when she got home at night. She rarely had anyone over. Once or twice a woman, skinny and with a homely face, came by and they would drink champagne, the other woman talking nonstop while Audrey listened, interjecting occasionally. But she was usually alone, and that was the way Alan liked to watch her.

"What's so interesting out there?" Quinn asked one night, when he thought she was watching the television.

"I thought I heard someone shouting in the courtyard, but it's probably just out on the street."

"Yeah, whatever," she said.

"What does that mean?"

"It means I see you looking out the window all the time. And I can't remember the last time you actually looked at me for more than a second."

"We ate lunch together today, remember? We were looking at each other the whole time. I helped you get that sesame seed out from between your teeth." Alan laughed.

Quinn shrugged from behind her cell phone. This was March, and Alan was pretty sure that Quinn had met someone new, some guy named Brandon who worked at her firm and who was always included in the group of coworkers who were inevitably getting together after work for a drink. It was something about the way she said his name, rushing through the two syllables in sentences such as: "Oh, and of course, Brandon was also there." Alan wasn't upset. He wasn't even jealous, really. He had Audrey.

As winter turned to spring, and spring turned to summer, she cracked her windows, and so did Alan. On quiet summer evenings, when the breeze blew in the right direction, he occasionally could hear music coming from across the courtyard. Audrey listened to classical when she was reading, and she read a lot, usually in the same position on her living room couch as the first time he'd spied on her. Sometimes she read in the bedroom, especially when the weather was hot, since her bedroom, like Alan's, had a ceiling fan in it. He never saw her fully naked, but he'd seen her in various stages of undress many times, usually as she got ready in the morning for work, or just after she came home, always around six in the evening. One hot night, Audrey left her curtains cracked, and Alan, chair pulled up to his own window in his unlit bedroom, watched through his binoculars as she read a paperback called *The Little Stranger*. She was naked except for a pair of black briefs. Alan imagined, for a moment, that if he opened his window all the way he could float across the courtyard and into her bedroom.

By late summer, Quinn had moved out—citing Alan's distance, although Alan had heard through the grapevine that she was now dating Brandon from work—leaving him with less than half the furniture and a monthly rent he couldn't afford. She'd also left him with more time to focus on Audrey. He'd formed a plan, a way to meet her that would seem natural and that would throw them together for a lengthy period of time. Alan had begun to occasionally follow Audrey when she left the apartment. He now knew where she worked—a small publishing house just over the river in Cambridge—and he knew that on weekends she liked to go and read at a low-ceilinged coffee shop in Harvard Square called Café Pamplona. His plan was to get there before her on one of those days, tell her she looked familiar, start a conversation. Eventually they'd figure out that they lived in the same apartment building in Boston, and wasn't it funny that they had actually met in Cambridge, and maybe they could get together sometime soon on their side of the river.

But he never got to enact this plan. Everything changed in February. A man had started appearing in Audrey's apartment. A tall jock in a suit, who always showed up with a bottle of wine. Alan knew who he was. His name was Corbin Dell, and he also lived at 101 Bury Street, right down the hall from Audrey.

CHAPTER 7

ALAN HAD MET CORBIN DELL shortly after he'd moved to Bury Street. This was before he'd begun watching Audrey Marshall, back when Quinn and he were an amorous young couple sharing their first apartment.

They'd met—Alan and Corbin—in the lobby of the building. Corbin was talking with the doorman named Bob and Alan was checking his mail on his way to play racquetball. The tape-wrapped handle of his racket poked out of his gym bag.

"Squash or racquetball?" Corbin asked Alan, noticing the racket.

"I've played both," Alan said, "but lately I've been playing racquetball. Do you play?"

"I do. Where do you play?" Corbin asked. He was almost impossibly square jawed. In fact, everything about him was square—his wide shoulders, his thick hands, his head, its sharp corners accented by a blond crew cut. Alan knew, just by looking at him, that he would be a far superior player.

"The Y," Alan said.

"Where? On the river?"

"Uh-huh."

"I didn't know they had racquetball courts. We should play some time. You could come to my club."

"I'm not very good," Alan said.

"I don't care about that," Corbin said. "The guy I play with now is so competitive it's stopped being fun."

They introduced themselves. Alan had a business card from the software company he worked at that had his e-mail on it, and he gave it to Corbin.

"You in marketing?" Corbin asked.

"I am. What about you?"

"Financial advisor. At Briar-Crane." Alan recognized the name. Of course he was in finance. Guys who looked like Corbin loved nothing more than currency speculation and talking about rates of exchange. They said goodbye, Corbin telling Alan that he'd be in touch about racquetball. Alan exited through the courtyard on his way to the Y, knowing that Corbin would probably never e-mail, but feeling a strange surge of pleasure that he suddenly lived in a building where men made racquetball dates in the lobby. This was his new life, now that he was with Quinn, who'd always had family money and always would have family money. She'd insisted on moving into 101 Bury Street, even though the rent was four times what Alan had been paying for a two-bedroom in South Boston.

Alan forgot about Corbin Dell, and was surprised when, a week later, he got an e-mail from him that read:

Let's play that game of racquetball. I can do Saturday morning if you can. I got a court for 10 am. Corbin

They'd played, and Alan had been right: Corbin was a far superior player, not just in skill level, but in fitness. After the game, Corbin looked like he didn't need a shower, while Alan, dripping with sweat, worked hard to form complete sentences. Still, after showering and walking back from Corbin's swank club to the apartment building, Corbin said they should play again.

And they did, but just once. It was right before Christmas week, and afterward they got a beer together at the Sevens on Charles Street. The drink at the bar felt to Alan like their racquetball games—Corbin in control and Alan scrambling to catch up. Corbin talked about great restaurants in Boston, mentioned his portfolio, and swiveled his head to watch a beautiful brunette walk across the room. Alan thought Corbin was overcompensating for something, although what that was he didn't know. Maybe it was that stupid, preppy name—Corbin—that he'd been saddled with, or maybe he was secretly gay and trying desperately to hide it. After the beer they walked together down Charles Street. It was just past five but dark already, the store windows festooned and glittery with Christmas lights. "I hate Christmas," Corbin said, almost to himself, then quickly laughed.

"I'm ambivalent. I don't celebrate it," Alan said.

That had been their last time hanging out, except for occasionally running into one another in the building's lobby or courtyard. Alan registered guilt on Corbin's face during those brief run-ins, as though the fact that they no longer played racquetball was a breakup perpetrated by Corbin. Alan wanted to tell him that the breakup was mutual.

Then Audrey entered Alan's life and Alan forgot all about Corbin, all about other people, really. He'd forgotten Corbin so completely that it actually took him a moment to identify him when he first saw him in Audrey's apartment. His blond hair was a little longer, but nothing else had changed. Tall and muscular, dressed in a suit or workout gear. He settled into Audrey's apartment as though he owned it, sprawling on her couch, watching her television. They were always sharing wine. They were rarely physical with one another, although Alan had watched them enter the bedroom together several times and pull the curtains closed. He'd also watched, once, as Corbin lifted Audrey into his arms, her legs around his waist, and kissed her. One of Corbin's massive hands slid under Audrey's skirt and Alan had to look away. Alan told himself that his disgust at seeing Corbin and Audrey together was a good thing, that it might cure him of his need to watch Audrey at all hours. If nothing else, Audrey was not the woman he thought she was, not if she was dating someone like Corbin.

Still, despite these thoughts, Alan found himself watching

Audrey as much as he ever had, cherishing those moments when she was alone in her apartment, reading on her couch like she always had. She'd started a new book, *Gone Girl* by Gillian Flynn, and Alan, on his way home from work, stopped at a Barnes & Noble and bought a copy, just so they could read it at the same time. Days would go by with no appearance by Corbin, and Alan would begin to hope that the relationship was over, but then Corbin would show up on a Friday night, always with a bottle of wine. They rarely seemed to go out together. Alan wondered if they'd come to some kind of sex agreement—neighbors with benefits. The thought bothered him. What did she possibly see in him? Even as someone just for sex.

On one of the nights when Corbin was in Audrey's apartment, Alan, after several beers, decided to send an e-mail to Corbin. It had been nearly a year since they'd last had contact. Alan composed the e-mail, working hard to make it sound dashed off, apologizing for how long it had been, then asking Corbin if he wanted to get together for a quick game followed by another beer at the Sevens. "Or we could skip the racquetball and just grab a drink, if you want," Alan added, thinking that having a conversation with Corbin was his only goal. He hit send as soon as he'd written the e-mail, so as not to give himself time to reconsider. Alan sat back and sighed. If Corbin took the bait, then he'd be able to quiz him about Audrey, maybe find out what was happening in the relationship. Maybe Corbin and Alan would become friends, this second time around, and that would allow Alan to formally meet Audrey, get to know her. Alan found his mind galloping forward, toward scenarios where Audrey would leave Corbin to be with him. He stopped himself from going too far with these fantasies, got up from the computer, and returned to the window. Corbin was looking at his phone. Alan wondered if he was reading the e-mail he'd just sent. If so, he didn't respond until the following day:

Hey man. Nice to hear from you. I actually stopped playing
racquetball, and only play squash now. But let's get that drink
anyway. I'm free Wednesday next week.

Alan replied that he was free as well. As the day neared, he
began to wonder if there was any chance that Corbin would bring
Audrey along. Because of this slight possibility, Alan dressed in
his best pair of jeans and his Rag & Bone blazer. But when he arrived at the Sevens at the appointed time, Corbin wasn't there. And
when Corbin finally showed, twenty minutes late, he was alone.

They small-talked through half a beer, Corbin checking his
cell phone at two-minute intervals. Realizing he had limited time,
Alan asked, trying to sound casual: "Who you seeing these days?"

"Seeing?" Corbin replied. "No one, actually. Well, there's this
girl at work. Married, unfortunately—"

"I thought I heard from someone that you were seeing someone
in the building. That girl who lives across from you—I don't know
her name . . ."

"Audrey?"

"Yeah, that might be it."

Corbin took a long pull at his Smuttynose beer, a thin line of
foam clinging to his upper lip. "I barely know her. Why? Who'd
you hear that from?"

"I must have dreamt it, I guess. Or seen you two together."

"Nah, man. I really don't know her. I've seen her, and wouldn't
mind knowing her, but nah. How 'bout you? Your girlfriend
moved out, didn't she?"

Alan gave Corbin the short-story version of his breakup with
Quinn and his plans to either find a new place soon or get a house-
mate to split the rent. They each finished their beer. The busy bartender swung past, asking them if they wanted another. Alan, not
done interrogating Corbin about his love life, was about to say yes
when Corbin jumped in and said he had to take off. "Sorry. I've

got somewhere to be, unfortunately. Let's do this again, though," he said, unconvincingly.

Corbin left, but Alan stayed, ordering a rye and ginger ale, and wondering why Corbin would deny knowing Audrey. It didn't make any sense. Even if they were trying to keep the relationship a secret for some reason, why would it matter if Alan knew about it?

When Alan returned to his apartment from the Sevens, he went straight to the window. Audrey's apartment was dark.

But the following night she was there, on her couch, reading a *Vanity Fair* and occasionally checking her phone. She seemed jittery, twisting a strand of her short hair around a finger.

Alan went to make himself a drink, something he had learned to do in complete darkness, and when he returned, Corbin was now in Audrey's apartment. They stood talking near her door, and Alan thought it looked like an impromptu visit. There was no bottle of wine, and Audrey was dressed in the black tights and oversized hoodie that she often wore when she was alone. Alan stood back a little from the window, even though he knew there was no way he could be seen. He watched them talking and knew that something was up. Corbin swung his head in the direction of Audrey's window, and Audrey's gaze followed, a frown creasing her face.

Both of them were staring directly across in Alan's direction.

Alan turned cold. He took another step backward. His binoculars were on the end table next to the couch, and he went and got them, continuing to watch from deep within his apartment.

Corbin and Audrey talked some more. At one point, Audrey shrugged, a smile on her face. Then Alan watched, his skin flushed, as Corbin crossed Audrey's living room and pulled her curtains all the way closed.

Alan lowered the binoculars. He hadn't been spotted, but it was just as bad. He'd been figured out. Corbin had realized that the only way Alan would know that he and Audrey were seeing each other was if Alan had been spying from across the way. Had it occurred to him immediately after the drink? Had he returned to the apartment, checked to see where Alan lived, the location of the apartment, and then realized that it was the exact mirror apartment from across the courtyard? Alan felt physically sick, his stomach clenching. For a brief, horrible moment he wondered if Corbin, and maybe Corbin *and* Audrey, would come over to his apartment to confront him. He instinctively pushed the binoculars down between the sofa's cushions. The lights were out. He wouldn't have to answer the door.

Then Alan told himself to relax, to take a deep breath, to begin to analyze the situation. Even if Corbin had figured out that they'd been spotted through the window, it didn't necessarily mean that they knew that Alan had been obsessively spying on Audrey. What if Corbin did confront him about it? All Alan would have to say would be something casual, like *Oh yeah, maybe that's where I saw you two together. Audrey never pulls her curtains all the way shut.* That thought relaxed him, and he stood again, walked toward the window to look through it. Audrey's curtains were still pulled shut.

Over the next few months, Alan gave up on the fantasy that he could somehow meet Audrey in the flesh. He knew it would never happen. He also knew that if it did, Audrey would recognize him as the creep from the other side of the building, the one Corbin had accused of spying. She must have taken Corbin seriously that night, because she became a lot more vigilant about pulling her curtains all the way shut, especially in the evenings. She did occasionally leave them open, but Alan had decided to attempt to curb the amount of time he spent looking out of his window. He knew it was unhealthy, and definitely immoral, along with probably being illegal.

He reconnected with some friends he'd lost touch with and accepted invitations from coworkers to get drinks after work. On one of those nights he wound up kissing an intern from Suffolk University. Bella was an avid softball player with long blond hair who photographed everything with her phone. Even though Alan was still in his late twenties, he felt like Bella came from another generation. They went to a movie, and afterward back to Alan's place. He realized she was the only other human who had set foot in his apartment since Quinn had left. The sex was bad, perfunctory and awkward, and Bella talked nonstop out of embarrassment. After she'd fallen asleep—"Is it okay if I spend the night, even though I totally know this is just a hookup?"—Alan, wide awake, had gone into the living room. It had been a few days since he'd checked on Audrey's apartment, but he pulled his curtains apart by an inch and looked across the way. She'd left her curtains slightly open as well. She was on the sofa, curled up asleep, her book facedown on the floor next to her. He'd seen her sleep on the sofa before. Her right hand was curled, palm out, along the center of her chest, her index finger grazing the soft skin under her chin.

Alan went to his own sofa, buried his own face into a pillow, and cried for the first time in years.

No more Audrey, he told himself.

He needed to erase her from his mind. And he'd succeeded lately. For the most part.

Then, on Saturday morning he'd found a stale, brittle cigarette and gone outside to smoke. He'd spoken to the pretty English girl—Kate something, maybe she hadn't told him her last name— and she told him that Audrey was missing. It had been a strange and unsettling conversation. In some ways, Kate had reminded Alan of Audrey. Not the way she looked, although they shared the same pale coloring. Kate—and maybe it was just because he was meeting her face-to-face—had seemed more grounded, while Audrey had always been more ethereal. Pixieish, with her small features, long limbs, and that still quality, as though she'd never move unless it was absolutely necessary. To flip a page of her book, or take a sip of her tea. That was the difference, Alan thought. Kate, almost as pretty as Audrey, with a face that was rounder and hair that was a shade darker, was definitely *not* still. She shifted her weight from leg to leg when they talked. When she pushed a loose strand of hair back behind an ear, Alan noticed that her unvarnished fingernails had been bitten down to the quick.

Then the police had arrived, and Carol, Alan's elderly neighbor from across the hall, had confirmed that a body had been found.

That evening a police officer, a woman who identified herself as Officer Karen Gibson, came to take a statement. He told her the truth. He knew Audrey Marshall by sight, but he didn't *know* her.

That night Alan had slept, but it had been fitful, punctuated by thin dreams in which Audrey was with Alan in his apartment, touching him, speaking with him, whispering in his ear. He'd woken before dawn and gone to look toward Audrey's apartment. It was dark, but he could tell that the curtain was open. He caught a flicker of movement and stared for a long time. The sky was lightening from black to orange, but the interior of Audrey's apartment stayed dark. Still, he watched, scared to even blink too much. Then there was another suggestion of movement, a trace of light as Alan was sure he saw Audrey's door open and shut quickly, a figure leaving the apartment.

CHAPTER 8

By noon on Sunday, Kate, after beginning but not finishing a lengthy e-mail to her mother, paced the perimeter of the vast apartment. She'd been awake since dawn, when she'd snuck into Audrey Marshall's apartment and seen Alan Cherney through his window. Now, as she paced, she looked out her own windows. The sky was a milky white and the surface of the river was still and glassy. The stretch of Bury Street that she could see from the west-facing windows was quiet. She was hungry, but tired of eating bread and cheese. In the kitchen she opened the door of the massive, stainless steel refrigerator and stared at its meager contents.

Go outside, she told herself.

And before she could change her mind, she was pulling her boots on over her jeans and grabbing her black-and-white polka-dot jacket. A quick walk around the block, maybe find a place to eat lunch, or maybe even buy something to cook back at the apartment.

It was colder than she thought it would be outside, the air raw and damp. Walking across the courtyard, she buttoned her coat up to her throat, wishing she'd brought her gloves.

There was a man pacing on Bury Street, his own hands deep inside his navy pea coat. As she came through the archway, he looked up, expectantly, and their eyes met. He had medium-length reddish hair that was sticking up at the top, and his eyes behind his wire-rimmed glasses were bruised looking, their surfaces wet and shiny. Kate went to cross the road, pausing for a moment to look for oncoming cars, as the man approached her.

"Hi," he said, awkwardly. "Hi, hello there. You live here?"

"I do," she said, her hands instinctively going toward the throat of her jacket, already buttoned up.

"Sorry. I don't mean to frighten you. I was a friend . . . I'm a close friend of Audrey Marshall, and I've talked to the police, and I spoke to your doorman here in the building, and I'm just hoping to get more information."

"I'm sorry. I really don't know anything. I just moved here. I didn't know Audrey."

The man seemed undeterred. His cheeks were mottled and red and she wondered how long he'd been standing out in the cold, waiting for someone to come out of the building. "Have the police talked with you?" he asked.

"They took a statement. I think just because I'm right next door."

"You're right next door? On her floor?"

"I am, but I literally just moved in and don't know anyone. I'm sorry I don't have more information." Kate took a tentative step down the sidewalk in an attempt to escape.

"Do you mind if I walk with you a bit? I need to go get a coffee. I'm Jack, by the way." He removed a glove, and Kate took his dry, warm hand in hers. "Jack Ludovico. I've been friends with Audrey since . . . since—"

Trying to channel her mother, who was always kind, but a master at avoiding unwanted social situations, Kate said: "Jack, nice to meet you, but I'm in a hurry, and I don't think I can help you at all."

"You're not Corbin Dell's cousin, are you? Audrey told me that he was going to London, and you were going to come and live in his apartment."

"I am. I just arrived. Audrey told you that?"

"Yes, I know all about Corbin and Audrey. I don't mean to keep you, but let's walk. I'm cold."

They began to walk together, Kate curious that there had apparently been a "Corbin and Audrey."

"I'm Kate," she said.

Jack introduced himself again, realized he'd already done it, and rapidly shook his head, embarrassed. "I'm a mess."

"You were close?"

"Yes and no. Yes, for me, anyway. We dated in college but it didn't work out, and then, when she moved up here, we got back in touch, just as friends, really, and I can't believe . . ." He stopped walking, put his face in his gloved hands, pushing his glasses up to his forehead, and began to sob, his shoulders hitching up and down.

"It's okay," Kate said, not knowing what to do. She put a hand on his shoulder, and they remained frozen in that tableau for what seemed an eternity. After he removed his hands from his face and wiped his gloves along the thighs of his jeans, he asked: "Who identified her, do you know?"

"No, I have no idea. Let's keep walking, okay?" Kate said, taking his arm and moving him down the street.

"Okay," he said. "Sorry about dumping this on you. You must have just gotten here, and now there's been a murder next door to your new place, and I'm here pestering you." He laughed, an unnerving staccato rattle, his shoulders hitching again like they had when he'd been sobbing.

"It's fine," Kate said. Then asked: "How did you find out . . . How did you find out about what happened?"

"It was in the *Globe* today. I was worried already, because I hadn't heard anything from Audrey for a few days, which was strange, and then I saw a headline that said a woman had been found dead in Beacon Hill, and I knew it was her even before I read the rest of the article."

"What did it say?" Kate asked.

"Just that her body had been found, and that the police were treating it as a suspicious death, and there was a number to call with any information, so I called it. I went into the police station, and they questioned me, but they wouldn't tell me anything, except that she'd been positively identified. Do you know who did that? Do you know who identified her?"

Jack's voice was rising in pitch. Kate, recognizing panic in someone else, felt, as she usually did, comparatively calm. She said, "Jack, I don't know anything. I'm sorry. I just got here. But I'm sure the police can't talk about it because it's an ongoing investigation. Is there someone else you can talk with? One of Audrey's friends? Or her family?"

He nodded. "I will. I don't really know her family, but I can talk with her best friend, Kerry. I know her."

"She might have been the one who alerted the police that Audrey was missing. There was a girl here when I arrived, knocking on Audrey's door."

"Yeah, that was probably Kerry." Something in Jack's voice made Kate think that he wasn't fond of Audrey's best friend.

"You should talk with her," Kate said. "I'm sure she knows more than I know."

"I will." They continued to walk, Kate picking up the pace a little, Jack keeping up. They passed Brimmer and were approaching Charles Street. "So does Corbin know yet?" he asked.

"I gave his e-mail to the police and I think they were going to do it, just in case he had any information. I didn't want to e-mail him myself yet because I didn't know if he'd heard."

"Do you think the police suspect him?"

"I don't. I didn't. They said they didn't. Why, was there something strange between him and Audrey?"

"Well, they had a thing."

"What kind of thing?"

"I don't know exactly. It was an on-and-off thing. Audrey told me that they slept together but that they weren't going out, that he just wanted to keep things between them strictly in the apartment." It was clear from Jack's tone that he hadn't approved of the situation.

"What do you mean in the apartment?"

"In the building. I guess they were hooking up, and Audrey wanted more, more of a relationship, and Corbin didn't. She didn't have particularly nice things to say about him. I'm sorry. I shouldn't be telling you this. I didn't get the sense that she was scared of him or anything. It wasn't like that. Just that he was an asshole."

"I don't really know anything about it," Kate said. They'd reached the corner of Bury and Charles, and were now facing each other again.

Jack's jaw was clenching and unclenching. "I don't think Corbin had anything to do with what happened."

"Well, he was already in London—"

"When did he leave, exactly, do you know?"

"He took a night flight on Thursday, because he got in early on Friday morning. That was the day I left to come here. We almost had time to meet one another, but not really."

Jack said nothing, and Kate watched as he seemed to be calculating whether Corbin could have had something to do with Audrey's death. "When did you last talk with Audrey?" she asked.

His eyes snapped back toward her. "Oh, I'm trying to remember. Sometime Wednesday evening, I think."

"So you think Corbin . . ."

"No, I don't think anything. I guess he could've had something to do with what happened. It's a possibility, right?" He looked almost hopeful.

"I don't know. Maybe someone else heard from her. You should really ask the police about that. I don't know anything."

Jack rapidly shook his head, as though he had water in an ear. "Jesus, I'm sorry. This has nothing to do with you. I'm just freaking out—"

"No, I get it. It's just that I can't help you. I don't know Corbin, and he didn't tell me anything about anyone else who lived here. I hope he had nothing to do with it. What do you know about what happened to her, to Audrey?"

"What do you mean? Like how she was killed?"

"I guess."

"They wouldn't tell me anything. They said they were treating the death as suspicious, which is just what the newspaper said."

A tear bubbled up in one of Jack's puffy eyes, and Kate decided to not ask any more questions about Audrey. She wanted to leave, but Jack looked lost, reminding her of a child suddenly separated from his parents.

"What do you do, Jack?" she asked.

"What do you mean?"

"For work?"

"Oh, I work in hospitality."

"Uh-huh."

"I'm an events coordinator at a conference center. It's not as exciting as it sounds, but I'm busy all the time. The last two weeks . . . I didn't even have time to see Audrey."

The tear slid down his cheek, and he wiped it away with the back of his gloved hand.

Kate, trying again to channel her mother's bluntness, said, "Jack, I really think you should go talk with someone who knew Audrey."

He nodded, and she continued: "Find that friend of hers, or her family. Where was she from?"

"Her family's from New Jersey. I never met them."

"They've probably come up here, don't you think? You should find them and talk with them."

"Yeah, I think you're right." He stayed rooted to his spot on the sidewalk. A family of tourists, the two youngest kids wearing lobster claw hats, maneuvered around him.

"I think I was still in love with her," he said. "I don't think she felt the same way. No, I know she didn't feel the same way. Because of what Corbin did to mess her up, but . . ." He stopped, his eyes settling on some unknown spot in the middle distance.

"It was nice meeting you, Jack," Kate said, and they shook hands again. He kept his gloves on this time. "I'm sorry, but I need to get some shopping done."

She left him on the street corner and walked, at a pace she hoped wasn't too noticeably brisk, toward the small grocery store she'd been to the day before. She felt guilty, but she also knew that she couldn't really do anything to comfort him. He needed to find someone else who knew Audrey. She also wanted to be on her own to think about what she'd learned. Corbin *had* been involved with Audrey. They'd been sleeping together, and it had turned sour, at least in the eyes of Audrey. Maybe in his eyes as well. Kate's mind spun out possibilities. Audrey becoming possessive and Corbin panicking, trying to get away from her. He accepted the job transfer to London. But, then, on his last night in Boston he thought he'd go and say goodbye to Audrey, tell her that he was leaving town. And maybe she freaked out on him, attacked, and Corbin, defending himself . . .

Kate pushed the escalating thoughts out of her mind and opened the glass door of the grocery store. But with a single look at the narrow, crowded aisles, panic flooded over her, hollowing out her insides. She backed away from the fragrant warmth spilling from the inside of the store, and bumped into a couple in running gear, trying to push past her. "Sorry," she said, eyeing an empty bench in front of a store that sold vintage prints.

She sat down and did her breathing exercises.

Face it. Accept it. Float with it. Let time pass.

A plane went by overhead, too low, she thought, and the sound of its engine made Kate's scalp prickle and tighten. She began to tap her finger pads together, then made herself stop, and stood up. She was no longer hungry but knew she had to eat. Across the street was a small, walk-up pizza place called the Upper Crust, where she bought herself a slice of pesto pizza and a cream soda. She went back to the bench to eat. It was cold, but the open air felt better than being inside.

Walking back home, she half expected to see Audrey's lovelorn friend still at the corner where she had left him, but he was gone. He wasn't stalking the front of 101 Bury Street either, and Kate was relieved to make it back up to her apartment without encountering anyone else.

Back inside, she studied the walls around her. Was this the apartment of a killer? If it was, would she be able to tell? There was so little of Corbin here. Besides being luxurious and spacious, it didn't feel like anything. No, that wasn't entirely true. It felt like a dead man's apartment. It felt like Corbin's father's place. The furniture was beautiful but slightly dated; one of the sofas was up- holstered in a floral print. And the artwork on the walls—most of it original—was abstract oil paintings, interesting (Kate thought) but dated somehow. No, very few, if any, of the furnishings in the house belonged to Corbin. He'd inherited his father's place and kept it exactly the same, even down to the framed photographs.

Kate, starting to relax a little, sat down and thought about what it meant. What would she have done if she inherited this place? Probably the same. It looked nice—why change it? And maybe Corbin had been particularly fond of his father, and keeping every- thing the same was a way to honor him. It was a possibility. But it was also a possibility that there was nothing of Corbin's around be- cause he wanted to hide, because he didn't want people to see who he really was. And if that were the case, was there a place where he did express himself? Where was the real Corbin?

Kate went to the window with the best view of Bury Street. It was still quiet. She'd expected to maybe see Audrey's lovelorn friend again, watching the building for any sign of another in- habitant he could grill. Hadn't she read somewhere that criminals liked to return to the scene of their crimes? *No,* she thought. Jack

Ludovico had been strange, but one thing he hadn't seemed was guilty of a crime. For once, her mind was not unspooling toward the worst possibility. He was what he seemed. An old boyfriend grappling with disbelief and grief. Easy to read, not like Corbin, who had an apparently complicated relationship with Audrey, plus a key to her apartment.

Thinking about the key made her remember that she needed to call the detective.

She went to the bedroom where she'd left Detective James's card, then thought of her sketchbook under the bed. She was suddenly sitting on the carpet, the sketchbook open to a new page, drawing Jack Ludovico's face, her hand moving automatically and without thought over the page. She drew him with his head cast down slightly, eyes looking up. When she finished, she pulled the charcoal pencil back and knew that she'd got him on the first try. It was a perfect rendering. She dated the picture and put his name under it.

She sat for a moment more, trying to remember why she had come into the bedroom. The detective's card. She was going to call her. She walked to the phone in the living room. The detective picked up after two rings.

"Hi. It's Kate Priddy. You left me your card."

A slight pause, then: "Hi, Kate. What can I do for you?"

"It's about Audrey Marshall. I found a key in my apartment, in Corbin Dell's apartment, really, and it has the initials 'AM' on it."

"You think he might have had a key to Audrey's apartment?"

"That's what I was thinking."

"Did you test it?" the detective asked.

Kate was surprised, not expecting to be asked that, but something about the detective's casual nature caused her to own up to the truth: "Actually, I did. It's the key. It's Audrey's key. I mean, he probably just had it so that he could water her plants when she was gone, or something."

"Yes, I'm sure you're right. We're in contact with your cousin and he's been helpful. I'll ask him about the key."

"Oh, he knows now?"

"He does. He's been helpful but said that he didn't know Audrey particularly well. He sounded most concerned about you."

"He said he didn't know Audrey well?"

"That's what he said. Excuse me a moment . . ."

Kate listened to muffled voices for a moment—the detective speaking with someone else.

"Sorry, Kate, I'm back," Detective James said. "Was there anything else?"

"No, just the key. And I talked with a friend of Audrey's. Jack Ludovico."

"Oh yeah?" She sounded interested. "How did you meet him?"

"He was in front of the building, said he was coming from the police station—that he'd talked with someone there, and he was hoping to get more information."

"What's the name again?"

"Didn't he come to the station?"

"He might have, Kate. I just got here myself and I haven't checked in with all my colleagues yet."

"It's Jack Ludovico. He actually had a different story about Corbin and Audrey. He said they were involved."

"I'd like to follow up with you about this, Kate, if I can. Can I call you back? Is this a good number to reach you?"

"Sure. Yes, I'm calling from the apartment."

"And thank you for letting us know about the key, and don't hesitate to call again with anything, okay? Even if it seems insignificant."

Kate hung up the phone. She sat quietly for a moment, thinking: *Did I make a mistake by not telling her that I'd seen the man from across the courtyard peering into Audrey's apartment?* She decided, swiftly, that not telling the detective about Alan Cherney was *not* a mistake. Of course he was looking across and into the apartment. There'd been a murder. He must have heard about it, and he was curious. Curious and upset, probably. It was natural.

When bad things happened, the world always looked. Kate knew that more than most people.

CHAPTER 9

K ATE FINISHED HER LONG E-MAIL to her mother, detailing what had happened since she'd arrived in Boston. She knew that as soon as she sent it, her mother would ask her to come home. Not so much for the sake of safety—although that would obviously be part of it—but because of what Kate had gone through with George Daniels.

She'd met George her first year at university. He was in earth sciences, and she was in the arts, but they'd ended up in the same beginning Greek course. Kate struggled in the course and ended up asking George for help. She'd only asked him because he looked studious and trustworthy. He wasn't bad looking, but at eighteen years old he looked like a fully licensed chartered accountant. He was tall and lanky, most of his height coming from his long legs. He wore plain spectacles, always dressed in corduroys and sweater vests, and was beginning to lose his hair. But the hair loss had left George with a prominent widow's peak that she found attractive. After several study sessions, he nervously asked Kate if she'd like to go to dinner sometime; he suggested an Italian place that he'd heard was very good.

She said yes, intrigued about what it would be like to go on such an old-fashioned date instead of just meeting up with some boy at the student union pub. And it *had* felt like an old-fashioned date. George even wore a tie under one of his sweater vests. It should have been awkward, but it wasn't. George and Kate had lots in common; both were secret poetry fans, and both were obsessed with *Twin Peaks*. That weekend they spent all of Saturday and part of Sunday in George's room watching the entire first season on George's laptop in his bed. By Monday they had each lost their virginity, and Kate was certain that she was in love. George, she knew, felt the same way.

They were together for a year, safe in the bubble of their relationship. Kate felt safe, anyway. Her whole life had been colored by her conviction that tragedy was always about to strike. The therapist her parents had brought her to when she was eight had asked her to name the three things she was most frightened of, and Kate had burst into tears, overwhelmed by having to reduce a world of strangers, spiders, gas leaks, bullies, invisible germs, and violent weather into just three simple fears. She was diagnosed with an anxiety disorder—to the surprise of no one—but also with fantasy-prone disorder. She was simply too imaginative.

What was comforting about George was that he planned everything, down to the little details. Kate still worried—her mind one of those rattling filmstrips that only showed lurid safety films from health class—but her worries would never change George's mind, and it took some pressure off her. For summer holiday after that first year of university, he booked a trip around the Greek islands. They were to fly from London to Athens, then take ferries to Santorini, Crete, and, finally, Rhodes. Kate had only flown once, as a thirteen-year-old, to the Azores, and her parents had promised her afterward that they'd never make her do it again. She remembered the feeling well, the plane taking off and her conviction that death was swallowing her whole. The feeling had gone beyond panic and into the cold vacuum of pure terror. Kate told George about it, told him she didn't think she could fly to Athens, but he'd looked at her calmly and told her he'd already planned it. "It's all booked, Kate," he'd said, his voice telling her that there wasn't going to be a conversation.

In a way, it made things easier. The days leading up to the flight Kate felt like she was moving through air that had solidified into something without oxygen. Her chest ached, and she'd begun chewing the insides of her cheeks again, her mouth constantly tainted by the taste of blood. But she knew she couldn't cancel, simply because it had been booked, and George had booked it, and when he made a plan he stuck with it. And in the end, she took the flight, helped along by several gin and tonics. It was bad, but she survived, and once the plane had safely landed and she had been disgorged into the chaos of Athens International, a giddy sense of possibility came over her. That sense carried over into the entirety of the trip. She thought she'd hate the ferries, but she was okay with them, the open sky and long vistas helping her to relax. It was a happy trip for the first few days, and then George's jealousy and paranoia kicked in.

He'd always been possessive, ever since that first weekend they'd spent together. He'd quiz her regularly on whether she found any of her fellow students attractive. She quickly learned to say no. If they went to a party together—a rare occurrence—Kate learned to talk only to other women, or George would sulk for days. She even learned that if they went to a movie together—something with Brad Pitt, say—that she shouldn't even mention that she found *him* attractive. She learned that the hard way. "He's Brad Pitt. I'd never in a million years meet him, you know."

"And I suppose if you did meet him, you'd just up and fuck him?" George answered.

"Of course not."

"But you find him attractive. Obviously, you want to fuck him, so why wouldn't you if he offered?"

"God, George. I wouldn't be with him because I only want to be with you."

"Then why would you be attracted to him?"

It went on like that for several days, and Kate learned to never mention any man's name—famous or not famous—again.

It got worse in Greece. Maybe it was the beaches, and all that tawny flesh on display. Kate kept her eyes on her book, or off into the blinding distance, but it was impossible to not occasionally glance at the parade of bodies, the men in briefs and the women mostly topless. Kate was self-conscious in her sea-green one-piece, and her pale skin that reddened instead of tanned. One afternoon she found herself watching a teenage girl dart in and out of the Mediterranean. Her bikini bottoms were the color of light brown skin, so that she seemed entirely naked. Even though she was past puberty, she still acted like a young girl, running in and out of the foaming surf. Kate wondered if she'd ever felt that giddy or free, even when she was very young.

That night, at dinner, George, after ten minutes of silence, asked Kate if she was a lesbian. She tried to laugh it off, but George wouldn't let it go, and Kate, for the rest of the trip, tried not to look at anyone.

But the worst incident happened on their last night, in Heraklion, Crete. On the other side of the road from the beach was a long line of competing cafés and restaurants. By late afternoon the restaurants would each send one of their waiters out toward the sidewalk to try to lure the tourists. "Look at the menu," they'd say. "Freshest fish in Heraklion." On the bad night, George and Kate had been coerced into looking at the menu of a pizza place, and then agreed to take a seat outside on the patio. Seating them, the handsome waiter had said: "We'll put the beautiful English lady facing the street so all the men will want to come here." Kate laughed, and to her horror, felt a blush suffuse her cheeks. George got quiet. They ordered a carafe of the terrible Greek wine and a seafood pizza. Halfway through the meal Kate said, "You're not upset about what that waiter said, are you? You know he says that to every woman he seats?"

"So is that why you keep looking at him?" George replied.

"I haven't looked at him once since we sat down, George."

They were silent for the rest of the meal, but continued the conversation later in their inexpensive hotel room three blocks away.

"I would never have brought you to Greece if I'd known what

it would do to you," George said. He was so angry that flecks of spit flew from his lips.

"It's not doing anything to me, George. It's doing something to *you*."

"You're honestly telling me that you're not going to lay in bed tonight dreaming of what it would be like to fuck that Greek waiter. I saw the way you looked at him. Why don't you just go back, go be with him . . ."

"Maybe I will," Kate said, and knew immediately she shouldn't have.

George grabbed her by the shoulders and started to push her toward the door. "Go, then," he shouted, his fingers digging into her sunburned flesh. Not knowing what else to do, Kate stopped resisting and dropped to the uncarpeted floor. She began to sob as George repeatedly punched the wall until a crack appeared and his knuckles were bloody.

"DOES DADDY GET JEALOUS?" KATE asked her mother the first time she saw her after returning from Greece.

"Jealous of what?"

"Of you, and other men?"

"God, no. Why?"

"What about when you were first together? When you were dating?"

"Maybe a little, but only because when I started dating your father I was still stepping out with Robert Christie." She took a sip of her wine. Rain slashed against the glass of the conservatory.

"That must have driven him mad?"

"I don't know about it driving him mad, exactly, but it spurred him to action. He asked me to marry him a lot sooner than I think he would have done otherwise. Not that Robert Christie ever would have asked me to marry him."

"And since then?"

"We're married, darling, and your father's not the jealous type. Why are you asking all these questions?"

Kate told her mother about George's jealous streak. She told her pretty much everything, only omitting the night in Heraklion that ended with him cracking the hotel wall with his fist.

"That doesn't sound good, darling."

"It isn't. I love George, but I feel like I'm walking on eggshells all the time, making sure I don't slip up and mention another man's name."

"That's ludicrous, dear. What does he think, that just because you're together you're not going to find other men attractive?"

"That's exactly what he thinks."

"Good lord, Kate."

"I know, I know. I think I need to end it." It was the first time she'd said these words out loud, and saying them made tears start to roll down her face.

"I think you do, too," her mother said.

IT WASN'T EASY. KATE DECIDED to write a long letter to George, explaining her reasons in detail, and trying her hardest to ensure him about how much he had meant to her. She left the letter under his residence door before leaving for summer vacation. A week later she tried to call him and he didn't pick up. She worried, but knew it was for the best. By August she still hadn't heard a word, and that was when she made her mistake. She posted to Facebook that she was spending a week at her uncle's cottage in Windermere. She simply wrote: "Walking holiday. Lake District. Bliss."

George didn't have a Facebook profile, and even though she did, she rarely posted. It never occurred to her that he might read the post. In retrospect, she knew that she'd been stupid, but what she had really been was hopeful. Hopeful that George was moving on, like she was. But George *did* read her post. He knew the cottage because they'd been there together before, on a minibreak holiday with her family. Years later, Kate wondered how long he'd been in Windermere watching her and following her before he made his appearance. She never sensed him, exactly, although it had been a blustery, dark-skied week, and Kate had had premonitions of death in her troubled sleep. For the first few days of the trip, Kate had shared the cottage with Sadie, her younger cousin, visiting from two villages over. George had probably been watching them, waiting for a moment when Kate was alone. He'd been sleeping rough in a wood nearby. Afterward, after all that had happened, they'd found his tent and a sodden sleeping bag hidden in a copse.

Midway through the week, and the first night that Sadie hadn't slept over in the cottage, Kate woke at just past midnight to find George seated next to her bed, the rifle lying casually across his lap. Kate had opened her mouth to scream and George had leapt on her, his knees on her chest, and pushed the oily barrel of the gun hard against her mouth, splitting her lip and breaking a tooth.

He held her like that on the bed for over an hour, telling her in a strange, flat monotone how she deserved to die for what she'd done to him. The way he spoke, the words he used, felt like they were coming from an entirely different person than the George she had known.

Kate quietly wept the whole time, her mind telling her that the death she'd always feared was now here, crouched on her chest. She didn't try to bargain or appeal to George's humanity. She submitted, her body going limp like a bird caught in the jaws of a cat. Her bladder released and she didn't even realize it till she smelled the sharp smell of her own urine. Her submission probably kept her alive. If she'd fought back, tried to convince George to not kill her, her words would probably have been enough to allow him to pull the trigger. Instead, he dragged her across the floor and pushed her into the small, cramped closet, shutting the door and jamming it with a wooden chair. Maybe he did it because he knew the dark, tight closet was a fate worse than death for Kate. Maybe he did it because after being unable to kill her, George simply wanted Kate out of his sight. Trapped in the closet, Kate began to scream uncontrollably, violently, till her vocal cords were raw. And then she wept until, finally, she stopped weeping, curled into a tight ball, and felt nothing.

It could have been two hours or twelve hours later when she heard the explosion of the rifle on the other side of the closet door.

Two days later, Kate's cousin returned to find her. The front door of the cottage was unlocked, and George's body was on the floor in front of the barricaded closet. The contents of his skull were spread across the rug.

It was the police who pulled Kate from the closet. She was conscious but unresponsive. Her eyes were squeezed shut, so she didn't see the remains of George Daniels as she was carried from the house. She spent three months in rehab—half of that time unresponsive—before she went home to her parents.

She never returned to university.

FIVE MINUTES AFTER SENDING HER mother the e-mail about Audrey Marshall, she received a reply:

> Terrible, darling. Your father and I say come home. Has someone told Corbin?

But it has nothing to do with me, Kate began to write back, then stopped herself. Her fingers rested, unmoving, on the keys of her laptop. She deleted the words. She'd reply to her mother later. She'd reply after she figured out what to do, and she hadn't done that yet. She wanted to stay, and begin her course tomorrow, because Audrey's murder (did she even know it was a murder?) really did have nothing to do with her.

You don't believe that, do you? George's voice, but also her own.

Maybe it has something to do with me. Because it has something to do with Corbin, and I'm in his apartment. The police have been here, and Audrey's friend knew something about what might have happened.

Suddenly, the high-ceilinged apartment felt cramped and too warm. And was it her imagination, or had it turned darker? She turned to the tall windows and saw that an inky cloud had crossed in front of the sun. She watched it continue on its path, till the sun was shining again. Still, the sun was lower in the sky than it should be. She checked the time on her cell phone and discovered it was almost five in the afternoon. How had it gotten so late so fast? She'd been thinking of George, of course, and sometimes when she did that time would slip away. Like it had in the closet when she'd been eaten by the darkness and by time itself. She didn't even think of it as a closet. It had been a room, the smallest room, and she had never left it. It was dark, and all four walls pressed against her.

Go outside, she told herself, and eat a proper meal. And she found herself standing, her head light with lack of food. Before she had too much time to think about it, she grabbed her coat, and an umbrella just in case, and forced herself to leave the apartment.

CHAPTER 10

ALAN HAD BEEN PACING BACK and forth across his apartment, steeling himself to go over and talk with Kate, Corbin's cousin who was staying at his place. He wanted to find out what she knew about Audrey and Corbin, even though he knew that the very act of speaking with her was going to reveal his own interest. He'd already told her that he barely knew Audrey. What would he tell her now? The truth? Part of the truth?

He looked out his window, as he'd been doing all day long. The police had not returned. The courtyard was quiet.

He walked to the mirror that Quinn had hung next to the front door. He rubbed at the skin below his eyes as though he could rub away the dark hollows. He wore his favorite vintage blazer and a knotted cashmere scarf. He'd put the scarf on so long ago—preparing himself to leave—that his neck had gotten sweaty. He took it off. Why would he need a scarf just to go across to another apartment?

He paced back to the window and saw Kate crossing the courtyard toward the street. Without thinking, he bolted to his bedroom, grabbed his wallet, then raced out his own door, taking the stairs down to the lobby three at a time.

By the time he reached the courtyard Kate had disappeared, but when he reached Bury Street he spotted her a block and a half away, making her way toward Charles. He began to follow. It was cooler than he thought, and he regretted taking off his scarf. He buttoned all three buttons on his blazer and turned the collar up. The clouds were building up in the sky again and he wondered if it might rain.

When Kate reached Charles, she stopped for a moment. Alan

slowed his pace. He was only about half a block away, close enough to see that she held a small orange umbrella in her left hand. She turned left. Alan wondered if she was looking for a place to eat, or if she was just taking a walk. Either way, he'd follow her. It would be easier to approach her in a restaurant, pretend that he was also there for dinner. It might look suspicious, but he *did* live in the neighborhood.

Charles Street was quiet, mostly dog walkers and mothers pushing strollers. A man with a stricken face hustled past carrying a bouquet of expensive-looking flowers. A husband who'd forgotten an anniversary, Alan thought. Kate was walking slowly, pausing to look through the windows of the many small bistros that lined this stretch of Charles. She was clearly looking for a place to eat. Alan forced himself to walk slowly as well, pausing at one point in front of an old carriage house that had been converted into a swank residence. He bent and tied his shoe. The brick sidewalk was still wet from an earlier shower, and he could smell an earthy scent, the smell of spring. Winter, always long in New England, had been particularly brutal this past year, dumping over four feet of snow in a two-week stretch at the end of January.

Alan watched Kate cross the street. She was hesitant, looking to the right and left as though she couldn't remember which way the cars would be coming from. Alan followed her across Charles, then up a narrow gaslit side street where she entered a place called St. Stephen's Tavern that Alan had never been to, even though he'd passed it frequently.

He kept walking, not wanting to look like he was following her. She was probably eating, which meant she'd be there for at least an hour. Alan decided he had time for a quick drink down at the Sevens before showing up at St. Stephen's. He walked fast, down the impossibly steep side street, then back onto Charles, where he pushed through the door into the narrow interior of his favorite bar. He ordered a rye and ginger ale, and drank it standing up, elbow perched on the wooden bar.

He was in a state of nervous excitement, he realized, from following this woman he barely knew. What was wrong with him? Maybe his obsession with Audrey had had nothing to do with Audrey herself and everything to do with the fact that he could watch her from afar.

Not for the first time, an uncomfortable memory resurfaced. He'd been thirteen years old, and his sister, sixteen at the time, had a summer job as a camp counselor in Maine. His parents had put him on a bus to visit her one weekend, and he'd been given a spare room in the counselors' area, a row of dorm-style rooms on the second floor of the main lodge. On his first night there, he'd discovered a knothole in one of the planks of wood that allowed him to see into the adjacent bedroom. With his own lights off, he'd watched a female counselor, a chubby girl with small breasts, about his sister's age, undress. She put on an oversized T-shirt with the logo from the camp on it, and got in bed to write in her diary. After only about three minutes of writing, she laid the diary on her chest and, with her lamp still on, began to touch herself between her legs. Alan watched, rapt and fascinated. He knew what masturbation was, and had shamefully done it himself, but hadn't known that it was something girls did. The girl began to rub more furiously, then stopped suddenly, closed her diary, slid it under her bed, and turned off the lamp.

Alan lay in the blackness, straining to hear anything through the pine walls. He thought he could hear the rhythmic squeak of cheap bedsprings, but then it stopped. He heard a long sigh, the girl letting her breath out as though she'd been holding it. Then nothing.

The next day he spotted the counselor in the dining hall at a table with some of the younger campers. He'd barely looked at her face the night before, but he studied it now. It was all circles.

She had full cheeks and round eyes, and Alan even noticed that her small ears, unpierced, were perfectly round as well. She was laughing uproariously at something one of the campers, a girl with red hair, had just said. The girl flushed, and the counselor put her arm around her, pulling her against her side. She was pretty, the counselor, especially when she smiled, and Alan could hardly believe what he had seen her do the night before. It didn't exactly fit in with the way she was acting now.

"You okay there, little brother?"

Alan was eating at the visitor's table, but Hannah, his sister, had come over to see him. "Fine," he said.

"You looked like you'd been hypnotized. You wanna go on a blueberry-picking trip with cabin five today, or would you rather just hang out by the beach?"

Alan picked the beach, bringing a copy of *Red Dragon* that he'd found in the counselors' quarters. He could swim in the shallow, roped-off section of the lake, but since he hadn't taken his deep-water test, he was banned from swimming off the pier. It was fine with him. He was happy to sit on the beach with his book open in front of him, hoping to see the counselor from the adjacent bedroom. He never saw her by the water, but spotted her later giving tennis lessons to several campers and then at dinner, which was an outdoor barbecue. Each time he spotted her he felt a sickening but addictive rush of adrenaline. He could barely wait for nighttime, when he hoped to see her through the knothole again. He told his sister he had a stomachache and got back to his room early. He turned off his light and waited, feverishly imagining what she might do when she returned to her room.

But when she did show up, she grabbed her robe and a shower caddy and disappeared to the showers. When she returned she was wearing her nightshirt under the robe and slipped immediately into her cot. She was less than a foot away from the wall, and Alan could see the fine blond hairs on the tops of her thighs. She took a deep, yawning breath that turned into a coughing fit, then turned the light out. Alan lay back on his bed and listened to hear if she was touching herself again, but he heard nothing. He thought he could smell the faint, stale odor of cigarettes. She began to breathe deeply. Eventually, he fell asleep.

He never saw her again. If she was at breakfast the following morning he couldn't find her, and after breakfast Hannah drove him to the bus station. Alan still remembered the gutted feeling he'd had as the bus chugged away from the station. He would never see the nameless counselor again. She was gone forever.

He finished his drink, paid, and walked out of the Sevens.

Outside, Alan noticed that the trees, starting to blossom, were newly wet. There must have been a passing shower while he'd been in the bar. The air smelled clean, and all the brick sidewalks had darkened.

He walked up the hill toward St. Stephen's and entered through its frosted glass doors, telling himself to look casual and go straight to the bar, which he did. He ordered another rye and ginger from the pretty bartender in a tight Bruins T-shirt, then leaned back a little on the swivel stool and glanced around. St. Stephen's was not a whole lot bigger than the Sevens. There was room enough for a long wooden bar and about a half-dozen booths. At the bar were two men, each drinking stout and each looking at their cell phones. Alan couldn't tell if they were together or simply seated next to one another.

Most of the booths were empty, but one held a husband and wife with their two kids, and at another was a lone woman looking at a laptop. She had dyed red hair, and was so short that her feet dangled from the booth's wooden seat.

Alan turned as the bartender was placing his drink in front of him. He thanked her and took a sip. He drank from his straw, and the first sip was pure alcohol. He stirred the drink and removed the wedge of desiccated lime. There was no sign of Kate. Maybe she'd just come in for a single drink and then left. Or maybe there was a back dining room that Alan couldn't see. He was about to ask the bartender when the ladies' room door swung open with a harsh metallic screech. Alan turned, and there was Kate.

CHAPTER 11

AFTER USING THE DINGY TOILETS, Kate pushed her way back into the restaurant. There, sitting at the bar, was Alan Cherney, looking in her direction. Their eyes met. A warning went off in her head. Had he followed her here? And if so, why?

He swiveled minutely on his bar seat, scrunching his brow as though trying to place her. She stepped forward.

"Hiya," she said.

"Hello," he answered. He wore a beautiful tweed coat, and under it, a shirt with a frayed collar.

"Kate Priddy. I'm in your building. In Corbin Dell's apartment."

"Oh right. Right. I know that. It's Alan."

"Yes, I remember you. You just here for a drink? Is this a place you come to a lot?" Kate inexplicably laughed after asking this question. Whatever ease they had had when they first met had disappeared. Maybe it was because Alan, in the dim light of the tavern, looked like a nervous public speaker facing a massive audience.

"No, no," he said. "I've come here before, maybe once, but not too often. How did you even know about it? I lived here for a year before I found it."

"Corbin recommended it. I'm eating dinner." She indicated with a turn of her head the farthest booth, directly underneath the tavern's lone television, silently showing highlights from a golf match being played somewhere sunny and warm.

"Well, I don't want to interrupt you—"

"No, join me," Kate said, surprising herself. "Unless you have—"

"No, I'd love to."

Alan brought his drink over and sat across from Kate, who was halfway through her second glass of wine. Her bowl of chicken chili had arrived while she'd been in the toilets. It was enormous, on a plate that was festooned with multicolored tortilla chips. "Have you eaten?" Kate asked.

"No, I haven't, but . . ."

"But you took one look at my dinner, and . . ."

Alan laughed. "No, I'm just not that hungry. I keep thinking about Audrey. Remember, we talked about her."

"I know. It's terrible. The police came and talked with me."

"Yeah, me too. Well, they took a statement."

"Did they search your place?"

"No, did they search yours?"

"Briefly."

"Huh." Alan shifted in his seat, crossing his legs under the table and bumping a knee.

Kate then told him about Jack Ludovico, Audrey's friend, who she'd talked to on the street. Alan listened intently, sipping at his drink.

"What did he look like?" Alan asked when Kate had taken a break from talking to eat her rapidly cooling chili.

Kate hesitated. Alan's rapt attention was unnerving somehow. Maybe she shouldn't have invited him to join her. "Only if you tell me why you're so interested," she finally said. "I know you said you barely knew Audrey, but I don't know if I believe you."

She watched as Alan made up his mind. His expressive face seemed to register everything, and Kate wondered if he knew that about himself, knew how easy it was to read him. "Okay," he said. "I didn't actually know Audrey Marshall. We never met, but I could see her through my window in my apartment. I have the place opposite her and we both look over the courtyard, so sometimes I watched her—I know that sounds incredibly creepy, but it wasn't like that. I couldn't see into her bedroom, or anything, but sometimes I watched her reading in her living room. She just seemed very nice."

"You could tell that from looking through a window?"

"No, I couldn't tell that, obviously, but I *thought* that. I imagined that. Look, I do know it's creepy. It *is* creepy. I guess I became a little obsessed with her."

"In what way?"

"What do you mean?"

"In what way did you become obsessed, like what did you imagine might happen?"

Alan pressed his lips together, hard enough that they became colorless. He ran a finger along the rim of his glass. "I imagined that maybe we could meet and be together. That was it. I actually formed a plan that we could run into one another, but then she started seeing your cousin, Corbin."

"Yeah, I heard that. From the friend."

"He knew?"

"He did. Yeah. He said they were an on-and-off thing, and he sounded suspicious of him. I think he thinks Corbin has something to do with what happened."

"What did this guy look like?"

"Who, Jack?"

"Yeah."

Kate described him. His red, unkempt hair, the wiry frame, his flushed skin.

"I don't know him," Alan said. "I never saw him at Audrey's place."

Kate almost responded by saying that that hardly meant he wasn't there, but she stopped herself. Something about Alan's certainty made her realize that he really had been obsessed with Audrey, and had probably spent an enormous amount of time watching her through the window.

"It's possible he didn't spend time at her place," Kate said.

"Yeah, it's possible. I used to see Corbin there, though."

"At Audrey's place?"

"Yeah, that's how I knew they were seeing each other. He used to be over there a lot."

"How'd you know they weren't just friends?"

"I saw them kissing a few times, I guess," Alan said, clearly embarrassed.

"Did you know Corbin?"

"I did, a little," Alan said. "I used to play racquetball with him. Not a lot, but a few times, and one of those times I asked him about Audrey, about whether he was seeing her, and he denied it. It was strange, at the time, because I'd seen them through the window, and knew that there was something between them. I just didn't understand why he would deny it."

"There could have been many reasons," Kate said, having finally had a few bites of her chili, grown cold in the wide bowl. "Maybe he was seeing someone else at the same time, or maybe Audrey was. Who knows, maybe Corbin just thought you were being a nosy git and didn't want to confide in you."

Alan smiled his beautiful smile, so at odds with the gauntness of his face. "Probably that one," he said.

"Which one? The nosy git?"

"Yeah, that one. I don't know. I think I've just gotten paranoid. It seemed shifty at the time that he wouldn't admit to seeing Audrey even though I knew he was."

"So, you suspect Corbin, too? That's what you're saying?"

"When did he leave for London? Exactly?"

"That's what Jack wanted to know. He took a night flight on Thursday night. I don't know what time exactly, but he got to London early in the morning, so, in theory . . ."

"In theory he could have killed Audrey."

"I suppose so."

"And the police seem interested," Alan said, then tilted his glass to get the last sip of his drink. "They searched your place—his place. What's it like, anyway, his place?"

"Like something from a design magazine, but dated. It was his father's apartment—that's why he's living there."

"I didn't know that."

A waitress swung by to see if they needed anything else. Alan ordered another drink and Kate asked for a water. "My jet lag's been terrible," she said. "I've lost all sense of time since I've been here. I'm exhausted all afternoon and wide awake before dawn."

"Quick. What time is it now?" Alan asked, a slight smile on his face.

"It feels like midnight, but I think it's only around six."

Alan pulled his phone out of his pocket and looked at its screen. "It's just past six." He put his phone down on the scarred wooden table and Kate noticed that his screen image was the purple and black movie poster from *The Exorcist*. It was one of her favorite films, but she didn't say anything. She'd always loved horror movies, despite the traumas of her past and her own fervid imagination. They calmed her, in the same way that genuine apprehension calmed her. And they showed her that nightmares existed for other people, as well, even if those other people were fictional. Alan's screen went to black, and Kate realized she'd been staring at it.

"I'm fading," Kate said. "I think I'll go back soon. I'm not trying to run away from you."

"That's okay if you are," Alan said, and grinned. "I'd understand."

"Why do you say that?"

"Because I just told you how I used to spy on my neighbor through my window and became obsessed with her."

"No. I really am tired. And I wouldn't judge anyone for being obsessive. I've been thinking about Audrey Marshall ever since I got here."

"Because she was murdered in the apartment next to yours."

"No, even before that. When I first heard she was missing, I knew something bad had happened. Well, I always think that—it's my nature—but I was right this time."

The waitress appeared with Alan's drink and asked them if they wanted anything else. Kate asked for a check, then Alan did as well.

"Can I walk back with you?" Alan asked.

Kate pictured the long narrow street that led from the tavern back to the well-lighted busyness of Charles Street. Was Alan a murderer? He'd clearly been obsessed with Audrey. And from afar. But if he was, then why come to her and confess all that he'd confessed? Was it to get information? Find out what she knew?

"It's totally fine if—" Alan started to say, as though reading Kate's mind.

"No, we can walk back together. Sorry, I'm spacing out."

After paying their separate checks, they exited onto the dark street, Alan leaving half his drink behind. The rain had stopped but the trees still dripped, and the sidewalk was covered with fallen magnolia blossoms, the air heavy with their cloying smell.

If we get to the end of this street, and Alan hasn't strangled me, then he never will, Kate told herself. She began to count the steps silently to herself, but Alan said, as though reading her mind, "I had nothing to do with what happened to Audrey."

"I know," Kate said.

"Do you think I should go to the police and tell them what I know?"

"You mean, what you know about Corbin?"

"Yeah."

"You should, probably, unless Corbin already told them. It's not as though you have crucial information. You might just have information they already have. I'll find out for you. I'm definitely e-mailing Corbin tonight. I was putting it off because I didn't know whether he'd heard from the police yet or not."

"You'll let me know?"

"I will," Kate said. They were halfway down the steep side street, Kate walking slowly in her boots because of the slipperiness of the fallen blossoms and the recent rain. She imagined herself falling, sliding onto Charles Street and getting crushed by some huge American SUV. But they made it all the way down and walked the rest of the way back to Bury Street. They talked some of the way, and Kate felt again the same ease with Alan that she'd felt the first time they'd met, as though they'd known each other for years and years. She reminded herself that she'd once felt the same thing for George Daniels.

They parted ways in the lobby of the building, Kate promising to let Alan know what she found out from Corbin.

"Come by my apartment and let me know. You know where I live." He smiled, a little crookedly.

"Is your side the exact same as my side?"

"Exactly." They said goodbye.

Sanders the cat was in the lobby, and he followed Kate up the stairs and down the hall to her door. She opened the door fractionally and placed her foot near the jamb to block him, but he quickly leapt over her foot and into her apartment. She entered and shut the door behind her. The cat was nowhere to be seen, but she decided to not worry about him; it was clear that he belonged to the entire apartment building.

She went straight to her laptop and opened her e-mail account. Corbin had written her:

Just heard about what happened from the police. I'm totally shocked. I didn't know her that well, but I knew her, of course, a little bit. Do you know what happened? The police only told me that she was dead. Was it a suicide? And how are you doing? I'm

sorry that your first few days in America have been stressful, and I
understand if you want to come back. It must be scary to arrive in
a new place and find out that your neighbor has died. Trust me, it's
a safe apartment building.

Not that it matters much, but I'm loving my time in London, and
your flat is in good hands. Write to me with any news. Sorry, again.
Corbin

Kate read it twice. Why would he deny that he had been involved with Audrey Marshall? Why didn't he use her name?

Before writing him back, Kate looked through her other
e-mails. Mostly junk, but there was one from Martha Lambert,
who lived on the first floor of her building in London. When Kate
had first moved in—nearly a year ago—Martha had immediately
assigned herself the role of new best friend. Kate hadn't minded,
even though Martha's sole interests were going to the pub and
landing a man. When Kate moved to London she'd been determined to be a little bit social, and Martha, with her constant in-
vites, had at least made that part easy. Her e-mail, not surprisingly,
was about Corbin:

Miss you, Kate, but I am v pleased with your replacement. He's
gorgeous, as you know. You should have seen Michael's jaw drop
when he saw him down the pudding. He's friendly, too, but I won't
go too much into that right now. How is it over there? What's his
flat like? Kisses, darling, I really do miss you. Martha

Kate opened up a reply window and stared at it for a minute, not
knowing what to write. Should she warn her? Something moved
in the periphery of her vision, and her heart stutter-stepped. It was
Sanders, returning to the room from his tour of the premises. He
sat back on his haunches and looked quizzically at Kate.

"He's not here," she said aloud.

To her surprise, Sanders answered back, a querulous meow.

She got up and went and opened the front door, and Sanders pranced off, brushing his tail against her leg on the way out. She shut the door and pressed her eye against the peephole to see where the cat went, but he was already gone from the hallway.

She returned to the e-mails. Should she tell Martha to be wary of Corbin? She should, of course, but she knew Martha well enough to know that it would totally fall on deaf ears. Instead she wrote:

> Don't you dare do anything in my bed, that's all I ask. Boston is nice, and Corbin's flat is bigger than mine. More later. Still jet-lagged. Kate

She didn't want to say too much more about the flat. If Martha knew how rich Corbin was, her predatory instincts would become even more heightened.

Kate opened up a response box to Corbin, then paused. What should she tell him? She decided to tell him the basic truth, leaving out what she'd heard from Alan, leaving out Alan altogether. So she wrote him back, telling him that the police had asked to search his place and she'd agreed, and she mentioned the key. This information, at least, would give him a chance to let Kate know that he didn't want the police in his apartment without a warrant. She hit send. It would be past midnight in London, and she wondered if Corbin was even up.

Before putting her laptop away, Kate searched for any new information on the death of Audrey Marshall. She found a story that indicated that the body removed from 101 Bury Street had been positively identified as Audrey Helen Marshall, and that her death was being treated as suspicious by the police.

Kate finally put her laptop away after clicking on several other news stories that all had the same, limited information. She went to the bedroom and got her datebook. Even though she knew that her first design class in Cambridge began the following day at one in the afternoon, she double-checked it. She'd already decided to leave early, give herself time to figure out the public transportation, and how to get to the school from the Porter Square T station. She sat on the edge of the bed, exhausted suddenly, but instead of leaning back, tucking herself up under the covers, and going to sleep, she grabbed the Dick Francis she'd started earlier, plus her well-worn copy of *I Capture the Castle,* a book she'd read many times.

She brought both of the books, plus the quilted comforter, across the expanse of the apartment to the leather couch in the den. She stretched out and opened the Dick Francis novel. She read one paragraph, then her eyes closed, the book still propped on her chest.

She was back in Audrey's apartment, and Alan was there, crouched on the floor, his head tilted up and back, and looking at her. *That's not Alan,* Kate thought. *That must be George.* But it *was* Alan. His fingers dug at the floor of Audrey's apartment, as though he was trying to find something buried in the wood. He opened his mouth, and a cat's meow came out. He dug some more, his nails making plucking sounds against the floor. Then he meowed again, louder, almost a keening sound. Kate woke with a jolt, both books sliding with the comforter to the floor.

Sanders was back in the apartment, scratching at the couch's arm.

CHAPTER 12

CORBIN DELL EMERGED FROM THE taxicab into the cool air of late morning. It wasn't raining but the atmosphere was damp, the sky low and white. Corbin hadn't been to London since the spring semester of his junior year, which he'd spent at the Hutchinson School of Business and Economics, and because of that, he wasn't sure how he'd feel arriving back in this haunted city. But he felt okay. Tired, because he'd only slept for about one hour during the flight from Boston to Dublin. He'd drunk some bad coffee during the lengthy layover and now he was jittery and slightly nauseous, his mouth coated with a bitter taste. The outside air was nice after the long ride from Heathrow.

The driver removed Corbin's matching luggage from the cab and placed it on the sidewalk. Sheepscar Lane was long and gray, the sidewalks lined with pollarded trees. Workmen were fixing a portion of the road, and the air smelled sharply of warm tar. It was that smell, more than anything else, that brought London flooding back. As a student, Corbin had lived in Camden Town, also in North London, and that sticky, slightly sweet smell of tar had always been in the air. He'd forgotten all about it. He felt twenty years old again, walking back in a cold dawn from Claire's flat on the other side of Regent's Park, having finally lost his virginity. He had been happy, exhilarated almost, but the memory of it was painful, for so many reasons. Maybe he shouldn't have come back after all, Corbin thought.

Kate's flat was in a squat stone building with a patch of front garden large enough for one midsized bush. The trim was white, and the front door was painted a deep shade of blue, edged by small panes of glass. There were three mailboxes affixed to the inside of the entryway, and Corbin pulled the envelope from the box for apartment 2. He could feel the contours of the key inside. He slipped it out, opened the outside door, and hauled his giant Victorinox suitcase over the threshold into a narrow, high-ceilinged foyer. When the outside door rattled shut behind him, it was dark inside, even with the multiple small windows. Corbin found a switch; it turned on a hanging lamp that cast a yellow light. The floor of the foyer was covered in black and white linoleum and the walls were thickly painted in a light blue. He carried his luggage up the steep stairwell to the second-floor entrance and walked into the flat.

Kate had described the place in one of her e-mails, but the layout was still surprising. The exterior door opened into the bedroom, then a short stairway led to the bathroom, halfway up the stairs, while the rest of the rooms, a kitchen and a bay-fronted living room, were located at the top of the stairs. There were windows overlooking the street from the living room, and windows down the stairs in the bedroom that looked out over a paved back patio, but that was it, since the building was attached on either side. It should have felt claustrophobic, but it didn't to Corbin. It felt comforting, almost, and it was decorated, not in a feminine way, but in a way that seemed cozy. There were throw rugs in bright colors and large pillows on both the bed and the living room couch. The walls were painted white and hung with graphic prints.

Corbin used the bathroom, then unpacked all his clothes, putting them in an empty drawer that had been marked with a sticky note from Kate, indicating that it had been emptied for him. He thought of showering, but he was too tired. A low, throbbing headache was starting up in his temples, and his shoulders and neck were stiff from the flight. He swallowed four ibuprofens. The tap water was terrible, and he made a mental note to buy a case of bottled water as soon as possible. He stripped out of all his clothes but his boxer briefs and his T-shirt and stretched out on the living room couch with Kate's long, handwritten letter. Annoyance flared up inside of him that she had taken time to write out a comprehensive guide to the neighborhood pubs and restaurants. He was only annoyed, though, because he hadn't done something similar. Well, he could write her an e-mail and suggest some places. And he'd left her that bottle of champagne in the fridge—that would count for something. Besides, wait till she saw his place. She'd be impressed, he was sure of that.

Kate would be on the plane now, pocketed somewhere above the Atlantic. He tried to picture her, but had trouble. He'd only seen a couple of photographs of her before, both from a few years ago. One was a photo that his father had taken during a trip to England a year before he died. He'd gone over for a large family wedding. Corbin remembered that he'd tried to talk both Corbin and his brother, Philip, into coming. Philip never would have come because it would have disappointed their mother, and Philip would never do anything to disappoint her. Corbin hadn't gone because of work. When Richard Dell returned, he'd printed the digital pictures he'd taken and cut them into the size of regular photographs to fit them into an album. Richard showed Corbin the book, pointing out myriad English relatives. That was when Corbin had first seen Kate, bracketed on either side by her father and her mother, Richard's cousin. "My favorite cousin," he told Corbin. "We were more like brother and sister, really, and this girl, this Kate, is the spitting image, the, the . . ."

He trailed off. Richard had retired a few years after the divorce, and since retiring, he'd aged noticeably. Not just physically, although there was that, but mentally. He seemed frail, and even sometimes weepy.

"Maybe I should never have left," Richard said, after they'd looked at every picture.

"Well, then—"

"Well, then, yes, I'd never have had you lovely boys, but your mother . . ."

Corbin didn't need to hear about her. He'd heard plenty already.

The only other picture Corbin had seen of Kate was one that was attached to her e-mail account, a small square color photograph in which Kate's face was three-quarters obscured by a book she was reading. Only her eyes peered at the camera.

There must be pictures here, Corbin thought, and almost got off the couch. There's time, he told himself. I'm here for six whole months, he thought, and the thought scared him a little. He yawned several times, his jaw popping. A spatter of rain hit the pane of glass above him. He fell asleep.

He woke, as he always did, suddenly—his eyes opening on their own, his mind fully conscious, any dreams he might have had already expunged and gone, like blackened matches. He sat up. The headache was gone, but in its place was a ravenous hunger. He checked his phone. It was midafternoon.

He went to the kitchen, found an apple, and devoured it till it was nothing more than a pencil-thin core. He opened drawers looking for something else to eat, but there was very little. Everything in the kitchen was small, including a refrigerator not much bigger than a dorm fridge, a tiny porcelain-topped table pushed into a nook, and what looked like a dishwasher but turned out to be, in fact, a laundry machine. Corbin looked, but couldn't find a dryer. It was something he could ask Kate about in an e-mail. He should check his account, anyway, especially since he hadn't heard yet from the office he was supposed to be reporting to on Monday. He went back to the living room and found the part in Kate's welcome letter where she gave him instructions on how to get onto wireless. He opened his laptop and checked messages, his mind rapidly seeking out Audrey Marshall's name even though he knew that a message from her wasn't a possibility. His brother had written to ask him when he was heading to London, because his mother wanted to know.

Corbin checked the Red Sox box scores from the night before, then jotted off a message to Kate, thanking her for the lengthy letter and mentioning the dryer. Then he shut the laptop down, got dressed again, and went out to find some food.

It wasn't even four thirty yet, but the Beef and Pudding, the closest pub and one that Kate had recommended, was filling up. Corbin grabbed an upholstered bench with a low table in front of it, waited for a few minutes for a waitress to appear, then remembered than in England you ordered at the bar. He left his jacket on his seat and shouldered his way into the crowded bar area. He ordered a Guinness Extra Cold, and when he asked about food, was directed to a large blackboard, menu items written out in green chalk. He ordered a spaghetti Bolognese and went back to his seat.

He nursed his Guinness and when the food came he ate it as slowly as he could, even though what he wanted to do was to bolt it like a dog. Done eating, he went back to the bar for more beer, deciding to try cask ales he hadn't tasted before. He sat back down with something called Greene King Abbot Ale, and had finished half of it when a woman in tight jeans and a patterned sweater said hello and asked if he was Kate Priddy's cousin. "I was next to you at the bar and heard your American accent. I live upstairs from you."

They had several drinks together and she introduced him to some of the bartenders, plus a few of her friends. Her name was Martha, and every time she went to the bathroom, she came back with reapplied bright red streaks of lipstick across her mouth. He kept drinking the Abbot Ale and she drank white wine, switching to something with vodka at the end of the night. They walked home together through a light, misty rain, and outside of 684 Sheepscar they wound up pressed up against a temporary Dumpster, kissing and groping at one another. She bit the lobe of his ear and told him she liked his accent. He slid fingers down the back of her jeans and touched the thin floss of her underpants, and that, more than anything else, sobered him up. He could feel that combination of fear and disgust spreading across his body. And even though he knew there was little chance that someone was watching them, it was still in the back of his mind. The way it always was.

It took all his will not to push the drunk girl away. Instead, he stopped kissing her.

"I'm exhausted," he said.

"You must be, poor thing," she answered. Her mouth was ringed with smudged lipstick, and her eyes were slightly out of focus. Corbin could hear the sound of distant laughter carrying through the rain; other drunk people returning from a night out. A drip of cool rain slid underneath his collar and down his back, and he shivered. Then, for one awful moment, he could taste the spaghetti at the back of his throat, and he thought he was going to be sick. It passed, and he told Martha that he really needed to get some sleep. They entered the house together, and Martha kissed him again on his landing. He kept his lips tightly closed even though he could feel the tip of her tongue flicking past her teeth.

Inside, he chugged some of the tepid water in the kitchen and took four more ibuprofens. He actually wasn't tired. He'd slept too much that afternoon, and now, even though it was midnight in London, it wasn't even eight o'clock yet in Boston. Kate would be at his place by now, probably trying to stay awake. He tried to picture her in his apartment in Boston, but couldn't. It felt wrong, somehow.

After doing a hundred push-ups on the orange area rug in the bedroom, Corbin took a shower, carefully stepping over the high lip of the bathtub, then standing under the stream of almost-hot water. He closed his eyes, letting the low-pressure spray hit the back of his neck, and stood so long that the water eventually lost its warmth. He was shivering by the time he pulled on his cotton pajama bottoms and got under the covers of Kate's bed. The sheets were soft flannel, tucked tightly under the corners of the bed, and he kicked his feet out from under them. It was the only way he could sleep, even when he was cold. The bed was softer than he liked. He turned off the bedside lamp, but the room, with the curtains open, was relatively light, and his eyes eventually adjusted so much that he could read the print on the framed poster across from the bed. THE FACE IN THE CORNER: ANIMAL PORTRAITS, NATIONAL PORTRAIT GALLERY, LONDON, 1998. There was a painting of a lady, and in the foreground, a black cat dipping a paw into a goldfish bowl. He thought of Sanders, the cat that was always in his apartment. Thinking of Sanders made him think of everything he'd left behind, but he shut down those thoughts. Instead, he closed his eyes, trying to will himself to sleep. Despite the shower, he could still smell Martha, the girl from the pub, all over him. He thought of her upstairs, now, wondering if she was thinking of him. Of course she was. He could go upstairs right now and fuck her if he wanted to. The thought filled him with sadness, more than anything. He pictured her drunken, excited expression as she opened the door, the way she'd lift her hips to let him take off her tiny underpants, the awful expectant look in her eyes. Then he imagined the look of fear in those eyes.

He turned the thought off as he shifted over onto his stomach. He pressed his face into the unfamiliar pillow that smelled of floral dryer sheets. He hadn't had a thought like that for a while. Maybe it was being in London. Maybe coming here had been a big mistake. He'd thought fifteen years had been enough time, but clearly it wasn't. She'd been on his mind all day. So he allowed himself to think of her, to think of Claire Brennan, the girl who changed everything.

CHAPTER 13

THE HUTCHINSON SCHOOL OF BUSINESS and Economics, where Corbin Dell studied during the second semester of his junior year, was situated in an ugly block of Georgian flats just south of the Mornington Crescent tube station. The school also owned and operated the Three Lambs pub, a wood-paneled drinking hole in the student union. It was there that Corbin met Claire Brennan, who was serving that night at the bar.

"What's good here?" he'd shouted above the overloud Coldplay song coming from the speakers.

She pushed a strand of her raven-black hair behind an ear and leaned across the bar. "Sorry. What'll you have?"

Corbin almost asked her again what was good but her cold blue eyes stopped him. He glanced across the beer pumps, selecting one at random.

"Pint or half?" she asked. Her accent was thick and lilting.

"Half," Corbin said, not knowing what it even meant.

After being served, Corbin sipped at his small glass of malty-tasting liquid. It was his second night in London. He'd gone to an orientation earlier that day with other visiting American students. Most of the orientation had been centered on how to find a flat in the city, and afterward, the other American students, gripping their list of real estate agents, had anxiously formed small groups to hunt for lodging. Corbin already had a place to stay, however, so he walked out of the orientation not having met anyone. His father had set him up in the spare room of a friend's apartment. It was a tiny flat on the third floor of a narrow brick building on a residential street south of the river. The spare bedroom was closer in size to a closet, and judging by the sparse furnishings in the rest of the flat—a stereo system, a loaded bar, a bed with satin sheets in the master bedroom—it was clear that the flat was probably nothing more than a sex hideaway for his father's business colleague. "He's never there," his dad had said. "You'll have your own bachelor pad in London."

Corbin hated the place already, and had gone to the Three Lambs in hopes of meeting other students. After getting his drink he leaned against the bar and surveyed the room, half populated with students, most in groups of three or four. He noticed, with a stab of shame, that the only students with small glasses of beer were female students, and that all the men had full pint glasses. He felt sudden, deep hatred for the bartender for even asking him what size glass he wanted. It should have been obvious he'd wanted a full pint glass.

He turned his back to the room and drank the warm beer down in two gulps. The bartender was now serving three male students, all of whom were getting pint glasses of Foster's. Corbin decided to get one of those as well. He waited patiently for her to serve the other men. She kept dumping the foam off the top of the beer and refilling them. When she was finally done, she turned her attention to Corbin and he ordered a Foster's as well, adding that he'd like a big glass. She'd smiled at that, and Corbin felt the urge to punch her in the teeth.

He took the Foster's—so much better than the other beer—to a high stool along a paneled wall near the bar, and tried to look bored and uncaring. He scanned the room, not recognizing any of the students as Americans. There was a lull at the bar, and the bartender came out to pick up the empty glasses scattered around on tables. Coming back past Corbin, she stopped and asked if he was American.

"I'm a visiting student, yeah," he said.

"D'you know anyone looking for a room in a flat? I have a friend who's looking to sublet out a room."

"Where?"

"Camden. Not far from here."

Corbin told her that he might be interested, that he had a place already but hated it. He told her it was his dad's friend's sex flat, and made up that it was filled with dildos and bowls of condoms. The bartender threw her head back and laughed, exposing her creamy white throat. "You'll look at this other flat, then?" she asked.

Corbin agreed, was given an address, and by the second day of classes had moved into an equally scuzzy apartment that was at least a lot closer to his school. He shared the flat with a morose Irish girl, whose main advantage was that she was never there, and when she was, she was in her bedroom, weeping on the phone. The other advantage was that she was an acquaintance of the dark-haired, blue-eyed bartender, whose name was Claire Brennan, and after the brief conversation at the Three Lambs, Corbin's initial hatred had turned into a deep infatuation.

Before coming to London, Corbin had told himself that there was no way he was going to get romantically involved with anyone while overseas. The previous semester—his first of junior year— he'd been seeing a freshman girl named Sarah Scharfenberg, who lived down the hall in his dorm. She was a rarity at Mather, a midwestern girl who didn't spend freshman orientation week trying to fuck every frat brother she met. She told him she was practically a virgin and wanted to take it slow. It was okay with him. He even drove her to see his mother's home in New Essex on a weekend when he knew none of his family would be there. She'd been impressed. He'd loved seeing the expression on her face as she took in the enormous house, the view of the ocean, his mom's art collection.

Back in his dorm that night, she'd produced a condom and whispered into his ear: "I want to make love with you. Right now." The words sounded rehearsed, and her voice theatrically breathy. They stripped naked, but all Corbin felt was disgust. In the bad dorm lighting she suddenly looked cheap and pudgy, and Corbin noticed a discolored tooth he'd never seen before. He couldn't get hard and told her that he wasn't in the mood. She made it worse by repeatedly telling Corbin that it was okay. She even tried to rub his neck.

He'd stopped seeing her after that, although on the last night of first semester, he'd gotten drunk and pounded on her dorm-room door. He'd decided to give her what she wanted, after all. Her roommate answered, told Corbin that she was probably spending the night at her boyfriend's dorm. The way the roommate looked at him it was pretty clear that she'd heard the whole story. "Fucking whore," Corbin said before going to his own room to pass out.

And now he was in London, where he'd already decided to have nothing to do with girls and sex, and where he'd already fallen for Claire Brennan.

She was easy to find, because she worked most nights at the Three Lambs. Corbin would casually swing by, usually by himself. It turned out that he and Claire were in the same class—Intro to Macroeconomics—and some nights he'd bring a textbook, and they'd talk about it together, Corbin drinking Foster's and Claire drinking wine behind the bar. Even though she was Corbin's age, twenty, she seemed grown-up and sophisticated in a way that American girls didn't. For one, she was working to put herself through school, and she despised most of the American students, who came over each semester and boozed their way through their three months in London. "Not you, Corbs," she said. "You're one step up from those arseholes, but a very small step." She held two fingers minutely apart, a wide grin on her face.

They rarely saw each other outside of the Three Lambs and the one class they shared, but with the first exam coming up, they wound up studying together at Claire's place in Queen's Park. It was a tiny studio flat, big enough for a bed, a desk, and a chair. They studied on the bed together. "Just sleep here," she'd said, when they'd finally decided to quit. It was past one in the morning, and the Underground was no longer running.

"I can get a taxi," Corbin said.

"Don't be an idiot"—she pronounced it like *eejit*—"just stay here."

"I kind of made a pledge to myself that I wasn't going to get involved with anyone while I was here in London."

She laughed. "Jesus, it's not like that."

They fell asleep without touching each other, but just past dawn, they wordlessly began to kiss, and before Corbin had a chance to tell her that he really meant what he said about becoming involved, they were having sex. It happened so fast that Corbin didn't have time to think about it, didn't have time to panic. Afterward, they kissed more, and Claire fell back asleep. Corbin didn't tell her that it was his first time.

Walking home through the cold, dewy morning, he'd felt not just elated, but somehow vindicated. It hadn't been *him*. It had been the string of pathetic, inexperienced girlfriends he'd had that had been the real problem. He'd just needed to find a real woman, and he'd finally found one.

He aced the exam—no surprise there—and continued seeing Claire, their relationship completely different from anything Corbin had experienced before. For one, they rarely talked about what was happening between them, not because Corbin didn't want to, but because she didn't. Anytime he'd bring up their situation, she'd make a joke or call him an idiot. Corbin became fixated on what she was thinking, obsessing over the smallest of clues that might indicate her frame of mind. It made him angry with himself, but at the same time, he knew he was in love. He told her once, drunkenly, after returning from a school-sponsored booze cruise on the Thames. It had begun to pour on their walk home, and they'd ducked under the awning of a closed bakery and stood kissing.

"You reek of beer," she said.

"I love you," he responded.

She laughed, not entirely unkindly, then had ferociously kissed him. "You're my favorite American," she said, laughing some more.

"Thanks," Corbin said, telling himself to never again let her know how he felt.

He didn't, and the relationship—at least that was what Corbin was calling it in his own head—continued up until the final week of that term. Corbin fretted over the state of their affair, wondering if he should ask her if she wanted to visit him in America during the summer break. But before he'd steeled himself to initiate that conversation, everything changed. It was a Thursday, and Corbin was nursing a pint at a large anonymous pub near where he lived and rereading one of his texts, when Henry Wood, another American student in his program, came up to his table.

"You studying?" Henry asked.

"Yeah." Corbin held up the cover of the book.

"The classes here are ballbusters, eh?"

"Yeah, they are," Corbin said.

Corbin hadn't gotten to know too many fellow students during his time in London, but he'd gotten to know Henry, because everyone knew Henry. He was one of those effortless socializers, someone who remembered everyone's name, someone who always kept the conversation going. Shortly after orientation week he'd thrown a party at his rental, a sprawling ground-floor flat in Hampstead. It was a cold, raw night, but Henry had strung lights in the shared garden and even somehow purchased a keg. It wasn't just Americans at the party but English neighbors as well, sudden lifelong friends that Henry had made during his short time in London.

It had begun to snow that night, small white crystals that melted as soon as they touched a surface, but everyone stayed, huddled in the fenced-in garden till long past midnight. The first two hours of the party were awkward for Corbin, but the beer kicked in, and before he knew it, it was two in the morning and he was talking college football with a girl from the University of Richmond and a beefy student from Baylor who had his bare, tattooed arm draped over the shoulders of the girl. Corbin excused himself, deciding it was time to leave. He wandered back into the flat, looking down a side hall for a bathroom. Henry was in the frame of his bedroom door, an unlit cigarette between his lips. Corbin generally hated long hair on men, but Henry's dark hair—two inches below his shoulders, at least—suited him. He was on the short side, strong looking through the chest and shoulders, and with small facial features. Corbin thought of a fox, anthropomorphized, cocky and handsome.

The bathroom door swung open and a tall redhead in a short skirt emerged. She brushed past Corbin on the way to Henry's bedroom, trailing a hand across Henry's shirt as she entered.

Henry smiled, the cigarette still between his lips, and cocked his head toward the interior of the bedroom, raising an eyebrow. Corbin was confused for a moment, then realized that Henry was asking him to join them. Casually, Corbin held up both hands and shook his head. He could feel the blood rushing to his face and ducked into the bathroom. When he emerged Henry's bedroom door was shut.

Corbin had seen Henry several times since the party, and there was never any indication that Henry remembered the incident in the hallway. Corbin began to doubt what he'd seen. Had he really been asked into the bedroom for a threesome? The details of the night had blurred and now he wasn't so sure. But every time Corbin saw Henry, he felt a click of anxiety in his chest and found himself stumbling over his words. Not that he needed to say much in the presence of Henry, who liked to talk and prided himself on knowing everything about everyone. Corbin tried to convince himself that Henry was a boorish attention seeker, but every time they were together he found himself hoping to please Henry in some way. With a joke, or by telling Henry something he didn't already know. And when that happened, Corbin felt an embarrassing surge of pride. He wondered if other people felt the same way.

Henry, surprisingly, was alone in the pub, and even though Corbin was half panicked in anticipation of his Game Theory exam, he was happy to see him and invited him to sit down.

"You know, I can help you with that exam," Henry said, sprawling on a chair across from Corbin, pint glass in his hand.

"You're not in this class, are you?"

"No, but I got the scoop on it. Same exam every year. Your professor never, ever changes it. Wanna know the questions?"

"Sure."

Henry told Corbin what he'd heard, apparently from a student who'd come to this program the year before. "I memorized all the questions, then ended up not taking the class because it filled up. So that'll help you out, right?"

"You positive about this?"

"Ninety percent sure. Ninety-five percent. Don't worry, dude. Let's have another pint."

Corbin went and bought a round. The questions did sound legit; all of them were around subjects that Professor Hinchliffe—one of those old men with a spiderweb of broken veins on each cheek—had expounded on at length. Corbin decided to trust Henry—it would make his life a lot easier.

Corbin put the book away, and he and Henry had several pints. It was the longest amount of time they'd ever spent in each other's company.

"Where've you been all term?" Henry asked.

Corbin, who didn't think he'd exactly been hiding, said, "I didn't need housing during that first week so I didn't really meet anyone right off the bat. I've been hanging with some of the English students."

"Traitor. You know you're not supposed to meet anyone foreign during your foreign studies program."

"I didn't get that memo."

"No? It's a requirement. Come to Europe as an asshole, make sure you don't meet anyone but other American students, and then return as an even bigger asshole. Spend senior year beginning stories with the words, 'When I was in Europe last summer . . .' Hey, you traveling this summer after classes end?"

"No, I wish," Corbin said. "I have an internship in New York. Starts first week of June."

"Hey, no way. Me too. Where?"

They compared notes on their summer internships. They were at different companies but on the same block in Midtown Manhattan.

"Excellent, dude," Henry said. "We'll be best friends. I already know what bar we should hang out at."

As they discussed the various bars and restaurants they knew in New York City, the phrase *best friends* echoed in Corbin's head. He knew that Henry was just using the words casually, but Corbin, although he'd always had friends, felt he'd never had a best one. He could picture Henry and himself haunting the same bars every night, meeting up without making plans in advance.

"It'll be epic," Henry said. "I mean, I love London, but we need a break, don't you think? Drink in cocktail lounges instead of pubs, meet some tanned women."

They laughed together, then each took a sip of his beer. Henry leaned in, dropped his voice a little.

"You know, Corbs, I think you and I have something in common."

"Oh yeah?"

"Claire Brennan." Henry smiled, lips spreading thinly over his teeth.

"Yeah, I know Claire." Corbin felt like he'd just swallowed a tennis ball.

"Yeah, I know you do. Intimately, I believe."

"Why?" Corbin asked.

"Yeah, I thought that was the case. It seems she's been two-timing the both of us."

"What do you mean?"

"Exactly what you think I mean. Jesus, look at you. Don't have a heart attack, dude."

CHAPTER 14

"Is that why you came over here to talk with me? Because of Claire?" Corbin asked, some time later.

Henry paused. "No, I just came over to talk. I did think I'd bring up the Claire situation, though. Seemed the right thing to do."

Corbin had regained some composure since Henry had dropped his bombshell about Claire. The sickening gut-wrench of betrayal had been replaced by a mounting feeling of rage. Henry shared the feeling.

"Bitch lied to us both," he said.

They'd gone back over events in their own personal time-lines, trying to figure out how she'd gotten away with it exactly. It turned out that Henry and Claire had first hooked up over a month earlier when Corbin had gone for a long weekend to Amsterdam to meet up with two of his Mather friends. Henry, like Corbin, had met Claire at the Three Lambs. He'd asked her out for dinner, and she'd agreed. The dinner had gone well, and Henry had been seeing her off and on for the past few weeks.

"How often do you see her?" Corbin asked.

"We have a standing date on Tuesday nights."

"I have my seminar on Tuesday nights."

"And Sunday afternoons we sometimes go to a pub on the river."

"She told me she always spends Sunday catching up on her studies."

"We got duped, buddy," Henry said, shaking his head. "Did she tell you to not act like her boyfriend in the Three Lambs? That she didn't want people there to know she was dating a customer?"

"Yep. She told me that. Jesus."

Henry finished his current pint in one long sip, then wiped his lips with the back of a hand. His lips curled slightly on one side, as though he were enjoying himself.

"You don't seem as upset as I am," Corbin said.

"I am, trust me. I've just had a lot longer to think about it, and now I'm more pissed than upset."

"How did you find out?"

Henry explained how he'd accidentally spotted Claire the previous Saturday night, coming out of the Camden tube station. He'd waved at her but she hadn't spotted him. She was in a rush, and on a whim, Henry had followed her, along the market stalls and to an Indian restaurant. Corbin was waiting outside, and they had kissed on the street.

"And you didn't tell her?" Corbin asked.

"I gave her a chance to tell me. I saw her the next day and asked if we were exclusive, and she said, yes, that she hoped so. That's when I got angry instead of just disappointed. And I decided I'd just stop seeing her, not give her a reason, and make her stew over it. And then I saw you here tonight. I almost didn't tell you, you know. I mean, you never would have found out, and maybe it wouldn't have made any difference in the big scheme of things. But you seem like a nice guy, and I figured you should know."

"I'm glad you told me. I feel like a fucking idiot."

"You're not an idiot. You just trusted a woman. I'm serious. Don't ever do it again."

"I won't."

"So what are we going to do?" Henry asked.

"What do you mean?"

Henry was playing with his empty pint glass, turning it upside down and making damp rings on the wooden table. "What are we doing to do to get back at her? Ball's in our court. She has no idea that we know."

"That's true."

Henry jumped up. "One more pint, okay, then we'll figure out the best way to fuck her up." He went to the bar before Corbin could answer.

THEY CONCOCTED A PLAN. HENRY knew a disused graveyard north of Hampstead Heath called Boddington Cemetery. He'd discovered it in his first week in London on a Sunday afternoon walk. The gravestones were mostly vandalized, and it was completely overgrown with trees and shrubs. Henry had already mentioned it to Claire, telling her that he wanted her to come back there with him before he returned to America, that he wanted to bring his camera and take pictures. She agreed, and they settled on a Wednesday afternoon. Henry hadn't seen anyone there on a sunny Sunday and didn't expect anyone there during the middle of the week. Except for Corbin, who would be waiting in the center of the cemetery, where they'd scare her enough to make her never want to get involved with two men at the same time again. Or one man, for that matter.

Henry gave Corbin a detailed sketch of the park. Near the center, the terrain dipped into a shallow valley. On one of the graves was a moss-covered statue of an angel, the head missing. Henry had written DECAPITATED ANGEL on the sketch, and had designated it as the perfect place.

"What if someone else is there?" Corbin had asked.

"No one will be there. And so what if they are? We're just scaring her."

Wednesday turned out to be typical London weather, the sky filled with low, fast-moving clouds, the cool air peppered with occasional rain. Corbin found the entrance to the cemetery and slid past the broken gate. There was still a discernible path, littered with rotting leaves, and he followed it into the heart of the cemetery. Henry had been right. There wasn't going to be anyone here today. Maybe on a sunny weekend a photographer might turn up, but not on a rainy weekday. He felt confident that he was alone.

Following Henry's sketch, Corbin found the split in the path and turned left, having to push his way past damp branches to reach the hidden clearing. He spotted the decapitated angel right away. She was robed and holding a garland of leaves. The stone was entirely covered in lichen, and she wasn't just missing her head, but both tips of her wings, as though they'd been clipped. A shudder of apprehension passed through Corbin. Were they going too far? But then he pictured Claire going back and forth between his bed and Henry's, and the anger flared up again. Maybe they weren't going far enough.

He took off his backpack, placed the retractable shovel on the damp ground next to the statue, then took out the water bottle that was now filled with the fake blood that Henry had mixed up. "It's awfully brown, isn't it?" Corbin had asked when he'd first seen it.

"Yeah, it's perfect. Blood turns brown after it's been exposed to the air. We don't want you to look like you've just been offed twenty minutes ago."

"I guess not."

Corbin checked his watch. He had half an hour until Henry was supposed to show up with Claire. He sat on the ground in front of the angel, leaning against its base, and smeared the fake blood across his neck and down his T-shirt, pooling the blood in the shirt's folds. He took the knife from the backpack and smeared that with the blood as well; it was Henry's knife, a folding buck, and it was incredibly sharp. He ran its edge along the pad of his finger and it sliced through a single, translucent layer of skin, not drawing any blood. He dropped the knife onto his lap.

He put the water bottle back into the backpack, nestled among the change of clothes he'd brought, then he tucked the backpack behind his lower back and out of sight. When Claire arrived, she'd see his dead body, laid out in front of the statue like a ritual killing. He began to giggle at the thought, couldn't stop himself from giggling, and he was soon laughing out loud, his shoulders shaking uncontrollably. *Jesus, get a grip,* he thought, then decided to let it out of his system. He let out a yelp of laughter that sounded strangely animalistic in his own ears. He stopped laughing, worried that someone might hear him. What if some stranger did come along, wanting to photograph the statue? He laughed some more, nervously, then told himself that no, it would be Henry arriving with Claire, promising that he wanted to show her something that she'd like to see. How would she react? Would she faint? Or scream? The thought made him giddy again, the way he'd felt years ago when he'd shown his brother the photographs he'd found hidden in the attic, the ones with naked girls being whipped and spanked by men in leather hoods. His brother had gone running to their mother, of course, and she'd punished Corbin by not letting him shower for over two weeks. He'd been a fastidious kid and hated the idea of not being clean. Being told he couldn't shower had been torture. "You can shower when your outsides look as dirty as your insides," his mother had told him. He'd asked her every day when that would be, and she'd told him every day that he wasn't dirty enough on the outside yet. She eventually let him take a shower only after his teacher sent him home with a note suggesting that he wasn't properly washing himself. Where had Corbin's father been during all this? His parents weren't divorced yet, but they were, for all practical purposes, separated, his father primarily staying at his apartment in the city. Corbin had wondered if it was because of the photographs; maybe his father was being punished as well for looking at them. It never occurred to Corbin, until much later, that the pictures might have belonged to his mother.

Wind shook the trees, and drops of rain pattered down on Corbin. It was almost time for Henry to show up with Claire. Thinking about the incident with the pictures and his mother had taken some of the giddiness out of him, but that was fine.

It was time to get serious. He channeled his nervousness and his anger until he felt only a sense of detachment, the way he used to feel during an at-bat when he played high school baseball, as though he was floating at a slight remove from himself. He began to focus.

He heard a rustling from the undergrowth and watched as a large pigeon with a ring around its neck stepped out into the clearing, then flew away. More rain pattered down, this time from the sky. Corbin stared straight up at the mass of cloud cover, and at the one swollen, ink-colored cloud in the middle that looked like it was about to unleash a deluge. Where was Henry? Maybe Claire had refused to come into the cemetery with him when it looked like it was about to rain? Corbin shifted his position, sitting a little more upright, so that he could watch the path where they would emerge, if they came at all.

He heard them before he saw them, Claire emitting a surprised yelp followed by laughter. She'd probably slipped coming down the incline. The laughter felt like sharp pricks against Corbin's skin. He hadn't seen her, or talked to her, since finding out who she really was; they'd only e-mailed, Corbin claiming he was suffering from a vicious flu and that he was unable to see her.

Henry came first into the clearing, and Corbin caught him glancing in his direction before turning back toward Claire, who was moving gingerly down the slippery path, her eyes angled down.

Corbin closed his lids, pulled in a deep breath of the damp, earthy air, and tried to be as still as possible. The rain was coming down harder, and it made listening difficult. They must be looking at him now. He heard a voice—Henry's—saying something like: *I brought you here to help me.* Then it was quiet for a moment, just the sound of the rain on the leaves, then he heard Claire's voice: "What have you done?"

"I did it for you, Claire," Henry said back. They were closer now. Corbin desperately wanted to open his eyes, to see the pained shock on Claire's face, but he kept them closed. Rain was pooling under his collar, and he could smell the dye from the fake blood.

"What have you done, Henry?" Her voice pitched right on the edge of hysteria.

"I brought you here for two reasons, Claire. I wanted you to see what happens to your other boyfriends. And I need you to help me bury the body." Henry's voice was calm, almost placid, and Corbin was amazed at the performance. He could only imagine the look on Claire's face, the panic in her eyes. He heard her say something but couldn't make it out. It was one word.

"No, Claire. You stay right here," Henry said, and Corbin heard the sound of movement. He opened his eyes a fraction, rain obscuring his vision, and saw Henry gripping Claire by the shoulders. Her face was down, chin burrowing into her chest, head shaking back and forth. Corbin sat up, rain streaming from his hair.

Look up, Claire, he thought. *Look up and see me.*

She didn't look up, but Henry took hold of her face in his hands, pushing her head back up. "Shhh," he said. "Calm down, Claire."

With her face in Henry's hands, her eyes found Corbin. He was sitting fully up now, looking back at her. Her eyes went wide, and what remaining color she had in her face disappeared. Her scream was high-pitched, birdlike. Henry turned to Corbin, then let go of Claire and burst into laughter, putting his hands on his knees. Corbin just stared. He couldn't take his eyes off Claire, who was stumbling backward like a boxer who has just been punched in the jaw.

Henry, done laughing, said to Claire: "Payback's a bitch, eh?"

She turned to leave, took a step on the slippery ground, and went down on one knee.

Corbin stood, the knife slipping from his lap. Henry turned back toward him, grinning wildly, as Corbin stepped forward. Henry reached out the palm of his hand, and Corbin took it. Their eyes met over the handshake. Henry seemed like he'd just won a trophy. "Fucking A, man," he said to Corbin. "Fucking A." Accenting every syllable equally.

"Assholes!" Claire yelled. She was back on her feet, looking at them. "You assholes!"

Henry and Corbin released their hands.

"No, Claire, *you're* the asshole," Henry said.

"Whore!" Corbin yelled.

Her eyes jumped to him, her head shaking. "Jesus, Cor. How'd you get talked into this? You're a decent guy."

She wore a scoop-necked white shirt, and the rain was pulling it down, the edges of her beige bra showing. The exposed skin of her chest was wet and pale. "Yeah, I am a decent guy, and you're a fucking whore," Corbin said, his voice gone shrill.

Claire took a breath and hitched her shoulders back. "Okay," she said quietly. She pushed her wet hair back off her forehead, then tugged her shirt back in place.

"Nice knowing you, Claire," Henry said, and Corbin envied his normal voice, how calm he sounded.

Claire looked at Henry, then back at Corbin, and shook her head. Corbin watched as a slight, sad smile appeared on her face. *She* pities *me,* he thought, *she fucking* pities *me.* As she turned to leave, Corbin ran and shoved her as hard as he could in the center of her back. She jerked forward, feet stumbling, then hit the ground, her head bouncing. Corbin was on her, spinning her onto her back. Her head had hit the edge of a sharp rock, and bright-red blood was running from a flap of skin, mixing with the rain. "How's it feel?" Corbin said, and shook her. She groaned and pressed a hand to the wound. She wore a Claddagh ring—she always had—and the heart was pointing toward her. Corbin had thought she'd done that for him. A surge went through his body, like a ripple going through a whip. He shook her harder, her head repeatedly hitting the ground.

"Hey, hey. My turn." It was Henry, touching Corbin on the shoulder. He was holding the knife.

CHAPTER 15

THEY DUG A GRAVE IN the clearing. The rain had turned the ground soft, the shovel making sucking sounds as they pulled out black clods of earth. When Claire's body was in the hole, but before they covered it, Henry said, in his calm, measured voice: "I think we should take a picture. One of you with her body, and one of me."

"What do you mean?" Corbin asked.

"We need to memorialize this moment."

"Are you crazy?"

"No, listen. It will be a symbol of our trust. We'll each hold proof on the other, and then we'll know that we're forever in this together. Think about it."

Corbin was still in shock, trying hard to comprehend what had just happened. They had actually murdered Claire. The two of them, together, had ended her life. He'd started it, hadn't he, by hitting the back of her head against the ground as hard as he had? He remembered how furious he'd felt, the adrenaline pumping through him, how good it felt to cause her pain. He'd wanted her to die, hadn't he? Or had he just wanted her to feel pain and fear? Had he wanted her to feel the hurt that she'd caused him? He didn't know now. But then Henry had come in with the knife, cut Claire's throat, and when Corbin saw the spray of blood arcing high above her body, a sense of unreality had come over him, like he was suddenly watching everything through a distorted lens. It was a dream. But it wasn't. It was real, all of it. The rain, the blood, the body twisted awkwardly on the ground, water pooling in her eye sockets, the eyes still open.

Henry pulled a Polaroid camera from the backpack he was wearing.

"Why do you have that?" Corbin asked.

"I told Claire I wanted to come here to take photographs. I needed a camera, didn't I?"

It bothered Corbin that it was a Polaroid camera, somehow. Such a perfect camera for taking pictures of a murder. Still, he posed, and Henry took a picture of him standing over the grave, and then they changed positions, Corbin taking a picture of Henry. The plastic camera was yellow and black. It spit the picture out and Corbin watched the image develop. Henry's shoulders were back, a toothy grin on his face. He looked proud.

Corbin handed the camera back to Henry, holding onto the picture. His hands were trembling, the tips of his fingers white as bone and starting to prune. He almost asked to see the picture that Corbin had taken of him, but decided he didn't want that image in his mind.

Henry folded the camera back into its closed position and put it in his backpack, then they covered her, smoothing the dirt down and adding a layer of wet leaves. It looked untouched, like no one had ever been there. It was a relief that the body was no longer visible, that all traces of Claire had disappeared.

"Like no one was ever here," Henry said, echoing Corbin's thoughts. "Let's go."

They walked in single file along the path, each carrying his things. Corbin felt a little better now that they were moving, and talking about what to do next. The rain had even lessened, the clouded sky lighter than it had been. At the cemetery gate they stood for a moment before going their separate ways. "No contact," Henry said. "Unless it's absolutely necessary."

"I agree," Corbin said.

Henry smiled. "I can't believe we did that, dude," he said, and there was true joy on his face, like they'd just won the big game. Corbin smiled back, wanting to let Henry know he felt the same way.

Once Corbin was on his own, walking among the normal pedestrians—returning home from work or heading to early dinner dates—the enormity of what he had done filled him with mounting panic and disbelief. Claire was dead. This morning she'd been alive, going about her life, and now she was buried in the ground. Corbin stopped walking, and a man with an open umbrella bumped into him from behind. "Sorry," Corbin said, ducking into an alley, where he put his hands on his knees. He was nauseous, and his heart fluttered in his chest. He took deep breaths, trying to fill his lungs with the sooty city air.

After a minute he began to feel better. He thought back to what Claire had done, trying to conjure up the rage he'd felt. It began to work, especially when he remembered the pitying look she'd given him in the cemetery, as though he were the asshole. He kept those thoughts in his head as he walked home. He needed to shower.

It was two days later when Corbin first heard about Claire.

"You knew Claire Brennan, didn't you?" one of his fellow students, a girl from UCLA, asked.

"Yeah. I *did*. Why?"

"I heard she was missing."

"Seriously?" Corbin had been terrified of being asked questions about Claire, but now that it was happening, he felt okay. His voice sounded natural.

"Yeah. She didn't show up at the Lambs, and someone went to her place and she wasn't there."

"Maybe she went home early."

Corbin braced himself for a visit from the police, but it never came. A few days later he was on a plane going home, drinking beer after beer in first class, and feeling the muscles in his chest and stomach finally unclench. He hadn't realized how tense he'd been those last few days in London. He'd barely slept, and when he had, it was in that thin realm where dreams and memories overlapped. He'd wake, sweat filmed and guilty, unsure whether what had happened in the cemetery was real or imagined. When he realized it was real, a dread would settle over him, far worse than what his nightmares had conjured. Being on the plane, leaving England, was an overwhelming relief. Was he free now? Had they gotten away with it? Eventually, the body would be found, of course, and then there would be a murder inquiry. Would they come looking for him, and for Henry as well? It depended on what Claire had told her friends about her life, how much she had shared. Did she keep a diary? Corbin and Claire had e-mailed, but only a few times, and nothing that personal. Most of their dates had been arranged face-to-face at the pub. It was entirely possible that no one but she knew about her love life. She'd been secretive, obviously, hiding one boyfriend from another. Maybe there'd been other boyfriends. Maybe she'd been secretive with everyone in her life.

Back in Boston, Corbin stayed with his father in Beacon Hill for a week. His mother came and took him out to lunch; he hadn't seen her in so long, and it was clear that she'd had more work done to her face. Her lips were fuller, her forehead unlined. She asked him, as she always did, for information about his father. He declined to tell her anything, except that he thought his father was happy, the opposite of what his mother was hoping to hear.

He moved to New York City and began his internship at Briar-Crane. He was sleeping better, the images from that cemetery in London receding slightly. He kept a constant eye out for Henry Wood, knowing that he was also in New York for an internship. They'd agreed to have no further contact after parting ways. In fact, they'd agreed to say they barely knew each other if questioned by the police, that they'd chatted once or twice at a pub. Corbin was eager to know whether Henry had been questioned by the police. He didn't think so. If they hadn't known enough to question him, then chances were they hadn't gone to Henry either.

And it wasn't just that he wanted to find out if Henry had been questioned. Corbin desperately wanted to see Henry again. He didn't know exactly why. Part of it was that they had shared something so transgressive and intimate that Corbin needed to know what effect it had had on Henry. Was he haunted by the image of Claire's lifeless body? Was he sleeping? Was he regretful at all about what they had done?

Corbin had Internet at his sublet in Manhattan, but he never searched for stories about Claire online, telling himself that search histories were evidence. Instead, every day he went to a newsstand near his apartment that sold foreign newspapers, and he bought the *Times* and scanned it for anything on Claire. On June 15, her body was discovered, dug up by an Irish wolfhound that was being walked through the cemetery. It was big news. There were pictures of Claire, looking rosy-cheeked and beautiful, plus a published shot of Claire's parents arriving in London to identify the body. There was no mention of suspects, no mention of Claire having dated an American student. Done reading, he threw the *Times* out in a public trashcan as he always did.

In early July, drinking with coworkers at Jimmy's Corner, Corbin spotted Henry, sitting in a booth with an older woman in corporate clothing. Henry was wearing a light gray suit, his maroon tie loosened, and his hair had been cut short. Corbin had been midsentence with Barry, a fellow intern, but stopped speaking the moment he saw Henry.

"You okay?" Barry asked, casting a look back toward where Corbin was looking.

"Yeah, yeah. I thought I saw someone I know. What was I saying?"

For the rest of the conversation, Corbin kept an eye on Henry, not sure what to do. Should they still pretend they didn't know each other? When his coworkers decided to move on to another bar, Corbin stayed, still unsure about whether he should approach Henry, but desperate to find out how he was doing. He finished his old-fashioned and ordered another. He took one sip, and felt a hand clap onto his shoulder.

"Dude. I've been wondering when I'd run into you."

"Hi, Henry. I saw you, I just didn't know if I—"

"You should've come over. Met Anna. She had to leave, and I was all set to go myself when I saw you, lurking here." He laughed, and Corbin smiled. "This seat taken? Look at you, drinking—what is that?—an old-fashioned. Dude, a few weeks in the city . . ."

Henry ordered the same, and they clinked glasses. "To us," he said, then he lowered his voiced and added: "And to getting away with it." He touched a knuckle to the wooden bar.

THEY SPENT THE SUMMER IN each other's company, developing a routine, meeting every evening after work for a cocktail at Jimmy's Corner. Sometimes there were other people there—coworkers, college friends—but more often than not, they were alone. They usually had a martini, altering the ingredients on a nightly basis in a quest to discover the perfect concoction. After that initial cocktail they'd move on to other venues, other drinks. Henry had rules. "Always head downtown as the night progresses." "Never have more than two drinks at any given bar." "Don't waste everyone's time talking to girls before midnight."

They'd break these rules, but not often.

Their nights together blurred into one long shimmering party. Henry made friends at every bar they frequented, yet he never abandoned Corbin. They'd always find one another toward the end of the night. Sometimes, of course, Henry would wind up going home with someone. But it was always a one-night stand, and never turned into anything serious. On one sweltering night in July, at a bar called Balcony, Henry left with a couple he'd met, an older man with a younger woman, and Corbin remembered the party in London when Henry had beckoned him into the bedroom. He wondered if there'd be another similar invitation, a night that would end with Henry and Corbin in bed together with the same woman. Corbin hadn't been with anyone since Claire, and the thought of any kind of sex made his stomach buckle with a combination of anxiety and lust. But it never happened. Henry, for all his success with women, seemed, conversationally at least, uninterested in sex. He was, however, always interested in talking about murder.

When they were alone, they often recounted the story of what had happened with Claire, telling it in the same way that new lovers tell each other the story of how they met, going back and forth, remembering every detail.

"And then there was that look she gave you, dude, like you were some little boy who got talked into doing something he shouldn't have done," Henry would say.

"I remember that look very well."

"She read you wrong, that's for sure."

The conversations made Corbin feel infinitely better, more at ease with what they had done. He still thought back with horror about what had transpired in that cemetery, but talking about it, especially in the way that Henry talked about it, well, it normalized it a little. They had been wronged, and they got their revenge. And now they'd gotten away with it. And that was the whole story.

"Think of all the men we've saved from Claire Brennan," Henry liked to say.

"A lifetime's worth. God knows how many."

Toward the end of the summer, just before their senior years began, Corbin took Henry to his mother's house in New Essex while his mother and his brother were touring Europe. They had the house to themselves for three warm days, punctuated by bouts of rain. They watched movies—thrillers, mostly, from the 1960s and '70s—and because of the rain, had the beach to themselves, swimming in any weather, including a thunderstorm at dusk during a slack tide, the water frothing around them from the tor-rential downpour.

On their last night they watched *Knife in the Water,* then sat on the deck, drinking a bottle of Corbin's mother's expensive Bor-deaux and sharing a joint. Henry said: "We should do it again."

"Do what? Come back here? Sure, man, anytime."

"No. I'm talking about Claire, and what we did to her. We should do it again someday."

It was sunset, and the house cast a long, narrow shadow across the dunes and onto the flat of the beach. "The right person, though," Corbin finally said, when he'd realized what exactly Henry was proposing.

"Fuck yeah, the right person." Henry slid forward in his chair, pulling a Parliament from his pack and lighting it. "Some-one like Claire. Someone who would get involved with two guys, with both of us, and think she was getting away with it. I was thinking about it with Anna this summer till I realized I couldn't spend another moment with her. You could've hit on her some night, see what she would do—well, we know what she would do—and then we'd punish her, the way we punished Claire."

Corbin's stomach had tightened, but there was something about Henry's excitement that was contagious. And the longer he'd known Henry, the more he wanted to please him. "We'd have to be careful. We lucked out with Claire."

"I know that. I think about that all the time. But don't forget—we have each other. We could always be each other's alibis. We'll always have each other's backs."

Below, on the beach, a middle-aged woman was speed-walking near the surf and for one terrible moment Corbin thought that his mom was back at the house. His eyes adjusted and he realized that it didn't look remotely like her. He plucked the lit cigarette from the ashtray and took a long drag before realizing it was Henry's.

"Sorry, man. I just took a drag off your cigarette." He put it back next to the stub of the joint they'd smoked.

"Don't worry about it. It's not my cigarette, it's our cigarette."

"I don't even smoke. I think I'm just stoned."

"Dude, I know," Henry said and started to laugh. Corbin joined him, their laughter mixing with the perpetual squawk of gulls.

IT WAS TEN MONTHS LATER when they found a candidate. Her name was Linda Alcheri, and Henry had met her in Hartford when he moved there after graduation from Aurelius College. Corbin was back in New York City, where he'd been offered an entry-level job at Briar-Crane.

"Thing about her," Henry said on the phone, "was that she started telling me how much she loved me about a week after we started seeing each other. It's bullshit, though, I know it. For one, she started saying it the night I took her to a really expensive restaurant. Not a coincidence, I'd say."

"Doesn't mean she's being unfaithful."

"Oh, I think she'd hook up with anyone if she thought there was something in it for her. I think she'd take one look at the way you wear a Brooks Brothers shirt and drop me like a hot potato."

So, Corbin came up during a weekend when Linda Alcheri was throwing herself a birthday party at her apartment. Linda lived in a complex in West Hartford, and the party was taking place on a shared roof deck. Henry begged off early, but Corbin stayed late into the night, until only he and Linda were left. "How are you getting back to Hank's house?" she asked Corbin. She had to put one of her hands against the railing of the roof deck in order to stay standing.

"You call him Hank?"

"Don't you?"

"No, I call him Henry."

"Henry. Hank. Whatever. Where is he, anyhow?" She looked around as though he might still be somewhere on the roof.

Corbin walked her to the bedroom, Linda leaning heavily against him. "Thank you, Corbin," she said, and gave him a sloppy kiss on the side of his mouth. She entered the room and shut the door behind her. Corbin called Henry on his cell.

"So?" Henry asked.

"She kissed me good night, and now she's passed out in her bedroom."

"What kind of kiss?"

"Pretty innocent."

"You should go crawl into bed with her, see what happens."

"She's pretty drunk."

"Exactly."

"Nah, man. Come and get me."

"I'll come early in the morning. Sleep on her couch."

Corbin stripped to his boxers and lay on the couch under a fleece blanket. He never slept particularly well, and drinking too much made it worse instead of better. He lay awake, staring at the ceiling of the old apartment. There was glitter in the textured stucco. He worried a little about Henry's plan to kill again, but he worried more about losing Henry's friendship. The few times he'd expressed reservations about their plan Henry had looked so disappointed.

"It's who we are, Corbs," Henry had said. That was during the winter break, when they'd spent a long weekend skiing at Sunday River. "Besides, how much time do you spend worrying about what happened to Claire Brennan?"

"I don't," Corbin said. It wasn't true. He did think of Claire, but not as often as he used to, and when he did think of her, he reminded himself that Claire had brought him together with Henry. Claire had given him that one thing. A best friend.

"Exactly," Henry said. "We'll pick someone else like Claire, someone the world will hardly miss. It'll be like stepping on a bug."

Just as the sky outside was getting light, Corbin felt his eyes grow heavy. He closed them, twisting onto his side, and was about to slide into sleep when the sound of bare footsteps on the parquet floor woke him up. Linda was standing above him, wearing an old Whalers jersey that hung halfway to her hips and nothing else. She took Corbin by the hand and led him back into her bedroom. "You're shivering," she said, when they were under the sheets together.

"Why don't you warm me up?" Corbin answered, knowing that her fate was now sealed.

Two weeks later, Henry lured Linda to an abandoned Boy Scout camp on a swampy pond forty-five minutes west of Hartford, telling her he was bringing her to a friend's luxurious cabin. Corbin was waiting there, posed as before, like he'd been stabbed to death. It felt so similar to being in the cemetery in London, but it also felt completely different. Lying there, the dampness of the ground spreading through his clothes, the fake blood drying along his collarbone, Corbin knew what they were planning, knew that Linda was about to die a painful, scary death, and something close to terror swept through him. It was a cold, paralyzing terror, the kind he used to get as a small child when the lights were turned off, but he couldn't sleep, and the monsters that hid in the walls began to whisper. He felt light-headed—he hadn't slept or eaten in the last eighteen hours—and sat up to take a deep breath of the piney air.

Henry and Linda were ten yards away, Henry's hand on Linda's arm.

When she saw Corbin sitting up, blood-splattered, she tore away from Henry's grip and ran, screaming, into the woods. Henry took off after her. And Corbin, once he stood on his weak legs, followed. Maybe it wasn't too late to tell her it was just an awful joke? But when he caught up to them, Henry had already killed her, using a large sharp-edged stone. "Sorry, man, I think she's dead," he said, smiling, looking down at her caved-in skull. Corbin's skin broke out all over in cool sweat, and for a moment he thought he was going to faint. Henry snapped his fingers. "Dude, you okay?"

"Yeah, man," he said back. It was done. Linda was dead.

Together, they dragged her body back out of the woods, and Henry sent Corbin back to his SUV to grab the shovel he'd brought.

It was a quarter-mile hike to where Henry had left his vehicle—Corbin telling himself that what they'd done was what made them special, better than the rest of the world—and when he got back to the camp, shovel in hand, he was ready to embrace the ritual act of burying the body. But he was stopped by the sight of Henry standing over Linda's body, grinning, his hands palms out as though he were presenting a gift. Corbin looked down. Henry had sliced Linda with his knife, a deep cut from her hairline down the center of her face, that continued down her torso, her clothes and skin split open.

Corbin turned, dropped to his knees, and emptied his stomach onto the weed-choked gravel.

"Sorry, man," Henry said. "I thought you'd like it. Half for you, and half for me. We split everything right down the middle."

"It's just . . ." Corbin began but couldn't finish.

"A little theatrical?" Henry said and laughed.

Corbin looked up. Henry was holding out a pair of rubber gloves, the same flesh-colored style that he was wearing himself. Corbin noticed that he was also wearing a thin ski cap that he hadn't worn before.

"Let's bury her and get the fuck out of here," Corbin said as he took the gloves.

Corbin tried as hard as he could to not look at her while they dug her grave, then rolled her body into it, but that single glance, her skin pulling away from the center of her face, black flies beginning to gather in the bright July sunshine, stayed with him after Henry and he cleared the crime scene and went their separate ways. It stayed with him—permanently burned onto the undersides of his lids—for weeks after that afternoon. Every time he shut his eyes, every time he blinked, there she was. His insomnia got worse, and so did his paranoia. He kept waiting for the police to show up at his door, especially since he'd learned from Henry that Linda Alcheri never knew Henry's real name. He'd told her it was Hank Bowman, and lied about where he worked and where he was from.

"I gave her my *real* fucking name at the party," Corbin said over the phone.

"Dude, she's not going to tell anyone."

"She could've told one of her friends, written it down somewhere, Jesus . . ."

"Sorry. I should have told you to use a false name. But you just told her 'Corbin,' right? Not your last name? You have got to relax."

"She had friends there who met me."

"Same with me. We're in the same boat, but it's not a bad boat, man. Not at all. They haven't even found the body yet. It's going to be like last time. They'll never connect her to us."

It turned out that Henry was right.

Like Claire Brennan in London, Linda Alcheri became a well-covered missing-persons case. Her body was discovered in early August, when a group of teenagers caused a small brush fire on Eel River Pond that needed to be put out. But in all the articles and reports that Corbin read, none mentioned Henry Wood, or Hank Bowman, for that matter. And no detective showed up at Corbin's door in New York. They'd gotten away with it again, even though that fact did little to alleviate the fist-sized knot in Corbin's stomach. It had been different with Linda—so different from when they killed Claire. With Claire, Corbin had been propelled by her wrongdoing and his enormous rage. She knew how much he'd been in love with her, and she let him believe she might feel the same way. And they hadn't even planned on killing her. It had just happened, and it only happened because Claire had smiled at him. That half smile of pity directed toward Corbin.

No, with Linda it had been something else. Premeditated, for one. And more like a sick, twisted game. Corbin began to wonder if Henry had ever really been that involved with Linda in the first place. He'd said they were, but maybe he had lied.

Corbin kept thinking back to the night of the party, to the way that Linda had acted toward Henry before he'd left the roof deck. She'd seemed glad to see him, giving him a kiss when he arrived, but she hadn't acted clingy, or even particularly affectionate toward him. She'd flitted around with her other guests. Maybe Henry was just someone she was hooking up with, a casual thing. And if that were the case, then what she did with Corbin that night wasn't straight-out cheating. Henry had rigged it, lying to Corbin about the extent of his relationship. Or had he?

With obsessive regularity, Corbin struggled to remember all the details that had led to Linda's death. He tried to remember what had happened after she woke him from the couch, then pulled him with her into the bedroom.

"I hate sleeping alone," she'd said. "Does that make me a slut?"

Corbin remembered the strong smell of alcohol coming from her pores, how she'd reached down and touched him, then told him maybe they could just cuddle.

"What about Henry? Hank, I mean."

"Oh," she'd said, sounding a little surprised to be asked the question. "He'll be okay."

"She was the life of the party, that's for sure" was what a lot of her friends said about Linda Alcheri after the body had been found. That was the most common quote. There was never any mention of a boyfriend.

The more Corbin thought about it, the more he realized that

Henry had desperately wanted them to kill again, to replay the events in London, and he'd made it happen, lying to Corbin, making sure he spent the night with a girl who probably slept with everyone. It had been an entirely different situation than what had happened with Claire.

He'd planned everything, even knowing ahead what he was going to do to Linda's face after she was dead.

Maybe Henry had planned the murder of Claire in London, as well?

He suggested they bring the knife and the shovel to the cemetery?

But the knife and shovel were there for a reason, Corbin told himself. They were there to fool Claire into thinking that Henry had killed Corbin.

Why had that knife been so sharp?

No, Corbin thought. Henry hadn't planned on it all, because it was Corbin who had started it, who shoved Claire, then banged her head against the ground.

Still, in midsummer, after a night of drinking, Corbin called Henry on his cell phone.

"Hey, man. Great to hear from you," Henry said.

"We're done," Corbin said. "It's done. I don't want to do it anymore."

"Okay. Relax. What are we talking about?"

"You know what we're talking about."

There was a pause. The air-conditioning in Corbin's Midtown one-bedroom clicked on and began to hum. "Dude, let's not have this conversation over the phone, okay?" Henry said.

"The conversation's over. You know what I'm talking about, and I don't want to be part of it anymore."

"Fine. I hear you. We'll, uh, not find any more girls to play with."

"And I don't think we should hang out together anymore. It's risky, and . . ."

Henry was quiet.

"You there?" Corbin asked.

"Yeah, I'm here. I'm trying to understand what it is that you just said."

"I think . . . I think, for now, at least, we are no longer friends. I don't want to be your friend."

"Whatever the fuck you want, man. I hear you, but keep your head, buddy. Don't forget about the Polaroids." Henry's voice was different. Calm, almost.

Corbin ended the call. His palms were sweaty and he wiped them on his shirt.

He hoped he'd never hear from Henry again.

And he didn't, not for a long time. Not until after he'd met Rachael Chess.

CHAPTER 16

CORBIN WOULD NEVER HAVE MET Rachael if he hadn't decided, shortly after his father died, that he needed to have a better relationship with his mother and his brother. They were both planning on spending the months of July and August at the New Essex house on the North Shore of Massachusetts, and Corbin, now living in his father's apartment in Boston, asked if he could join them for two weeks.

His brother Philip's response: "Dibs on the front bedroom, Corbin. I always stay there now."

His mother's: "I thought you hated the New Essex house. There's greenheads on the beach, remember?"

He'd gone anyway. The day he arrived he knew it had been a mistake. Philip had taken the boat out—in a transparent attempt to avoid Corbin's arrival—and while his mother had made an attempt at civility, he caught her looking at him in a mirror while she mixed gin and tonics. She wore an expression of visible disgust, her wrinkled mouth turned down at the corners, translucent nostrils slightly flared. She'd never loved him. He'd known this from a very young age, and accepted it the way that children will always accept the rules of their universe. As he got older, he realized that his mother despised him because he reminded her of her husband, and that she loved Philip because he reminded her of herself. One of the reasons that Corbin wanted to visit his mother after the death of his father was to see if she'd softened at all, if her attitude had changed. It hadn't. He felt it immediately, and in a strange way it comforted him. If his mother had become affectionate, the way she was with Philip, well, the thought of that almost made him physically sick.

He stayed for the two weeks, anyway, determined to enjoy the house, with its views of the Atlantic, and spend as little time with his family as possible. On his second night in New Essex, he ate dinner at the Rusty Scupper—a bar and grill walking distance from his mother's house—and that was where he met Rachael Chess. She was escaping from her family as well, having just begun her annual two-week stay at their year-round house just off the town beach in the southern part of town. He walked her home, and they sat talking on her front porch for hours. He told her about the recent death of his father and the awful members of his remaining family, and she told him how she'd been sleeping with one of her teachers, a married man, at the nursing school she was attending.

By sunrise, they were kissing, and they'd agreed to a two-week fling, no strings attached. He walked home along the beach in the milky light of dawn and felt a strange sense of calm, as though the world were shifting in his favor.

He and Rachael had made plans to meet for lunch the next day, and when she was late, he wondered if he'd dreamt her. But she showed up, and they spent almost every moment of the next two weeks together. Rachael was an open book, telling Corbin intimate details from her complicated life. Corbin, in turn, told her about the way his mother had paraded her sexual affairs in front of his father, and Philip and him, for years before his father finally left. He even told her about some of his own sexual problems during college; she was sympathetic without being pitying, and Corbin found himself desperately wanting to tell her what had happened with Claire in London, and then with Linda Alcheri in Connecticut. He knew that he couldn't, of course, but it was the first time he had ever wanted to talk about those events with another person. And because Claire and Linda were on his mind, he suddenly found himself plagued with terrible dreams, conflations of the two murders he'd committed, mixed in with images of chasing Rachael along the beach, a buck knife in his hand. At the end of the two weeks, when both Rachael and he returned to their normal lives, he felt heartsick but relieved.

Two months later, Rachael texted Corbin to tell him she was going to be back at her parents' house over Columbus Day weekend, and did he want to come up. He told her he'd be away for work—the truth, since he was going on a company retreat to the Cayman Islands. But even if he wasn't going to be away, he wasn't sure he wanted to see Rachael again. He remembered the dreams.

When Corbin returned from the retreat, he found out, while watching the local news, that Rachael Chess had been murdered, her body discovered in the dune grass by a beachcomber on Monday morning.

Corbin called in sick to work for a week, not leaving the apartment in Beacon Hill that his father had left to him. His boss had joked that the Caymans had done him in. Corbin didn't let on that he'd known the girl on the North Shore who'd been killed, even though the police had taken a statement, having found out from one of Rachael's friends that she and Corbin had been involved. An officer had interviewed him over the phone, then presumably checked his alibi through the Briar-Crane offices. Corbin said they'd had a casual fling and that they'd had minimal contact since.

He didn't tell them that he knew who had killed Rachael Chess. She'd been killed by Henry, of course, sending Corbin a clear message. He knew this with a certainty, even before the police released the information that Rachael Chess had postmortem wounds. They didn't specify what they were, but Corbin knew: Rachael had a single, deep cut down her middle, same as Linda Alcheri.

How had Henry even known about Rachael, about Corbin's relationship with her? Had he been up in New Essex watching Corbin in August? The thought terrified him. He googled Henry Wood and found nothing. The most recent mention he was able to locate was some cross-country track times when Henry had been at Aurelius. He tried Hank Bowman, the name that Henry had used when he'd been dating Linda Alcheri, and found nothing under that name either. He considered, for the first time ever, going to the police and confessing everything, showing them the Polaroid he still had of Henry standing over the body of Claire Brennan in the London graveyard. But what would happen to him? Even if he lied and said he'd only ever been an accomplice in the murders, he'd still go to jail for a long time. He'd still become a public figure, known for his atrocities, and also for his cowardice.

No, he could never confess. Corbin realized that Henry, by killing Rachael Chess, by making himself known to Corbin, had trapped him. He was being watched and he couldn't see his watcher. He felt a hatred toward Henry deeper than any hatred he'd felt before. Corbin decided on the only option he felt was available to him. He would lay low, and he would never become involved with a woman again. If Henry Wood ever showed himself, or if Corbin was ever able to track him down, he would kill him himself. He'd done it before and he could do it again.

CHAPTER 17

SOON AFTER THE DEATH OF Rachael Chess, Audrey Marshall moved into a vacant apartment on Corbin's hall. 101 Bury Street was mostly occupied by older couples, and it was a shock when he first saw Audrey carrying boxes into Apartment 3C. She was not the type of woman he was naturally attracted to; she was a wispy blonde, fragile looking, with milk-white skin, but seeing her wrestle with her door, her thin arms straining to hold on to the box, Corbin felt a jolt of longing. He offered to carry up some of her things from the moving van parked on the street, and to his surprise she'd happily accepted. It was box after box of books. She told him she'd been working as a literary agent in New York, but had moved to start a job in editing at Boston's biggest publishing house. After emptying the van, she'd said: "Now I owe you. As soon as I get settled let me make you dinner. I can't wait to use the kitchen in this place."

"You don't owe me anything," Corbin had said, and returned to his own apartment. He hoped that his coldness would eliminate any further contact.

It did, for a time. He passed Audrey in the hall and in the courtyard, and they were always civil, if not overly friendly. Whenever he saw her, she was alone, usually carrying a manuscript or a book. He began to imagine her life, alone in a new city, and felt a little bad for his aloof behavior on the day she'd moved in.

The second winter after Audrey's arrival was one of the worst in Boston's history, snow piling up and day after day of subzero temperatures. The largest of the storms began on a Thursday night in January and paralyzed the city all through the weekend plus most of Monday. It was during that weekend that Audrey, after saying hello to Corbin in the front lobby, showed up twenty minutes later at his door.

"I'm so stir crazy that I made enough chili to feed the entire building. Please come over and have some."

"I . . ."

"I'm not taking no for an answer—unless you have other plans—*and* I'm not hitting on you, I promise. You don't have to stay long."

Corbin agreed to come over at six. He found a good bottle of red wine and changed out of his workout clothes into jeans and a flannel shirt. He knocked on Audrey's door at five minutes past six and she let him into her place, considerably smaller than Corbin's massive end apartment. NPR was playing through her speakers, and Corbin wondered if that was a deliberate choice, so that their eating dinner together would seem less romantic. If it was, it backfired. Something about Audrey tending to the chili while Corbin made a salad, the news of the day prattling on in the background, made them seem like an instant couple, comfortable with each other and comfortable in their own skins. Corbin stayed till midnight. They finished his wine and drank another bottle that belonged to Audrey. She admitted that she'd been lonely in Boston, but not unhappy. He told her that he loved his solitary lifestyle. Back in his apartment, while brushing his teeth, Corbin felt a sharp pain in his chest. He thought it was heartburn and pressed a hand against his pectorals. To his shame, tears filled his eyes. The night with Audrey had made him realize how lonely he'd become.

They didn't see each other for over a week, not till Corbin was opening his door to let Sanders, who'd been scratching for at least ten minutes, into his apartment. Audrey was walking down the hall, stripping off a long, padded jacket that was damp with the latest snowfall.

"Hey, stranger," she said.

He'd invited her in, since she hadn't seen his apartment yet, and they ended up drinking wine and ordering a pizza.

"I like you," she said to him at the end of the night. "Even though I can't read you at all. You're a complete mystery."

"I'm not, really," Corbin said.

"No, you are. Are you going to kiss me?"

He did, and Audrey stayed the night. After she fell asleep, Corbin went to the bathroom on the distant side of the apartment, sat on the toilet lid, and cried again; his chest felt like there was a knife in it. Several knives.

"Do you mind if we talk a little bit?" Corbin asked Audrey as she was getting dressed the next morning. He hadn't slept at all.

"That was soon," she said. "You have a girlfriend? You're gay? You just got out of a really damaging relationship?"

"None of those," Corbin said. "But I have a strange request, and I will completely understand if you want nothing to do with me after I request it."

"Okay," she said, her voice wary. Audrey stood in just her jeans and a thin pink bra that she hadn't clipped at the back yet. Corbin noticed the faint scar from an appendectomy above her right hip.

"I'd really like to continue seeing you, but I think we should only see each here in this apartment building. At my place or your place, but not in public. I know that sounds horrible, but I have a reason, and it's a reason I can't tell you."

"Obviously, you have a girlfriend," Audrey said.

"I don't. I know you won't believe me, but I really don't. It's something else that I can't tell you about it. The closest I can say is that I've had girlfriends in the past and things went wrong, and I swore I wouldn't become romantically involved again. But this feels right, but only if it's here, just here, in this building."

She hooked her bra and took a deep breath. "Okay," she said. "I guess it's convenient." She laughed, but Corbin thought it seemed a little forced.

The arrangement actually worked for a while. Most of the time Corbin would go to Audrey's apartment. He'd bring wine, and they'd watch a movie on television, or they'd cook together. There were so many elements of Audrey that attracted him. She was matter-of-fact, not duplicitous at all, always telling him how she felt. In the bedroom she was responsive but not overly eager. She never said dirty things, and she preferred the lights off, like he did. Periodically, however, she would bring up the arrangement. Sometimes as a joke: "So which one of us is going to walk down to the 7-Eleven for ice cream, since we can't walk together?" Sometimes not: "My sister is coming to visit, and it's ridiculous that I can't introduce you to her. You realize that?"

Corbin always responded the same way. He said that it was unconditional that they never be seen in public together, and that it had everything to do with him and nothing to do with her. But every time he was forced to say those words to Audrey, his anger and resentment at Henry grew. Henry had made Corbin a murderer, and as though that weren't enough, he was now out to destroy Corbin's life, to destroy any possibility of happiness. Because why? Because they were no longer friends?

In his spare time, Corbin hunted for Henry Wood across the Internet, even contacting some fellow classmates from the semester in London to see if any of them knew what had happened to Henry. One of them said he'd run into him in New York City, but that was two years ago. The thought of finding Henry, and making him pay for what he'd done, consumed Corbin, especially now that he was with Audrey. If Henry were dead, then he could be with her without the constant fear of being seen together. And that was what it was: a constant fear. As much as he wanted to be with Audrey, he wondered all the time if he would come home some day to find out she'd been killed, that Henry, the invisible monster, had found out about them and made Audrey pay for it with her life. It was nonstop paranoia.

The worst moment came when Corbin was having drinks with the only other young resident of the building, a guy named Alan Cherney with whom he'd played racquetball a few times. Alan point-blank asked him if he was seeing Audrey—he'd heard rumors, he said, although he didn't say where he'd heard those rumors from. Corbin had played it cool, but the conversation kept replaying in his head over the next twenty-four hours. If Alan knew they were seeing each other, then other people could know. And if other people knew, then Henry, wherever he might be, might know, and he would come for Audrey the way he had come for Rachael Chess.

Even though they didn't have plans, Corbin barged in on Audrey the following night and accused her of letting someone in the building know about their relationship.

Audrey's eyes went large in disbelief. "Jesus, Corbin," she said, shaking her head.

"It's not funny. I was out having a drink with a guy from across the way and he asked me about the two of us. He knew."

"So what?"

Corbin made himself wait two seconds while he unclenched his jaw. "I know that you don't care because I haven't told you my reasons, but you *do* know how important it is to me that no one knows we're together. Don't pretend it's no big deal."

"No, trust me. I know it's a big deal. What do you want me to say? I haven't told anyone. We don't go out in public together, so I have no idea how he knows about us."

"Well, he knew."

"Who is he? Do I know him?"

"Alan something. He lives on the other side of the building."

Audrey looked out her window. "He lives across from me. I've seen into his apartment. He's probably seen into here, and seen you. That's all."

Corbin looked through Audrey's living room window and

across at the dark windows on the other side of the courtyard. "You think?" he said.

Audrey smiled, for the first time since Corbin had entered her apartment. It wasn't much of a smile, but it was a smile. "Yeah. What else could it be? He probably watches me and he's seen you come over. Big deal."

"You don't care that he's watching you?"

"I don't know. Maybe it's exciting. Maybe I should be going out with him instead of you." She was still smiling. Corbin went and pulled the curtain across Audrey's window.

That night, that conversation, was the beginning of the end.

It wasn't surprising to Corbin. He knew it was never going to last. They spent a few more nights together, but Audrey kept pressing him about his reasons for keeping the relationship private. He couldn't answer her, except to say, "It's to keep you safe, you have to believe me on that."

"Do you have any idea how creepy that sounds?" she said.

When it was officially over, Corbin, in a way, was relieved. He went back to a solitary existence, working long hours, going to the gym every day, but at least it was an existence in which Audrey wouldn't be hurt. He occasionally fantasized about opening a newspaper and seeing an obituary for Henry Wood. He pictured himself finding Audrey on the street in broad daylight and kissing her there in front of everyone. It would be like one of those films he hated, but he wouldn't care. He couldn't get the image out of his mind.

When the opportunity to transfer to London came up, he jumped at it. Six months away from Bury Street, from living next to Audrey, would be good for him, and good for Audrey, as well. It made him nervous to return to the city where he had fallen in love with Claire Brennan and first encountered Henry Wood, but it was also the city his father was from. Maybe he'd reconnect with that side of his family. He remembered the pictures his father had shown him from that trip he took to England the year before he died. There'd been several of his cousin Lucy and her husband and daughter. Something had happened to that daughter since those pictures had been taken; she'd been stalked and nearly killed by an ex-boyfriend. At least that's what Corbin's mother had told him, although how she found out he didn't know. Corbin wrote to his father's cousin, Lucy, and told her he was probably coming to London, and said that maybe they could meet. She was the one who suggested a possible switch of apartments with Kate. She said that an adventure would do her daughter good. It had all been arranged so easily. The thought of Kate moving into his place made Corbin somehow feel comforted. Maybe she'd become friends with Audrey and report back. It would be a connection, even the tiniest one.

For his first full day in Kate's cozy flat, Corbin only left once, walking to the nearest grocer for food and bottled water and wine. During this excursion, he was enormously relieved to not run into his new upstairs neighbor Martha. It had been a mistake getting drunk and making out with her the night before. She'd be hard to avoid but not impossible.

The rain came and went all day, battering at the large bay windows at the front of Kate's flat. He watched English television while doing push-ups and squats, then cooked the chicken breasts he'd bought. He checked his e-mails. Audrey still hadn't responded to the last one he'd sent her, the one in which he said he hoped things were easier now that he was out of the country, and he hoped she met someone who was worthy of her. He wrote an e-mail back to Kate thanking her for recommending the pub down the street, and he even mentioned meeting Martha, curious to see if she'd have anything to say about her. Martha had claimed that Kate and she were best friends, but somehow Corbin doubted it.

By Sunday afternoon he still hadn't heard back from Kate in Boston. For some reason it worried him. He took a long run, even though it was still raining, and wound up at a park called Primrose Hill with a hazy, distant view of central London. The wet soil in the park sucked at his running shoes, and he thought of that day in the cemetery with Henry, digging a grave. He ran home, showered, then checked his e-mails again.

Still nothing from Kate, but someone named Roberta James from the Boston Police Department had written to inform him that his neighbor Audrey Marshall had been found dead under suspicious circumstances, and would he get in touch with them as soon as possible.

CHAPTER 18

KATE SAT UP SO FAST that Sanders, startled, bolted from the room.

How did he get back in? She'd let him out, hadn't she? Her mind scrambled to remember. She'd opened the door for him after he'd meowed at her. She'd watched him leave, hadn't she? But then she remembered that she'd looked for him through the peephole and she hadn't seen him in the hallway. She thought it had been strange at the time, but had just assumed that Sanders had raced down the hallway and out of sight before she'd had time to see him. But maybe he'd never left at all. Maybe that was it. That possibility allowed her to breathe, pulling in several lung-filling intakes of breath.

She stood, walked on tingling legs to the den door, and switched on the recessed lighting that ran along the shelves and cabinets. "Hello, there!" she shouted, trying to make her voice sound rational. She'd still look around the place, make sure no one had opened a door, make sure that no one was inside the apartment. Just in case. She told herself that Sanders must have not actually left.

No, he left. You saw him. It was George's voice in her head. He giggled. It was something the George inside of her sometimes did, even though the real George, the *dead* George, had never giggled.

I didn't see him, she told George's voice. *I just opened the door and thought that he brushed past my leg on the way out. I was wrong.*

She stepped from the den into the hallway and walked toward the living room, turning on lights as she went. Sanders stood at the front door again, staring at it, as though it might magically open of its own volition.

"Sneaky kitty," Kate said to Sanders as she walked toward him. "I thought you'd left."

He meowed back at her, and Kate cracked the door open, watching as he left this time, his tail twitching. She locked the door behind her and pressed her back to it, looking at the living room, trying to sense whether someone was in the apartment. *No, she told herself. I'm alone. Sanders must have been here all along.* Still, she walked across the living room to the fireplace, its grate stacked with real wood, and picked up the fire iron that leaned against its brick exterior. She immediately felt better with its weight in her hand. Moving swiftly, she searched the apartment, turning on every light she could find and peering into every room. The place was empty, as far as she could tell. The front door was locked, and so was the door in the kitchen that led to the back stairwell.

She returned the fire iron to its place. Her hand was sweaty where she'd gripped it, and there was a faint line of soot across her palm.

Leaving all the lights on, she returned to the den, telling herself that she was alone in the apartment, that Sanders had not been let back in by some mysterious stalker, that he'd never left. She was overtired. She needed to sleep. She bent and picked up the comforter from the floor in front of the couch. Her copy of *I Capture the Castle* flopped out and banged onto the floor, a photograph sliding out of its pages. She picked it up and looked at it; it was a picture from a holiday she'd taken with her parents and some family friends to Torquay many years ago. The picture was of Kate and her mother, sitting next to their luggage on the steps of the guesthouse they'd stayed in. She couldn't remember if they were coming or going. The sliver of sky that had been captured in the photograph was dark and ominous. Kate remembered it had rained all week. She also remembered that it was during that holiday—Kate was thirteen—that she'd gotten her first period. Her mother had announced this fact over a full English breakfast in the crowded dining room of the guesthouse, and her father had beamed at her like she'd won some kind of prize. It had been a mortifying week.

But she did like the picture of her and her mum. They were shoulder to shoulder on the wooden steps, and they were smiling, but not toward the camera. They'd clearly been talking about something amusing. Kate liked the picture because she didn't look anxious in it (it must have been taken at the *beginning* of the week), and that was probably why she'd kept it and hidden it away in the pages of her favorite book. It was something she often did with photographs that she didn't know what to do with. Put it in a book, and maybe discover it later on. Or maybe not.

Kate had a thought, wondering if Corbin put secret pictures in books to discover later, as she did, or even to hide them. And as soon as this thought passed through Kate's mind, she knew that she would have to look through every book. It was the way she was. Once she fixated on something, she would need to see it through to the end. A year ago, she'd half recalled a quote from an Agatha Christie book, something about how all killers are someone's oldest friend, but couldn't remember what book it came from. Over Christmas, back in her childhood room, she'd scoured obsessively through every Christie book she had till she found it.

Kate stood and went to the television, surrounded by its wall of books. The shelves were filled with airport thrillers and business books. Here and there was a stack of coffee-table books, stacked on top of one another so they'd fit on the narrow shelves. Like the books in the living room, these looked like they belonged to Corbin's father, not to Corbin himself. Still, she wondered what she might find if she looked through the pages. There were a lot of books, but she had a lot of time. She knew she needed sleep, but she wasn't really tired, not since being woken up by Sanders.

She had to stand on an ottoman to reach the first book on the far left of the top shelf. It was a hardcover copy of John Grisham's *The Firm*. Using her thumb she fanned through the pages, then tipped it upside down and shook it. Nothing. She replaced it and checked the next book.

By the time she'd finished going through all of the books on the den's shelves, she'd found many bookmarks, five receipts, all from at least ten years ago, and one cut-out magazine picture of Ashley Judd in her underwear that was folded up inside a paperback copy of something called *Who Moved My Cheese?*

Kate sat on the leather ottoman. What was she looking for? A picture of Audrey Marshall with the words KILL HER in red ink across her face? No, but maybe something to prove that Corbin had some kind of personal life that he kept hidden, and possibly one to do with Audrey. So far, Kate had three accounts of that particular relationship. Corbin said they barely knew one another. Audrey's friend said that Corbin and Audrey were casual hookups. And then there was the third account, from Alan Cherney, who claimed that Corbin was over at Audrey's place a lot. Why would Alan lie about that? Kate believed him, or at least she believed that he believed it. He'd clearly been obsessed with Audrey Marshall, but she trusted him. And not just because she found him attractive and easy to talk to.

She left the den and walked into the living room, now filled with milky morning light. It was dawn already. She checked her e-mails. Martha had written a long detailed e-mail back about Corbin. They'd met at the Beef and Pudding, then snogged, "just a little," on a walk back to their flats, but Corbin told her he'd been tired and went alone into Kate's flat. Martha hadn't seen him since. "Does he have a girlfriend back there?" Martha wrote. "E-mail him and ask him. Pretty please."

That's what I'm trying to find out, Kate thought. She was relieved to hear that Corbin seemed to be avoiding Martha, and that she probably didn't need to warn her friend that the hot American might be a girlfriend murderer.

Kate needed coffee but thought she'd get a start on the books in the living room first. There were many more in here than in the den, and the shelves stretched all the way to the very high ceilings. There was a sturdy-looking desk by one of the windows, and she pulled it over to stand on. Standing on the desk, she was just able to reach the top shelf, and pulled out the first dusty hardcover. As she riffled through its pages, Kate was struck by a wave of déjà vu that felt almost physical. Her knees buckled. She had a clear memory of going through the books on these shelves before. Of standing on this desk, and of the way her bare feet felt against the grain of the desk's wooden surface. A bubble of anxiety formed in her chest. She said her mantra to herself and did her breathing exercise. The déjà vu passed, and in its place, Kate was flooded with the dreams of the night before. In her dreams, she'd searched through these books, as well. At least, that was what she remembered. Tipping the books upside down, their pages sliding out and covering the floor of the apartment, the pages filling the rooms like snow fills an empty swimming pool.

Did I really dream about searching all these books, and now I'm doing it? Kate thought. And for one terrifying moment, she thought she was still dreaming. Then the feeling passed.

She made herself coffee before going through the rest of the books. She must have checked hundreds before she finally found something of interest.

She had reached a stretch of books on one of the low shelves that felt different, and Kate felt that these books—a lot of Stephen King, *The Wheel of Time* series by Robert Jordan, two Chuck Palahniuk novels—had belonged to Corbin. She went through these books more carefully than she had with the others, and it paid off. In a paperback copy of something called *Ender's Game* by Orson Scott Card, she found three photographs of the same girl. It might have been the same girl from the photograph Kate had found earlier in the closet off the den, although it was hard to tell because these pictures were slightly out of focus, taken on a narrow bed in what looked like a narrow bedroom. The walls were white, and an un-framed poster—a Picasso print?—was taped to the wall.

In the first photograph, the girl, laughing, was striking an exaggerated pinup pose, propped up on an elbow, the pho-tographer above her. She was wearing faded jeans and a pink camisole. In the next one she was laying back on the bed in a more natural position, her face now serious. Kate imagined Corbin's—these must be his pictures—instructions: *No, don't be silly, just be natural. You look beautiful.* She did look beautiful, es-pecially in the third and final photograph. It was a close-up, her skin dotted with freckles, her mouth slightly parted. Looking at the pictures, Kate felt as though she was spying on something incredibly private, prying into a shared, and sexual, moment. She placed the pictures back in the book and replaced the book on the shelf, then quickly looked through what remained of Corbin's novels, finding nothing.

She leaned back against the shelf and closed her eyes briefly. She was exhausted, and not sure how much time she'd spent ran-sacking the apartment. And all she'd found was evidence of an old girlfriend tucked away in a forgotten book. What had she been expecting?

There was a clock on the fireplace mantel, and Kate checked the time. Just past seven. Maybe she should get a quick nap in since she had her class today. She curled up on the nearest sofa in the living room, her head on a satiny, embroidered pillow. She closed her eyes and was almost immediately into a dreamless sleep.

THERE WAS A KNOCK ON the door, three sharp raps, and Kate bolted upright. She stood, still half asleep, and walked toward the door. There was a mirror near the door and Kate looked at herself. Her hair, unwashed for a couple of days, hung lifeless and lank. She pushed it back behind her ears. She looked through the peep-hole; it was Mrs. Valentine, the older woman who had shown Kate the apartment when she'd arrived on Friday. Kate swung the door open.

"Oh, Kate, did I wake you?"

"No, no. Come on in."

Carol Valentine was swathed in a complex white sweater belted across the middle. "I won't come in, but I wanted to invite you to our apartment for that drink. Any chance you're free tonight?"

Kate's mind quickly ran through a number of excuses, but then she heard herself say: "Tonight's perfect. I'd love to."

They agreed on seven o'clock, and Carol Valentine departed down the hall, leaving behind the scent of Jean Naté. That after-bath smell reminded Kate that she should probably take a shower at some point in the day, then she suddenly remembered that her class was starting that afternoon. She ran to her phone to check the time. It was just eleven. How long had she been sleeping?

She showered quickly, then dressed in her best pair of jeans and her favorite sweater. The only good thing about wasting the entire morning napping was that she now had less time to worry about her first class, and less time to worry about the subway trip. She ate a hunk of untoasted bread with honey and butter, and had a second cup of coffee, even though she knew it was a mistake. Her skin was already rippling with anxiety, and she had begun tapping the pads of her thumb and index finger together in anticipation of the afternoon.

She went to the bedroom and pulled her empty backpack from her larger bag. In her class confirmation e-mail, the instructor had said that there was no need to bring anything, that there were computers on site. Still, Kate wondered if she should bring her laptop. She decided against it, but grabbed her sketchbook from under the bed and put it in her backpack along with her pack of charcoal pencils. If she had time to kill, she could sketch, an activity that always calmed her down.

She had to walk several blocks down Charles Street to get to the station she was looking for on the Red Line. The sky was half filled with fast-moving clouds, and when the sun shone through the day felt warm, like early summer. But when a cloud covered the sun, and the wind picked up, the temperature seemed to drop about twenty degrees.

Charles Street Station was a massive structure made of glass, across a hectic intersection from Kate. She waited for walk signals, even though pedestrians in Boston darted across busy streets when there was any kind of pause in the traffic. Inside the station she bought a CharlieCard and put twenty dollars on it. It was easier than she thought it would be, and as she took the escalator to the outside platform, she was filled with a sudden surge of well-being. Here she was, in Boston, about to attend a class on InDesign. Life was good. And now that she was outside of the apartment, it suddenly seemed ridiculous how much she'd been obsessing about Audrey Marshall's death and Corbin's part in it. If he had been a genuine suspect, the police would have been back to search the apartment again.

A train approached, rumbling to a protracted stop on the tracks. Kate stepped into the car and took an end seat closest to the sliding doors. About half the seats were taken, mostly by lone commuters wearing earbuds and staring at their phones. Two women in baggy, light-blue nurse's uniforms had gotten onto the car with Kate. As the train pulled away from the station, one of them said something to the other and they both broke into a laughing fit. The train went over a bridge and Kate got a good view of the river and the Back Bay. There were sailing boats on the river, circling an inlet. Then, in a flash, the train entered a tunnel, the lights flickering. Kate shivered.

The train stopped at Kendall Station. Three more stops and she'd be at Porter, her destination. Very few of the passengers departed at Kendall, however, and many got on. A man who smelled like fast food settled down next to Kate, his large thigh pressed against hers. She pulled her leg in and squeezed up against the barrier. A woman with graying hair but a relatively young face took hold of one of the grimy-looking bars in front of Kate. How old was she? Kate wondered if she should give up her seat and offer it to this woman, or would that be an insult. She decided to stay put. The doors shut with a hiss and the train rattled forward. She took a deep breath, but the air seemed thin, and she immediately began to tell herself what she always told herself in these situations. Let the panic come. It cannot hurt you or change you. She felt a little better. To do something with her hands, she unzipped the backpack on her lap and pulled out her sketchbook. She wanted to look at the drawings she'd done so far. She cracked the book. There was Alan Cherney, her first impression of him, and she thought she'd done a good enough job. Having spent more time with him the previous night, she now thought that his cheekbones were a little more pronounced, his lips just a little thinner. Later, she'd draw a new picture of him.

She flipped the page and looked at the self-portrait she'd drawn, then quickly flipped the page again to look at Jack Ludovico. She stared. It no longer really looked like him, at least not the way she remembered him in her mind. Close, but the eyes were wrong, and the face had a different shape. How had she drawn him so wrong? Or had this been the way he looked, and she was remembering him wrong?

She really studied the picture, her heart beginning to race in her chest. Now she was sure it was not the picture she had originally drawn. Someone had gotten hold of the book and changed it. *No, she told herself, not possible.* And if that wasn't possible, then she'd changed it herself, gone back in and altered the features somehow. But why would she do that? And why couldn't she remember doing that if she had?

The train came to a rasping halt. There was an indiscernible announcement over the loudspeaker that could have been saying something about Porter. Kate stood and looked through the grimy window of the train. They were at Harvard Station, one stop away. Even more people were squeezing their way into the car. Why was no one getting off?

Her heart hammering, Kate pushed her way through the herd of passengers and out onto the platform. Clutching her sketchbook, she gulped at the air as the doors shut and the train moved away.

CHAPTER 19

K ATE MADE IT TO HER class with five minutes to spare. After leaving Harvard Station, she was able to navigate down Massachusetts Avenue toward the Graphics Institute, housed in several rooms of a gray Victorian mansion. It wasn't too far to walk, less than a mile. Walking briskly in the open air cleared her head a little, and she decided she'd overreacted to the drawing of Jack Ludovico. So she'd got his face a little wrong, after meeting him briefly. That was all. She'd just come to a new country, and she was jet-lagged.

The class was easier than she'd predicted. She was worried that the instructor would have the students go around the room and introduce themselves, but as soon as she walked into the second-floor classroom filled with twelve stations, each with its own Mac, she was simply told to take a seat. The instructor, who had a southern twang and a large ginger beard, jumped right into an explanation of the tools of InDesign. Kate was slightly familiar with the program, having been shown the ropes by the art teacher from the hospital she'd been held at after George Daniels's death. Kate had always been artistic. Her first great love had been coloring books, and she sometimes wondered if that would be how she'd spend her declining years as well, an old lady doing paint-by-numbers morning to night. Even from a young age, she realized that being lost in an art project, or even simply doodling in the margins of a notebook, was the one sure way she could relax. It turned out to be the same with computer graphics, once she got past her initial fear of not understanding the programs. She had become very good at Photoshop, and picked up some freelance jobs through a graphic design temp agency in South London. She'd decided that, for better or for worse, she'd make it her career. It was a far better option than becoming a portrait artist, which is what her mother had been pushing her to do. Doing someone's portrait was inherently intimate, in a way that made Kate nervous just to think about. Plus, the chances of disappointing a client were somehow much higher when doing their portrait.

After class, the girl sitting next to Kate, who was so tiny that Kate initially thought she was a child, introduced herself.

"My mother's English, too," said the girl after hearing Kate's accent. "English by way of Pakistan."

They walked from the classroom to the street together, then stood for a while, talking. Kate told the girl, named Sumera, about the apartment swap and the plan to live in Boston for six months.

"Do you have friends here?"

"No," Kate said.

"Oh my God. You are so brave. I'd never do something like that."

Kate laughed. "That's the first time, and probably the last time, anyone's called me brave."

"No, you really are," Sumera said. "I mean it."

"Okay. I'll accept it."

"Where's your apartment?"

Kate told her that she was living just off Charles Street near the river, and Sumera said: "Did you hear about that murder over there? Some girl was killed in her apartment."

"It happened in my building," Kate said, deciding to not add that it happened in the apartment next to hers.

Sumera covered her mouth. "Oh my God. That's terrible."

"How did you know she was killed? I thought the papers only reported that she'd been found dead."

"It was on Reddit," Sumera said. "Check it out. It's awful. Someone said she'd been split open."

"What do you mean?"

"I don't know if it's true, but they said she'd been cut open

down the middle, like maybe it was some kind of surgery thing.
It's obviously some kind of serial killer thing. I mean it's Reddit, so
who really knows—"

"I don't know what Reddit is," Kate said.

As Sumera explained, Kate tried to shake the image of Audrey
Marshall cut open. Until this moment, she'd not imagined the specific details of Audrey's death for the simple reason that there were
too many possibilities. But now that she knew what had happened,
her mind was picturing it, and she wondered why she'd seen
nothing—no bloodstains at all—when she'd snuck into Audrey
Marshall's apartment. Had that been a dream?

"Look, I don't know if you should stay there. In the same building."

"I think it will be fine," Kate said. She suddenly wanted to
leave. Sumera's face, ever since they'd started talking about the
murder, had been wide-eyed in alarm, and it was starting to make
Kate nervous. "It was nice meeting you, Sumera. My neighbors
invited me to their apartment tonight, so I should probably get
going."

"Maybe they'll know more about what happened."

"Maybe. I'll see you back in class on Wednesday."

"Okay. Are you walking to Porter T?"

She'd been planning on it, but Kate said, "I'll probably walk to
Harvard. I have some things . . ."

Sumera, finally sensing Kate's discomfort, let her go, and Kate
began the walk back along Massachusetts Avenue. The wind had
lessened, but the sky was now entirely filled with clouds, so that
the light seemed to blur. She wondered if she could walk the entire
distance home; she was pretty sure that the wide, busy avenue that
she was currently on extended all the way into Boston. But as she
approached Harvard Square and spotted the T station, she decided
that it was important she rode the subway again. It was only a few
stops. Her panic earlier had had more to do with the sketchbook

than with the claustrophobia of the train. And she'd be heading home this time, back to the relative safety of her apartment.

Without hesitating, she entered the subway station, weaved through a disembarking crowd, and got onto a nearly empty car. It was a much easier ride on the way back. She was anxious to get back and see what she could find out on the Internet about Audrey Marshall. She wondered if Sumera had even known what she was talking about. Was there genuine information out there about the nature of Audrey's death? Before she knew it, she'd made it to Charles Street Station. On her walk home, she stopped for more provisions. Her next class was not until Wednesday, and she wanted to at least give herself the opportunity of spending all of Tuesday inside.

Back at the apartment, Kate climbed onto her bed and pulled her sketchbook from her backpack to take one more look at the sketch she'd done of Audrey's friend. Maybe she'd overreacted on the subway earlier. But, no, looking at the drawing again it seemed significantly wrong, maybe even more so in the better light of the apartment. The eyes had completely changed.

Someone else drew those eyes. George's voice again.

She tried to ignore him, flipped a page, removed a charcoal pencil from the pack, and quickly sketched Sumera, her round face and thick, unplucked brows, hair parted in the middle. She didn't know how to spell *Sumera,* so under the picture she wrote, GIRL IN GRAPHIC DESIGN CLASS, CAMBRIDGE, MA, and then the date. She flipped to another page and started to draw a new sketch of Jack Ludovico, but it wasn't coming out right. She had lost confidence in what he looked like. She did something she rarely did, and sliced that page out with the razor blade she kept with her art supplies. She crumpled the page into a tight ball and threw it out.

She got off the bed and went to the computer, searching for any new information on the murder, but could find nothing. She even went to Reddit and tried to find out something there, but she could barely comprehend the Web site, let alone figure out how to navigate it.

She checked her e-mails. No response from Corbin, even after telling him that the police had searched his apartment.

At seven o'clock, after changing into a summery dress and a cardigan, Kate walked out of her apartment, down the stairs to the lobby, then up the stairs to the other side of the building. She wondered if maybe Carol Valentine or her husband would know something about the Audrey Marshall investigation. She assumed it would be part of the evening's conversation.

As she rounded the corner onto the Valentines' hallway— decorated on this side in a wallpaper of black and silver—Alan Cherney was coming out of his apartment, locking the door behind him. He turned, and Kate noticed he was holding a bottle of wine. She wondered briefly where he was going before realizing that he was probably invited to the Valentines' apartment as well.

"I'm crashing your welcome party," he said as she approached him.

"I didn't bring anything," Kate said, her eyes on the wine bottle. "I didn't even think of it."

"Here." Alan held the bottle out toward Kate. "I've already blown my first impression on them, months ago. You bring it."

"No, no," Kate said.

"They only invited me because I ran into Carol in the lobby this afternoon, and I told her that I'd gotten to know you a little."

"Is it going to be a big party? I thought it was just me having one or two drinks."

"No, it'll just be you, and maybe Mrs. Anderby who lives downstairs. And now me. I think it's kind of a Bury Street tradition. All new tenants get invited to the Valentines'. I'm only bringing wine so I don't come empty-handed, but they'll serve martinis, and you'll be expected to drink one."

"Really?"

"They did when Quinn and I were invited over."

"We should go in, don't you think?"

"We should."

Alan knocked and the door was opened by Mr. Valentine. He was a short man with beautiful white hair. Whether he'd always been short, or it was a function of his extreme old age, was hard to tell. He wore suit pants and a pale blue cashmere V-neck, and he beckoned them in with a long, thin silver spoon. "Olive or a twist?" he asked.

Kate, confused, thinking he'd said "Oliver Twist," turned toward Alan.

"I'll have a twist, please," he said to Mr. Valentine, then turned to Kate, and asked, "Do you want an olive or a twist of lemon in your martini?"

"Oh, an olive, please," Kate said, as Mr. Valentine turned and departed, just as Carol appeared. She was still wearing the wrap-around white sweater she'd been wearing that morning, but her gray hair, which Kate had only ever seen up, was down, swept back off her forehead, and stiffly held in place by some sort of hair product.

"Come in, you two. Kate, what a lovely dress. Please excuse Bill. He doesn't talk until he's had his first martini of the night, and then you can never shut him up."

They followed Carol into the elegant living room, the furniture mostly white and the walls papered in pale gold. Alan, as they followed, whispered to Kate: "She said the exact same words last time I was here." As he whispered, their bodies bumped together, and Kate found herself glad that he had come as well.

In the living room, Bill Valentine was at a sidebar stirring a pitcher of martinis with the long spoon he'd held when he greeted them. Weaving between his legs was Sanders the cat, who stopped and stared at the new guests.

"Oh, Sanders," Kate said.

"Is he in here?" Carol said, spotting him. "I'm sure he's already tried to get into your apartment. You don't have to let him, you know, if you don't want to. He thinks the entire building is his house, and everyone's his staff."

"I haven't met the woman who owns him," Kate said.

Alan and Carol both said "Florence Halperin" at the same time.

"No one sees her," Carol continued. "As far as I know, she doesn't leave her apartment. Her groceries are delivered."

"I've never seen her," Alan said.

There was another knock on the door, and Carol said, "That must be Mrs. Anderby. Please excuse me."

Left alone, Alan walked toward the bar to see if Bill Valentine needed any help, and Kate wandered farther into the opulent room. There was the sharp, unpleasant smell of lilacs, and Kate turned and spotted a large bouquet on a waist-high, marble-topped table. Above the table was a tall oil painting, a portrait of Bill and Carol that looked like it had been painted about twenty-five years ago. Bill was seated, and Carol stood behind him, a hand on his shoulder. They looked the same except for their hair, Bill's dark and just beginning to be streaked with gray, Carol's fully blond. Alan appeared beside her holding two martinis, one with a lemon twist and one with an olive. He handed Kate her drink. Her hand shook a little, and the surface of the drink, poured right up to the lip of the glass, spilled over. Kate dipped her head and took a slurping sip of the ice-cold gin, some of which dribbled down her chin.

"God. I'm glad you were the only one to see that."

Alan laughed, then turned as Carol came in with Mrs. Anderby, older than either Bill or Carol. She was short, with a slight dowager's hump and hair that was thinning on the top, revealing her pink scalp. Carol introduced her to Kate, who was surprised by the firm grip of Mrs. Anderby's plump hand.

"Yes, she is pretty," Mrs. Anderby said.

"No," Kate said. "It's my name. It's Kate Priddy. P–R–I–D–D–Y."
It was something she was used to having to explain.

"Oh, I see. Well, you're also pretty, dear."

"Thank you."

It took a while, but eventually all the guests were settled in various seats around a white lacquered coffee table that held several small bowls filled with nuts and olives. Kate had finished half her martini, just to keep it from spilling, and she already felt the effects. She'd had plenty of gin, but never without tonic in it, and she decided that she liked this concoction, despite the little shivers she got every time she took a sip.

Bill Valentine was halfway through his martini as well, and explaining to Kate the history of the building they were in. "It's the Italian courtyard that really sets this building apart from other similar buildings in the Flat of the Hill."

"What's the Flat of the Hill?" Kate asked.

"That's our neighborhood—"

"Beacon Hill, really," Carol said.

"No, not really. People say we live in Beacon Hill, but we're not on a hill, are we? What we're actually on is landfill that pushed the river back so they could create more housing. That's why it's flat."

"Whatever it's called, it's the most beautiful neighborhood I've ever lived in," Kate said.

Bill continued to tell Kate about the local history, including a long list of famous residents, none of whose names Kate recognized. Carol, meanwhile, grabbed Alan's attention and began to talk with him and Mrs. Anderby. As Bill monologued on, Kate could hear snippets of the other conversation and realized they were talking about Audrey Marshall. She tried hard to stay interested in what her host was saying, but she kept straining to hear what Carol was saying—something about the incompetence of the police. There was about a half ounce of gin left in Kate's glass, and she drank it down—it had warmed and now tasted harsher—and then ate her olive, hoping Bill would notice her empty glass and offer her a refill. His eyes flicked to her empty glass, and he swiftly finished his own. Kate asked him if he wanted another and began to rise, but he quickly stopped her and said he'd make them. He pushed himself with some effort up off the couch, and took both empty glasses back to the bar. Kate felt a pang of guilt, but she really wanted to hear what the others were saying. She slid along the couch so that she was closer to them.

Carol turned to Kate and said, "We're talking about Audrey Marshall. I hope that doesn't upset you. Nothing like arriving in America and finding out your next-door neighbor's been murdered."

"It's officially a murder, then?"

"Oh yes, I think so." Carol's eyes darted from guest to guest for confirmation.

Mrs. Anderby, speaking in a deep, masculine voice, said, "Oh, it was murder. Sex crime, probably. It's just not safe in the city anymore, even with a doorman. I told my son that I'll have to hire a full-time dog walker for Scout because I don't know if I can safely walk the streets. I don't even recognize my own neighborhood anymore."

"Lila, I don't think these streets are any more dangerous now than they've ever been," Carol said.

"Well, I just don't know."

"Has anyone heard anything about how Audrey Marshall was killed?" Kate asked. She was hoping to get some confirmation of what she'd heard earlier from the girl in her class.

"No, even Bob said he wasn't sure, and if Bob doesn't know . . ."

"With a knife, and she was mutilated," Alan said, as casually as though he'd just revealed that the five-day weather forecast was looking good. All eyes turned to him.

CHAPTER 20

Mrs. Anderby actually placed a hand against her chest and gasped a little after what Alan had said. "Well, that's what I read," Alan continued. "Online."

"Was it on Reddit?" Kate asked.

"No, it was in the comments section of a *Globe* article. I realize that doesn't sound very reliable, and it probably isn't, but one of the commenters said he knew the ambulance driver who took her to the morgue. He said it was the worst crime scene he'd ever seen."

"Good lord," Carol said.

"I heard the same thing today," Kate said. "Not from online but from this girl in my class. She said she read it on Reddit. I don't even know what that is."

"Well, let's hope that it's not true," Carol said. "If that gets out we'll be absolutely swarmed with gawkers and reporters. It'll be just like what happened over in Charlestown after the, after the . . ."

"Have they arrested anyone yet?" Mrs. Anderby asked, directing the question midway between Kate and Alan.

"No," Alan said. "At least not that I read about. I really don't know much of anything."

"Did you know her?" Carol asked.

"Um . . ." Alan glanced in Kate's direction. "I didn't really. I mean, I saw her around like everyone else, but no, I didn't know her."

"We had her over here, right after she moved in, didn't we, Bill?"

Bill Valentine was settling back into his seat after handing Kate her fresh drink. "She was very pretty," Carol continued, "but I can't say that I came away from the evening with any real sense of what she was like. What was it she even did, Bill, was it publishing, or something like that?"

Bill shrugged and shook his head.

"I got the feeling that she was—"

"I don't understand what he means by mutilated," Mrs. Anderby, her voice a deep croak, interrupted Carol.

"Honestly, it's just a rumor," Alan said. "I'm sure it's actually not true."

"They did spend an awfully long time at the crime scene," Carol said.

"Have the police come and spoken with you yet?" Kate asked.

"They came and took a statement. They took a statement from everyone in the building."

Kate told the group how her place had been searched immediately after the police had first arrived on the scene.

"Did they have a warrant?" Bill asked.

"They didn't. I didn't know what to do. I'd just arrived here, and I wasn't sure—"

"Oh, I'm sure Corbin has nothing to hide," Carol interjected. "He wasn't even here when it happened, was he? But I wonder why they searched his place and no one else's."

"It was probably just because he was the direct neighbor," Alan said.

"I'm sure that was it. Did they know one another, Kate? Audrey and your cousin?"

Kate glanced at Alan. "They did know one another. I don't know exactly how well, but the police e-mailed Corbin to let him know what had happened. I don't think they've asked him to come back to Boston, or anything." Kate took another sip of her second martini and told herself to slow down, even though it tasted far more delicious than the first.

"I still don't understand about this mutilation," Mrs. Anderby said.

"No one does, Lila," Carol quickly said. "We don't even know if it happened. But maybe we should change the subject to something else. Kate, tell us all about yourself."

All eyes turned to Kate, and she felt her cheeks flush red. She put her martini down on the coffee table and opened her mouth to say something, although she didn't know what. Carol prompted her further, asking what part of England she was from.

"Braintree, Essex," Kate said, "but don't hold that against me." Judging from the blank stares, she didn't think any of the guests had any opinion whatsoever of Essex. Kate talked a little about her upbringing, and how she'd done some portrait painting and now wanted to get into graphic design. As usual, when talking about herself, Kate was overly aware of the blank years in her biography, the time after university, after what had happened with George Daniels, when she was either hospitalized or home with her parents, unable to leave their house.

"And is this your first time in America?" Mrs. Anderby asked.

"It is."

"We should make Kate a list of things she has to do while she's here." This was from Alan, and Kate immediately recognized the suggestion as a tactic to remove the focus from her. It worked. Everyone started speaking all at once, throwing out suggestions as to what Kate absolutely *must* do during her time in Boston. Kate glanced toward Alan, hoping to thank him with a look, but he wasn't looking at her. She studied his profile for a moment, noticing for the first time how full his lower lip was. She felt a surge of affection that he'd sought to protect her. They'd met three times and she felt as though she'd known him her entire life. Self-conscious suddenly, she stopped looking at him and picked up her martini again from the table to take another sip. She was drunk, she realized, her fingertips numb against the still-cold glass. She scooped a number of cashews from the small dish on the table and began to eat them, one by one.

After about twenty minutes, the guests, orchestrated by Alan, had assembled a definitive list of things Kate had to see or do during her time in Boston. They included the Isabella Stewart Gardner Museum, a Red Sox game at Fenway Park, the lobster roll from Neptune Oyster, taking the ferry to Provincetown, and visiting the Athenaeum, a private library, on the other end of the Common. The latter suggestion was Alan's, and after he'd made it, he told Kate that he'd be happy to take her there himself.

Bill stood, asked, "Who here wants one more for the road?"

Mrs. Anderby raised her hand, as Carol said: "Bill, I'm sure the young people have dinner plans."

Alan turned to Kate, a question in his eyes. Kate, who hadn't spoken for a while, said to the room: "I think two martinis is my martini limit." Everyone laughed, and she wondered if she'd slurred her words.

Carol walked Alan and Kate to the front door as Bill made another drink for Mrs. Anderby. "I'm sorry we had to cut short the conversation about Audrey Marshall, but Lila won't sleep for days," she said. "Kate, I've spoken to the building manager, and individually with both Bob and Sanibel and, who's the new one . . . ?"

"Oscar," Alan said.

"And Oscar, and all three are going to be *extra* on-their-guard in the coming months."

When Alan and Kate were left alone in the hall—Carol having insisted that they come back soon, maybe even for dinner—they stood for a moment, quietly, each looking at the other. The pause in conversation made Kate all the more aware of how drunk the two martinis had made her, the walls of the hallway shimmering as though they were underwater.

"I think I need to eat something," she said.

"Those were big martinis," Alan said.

"How many did you have?"

"I had two, but I'm a professional."

"Yeah, I think I'm an amateur."

"I'm not much of a cook," Alan said, "but I'm good at breakfast food. I can make you an omelet."

"That sounds lovely."

Alan's kitchen, like Kate's, had a large granite-topped island. She sat and watched him make the omelet. He'd offered her a glass of wine, but she asked for water instead. He'd already whisked the eggs, and was now shredding a block of Jarlsberg cheese. "I'm sorry I don't have any vegetables," he said.

"Please. I'd be happy eating that block of cheese."

"I can make you some toast, too, if you'd like?"

"Yes, please. And I can make it if you point me toward the bread."

As Kate made the whole wheat toast, Alan went to the living room and started playing music, some sort of jazz that was vaguely familiar to Kate. Tenor saxophone, piano, drums. He came back and started the omelets, sliding a large pat of butter onto the hot surface of the pan. He had a look of intense concentration on his face, and Kate instantly saw what he would have looked like as a small boy, hovering over a spelling test at school. It was then that she decided to definitely sleep with him.

She hadn't been with anyone since George Daniels. Over five years. The thought of being intimate with someone again terrified her, although she'd known for a while that it was something she needed to do. She had no intention of exiting this realm having only ever had sex with a man who'd tried to kill her. But the timing had to be right. She was worried about picking the wrong person and the wrong moment, and winding up traumatized again. But now—right this very moment—the conditions were perfect. She was drunk, and in another country. If she needed to suddenly escape, her own apartment was in the same building. And she was attracted to Alan, and he seemed to be attracted to her. And even though there was something a little off about him—his obsession with Audrey, for one—he seemed kind. And it was time, she told herself.

Knowing what was probably going to happen next, Kate lost her appetite. Still, she ate her omelet and the buttered toast, while they talked about Carol and Bill. Alan told her that Bill had run a major airline once upon a time, and that they spent their winters in Palm Beach. They'd had one son, who had committed suicide nearly twenty years earlier.

"How do you know all this?" Kate asked.

"Quinn, my ex-girlfriend, found out. We'd had drinks with them—an exact replica of tonight's evening, by the way—and Quinn had apparently passed the test, and I did not, because Carol and Quinn became sort of friends. Well, they had lunch on one of Bill's golfing days, and I wasn't invited to play golf."

"Do you play golf?"

"No."

"So what makes you think you made this bad impression?"

"I made a comment about how unnecessary a doorman was in a building in Beacon Hill. Something like that. I got a lecture. And I'm not sure they liked the shape of my nose."

"Seriously? Really?" Kate said.

"No, not really. I mean, because I'm Jewish."

"Oh."

"Did you know I was Jewish?"

"No, I never even thought about it."

"Maybe I was being paranoid, but the whole night I was sitting there, I kept thinking that all they were seeing was this ugly Jew with a beautiful shiksa, and wondering how I'd made it into their building. They were probably thinking it again, tonight."

"I think you sound paranoid."

Alan laughed. "No, I'm definitely paranoid. Doesn't mean they didn't think it, though."

"And I don't think you're ugly," Kate said. "Not at all."

They cleaned the dishes, and Kate accepted a glass of white wine. The food had sobered her up, and she wanted to regain a little bit of the feeling she'd had earlier. After the kitchen was clean, Alan went into the living room to put on a new record, Kate following him. The music started—jazz again, but with a female vocalist—and Kate put her glass down on a wooden side table. Alan put his glass down next to it, and with only a little hesitation took Kate into his arms and kissed her. Kate froze a little, then relaxed and parted her lips. The tips of their tongues touched, and Kate's legs weakened. She pulled away a little.

"You okay?" Alan asked.

"It's been a very long time since I've done this."

"Okay."

"And there's a reason for that. I have baggage."

"Okay. We can talk about it if you like."

"No, I don't want to talk about it. I just wanted you to know in advance in case it got weird."

Alan smiled. "Thanks for letting me know." His voice sounded a little hoarse. "Forewarned, forearmed."

They kissed some more, standing next to the record player. Kate recognized one of the songs: "Bewitched, Bothered, and Bewildered." It was an old song, and it made her feel as though they were kissing in a different era. Years earlier. It helped Kate pretend she was someone else, someone who wasn't scared all the time, someone who slipped in and out of passionate affairs on a weekly basis.

"Do you want to . . . ?" Alan began to ask.

"Stay?"

"Yes."

"Okay."

They moved to the bedroom, which was as neat as the rest of the house, the double bed tightly made, no clothes lying on the floor. Above the bed was a framed print that Kate recognized as a Chagall. She wondered if it was Alan's or a memento from his failed relationship. Alan used the bathroom first, then Kate did, and when she returned Alan was already in bed. She now felt entirely sober, and nervous, but she wasn't panicking. She felt ready. George Daniels crept around in the back of her mind, of course, watching them, but Kate could handle it. He was always there, and she was used to him.

Kate noticed a T-shirt and what looked like a pair of pajama bottoms neatly folded at the foot of the bed. Alan said: "In case you wanted something to wear." She realized that Alan, ever since she'd confessed to him that she hadn't done this in a while, had been overly careful with her. She pulled her dress over her head, unhooked and took off her bra, and slid next to him. The sheets were crisp and cool, and Alan pulled her in close to his thin, warm body. His hand slipped around one of her breasts. His mouth still tasted like wine.

SHE WOKE AT DAWN, THE bedroom's only window suffused in a pearly gray light. Alan was snoring lightly, one of his hands resting on her hip. Standing over them was George Daniels. He was holding his hunting rifle in one hand. With his other he was unzipping his pants. He smiled at her, his mouth a gaping hole, without teeth. Kate wondered where his teeth were, then realized they were in her own mouth, a pile of them, rattling around like little sharp-edged marbles, choking her.

SHE WOKE AGAIN. THE WINDOW looked the same, glowing dimly in the dawn, but there was no George, and Alan's hand was no longer on her hip. Her heart was skipping a little too fast, and her skin was damp with sweat. It was just George, in her dreams again, the only place he could reach her. She slid out of the bed and walked naked to the bathroom. She flipped the switch, and a harsh, bright light—four oversized bulbs above the vanity—flooded the bathroom. She closed her eyes, then opened them slightly to allow them time to adjust. Her mouth was dry, and she drank cool, tinny water directly from the faucet. Then she looked at herself in the full-length mirror, her nakedness making her acutely aware of what had just happened. It had been good. More than good, really. They'd kissed for a while, touching each other shyly under the sheets. It was very clear that Alan was taking things slow, and she'd started to regret telling him she had baggage, but after she removed her own underwear and asked him if he had a condom, he took charge, slowly at first, then, after he was inside of her, with a sense of purpose that George, awkward and needy, had never had. She'd enjoyed it, even though she'd felt at a remove, watching the proceedings, desperately happy that it was happening, but never entirely in the moment. Afterward, Alan had buried his head in the space between her neck and shoulder and let the full weight of his body press against hers. She could feel the breath moving in and out of his lungs, and the sticky warmth between their skin. It had been her favorite moment. She'd touched the tip of her tongue against the side of his neck just to taste him. Thinking of it now, she still felt relief that she had finally been with someone besides George Daniels, but she was also anxious. Despite the way that Alan made her feel, she barely knew him.

She turned the light off, and the bathroom went black. She found the doorknob and stepped into the dimly lit hallway. Back in the bedroom, Alan still slept, his face planted into a pillow, one leg kicked out from under the comforter.

Quietly, Kate collected her clothes and left to dress in the bathroom. Seeing him lying there—innocently asleep—had caused a flutter of fear in her stomach. It was the way George Daniels had always slept, flipped onto his stomach, a hand tucked under his chin.

It's just the way Alan sleeps, she told herself. *He's not George.*

But she could feel the good feelings she'd just felt about Alan evaporating away. It was like a rapid change in the weather.

She dressed and left his apartment, walked to her side of the building. She didn't see anyone, but the sound of her shoes on the tiled floor made her feel as though the entire apartment building knew where she had been.

Back behind her closed door, she felt her mind starting to race out of her control. She barely knew Alan. He'd been obsessed with a woman in the building who was now dead. After meeting her once in the courtyard, he'd showed up at the restaurant where she was eating dinner. He'd probably followed her there, and he'd probably also made sure to get himself invited to Bill and Carol Valentine's apartment for drinks. At best, he had decided to seduce her—and succeeded, almost instantly. At worst, he was a psychotic murderer. She caught herself rapidly touching the pad of her thumb to each fingertip, three times on each finger, then made herself stop.

There was a knock on the door, light, almost hesitant. There was no need to look through the peephole. *It's Alan,* came George's voice. *He's chased you down.* Still, Kate looked. And there was Alan's face, serious, almost haunted. And was there something else? A little bit of anger, maybe.

Kate slid the shoes off her feet and backed away from the door, as quietly as she could, George still whispering in her ear.

CHAPTER 21

KATE TRIED TO SLEEP SOME more, and when that didn't work, she showered and got dressed, even though she had no intention of leaving her apartment that day.

She opened up her e-mail account, saw that Martha was also online, and sent her a message: Hiya.

Five minutes passed, during which Kate read an e-mail from her father telling her that he hoped she wasn't becoming too stressed. She knew that the e-mail had been dictated to her father, or flat-out written, by her mother, who didn't want to write the same message herself. She was about to google Alan Cherney when Martha wrote back: Hi.

KATE: How's life? Haven't snogged with my cousin again, have you?

MARTHA: I wish. he scampered

KATE: What do you mean?

MARTHA: Haven't seen him, or heard him. Not that I've been trying to (complete lie), but he's not around

KATE: Since when?

MARTHA: Since the last time I saw him. I don't know. Heard him Saturday, I think.

KATE: Strange.

MARTHA: He ask you about me? Did you tell him to run for the hills?

KATE: I recommended he get as far away as possible.

MARTHA: You probably did, you dirty bitch

KATE: He probably rented some glamorous flat to get out of mine. If you see him, let me know, though.

MARTHA: What's going on?

KATE: Nothing. Just being nosy. Gotta run.

Kate logged out of her e-mail account. Where did Corbin go? Was he on his way back here? And if so, why hadn't he let her know?

Kate went back to googling Alan Cherney, finding very little. It looked as though he'd been a fencer, and his name showed up on tournament results, plus one photograph from the Tufts varsity squad, a picture that was ten years old. She remembered what he'd said the night before at the cocktail party about how he'd found out Audrey Marshall had been mutilated from a *Boston Globe* article. No, not from an article, but from the comments section of an article. Kate went to the *Globe*'s Web site and found an article on Audrey Marshall. There were a few comments, but nothing mentioned how she'd been killed. She checked every article she could find, and all the comments. Nothing. Either it had been deleted—pretty likely, if you thought about it—or else Alan knew what had happened to Audrey for some other reason.

Kate slid the computer off her lap and stood quickly, felt lightheaded, then sat again. Her mouth was still dry from the night before and all that gin. She stood again, slower this time, and went to the kitchen. She drank orange juice straight from the carton. Once she began, she felt as though she couldn't stop, chugging it till it ran down her chin. Then she ate a vanilla yogurt. She started to feel a little better.

She went back into the living room and looked out the window at the day. It was bright and clear, not a cloud in sight, the first day she'd seen like that since coming to Boston. The part of the river she could see, however, rippled with wind, and a nearby tree, filled with new leaves, was bending and unbending. She pressed the palm of her hand against the glass of the window; it was cool to the touch, and she could feel the wind's vibration through her hand.

Maybe she would take a walk today, she thought, then dismissed it. She felt okay behind the locked door of the apartment, and out there in the world—out there somewhere—was

Audrey's murderer. And maybe that murderer was now interested in Kate.

She tried to tell herself she was being paranoid, but it wasn't working. What had happened to Audrey had something to do with her. Maybe not at first, but now it did. Corbin had been involved with Audrey and was now lying about it. And here she was, in Corbin's apartment. Even the police were interested in Corbin.

And there was Alan. What had she been thinking, sleeping with Alan? Even if he had nothing to do with what had happened to Audrey, he'd spied on her for months and months, obsessed with her, plotting a way to get to know her. *Normal people don't do that,* Kate thought. But maybe Kate just wasn't attracted to normal people. Maybe she was attracted to psychopaths. George Daniels hadn't gotten her psychopath attraction out of her system. She needed to go to an entirely different country and find another one. She pictured Alan's distorted face through the peephole just a few hours earlier, and she was scared. He was probably at work now, but he'd be back at her door later that evening. She was sure of it.

The phone in the living room rang, a sharp jangling sound. Kate walked toward it, her heart speeding up a little. Would Alan have this phone number? It was possible. Maybe it was even listed. She let it go till it stopped ringing. A few seconds passed and it started again. It was definitely Alan, Kate thought, and told herself to pick up. If she was going to have to speak with him—and she'd slept with him, so, yes, she needed to speak with him—it would be easier to do that on the phone than in person.

She cleared her throat, picked up the handset, and said, "Hello?"

"Is this Kate Priddy?" It was a woman's voice.

"Uh-huh."

"It's Detective James calling. I was wondering if we could come by this morning and take another look at your apartment?"

"I guess so. Do you, uh, have a warrant?"

"I don't, although we can get one if you'd prefer."

"I think it will be okay."

"I'm bringing Audrey Marshall's parents to Audrey's apartment so they can collect what they want. I thought it would be good to leave them alone for a little while. It would give us an opportunity to talk, and for one of my officers to take a better look around Corbin's apartment. Your apartment, now, of course."

"Oh. Okay. Is Corbin a suspect? Have you talked with him?"

"I can answer your questions when I get there, Kate, okay?"

"Okay."

Kate hung up the phone. She wondered if they were coming back with an enormous team, with men in rubber gloves with little baggies to collect evidence. It didn't sound like it, if they hadn't gotten a warrant. Still, they clearly knew that Corbin had been in some sort of relationship with Audrey. As before, the imminent arrival of the police was making Kate want to search the apartment again herself. But she also wondered if she should be careful about touching things. She stood frozen by the phone. They'd want to see the key to Audrey's apartment, she imagined. Where was that key? Kate, for a moment, couldn't remember, then had a vague recollection of putting it back in the drawer where she had found it. She walked to the kitchen to check. It wasn't there. There were several unmarked keys, and then the few that were labeled, although she couldn't find the one that was labeled AM. Kate thought hard. Maybe it was still in the pocket of the jeans she'd been wearing the night she went to Audrey's apartment. She raced to the bedroom, searched through her clothes, and couldn't find the key. She returned to the kitchen and searched the drawer again, lifting out the cutlery tray to make sure that the key hadn't slid beneath it. She racked her brain but came up with nothing. The last time she remembered having the key was when she returned from looking at Audrey's apartment. She'd watched Alan across the way. She shivered a little, then pushed him out of her mind.

She looked through the labeled keys again, picking up the one that was marked STORAGE. She'd seen that key before, and assumed at the time that it was for some storage unit that either Corbin or his father had rented, but what if it wasn't? What if it was for a storage unit in the basement of the apartment building? It didn't seem likely that with apartments so large there'd be extra space for storage, but the more she thought about it, the more she realized that of course there would be. She gripped the key tightly between her fingers. Maybe that was why she'd found so little evidence of Corbin's personal life in his apartment; it was all in his storage unit. Detective James had said that she'd be at the apartment in about an hour. Kate decided she had time to quickly check the basement and see what was down there. As soon as the idea entered her head, she knew she had to do it. It was a compulsion she was familiar with: if she didn't look, then there was something terrible in the storage unit. She needed to look to make that terrible thing go away. And what was that terrible thing? The halved remains of endless murdered girls?

Kate tapped her fingertips together, dropping the key. It hit the slate floor with a snapping sound.

She picked it up and unlocked the kitchen door. Mrs. Valentine had told her, when she'd first given Kate the tour of the apartment, that the door in the kitchen led to the basement. Kate swung the door open, then found the switch, and a dim yellow light flooded the narrow, steep stairwell. Testing first to make sure that the door wouldn't swing closed behind her of its own accord, Kate took the stairs down the three levels, the air cooling as she descended. At the bottom of the stairwell was an unlocked door. She pushed through and into the basement. She was expecting dim lighting and damp walls, but it wasn't like that at all. It was a wide, uncluttered, well-lit space. The floor was spotless poured concrete, and the finished walls were painted an industrial gray. Along one wall was a row of water heaters, and opposite them was a series of wooden doors constructed from particleboard. The doors all had stenciled letters on them and were padlocked. Storage units. Kate found the door marked 3D and tried the key. It slid into the padlock. Kate turned it and the lock snapped open.

This is it, Kate thought, her mind careening down its path of atrocities. She touched her upper lip with a dry tongue.

She swung the door open on its well-oiled hinges. It was dark inside but not so dark that she couldn't see what was in front of her. There wasn't a shrine to Audrey, splattered in blood. There wasn't a corpse, or even a pool of blood. There were stacked boxes, plastic crates of sporting equipment and CDs. Kate stepped into the space, let her eyes adjust. A barbecue with a bubbled metal lid gave the space the smell of dusty charcoal. Stacked along one wall were half a dozen cheaply framed posters. She flipped through them. One was a crude picture she recognized as an album cover for a band called Ween. It was a photograph of a woman's torso. She was wearing a plastic belt with the band's logo, and a shirt that just barely covered her breasts. Kate stared at it, transfixed but not knowing why. The other posters were primarily of Italian sports cars, the types of posters that would seem pretty cheesy even on the walls of a university dorm room. There was also a poster for *Fight Club,* and a poster that listed the Twelve Reasons Beer Is Better Than a Woman.

Kate opened the nearest box. It was filled with comic books in plastic sleeves. She pulled one out—*The Fantastic Four*—and put it back. The rest of the boxes contained comic books, as well, all preserved in plastic sleeves. One box also contained a stack of sports car magazines, and hidden within them, a well-thumbed issue of *Penthouse.* Kate had a moment of guilt, prying through Corbin's things. She thought of her own closet in her flat, the box that contained all her old sketchbooks, including one that was dedicated to drawings of boy bands and unicorns. She hoped he wasn't looking through those. Then again, Kate wasn't looking just to satisfy a prurient interest; she was looking for evidence. And suddenly, having that thought, she felt ridiculous. The police would be here soon, also looking for evidence, and they actually knew what they were doing. And there was nothing here in the storage unit to see. It was just items that Corbin wasn't quite ready to throw out yet. Everyone's storage unit looked like that.

She left the unit and swung the door shut behind her, and felt a splinter from the cheap wood slide into her thumb. She immediately put her thumb in her mouth, then took a look. The dark splinter was visible under her translucent skin. She felt for its bottom ridge with her index finger and tried to push it out, but it was in deep. I'll deal with it upstairs, she thought, and was about to relock the padlock, when she felt a sudden compulsion to look again at the posters. There had been something odd about the one of the girl with the large breasts. She opened the door and went to the posters, pulling it out. The frame was incredibly light. There was a darkish line that ran down the center of the poster. That was what had brought Kate back. The sides of the posters were held by thin plastic frames—Kate pulled the top one off, and the sides fell away. The thin transparent plastic covering the poster slid away as well, and Kate saw that the poster had been sliced down the middle. The line she'd seen had been a cut, and half the poster fluttered to the floor, landing face up so that Kate was looking at half a woman, severed down the middle.

The blood rushed from Kate's head and she felt cold all over. She crouched, instinctively, to pick up the poster half and try to put it all back together, then abandoned the idea and decided to get out of the storage unit, out of the basement.

She backed away, shutting the door, and locking it this time.

She turned to go, but a flash of movement from the shadows behind one of the water heaters caught her eye. She stopped and listened, heard scratching noises, then crouched and saw Sanders emerge, something in his jaws. He turned toward her, his eyes two buttons of reflective yellow. She tried to make out what he had caught. It was either a small rat or a large mouse. He dropped it to the floor and it moved sluggishly away. Sanders leapt and pinned it under his paws. Then Sanders looked directly at Kate and hissed loudly.

Kate left the basement on hollow legs. What did the mutilated poster mean? Was it possible that the poster had been folded and had, over time, separated at the crease? No, not really possible. The poster wasn't torn, it was deliberately cut. Deliberately cut, then reframed. Did Corbin have some kind of sick fantasy about mutilating a woman? A fantasy that he had finally enacted with Audrey Marshall? Kate reentered the apartment and stood for a moment, thinking, tapping her fingertips together in a deliberate pattern.

Back in her living room, Kate heard a commotion in the hallway. She looked through the peephole, just in time to see Detective James removing the police tape from Audrey Marshall's door while a middle-aged couple—Audrey's parents—waited quietly. They looked older than Kate would have imagined. The woman used one of those canes with a large four-pronged base. Maybe they'd had Audrey late, or maybe these were grandparents. With the tape clear and the door open, the detective led the couple into the apartment while two uniformed officers remained in the hall. Kate stopped watching, went to the kitchen to get a drink of water.

A knock came at the door, sooner than she expected, and she let in Detective James, plus one of the uniformed officers.

"I need to talk with you," Kate said to the detective as she crossed the threshold.

"Okay. Let's sit."

The uniformed officer—a young black man with a shaved head—seemed to know what to do without being told. He went toward the kitchen, pulling on gloves. Kate tried hard to not look at the holstered gun on his belt.

The detective sat on the edge of the couch, smoothed out the legs of her black pantsuit, and said, "Are you okay? You look a little upset."

"Was Audrey Marshall mutilated?"

The detective's face didn't change, but Kate thought she saw an alteration in her eyes. A look of interest, and also concern. "Where did you hear that?"

"I met a woman in a class I'm taking, and she told me that she'd read it on the Internet. And then I heard from someone else that he'd also seen it online, in the comments section of an article that he'd read." Kate was aware that she hadn't mentioned that one of the sources of her information was Alan Cherney, but if the detective asked, she'd tell her. She'd decided to tell her everything.

Detective James nodded slowly at the information. She seemed to be considering her options. "Without going into too much detail, Kate, yes, Audrey Marshall, after she was dead, was cut in several places. I'm going to ask you to keep that information to yourself since we haven't released it to the press yet. Although clearly someone has."

"Okay, I promise," Kate said. "How was she cut? I mean, where was she cut?"

"Why do you want to know that?"

"I'm pretty sure that Corbin, that my cousin Corbin, had something to do with Audrey's death. I went down to the storage units in the basement—"

"In the basement here in this building?"

"Yes."

"When did you do this?"

"Just this morning. Just now, before you got here."

Kate told her what she'd found, describing the poster of the sexy girl, and the way it had been sliced down the middle, and then reframed. As she explained it, she wondered if she sounded paranoid, but the detective was interested, noticeably sitting a little taller on the edge of her seat. When Kate was done, the detective thanked her, then said she wanted to make a quick phone call. She stood, pulled out her cell phone, and walked over to the window. Whoever she called, they talked for less than a minute, the detective pocketing the phone as she walked back toward Kate.

"Audrey Marshall's cause of death was a knife wound to the throat, but, there were also postmortem wounds, a slice from her head down the length of her body." The detective ran her finger down her own center.

"Oh," Kate said, her mind immediately picturing the skin folded back, a skull revealed. She tasted bile at the back of her throat.

"Why did you go to the storage unit in the first place?" Detective James asked. "Are there other reasons you suspect your cousin?"

Kate filled her lungs with one long, deep breath, then let it out. She knew she had to tell this detective everything. She began, first telling her about what she had learned from Alan Cherney, how he was able to see into Audrey Marshall's apartment, and how he had become convinced that Corbin was dating Audrey. How he'd seen them kiss.

Kate thought the detective would want to know why Alan Cherney was spying on Audrey Marshall, but, instead, she asked: "Even if Corbin was romantically involved with Audrey, why would that make you so suspicious? There must have been something else."

"Well, it was because he denied it. And Alan says they were involved, and so does Audrey's friend, Jack—he seemed to think that Corbin had something to do with what happened, as well."

"I definitely want to get back to Jack Ludovico, and hear more about that conversation, but first, is there anything else that has caused you to suspect your cousin? Obviously, you've been looking around . . ."

"I told you about the key that he had to Audrey Marshall's apartment."

"Yes."

"There's that. Although that could mean anything, of course. He was her neighbor, after all. And, then, there was what I found in the storage unit. The cut picture."

"Do you have the storage unit key with you now?"

"Yes, here," Kate said, reaching into the front pocket of her jeans, but not finding the key. She stood, searched her other pockets. Nothing.

"Did you put it back in the drawer?" Detective James asked.

"God, I must have," Kate said, and turned to walk to the kitchen.

"That's okay," the detective quickly said. "We'll find it."

Kate sat back down. Yes, now she remembered: she'd put the key back in the drawer of the kitchen. "I'm sorry," she said. "I haven't been sleeping, and I've been freaking out about what happened in this building."

"Totally understandable," Detective James said. She reached out and briefly placed two fingers on Kate's knee to reassure her. Kate recognized the gesture, and the detective's half smile, from the dozens of psychiatrists and counselors she'd had contact with in the course of her short life. She wasn't crazy, though. Not right now. The police presence proved that. There had been a murder next door. And Corbin was somehow involved.

"Tell me more about Ludovico. Do you know how he spells his name?"

"I don't know. The way it sounds, I guess," Kate said. "Why?"

"Because after I talked with you last, and you told me that you'd talked with him, I tried to look him up, and didn't find anything."

"Didn't he come by the police station?"

"He didn't. Did he tell you that he had?"

Kate tried to remember. She was still frazzled by not remembering where she'd put the key, and suddenly all of her memories felt unreal to her. "He did," she said at last. "I'm sure of it. He came

here to the building to get information. He said that he'd been
to the police but that they'd told him nothing. He said he'd been
questioned, I think."

"Did you tell me everything about your conversation?"

Kate thought back. "I did. He was a friend but he clearly had a
thing for Audrey. He said he worked in the hotel business."

The detective was rapidly writing in her notebook. She looked
up, and asked, "Can you describe him for me? What he looked
like?"

Kate thought hard. She kept picturing the sketch she'd done
that had changed somehow. She almost went to get it, then said, "I
can draw him for you, if you'd like," she said. "I'm better at drawing than describing."

"Sure," Detective James said, and passed Kate her notebook and
pencil.

She quickly sketched Jack Ludovico, his smallish features that
made him look more like a boy than a man, the hair that stuck up.
The strange picture from her sketchbook kept jumping into her
mind as she drew, getting in the way of her memory, so that his
eyes came out wrong somehow, in a way she didn't quite understand. Still, she handed the notebook back to the detective.

"His hair is red. I should have indicated that."

"I'll remember. You're a good artist. This is helpful," the detective said.

"It's not perfect. I only met him the once."

"It's good. Thanks. Can I ask you one more thing? When did
you and Corbin make the decision to swap apartments? Do you
know when he first contacted you?"

Kate thought back. She remembered her mother broaching the
idea of the swap after dinner on a Sunday. It was late February, she
thought, or early March, the days still short.

"Sometime in late February," she told the detective.

"Any chance you can be more specific than that?"

"Oh. I would say either the last Sunday in February or the first Sunday in March. I can ask my mum. She'll remember, and if she doesn't, she's probably written it down somewhere."

"That would be great." Detective James closed her notebook, rocked backward a little in preparation for getting up. Kate noticed how perfect the detective's posture was, her back straight, her wide shoulders back, and sat up a little straighter herself.

Before the detective had a chance to get up, Kate asked, "So Corbin was involved with Audrey Marshall? That's why you're here, right?"

"He was. Audrey kept a diary, and he's mentioned in it. And we've confirmed from one of Audrey's friends that they were involved for a period of time over the past couple of months."

"Oh." Even though she'd suspected it—known it, really—the blunt fact still surprised her. "So they were definitely involved. So he's a definite suspect."

The detective smiled and scratched at her wrist, underneath the strap of a chunky watch. "He is a definite person of interest, Kate. We'd very much like to talk with him."

"I thought you had."

"There was an e-mail exchange, but a London police officer went to question him at your flat and he wasn't there."

"No. He's gone missing from there, I think."

"How do you know that?"

Kate told the detective about her friend Martha, and how she hadn't seen him around.

"If you communicate with Martha again, please ask if she's seen him come and go."

"I will. Are you going to arrest him?"

"We just really want to speak with him. Sooner rather than later."

The detective's phone rang, and she pulled it from her pocket. "Good, you're here. Just come straight up. It's one down from

Audrey Marshall's, the door at the end of the hall." She ended the conversation but kept the phone in her hand as she said to Kate, "My colleague from the FBI will be coming up, as well."

"Why the FBI?"

"There's a chance, Kate, that this crime is connected with two previous crimes, one of which occurred in Connecticut, and that was when the FBI became involved. We're following every lead, and I am very interested in seeing what you found in the storage unit downstairs."

There was a knock on the door, and the detective jumped up to answer it. An Asian woman wearing a black leather jacket over a white top entered. She didn't look a whole lot older than Kate. The detective introduced her to Kate as Abigail Tan, then asked, "Kate, can you come with us to the storage unit, show us what you found?"

CHAPTER 22

WHEN ALAN WOKE TO FIND Kate gone he knew that something was wrong. She'd obviously had a change of heart, otherwise she'd have at least said goodbye. Alan went to his phone to text her before realizing that he didn't have her number. He got out of bed, pulled on a pair of jeans and a T-shirt, then walked through the quiet apartment building to her side and knocked on her door. She was there, he knew it, on the other side. He couldn't hear her, but he sensed her. The dark peephole stared at him, and he was suddenly angry at himself for chasing her down. He returned to his apartment, shucked off his shoes, and tried to decide what to do next. He was up hours earlier than he usually was, but he was far too wired to consider going back to bed. His stomach had a queasy hollowness, and there was a dull thudding somewhere in his head. He drank two glasses of water and swallowed some aspirin.

If he was slightly hungover, Kate was probably hungover as well, maybe worse than he was. Maybe she'd woken up, felt sick, and returned to her own place. Or maybe she'd woken up and felt ashamed of what they'd done. She'd told him that she had baggage, and that she hadn't been with anyone for a long time. He'd been sensitive to that fact, going slow, even though he'd been overcome with not just intense physical longing, but something emotional as well. Afterward, with their chests pressed together, their breathing synced, he felt healed of an injury he hadn't known he had.

And now she'd run away.

For something to do, he made a pot of coffee, then nuked some instant oatmeal even though he wasn't hungry. He went to his computer, opened his work e-mail account, and sent a message to his boss that he'd woken up with some sort of stomach ailment and planned on staying home. He drank a cup of coffee, sitting by the window, with its view of the courtyard. It was strange to sit there and not be fixated by Audrey Marshall's window. She'd been dead less than a week, and her importance in Alan's life was already diminishing.

The day was bright but windy. A plastic bag spun in circles around the apartment building's courtyard. At just after seven the lobby's doors swung open and a man in a business suit emerged, a newspaper tucked under one of his arms. Alan recognized him but couldn't remember his name. A financial analyst, he thought, who lived on the first floor with a wife who never appeared. The plastic bag snagged on the man's right shoe as he traversed the courtyard. He bent and pulled it off, holding it at a distance as though it were toxic. He hesitated in that pose for a moment, and Alan knew he was weighing his options. Should I drop it back into the courtyard for someone else to deal with, or should I throw it out myself? He dropped it, wiped his fingers on his suit pants, and continued on his way.

Alan kept watching. If Kate emerged from the apartment that day—and it was definitely an *if,* not a *when*—then Alan could race down and confront her. She'd have to talk with him. She'd have to tell him what had happened to make her run from his apartment. He knew how it would look, him tracking her down, but he didn't care. Besides, it would be better than returning to knock at her apartment and knowing that she was on the other side, not answering the door. Was it just shame on her part? Or had he done something wrong? He scoured his memories from the night before, looking for clues, but finding nothing.

He only left the window once during the morning, to quickly race to the bathroom, wash up a little, brush his teeth, and pull on clean clothes. On his way back he stopped in the kitchen, peered at the uneaten oatmeal congealing in a bowl, then rolled a piece of turkey up with a piece of Swiss cheese and brought it back to his post by the window. He watched the mailman arrive, trudging across the courtyard while pulling out a large parcel of mail from his saddlebag. Several other inhabitants from the building passed by, all on their way out into the brightness of Tuesday morning. He watched as Mrs. Anderby stepped into the courtyard with her pug, letting him off his leash to go sniff around the shrubbery for a place to urinate. There was a large burst of wind, and Mrs. Anderby stutter-stepped a little, so she wouldn't fall over.

At around eleven, Alan watched as two gray sedans pulled up on Bury Street, parking side by side at an angle, both cars jutting into the street. He knew it was police, even before he watched a tall woman in a dark suit emerge from one of the vehicles and two uniformed cops from the other. The three conferred briefly, then crossed the courtyard and entered the lobby. Alan recognized the female detective from before. He assumed that they were returning to Audrey Marshall's apartment for whatever reason. His eyes went to her windows, the interiors dark. Even so, he caught a flutter of movement, as though someone had just let go of the curtain in the bedroom window. He sat up straighter and stared hard at where he thought he'd seen the curtain move. He could make out a reflection of the enormous rustling maple that loomed behind the apartment building. Was that what he had seen? The movement of a reflected tree?

He shifted his eyes back to the living room window that was directly across from him, the curtains partway pulled. He waited for the police to enter. If there was already someone in there, then they'd find him or her. Most likely, if there was someone in there, then it was probably another police officer. Alan told himself to be rational, even though he wasn't feeling particularly rational.

After a few minutes, it became clear that the police had not arrived to re-search Audrey's apartment. So where were they? Were they back at Kate's place, maybe searching it again?

Alan was so fixated on Audrey's windows that he almost missed the man coming out from the lobby and walking briskly across the court-yard. Alan didn't recognize him as someone who lived in the building. His hair was red, and he was wiry and small. He fit the description of Jack something-or-other that Kate had given him. The man who claimed he'd been Audrey's ex-boyfriend. Had he been the one in the apartment? Still, he'd been moving too fast for Alan to catch up with him, even if he'd wanted to. He turned his attention back to Audrey's windows. Still no activity. Alan looked out toward the street, where the police vehicles had left just barely enough space for a passing car. Near the vehicles was the man he'd just seen coming out of the apartment building. He was standing on the sidewalk and staring up at the build-ing, staring up at exactly where one of Kate's windows would be.

Alan pulled his shoes on, grabbed his keys and his leather messenger bag, and went out the door. Even though he hadn't decided yet exactly what he planned on saying to this guy, it felt better than just sitting by a window waiting for something to happen. He bolted down the steps but walked casually through the lobby and courtyard, not wanting to look insane. On Bury Street he turned right, but Jack had disappeared. He looked toward Charles Street and spotted him loping along the side-walk. Alan followed.

Jack—if it was Jack—turned left onto Brimmer Street instead of continuing all the way down to Charles. Alan sped up a little so as not to lose him, but when he turned left on Brimmer there was no sign of anybody. Alan continued to walk, looking left and right in case he'd ducked between one of the buildings, but Brimmer was almost entirely lined by redbrick apartment buildings. There was nowhere to hide.

"Are you looking for me?"

Alan turned at the sound of the voice. Jack was behind him, and Alan scanned the street to see where he might have been hiding. There was one large tree—a ginkgo—and maybe Jack had been behind it.

"I am," Alan said, and was embarrassed to hear that his voice quavered a little. "Can I ask your name?"

"You can ask me, but I don't know if I'll tell you." He smiled, showing off prominent canines. His short messy hair moved in the wind.

"It's Jack, right?" Alan asked. "You were Audrey Marshall's friend."

"How did you know that?" Jack asked, still smiling, but now with a perplexed look in his eyes.

"I guessed. I saw you leaving the apartment building. I live there, too, and I'd heard about you. You've come to the building before, right?"

He hesitated a fraction. "Yeah. A couple times."

"Right. I'm Alan."

Jack held out his hand, and Alan took it.

"Did you know Audrey, then? I don't remember her mentioning you."

"I didn't, no. I know Corbin a little bit, and I'm friends with Kate, Corbin's cousin, who's now living in his place. She told me she'd met you. How long did you know Audrey?"

"Since college, but we fell out of touch. We reconnected when she moved here. When she moved to Boston." Jack blinked several times, as though the wind had blown something into one of his eyes.

A car pulled around the corner, moving slowly, as though the driver were looking for a specific address. Jack watched the car as it departed down the street, then turned his dark, questioning eyes back to Alan. "So are you going to tell me what you want? You did follow me from the building, didn't you?"

"What were you doing there?"

"Doing where? At Audrey's apartment? That's not really any of your business."

"So you *were* in Audrey's apartment?"

"Again, that's not really your business." Jack's words were aggressive, but his manner really wasn't. He still had that frozen, wolflike grin on his face. Alan felt himself struggling to remember his reasons for following Jack.

"Fine," Alan said eventually. "Then you won't mind if I report that I saw you to the police."

"Please, go right ahead. I'll tell them myself, if you want. I have nothing to hide."

Alan, his embarrassment growing, said, "Look, I'm not accusing you of anything. But there's been a murder in my building, and then I saw you lurking around . . ."

"No, I understand. Sorry to give you a hard time. Feel free to tell the police you saw me there. I was just going, because . . ." He trailed off, and Alan watched as his eyes turned glassy and wet.

"Sorry, man," Alan said.

Jack turned his head away, into the wind, and rubbed at one eye with a knuckle. They stood quietly for a moment, Alan trying to conjure up something to say that would end the conversation.

Jack finally said, "Have you heard anything from the police? Are they bringing Corbin back from England?"

"No, I haven't heard anything. You think Corbin had something to do with this?"

The puzzled expression returned to Jack's face, as though Alan had just asked a simplistic, obvious question. "Yeah, he did it. Audrey told me all about their relationship, how he wouldn't let them go out in public, how he was always lying."

"You told the police this?"

"Yeah, I told the police this, and I told that girl living in his apartment now. She better get out of there before he comes back, because when he does . . ."

"You think he'll come back."

"I guess not," Jack said. "I mean, yes, he'll be back because the police will bring him back, but I doubt he'll come back on his own. I wouldn't. If he does, I'll be waiting for him. I don't really care who knows, but if he comes back I'm going to kill him myself. I'm not even joking."

The odd, humorless grin was back, and Alan thought that Jack looked more like a young suburban dad telling a mildly dirty joke at a cookout than someone in a murderous rage.

CHAPTER 23

IT WAS LATE AFTERNOON BY the time Kate was alone again in the apartment. After she'd shown Detective James and the FBI agent the storage unit, and the slashed poster she'd found, they'd sent her back up to the apartment. She'd waited in the living room, looking at her laptop while the two officers upstairs had thoroughly searched each and every room.

"Is it okay if I continue to stay here?" Kate had asked Detective James before she left.

The detective looked Kate directly in the eyes and said, "Like I said before, Corbin Dell is a serious person of interest. According to Audrey's diary they had a relationship that didn't end particularly well. When we spoke with Corbin he told us that he barely knew her. Obviously, that's rung some bells around here, and since we don't have another suspect, he moved up on the list. That said, Kate, there is nothing else—no real evidence—to link your cousin to what happened next door. If Corbin were on his way back here, and he's not, then I would be the first to let you know. He can't use his passport without us knowing it. So I would say it's okay for you to stay here, as long as you don't mind staying in the apartment of a murder suspect." Detective James smiled, just enough to show a small portion of her very white teeth.

"Why do you think he's claiming he didn't know Audrey?"

"That's what we're trying to figure out."

"It doesn't make sense. It makes him look guilty, so, if he is guilty, why would he lie? He'd just be caught out."

"Welcome to my world," the detective said, then added, "Look. I won't leave you in the dark. If anything happens with Corbin you'll be the first to know, or one of the first, I promise."

"Thank you."

"Do you have a phone number for the woman who lives in your apartment building, Martha . . ."

"Martha Lambert, yes."

Kate got her cell phone and gave the detective Martha's number.

After the detective left, Kate wandered the apartment, looking to see what had been disturbed. But everything, except for maybe the looted den closet, looked the same. She stared through the window out onto Bury Street and caught the detective's car pulling away toward the river. The day was darker, and the wind had picked up, buffeting and rattling the window. Kate stood frozen for what seemed like several minutes, unable to decide what to do next. The longer she stood, the more anxious she felt. She knew that she needed to do something, but still didn't move. She could make herself lunch, or do the assignment she'd gotten from her class, or go sketch for a while. Maybe do a portrait of the detective—what was her full name, Roberta James?—while her face was fresh in her mind. And what about Alan? What was she going to do when he came back from work and tried to see her again? He would, wouldn't he? She couldn't just hide from him in her apartment. She couldn't hide forever, could she?

Finally, she willed her feet to move and went and got her laptop. Maybe Martha would be online, and she could ask her again if Corbin had made an appearance at her flat.

She took her computer to the bedroom. She was cold, and got under a blanket on the bed.

She opened her e-mail account, looked for Martha's name on her list of contacts, but she wasn't online. Instead, Kate sent her a short e-mail: Any sign of Corbin, or has he totally disappeared? She looked through some of her other e-mails, mostly junk, and considered sending another one to Corbin, when she noticed that his name, down the left bar, had a green dot next to it. That meant he used the same e-mail service as she did, and was currently online. She opened a chat box to him, wrote: Hello there.

And waited. Minutes passed.

She opened another browser page and googled *woman cut down middle*. Most of what came up had to do with middle-aged women's haircuts, for some reason. She tried *woman cut in half,* and there were links to several videos—none that Kate watched—of train and elevator accidents. There were a few links to stories about magicians. Kate tried *postmortem mutilation* and looked through news stories. There were too many, but she kept scrolling, eventually finding a newspaper article from three years earlier titled "Mutilated Body Identified as Rachael Chess, Nursing Student from Portland, Maine." Kate clicked on it. It was a local story, from a Gloucester newspaper. The body had been found on a New Essex beach by an early-morning shell collector. Police had not released all details, except to say that they had found postmortem wounds. Kate's mind immediately flashed to the picture she'd found in Corbin's box when she'd first searched the apartment. A brunette woman on a beach. Her name, written on the back of the photograph, had been Rachael.

Kate wrestled the blanket off her and got off the bed. She ran across the apartment to the closet in the den, pulling open the door. The boxes were gone, including the one with the photograph. She'd suspected this, having seen a bunch of boxes being toted off as evidence. If the woman in Corbin's photograph was really the murdered Rachael Chess, then the police would figure that out, as well. She walked back through the living room, then remembered the other photographs she'd found, the ones in the copy of *Ender's Game.* She found the book again, took the photos from it, and fanned them out in her hand, the pretty woman with the freckles staring into the camera as it got closer. She carried the photographs back past the kitchen, and heard a scratching sound that made her stop. She went to the kitchen door that led to the basement and listened. Another scratching sound, plus an audible meow. She opened the door about two inches, and Sanders squeezed through, making a beeline to toward the living room. Kate shut the door and locked it. She was happy that Sanders didn't still have that dying mouse in his jaws.

Back in the bedroom, she read more about the case of Rachael Chess. No one had ever been arrested, even though it had been discovered that she was having an affair with one of her married instructors at nursing college. But that instructor, Gregory Chapel, had a solid alibi for the night that Rachael had been murdered. There was no mention anywhere of a Corbin Dell. There was also a notable lack of good pictures of the murder victim. Most of the news stories used the same one, a highly pixelated black-and-white picture of a girl in a graduation gown and mortarboard, smiling widely into the camera. It was probably the picture that Rachael's parents had provided. Kate studied it, comparing it to the pictures from the book. She didn't think it was the same girl. Same dark hair, but the faces were different. She tried to remember the picture of the girl on the beach. All she could remember was windblown dark hair, jeans, and a sweater. The beach had been named on the back of the picture, as well, Kate thought, but she couldn't remember it. But that picture must have been of Rachael Chess. It was the same unusual spelling of her first name. And the beach, a cold New England beach, connected them as well. Didn't it?

A loud beep emanated from her laptop, and Kate toggled back to her e-mail page. She'd gotten a response in the chat box from Corbin. Hi, he'd written back. Her heart fluttered a little, as though he'd suddenly shown up at the door, not just on her computer screen. She took a moment, then wrote: Did you kill Audrey Marshall?

Then deleted it.

Then wrote it again, and pressed send. There was a lengthy pause, a series of dots flashing next to Corbin's name, indicating that he was composing his answer.

CORBIN: I didn't. I promise you. Do the police think I did?

KATE: They've been back here. They say you were in a relationship with her. Were you?

CORBIN: I was.

KATE: Why did you lie about it?

Another pause. Then: Habit, I guess. When we were seeing each other, it was a secret, so I just got used to not talking about it. I didn't kill her.

KATE: Do you know who did?

CORBIN: No. I wish I did.

KATE: Where are you now?

CORBIN: Home. Your home, in London. It's rainy here. What's it like there?

KATE: Nice. Windy and nice. The police are going to send someone to talk with you.

CORBIN: That's okay. I'll talk to them.

Another chat box suddenly appeared. It was Martha. You there? Kate wrote back to Martha: Yes. Do me a big favor. Are you home?

MARTHA: yes

KATE: Can you go knock on my door and find out if Corbin's there? Don't say anything about me.

MARTHA: okay, but I don't think he's there, haven't heard anything from your flat for days

KATE: Please check.

Kate turned her attention back to Corbin's chat box. He'd written: Everything ok with you?

KATE: Everything's fine. Sanders says hello.

CORBIN: Ha!

Kate almost asked a question about Rachael Chess, but stopped herself. He'd know that she'd been snooping around his place, trying to discover if he was a murderer.

Instead she wrote: What was Audrey Marshall like?

CORBIN: She was great. It's awful what happened. I can't stop thinking about it.
KATE: Did you know her friend Jack?
CORBIN: No, I didn't. Who's that?
KATE: A friend from college. He knows about you.
CORBIN: Jack what?
KATE: Jack Ludovico.
CORBIN: What did he look like?
KATE: Pretty ordinary. Short, reddish hair. Glasses.
CORBIN: And you talked with him?
KATE: He came here, looking to find out what had happened. He stopped me on the street and asked me all these questions.
CORBIN: Did you tell the police about him?
KATE: I did, but I don't think they've talked with him yet.

Martha was back in the other chat box, and she wrote: not there. Kate responded to Martha: You sure?

MARTHA: I pounded on the door. maybe he's hiding, but no, he's not there. I'd have heard him come in and out
KATE: Thanks. How's the weather?
MARTHA: sun's out this morning for the first time since you left. didn't even know what it was at first
KATE: Martha, I have to run. Kisses.

Corbin had written: I should go.

KATE: Say hi to Martha for me.

CORBIN: Have you talked with her?
KATE: A little. She said you were an upgrade from me.
CORBIN: She seemed nice.

Kate didn't write anything back, not immediately. Neither did Corbin, and it felt like an awkward silence, if you could have an awkward silence during an e-chat.

Kate finally wrote: I'll let you know if anything happens here.

CORBIN: Okay. Bye.

Kate logged out of her e-mail browser. She was still cold, despite the blanket, and shut the laptop, pressing its warm plastic against her chest. Why had Corbin lied about being in her flat in London? Unless he was hiding in there, the blinds pulled, refusing to answer the door. It was possible, of course. Martha could be a little aggressive.

Sanders came into the bedroom, jumped up onto the bed, and meowed. Kate sat up, and Sanders leapt to the floor, racing toward the front door. She followed him and let him out, then went to the kitchen for a drink of water. The digital clock on the microwave read 6:25. It seemed late. Had she fallen asleep on the bed?

After drinking two glasses of water, she realized she was hungry, made herself a piece of toast from the stale sourdough bread, then slathered it with butter and honey. She carried the toast with her across the apartment, turning on lamps and pulling curtains halfway closed. The door to one of the spare bedrooms was open wider than she'd remembered, and she went inside. It was that time of night when the fading light outside made the inside seem darker than it was. She turned on a bedside lamp and finished her toast, having to lick honey from her fingers. This bedroom was vaguely feminine, with flower prints hung on the wall and a cream-colored blanket on the bed. She noticed a slight indentation on the blanket, and looked closer. There were white hairs—Sanders's hairs—and Kate pressed her hand on the bed; it was still a little warm from where he'd had his afternoon nap. That was why the door was ajar. She breathed a little deeper and left the room, leaving the light on.

She peered into the dark, windowless cave of the den, considering trying to watch some television, but she felt too jumpy. Instead, she decided to sketch, getting the sketchbook and pencils from the bedroom and bringing them to the living room. She stretched out along the couch and opened the book. She was prepared for the picture of Alan that she'd drawn on her first full day in Boston. It was less than a week ago, but felt like a year. She studied it. She'd caught his likeness, she thought, except for the eyes. They were vague, a little glazed, instead of intent. She stared at them, her scalp prickling. Had his eyes been changed, maybe a little? No, she told herself, but they seemed smudged. Maybe it just happened on its own.

Yeah, his eyes got smudged but the rest of his face didn't.

Did I do it? she thought. *Of course not,* George said, but she ignored him. Her days and nights since she'd arrived in Boston had been so fuzzy that it was hard to remember. It wasn't unheard of that she went back over drawings she'd done and altered them slightly, usually with a fingertip. Cleaning up lines, adding texture. She flipped past it, determined not to make herself insane, and found a fresh, unmarked page. She quickly sketched Alan again, trying to get the eyes right this time. When she was finished, she held the book at arm's length and looked. It was Alan, but she'd tried so hard to get the intensity of the eyes right that he looked pissed off, a little bit scary. Then she realized that that was exactly how he'd looked when she'd peered through the peephole earlier in the morning, when she hadn't let him in. Had she made a mistake? He'd probably just been worried that she'd left without saying goodbye. But, no, the sketch was accurate—he'd been upset. She'd made a *big* mistake, not just in sleeping with someone she barely knew, but in sleeping with someone who, at the very least, was a voyeuristic creep, and maybe a whole lot more. She turned to the next page, and quickly drew Detective Roberta James's face. She did a pretty good job, nailing the high cheekbones, the dark eyes. It was the mouth that wasn't perfect. Too severe, the lips not full enough. She smudged it out and gave the detective a half smile. Satisfied, she labeled the sketch and dated it, and then started another drawing.

It was fully dark outside by the time Kate had finished sketching Mrs. Valentine, Mr. Valentine, the other woman at the drinks party (she'd forgotten her name), and, finally, a picture of George Daniels. She'd never stopped drawing him. A number of counselors had suggested that it wasn't healthy to dwell on his likeness, but she couldn't help herself. He was always somewhere in her head, and it felt good to pull him from inside of her and put him on the page. In today's picture, she drew him as she'd seen him in her recent dream, his mouth toothless and grinning.

It was a good drawing, the best she'd done that day. She used the flat of her thumb to smudge the forehead lines, and felt a sharp prick where she still had the splinter from the storage unit door. She'd forgotten all about it, and took a look, the swollen skin around the splinter now a pinkish red. She went to the kitchen and washed the charcoal off her hands, then searched through drawers until she found a safety pin and a book of matches. She burned the sharp tip of the pin, then returned to the living room, where the light was better. There, she picked at the opening in her thumb, widening the ragged skin so that she could see the splinter and prod at it with the pin. It was pretty deep. She sucked on it, tasting her own blood, but it didn't budge. She'd have to look for tweezers, but the thought exhausted her. What would happen if you left a splinter in your thumb? Would it eventually work its way out on its own, or would it stay there forever and become a part of you?

A scratching sound from the kitchen startled her. She'd let Sanders out, hadn't she? She put the safety pin down on her sketchbook, got up, and returned to the kitchen. She heard the sound again. It was coming from the door that led to the basement—Sanders again, having looped around through the basement. She opened the door, and there was Alan, holding his palms toward her, his eyes bleary and wild looking. "Please let me in," he slurred, taking a step into the kitchen before Kate could slam the door.

CHAPTER 24

ALAN WASN'T EXACTLY SURE HOW he'd gotten so drunk, but it had happened, almost accidentally, and now he was walking back through the darkness, determined to see Kate, even if she didn't want to see him.

After encountering Jack on Brimmer Street earlier in the day and hearing from him that he thought Corbin Dell had murdered Audrey Marshall, Jack had become chatty, suggesting they go somewhere and talk more. Alan, more than anything, wanted to turn around and go home, in hopes that he'd spot Kate in the courtyard, but decided instead to spend some time hearing what Jack had to say. Alan suggested St. Stephen's. When they got there, settling into one of the high-backed booths, Alan ordered a large Coke and Jack ordered a bottle of Heineken. The waitress spun on her heels to get their drinks, and Jack immediately started talking about a woman named Rachael Chess, who had been found murdered on a beach in New Essex a few years earlier.

"She was mutilated," Jack said, "just like Audrey was." His voice cracked every time he said Audrey's name.

"How did you hear that Audrey was mutilated?" Alan asked.

"It's all over the Web, and so I started to search other cases, other cases where someone had been cut down the middle, sliced open, and I found Rachael Chess."

"And what does she have to do with Corbin Dell?" Alan was interested in what Jack had to say, but also a little wary. Jack was becoming increasingly animated, almost manic, in the way he was talking. The waitress returned with their drinks. Jack took a long pull from his bottle of beer.

"Get this," he said, setting down the beer hard enough that

foam spilled over its lip and rolled down its side. "Corbin Dell used to live in New Essex, and his mother still does. She has a place right on the beach—"

"How do you know all this?"

"Audrey told me some, and some of it I just looked up online. That's not the point, though. The point is that Rachael Chess's parents also lived in New Essex, not right on the beach, but close. It's how Corbin and Rachael met, obviously. He's a psychopath. Audrey told me that when they were together he was paranoid about being seen in public with her, that he always wanted to stay in. It's because he didn't want to be associated with her, because he knew he was going to kill her. But then she started to see me, and wanted nothing to do with Corbin anymore, and that was why he killed her. It's him. I know it." Jack scratched at some raised welts on a reddened arm.

"You okay?" Alan asked.

"Hives, I think. I hate the spring."

"Have you gone to the police with all this?" Alan asked.

"I will. I promise. But I want to get all my ducks in a row. He's not getting away with this."

Alan knew that he hadn't gone to the police because he was playing amateur detective, maybe even hoping to get revenge on his own.

"I think you should go to the police. They'll probably know if there was ever a link between Corbin and this Rachael person."

"Another thing that he always told Audrey was that he wasn't any good for her, almost like he knew what he was going to do. You want to get something to eat? It's lunchtime."

Alan had already finished his Coke, and agreed to get lunch. Jack waved the waitress over and they both ordered cheeseburgers. Jack asked for another beer, and Alan decided to have one as well.

"Jack, how often did you see Audrey?" Alan asked, after they gave their orders. He was hoping to get some information on why he'd never seen him before through Audrey's windows.

"About once a week," Jack said. "We'd get together for coffee or for drinks. I think at first she thought I was trying to date her again."

"But you weren't?" Alan asked.

"I don't know. Yes. No."

"I never saw you at the apartment building. Were you ever there, or . . . ?"

"A couple times."

Alan thought he was lying about being in Audrey's apartment. He guessed that in Jack's mind, the friendship with Audrey— maybe a couple of coffees, a few text messages—was much more important than it had been to her. The beers came and Alan took a sip. It was so cold it made his teeth hurt.

"Just this one beer and then I should go to the office," Alan said. "It *is* a Tuesday."

"Thanks, man," Jack said. "Thanks for spending time with me. It's nice to talk with someone who doesn't think I'm crazy. You don't think I'm off the rails about Corbin, do you?"

"I don't."

"So you agree with me?"

"I agree that Corbin had a motive, and he probably had a key to Audrey's place, and he left town right after she was murdered."

"Why do you think he had a key?" Jack asked.

"Just thought it was probably likely. They went out. They lived next to one another." He didn't want to mention what he'd learned from Kate. He wasn't exactly sure why, but somehow he wanted to keep her out of it.

"I can see that," Jack said.

The food came and Alan listened as Jack explained, again, the reasons he was sure that Corbin had killed before. Everything he was saying made sense.

Alan and Jack stayed at St. Stephen's till late afternoon, each drinking several more beers. It had been a strange few hours. Alan found himself telling this man all about his relationship with Quinn. He almost found himself telling him about the previous night with Kate, but stopped himself just in time. Why was he talking so much? He went to the bathroom, stared at himself in the mirror, and didn't like what he saw. Why was he drunk in a bar with a stranger on a Tuesday afternoon? He decided he needed to leave.

As they stood outside the bar, saying goodbye, Jack's eyes filled with tears. "Thank you, thank you, for hanging out with me. I know . . . I know it wasn't . . ."

"It was nice," Alan said, and put a hand on Jack's shoulder.

Jack removed his gloves and wiped at both eyes, then held out his hand to shake Alan's. Alan was relieved that there had been no hug; the handshake, long and aggressive, had been enough. "Which way you headed?" Jack asked, and Alan, suddenly desperate to escape, tilted his head east, since Alan was already taking a step down the hill back toward Charles Street. They parted ways, and Alan walked through a residential neighborhood he had never walked through before. The wind had died down a little, but the tops of the trees still rustled, and Alan's T-shirt flattened out against his body as he walked aimlessly. He was hungry again, and needed to pee. He spotted the State House and walked toward it, knowing there'd be bars nearby. The first one he passed was a faux-Irish pub on the corner called Rosie McClean's that was empty except for a table of Japanese tourists eating an early dinner. Alan sat at the bar and ordered fish and chips and a large Coke. After drinking the Coke, he asked for another, but with Old Overholt in it. He knew enough about day drinking to know that if he quit now, he'd wind up with a splitting headache for the rest of the night. The fish and chips came and the food made him feel better, less drunk, and he ordered another rye and Coke and thought about his conversation with Jack.

Alan's phone rang. He pulled it out of his bag and checked the screen. His sister. He was all set to hit Ignore, but then decided to answer, just in case she had a real reason to call and wasn't just checking up on him.

"Just checking in," Hannah said after they'd said hello.

"I'm fine."

"You sound funny. Have you been drinking?"

"A little bit. I'm eating, too. My mouth was full."

"Don't forget to call Mom on her birthday."

"Uh-huh. That's why you called?" Alan was annoyed, even though he probably would have forgotten.

"No. I'm worried about you. I had this crazy dream."

Alan listened while Hannah described, in detail, the dream she'd had where she found Alan dead in his apartment, a rotting corpse, after not hearing from him for years. During the description, Alan finished his drink and ordered another one by catching the bartender's eye and pointing at his empty glass.

"Hey," Alan said after Hannah stopped talking about the dream, "do you remember that time you were a camp counselor and I came up for the weekend?"

There was a pause. Alan could hear one of her kids—it sounded like Izzie—laughing in the background. "I guess so. I think so. Oh yeah, Mom and Dad made me take you so they could go to the Cape alone."

Alan didn't remember that part. He said, "You know, that was the first time I saw a naked girl. I spied on her through a hole in the wall."

"What? A counselor?"

"Uh-huh."

"Ha. Do you remember who it was?"

"I don't know if I ever knew her name. She was kind of chubby."

"Was it Allie something?"

"I never knew her name, but I think she turned me into a pervert."

"What are you talking about?"

"Because I was spying on her, without her knowing I was doing it."

"Oh God. You and everyone else at that pervy camp. All the walls had knotholes in them. She probably knew she was being watched. Look, as much as I'd love to hear more creepy stories from my drunk brother, I've gotta go. Call Mom, and don't be a fucking stranger."

When Alan finally left the pub, it was filled with after-work drinkers. The darkness outside somehow shocked him. It was colder, too, and Alan, wearing only a T-shirt, was nearly shivering by the time he reached 101 Bury.

Maybe because he was drunk, or maybe because of the peculiar light that night, the apartment building seemed taller than usual, towering behind its gate. Moonlight reflected on the slate roof of the next building over, and across the street, a homeless man was trying to keep warm in a doorway. Low lights were on in Kate's apartment. During the walk, he'd decided that he needed to see her no matter what. He needed to find out why she'd left his apartment without saying goodbye. He needed to tell her what he'd learned from Jack, and he even wanted to tell her how his sister had called, and he'd finally told her the big secret about what he'd done at her summer camp, and she'd barely cared. He walked across the courtyard and through the lobby, nodding toward Sanibel, and wondering if the doorman even noticed that he was taking the stairs toward the north wing and not the south. He walked down the hallway, aware, peripherally, of Audrey's door and of what had happened in that apartment, but focusing on Kate's door. He was about to knock, but stopped himself. What if she didn't answer? In fact, why would she answer? She hadn't earlier in the morning, when he'd known she was just on the other side, probably looking at him through the peephole. Alan formed a different plan.

He went back to the stairwell and walked all the way down to the basement level. He passed through the fluorescent-lit basement, thankful that it was empty, then found the back stairwell that would lead to the kitchen entrance to Kate's apartment. At least, he thought it would. He was always leaving that entrance unlocked in his own place and was hopeful that Kate had as well. At the very least, he could talk with her through the door without having to stand in the hallway. He could say his piece.

He climbed to the top of the steep, narrow stairwell and quietly tried the knob. It was locked. He was about to knock when he had an idea. Sanders the cat was always scratching at his own back door, trying to get into his apartment. He wondered if he'd done the same here. Knowing it was a terrible idea, but deciding to do it anyway, Alan half knocked, half scratched at the door. And waited.

He heard faint footsteps in the kitchen, and then the door was being opened, and he was looking at Kate's horrified face. He quickly put his hands up, stepping across the threshold with one foot. "Please let me in," he said, willing his voice to sound harmless.

Kate pressed a hand against her chest. She was pale, as though all the blood had drained from her face.

"I need to talk with you. I can do it from here, but we need to talk. I don't think you should be in this apartment. You should be in my apartment." The words weren't coming out the way he'd planned.

"You're really drunk," Kate said.

"I know. I know. I met Jack, and he told me all about Corbin and he got me drunk."

"Who's Jack?"

"Jack. *Jack.* That guy who was friends with Audrey that you told me about. On the street. You met him on the street."

Before answering, Alan began to move farther into the kitchen. Kate jumped back, said, "No, no. Stay there."

Alan took a step back. "You're not scared of me? Oh no, you're scared of me." He felt terrible, and kept apologizing.

Kate said, "It's okay. I know you're sorry. Tell me about Jack."

"I saw him this morning coming out of the building—"

"Coming out of where? Out of here?"

"Yes. Right after the police arrived. I didn't recognize him, but he was looking up at your window, so I followed him and he caught me and then we were talking. We went to that bar you and I . . . St. Stephen's, and he told me about his theory, how Corbin's a serial killer."

"What do you mean a serial killer?"

"He said that there was this other girl that Corbin murdered. She was also mutilated, and he's sure that Corbin killed Audrey, and I just don't think it's safe for you to be in this apartment all by yourself."

"If Corbin killed Audrey, then he's not going to come back here, is he? That wouldn't make any sense."

"Then you're going to stay here? Tonight?"

"Alan, I'm sorry. I think we rushed into things last night, and it was . . . for me, it was a mistake. No, let me talk. Let's meet tomorrow, okay? For coffee or something in the morning, and we can talk about all of this. But not now. Not while you're like this. Okay?"

It was the expression on Kate's face as she said *okay* that made Alan realize he needed to leave. She looked like she was about to cry. Alan, without saying anything, turned and walked back down the stairwell, pressing his palms against the walls to keep himself steady.

Back in his apartment he lay on his bed, shoes kicked off, jeans and T-shirt still on. When he closed his eyes, the room tilted.

When he opened them, the world stood still. He kept them open as long as possible, trying to reassemble in his mind everything that had happened that day, everything that had happened recently. He closed his eyes. The room tilted again, but backward, and Alan slid into a deep, troubled sleep.

CHAPTER 25

IT'S TIME TO GO HOME, Kate thought, after Alan had finally left. Back to England. She placed a hand on the kitchen countertop to steady herself.

She felt George's voice rising in her head, his words starting to form, and she managed to stop him from speaking to her by pacing the kitchen floor.

I should never have left the country. I should never have left my parents' house. Not to go to university, not to go on holiday in the Lake District, not to go to London, and *definitely* not to travel to Boston. Bad things happen to me.

Bad people happen to me.

Kate poured wine into a water glass. She carried it from room to room in the apartment, checking window locks and looking into closets. Her hands shook with adrenaline, and her heart tripped along in her chest, but she was okay. One more night in this cavernous apartment filled with shadows, and she could head home—back to her parents' house—never to leave again. She checked the front door lock and looked out into the quiet hallway. A murderer had stood outside Audrey Marshall's door with the intention to kill her. And then he'd gone inside and done it. Killed her with his knife. Mutilated her.

She looked for a long time out into the hall, contorted by the peephole into a tunnel with curved walls. She expected someone to turn the corner and make an appearance at any moment. Sanders the cat. George Daniels back from the dead. Corbin Dell back from England. Alan stalking her from the front door instead of from the back. But nothing happened. The well-lit, carpeted hall remained empty.

She went online and looked at airfares for returning to London. She began an e-mail to her parents telling them she was coming home, but didn't finish it. She could do it tomorrow, after she booked something, when it was all finalized.

She looked at the Rachael Chess articles again online. That must have been who Alan was talking about when he mentioned the other woman who had been killed. So Jack had been doing his research as well.

She went back to the kitchen to get more wine, but the bottle was empty, and she poured herself a glass of milk instead. She brought it to the den and turned on the television. The old movie channel was playing a film that she knew pretty well, because it was one of her father's favorites. *I Know Where I'm Going!* starring Wendy Hiller and Roger Livesey. She curled up on the couch, rested her head on two oversized pillows, and attempted to let the black-and-white images soothe her. She kept thinking of Alan, though, behind the door in the kitchen. Seeing him, visibly drunk, standing there, Kate thought she was about to die. It was George Daniels all over again—another man come to kill her. Although George, for all his rage and craziness, had never been a drinker. In fact, whenever Kate had more than a couple of glasses of wine, he'd start to get mad at her, asking her repeatedly why she needed to drink so much.

In the film, the woman played by Wendy Hiller was desperately trying to get to the Scottish island where her fiancé was, but a storm had trapped her on the coast, where she'd fallen in love with another man. She was trying anyway, in a small boat, and a whirl-pool was pulling her to her death. Kate pulled the comforter on top of her. The movie ended, and another immediately started up. *Pygmalion.* Another Wendy Hiller. She thought of her father, who would love this movie channel that only showed old films. She started watching the film, but she had to pee, and her jeans were uncomfortably tight. She forced herself to get up and walk through the living room and past the kitchen to the bedroom, where she changed into pajamas, peed in the en suite bathroom, and brushed her teeth. She passed back through the bedroom, where the strong moonlight through the window cast strange shadows in the twisted sheets of the bed. This apartment is haunted, she thought, and walked briskly back toward the den, lit in flickering black and white from the massive television.

Leslie Howard was standing in the rain, secretly listening to Wendy Hiller's cockney accent as she was selling flowers.

Kate didn't remember falling asleep. It felt as though one minute she was watching the television, wondering if any of the actors were still alive, and then her eyes must have shut, and she was suddenly in the world of the film, the voices part of her dream. The couch was swallowing her, and she was on the brink of sliding into the true blackness of sleep when the dream shifted, and there was a hand pressed against her face, and she felt herself rising back up from the depths, jerking awake, but the hand was still there, pressed hard against her mouth, another hand gripping her shoulder.

This is real, she thought and began to struggle, fully awake.

The room was dark, the television still on, and the man who held her was making shushing sounds. It wasn't Alan. She could see razor-cut blondish hair and the line of a square jaw, and she could smell his sweat, stale and powdery. Her heart was beating so fast that her chest hurt, and tears sprang to her eyes. The man about to kill her was a stranger, although he was vaguely familiar, as though she'd passed him on the street or seen him in a dream.

He was speaking in a low whisper. "Kate, please listen to me. It's Corbin. It's your cousin. I am not going to hurt you. I need you to be very quiet. There's a man in this apartment and he's a very bad man. Shhhh. If you scream, or make a noise, he's going to come in here. I need you to hide, and then I can go deal with him. Nod if you understand."

Kate shook her head. Only half the words had made any sense

to her. Was it really Corbin, or was he lying? How was he here, in the apartment? She thought of trying to bite his hand, but it was pressed hard against her mouth, her lips flattened against her teeth. She could see the man's eyes, darting furiously over the edge of the couch toward the dark interior of the rest of the apartment. He looked scared. *It is Corbin,* she thought, recognizing him from pictures she'd seen.

"Shhh," he said again. "You *have* to trust me, or we are both going to die. Do you understand?" His voice had become more urgent, cracking almost, and Kate nodded this time, deciding that she needed to do what he said. He'd either kill her or he wouldn't. It was happening again—not with Alan, the way she'd thought earlier—but with some man she had never met.

After feeling Kate nod, Corbin looked her in the eyes. He loosened the hand around her mouth, but didn't remove it. "Do you believe me? You have to believe me."

She nodded more, and took a deep breath.

"Everything's going to be all right," Corbin said, but his eyes were still darting toward the hallway. "Do you know about the closet in here?"

"No," Kate said in a cracked whisper through his hand.

"There's a false back in it. It's where my dad kept valuable things. Press your hand all the way to the right and push. You'll hear a click and it will swing open. There's enough room for you to hide there."

Kate, not even realizing it, was shaking her head again, saying "no" into Corbin's hand. He continued:

"Just stay there until I come back to get you. If I don't come back, then just stay there longer. He won't find you, and eventually he'll give up. You have to trust me, okay?"

"I can't," Kate said. She felt tears sliding down her face. She breathed in deeply through her nose, her chest swelling. She thought for a moment she might start laughing.

"You have to," Corbin said. "You'll be safe. I promise."

She looked at him and for the first time they made eye contact. It was like finding a handhold on a sheer cliff. Making a decision, she nodded, calmly, and Corbin took his hand all the way off her face.

"Who is it?" she asked. "Who's here?"

"It doesn't matter. We don't have a lot of time."

She followed him to the closet, her numb legs somehow operating independent of the rest of her body. He gently pushed her into its interior, filled with dry-cleaned suits hanging in plastic. "Just push, all the way to the right. You'll hear the click," he repeated.

"Okay," she said, the sound of her voice coming from far away.

Before shutting the door, he whispered: "I am going to save you." And then she was enveloped in darkness. She did as he said and pressed her hand against the back wall. It gave a little, clicked, and swung open. She stepped inside and felt around. There was a small metal handle and she pulled the door back in toward her, but not all the way. The small enclosure smelled of untreated wood and musty paperbacks. She felt as though she'd stepped back through time, into that other closet in another country, another madman on the other side, only this time she was calmer. No, it wasn't exactly a sense of calm. It was resignation. It was over. The world had been trying to kill her in the worst way possible, and now it was finally going to do it. She gave in, the calmness spreading through her. She even pulled the false door all the way closed; the handle turned and she knew she could get out again, but maybe it didn't matter. She slid her hands along the wood. The space was the width of the closet, wider than her outstretched arms, but it couldn't have been more than a foot deep. With her back pressed tight against the rear wall, her breasts grazed the false door. A wave of unreality passed over, and she welcomed it. And she waited.

She listened. She could hear her own breathing and her heart in her chest, but nothing else.

How had Corbin gotten back to America? Or had he never left? No, he had left and gone to London, because Martha had seen him, hadn't she?

He'd come back because he'd killed Audrey and now he was going to kill her, and this hiding in the closet, this other man, was all part of some elaborate game he was playing.

Or could there really be someone else in the apartment?

Was it Alan, still drunk, who'd found another way to sneak in?

Or was it finally George Daniels? Kate felt the laugh again, rising up through her lungs, and she held it down by tensing her jaw, her neck muscles almost seizing up. George Daniels back from the dead, and in another country. In some ways, she wouldn't be surprised. As she always said to herself: he was always with her, always along for the ride.

His voice in her head: *You are going to die in a closet, Kate.* Giggling.

She closed her eyes, and nothing changed. The world was still black.

She tried not to think of her parents and how they would feel when they heard she'd been murdered.

She thought of Alan. Twenty-four hours earlier she'd been in his bed, allowing herself to feel something. She'd been happy, celebratory almost, that she was finally with another man. Maybe that was what George Daniels had been waiting for all along, waiting for her to finally cheat on him, so that he could finally give her what she deserved. Maybe he really was alive, and the police, and her parents, and everyone else had lied to her. For a horrible instant, she believed it.

And then she heard something. A human sound, like a grunt. Or maybe it was a scream that had suddenly been cut off. She waited, barely breathing, but there was nothing else, just the sound of the building humming and sighing around her. And suddenly she wondered if she'd heard anything at all. She allowed herself to take a breath, sipping at the thin air in the closet. She cracked the false door open a little, relieved that it hadn't locked her in. She tapped her fingertips together, felt a sharp pain when she tapped her swollen thumb, the splinter still embedded deep in the pad. She put the thumb in her mouth and tore at the skin with her teeth, eventually sucking the splinter out. She wiped the blood down her shirt. Removing the splinter had made her feel sane for a brief moment, but now she wondered how much longer she could stay in this closet. What was happening out there?

She formed a plan, just to see how it would feel in her head. She would push her way out of the closet and move as swiftly and quietly as possible from the den to the hallway, then from the hallway to the living room and foyer, then she'd go through the door and run as fast as she could to the front desk. It was a big apartment. Corbin, or whoever else was in here, might be somewhere else. She might get free. And if she didn't? Then at least she wasn't cowering in this closet anymore.

Her thumb continued to drip blood, and she sucked at it some more, actually savoring the taste in her mouth.

She'd often wondered about the night that George Daniels had tracked her down in the Lake District and sealed her in the closet. She wondered whether, even if the door hadn't been blocked, she'd have been able to leave. Not while he was still out there, but after she heard the gun go off. She'd been trapped, and there was nothing for her to do but wait, but even if the door had been open, Kate sometimes thought that she'd have stayed there forever. She'd crouched into a ball, like an injured animal, and hadn't moved, not even when the frightened copper had opened the door and reached in to take her out. But now she had a chance to run, and she knew she needed to take it, for better or for worse.

She swung the false back door all the way open and stepped into the main space of the closet, pressing her ear to the door. She listened for a minute but heard nothing. She put her hand on the knob. She breathed in through her nose and blew out through her mouth.

She tried to remember a prayer from childhood, but all she could remember was what she learned from her grandmother to say at bedtime. She said it now, to herself, her eyes closed:

From ghoulies and ghosties
And long-leggedy beasties
And other things that go bump in the night,
Good Lord, deliver us

Calmed by the words, her grandmother's voice in her head, she swung the door open and stepped out of the closet into the still-flickering light of the den.

CHAPTER 26

ON MONDAY MORNING, AFTER CALLING the London office and letting them know he was deathly sick, and asking if he could start the following week, Corbin Dell took out fifteen thousand pounds in cash from the local branch of the Royal Bank of Scotland. He'd opened an account online before his departure to avoid having to pay transaction fees on all his withdrawals. The teller, an Indian woman wearing a head scarf, registered almost no reaction to the request, but she did spend close to fifteen minutes making calls and typing into her computer before finally handing over the money in hundred-pound notes.

With the hefty packet of money in the inside pocket of his raincoat, Corbin took a taxi to Camden Market and began to wander the stalls, looking for a candidate. He wasn't going to rush it; he had all day, and knew his chances were best when the pubs opened. But he had a plan. He was going to find Henry Wood and he was going to kill him. And this was the best opportunity he was going to have.

It was almost two in the afternoon when Corbin spotted the first promising match. It was in a dingy pub several blocks from the market area. The man had a beard and longish, greasy hair, but other than that, he looked a lot like Corbin. Same coloring, similar features, prominent jawline. And he looked mildly down and out, drinking a pint glass of cider over ice in the middle of a rainy Monday afternoon.

Corbin ordered himself a pint of Stella and another cider, and brought both over to where the man was seated, at a table near the grimy windows. There was just enough light coming through for the man to read his Charles Bukowski novel.

Corbin sat and pushed the cider over to the man, who looked alarmed as he lowered the well-thumbed paperback. He really did look like him, enough anyway.

"Can I ask you something?" Corbin said. "Do you have a passport?"

"The fuck you want?" the man answered. The words were clear, but Corbin didn't recognize the accent.

"I have a proposition for you, but I need to know if you have a passport first."

"Yeah, I've got a passport." Maybe it was a German accent.

"I'd like to borrow it, plus any other identification you have. It will be no more than a week, I promise. I can give you eight thousand pounds in cash right now, and I'll give you another two when I return everything. There'd be no risk for you, at all."

The man laughed. "Go away."

"I'm telling you. It's ten thousand pounds and no risk."

"No risk? It's my fucking passport you'd be using."

Corbin took a sip of his beer. He'd sold enough financial opportunities over the years to know that this guy was already hooked. Getting his passport was not going to be a problem. "How tall are you?" Corbin asked. "Do you mind standing up?"

The man didn't answer the question. Instead, he said: "What if you don't come back?"

"Then report your passport stolen. It happens all the time. Where are you from, anyway? I don't recognize your accent."

"I'm from Rotterdam. I'm Dutch."

"What's your name?"

"It's Bram. I haven't decided to do this, you know."

"Listen, Bram. It's ten thousand pounds. In cash. All you have to do is hand over the passport, and help me book an airline ticket with your credit card. I'll pay you in cash for that as well. I need to take a trip but don't want someone to know where I'm going.

That's all there is to this. In one week I return everything. If something goes wrong, you just have to say that your passport and credit card were stolen and you didn't notice right away. There's no downside to this."

Bram thought for a moment, then said, "I'll do it for fifteen thousand pounds."

Corbin stood up. "I'll keep looking. There'll be someone else 'round here that looks like me."

Corbin returned his empty pint glass to the bar and exited the pub. Bram caught up with him on the street. "Okay, okay," he said. "I'll do it."

Bram Heymans was squatting in a large nearby flat that was under construction, sleeping on a rollout and living out of a back-pack. Despite this, he had an Apple laptop and a portable wire-less router. Corbin studied Bram's maroon passport. In the picture Bram was clean-shaven, his hair swept back off his forehead. Corbin had been hoping that the picture would have the bearded version of Bram, but the clean-shaven picture was good enough. Corbin would pass as Bram, so long as he didn't draw too much attention to himself. There were no flights going to Logan for the remainder of that day, so Corbin, using Bram's Visa card, booked an early morning flight for the following day. He gave Bram the eight thousand pounds, plus an extra eight hundred for the ticket, and took possession of the passport.

"You'll still be here in a week?" Corbin asked Bram, who was flicking through the bills with a nicotine-stained thumb.

"What, here? In this flat?"

"Yeah."

"Yeah, I'm not going anywhere."

"So one week from today I'll be back here with your passport and ID. At noon. You'll be here?"

"I'll be here," Bram said, still looking at the bills.

———————

THE LINE AT THE GATWICK security gate was at least a hundred travelers long, but Corbin was early. He was happy to see the crowd; it would hopefully mean that whoever looked at his passport might rush the job, not studying the picture too hard. Corbin had been anxiously analyzing the small photo all through the night and into the morning, trying to decide if it was going to work. He thought it would, especially since the picture was seven years old. He had been trying to decide whether it would be better to keep his current style or to imitate the hairstyle in the photograph, and decided to keep his current style. If the hairstyles were perfect then the security agent, or the customs agent in Boston, might look too closely at the facial features, realize that the eyes weren't quite right, the ears entirely different.

The hungover-looking agent at the end of the line barely looked at the passport after placing it on the scanner, just perfunctorily moving his eyes from the picture to Corbin's face, then ushering him through toward security.

It was a little rockier in Boston, where they'd recently installed Automated Passport Control. Corbin stood in front of a computer screen, scanned his passport, then stood still and stared at a camera, waiting to have his photograph taken. He hadn't been prepared for this, and his heart sped up as he waited for the camera to flash. Instead, words appeared on the screen—the machine had failed to capture a recognizable face—and Corbin thought he was finished, that some software program was figuring out that the face in front of them didn't match the face on the passport. Corbin tried the picture again and got the same message. A customs agent drifted over, adjusted the height of the machine, and it worked. A light flashed, and a slip of curled paper slid from the machine—a black-and-white image of Corbin's alarmed face. He brought the slip of paper and his passport to another agent, a young acne-ridden man with a military-looking mustache, who grilled Corbin about his trip to the United States, asking him where he was staying and how long he planned to stay, and studying the passport, although paying relatively little attention to the picture. Finally, the customs agent stamped Bram Heymans's passport and Corbin, armpits damp but otherwise okay, walked through the double doors into Logan airport. He could see through the terminal, and the large sliding doors, to the taxis idling on the curb outside; he was free, unmoored. He was in America and no one could ever prove it. As long as he wasn't caught, he had a perfect alibi. He had tremendous power, he realized, so long as he could find Henry.

He was suddenly nervous that someone would recognize him now that he was back in his hometown. Should he disguise himself? Where was he going to stay? He hadn't thought everything through since he'd been so concerned with whether he could return to America without using his own passport. Now that he'd done it, what was next?

He took a taxicab to a boutique hotel on Beacon Street and checked in using Bram's passport and cash, claiming, with a terrible Dutch accent, that his credit card had been recently stolen. The clerk said they needed a credit card for incidentals, but Corbin offered a cash deposit of two thousand dollars (he'd traded in nearly five thousand pounds at the cash exchange at Logan, using Bram's ID), and the hotel manager finally agreed. Alone in the room, Corbin stripped off his clothes and stood under the shower for nearly half an hour, trying to will his body to relax. Ever since he'd received the e-mail from the police, Corbin had felt like a man possessed, finally knowing what he had to do. What he hadn't yet allowed himself to feel was the pain of what had happened to Audrey, the sadness that she was gone forever. But now the thoughts came anyway, along with uncontrollable tearless sobs, Corbin's jaw clenched so tight that he worried his teeth might shatter. The only thing that calmed him was the thought of getting to Henry and crushing him in his hands, making him pay for what he'd done. Henry had been in Boston less than a week ago. *There's a chance I can find him,* Corbin told himself. As soon as it got dark he would walk to his apartment building and wait in the bushes, to see if anything happened, if Henry, for whatever reason, made an appearance.

It was almost noon. He had barely slept or eaten since hearing about Audrey, but now his stomach was growling loudly, and his head was light with lack of food. He pulled on jeans, a T-shirt, and the hooded Jack Wills sweatshirt he'd bought at Gatwick. He pulled the hood tight around his head, tightening the strings so that it wouldn't come loose, and left the hotel, turning right and walking toward the hospitals. He passed a barbershop he'd never really noticed before, doubled back, and pushed through the doors. There were two barbers, one old and bald, and the other young and bald, clearly the son. The dark interior was about as wide as a train car and smelled of pomade. The young barber was free, and after being seated, Corbin asked for a buzz cut.

"How short?" the barber asked.

"As short as you can go."

The barber set his clipper to the lowest setting and began taking off almost all of Corbin's hair. Sports talk radio was playing from an old boom box high up on a shelf, and Corbin was able to turn his mind off for a moment, listening to callers complain about the lousy relievers the Red Sox had this season.

"You want a shave as well?" the barber asked after finishing.

Corbin ran his hand across his chin. He hadn't shaved in over a week, and his beard was thicker than it had ever been. "Sure," he said. "Shave everything but the mustache." He'd read or heard somewhere that if a man wanted to change his appearance he should shave his head and grow a mustache. It was one of those things that had stuck in his head for years, even though he'd always wondered if it were true. But when the barber was done, and Corbin stared at his nearly bald head and the beginnings of his reddish mustache, he did think he looked different enough to possibly fool someone who happened to glance at him. It was enough.

After leaving the barbers, Corbin walked down toward Mass General Hospital and found a Greek pizzeria he'd never been to; he ate a large meatball sub and drank two Cokes. Then he got a turkey sub to go and brought it back to the hotel. Who knew when he'd get a chance to eat again? Back in his room, he cracked the window that looked out over slate roofs toward the Common. It was a windy day, and it felt good to let some of the blustery, cool air into the stuffy room. He opened his laptop, keyed in the wireless code, and checked his e-mails. He'd left his phone behind. Even with GPS turned off, it would still make him nervous, but he felt okay with using the laptop, fairly certain it wouldn't give his location away. There was nothing new from his cousin Kate, just the e-mail she'd sent him on Sunday night that the police had asked to search his apartment. He was still wondering about that. There must have been some way they'd connected him with Audrey, although he didn't know how. Maybe they'd interviewed other residents in the apartment and Alan had said something. It didn't really matter. They weren't going to find anything in his apartment.

Corbin opened a browser window and, for the thousandth time, searched for anything related to a "Henry Wood," or "Hank Bowman," or "Hank Wood." There was nothing. He lay back on the bed and stared at the high ceiling, the ornate molding. The wind whistled through the room, fluttering the curtains, and Corbin closed his eyes, pretended he was a kid again, lying on Annisquam Beach, the salt air moving over him. He fell asleep and dreamed that he was innocent, that the murderers were coming for him, and that he wasn't one of them.

CHAPTER 27

A BEEP FROM HIS COMPUTER woke Corbin. The hotel room was cold, and he was shivering. He sat up and looked at his computer screen. He had left his e-mail account open, and Kate Priddy had sent him a message in a chat box. Hello there, it said. He stared at it for a long time, his teeth now starting to chatter from the cold. It felt as though she could see him through the computer screen, see where he was. He got up and shut the window, pulled his hoodie back on. Hi, he wrote back.

Did you kill Audrey Marshall?

Corbin, barely breathing, put his fingers on the keyboard. He wanted to write that he knew who killed her, but he wasn't brave enough. Instead, he wrote to Kate that he hadn't killed Audrey, and asked if the police thought he had. They say you were in a relationship with her, Kate wrote, and Corbin admitted that he was. He told her their relationship had been secret and that's why he hadn't brought it up. He knew how lame it sounded, of course. Why *hadn't* he just opened up about his relationship with Audrey as soon as he'd found out she was dead? It wasn't to protect her anymore.

He promised Kate he hadn't killed Audrey. It seemed to work, since they were now chatting about the weather and Sanders, the cat. She asked what Audrey was like, then mentioned a friend of Audrey's who she had met.

Corbin's skin prickled. He asked her who the friend was.

Jack Ludovico.

Corbin asked what he looked like and she told him he had reddish hair and glasses. It didn't sound like Henry, but he could have easily dyed his hair.

Corbin quickly googled the name. Nothing. Then googled the name with *Henry Wood*. Still nothing. They chatted a little more and said goodbye. He felt nauseous at the thought that Henry had possibly met Kate. Corbin had to find him.

Why Ludovico? It sounded familiar to Corbin, and he googled it. The first item that came up was the Ludovico Technique, the aversion therapy from the scene in *A Clockwork Orange* in which they pry Alex's eyes open and make him watch violent pornography. It had been Henry's favorite film, or one of them. He loved all of Stanley Kubrick's films, and Corbin and Henry had watched many together that summer in New York City when they had been so close. It felt like decades ago. Henry obviously had gotten that particular pseudonym from the film; what about his other false name—Hank Bowman—that he'd used when he lived in Hartford? Corbin punched *Kubrick* and *Bowman* into the search engine, and the film *2001* immediately came up. Corbin's heart began to race, and a flush of excitement went across his skin. He looked at the list of all of Kubrick's films. They'd watched *The Shining* together several times. What was Jack Nicholson's character's name? Corbin looked it up. It was Jack Torrance. He punched in *Henry Torrance*. There were a few hits. An actor who'd been in a bunch of B movies. Corbin added Boston, and a mediation consultant came up. There was a Web site, and even though there was no picture of Henry Torrance, Corbin somehow knew right away that he had finally, after all this time, found him. The biography listed Aurelius College and Columbia University for a master's degree in conflict resolution. It was definitely Henry. There was a phone number and an office address in Newton.

He'd found him.

Even though it was nearly five, and the chances of Henry's still being at work were slim, Corbin hailed a taxicab on Charles Street and gave the address of Henry's office in Newton. It took forty-five minutes to get there through stop-and-go Boston rush hour traffic. The office was in the village of Newtonville, above a bakery on a tree-lined street that ran parallel to the turnpike.

There was a bench across the street, and Corbin sat there, keeping an eye on the building. He needed a moment to think. He couldn't quite believe how close he'd finally gotten to Henry. It was entirely possible he was up in his office right at this moment. The thought filled Corbin with equal amounts of hope and fear. If Henry actually was up there, he had no doubt that he could kill him with his bare hands, choke the life out of him. But what if there was someone with him? Or someone on the same hall who heard the commotion? What if Henry had a gun?

Corbin stood, the seat of his jeans now slightly damp from the wooden bench, and looked up and down the commercial block. There was a tavern, a sub shop, two banks, a jewelry store, and down at the far corner, what looked like a mom-and-pop hardware store. It was exactly what he was looking for. He walked briskly to its entrance, pushing through the door, jumping a little as it set off a bell to let the owners know they had a customer. The place was dark and narrow, its aisles just wide enough for one person.

"Can I help you?"

Corbin didn't immediately know where the voice was coming from. He swiveled his head and spotted a woman with tightly curled gray hair behind the register. He thought for a moment that she was kneeling, because her head barely rose above the countertop, but then watched as she scooted up onto a tall chair. She was incredibly short, possibly with some dwarfism.

"No, thanks," Corbin said. "Just looking around." His voice, to his own ears, sounded nervous and disingenuous.

"Just holler if you can't find something you're looking for."

He entered a random aisle that turned out to have plumbing

supplies, shelf after shelf of plastic pipes and fittings. *What am I looking for?* Corbin thought. He found another aisle filled with hand tools—hammers and screwdrivers and wrenches. There was a smallish hammer, its rubber handle only about five inches long. It fit nicely in his hand. He could easily knock Henry out with it, then either strangle him or hit him till he was dead. But even though it was small for a hammer, it would be awkward to carry, too noticeable in his jacket pocket. He kept browsing, considered a chisel that really wasn't sharp enough, then found what he was looking for, a heavy-duty box cutter with a rubber grip. It was small enough to fit in his pocket with the blade retracted. He could even carry it in his fist without its being too visible.

He was about to take it up to the register, but paused. If Henry was in his office, and Corbin killed him with the box cutter, then wouldn't the woman working at the neighboring hardware store remember the shady man who bought the cutter just before the murder occurred? He glanced at the ceilings, looking for mounted cameras, but saw none. He slid the box cutter into his sweatshirt pocket, wandered over to the next aisle, picked up a cheap bottle of rubber cement, and brought that up to the register.

The woman put down her Dean Koontz paperback and rang up the rubber cement on a cash register that looked as old as she did.

"Found something you couldn't live without, I see," she said and smiled.

"Can never have too much glue," Corbin responded, trying not to make eye contact. Maybe he should have just walked out of the store with the box cutter in his pocket. Now this woman would definitely remember him.

Back outside, carrying the small plastic bag with the rubber cement, Corbin walked with purpose down the street toward the sub shop. There was a large garbage bin on the corner, and he dropped the rubber cement into it, then stripped the box cutter of its flimsy paper packaging and threw that out as well. There were people around, mostly commuters, a few preteens on skateboards, but no one was paying any attention to Corbin. If Henry was in his office—and that was a big if—then Corbin needed to take advantage of that fact. It didn't matter that the woman from the hardware store might remember him. The only thing that mattered was getting to Henry.

He crossed at the crosswalk and made his way through the glass door into a small vestibule with water-stained walls and linoleum floor. The cramped space smelled of fresh bread and industrial cleaner. On the largest wall were three buttons, and three businesses listed. Corbin pressed the buzzer next to HENRY TORRANCE, MEDIATION SPECIALIST, and waited. What would he say if Henry's voice came through the speaker on the wall? Corbin could feel the adrenaline in his blood. He decided to say nothing. If Henry was here, he'd simply bolt up the stairs, break down his door if necessary, and slit his throat with the box cutter. His fingers twitched at the thought.

But there was no answer to the buzzer. He pressed it again, held it longer. No one was there.

Corbin went up the narrow stairwell anyway. Off the landing was a short, poorly lit corridor with three closed doors. MELANIE GELLAR, LICENSED THERAPIST. JOSEPH HAHN, CPA. And then simply HENRY TORRANCE. That door was locked, but the knob felt flimsy in Corbin's hand, like a tin can that he could crush. He considered busting through into the office for a lead on where Henry lived, but then he heard a phone ring in one of the other offices and a man's voice answer it. Corbin took his hand off the doorknob. No, now he knew where Henry worked, and if he broke into his office, then Henry would be alerted. It was better to leave now and come back early the next day, stake out across the street, wait for Henry to show up.

Back outside, Corbin realized he didn't have a way to get back to his hotel. Newton, although just on the outskirts of Boston, was still a suburb, and not an easy place to flag a cab. He spotted a bar across the street called Edmands Tavern. Inside, a small after-work crowd was filling up the padded leather seats around the horseshoe bar. Corbin leaned against the bar, ordered a Lagunitas Pils, and asked the bartender if she'd call a cab for him. She was young— college age at the most—with an arcane symbol tattooed onto the back of her long neck, and she looked at Corbin as if he'd just asked her if he could tie his horse out back for the night.

"I lost my cell phone," Corbin explained.

She pulled out hers, and with rapidly moving thumbs, located a cab company and called them, handing the phone over to Corbin. He named the bar he was in and was told to wait ten minutes.

"You should get Uber," the bartender said when he handed the phone back to her.

"I have it, but it's on my phone."

"Oh right." She laughed, sliding down the bar toward a pair of bearded men in polo shirts who had just arrived and were studying the beer list.

Instead of having the cabdriver take him back to the hotel, Corbin gave 75 Bury Street as his address, then he leaned back on the worn vinyl of the backseat and closed his eyes for a moment, willing himself to relax. He started with his face, forcing his jaw muscles to slacken, then worked his way down his body. He was so close to getting to Henry, and because of that, he allowed himself the briefest of fantasies, one that he'd had a few times. If he could kill Henry and get away with it, then he'd have his life back. Some semblance of a life, anyway. Maybe over time he could learn to forgive himself for what they'd done to Claire and to Linda, and the part that he'd played in Rachael's and Audrey's deaths. No, he could never truly forgive himself. But maybe he could atone. He didn't know exactly how he would do that, but the image that sometimes came to his mind was an image of himself with a family, daughters of his own that he would protect. As soon as that image came into his mind, he pushed it away, knowing it was far too optimistic. No, if he could kill Henry, then the most he could expect from the rest of his life was to not hurt anyone else, to get through the days and years unscathed. That would be enough.

THE TAXI LET HIM OUT a block away from his apartment building. It was now dark, the wind lessening but the temperatures dropping. He pulled his hood up over his head and tightened the strings. With his hands pushed into his jean pockets, he walked toward 101, but before he reached the gated entryway, he crossed the street, not wanting to bump into a resident face-to-face. He moved slowly, looking for a place where he could hunker down and keep an eye on the building. If Henry had visited Kate already, he might visit again. He'd feel better watching his apartment building than he would in his hotel room, waiting for morning to arrive.

Bury Street was primarily redbrick and residential, the entryways well lit, but 106 Bury Street had retained its old stable doors, slightly recessed so that Corbin could sit on a low stone riser. It wasn't a hidden spot, but he was halfway between streetlamps and relatively in the dark. More important, he could see the entryway to his building and also the living room windows of his own apartment. They glowed with lamplight, the curtains halfway pulled. Corbin pulled his legs up tight, pressing his back against the wooden stable doors, and tried to make himself as unnoticeable as possible.

Over the next two hours, Corbin watched several people come and go from the building. Most of them he recognized. There was the old woman who was friends with the Valentines, out walking her small asthmatic pug. She took the dog just beyond the gates, toward the short hedge that bordered the neighboring property. The pug snooped around and eventually peed on the sidewalk. The woman cast a glance in Corbin's direction. He raised his head slightly, hoping she'd see that he was Caucasian. Otherwise, she just might call the police. A short time later, Corbin watched Mrs. Heathcote get out of a taxicab in front of the building, the driver carrying her two bags of groceries across the courtyard for her. A few other people Corbin didn't recognize came and went, but none of them was either his cousin Kate or Henry Wood.

As the night darkened, the streetlamps seemed to cast brighter, wider circles of light, and Corbin wondered how long it would be before some paranoid neighbor called the police to report a loiterer. If the police did come, he could simply say he was resting. He could use a Dutch accent and provide Bram's ID. They'd move him along, but they wouldn't take him in. At least, he hoped not.

Corbin heard loud, irregular footsteps and watched as a man who looked about his age stopped in front of the courtyard. He swayed slightly, as though drunk, then looked up, directly at the windows of Corbin's—now Kate's—apartment. Was it Henry? It didn't look like him from behind—too tall and solid—but maybe it was. Then the man turned his head, and in the light from the moon and the streetlamp, Corbin recognized Alan, the guy from the other side of the building who had asked Corbin once if he was seeing Audrey Marshall. Why was he looking up at Kate's windows? Maybe that was just his thing—a weirdo who liked to look into windows. Hadn't he decided that that was how Alan had found out about his relationship with Audrey? Corbin pulled his legs in tighter and lowered his head, as though he was trying to keep warm. Alan lurched through the gates into the courtyard; with each step he looked as though he was about to fall, just managing to get a foot down before it happened.

The street was quiet again, and Corbin started to stand, wanting to stretch his legs, when he saw another figure rounding onto Bury from Brimmer Street. He quickly sat back down, pressed against the door into the shadows.

It was Henry.

Corbin was almost sure of it. His whole body was pulsing in time with his heartbeat. Even though he couldn't see the man's features, the way he was walking—fast clip, shoulders back—was so familiar. He was so sure it was Henry that he was baffled when the man walked straight past the entryway to 101, not even turning his head, and kept walking toward the river. Corbin stood and watched. The man—now he was unsure whether it was Henry or not—walked past the next building, then suddenly cut right and out of sight. Corbin crossed the street, breaking into a jog, holding onto the box cutter that was still in his sweatshirt pocket. He slowed when he got to the place where the man had disappeared. There was a narrow, almost impassable alley between two buildings, and just enough moonlight to see that the alleyway was now empty. Corbin stepped into it, each side brushing a shoulder. The pavement below his feet was slippery, and a smell like spoiled milk reached his nostrils. Without thinking too much about it, Corbin turned his body slightly and briskly walked the length of the buildings, coming out on another alley, much wider, that ran behind the backs of Bury Street residences. There was no sign of the man he was following, but he must have turned right, since the alley dead-ended to the left. Corbin walked slowly and carefully toward the back of his apartment building. He'd never seen the rear of 101 Bury, and was surprised to find a wide metal door built into the brick wall, a door that more than likely led to the apartment building's basement. There was a security camera bracketed to the wall above the door, but it was angled toward the entrance to the alleyway.

Now there was no doubt: that had to have been Henry he was following, and Henry had come back here to enter the building. But why? And how did he get in?

Corbin's apartment keys were in his hotel room. Now was his chance. If Henry was still in the basement he could kill him there. If Henry wasn't in the basement, then where was he? No matter where he was, Corbin would find him.

Back at the hotel room, a little breathless from the speed with which he'd walked, Corbin got the apartment keys from the zippered pocket on the outside of his carry-on luggage. There were three on the metal ring: one for the apartment, one for the storage unit, and one that opened the front doors, even though he'd never used that key, since a doorman was always present and the front doors were never locked. Still, he wondered if that same key also opened the back door that led to the basement. It was worth checking.

Before leaving, Corbin chugged three short glasses of water in the bathroom. He looked in the mirror. The short hair and the half-grown-in mustache *had* changed his appearance, but only superficially. He stared into his own eyes. He was scared but also certain. Henry needed to die, and he was going to kill him.

CHAPTER 28

BACK AT 101 BURY, CORBIN tried his key in the rear door's lock. It stuck at first, then turned after he jiggled it for a while. He swung the heavy door open. He'd been right; concrete steps led down into the storage area of the building. He hesitated at the top of the steps, listening to hear if anyone was in the basement. The worst thing would be for some other resident to see his face, especially before he had a chance to find Henry. After listening for a minute, he tightened the hood around his head and stepped down into the harsh white fluorescence. There were very few places to hide in the main room of the basement area; locked storage units dominated one wall, boilers and water tanks the other. Corbin, hugging the wall, crept toward where he could see behind the water tanks. There was no one there.

He crossed the room toward the corridor that led to the back stairwells. His shoes tapped on the poured-concrete floor and he wished he'd changed into the sneakers he'd brought. He opened the door and peered into the empty corridor. Henry, if he had entered the building, must have gone up toward one of the back entrances to an apartment. It was possible he had gone to Audrey's apartment, revisiting the scene of the crime. But it was also possible he had gone up to Corbin's own apartment, that he was stalking Kate, for whatever reason.

He walked the length of the corridor to the stairwell that led to his apartment. He'd gone up and down the narrow stairs toward his place many times, but he'd never been so aware of how the low-wattage bulbs on each landing barely illuminated the steps. He felt almost blind, his hands on either banister. When he reached the back entrance to his apartment, he pressed an ear against the door, straining to hear anything, but there was no sound. He honestly did not know what to do. Henry had disappeared. If only he'd had his keys on him earlier, then he'd have been able to follow Henry into the basement. Henry could be anywhere now.

Corbin decided that the best course of action would be to return to the basement, hide behind the water tanks, and hope that Henry reappeared.

He was about to start down the steps when he heard something, a sound from below. He stood perfectly still. It was footsteps, quiet but steady. Someone was coming up the stairs.

In a panic, Corbin fumbled for his keys, feeling for the one that opened the doors to his apartment. He slid the key into the knob and, quietly as he could, opened the door, stepped into the dark kitchen, and closed the door behind him.

He stood, still as possible, listening for sounds from the stairwell, but also listening for any sounds coming from within the apartment. His eyes adjusted until he could see the kitchen in the moonlight streaming in through the window. For a moment, there was pure silence, then he heard the approaching footsteps, slow and careful, on the other side of the door. They stopped on the landing. Corbin gripped the box cutter, using his thumb to slide out the blade. Suddenly, the weapon felt inadequate, the blade sharp enough but too small. He'd have to take a perfect shot at Henry to do any damage. Moving slowly, his eyes on the glint of the doorknob, he backed toward the nearest counter, pressing up against it. He slid his left hand along the granite countertop and found the block where the knives were kept. He felt with his fingers for the largest handle and removed the knife. He put the box cutter back in his pocket and switched the knife to his right hand.

What was happening on the other side of the door?

If it was Henry, and he was waiting, for whatever reason, to enter the apartment, Corbin would wait as well. With his free hand on the edge of the countertop, he slowly and quietly moved farther back so that he was partially hidden in the alcove next to the refrigerator. He concentrated on his breathing, making sure it was steady and silent.

He heard something, not from behind the door, but from the interior of the apartment. The rustle of clothes, bare feet on the wooden floors, and Kate was suddenly walking past the kitchen toward the bedroom. If she'd entered the kitchen, or even just turned to look in, she would have seen him. He remained perfectly still, listening. The toilet flushed, and he heard the familiar clunk in the plumbing, the tap being turned on. Moving quickly, Corbin left the kitchen and entered the large living room, lit by a single lamp; he crossed to the darkest part of the room and hid behind the curtain. A few minutes passed and Kate crossed back through the living room. He only heard her steps, and not the rustle of her jeans. She must have changed into whatever she slept in.

After five minutes, he stepped halfway out from behind the curtains. He could hear the faint sounds of the television in the den. At least now he knew where Kate was; it was only a matter of waiting to see if Henry appeared. He stayed where he was, listening intently. An hour, or what felt like an hour, passed. Corbin began to wonder what he was doing there, what he hoped might happen. He even began to wonder whether he'd really heard anything on the stairwell below him. Maybe he'd imagined it. These were the thoughts that were going through his head when Henry Wood, casually, as though he lived there, walked into the living room. Corbin, frozen, watched him, his fingers numb where they held the knife. It was definitely Henry, his hair cut short and dyed, wearing a dark midlength coat with an upturned collar. He was headed toward the den.

Corbin dropped to one knee and yanked his shoes off, one by one. Why hadn't he done that earlier?

In his socks, being careful not to slip, he moved down the hall and entered the den. A black-and-white movie filled the screen.

Kate was under a blanket on the leather couch, clearly asleep. There was no sign of Henry. He spun, looking back down the hall that culminated in the living room. Henry was in one of the two spare bedrooms, the second bathroom, or the laundry room. Kate shifted on the couch behind him, emitting a tiny snort. Corbin thought of the hideaway in the closet in the den, the secret place that his father had had built in when he'd first bought the apartment. He needed to wake Kate and tell her to hide there. That way, if he couldn't find and kill Henry, or if Henry killed him, at least Kate would be safe. It would be all over for him no matter what happened, but he could accept that.

Keeping Kate alive was all that mattered now.

He dropped to her side, put the knife on the floor, pushed the hood off his head, and pressed his hand against her mouth. She woke, struggling, and he put his other hand on her shoulder to hold her in place. He told her—using what he hoped was a reassuring voice—who he was.

"You *have* to trust me," he whispered, "or we are both going to die. Do you understand?"

Kate finally nodded, and Corbin felt like maybe she'd begun to listen to him. He told her about the hidden back in the closet—the one his father had put in to hide gold after the collapse of the technology bubble—and how she'd need to go in there and stay in there until he came to get her. She seemed to get frantic again, but she was struggling less. He kept telling her that she needed to do this, and finally he felt her body relax. She nodded, and he took his hand away from her mouth. Strands of hair, wet with tears and saliva, fanned across one of her cheeks.

"Who is it?" she asked. "Who's here?"

Corbin told her it didn't matter, that she needed to go to the closet. Obediently, she followed him. He felt as though her will had been broken. He desperately wanted to pull her close to him, to hug her. They were family, after all, even if they didn't know one another. He resisted, but right before she stepped toward the back of the closet, he said, "I am going to save you." For that moment, he believed it.

With the closet door shut behind him, he went to the foot of the sofa and picked up the kitchen knife. The film still played behind him, something in black and white, with English accents. A man and a woman at a fancy ball. He was glad for the sound of the television; hopefully, Henry still had no idea that there was someone else in the apartment besides Kate and himself.

Corbin looked down the hall. The doors to the bathroom and the laundry room were closed, but both of the doors to the guest bedrooms were slightly ajar, one more than the other. It was more than likely that Henry had gone into one of the bedrooms. Corbin crept along the hallway's Persian runner and was about to peer into the first bedroom, when movement from the living room caught his eye. He turned and looked. And there was Henry, looking back at him. The light from the single lamp was enough so that Corbin could read his expression. Surprise, mostly. Maybe even some amusement.

Corbin pressed the flat edge of the knife along his jeans to hide it and walked toward Henry.

"You came," Henry said, and smiled, his upper lip pulling back to reveal the large white canines.

"What are you doing here, Henry?" Corbin asked, his voice sounding calmer than he was.

"I'm here because of you, dude. You didn't think . . ."

Knowing he couldn't get into a conversation with Henry—knowing he needed to act—Corbin took two large strides and lunged with the knife, but he wasn't quick enough. Henry pulled his stomach in, hunching his shoulders, like a kid trying to avoid getting tagged in the playground. Then, with Corbin off balance, Henry tackled him, bringing them both crashing down onto the floor, the air punched from Corbin's lungs. Henry pinned Corbin's hand that still held the kitchen knife, and with his other hand tried to twist the knife, slicing open his palm. He hissed in pain, and Corbin, his lungs beginning to work again, managed to hold on to the handle of the knife while toppling Henry off his body and onto his back on the floor. Corbin took a wild shot at Henry's head, stabbing the knife's tip into the floor next to Henry's cheek. Henry's eyes were wide with adrenaline and what Corbin hoped was fear. Corbin began to pull the knife out of the hardwood plank, but his hand, slippery with sweat, slid off the handle. The motion caused him to rock backward a little, landing off-balance on the palm of his left hand. The knife vibrated like a tuning fork. Corbin watched as Henry quickly got to his feet, grabbed the handle of the knife, twisted it out of the floor, and lunged. All Corbin could do was put up his right forearm for protection and kick out with his legs. It wasn't enough. The knife found his throat.

Corbin rolled onto his back, both of his hands instinctively grabbing at the wound, warm blood oozing out between his fingers. He heard scrabbling along the floor, but couldn't raise his head to look for Henry. Instead, he stared up at the coffered ceiling, all feeling from his body beginning to dissolve. He was ready to close his eyes when he saw Kate crouched above him. *You look a little like my father,* Corbin said, but all that came out was the sound of his own blood gurgling in his throat. *You have his eyes.*

CHAPTER 29

ALAN WOKE, THE ALARM CLOCK rattling in his ear. He gingerly turned his head toward the digital numbers. They were telling him it was ten thirty. For a moment he didn't know if it was day or night, then he realized it was dark outside. He thumped at the clock and closed his eyes again. His temples throbbed as though his skull were pinched in a vise.

The alarm went off again. He sat up this time and looked around. It wasn't his clock. It was the door buzzer. He jumped off the bed, surprised that he was still dressed, and walked sloppily across the living room to the intercom. *Kate,* he thought. Fragments of the evening came flooding back to him. There was Jack, and the long, rambling monologue about Corbin having killed before. There was the walk back across Boston, and the Irish pub, and then it started to get hazy. Still, he remembered seeing Kate. They were arguing and she looked scared. It was in a kitchen, he thought, but he didn't remember how he'd gotten there, or how he'd gotten back to his own apartment.

He pressed the button that answered the intercom.

"They're on their way up," the doorman said.

"Who?"

"The police. They showed me a warrant."

There was a loud rap on the door. Alan felt a wave of nausea but went and opened the door.

"Alan Cherney?" It was the woman cop he'd seen before. Behind her were two uniformed officers, both male, both shorter than she was, plus another woman in plain clothes, who looked like an intern along for the ride.

"Yes."

"I'm Detective Roberta James, and this is Agent Abigail Tan from the Federal Bureau of Investigation, and we have a warrant to search your premises." She handed Alan a piece of paper that looked as though it had been folded and unfolded many times.

"Okay," Alan said, and took a step backward to allow all four into his apartment. "Does this have something to do with Audrey Marshall?"

"It does, actually," the agent said, her voice sounding as young as she looked. She removed two pairs of latex gloves from her jacket pocket and handed them to the uniformed officers. "Is there anything you'd like to tell me about your relationship with the deceased?"

Alan rapidly shook his head, aware that he was having trouble meeting her stare. He felt another sharp wave of nausea. "Excuse me," he said, and bolted for the bathroom.

He managed to get the door shut behind him before kneeling on the hard tile, vomiting until there was nothing left but bile. Then he splashed cold water on his face and brushed his teeth. He studied himself in the mirror. His eyes were bloodshot, the lower lids wet with tears from throwing up. His skin was the color of chalk. Wiping away the tears, he felt a terrible sense of dread, not just because the police were searching his apartment, but because he knew something was very wrong.

He heard a police radio out in his living room. What were they looking for? Before heading back out, he opened his medicine cabinet to look for ibuprofen, grabbed his allergy medicine by accident, and putting it back on his shelf, got a sudden, jarring flash of Jack scratching at his forearm in the bar the day before. Hives, he'd said, something about springtime. Only they hadn't looked like allergic hives to him, and Alan suddenly realized what they were, and what that meant. A dizziness coursed through his body at the thought, and he felt an alarm go off that Kate was in terrible danger. He didn't know why, exactly. It was just a feeling, but a feeling as real as anything he'd ever felt.

He exited the bathroom, turning into the living room just as the young agent was crossing the room toward him. She was removing her gloves. Behind her, in the alcove kitchen, he could see the other cop bagging one of his kitchen knives. Alan began to speak, although he was not entirely sure what he was going to say. He stopped when he saw the agent remove her handcuffs from under her jacket. "Alan Cherney," she said, her eyes expressionless, "I'm arresting you on suspicion of the murder of Audrey Marshall . . ."

She read him his rights as she cuffed his hands behind his back.

PART II

AN EVEN SPLIT

CHAPTER 30

THE FRIENDSHIP—OR WHATEVER YOU wanted to call it—with Corbin Dell had been special. Henry Wood, for the first time in his life, imagined that he felt what normal people felt when they fell in love, or looked at a parent, or brought a new puppy home to live with them. Then the friendship ended—Henry getting the call from Corbin after they'd *both* murdered the insignificance that was Linda Alcheri—and Henry felt deeply hurt, another new emotional experience. Not just hurt, but shocked. After all, Henry had introduced Corbin to a new and better world. He'd taken him from Kansas to Oz, and now Corbin, for some reason, wanted to go back to Kansas.

Had Corbin not realized that what had happened in the Boddington Cemetery was something beautiful? And that what had happened on Eel River Pond could have been even more beautiful?

That was how Henry thought of it, especially their shared moment in London with Claire Brennan. Some of it was probably the heightened nostalgia of college memories, but, no, he had felt the incredible beauty at the time, as well. For the short time after the murder that Henry was in London, and then all during that incredible summer in New York, the world was composed of new colors. Henry, every night as he fell asleep, replayed every detail of what had happened between Corbin and Claire and him on that wet Wednesday afternoon. It had been a spontaneous dance in which each participant knew their dance moves without having practiced them before. That was how he remembered it. Claire's death was the climax, and her spilled blood was shared, in perfect equal measures, by Corbin and him. Even the rain, coming when it did, had added to the beauty, washing the blood away, cleaning the air.

Occasionally, Henry altered what had happened, tweaked it to make it a little bit better. For instance, he always took away that awkward moment when he'd slipped on the slick ground and fallen to one knee, the knife slipping from his fingers. He also always reduced the amount of time it had taken to dig the grave, Corbin beginning to panic that someone would come along. And sometimes he allowed himself to add a scene, one in which they'd slice Claire's body down the middle before burying it. *One half for Corbin, and one half for me,* Henry thought. *An even split.* It would have been a way to memorialize why Claire had died; that she'd foolishly shared her love and paid the price. But it would also have memorialized what had happened between Henry and Corbin.

Of course, Henry found out, after Linda Alcheri, that Corbin didn't really understand, and never would really understand. Cutting Linda had been a present that Corbin didn't appreciate.

Still, when the phone call came—Corbin telling him that their friendship was over—Henry was shocked.

And then he got angry.

What did Corbin think? Did he think that after what they'd done together, he could just somehow stop? Did he think he was going to go back to a normal life? Did he want to get married? Have children? Did he actually think he'd be happy back in Kansas, living in a world drained of all color? And Henry decided that, if nothing else, he would make sure that none of that ever happened. That was not how the world worked. Corbin was like him. He could pretend he wasn't, but that wasn't going to change facts, and Henry would make sure that Corbin never forgot it.

Henry Wood became Henry "Hank" Torrance, mediator specializing in business disputes in St. Louis, Missouri. It was easy work. There were so many simple ways to manipulate people, especially people weakened by grievances. Especially stupid people.

He met a woman named Kaylee Buecher who reminded him of Claire, the way she looked and moved, and the smuttiness behind her eyes. He took her to dinner and listened as she told him, in that ugly midwestern accent, how she was the first one in her family to go to college, and her parents didn't appreciate her, just wondered why she hadn't gotten married yet. He never called her back but stalked her for half a year. She lived in a single-family in Webster Groves, a rental. He followed her, learned her schedule. He bought a set of picklocks, taught himself how to use them, and broke into her house whenever he felt like it. He liked to rearrange her things, spit in her leftovers, read her pathetic diary ("Hi Future Me!"). One afternoon, she came home early from work with a man from her office. Henry hid in the bedroom closet and listened to them have sex. Afterward, the man cried, moaning that he was married and he'd never cheated on his wife before. Or that's what he said, anyway. After he left, Kaylee got on the phone and told some friend of hers all about it, then she called her office to tell them she'd be at home the rest of the day with a migraine. Henry stayed in the house all that evening and through half the night, leaving at three in the morning after standing over Kaylee's bed and watching her sleep.

Being alone in the house with Kaylee was the best feeling he'd had since spending time with Corbin.

He visited as much as possible. He learned every hiding place in Kaylee's Dutch Colonial, memorized every creaking floorboard and unoiled hinge. He found he could move around the house at ease with Kaylee in it. He was nearly caught only once. He was in the downstairs bathroom, the one Kaylee never used, when she came home from a night out, bolting into the bathroom to pee. Henry had time to step into the shower stall but not to pull the curtain all the way across. Kaylee sat on the toilet, ferociously emptying her bladder, and if she'd looked up and into the mirror she would have seen Henry's face from behind the shower curtain. But she never looked up, never taking her eyes off her phone. It was what had saved her, some text she was reading that was making her laugh and cry at the same time.

Eventually, the owners of Kaylee's house put it on the market because of the real estate boom, and Kaylee decided to move back into the city with a girlfriend. On Henry's last night with Kaylee in the house, he cut a deck of cards in the living room while Kaylee slept upstairs. Red and he'd kill her in her bed, black and he'd let her live. It was a seven of clubs. Before leaving, Henry got a pair of scissors and cut every picture of Kaylee Buecher that he could find in half, replacing the two pieces back into the frame, or taping them together and putting them back up on the fridge. Then he stole a hand-signed screen print of Andy Warhol's portrait of Mao that was probably worth tens of thousands.

Being with Kaylee had been fun, but also somehow lonely. Even though he'd left her the photographs he'd improved, she would never know it was he that had done it. It would just be a mystery in her life.

Henry decided it was time to find Corbin. Time to get revenge.

It wasn't hard. According to LinkedIn, after a few years in New York City, Corbin had moved back home to Boston to work at the headquarters of Briar-Crane. During his summer vacation, Henry flew to Boston to look for Corbin. He shadowed Briar-Crane's small South End offices; it was clear that Corbin was away. Henry left a fake business card with the chatty Briar-Crane receptionist and learned that Corbin was on the North Shore with family for most of August. Henry rented a car, drove north, and checked into the New Essex Motor Court, the only hotel with a vacancy at the height of the summer season. He tailed Corbin and his beautiful, dark-haired girlfriend for the week. Corbin was tan and muscled. He ran on the beach every morning. And he seemed genuinely happy in the presence of the townie he'd picked up. Henry learned her name. Rachael Chess. She had long, dark hair like Claire Brennan had, and she was always smiling in the presence of Corbin, or draping an arm around his shoulders, or wrapping her legs around him when they were in the ocean together. Wrapping those legs around him every night, as well, Henry imagined. And never suspecting that her golden god had once pounded a woman's head into the ground till she was unconscious. Henry's rage almost made him want to just take Corbin out, sneak into his bedroom some night and slit his throat, stare him in the eyes as he bled out. But, no, that was too good for Corbin. He decided to have some fun first.

Rachael Chess had an active Facebook account, and when Henry learned that she was returning to New Essex over Columbus Day weekend, he flew back. Corbin was not around—surprising, but it made things easier. He managed to meet Rachael at a beachside bar called the Rusty Scupper. Not surprisingly, she was an uppity bitch who refused his offer to buy her a drink. He left the bar to wait in his car. She left at closing time. Some guy kept trying to kiss her in the parking lot, and she kept pushing him away until he stalked off, driving away in a pickup truck that needed a new muffler. She walked toward the beach. Henry removed his backpack from the trunk of his rental car. It contained the new filleting knife he'd bought at Walmart the day before, sharp enough not just to kill her, but to carve her body in a way that would leave no doubt in Corbin's mind as to who had killed his girlfriend.

A year later, more out of boredom than anything else, Henry moved to Boston, opening a walk-up office in Newtonville and renting a furnished apartment downtown. There was a coffee shop across the street from where Corbin worked, and sometimes Henry would wait for Corbin to appear, almost always at six thirty in the morning. Usually, he would go to the nearby gym after work; sometimes home. But he never met anyone, certainly not a woman. By now, he knew the consequences. He knew what had happened to Rachael Chess.

Henry wondered what Corbin thought of him now. Was it pure hatred and fear, or was there some admiration, as well? Was there jealousy? Regret?

When Corbin was at work, Henry would sometimes break into his apartment building, picking the lock at the rear entrance and going through the basement and up a back stairwell that led to Corbin's massive apartment. He didn't do it too often; he was scared of being spotted coming through the back entrance, although he never saw anyone in the basement at all. It contained storage space and not much else. Sometimes there was a cat down there that would follow Henry up the dark, narrow stairwell, meowing plaintively. He wondered if it was Corbin's, but doubted it, since there was nothing in Corbin's apartment—no litter box, no food bowl—that would indicate he had a cat. Sometimes Henry imagined how easy it would be to snap the cat's neck, then spread its guts all over Corbin's Oriental carpets. He didn't do it, though. He wasn't ready for him to know how close he was, and he enjoyed his time in Corbin's apartment far too much.

It was a Thursday afternoon when he discovered that Corbin was hiding a girlfriend. He'd been lounging on the sofa, drinking some of Corbin's Belvedere vodka, when there was a knock on the door. Henry moved quickly and silently to the door, pressing his eye against the peephole. There was a blonde who looked somewhat familiar. He heard a key in the lock and fled toward the master bedroom, just entering the hallway as the door swung open. He didn't panic; he'd had so much experience spending time with Kaylee in her house without her knowing he was there. He ducked into the kitchen and hid in the nook on the far side of the refrigerator, listening for any noise. Henry didn't hear a thing till the front door opened and shut again. He slowly emerged back into the hallway, then back into the living room. There was a note on the coffee table, pinned under his glass of vodka. She had confident, looping script:

Dear Cor,

Used my key and broke into your apartment because I have
a migraine coming on and that stuff you have is the best.
Didn't snoop, I promise. Don't come by tonight because I
might be under a sheet with my earplugs in, but maybe I'll
come over if the headache's gone?? It's been too long.

Audrey

Corbin had a girlfriend. A fuck buddy, anyway. And now Henry
remembered where he'd seen this girl. She lived in the building,
a cold-looking blonde with a man's haircut, always carrying a bag
that looked full of books. Always coming and going. She didn't
seem Corbin's type. Both Claire and Rachael had been dark-haired
girls with soft, curvy bodies. This one was hipless, all legs, looked
like she'd be knocked over by a warm breeze. But still, they were
involved. And it would be so easy to find out her name, what apartment she lived in, how seriously she and Corbin were involved.

Henry felt a great unloosening in his chest, an anticipation of
all that was to come. Corbin might be done sharing with him, but
Henry wasn't done sharing with Corbin.

CHAPTER 31

HER NAME WAS AUDREY MARSHALL. She worked in publishing. She'd moved to Boston from New York City. And she lived in the apartment right next to Corbin Dell's.

Henry got all this information off a simple Google search, preceded by one trip to the lobby of the apartment building with a fistful of leaflets advertising handyman services. The doorman took the leaflets, promising to add them to the residents' mail, although Henry doubted it. "You don't need to add one to Audrey . . . Audrey . . ." He snapped his fingers rapidly, as though trying to remember.

"Audrey Marshall," the sleepy-eyed doorman said.

"That's her. She has my info. I painted her walls a little while ago."

The doorman looked a little confused. "When was that?"

"Few months ago, I think," Henry said as he ducked out the door.

He began to follow Audrey on occasion. She worked strange hours, sometimes not going into the office until midmorning, often not coming back till nearly midnight. And occasionally, on a weekday, she'd stay home. Because of her erratic schedule, it made Henry nervous about breaking into her apartment, something he very badly wanted to do. It wasn't until he saw her leave one morning with a large piece of hand luggage, a taxi idling at the side of the curb, that Henry felt like the opportunity had arisen. He broke in that night, moving through the empty basement and up a different stairwell. Her back-door lock was a five-pin tumbler, and it took him a while to pick it, but eventually he got in. He kept the lights off, letting his eyes adjust to the dark, then moved through the sparsely furnished space, a lot smaller than Corbin's but still big for city living. There were books everywhere in the living room, stacks on the floor that formed a cityscape. The living room curtains were open, so Henry moved into the bedroom, where the curtains were drawn. He brought out his penlight and searched through her things. In the drawer next to her bed, he found what he was looking for, a red leather notebook with a rubber band around its middle. He removed the band and opened the book; it was a diary, page after page of the cursive that Henry had seen on the note she'd left for Corbin. He sat on the edge of the bed and began to read; she dated the entries, which were rarely longer than two or three sentences. It was boring mostly—books she'd read, phone calls with a needy sister—but then the mentions of Corbin began and it got a little more interesting. The first mention he found was from a few months earlier, in January:

Hot Neighbor came for dinner. I can't read him at all. It's like staring at a blank page, a very hot blank page. We drank two bottles of wine and I thought he was going to make a move but then he was out the door like I'd hit him with a cattle prod.

After that the mentions were more frequent, every few days:

Spent the night with Hot Neighbor in his ginormous place. Slightly weird, but nice. Gave me the Not Looking For Relationship speech.

Finally told Kerry about Hot Neighbor. She asked a ton of questions, natch, and I didn't have answers. I said I thought he just wanted to be with someone but didn't want a girlfriend. Because he already has one, Kerry said. I laughed, but it's not as though I haven't thought that a hundred times.

Thing is, I don't think he does. I think it's more complicated than that.

For better or worse, HN and I are now definitely a thing.
I just don't know what that thing is. The sex is nice, and I
have feelings for him and he has feelings for me, or pretends
to, and for the life of me I can't figure out why we're not
even allowed to take a walk around the block together.

Need to break up with HN, sooner rather than later. If I
thought we were just sex buddies, then that would be one
thing, but I know that we are more and he still won't tell me
what is happening inside of that big, thick skull. I need to
get out before I get hurt. We exchanged keys the other day,
more of a neighborly thing, but still, it seemed like something. Corbin, if you're in my apartment and reading this,
then fuck you, and stop doing that thing with your tongue
in my ear. It's gross.

HN is broken. Something is seriously wrong with him. If
he won't talk to me, then it needs to end.

It's over. He came over and accused me of—I don't actually know what he accused me of. Telling someone about
us. One of our neighbors! I'm beginning to think there is
something really wrong with him, and now I want out.

Cor is moving to London for six months, and his cousin is
moving into his place. I'm happy. Why wouldn't I be? If
only he hadn't looked so sad when he told me.

That was the last entry that mentioned him. It was dated a week
before. Henry was shocked. Corbin was moving to London. When

was that happening? Something about it pissed him off. London was their place, and now he was returning as though nothing of importance had happened there. As though it were just another city.

The next day, Henry broke into Corbin's apartment and found a folder on his desk that contained travel documents and copies of the work visa for his time in London. He was leaving in a week, a Thursday night flight. Henry made an easy decision—that same Thursday night he would break into Audrey's apartment again, and if she was there, he'd kill her.

It was time to fuck over Corbin for real, and let him know who had done it to him.

Henry stayed away from Beacon Hill and Bury Street for the next week. He knew he'd been pushing his luck by spending so much time in that neighborhood. Someone was going to notice. That week, he finished a job at a Cambridge nonprofit in which one of its internal groups was considering becoming its own non-profit entity. He also booked a new client, a small law firm in Waltham with a personnel dispute, and over the weekend took the executive assistant from the nonprofit out to dinner. It was a boring date, and an awful restaurant, so Henry amused himself by telling her a long, improvised story about an affair he'd had with a famous television star. Watching the woman's eyes light up with utter belief as he made up stories of the actress's pathetic behavior almost salvaged the evening.

When Thursday night arrived he filled his backpack with his favorite tools, pulled a tight synthetic ski hat over his hair, donned gloves, and walked all the way to Bury Street. It was a beautiful spring night, the air rain-washed and smelling of crushed blossoms, and Henry felt as if the muscles of his body were singing in unison. He felt as though he could kill Audrey Marshall and tear her in two with just his hands.

It hadn't worked that way.

After he entered through the kitchen, Audrey must have heard him.

"Corbin?" she said nervously as she stepped into the kitchen. Henry grabbed her from behind and stuck the knife in her neck before she could say another word. The spray from the artery went from the counter across the cabinets to the ceiling as she crumpled to the floor.

It was early morning before he left her apartment the same way he had entered it. He left her body arranged the way he'd wanted it. Split down the middle. *Half of her for Corbin, and half of her for me.* But it had been messy, hard work, and midway through the job, Henry had been stung with a surge of loneliness that almost took his breath away.

He felt better when the job was done, when he was walking home in the early hours. There was no doubt that Corbin would become a suspect, and if they pinned it on him, well, they wouldn't be wrong, would they? Corbin was as guilty of Audrey Marshall's death as Henry was. Just as he'd been guilty of what happened to Rachael Chess. It was half and half. Always and forever.

Henry got home just as the emerging sun was beginning to lighten the sky. There were fragments of mist on the roads and sidewalks. It would be light in London by now, midday. How long would it be before Corbin heard what had happened with Audrey, before he knew that Henry was still in his life, that Henry would always be in his life?

It wasn't until Saturday afternoon that Henry first read about the murder, an item appearing on the *Globe*'s Web site.

He'd done some thinking since then. Even though he was pretty sure that Corbin would become a suspect—the police would read Audrey's diary, for one thing—Henry wanted to make sure that it happened. He wanted Corbin's name dragged into it, and, ideally, he wanted him arrested. Corbin's pretty face would be splashed across the Internet; preppy, blond killer of innocent young girls.

The question was: Would the diary be enough to land Corbin squarely on the suspect list? It would, of course, but there needed to be more. And if Henry was going to play this game, he really wanted to play it. He needed to plant the idea that there was something suspicious about Corbin Dell, and he thought of a way he could do that.

The next day at noon he went to 101 Bury Street, waiting around outside on the street to see if anyone might come out of the building. It felt good being there and being untouchable. In his mind, he was a friend of Audrey's who had come to grieve. Maybe he was a friend who was secretly in love with her, although he couldn't admit it to himself. A man came out of the building in a fleece jacket and poorly fitting jeans. He stopped in the courtyard to find the song he wanted to hear through his headphones, then double-knotted both shoelaces before setting off on what looked like a habitual walk. He didn't glance in Henry's direction.

The next person to exit the building was a woman in a stylish black-and-white jacket, walking anxiously as though she were trying to escape from someone. As she neared, Henry felt a click in his chest. She looked like Corbin, not a lot, but enough to make him think she might be the cousin. At the street crossing, she instinctively looked right instead of left, then corrected herself. It had to be the English cousin. He stopped her, told her the story about being a friend and trying to get information. She kept trying to end the conversation, but he wasn't going to let that happen. For one, she had nervous, haunted eyes. Something had happened to her. She was damaged goods, and that was more beautiful to Henry than her lovely bone structure and her plump mouth.

He walked with her to Charles Street, telling lies. It was gratifying playing the bereaved friend. He wore his reading glasses, the ones that made him look sensitive and vulnerable, and even managed to squeeze out some tears. Before they parted ways, he made sure to tell Kate that Audrey had told him how weird Corbin had been. He then purposefully asked Kate exactly what time Corbin's flight to London had been. He'd done enough, he knew. He caught her tapping the fingertips of her right hand against her thumb, back and forth in succession. Kate would probably do one of two things. She'd either contact the police and tell them what she'd heard, or she would contact Corbin and tell him about the visit. Either way, Henry had alerted her that something was amiss. She was just an ordinary prey animal and she'd start to get nervous.

He returned to his apartment. He kept thinking of Kate, and how much he'd enjoyed talking with her, and how much he'd like to spend time in the apartment with her, especially if she didn't know he was there. He retrieved the hollowed-out copy of *The Monetary History of the United States* from the bedroom bookshelf. It contained his birth certificate, his certificate of name change when he legally became Henry Torrance, a lock of hair from Jenny Gulli, the first girl to really disappoint him, all the way back in high school, and the Polaroid he had of Corbin standing over the corpse of Claire Brennan. It was their insurance, of course, since Corbin owned a similar photograph of Henry, but Henry had always thought it was something more. A pact. A promise. He wondered where Corbin kept his Polaroid. Probably in a safe-deposit box somewhere. Henry knew that he should do the same, but he liked looking at it too much; he liked to have it close.

He paced the apartment with the photo in his hand. He hated being alone in his place; he'd hated it ever since his exciting visit with Audrey Marshall. Knowing suddenly what he was going to do, he logged onto his business e-mail account and canceled his meetings for the following day with the family law firm in Waltham. He packed his backpack with everything he needed. He was going to move in with Kate.

CHAPTER 32

Henry walked across the park in the dusk light. It had rained earlier, and there were puddles on the walkways and rain dripping from the trees. He crossed Beacon Street and then walked the one block of Charles that took him to Bury. He turned, and there was Kate, coming directly toward him. He lowered his head and kept walking. She never looked at him. Her eyes had that glazed emptiness of someone deep in thought. He almost followed her, just out of curiosity, but decided instead to take the perfect opportunity that had been given to him. He continued to walk toward the apartment, nearly bumping into a man about his age, hurrying along as though he was late for something. They each apologized at the same time, Henry catching a glimpse of a gaunt face, dark eyes.

He walked past the apartment building and through the two alleys that brought him to the back entrance. No one was in the basement, as usual. Henry's feet were wet and muddy, and left tracks on the floor. He found an old stiffened rag behind one of the water tanks and cleaned his shoes off, then wiped away the tracks. He took his time, confident at this point that the residents in this building rarely visited their storage units. Why did they need these units when their apartments were so massive? Some didn't even have locks on them since they were probably unused. Corbin's unit—the door stenciled with 3D—had a stainless steel padlock on its flimsy door. Could that possibly be where Corbin kept the photograph of Henry with the body of Claire? He decided to visit the unit when he got a chance. The lock would be easy to pick.

Henry entered Corbin's dark apartment, or Kate's apartment, since it was now hers. He removed his shoes in the kitchen, wrapped them in one of the plastic bags he'd brought, and put them in his backpack. He knew the apartment well, and had already decided that the best place for him to hide would be in the north-facing guest room, the larger of the two guest rooms. There was a relatively deep closet; one side had shelving that held linens and towels, but the other side was recessed slightly, and empty. Two suits, in plastic garment bags, hung on the closet rod, and if he positioned them carefully he'd be able to stand in the recess and be hidden, so long as no one moved the suits.

The guest bedroom was mostly covered by a large pile rug, beige and with a fleur-de-lis pattern. The bed was a four-poster with about two feet of clearance underneath. Henry thought he could comfortably sleep under the bed. He stashed his backpack in the closet and walked through the entire apartment, automatically picking out quick hiding places—behind curtains, a walk-in pantry—that he could use if he had to. He wasn't too worried about it.

He went into Corbin's obscenely large bedroom. He studied the framed pictures on top of the low bureau, even though he'd looked at them before. There were many of Corbin when he'd been young, and some of him when he was college age, the age when Henry had first met him. The pictures were almost humorously upper class; most were on boats, and the blond, tanned inhabitants were all holding gin and tonics and wearing the half-amused expressions of people so rich that they could hardly be bothered to smile completely for a picture.

After looking at the pictures, Henry searched the bedroom for signs of Kate; she'd barely unpacked. Her toiletries were spread around the bathroom, but a large duffel on the carpeted floor was still filled with clothes, some spilling out. The bed had been slept in, then half made again, the sheets and duvet pulled up, but not tucked in or smoothed. Henry pressed his face against the sheets and breathed in deeply through his nostrils. They smelled of detergent and not much else. He dropped to the floor to look under the bed; there was only about a foot and a half of space, enough to get under if he needed to, but not very comfortably.

There was a book under the bed with a black faux-leather cover. Henry opened it. There was a charcoal sketch of a man's face, a perfect rendering of the man that Henry had nearly bumped into on Bury Street earlier. Who was that man, and why had Kate—this had to be Kate's sketchbook—drawn him? He flipped over a page and there was a sketch of Kate herself, stunningly real, her wary eyes staring out at Henry as though she could see him. On the next page was Henry's own face, his name under it—JACK LUDOVICO (she'd spelled it right)—and today's date. It wasn't a bad drawing, and Henry found himself mesmerized, as though he was looking at himself through someone else's eyes. She'd drawn him with his head angled down, his eyes with a touch of sadness behind the lenses of his glasses. It was exactly what he'd been trying to convey, and she'd gotten it perfectly. He felt proud of himself, as he always did when someone entirely believed the mask that he was wearing.

He wondered if Kate tried to sketch everyone she met or just those people that she was interested in, people who affected her in some way. If that was the case, then who was this neighbor on the first page—ALAN CHERNEY, she'd written—and why was he walking behind her this evening? Had he been following her?

Almost unconsciously, Henry touched his tongue to the tip of his index finger and brought it down within an inch of the charcoal sketch. He very badly wanted to smudge the man's eyes, alter him somehow, maybe just enough to freak Kate out when she looked back at the sketchbook. What he really wanted to do was smudge the eyes entirely. He thought back to his sister's *Tiger Beat* magazines and how he used to meticulously go through them, whiting out the eyes of all her favorite boy bands, making the Hanson brothers look like eyeless zombies. Sometimes he'd get a red pen and draw blood coming from their eyes and mouths. After he'd done it to his sister's middle school yearbook, his mother made him go see a therapist—the only therapist in Stark, New York, a fat middle-aged woman who was so stupid that Henry was able to convince her that his sister had been the one tormenting him, and that he was only defending himself. He was eight years old at the time. His sister was twelve. The therapist must have gone to his mother and suggested that Mary was the problem, because all Henry knew was that he didn't have to go see Nancy the therapist anymore, and that his sister had started to go. Henry stopped mutilating Mary's things, but he did find ways to torture her that were never tracked back to him. Easy ways. He started rumors about her that wrecked her friendships. He got her fired from her first job at the pharmacy by making it look like she was stealing. For a time he added tiny amounts of antifreeze to her Gatorade, till she was hospitalized for over a week. She dropped out of high school junior year and left town with the local drug dealer. They had one postcard from Mary five years later—Greetings from San Diego—and that had been it.

It had been so long since he'd thought of his family, and as always, it filled him with a combination of amusement and shame in their mediocrity. His parents were still together, living in the same ranch house in Stark. On the few occasions when he spoke with them, he sometimes lied and told them that he'd hired a private detective to track down his sister, and they'd thanked him, and prayed that wherever she was she'd found peace. He could hear in their voices that they actually didn't want to find her, that they'd already accepted a life without their children. They didn't want him back. He knew that much. He hadn't laid eyes on them for ten years.

Henry refocused on the sketch in front of him. He decided not to smudge the eyes, as temping as it was. It would probably be too much; Kate would call the police, probably leave the apartment. Instead, he turned to the picture she'd drawn of him and used his finger to smooth out some of the lines that defined his face, then he allowed himself to dab at the charcoal eyes with a moistened finger, altering them just enough so that they looked out of focus. Satisfied, he shut the book and slid it back under the bed, wondering how long he'd been sitting there. Disoriented suddenly, he stood, the room swimming a little in his vision. He was hungry, and he went to the kitchen to see if there was enough food that he could take some. If not, his backpack was filled with granola bars.

Kate came home around eight that night. Henry was in the guest room, sitting in the dark. He didn't bother to hide. If she came looking, he'd have enough time to duck into the closet while she was turning on the light. And if he didn't, and she spotted him, well, Kate would have to die. Henry wondered how Corbin would react to that. Would it be more personal because she was family, his blood, or less personal because he'd never fucked her? Either way, it would flush Corbin out from his hiding place in London. He'd *have* to return to Boston. Henry was pondering this when the white cat he'd seen in the basement trotted into the bedroom and stared at him, eyes glowing yellow in the dark. Henry hissed and the cat cocked its head, then turned and left the room.

He waited and listened. He heard the front door open and close, and wondered if Kate had left, but somehow he doubted it, and he stayed where he was. Fifteen minutes later, she came padding down the hall, heading for the media room, or whatever Corbin called that dark-paneled man cave with the overstuffed leather sofa. Henry let five minutes pass, then stepped out into the hall. The lamp by the leather sofa was on, and even though its back was to Henry, he could see the crown of her head and hear the dry flicking sound of a page being turned. She was reading. Henry stayed where he was, still as he could be, waiting for another page to turn. She must be a slow reader, he thought, then he heard the book clunk to the floor and Kate shift on the sofa. She'd fallen asleep.

He stood behind the sofa. She was half covered by a lumpy

duvet, one of her hands turned so that the palm faced outward and the knuckles rested on her cheek. He watched her for a while, amazed that people were held together by something as fragile as skin. Even in the dull light from the lamp, he could see the blood moving beneath it. Her jaw moved, and with it, the delicate tendons of her neck. She began to snore, then shifted, her eyes squeezing shut as though trying not to see whatever it was that her dreams were showing her. Henry backed away, then turned and walked to the kitchen, where he drank milk directly from the bottle. Just to amuse himself, he thought of sleeping in Corbin's bed. There was a good chance Kate was going to stay all night on the sofa. No, he thought. He was having too much fun and didn't want it to end. He'd sleep under the bed in the guest room. It was the safest place.

He put the milk back in the refrigerator, then heard a soft scratching sound on the door that led to the basement. He opened the door and let in that idiotic cat. It actually rubbed up against his leg. He bent and picked it up, turning it over and holding its skull, not quite the size of a tennis ball, in his hand. The cat purred. Could he crush its head with just his hand? He thought he probably could. He began to squeeze, then decided against it and dropped the cat to the floor, where it scampered off toward the living room, unaware how close it had been to death. It would be more fun for Kate to find the cat in the house again and have her wonder how it got back in.

Henry returned to the guest room, slid under the bed, and closed his eyes. He wasn't tired, but long ago he'd figured out how to get himself to fall asleep at almost any moment. He imagined himself floating down an enormous river. In front of him were all the people he knew who'd been born before he was, growing older as they floated, and sinking one by one below the surface as time, or disease, or just bad luck, caught up with them. Around him were the people his age, the sheep he'd gone to high school with in Stark, the entitled kids from college who acted like they'd live forever, his workmates and clients, all of them treading water hard in the middle of their lives, just trying to stay afloat. And behind him were those younger than him, the ones being born, new bodies trying to enter the slipstream, growing more multitudinous as the people in front of him thinned in their ranks. Once the image was clearly in his mind—a phalanx of human bodies with Henry in the middle, moving constantly toward the front—he allowed himself to sink below the surface of the water so that all he saw were the legs churning in the froth of the moving river. And like a snapping turtle that pulls a baby duck down underneath the surface of a pond, Henry knew that he could take hold of someone's legs and bring them down to the dark, cold river bottom, where he could breathe but they could not.

Thinking this, he'd fall asleep. And never dream.

CHAPTER 33

HENRY STAYED UNDER THE BED until Kate left the apartment. It was around noon.

Kate had gotten up early, before dawn. The reappearance of the cat had clearly freaked her out. She'd yelled "Hello, there!" into the apartment; then, a little later, she'd turned the lights on in the guest room for ten seconds. He had held his breath, wondering if he was going to see her head dip down below the bedspread, but it hadn't happened. She turned the light back off, and for a few hours Henry could hear her moving through the apartment.

Then it was quiet for a while, and Henry wondered if she'd gone back to sleep, or maybe even left. Then voices—someone was at the door. Kate's distinctive, accented speech, and another woman's. An older woman with a raspy bark. He worried briefly that it was a detective, that Kate had called to have the place searched, but then the voices stopped, and shortly afterward, he heard the front door close. He was pretty sure Kate had left. Sure enough to slide out from under the bed.

He stood, knees popping, then swung his arms around to get the joints working properly. He rolled his head on his shoulders, then slipped from the room. He was fine. Kate was gone. He could sense it in the air of the apartment.

He washed his face in the guest bathroom, then changed his shirt, making sure to apply an extra amount of odor-free antiperspirant. If he was going to live here with Kate for a while, it was important that he smelled as neutral as possible. In the kitchen, on one of the top shelves, Henry found a half-filled box of Rice Chex. He filled a bowl, then covered them with the small amount of Kate's skim milk that he felt he could get away with stealing. The cereal was stale, but reminded him of Corbin. The last time he'd had Rice Chex had probably been their weekend together in New Essex, years and years ago. He hadn't had any since.

He washed out the bowl and returned it to its place, then wandered the apartment, forming a plan. He went to look at Kate's sketchbook, wanting to study the picture she'd drawn of him again, but it wasn't under the bed. She'd taken it with her.

He remembered the storage unit down in the basement. Even though he had his lockpicks, he went to the kitchen drawer where he knew Corbin kept spare keys. He grabbed the one with the label that said STORAGE and went down to the basement. He entered Corbin's unit, pulling the door shut behind him, and used his penlight to search the small space. There was box after box of comic books, neatly organized. There was a barbecue grill, and there were several framed posters, the type of posters someone in their early twenties might hang on a dorm-room wall or a first apartment. Car posters. Girlie posters. He wondered why Corbin had kept them. One of the posters was a large framed album cover: Ween's *Chocolate and Cheese*. A woman's torso, the bottoms of her meaty breasts hanging below a cutoff top. Henry felt for his pocketknife. He decided to do some surgery on the poster.

Kate was back for some of the afternoon, Henry hiding in the guest room, but she left again. He went to the bedroom, where her shucked jeans were on the floor, still a little warm. He sniffed at them, detecting almost nothing of her scent, just a faraway whiff of baby powder. Where had she gone that she needed to change out of her jeans? He looked in the bathroom; her toothbrush was recently used, still wet, and he put it in his mouth, sucked the minty taste out of the bristles.

Ever since cutting the poster, Henry, instead of feeling pleased, was agitated and anxious. He wanted something to happen, for Corbin to return or for the police to come, or even for Kate to discover him hiding in her closet, the pocketknife conveniently held between his fingers. He did his stretching exercises, then found a fresh bottle of vodka and cracked its seal, pouring half a tumbler's worth over crushed ice. Hours later, Kate was still gone, and Henry, his face numb and tingling from drinking the vodka, was pacing the apartment, hungry and annoyed. He decided to leave, stashing his backpack in the guest room closet and heading out into the night through 101's back entrance. Before he left, he returned the storage key to the drawer, but pocketed one of the other unlabeled keys, assuming it was a spare for the apartment, plus a key that was labeled AM—Audrey Marshall's apartment, probably. He had the picks, but they took time, and it was always better to have actual keys. He walked across the Commons to a dark bar he liked called the Proposition, ate two orders of wings, and drank several Heinekens.

"You've been away," the bartender said.

He looked at her, and it took him a moment to realize they'd talked before, but then it all came back. Samantha. Bay State College undergrad. She had to take a semester off from school because her grandmother had been paying her tuition but now her grandmother was in an expensive nursing home, and she hadn't squared away her financial aid package yet. Henry also remembered the things he knew about Samantha that she hadn't told him. The bulimia she'd been fighting on and off for years, evident by the puffiness of her face and the loss of enamel on her teeth. The way she'd sleep with any guy who was halfway nice to her, and plenty who weren't. How bad she felt about herself most of the time.

"Not away, just trying to eat better," Henry said.

"I hear you," Samantha said, and ended the conversation. Henry wondered if she sensed he didn't want to talk, and found himself annoyed that she probably had. He hated being read by anyone, even by stupid female bartenders. He cracked a chicken bone between his teeth and sucked at the marrow.

Henry returned to Bury Street, studied Corbin's windows from the sidewalk, and decided that Kate wasn't back. Or if she was back, she'd gone straight to sleep. He'd risk it, either way. He entered the basement, which was empty except for the cat that was always around. "Here, kitty, kitty," he said, pushing his fingers underneath its chin. The words sounded a little slurred in his own ears, and he wondered if he'd had too much to drink, if maybe he should just head home to the South End and sleep it off. He rubbed the cat's twig-like jawbone. It didn't purr, and when he pulled his hand away, it latched onto his forearm with both paws, its claws sinking into his flesh. Henry, shocked, pulled back, feeling his skin tear, and the cat hissed viciously, then turned and bolted before he had a chance to stamp it to death. He looked at the wound, the skin already beginning to puff up and little pinpricks of blood appearing, like condensation on a glass. He sucked at the wound, tasting his own salty blood. It was beginning to itch.

Instead of going up to Corbin's apartment, Henry went up the stairs that led to Audrey Marshall's place. He hadn't been there since the night he'd killed her. He picked the lock of the door and entered. The curtains of the apartment were open and the night was light enough that he could maneuver through the apartment. There were marks on the floor from the crime scene investigators, taped areas on the kitchen tile where he'd left Audrey's body. Had they noticed how her hand had been positioned, pointing with an index finger toward Corbin's apartment? Henry smiled at the memory. Arranging Audrey had been the most fun he'd had in years, the most fun he'd had since Corbin and he had killed Claire in the cemetery. After Audrey was dead, and he was free to arrange her as he wanted to, he'd contemplated trying to actually cut her in half, find a way to saw through her spine, but decided against it. Still, the image of it, the thought of her actually in two pieces—a perfect half of her for each of them—almost made him giddy. One day he could do it, but he didn't think he could do it alone.

He wandered the apartment. In the bedroom, some of Audrey's things—clothes, books—had been boxed up and left. Maybe the family had begun the process, then got overwhelmed and quit. Henry wondered what would happen if he died. Would his parents come to reclaim his things? Of course they wouldn't. They were never going to leave Stark, except maybe if Mary reared her ugly head, but not for him. They were a little scared of him, he knew that. He could hear it in their voices on the few occasions when he called home, that slight vocal hitch in the "Hello, Henry" after they'd picked up the phone, expecting nothing more than a call from their church deacon to let them know that the bake sale was going to be understaffed this year, and could they help.

In the living room, Henry stared down at the empty courtyard, then across into the opposite apartment. There was movement, a light on in an alcove kitchen. Henry watched. It was a man and a woman, the man crossing the dimly lit living room toward a woman with dark blond hair in the kitchen. Henry stared, and began to think that it was Kate that he was looking at, although he couldn't be sure. The man was in the kitchen again, a tall man with messy black hair who could have been the man that Henry had bumped into on the street, the man Kate had drawn in her sketchbook. That would make sense. Somehow they had met, and now Kate was fucking this guy. When had she got here? Three days ago? She'd wasted no time.

He watched for about twenty minutes. He couldn't see all the way into the kitchen, but it looked like they were eating around an island. The man came into the living room again, crouched in a corner—getting more alcohol, maybe—then returned to the kitchen. The light caught his profile, the blade of his nose. Jewish, Henry thought. He started to get bored, and the boredom made him a little angry. He wanted Kate back in their apartment, curled up and asleep in her nest of blankets on the couch. He wanted to watch her twitching face, and listen to her breathe, and know that somehow, some part of her, the animal part, would know she was being watched. They always do.

But at least now he had the place to himself for the night. He returned to Corbin's apartment, going straight to Kate's bedroom to look for the sketchbook. It was under the bed again, and he opened it to that first picture, confirming that it was the same man across the courtyard. He took his index finger and pressed hard against both of the eyes in the picture, trying not to overly smudge them. It felt good, and he liked the effect. The eyes looked different, but subtly different, just enough to make Kate wonder.

He used the bathroom, then went to his bedroom. He stared out the window, toward the river. The night sky was clear, a scattering of stars visible, a rarity for the city. He lay down on top of the bed, on top of the covers, folding his hands across his stomach, and let himself sink into a river of sleep.

Kate returned in the early morning. Henry thought of hiding beneath the bed, but decided not to bother. It was easier to listen from where he was. She answered a phone call midmorning, and he heard her asking whoever was on the other end if they had a warrant. If the police were coming then it was time to leave. It got quiet again for a while, and he hoped she was either napping or had left. He put his shoes on, gathered his backpack, and decided to go. He could come back that night and see Kate again. Or maybe he could come back and visit as Jack Ludovico, the bereft friend, see if he could get her to sleep with him. He thought it would be pretty easy.

He moved silently across the apartment, rubbing his arm where the cat had scratched him, but when he got to the kitchen he saw that the door to the basement was open. She must have gone down there, herself. He made a sudden decision to leave out the front of the building. It would be safe enough, especially since Kate was in the basement. He exited through the front door and walked down the hallway, then heard footsteps coming up the stairwell, plus the identifiable squawk of a police radio. His mind furiously considered his options. Walk casually past the police. Reenter Kate's apartment. Then he remembered the key that said AM on it and dug it from his pocket. He opened Audrey's door, ducked under the police tape, and was inside, breathing rapidly. He listened to the police lumbering down the hall. A woman's voice was giving instructions—he heard her say that they were looking for a thin knife. A man's voice came back: "Like a filleting knife?" He didn't hear the woman respond. They were knocking on Kate's door. *Yes, like a filleting knife,* Henry said to himself. He counted to thirty, then let himself out of Audrey's apartment and took the stairs down to the lobby, and he was outside in the bright, windy day. He filled his lungs, almost laughed out loud at how close he'd come to being caught by the police. Still, what would have happened? He'd have told them the same story that he'd told Kate. He used to date Audrey Marshall and had been coming to her apartment in order to grieve. Walking down Bury Street toward the park, he imagined the conversation with the police officers in his mind, how he'd make them believe he was some loser who'd lost the girl he loved, while Corbin was the creep next door.

The fantasy conversation was so enjoyable that he almost didn't notice that he was being followed. But he did notice. He could feel it, the way you could feel warmth on your skin when your eyes were closed and know that the sun had come out from behind a cloud. He took a sudden left turn onto another residential street. There was a tree half a block down the brick sidewalk. He briskly walked, then leaned against its trunk where he wouldn't be seen by someone coming from Bury Street.

Fifteen seconds later he heard the hurried footsteps coming his way, then watched as Kate's boyfriend—Alan was the name— raced past like a man who'd lost his dog.

"Are you looking for me?" Henry asked, and the man jerked around, like a fish that's been hooked.

CHAPTER 34

HENRY SPENT A VERY PLEASANT afternoon with Alan Cherney. He remembered his surname from Kate's drawing. They went together to a small neighborhood bar about three blocks from Bury Street. Henry did the grieving friend act and told Alan all about his theories that Corbin was a serial killer who liked to mutilate his victims.

He told Alan about Rachael Chess, found murdered on a beach in New Essex, the same place Corbin's mother lived. Alan was riveted, but slightly uncomfortable. Henry talked him into having a couple of beers, and that began to loosen him up. Color came back to his face. As they talked, Henry tried to get a read on this Alan character. He was about the same age as he was, successful enough, or rich enough, to live where he did on Beacon Hill. He was that typical Jewish intellectual who thought he was smarter than everyone in the room, but acted neurotic so no one would know it. He'd known the type well at Aurelius. But there was something else that he couldn't read, like a blurry line of text in an otherwise simple book. Alan cared too much about Audrey, for one thing, or maybe he cared for Kate. Either way, he cared about what Henry had to say, was hanging on every word. So Henry led him directly to Corbin, in the same way he'd led Kate to Corbin. He painted him as a psychopathic killer, and he painted himself as the unhinged boyfriend who was out for revenge.

Alan drank several beers, becoming more and more animated. Henry matched him, not just beer for beer, but also in his exuberance. They were like two college freshmen arguing philosophy in a dorm room. Alan kept sliding forward in the booth, one knee vibrating like a tuning fork. He *feels* too much, Henry thought, fascinated. And while they talked on, Henry formed an organized fantasy in his mind. He pictured Alan and himself killing a woman together, maybe Kate, maybe someone neither of them had met yet. And they were taking their time in killing her and arranging her. And they were splitting her down the middle. And no one ever would know why except the two of them. Corbin would know, though. Corbin would know exactly what was happening. Then the fantasy passed, and Henry felt a strange, unfamiliar sense of shame, as though those thoughts constituted not infidelity, exactly, but something like desperation. The need to take a singular experience and try and replay it with someone else.

"You okay?" Alan said.

"I am. Sorry," Henry replied. "I get these moments when everything seems normal, the world exactly as it should be, then I realize that she's not in it anymore. Audrey's dead. And the world hasn't stopped with her."

Alan's lips were pursed. He nodded his head in understanding. Henry straightened up, felt as though he was seeing Alan for the first time properly. He wasn't another playmate. He was a patsy. The perfect patsy. "Sorry, man," Henry said. "I keep talking about myself, and Audrey. What about you? You must have a girlfriend."

Alan hesitated. Henry wondered if he was about to mention what he had done with Kate the night before. Instead, he said, "Nothing much to tell. I had a girlfriend. We lived together, and she moved out. But you don't need to hear about that."

"No, please. I want to hear about it. I want to just stop thinking about my situation for a moment. Please, tell me."

Alan spoke while Henry thought. *Maybe this guy really should be the patsy.* All along, Henry had thought that he wanted Corbin arrested for the crime of murdering Audrey Marshall. Maybe not arrested, but suspected. It was all part of the game they were playing. But maybe he didn't really want Corbin arrested. And it wasn't just because Corbin would try and finger him for his part in the crimes. He could handle that. It wouldn't be easy to track down Henry Wood these days. Not impossible, but not easy, not since he'd legally changed his name. It would sound as though Corbin were making up a bogeyman. But, no, Corbin in prison was not really what Henry wanted. It was more fun to play with something when it wasn't in a cage.

Henry formed a plan, then turned his attention back to Alan, who was sputtering along about someone named Quinn. Their eyes met, and Alan suddenly stopped talking, as though embarrassed. He excused himself to go to the bathroom.

Henry moved fast. The bar was empty except for two men, both in button-down shirts, sitting at the bar and watching sports highlights on the television. He removed the knife, still in its plastic bag, from his backpack. It had been reckless to hold on to the murder weapon for so long, but now it was going to come in handy. He pulled it from the plastic bag, pinching the blade between the sides of his fingers so as not to leave prints. Alan had brought a leather bag with him, about the size of a briefcase. Henry opened it. Inside was a computer tablet, a book—*The Wind-Up Bird Chronicle*—and a thick wad of unopened envelopes, mail he hadn't dealt with yet. Henry dug toward the bottom of the bag. A small, black umbrella nestled there, and Henry slid the knife underneath it, returning the bag back to the way it had been, just as Alan came back into the bar. "I should go," he was saying.

"Sure. I understand," Henry said. They paid the bill at the bar, each contributing cash, then walked out together, Alan slinging his bag over his shoulder.

HENRY MADE THE CALL TO the Boston Police Department Tips Line from a pay phone near the Tufts Medical Center. He wore gloves to touch the phone, just in case.

"I know who killed Audrey Marshall," he said to the man who answered the phone.

"Can I get your name, please, sir?"

"I'd rather not say. I'm calling from a pay phone because I'm scared." Henry let his voice, pitched a little higher than usual, noticeably tremble.

"Can I ask you what you're scared of?"

"I'm scared of Alan Cherney. He lives in the same building that Audrey Marshall lived in, and I'm pretty sure he killed her."

"Can you tell me his apartment number?"

"I can't. I don't know it. But he lives right across from where she lived. It's not hard to find out. All you need—"

"Okay, of course. We'll look it up. It will be easy to find out. Can you tell me why you think Alan Cherney was involved in Audrey Marshall's murder?"

"Because he has the knife that killed her. It's in his bag."

Henry hung up and, keeping his head down, walked away from the phone. He hadn't seen any surveillance cameras around, but he couldn't be sure.

CHAPTER 35

W HEN HE GOT BACK TO his apartment, Henry put on New Order's *Brotherhood* as loud as he thought he could without getting a complaint. He'd known, as soon as he hung up the phone, that he'd made the right decision. It was time to take some of the heat off Corbin. Even if Alan wasn't convicted, Henry had muddied the waters. It was going to be fun to follow it from afar. His work was done, for now.

He took a long, stinging shower, then dressed, replayed the album, and lay down on his made-up bed. He was going to miss Kate. When he'd left the apartment that morning he'd only thought of it as a temporary absence. Still, it was best that he stayed away. He closed his eyes, flexing one foot in time to the music. He floated on his river, cool and refreshing, and fell asleep while he was still on the surface, bobbing along, contented, maybe even happy.

He woke in a dark apartment, cold and shivering. He'd slept too long, and when he sat up the air felt liquid and he nearly lay back down again. He was plagued with doubts. Had he gone too far with the call to the police? Alan Cherney didn't know his real name—he'd just said "Jack," hadn't he?—but he could describe him. And so could Kate. She could draw him, as he knew. Henry decided that his involvement with Kate and Corbin and Alan was now done. He'd set his traps, and it was time to walk away. He'd been extraordinarily lucky so far—the near miss with the police this morning—and for the next few weeks he wouldn't leave his apartment except to go to his office in Newtonville.

He made himself a cheese sandwich and drank a glass of milk, then went to unpack his backpack. He carefully laid out every-thing he'd brought to Kate's house. His extra shirts, the gloves, his outdoor hat, his antiperspirant, his granola bars, the empty bottle in case he ever needed to empty his bladder while hiding, his anti-slip socks with the rubber grips, his night vision goggles with the head strap, and his sheathed filleting knife, brand new. It was all accounted for except for the Lycra ski mask he slept in so as not to leave hairs behind. He searched the pockets of his backpack, then the pockets of his pants and his jacket. It was nowhere. He remembered pulling it on the night before when he'd been sleeping under the guest room bed. It had gotten warm in the night and he'd pushed it up to his hairline. That was his last memory of the ski mask. It must have slipped off his head in the night, and was probably still under the bed. Where else could it be?

He headed back out into the night.

Before returning to Kate's apartment to look for his ski mask, Henry visited Audrey Marshall's place one more time. He knew it was his last chance.

He stood in the dark kitchen, breathing the air, remembering . . .

Not the work of cutting her—no, that had been hard—but the way she had looked when she was done, cut open, an arm out-stretched to point toward Corbin's apartment. There was so much spilled blood on the floor that the floor simply looked red, a shining pedestal for a girl who got involved with the wrong man. Henry closed his eyes and stood absolutely still for a moment, savoring the moment. With his eyes closed, he felt invisible, the way a child thinks they're invisible because they can't see anything themselves. Except that children were wrong, and Henry was right. He was invisible. Almost, anyway. No one could see him but Corbin. And Corbin could do nothing about it.

He went back down the stairs to the basement corridor, then up toward Corbin's apartment. As he neared the top, he felt a tiny ripple in the air, and thought he heard the click of a door closing. He paused and listened for a while. Nothing. Then he climbed the remaining stairs and paused outside the door that led into the apartment. He listened for a long time. Just as he felt confident enough to open the door, there was the sound of movement, the pad of steps. Henry sat on the top step and waited. He could be patient. All he needed to do was enter the apartment, go to the guest room for his ski mask, and then leave.

He heard a flush, the sound of water moving through the building's walls. He thought he heard steps again, then it was quiet. He waited for what felt like twenty minutes before folding his hand around the doorknob and turning it. The door was unlocked. He was pleased, but wary. It was the first time he'd found it that way. Had Kate simply forgotten? He swung the door open and stepped into the moonlit kitchen. The apartment was quiet. He shut the door behind him and walked toward the living room, turning into the hallway that led to the guest room. Muffled sounds plus a flickering light at the end of the hall told him the television was on, which meant Kate was probably asleep on the couch in front of it. Henry ducked into the bedroom, lay down on the plush carpet next to the bed, and felt with his outstretched fingers along the spongy fibers for his lost ski mask. Shifting himself farther under the bed, he found the bunched-up hat. Relief swept over him. Once he was standing, he shoved it into his jacket pocket. He was about to leave the bedroom when he sensed movement in the hallway. Kate must have gotten up. But, no, it was coming the other way. Henry stepped back, watching shadows move along the doorframe. Whoever it was entered the room with the television. Henry, feeling trapped in the bedroom, moved rapidly the other way down the hallway toward the living room, where he stopped and turned. He felt better in the cavernous dark. There was a large armoire near the front door and he stood next to it, waiting in its shadow.

Who else was in here? He guessed it was Alan, coming over for a repeat of the night before. Still, he waited to find out what would happen, listening intently, but all he could hear was the muffled sound of the television.

And then Corbin appeared, unmistakable, even with short hair. He was in the hallway, coming forward, and something dropped down the center of Henry, like a rock sinking through water. It was fear, but it was also excitement.

"You came," Henry said to Corbin. It was something he'd said to him a hundred times in fantasies, wanting Corbin to know that he had summoned him, that he was the one pulling on his strings. It was all worth it, Henry thought, no matter what happens next.

"What are you doing here, Henry?" Corbin asked, sounding like a stern teacher disciplining a student.

Henry began to speak, to explain, when he realized that Corbin had a knife and was coming toward him. A surge of adrenalized joy went through Henry as he jumped back and avoided Corbin's lunge. Then he leapt, riding Corbin's body down to the wooden floor, pinning him and wrestling for the knife. He nearly had it when it sliced across the palm of his hand, and he instinctively jerked backward. Corbin came after him again, nearly stabbing him in the face, but the knife stuck in the floor, and Henry was able to get to it with his good hand, leaping onto Corbin, slicing with the knife at his throat, the skin parting the way skin does. So easily. Corbin fell to the floor. In the dim light the blood that came from his neck was an inky black.

Henry stood, stumbling backward. His hand thrummed, and he looked at it. Blood was oozing its way down into his sleeve, and his thumb hung loose, the tendon severed. He quickly looked around the room for something to stanch the bleeding, then remembered the ski mask in his pocket. He set the knife down, pulled the hat out with his good hand, and crouched down to dress his hand. He gingerly slid his dangling thumb through an opening in the slick material, then wrapped his hand, tucking the excess material so that it held. It would have to do for now. Corbin was still making sounds, soft, bubbling gurgles, and Henry turned his attention to him.

They were no longer alone. Kate had entered the living room and was now crouched over Corbin's crumpled body. She hadn't noticed Henry. He took the knife from the floor and stood. He watched for a moment, the world slowing down into this one frozen tableau. Corbin dying, and an angel in white already at his side.

Then Corbin's gaze shifted, and for a brief moment, his eyes made contact with Henry's, the two of them looking directly at one another after so many years. Corbin was gesturing with his blood-slicked hand, moving a finger, and trying to say something to Kate. It caused her to turn, and that was when Henry leapt, landing on her back. He heard the air leave her lungs, her head thunk as it hit the floor. He pushed the knife into her back, encountering a shoulder blade, pulled it out again, and stuck the entire blade into the softness high up next to her spine. Henry rolled off her and into a sitting position. Corbin's hand still clutched at his throat. Henry moved closer, looked at his eyes, open but unfocused now, blood bubbling from his mouth.

There was a loud knock at the door, followed by a woman's voice: "POLICE. OPEN UP."

Henry, in the seconds he had, began to calculate. Should he run for the basement? Then he watched, in amazement, as Kate, knife still protruding, stood up and wobbled toward the front door, opening it up as though a cocktail party guest had arrived. Henry pulled his small pocketknife from his jacket pocket, flicked out the blade, then took Corbin by the shoulders and yanked him toward him to act as a shield. The policewoman entered, gun drawn. Henry watched her eyes scan the scene, from Kate to Corbin and then to Henry, who was now dragging Corbin's body back onto his, holding the pocketknife to Corbin's damaged neck, the smell of blood thick in the air.

She took a step into the room, gun pointed at Henry. "Let him go, and let me see your hands." She took her left hand off her gun and fumbled for the radio at her belt.

Henry paused, holding on to the knife. He was grateful, in a way, that it had come to this.

CHAPTER 36

DETECTIVE ROBERTA JAMES TOOK CAREFUL aim, exhaled, and fired her Glock at a living target for the first time in her life. The .40-caliber bullet hit the smiling man in the upper lip, and his smiled collapsed inward as he fell backward and hit the floor. The knife that he'd been pushing into the neck of the bleeding man clattered to the floor.

While radioing in for immediate backup, she dropped to a knee and took a look at the man with the neck wound. The blood was coming fast, although it wasn't spurting. She turned to Kate and calmly asked for clean towels.

"Is he dead?" Kate asked. Her voice sounded too casual, as though she wasn't comprehending what was happening.

"I don't know. I need to get some towels and stop this bleeding." She stood, and that was when she noticed the handle of the knife that was jutting at a ninety-degree angle from the top of Kate's back, just behind a shoulder. "I'll get them, Kate. You just stay there. Where are they?"

"There's a bathroom right down there," Kate said. She swiveled, made a funny expression, and asked: "Is there something on my back?" She reached back with a hand and Detective James stopped her, gripping her forearms and bringing them down to her side. Kate's eyes were bright. The detective knew she was in shock. "I need you to have a seat, right here, and not touch your back. The ambulance is on the way."

She left Kate where she was and moved as fast as she could, located a bathroom, and pulled a towel from a rack. Returning, she was relieved to see that Kate had stayed where she was, her hands primly on her knees. "It's Corbin," she said to the passing detective.

"Who is?" Detective James asked while pressing the towel against the blood flow from the neck.

"He is. That's my cousin, Corbin Dell. He was trying to save me." Her voice was far too calm, the voice of someone speaking in their sleep.

James held the towel in place as it turned dark and damp from the blood. At least the knife hadn't severed the carotid artery, or he'd be dead already. Still, he had lost a lot of blood. She looked at his face; it did look like the pictures she'd seen of Corbin. His eyes were glassy, and she said, "Corbin, hang in there."

She thought she saw some comprehension in his eyes.

"Is he dead?" Kate asked.

"No, he's still alive. The ambulance will be here any moment. Tell me what happened."

"Corbin woke me up and made me hide in a closet. He was trying to save me. I should have stayed in the closet."

James heard a distant siren and silently prayed that it was the ambulance coming for them. She pressed two fingers underneath Corbin's chin. If there was a pulse, it was very, very faint.

"You saved her, Corbin," she said, in case he was listening.

"Hi, Sanders," Kate was saying, and James spun her head. A white cat went up to Kate and rubbed against her leg. Kate stroked its back, leaving a streak of blood on its pristine white fur. The siren got louder.

SIX HOURS EARLIER, DETECTIVE JAMES had entered her condo in Watertown, a little bit relieved that the FBI was officially taking over the Audrey Marshall homicide. She calculated that she'd slept a total of maybe twelve hours since the body had been discovered on Saturday. It was now Tuesday evening. She poured herself a Famous Grouse on the rocks and changed into the tank top she liked to sleep in and the Celtics pajama shorts she'd gotten for Christmas from her parents. She liked them, not so much because they were emblazoned with the Celtics logo, but because they were comfortable, and even in the coldest stretch of a Boston winter, she hated to sleep in full-length pajama bottoms. She lay down on her sofa and held the lowball glass on her stomach. The pajama bottoms weren't the only Celtics-related item she'd received this past Christmas. She'd gotten a mug, as well, from her niece who always got her a gift, and a pink long-sleeved T-shirt from her sister with the Celtics logo on it. It was clear what she was becoming—that relative who was only associated with one thing. *She's a Celtics fan, so get her something Celtics if you can't think of anything else.* She was like that old uncle who liked golf, so all he got was golf stuff. And the message from her sister was also very clear; the fitted pink shirt was suggesting that it wasn't too late to snag a man.

She sat up a little and took a sip of her scotch. Why was she thinking about this stuff? *Because I'm exhausted,* she told herself.

She closed her eyes. The image of Audrey Marshall on the kitchen floor, butchered like a piece of meat, swam immediately into her mind, as it had been doing, regularly and without mercy, for the past three days. She sat up on the sofa, had another sip of her drink, and stretched her back out, listening with satisfaction to the small popping sounds coming from her spine.

Her cell phone rang, and she knew instinctively that it was her captain before she even saw his name on the screen.

"Thought you'd like to know that we got an anonymous call right after you left. It came from a pay phone in the South End, from a man who claimed to be one of Audrey Marshall's friends, but he wouldn't give us a name. He said that Alan Cherney is the killer, and that Alan has a bloody knife in his possession."

"Jesus. How did he know that?"

"He didn't say."

"Probably knew because he planted it on him."

Mark laughed, and as usual, laughing made him cough. "Thought you'd like to know, even though I know you were going home to get some sleep."

"Strike that off the agenda. Tan's been told?" Abigail Tan was the FBI agent now assigned as lead in the case.

"Yes. She's off to get a search warrant."

"What did she think?" James asked.

"She didn't tell me, but she wanted me to tell you. What do *you* think?"

"It's our Jack, I'm sure of it. He's setting up Alan Cherney, I guess. I don't know why, exactly."

"Probably what Tan thinks, too."

"But let's execute the warrant, and if we find a knife, arrest Cherney. We can find out more about Jack, at least, and get something, anything—"

"Oh, gotta run, Roberta. I'll call you right back."

He'd rung off. James took a sip of her scotch but it was gone, and the ice tapped against her teeth. She paced the room, thinking.

Jack was getting bold, which meant he was probably about to screw up. Or that's what she was hoping for, anyway. He was now their principal suspect, despite the fact that Corbin Dell had gone missing from his borrowed apartment in London. Corbin was involved somehow, but James did not believe he had killed Audrey Marshall. The timeline made it a very remote possibility. She believed the killer was the man who was calling himself Jack Ludovico, and she believed that he'd killed at least two women before, one on the North Shore of Massachusetts named Rachael Chess, and one in Connecticut named Linda Alcheri nearly fourteen years earlier. Both women, like Audrey Marshall, had been cut down the middle after they'd been killed. Rachael Chess had been found on a beach in New Essex, not far from where Corbin Dell's mother had a house. James had studied the file, and Corbin's name had come up as someone who knew the deceased, but he'd been eliminated from the inquiry since he'd been out of the country when the murder had been committed. There was no connection that James could find between Linda Alcheri, the dead girl from Connecticut, and Corbin Dell. She'd been found dead at an old Boy Scout camp outside of the city. Cause of death had been a blow to the head from a rock, but before she'd been buried she'd been cut down the face, and her clothes and some of the skin on her torso was cut away. Why had no one made a connection with the second murder in New Essex? Cause of death had been different, but the postmortem wounds were the same, or at least they were extremely similar. Now that there'd been a third murder—another woman with the exact same wounds—the FBI had arrived. James heard that some of the police were now calling the murderer the Failed Magician. *He tries to cut his women in half.*

Abigail Tan, despite her age (she didn't look much older than twenty-five), seemed competent. Earlier that day, James told her what she'd found in the Alcheri files. "Two of Linda's friends mentioned in interviews that Linda had briefly been seeing someone named Hank. They both remembered a first name, but not a second. They never found this Hank."

"And you think this Hank is . . . ?"

"I think the person who called himself Hank back then might be calling himself Jack Ludovico now."

"What makes you think he's not just who he says he is, a friend trying to get some answers?"

"Then why didn't he come to us? And why doesn't Audrey Marshall mention him in her diary?" What James didn't say was that she just somehow knew. Both murders involved a shadowy figure who never came forward, and she knew that that person, probably not named Hank or Jack, was the same person.

"Okay, then, if he's the killer, then why is he hanging around? Why did he go and talk with Kate Priddy?"

"I think he's trying to pin this murder on Corbin Dell. Audrey

Marshall's arm was bent back over her head, pointing toward Dell's apartment. The coroner said her arm was placed in that position after death. He wants us to think it's Corbin, so that's why he's hanging around. Maybe killing Rachael Chess was his first attempt at framing him, and it didn't work."

"Should we publish the sketch that Kate Priddy did?"

James had thought of that. "Not yet. I don't think he lives locally, and if the sketch shows up on the front page, he'll leave town. He's being reckless right now, returning to the scene of the crime to talk with a neighbor. Let's wait him out and see if he pops up again."

And now he had, trying to frame Alan Cherney for some inexplicable reason.

James picked her phone back up to call the captain, but before she could call him, the phone was vibrating in her hand. Abigail.

"Did you get a warrant?" James asked.

"Not yet, but I talked with Dietrichson. He agreed to stay late."

"Want company?"

"That's why I'm calling."

They met at the courthouse, and got Judge Albert Dietrichson's fairly reluctant signature on the search warrant for Alan Cherney's apartment at 101 Bury Street. James had to convince him that the anonymous call that had been recorded that afternoon was not the sole reason for the search warrant.

"Did you get a statement from Alan Cherney after the body was discovered?" the judge asked, as he was packing his briefcase to go home for the day.

"We did. I didn't take it, myself, but Officer Karen Gibson did. She said he reported that he didn't personally know Audrey Marshall, but that he knew her from sight. She reported that he was acting strange."

The judge raised one eyebrow and looked at James. "Did she specify what she meant by strange?"

"She reported that he seemed visibly shaken by the death in his apartment building. She didn't know whether it was because of the proximity of the crime, or because he knew the victim more intimately than he was indicating. And one more thing, Kate Priddy, the cousin who is currently occupying Corbin Dell's apartment, has gotten to know Alan Cherney, and she indicated to us that he used to watch Audrey Marshall through her window."

"From where? The street?"

"No. From his own apartment. Their windows face one another above the courtyard of the building. It's shaped like a U."

"Got it," the judge said. His expression didn't change as he signed the warrant.

An hour later, James met up with Abigail Tan at 101 Bury Street, and together, along with Mike Gaetano and Andre Damour from the department, entered Alan Cherney's apartment and served the warrant. He had been sleeping, and he was extremely drunk, blurry eyed and slurring his speech. He'd gone to his bathroom to be sick; they'd located the leather courier bag that the anonymous caller had identified, and found and bagged the knife. Abigail made the arrest.

Back at the station, James got Alan, who had declined the offer of legal representation, a cup of coffee and brought him to an interrogation room. He was alternating between docility and panic. "I didn't kill Audrey Marshall," he said, as she walked him into the room. "You know that, right?"

"Agent Tan's going to be questioning you in just a few minutes, and you can tell everything to her."

Before leaving the room, leaving Alan alone to stew for a few minutes, he blurted out, almost near tears, "It wasn't hives." It was something he'd said earlier, when she'd first cuffed him.

James paused. She knew she should leave him alone, let him answer questions once the official interrogation began, but she turned back toward him anyway. "You need to go and check on Kate Priddy," he said. "He said he had hives on his arm, but it wasn't. It was Sanders who scratched him, but Sanders only scratches anyone when he's in the basement. He's a different Sanders down there, and that's where Jack got scratched. He's coming and going through the basement. I think he's after Kate. I have a bad feeling. It's a really bad feeling."

"Sanders?" James asked.

"He's the cat that's always around. He's friendly, but if you try and pet him when he's in the basement, he scratches you. Jack is coming through the basement. That's how he's getting in."

James said, "Someone'll be right here, Alan, okay?"

An hour later, James watched the beginning of the interrogation, watched as Alan, who seemed to be sobering up, said the exact same thing about the cat to Abigail Tan. Hearing the words again made James's scalp tingle.

She left the station and drove back to 101 Bury Street. She sat in her car for a moment, staring up at the blank windows of the apartment building. It wouldn't hurt to just check on the apartment. She'd knock gently on the door. She'd listen, and if she heard nothing, then she'd return to her own apartment.

"Hey there, Sanibel," she said to the doorman, no longer needing to show him her badge. "Just checking in on Kate Priddy in 3D. She's expecting me."

She'd only just reached the door when she heard scuffling sounds from inside, then what sounded like a bag of sand being dropped onto a concrete floor. She unholstered her gun and banged on the door. She should have gotten backup, but it was too late now.

CHAPTER 37

THE MAN DETECTIVE ROBERTA JAMES had shot in the face was pronounced dead at the scene by the EMTs.

Kate Priddy was taken by ambulance to Mass General Hospital, where on-call surgeons removed the five-inch knife that was buried high up in her back. Somehow, the blade had missed her spinal cord, plus all major arteries. There was bone damage, and she had a concussion, but the doctors and nurses who were present at the surgery would have a story to tell for many years about the girl who survived a knife wound that should have been fatal.

Corbin Dell was strapped to a gurney and taken to a separate ambulance. The EMTs managed to stop the bleeding, but he'd already lost too much blood. He was pronounced dead en route to Mass General.

Alan Cherney, his interrogation interrupted when Agent Tan was told what was happening at Bury Street, sat for several hours in the interrogation room, eventually putting his head down on the table and going to sleep. His interrogation was completed early the next morning, then all charges were dropped and he was released.

THE FIRST FACE KATE PRIDDY saw upon opening her eyes at midday on Wednesday was Detective James's.

"I'm alive," Kate said.

"You are."

James put her hand on Kate's shoulder and watched the young woman close her eyes and go back to sleep.

WHEN KATE WOKE AGAIN, a nurse was checking her vitals. "Hi, there," Vicky Wilson said, when she saw Kate's half-opened eyes. Vicky was secretly thrilled to be in charge of the celebrity patient, but tried to conceal it as she asked: "How are we doing this afternoon?"

"Thirsty."

"I can probably get you some ice chips, sweetheart. What else can I get for you?"

"The detective." Kate's voice was a faint croak.

"A detective?"

"No. Detective James. Roberta." Kate had to swallow after saying the words. Her throat ached.

"When I'm done here, sweetheart, I'll go find Detective James, okay?"

Kate closed her eyes again.

When she opened them, Roberta James was there, and Kate said: "Tell me everything."

James smiled. "I'll tell you what we know, okay?"

"Is Corbin dead?"

"Yes, Corbin Dell is dead."

"What about Jack Ludovico?"

James paused, enough so that Kate had one awful moment where she thought he'd somehow gotten away. "The man you knew as Jack Ludovico is dead as well. He went by a lot of names, and we're still trying to figure out what the real one is. Does the name Henry Wood mean anything to you?"

Kate shook her head, causing small detonations of pain in her neck and shoulder. She must have grimaced, because Detective James said, "We'll talk more about this later. You'll be glad to know your parents are en route from England."

"That's nice."

"And there's a man, Alan Cherney, who very much wants to see you. He's here, now, in the hospital."

"Not right now, okay," Kate said, closing her eyes.

"Of course. I'll let you sleep."

James was standing up when Kate opened her eyes again and asked, "How did Corbin Dell get back into America? I thought you said—"

"That we were monitoring his passport. We were. He used someone else's, a Dutch passport."

"Why?"

"We don't know everything yet, Kate. We think that the man you knew as Jack Ludovico, who also went by Henry Wood, had been targeting Corbin Dell, maybe trying to set him up, frame him for a murder."

"So Corbin's not a killer?"

"There's a lot for us to unravel, Kate. We just don't know the whole situation."

"They were both in the apartment. How did . . . ?"

"How did they get in? Corbin had a key, and we found lock-picks on Jack. We think he was coming in and out of Bury Street through a back entrance that led to the basement."

"How long had he been coming into the apartment?" Kate's mouth was getting drier the more she talked.

"We don't know that, but there's evidence—forensic evidence—that he'd been all over the apartment. I'm going to tell you everything as we learn it, Kate, but right now, I think you need some more rest."

"Okay," Kate said, and let her lids close. There was pain in her upper back and at the base of her skull, and that pain was spreading and joining, and becoming stronger. She heard the detective's chair scrape along the linoleum floor, then she knew she was alone. She tried to open her eyes, found she couldn't, and was asleep again.

JAMES RETURNED TO THE WAITING area where Alan Cherney sat, an unread book on his lap, a hopeful expression on his face.

"She's not ready to see you yet," she said to him.

"Okay," he said. "I'll wait a little longer."

"She didn't recoil in horror when I mentioned your name," James said, wanting to reassure him for some reason. She supposed she liked him, and not just because he had probably saved Kate Priddy's life by convincing James to return to Bury Street. He'd been right about the scratch on Henry's arm; the coroner said it had come from a cat.

Alan smiled. "That's something."

James moved out of earshot of Alan and called in to the station. The Bureau had descended in force, Abigail Tan replaced by a senior agent named Colin Unger, who looked like a model from a military recruitment catalog. James got through to her captain and reported on Kate's condition.

"I'll let them know she's awake and ready to be questioned."

"Let them know in a little while. She's going to be overwhelmed."

"You think she knows anything?"

"About what? Henry Wood? No, nothing. She knows what happened the night she was nearly killed, but that's it. She told us all about it while she still had a knife stuck in her back. Oh, she wanted to know if Corbin was innocent."

"What did you tell her?"

"Told her we'd talk later. She's still pretty fragile."

After hanging up with her captain, she thought of the Polaroid picture they'd found in the apartment that belonged to Henry Wood. It was of Corbin Dell, standing in the rain, above an open grave that contained the body of what looked to be a brunette woman. There was an old gravestone in one corner of the picture, suggesting that he was in a cemetery. Corbin, to James's eye, looked about eighteen years old. It was hard to read the expression on his face; his eyes were maybe a little shocked, but he looked relaxed, his mouth parted slightly. It was that image that had been haunting James for the past thirty-six hours, even more than what she'd seen in Kate's apartment, the bloodbath that was stopped when James took a man's life with a single bullet. It hadn't saved Corbin Dell, but her being there had probably saved Kate Priddy.

It was something.

Four hours later, Agents Unger and Tan arrived at the hospital to question Kate.

"You want me in there, as well?" James asked.

"We do," Unger said. He had a slight southern accent. North Carolina was James's guess.

"Okay. Happy to. We can't wake her, but we can wait till she wakes up on her own."

They didn't have to wait too long. In half an hour a nurse came to tell them that Kate had woken and that she'd asked for Detective James again. In that half an hour, Abigail Tan filled James in on what they'd learned. Corbin Dell and Henry Wood had studied at the same program in London fifteen years earlier. Not only that, but there was an unsolved homicide from the time, an English student at the same business school they'd both attended by the name of Claire Brennan. She'd gone missing at the time when Corbin and Henry had both been in London, and her body had eventually been found, buried in an old graveyard in North London. No one had ever been arrested for the crime.

"Was she mutilated postmortem?" James asked.

"She wasn't, no," Tan said.

"Still."

"Right, still."

"What are you thinking right now? They killed women together?"

"That's what it looks like," Tan said. "Henry and Corbin meet in London and kill Claire Brennan together. They take pictures, then maybe do it again here in America. First Linda Alcheri, and then Rachael Chess."

"Corbin Dell was out of the country when Rachael Chess was killed," James said.

"Corbin Dell is supposed to be out of the country at this very moment, according to flight records."

"Okay. Point taken. Then what? They kill Audrey Marshall together, and then Corbin Dell returns here so that they can kill his cousin? It doesn't make a lot of sense."

"No, I know. It doesn't," Tan said. "We're hoping Kate Priddy can help out."

"She told me what happened on that night. According to her, Corbin was suddenly in her apartment. He woke her up and told her to hide in a closet, that a bad man was there. Those were his words. When she came out, Corbin was bleeding out on the floor and she was attacked from behind."

"Then you showed up," Tan said.

"Yes, then I showed up."

After Kate woke, Agent Unger, with some assistance from Agent Tan, questioned Kate Priddy for about twenty-five minutes. She told them exactly what she'd told James before. Nothing more, nothing less. At the end of the conversation, when Kate's eyes were starting to close, she said: "It's me, I guess."

"What's you?" Agent Unger said.

"It's my fault. They come to me, psychopaths. I'm like a magnet."

"I don't know everything right now, Kate, but I do know that none of this is your fault. None of this." James decided that she liked Agent Unger, despite the flat-top haircut and what had to be a pretty serious gym addiction.

Back outside in the hall, Unger asked James what Kate had been talking about.

"She was attacked about five years ago by an ex-boyfriend. This was in England. He locked her in a closet and committed suicide, leaving her there."

"Goodness." Unger drew the word out, made it sound like a curse.

"Yeah."

"But there's no connection?"

"Not that we could find," James said. "I think it's just random, or maybe she is a psycho magnet, like she said."

She'd said it as a joke, but Unger frowned, as though he was considering it. "Either way, poor thing," he said, then added: "Are you going to tell her that it looks like Henry Wood had been hiding in her apartment for at least two days?"

James had already thought about this. The crime scene officers had found fingerprint evidence from Henry Wood all over the apartment: on food in the kitchen, in most of the rooms, on Kate's possessions. They'd also found hair and DNA evidence that suggested he'd been sleeping underneath one of the beds in a guest room.

James, remembering Kate's request that she be told everything, said, "Yeah, I'll tell her."

WHEN KATE'S PARENTS FINALLY REACHED the hospital, it was just past visiting hours, but James escorted them past a uniformed officer into a private room, where Kate lay sleeping.

They watched her sleep for half an hour, not willing to wake her. "Let's go check into the hotel, then come back," Patrick Priddy said in a whisper to his wife.

"You check us in, darling, and I'll stay here."

But before Kate's father had left, Kate opened her eyes, saw both her parents, and for the first time since she'd been admitted to the hospital, began to cry.

CORBIN DELL WAS OFFICIALLY IDENTIFIED by his brother, Philip Dell, who had driven down from New Essex to make the identification. Detective James hadn't met him, but she heard from the grief counselor who'd been present that he displayed no emotion whatsoever and kept insisting that he needed to return to his mother, who was not used to being left alone.

Philip Dell was questioned by the FBI. Abigail Tan told James that he'd never heard of a Henry Wood. When asked about his brother's semester abroad in London, Philip Dell said that he hadn't remembered his brother going to London at all. When asked about Rachael Chess, and Corbin Dell's relationship with her, Philip said that Corbin's sex life was no concern of his.

ON THE DAY THAT KATE Priddy was released from the hospital, she agreed to see Alan Cherney, who'd shown up that morning at the hospital the way he'd shown up every morning since Kate had been admitted. He entered Kate's room, pale and nervous and holding a bouquet of paperwhites. Kate was sitting up in bed, drawing in a new sketchbook that her parents had brought to her the day before. She'd already sketched four nurses and two doctors.

"Thank you for the flowers," Kate said as Alan handed them over. They were strong smelling, and Kate couldn't stop herself from making a face as she placed the vase on her side table.

"They smell terrible," Alan said. "Sorry."

"No, they don't. They smell better than this hospital room, anyway."

"I heard you were getting out today."

"That's what they tell me, but I'll believe it when it happens."

"What are you going to do?"

"My parents have a suite at a hotel around the corner, so I'll stay there tonight, I guess. Then I'll go home."

"You're not going to stay and finish your courses?"

Kate laughed. "No, I don't think so. Where would I even stay?"

"Well, you could stay with me, of course. It wouldn't be a problem. I'd like it . . ."

"Thanks, Alan, but I don't—"

"I totally understand. I just wanted you to know that there was an offer on the table. A real offer. I didn't expect you to say yes."

"What's it like there?"

"Where? At Bury Street?"

Kate nodded.

"It's insanity. For the first twenty-four hours they cordoned off the whole building because there were so many reporters. Now, it's just your whole wing, but there have been nonstop police officers coming in and out, and news vans parked outside almost all the time. You know I was arrested, right?"

"I know all about it. Roberta—Detective James—has told me everything. Or at least she's told me that she's told me everything. She said that after you were arrested she came back to the apartment because of you—because of what you said."

"Honestly, that whole night is pretty blurry for me. I remember going to your apartment—sorry, again, about that—but I don't really remember what we talked about. Then I went home and fell asleep and next thing I knew the police were there, arresting me, and all I could think about was that you were in danger. I was sure of it."

"He'd been hiding in my apartment. When I was there."

"I know. That's what the papers are saying. It's terrifying."

"What else are the papers saying?"

"You heard about the unsolved murder in London?"

"Detective James told me about it. Was it them?"

"It looks like it. There was preserved DNA evidence at the crime site, so if it was them, then I guess the police will find out for sure. This is a massive story, you know that? There's bound to be a TV movie ramping up in production right now."

"I'm getting that feeling."

"Reporters have been contacting me with requests for exclusive interviews. I've been offered money."

"Oh yeah?" Kate said. "What are you going to do?"

"Nothing. I don't care about that. I'm worried about you."

"I think I'm going to be okay, honestly. Maybe I'm still in shock, but for some reason I'm not as traumatized or frightened as I should be. I should have died—I should have died twice, really—and here I am still alive. I know this sounds strange, but I feel lucky. Tell me more about what you're reading in the papers."

They talked for a while more, Alan filling her in on everything that had happened since the night that Corbin Dell and Henry Wood had both died. He even told her how his ex-girlfriend Quinn had gotten in touch, wanting to know if he wanted to get a drink.

"You think she wants to get back together with you, now that you're famous?"

"I think she just wants to hear the details."

"You should take advantage of your fame. It's fleeting." Kate smiled, weakly.

The smile was enough to allow Alan to say what he wanted to say. He shifted forward a little on the molded plastic chair. "I have a speech," he said. "I apologize in advance."

"You don't have to make a speech," Kate said, but she was still smiling.

"I'm only going to make it once, then I'm done. It's short. I promise."

After the speech, Kate nodded and said she'd consider it. Alan thanked her and left the hospital room. At least he'd had his say. He'd told the truth, or close enough. Saying how much their night together had meant, how bad he felt about crashing into her apartment through the basement, and how he genuinely believed she should stay for a while in America and give their relationship a shot, was just a long way of saying what he really wanted to say. That even though they'd only just met, he knew he was in love with her.

JIM AND LINA WOOD DROVE eight hours from Stark, in upstate New York, to help identify their son. They were both surprised that they weren't brought into a basement morgue, Henry's body under a sheet, his face revealed. It was the way they'd seen it done on countless television shows, and they assumed it was the way it was done in real life. Instead, they were brought to a sterile, well-lit office, where they were shown photographs of Henry's face, surrounded by what looked like a blue sheet. It was their son, of course. Neither was surprised.

Jim had wanted to turn around and drive all the way back to Stark, but Lina talked her husband into spending the night. They found a Super 8 just west of the city. It was across the street from a diner that looked like it might be okay for dinner. Jim wouldn't admit it, but his driving skills, especially at night, were not what they used to be.

After dinner, they returned to the motel. Jim found a baseball game on the television. They hadn't talked about Henry. They'd talked about him plenty when he'd been younger. They'd prayed about him, too. That it had ended as it did was neither a shock nor a comfort to either of them. It was just a fact. Something had been wrong with him, and now he was in God's hands. It was terrible that they were saying he had killed those women, but at least now he couldn't kill anyone else.

Jim fell asleep with the game still on, and Lina turned the television off. Jim's breathing was labored and raspy. She was worried, but figured he'd be okay for one night without his apnea mask.

Before falling asleep herself, she allowed herself one selfish moment, one moment of remembering Henry when he had been an infant, just five or six months old. She used to put him on her thighs while she sat on the couch, hold his tiny chest in her hand, and gently shake it, and Henry would laugh and laugh, staring up into her eyes.

Then she let the memory go, and told herself she could never think of it again.

CHAPTER 38

"I'VE DECIDED I WANT TO stay here, just for a short while."
Kate said these words on her second night at the large hotel near to
the hospital. She was eating dinner with her parents at the restaurant called Foliage, the one restaurant of the three in the hotel that
wasn't squarely aimed at the business traveler with a hefty expense
account.

"Why?" her mother said, a quivering spoonful of crème brûlée
halfway to her lips.

"Where?" her father asked.

"Just for a little while. I can't explain it. I might take the ferry
over to Provincetown and spend a couple of nights alone. I haven't
been—"

"We could all go, darling," her mother said.

"No, I want to do this alone. I think if I go straight back to England, and back with you to your house, that I'll never leave again.
It's just for a few days."

To Kate's surprise, her parents agreed without putting up too
much of a fight. They went with Kate to the concierge and found
information on taking the ferry directly from Boston Harbor to
Provincetown, on the tip of Cape Cod. The concierge offered to
book Kate a hotel room for when she got there, but she insisted
that she'd find her own place to stay. Kate's parents offered to book
a return ticket to London, but Kate told them she'd book it herself
when she was ready to come home.

"Not too long, okay, darling?" her mother said.

"Your grandparents are not going to believe we've let you stay
here after what happened," her father said.

"Tell them I'm a grown woman, and I'll be back soon."

Kate's parents put her on the ferry on the afternoon of their return flight to England. Before leaving, Kate called Detective James from the hotel and told her where she was going to be, in case they needed to further question her. She doubted it, though. And there wasn't going to be a trial. Corbin Dell and Henry Wood had died together.

"Provincetown is nice," the detective said.

"I heard it was."

"Take care of yourself, Kate. You've been through a significant trauma."

"Story of my life," Kate said.

The midsized ferry chugged out of Boston Harbor toward the expanse of the Atlantic Ocean, sparkling under a cloudless sky. Kate stood on the front deck for the entire ninety minutes, her face tilted toward the sun, occasionally closing her eyes. She didn't really know what she was doing. She only knew that she didn't want to return home to the coddling of her parents, to questions from relatives and friends, or worse, silence. And she couldn't return to the apartment on Bury Street. And she still hadn't made a decision about Alan Cherney, even though he'd been right when he told her in the hospital that there was something special about their one night together. There had been. She had felt it. But she had also felt that enormous fear upon waking, the terror of putting your life and happiness in someone else's hands.

Kate spotted the long spit of Cape Cod, shimmering along the horizon. Then she could make out a tall stone monument and a water tower looming above a town packed tightly with houses. The ferry moved through Provincetown Harbor, studded with moored boats, and tied up at a concrete pier. She walked down the rickety gangway and onto solid ground, slightly nauseous from the boat trip but happy, suddenly, to be somewhere new. To be a stranger.

She got a fried clam roll at the first place she hit coming off the ferry, sitting outside at a wooden picnic table even though the air was cool. It was before the season, she knew, the calendar having just flipped from April to May, but there were lots of people about. She knew Provincetown was famous for its heavily gay population, but the residents and visitors who walked past Kate during her lunch seemed as varied as any place she had ever been to. There were heavily muscled young men in couples and groups, families of tourists, two old women still dressed in their winter coats, both pushing bicycles, a fat man in a business suit smoking a cigar, a group of twenty-year-old women in rugby jerseys. After lunch, Kate wandered, finally checking into a guesthouse up Howland Street. The Spartan room was perfect: painted wooden floors, four-poster bed, no television, and a narrow window with a view toward the water.

She stayed three days, taking long walks, reading several Barbara Pym novels that she'd found in a used bookstore in town, and eating most of her meals at the long curving bar of a Portuguese restaurant on the east side of town. The fear was still there. Walking home after dark, all the footsteps she heard were following her, and the shadows between houses were filled with murderers and rapists. During the day, Kate waited for some drunk driver to veer onto the narrow sidewalks of Commercial Street and crush the pedestrians. She watched the skies for storms that would rip the roofs off the salt-weathered houses. And she even watched for George Daniels, seeing him as she always did in the long-legged strides of distant strangers and in the haircuts of waiters. It was funny that it was still George who haunted her, now that he'd been joined by Corbin Dell and Henry Wood. She knew that Henry, or Jack, as she still thought of him, would show up in her dreams eventually with his twitchy body and his white teeth. It would be okay when he did. He couldn't hurt her anymore.

She wondered if Corbin would ever enter her nightmares. Even though she'd found out that there was strong evidence he was involved in at least two murders, the college girl in London and the woman from Hartford, Connecticut, Detective James had told her that they were now positive Corbin had not been involved in Audrey Marshall's death.

He had come back from London to save her. Whatever he once had been, he'd changed, hadn't he?

Packing up to leave Provincetown, a slip of paper fell out from between two sweaters that Kate hadn't worn on her trip. It was a note from her mom:

Darling, letting you out of our sights and not bringing you back home with us has been the hardest thing I've had to do, but Daddy insists you're okay, and I tend to agree. I want you to know how proud we are of you. We know that life isn't easy for you at the best of times, and you've weathered the worst. Twice. I've always been a little fretful myself, but I'm not worried about you now. You are going to be fine. We'll see you at home soon. Love you, darling, Mummy

Kate read the note several times, then placed it within the pages of the book she was reading.

It was early evening when she got back to Boston. It was warmer in the city than it had been on the Cape, but the skies were half filled with clouds, the air heavy with the possibility of rain. She took a taxi from the harbor to Bury Street, expecting the driver to make some comment about what had happened in the building, but he didn't. He merely helped her with her bag and left her on the sidewalk in the approaching dusk. The apartment building looked unchanged. There was no police tape, no news vans. The only thing she noticed was a young couple slowing down as they passed the building, the woman pointing toward the windows of Corbin Dell's apartment.

Kate entered the lobby, surprised to see the doorman named Bob at the station, since he didn't usually work evenings. He was more surprised to see her.

"Hello, miss," he said. "Nice to see you."

"Hi, Bob. I'm actually here to visit Alan Cherney. Do you know if he's in?"

"I'll check for you." He picked up his handset, and after a brief conversation, sent Kate up the stairs toward Alan's wing.

She had no plans, beyond wanting to see him again. Heart beating, Kate Priddy walked to Alan Cherney's door. It was open and he was standing there, a nervous grin on his face. She put down her luggage and stepped into the small circle of his waiting arms.

Date of Return

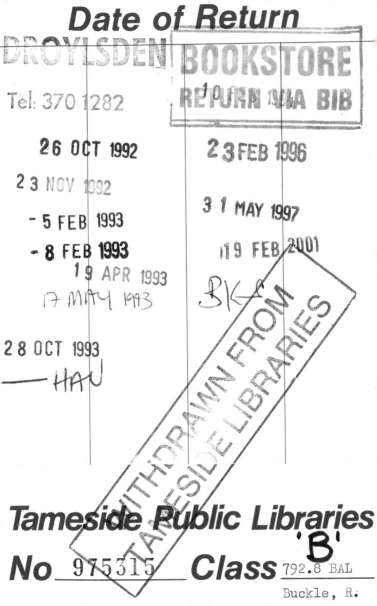

Nijinsky (1971)

Diaghilev (1979)

Buckle at the Ballet (1980)

The Most Upsetting Woman (1981)

In the Wake of Diaghilev (1982)

GEORGE BALANCHINE

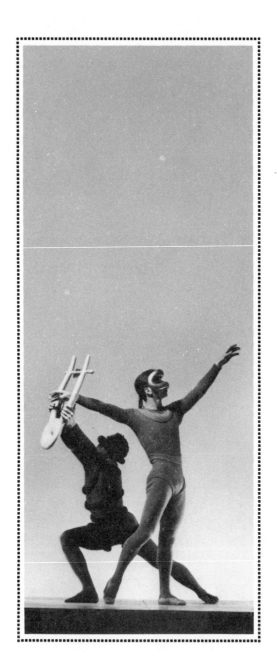

GEORGE BALANCHINE

B·A·L·L·E·T
M·A·S·T·E·R

A Biography by

RICHARD BUCKLE

IN COLLABORATION

WITH JOHN TARAS

HAMISH HAMILTON▪LONDON

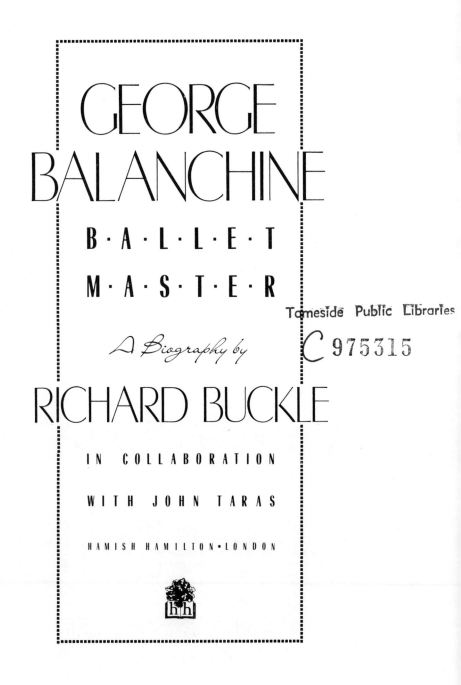

HAMISH HAMILTON LTD
Published by the Penguin Group
27 Wrights Lane, London W8 5TZ, England
Viking Penguin Inc., 40 West 23rd Street, New York, New York 10010, U.S.A.
Penguin Books Australia Ltd, Ringwood, Victoria, Australia
Penguin Books Canada Ltd, 2801 John Street, Markham, Ontario, Canada L3R 1B4
Penguin Books (N.Z.) Ltd, 182–190 Wairau Road, Auckland 10, New Zealand

Penguin Books Ltd, Registered Offices: Harmondsworth, Middlesex, England

First published in Great Britain 1988 by
Hamish Hamilton Ltd

First published in the United States of America 1988 by
Random House, Inc., New York

Copyright © 1988 by Richard Buckle and John Taras

Grateful acknowledgement is made to the following for permission to reprint previously published material:
Nancy Goldner: Excerpts from *The Stravinsky Festival of the New York City Ballet* by Nancy Goldner. Copyright © 1973 by Nancy Goldner. Published by Eakins Press Foundation.
Farrar, Straus & Giroux, Inc.: Excerpts from *Zorina* by Vera Zorina. Copyright © 1986 by Brigitta Lieberson, Reprinted by permission of Farrar, Straus & Giroux, Inc.
Alfred A. Knopf, Inc.: Excerpts from *The New York City Ballet* by Anatole Chujoy. Copyright 1953 by Anatole Chujoy. Excerpts from *Choura* by Alexandra Danilova. Copyright © 1986 by Alexandra Danilova. Excerpts from *Thirty Years: The New York City Ballet* by Lincoln Kirstein. Copyright © 1973 by Alfred A. Knopf, Inc. Copyright © 1978 by Lincoln Kirstein. Reprinted by permission of Alfred A. Knopf, Inc.
Limelight Editions: Excerpts from *Split Seconds* by Tamara Geva. Copyright © 1972 by Tamara Geva. First Limelight Edition, March 1984. Reprinted by permisssion of Proscenium Publishers, Inc.
Random House, Inc.: Excerpt from *Winter Season: A Dancer's Journal* by Toni Bentley. Copyright © 1982 by Toni Bentley. Reprinted by permission of Random House, Inc.
Simon & Schuster, Inc.: Excerpts from *Balanchine's Tchaikovsky: Interviews with George Balanchine* by Solomon Volkov. Copyright © 1985 by Solomon Volkov. Reprinted by permission of Simon & Schuster, Inc.

British Library Cataloguing in Publication Data
Buckle, Richard, 1916–
George Balanchine: ballet master.
1. Choreographers—United States—Biography
I. Title
792.8′2   GV1785.B32

ISBN 0–241–12180–9

Printed in the United States of America

Typography and binding design by J.K. Lambert

ACKNOWLEDGMENTS

JOHN TARAS knew Balanchine better and for much longer than I did, besides knowing most of his ballets thoroughly, so when we began to plan this book, shortly before Balanchine's death, we agreed that he would do the majority of the interviews. He obtained valuable information from, among others, Lew Christensen, who has since died, Alicia Markova, Tamara Toumanova and Diana Adams. A few interviews we did together. After Taras became associate director of American Ballet Theatre in 1985 and could no longer give so much time to our collaboration, I did most of the interviews. William Lawson taped seven, and Tom Lacy, one.

On pages 333–335 is a list of all those who were kind enough to spare the time to be interviewed or who answered questions. With Betty Cage, a friend for over thirty years, and Natalie Molostwoff, a friend for over twenty, I spent long hours of talk. Betty Cage also made available correspondence between herself, Balanchine and Lincoln Kirstein. Rosemary Dunleavy gave up several Saturday mornings to help me. Karin von Aroldingen and Barbara Horgan were wonderfully generous with their time and information.

My own intermittent conversations with Balanchine began in 1948, though my admiration for his work dates from the 1930s. In 1950 we became friends. In 1977, when I was writing the life of Diaghilev, he spared two mornings to talk to me about the 1920s, and, to my surprise, seemed to enjoy looking back.

Lincoln Kirstein made an invaluable contribution by allowing me to read and quote from his diary for 1933–34. Edward M. M. Warburg was generous in sharing his reminiscences of Balanchine's early days in America. Eugene R. Gaddis of the Wadsworth Atheneum Museum archives was helpful in describing the performances at Hartford. Alexandra Danilova not only talked to me for hours, but wrote detailed letters. I have quoted at length from her autobiography, as well as from those of Tamara Geva and Vera Zorina. Kyril Fitzlyon, the distinguished Russian translator, traveled with me to Russia to act as interpreter in my taped conversations with Balanchine's brother Andrei, who, with his whole family, gave us a warm welcome and provided much information on the choreographer's early days in St. Petersburg and on his first visit to Georgia in 1962. Boris Kochno produced fascinating early letters. The Dmitriev contracts and the cables between Kirstein and Balanchine are from the files at the School of American Ballet. A few letters from Balanchine to Diaghilev come from the Dance Collection, Library and Museum of the Performing Arts at Lincoln Center, New York; these were translated by Nathalie Gleboff. I have also drawn on the remarkable archive at Parmenia Ekstrom's Stravinsky-Diaghilev Foundation.

Musicians who helped me were Desmond Shawe-Taylor, Robert Irving and especially Gordon Boelzner. William Lawson worked out the evolution of *Agon* and gave me the benefit of his researches into Balanchine. At the New York State Theater, Edward Bigelow and Deni Lamont played videotapes of various ballets to refresh my memory; so did the helpful staff of the Dance Collection.

Nancy Lassalle and Jane Emerson of Ballet Society and Shields Remine of *Ballet Review* were tireless in assisting me with research on facts and photographs. Patricia Neary wrote and telephoned frequently in reply to questions and lent me a tape of Balanchine she had made in Zurich. Balanchine's two previous biographers, Bernard Taper and Solomon Volkov, were generous and helpful in answering questions. William Lawson did research for me in New York University Library, Sarah Woodcock and Philip Dyer in the

Theatre Museum, London, Jane Pritchard in the archives of London Festival Ballet and Elsa Lowry at Lincoln Center.

I would also like to acknowledge the assistance given by Robert Cornfield, Dr. David Brown, Tom Schoff, Nancy Goldner, Beryl Grey, Michael Somes, Kensington Davison, Natasha Spender, Charles Mackerras, Richard Rapp, Karl Reuling, Charles France, Morton Gewirtz, George Dorris, Robert Craft, Randall Bourscheidt, George and Patricia Harewood, Peter Heyworth, Denisa Beach, David Dougill, David Leonard, Molly Daubeny, Thilo von Watzdorf, Delia Peters, Tina Campt, Virginia Donaldson, Leslie Bailey and Maitland McDonagh. Jane Harriss typed several versions of each chapter as the book evolved and our descriptions of certain ballets were condensed by thousands of words.

Martha Swope and her staff were infinitely patient in helping me find the photographs I needed from their archive. At the Library and Museum of the Performing Arts, Nancy Shaweroff arranged for George Platt Lynes's pictures to be printed. The photographers of Tass in Tbilisi copied Andrei Balanchivadze's precious old pictures in the course of an afternoon.

Jonathan Galassi originally signed up the book, but later left Random House. Anne Freedgood, who took over from him, pruned the manuscript, suggested what was missing and oiled the wheels of narrative: her admiration for Balanchine gave her the strength to overcome every obstacle. Jean-Isabel McNutt worked on the text and notes with sympathy and understanding. It was with pleasure that I found the ideas of James K. Lambert, the designer, coincided closely with my own.

RICHARD BUCKLE
Wiltshire, July 1987

CONTENTS

GEORGE BALANCHINE

Chapter 1

··

A GEORGIAN IN

ST. PETERSBURG:

1904 - 1924

G EORGE BALANCHINE liked to say that he was Georgian. Although this was only half true—and he completely lacked the Georgian swagger—there is much in the Georgian character that may have shaped his own.

Georgia lies in the Caucasus, the mountain barrier extending from the Black Sea to the Caspian. The ancient Greeks believed it was on Georgia's Mount Kazbek that Zeus chained Prometheus as punishment for stealing fire from heaven; and it was to the western coast of Georgia that Jason sailed with his Argonauts in search of the Golden Fleece. Xenophon traveled to the region in 400 B.C., and it later came under the sway of Alexander the Great. Pompey established a Roman hegemony there in 66 B.C. Christianity was introduced in A.D. 303 by Nina, a slave girl from Cappadocia in Asia Minor, who was later canonized. The ancients called Georgia the end of the world, but its inhabitants have always considered it the center.

Present-day Georgians, many of whom remain devout Christians and who clearly have an Oriental strain, nevertheless regard themselves as the heirs of the ancient Greeks. "Georgians are Mediterranean people," Balanchine said late in life, having perhaps come to this conclusion on his first visit, at the age of fifty-eight, to the country of his ancestors. It struck me, when I was there, that they must indeed believe that they are descended from the gods, goddesses and heroes of Hellas: a chambermaid at my hotel in Tbilisi was called Persephone. The choreographer's grandfather was named Amiran—Georgian for Prometheus. Balanchine's father, Meliton ("sweet as honey") Balanchivadze, named the children of his first marriage Nina, after the saint, and Apolon, after the god Apollo. Those of his second marriage were Tamara, after a medieval queen of Georgia famed for her beauty; Georgi, after the saint; and Andrei, after the apostle.

The Balanchivadze family came from the village of Banodzha in western Georgia, five kilometers from the mountain town of Kutaisi—whose coat of arms is the Golden Fleece—where distant cousins of Balanchine still live. In the Middle Ages, a *balanchi* was a court jester; *balanchivadze* means "jester's son." These jesters were also bards or wandering minstrels, their function being not only to make princes laugh but to compose music and recite poetry. When, in 1962, the choreographer, by then an American citizen, came to Tbilisi and learned that the historian Arkady Shanidze had traced the origin of the *balanchini*, he was delighted because the plural sounded "so Italian." "The fools had to be ugly," explained Andrei Balanchivadze recently, twisting his amiable features sideways. He claimed to have detected a slight deformity of the jaw that was shared by his two sons and his elder brother, Georgi: one side was higher than the other. His Uncle Vassili, an actor as well as a painter, had, he said, a completely crooked face.

Amiran Balanchivadze, Balanchine's grandfather, was a priest. Priests of the Russian Orthodox Church are required to be married, and Amiran had three sons and a daughter. Some time after the birth of his daughter in 1873, his wife died, and he was entitled to become a monk. Only monks can attain the rank of bishop; Amiran changed his pagan-sounding name to Anton, and became bishop of Kutaisi.

The bishop's eldest son, Meliton Antonovich, born in 1862, sang from childhood in church choirs and from the age of eighteen in the chorus of the Tiflis (now Tbilisi) Opera, where he later became a soloist. His first wife, also a Georgian, bore him a daughter and a son. By this time he was already collecting the Georgian folk songs and sacred chants to which he was later to devote his life. In 1899, when he was sent to the St. Petersburg Conservatory to study singing, his marriage broke up, and he was divorced. He spent two years learning composition under Rimsky-Korsakov and wrote the first Georgian opera, *Perfidious Tamara*, parts of which were performed in St. Petersburg in 1897. His second wife, a pretty blonde with dark eyes, was twelve years younger than himself. Maria, the daughter of a Baron Nicholaus von Almedingen who abandoned his wife and child and returned to Germany, was given her mother's name of Vasiliev. The three children of Meliton's second marriage were therefore half Georgian, one quarter Russian and one quarter German.

Georgi Melitonovich Balanchivadze, two years younger than his sister, Tamara, two years older than his brother, Andrei, was born on January 22, 1904, in Kirochnaya Street, St. Petersburg, a long street running west–east from the fashionable heart of the city toward the Smolny Convent. (It is now Ulitsa Saltykov-Shchedrin.) On its north side lay the gardens of the Tavrichevsky Palace, built by Catherine the Great for her favorite, Grigori Potemkin. In 1905, this mansion was to house the Exhibition of Historical Portraits that Sergei Pavlovich Diaghilev, with whom Balanchine was so closely associated later, organized before he set off to introduce Russian painting, music, opera and ballet to the West. The show was in preparation at the time of Georgi's birth and was opened by the emperor a year after it.

Before her marriage, Maria Balanchivadze had paid a hundred rubles for a ticket in the state lottery; several years later, her number came up. She won 200,000 rubles (about $30,000). Meliton, who had no head for practical matters, set about enjoying this windfall. The family moved to a larger apartment in Bolshoya Moskovskaya, a charming street with a double row of trees bordering a strip of garden down the middle. One of Maria's first cousins, always called "Aunt Nadia," came to live with them and had her own separate corner in the apartment. Georgi was her special pet.

The newly affluent Meliton gave presents to his friends, financed Georgian restaurants—where very few customers were pressed to pay their bills—and bought a *dacha* in Finland. He also paid for the publication in 1907 of the composer Glinka's letters. But when a factory in which he had invested failed, he was put under house arrest as a debtor—according to Andrei, he was given a set of rooms and forbidden to leave them for four months. He did not go to prison, as has been stated—this was one of Balanchine's romantic exaggerations—and he was allowed to keep his house in Finland.

The apartment in Bolshoya Moskovskaya was near the church of St. Vladimir, an eighteenth-century building in the typical St. Petersburg style, painted pink and white and with a baroque-looking bell tower. (It is now a hospital.) Even though Georgi found the services at St. Vladimir's too long—at Easter the family stood on the stone floor for four hours—he later told Solomon Volkov that the liturgy made a wonderful impression on him; he thought the priests, with their gorgeous miters, looked just like saints, and he envied the choirboys, who sang with angel-like delicacy.

The Balanchivadzes' *dacha* was an isolated house in the woods near Lounatiokki, a village not far from Vyborg. It was here that Georgi first experienced the pleasures of country life and learned from his mother, who was a wonderful cook, the delight in good food that remained with him all his life. It was at Lounatiokki, while he was stumbling through a Beethoven piano sonata, that he suddenly recognized the power of music; as he told Bernard Taper fifty years afterward, it was a revelation. The awareness that something miraculous existed beyond the tedium of piano practice brought tears to his eyes.

Because Meliton was often away, traveling with his choir, the children saw less of him than of their mother. Maria Balanchivadze played the piano, but the children's regular piano teacher was a German lady, Elena Künze. The children also had a German nanny, and grew up speaking the language fairly well. When Meliton was at home, he taught his children Georgian three-part songs, which they performed when he entertained his friends. At Christmas, little Andrei was always delighted to dance for his father's guests, but Georgi stood in a corner and kicked at people because he hated anything to do with dancing. The two brothers were close, and Georgi was always kind to Andrei, but he was very reserved—an un-Georgian characteristic—and never showed his feelings. When he was punished, he used to hide, afraid that someone would see him crying.

Although the children of Meliton's first family were about twenty years older, they were on good terms with his second. Nina, married to Prince Shalva Kordzaya, had a son, Melkhizedek, three years senior to Georgi; Apolon had a daughter, Elizaveta. Because Apolon was a colonel in the police force, he suggested that Georgi, with his straight back and dignified bearing, should become a soldier. Tamara was intended for the Ballet School, Georgi for the Military Academy and Andrei for Technical School. As it turned out, Tamara became an artist, Georgi a choreographer and Andrei a composer.

The brothers' first visit to the theater, when they were about nine and seven, was to hear Rimsky-Korsakov's opera *Tsar Saltan* at the Maryinsky. Did this make a big impression? I asked Andrei. "Overwhelming!" The two boys spent hours afterward playing passages from the opera on the piano.

Their sister Tamara failed her first audition at the Ballet School, and when her mother took her for a second attempt in August 1913, Georgi went with them. One of the school officials who knew Maria asked, "Why is that youngster sitting there doing nothing? Why can't he take the examination, too?" Both sister and brother were accepted, but Tamara, it seems, had little talent for dancing, and she was later dismissed.

The Imperial Theater Ballet School was housed in one of the two long buildings the Italian architect Rossi built in the 1830s to form Teatralnaya Ulitsa (Theater Street), which led out into an open square opposite a bridge over the Fontanka Canal. Its magnificent exterior arcading and white columns stood out against the rosy ocher paint; within, austerity reigned. The boys' huge, bare dormitories were on the top floor, above the girls'. The boarders were allowed to go home only on Sundays, and Georgi became so homesick that he ran away after a week. Knowing his mother would send him straight back, he went to his Aunt Nadia, who managed to hide him in her corner of the apartment for several days before he was discovered.

The students learned the grammar of their art at the school every morning. Traditional exercises at the barre were followed by center practice, in which they performed turns, leaps and short combinations of steps improvised by their teacher; lessons in national and character dancing followed, so that the students could acquire the correct deportment for the stately polonaise, the controlled passion of the Polish mazurka and the alternating languor and frenzy of the Hungarian csárdás. Lessons in adagio—movements performed slowly, so that the dancers could learn control and balance—would come later. When the boys went downstairs to work with the girls, turning, lifting and supporting them, learning how to present them with the noble subservience of ballet cavaliers, conversation between the sexes was discouraged. In the afternoons, there were lessons in music, history, French and mathematics. To Georgi, this daily round was as dull as his piano practice had been until the moment of revelation. At the end of his first year, however, when less promising pupils were weeded out, he passed his tests.

He was sad and lonely if his mother or aunt was unable to bring him home on Sundays, because the school was almost deserted at weekends. "You'd go to the church and stand there for some time. . . . You had to kill time before dinner," he recalled. "I would go to the reception hall and play the piano." Georgi was good at mathematics and preferred theology to history and literature. As he told Solomon Volkov many years later:

I liked reading Jules Verne—*Twenty Thousand Leagues Under the Sea.* . . . I still remember the captions under the pictures. . . . We were also enthralled by the adventures of Sherlock Holmes, Nick Carter, and Pinkerton.

The children were sometimes asked to walk on—or even to dance small parts—in ballets at the Maryinsky Theater, a mile or so away, to which they were driven in closed carriages, six boys in each. One evening, ten of these carriages set off for the Maryinsky, where the children were herded into a dressing room, costumed and made up. The ballet was *The Sleeping Beauty.* This was probably not Georgi's first appearance onstage, but in later years he spoke as if it were that performance that had opened his eyes to the wonders of classical ballet. As he stood in the wings listening to the magical Tchaikovsky music, he perhaps saw part of the variations for the six Fairies before preparing to scuttle on as a little monster in the train of the wicked fairy Carabosse—to find himself facing the blue and silver auditorium, flashing with diamonds. Since he was also in the Garland Dance, he had a chance to watch the evening's Aurora perform her breathtaking Rose Adagio. He marveled at the enchanted forest as it grew to surround the castle, with trees ascending, branches weaving in and out, and at the fairy boat as it moved past the unfolding panorama to the harp arpeggios and pizzicato strings of Tchaikovsky's music. In the last act he may also have danced one of the seven brothers of Hop o' My Thumb. That evening he came to understand the goal beyond the sweat and monotony of ballet school. His vocation was determined.

.   .   .

MARIUS PETIPA, the choreographer of *The Sleeping Beauty*, was a Frenchman, born in Marseilles in 1818. Both his father, Jean, and his elder brother, Lucien, were dancers and choreographers, but Lucien achieved his greatest fame as a performer at the Paris Opéra, where he created the role of Albrecht in *Giselle* and part- nered not only Carlotta Grisi but most of the other principal ballerinas of his day. Jean Petipa's career was largely spent as ballet master of the Théâtre de la Monnaie in Brussels, but he was invited to America in 1839 and took Marius with him. The twenty- year-old Marius, suffering from the aftereffects of a broken leg, had little success in *La Tarentule* at the National Theater on Broadway. It is interesting, however, that Balanchine, who was often called "the heir of Petipa," should have been preceded by him in New York ninety-five years earlier. Had Marius Petipa met with success and remained in America, the history of both Russian and Ameri- can ballet might have been very different.

As it was, the two Petipas sailed back to Europe the same winter. After three more years at La Monnaie, Jean Petipa joined the Imperial Academy of Dancing in St. Petersburg as a professor, and Marius followed him. Perhaps something more than family feeling prompted Marius to go to Russia in 1847. Taglioni retired from the stage that year, and there was a general feeling that the golden age of what we now call the "Romantic ballet" was coming to an end. Apart from Marius Petipa's doubts about making a name or a fortune in France, he may also have felt political apprehension. Eighteen forty-eight was to be the year of revolutions throughout Europe, the year of Louis-Philippe's abdication.

During his early years in Russia, Petipa was eclipsed first by Jules Perrot and later by Arthur Saint-Léon. In 1881, however, Ivan Vsevolojsky was appointed director of the Imperial Theaters, and in 1889 his patronage of Petipa led to their triumphant collaboration with Tchaikovsky on *The Sleeping Beauty*.

Tchaikovsky had previously composed *Swan Lake*; and his last ballet, *Casse-Noisette* (*The Nutcracker*), in which Petipa collaborated with Lev Ivanov, was produced at the Maryinsky in December 1892, shortly before his death.

. . .

DANCING in *The Sleeping Beauty* gave young Georgi a new incentive to work. He liked Samuel Andrianov, his teacher, whom he remembered as a brilliant one, and a "marvelous Siegfried in *Swan Lake*" besides, but who died young, of consumption. Georgi also admired the elderly Pavel Gerdt, who, he later explained, was "the very first [Prince] Désiré in the ballet *Sleeping Beauty* and the very first Prince Coqueluche in *The Nutcracker*." Another link with Tchaikovsky was the old Italian composer/conductor Riccardo Drigo, a man "just the opposite [of Gerdt], small and friendly, easygoing, with a gray mustache. . . . He spoke a very funny Russian. Drigo had conducted the premieres of both *The Nutcracker* and *Sleeping Beauty*. He had discussed the music and tempi with Tchaikovsky himself! Even in our day he conducted ballet performances in the Maryinsky."

When dancers from the Imperial Ballet came to take classes at the school, Georgi watched them carefully. Felia Doubrovska, a young soloist, always remembered his silent scrutiny and thought to herself, "There's a little boy who doesn't miss a thing." Another dancer, only one year ahead of him in school, was struck by his singularity, by the way he kept to himself and by his charm. This was Alexandra Danilova.

When war broke out in 1914, shortly after his admission to the Ballet School, several artists who had worked with Diaghilev in Western Europe came back to Russia. Mikhail Fokine returned to stage his ballets at the Maryinsky. Georgi loved *Les Sylphides*, called in Russia *Chopiniana*, but was critical of others. He also said later that "Fokine didn't come out too well when he took Rimsky-

Korsakov's *Schéhérazade* and Liszt's *Préludes.*" The former, when
staged by Diaghilev in a setting by Bakst, with Nijinsky dancing
the Golden Slave, had been the sensation of Paris in 1910, but
Diaghilev himself soon began to find it ridiculous, and the young
Balanchivadze knew that the surging music of the last movement,
which in the ballet accompanied the massacre of the Sultan's
unfaithful wives, had been intended by the composer to depict a
storm at sea. Another of Fokine's ballets mounted at this time was
Eros, for which the choreographer used Tchaikovsky's Serenade
in C for strings—music that would accompany the first ballet
Balanchine choreographed in America.

Tamara Karsavina, who had also returned to Petrograd, as it was
now called, at the outbreak of war, was one ballerina Georgi
admired; another was Elizaveta Gerdt, the daughter of Pavel Gerdt
and the wife of Georgi's teacher Andrianov.

Georgi was for the most part unaware of the political situation—
politics meant little to the enclosed community of Theater Street.
Neither Russia's defeats in the West nor the sufferings of her
ill-equipped army affected the students. They had probably heard
that Nicolas II had himself taken over the supreme command of
the armed forces, but they could not have realized that as a result
political power had passed to the empress's ineffectual favorites,
and the country was disintegrating. They must, however, surely
have heard of Rasputin's murder in December 1916 and the czar's
abdication the following March. On April 16, 1917, Lenin arrived
in Petrograd. Bolshevik extremists soon overthrew Kerensky's
moderate socialist government. Revolutionary troops searched the
Ballet School for czarist agents and subsequently closed it. It was
then occupied by the army.

The Balanchivadze family remained together in Petrograd for a
while, but later in 1917 Meliton was appointed Minister of Culture
to the Georgian republic. The following year, he founded the
Balanchivadze School of Music in Kutaisi. The rest of the family
stayed in Petrograd.

In a letter to their father written during the first winter of separation, Georgi and Andrei told him that they had learned how to repair their own galoshes, which was "much cheaper." They then proceeded to scotch a rumor that had caused them—Georgi probably more than Andrei—a little anxiety. The brothers wrote alternate words:

November 27 1917

Dear Daddy,

 . . . Who has been saying in the Caucasus that Georgi is a composer and has written many pieces of music and is an excellent musician? But this is not true. When we go to the Caucasus everyone will ask us to play, but we can't play anything special, so you, Daddy, tell everyone that we play only for ourselves.

In the meanwhile all best wishes,
Your loving Georgi and Andrei

Food was more plentiful in Georgia, so in 1918 Andrei was sent to join his father. Maria stayed in the capital to take care of the older children. The husband of their half-sister, Prince Shalva Kordzaya, "disappeared" soon after the Revolution. Uncle Apolon was persecuted and banished because of his former high rank in the czarist police. He later became an accountant and finally a priest. Georgi, aged fourteen, had to take what jobs he could find. He worked as a saddler's assistant and played the piano accompaniment in a movie house in return for bread, soap or matches. He and another former student went on foraging raids, stealing from Red Army barges moored on the Neva. They also rounded up stray cats, took them to an attic, strangled and skinned them, then gave them to Maria to cook. The dispossessed ballet students used to meet outside the school in Theater Street to exchange news and keep in touch. One day in 1918 they found a notice fixed to the door: the school was to open again. Anatole Lunacharsky, the Bolshevik Commissar for Education, had persuaded Lenin that opera and ballet were not counterrevolutionary.

The school was cold, and the food was much worse than in the old days. At the unheated Maryinsky, which had lost its aristocratic audience, the pipes froze and burst. The corps de ballet wore long-sleeved undershirts beneath their costumes. But, as Balanchine described it, "What could the poor prima dancers do? They got pneumonia, one after the other." There was talk of closing down the theater, but once again Lunacharsky came to the rescue. Salaries, however, remained very low.

The breaking down of traditional hierarchies and barriers meant that the Ballet School now had to share its premises with the recently organized School of Russian Drama. This led to Georgi's making a new acquaintance, Yuri Slonimsky from Warsaw, who became a ballet historian.

A reminiscence of Georgi at this time comes from Vera Kostrovitskaya, who later became a senior instructor at the school:

He never teased us little ones . . . but acted as if we were equals, and of the same age, though in those early years a difference of three classes was enormous. . . . He could never pass with indifference any musical instrument. The minute he came down to our floor of the school the sounds of a piano would be heard. . . . Sometimes, in the evening, we would secretly climb the stairs to listen to Balanchivadze playing Liszt, Chopin or Beethoven in the boys' quarters. . . .

For the school performance of 1919 Georgi danced the pas de deux from *Paquita* with two girls who were a year ahead of him, Lidia Ivanova and Alexandra Danilova. Danilova thought that the school authorities must have had high hopes for their future, since they chose them for this important number. She considered Georgi "not yet handsome, but . . . interesting looking, with piercing eyes . . . somehow special . . . very serious for his years."

Most women were to find Balanchine handsome in later life, but his looks were unusual. He had a high forehead, from which his dark-brown hair was brushed back; his nose was Roman. The high cheekbones were Oriental, but his slightly projecting teeth made the upper lip curve outward, so that his chin appeared more receding than it actually was. His wide mouth, with its full lower lip, tended to turn down slightly at the corners. He held himself very straight, as he had done in childhood, but his habit of tilting his head back and looking down his nose may have come from youthful resentment at his failure to grow any taller than five feet seven inches. His eyes, large and dark brown like his mother's, were charming, and his normal expression was one of benign amusement. He had a tic that caused him to twitch his nose and sniff as he talked (at school he had been nicknamed "the rat"), but he spoke softly in a rather high, nasal and reedy voice.

One of the boys' schoolmasters, Grigori Grigorievich Grigoriev, took a particular interest in Balanchivadze. He invited him to stay in his apartment, gave him lunch on Sundays, talked to him about music and lent him books. He was probably in love with him. The world owes something to this jealous old intellectual; according to Danilova, it was he who suggested that Georgi study music at the Conservatory.

In 1920, the sixteen-year-old Balanchivadze made his first attempt at choreography. He asked permission, which was granted, to arrange a dance for the annual school performance (Baryshnikov says the ballet is still danced today in Russia). Danilova recalls the incident in her memoirs:

To a piece of music by Anton Rubinstein [the Romance in E flat], he made a pas de deux called *La Nuit,* which he danced with Olga Mungalova. It was what would today be called "a sexy number." The boy conquered the girl: he lifted her in arabesque and held her with a straight arm overhead, then carried her off into the wings—so, she was *his*! This was the first time we had ever seen a one-arm lift in arabesque, which is now almost commonplace. But the effect that pas de deux had on me was more than the surprise at seeing new steps. It awakened something in me as a woman. Until then, all my boyfriends at the school had been just friends—I had never felt the need for anything more. And then suddenly I thought, there is something else. . . .

Alexandra Danilova graduated that spring, along with Ivanova and three other girls in her class. The departing graduates asked all their schoolmates to write in their yearbooks. Georgi wrote some bars of music in hers. "When I went to the piano and played the notes, I discovered it was Lensky's aria from *Eugene Onegin*: 'I love you, I love you.' I thought it was a joke, just a nice thing to write. I didn't take it seriously."

In the summer of 1919, Balanchivadze applied for admission to the Conservatory of Music, of which Alexander Glazunov was director. He had already met Glazunov, who had once come to the school theater to play his *Raymonda* on the piano—and "played beautifully, fluidly, clearly . . . just right for ballet rehearsal." Although Georgi was accepted, it was almost impossible for an undernourished dancer to work simultaneously at the school and the Conservatory, and he never completed his music course. Georgi's brother, looking back, judged that, from the point of view of a professional musician, he played pleasantly, although his hands were not "set."

On April 4, 1921, most of Balanchivadze's entire class of eight girls and four boys was graduated with honors from the school and joined the company of the State Theater of Opera and Ballet (formerly the Maryinsky). At the graduation performance, Georgi danced the role of Jean in *Javotte,* a ballet to the music of Saint-Saëns.

There can be little doubt that his concentration on both dance and music—the foundation of his later excellence in choreography—coming as it did at a time of dire food shortage, damaged his health for life. By this time he had already begun to show symptoms of tuberculosis and to spit blood, but he never spared himself. His friend Mikhail Mikhailov, a student one class behind him in the school, remembers that during the first or second summer recess after his entry into the corps de ballet of the State Theater, Georgi was chosen by Elizaveta Gerdt, whose usual partner was suddenly indisposed, to support her in an afternoon performance at the outdoor theater at Pavlovsk, the country palace, sixteen miles south of Leningrad, built by Catherine the Great for her son Paul. They were to dance a pas de deux from *Swan Lake.* The flattering summons arrived on the morning of the matinee itself, and Georgi went off in search of a costume. The first half of the performance was over and the bells for the second had rung, and there was still no sign of him. At the very last moment the reassembling audience parted to let through a frantic cyclist, and Georgi arrived at the stage door clasping a parcel. He apologized to his partner. "I am late. Please forgive me. It took a long time to find a costume, and when I got to the railroad station I could see only the end of the train vanishing into the distance. There was nothing for it but to borrow a bicycle from some people I know." After his sixteen-mile bicycle ride, he partnered Gerdt in the *Swan Lake* pas de deux.

. . .

DANILOVA, among others, remembers that Balanchivadze's most sensational number was the Buffoon's dance in *The Nutcracker* (called Candy Cane in America), in which he jumped through a hoop. The Buffoon is a character role. A character dancer, who is often strong and thickset, is one skilled in national dances such as the mazurka or trepak, or in comic, grotesque roles. He is the opposite of the *danseur noble,* who is usually taller and must have a more elegant line, the better to support and show off the ballerina. A demi-caractère dancer is a good classical dancer who excels in allegro and has a gift for comedy. Danilova rated Georgi as an excellent demi-caractère performer. It is clear from a few surviving photographs that the choreographer destined to extend the vocabulary of classical dance had neither the legs nor the feet of a *danseur noble.* According to Danilova, however, his Candy Cane variation always brought down the house. "His distinguishing features . . . were speed, musicality, a big jump, and a sharp attack." He was assured of a good career in the State Ballet, but the authorities did not approve of his essays in choreographic innovation. Danilova realized that his musical training at the Conservatory had extended his horizons.

More choreographic experiments followed the Rubinstein pas de deux. Georgi was impressed by the odd, acrobatic choreography of Kasyan Goleizovsky, a dancer from Moscow whose erotic ballets shocked the die-hard classicists. The authorities at the State Theater disapproved of Goleizovsky; an original in life as well as in art, he fancied long hair, velvet gowns and earrings. Balanchine was later to describe his choreography as "plastic." By this he presumably meant that the Moscow innovator used sculptural poses that bore no relation to the geometry of classical ballet; that he tied groups of dancers into knots, then led them in and out of mazes formed by their linked hands and arms. Balanchine, who was to become celebrated for his own knots and mazes, also adopted Goleizovsky's so-called sixth position, a stance with toes as well as heels touching: this was a contradiction of the first position of classical ballet, in which the heels are placed together and the toes turned out at an angle of 180 degrees.

Fyodor Lopoukhov, a principal choreographer of the State Theater and one of the few who rebelled against tradition and encouraged experiment, also influenced the young Balanchivadze. Lopoukhov's sister, Lydia (whose name Diaghilev changed to Lopokova on English tours), had defected. In 1922, Balanchivadze and some of his friends gave up their summer holiday to work with Lopoukhov on a ballet to Beethoven's Fourth Symphony, a bold attempt to express the inexpressible in terms of dance. A feature of the choreography was the formation of chains of linked dancers, some standing, others kneeling or recumbent. The small group of eighteen must have been kept busy. When *Dance Symphony: The Creation of the World* (also known as *The Grandeur of the Universe*) was presented—without the approval of the Theater Council—at the State Theater as part of a benefit performance on March 7,

1923, "a mixture of hissing and applause" greeted it. The ballet was never repeated. The acerbic old critic Akim Volinsky, who had opposed Fokine in the past and who had recently opened a school, attacked the experiment. Balanchivadze wrote an article in Lopoukhov's defense, deriding Volinsky's school and sounding the call for reform.

The revolutionary spirit of the poets Mayakovsky and Esenin, of the painters Tatlin, Malevich and Kandinsky, penetrated the world of dance; anything new was irresistible. The awareness of dawning possibilities was akin to that which had inflamed young romantics in the Paris of 1830. Balanchivadze cultivated a cadaverous pallor and wore his hair long. Danilova attributed this to a passion for Chopin and a wish to resemble him. She remembers that he wore nail polish, a cameo bracelet and a black shirt. A photograph dating from this period shows him seated cross-legged in the center of a group of his favorite colleagues, three women and three men. He is wearing white trousers and appears to be their acknowledged leader. It is not easy to cut a romantic, dashing figure when both money and materials are in short supply, but an eager young rebel can be a dandy in rags.

Fired by the experiments of Goleizovsky and Lopoukhov, Balanchivadze decided to form a group of his own. "Group" is perhaps the wrong word, for dancers came and went. Danilova recalled that one of these, Piotr Gusev, was Balanchivadze's closest friend at the time; and later he tried to persuade Mungalova, who became Gusev's wife, to leave Russia and join the Diaghilev Ballet. In the 1970s, by which time Gusev was an Honored Artist of the USSR, he recalled how much he had enjoyed being the raw material for Balanchivadze's choreographic attempts, even to working out parts that were later given to others.

It was Gusev who conducted the first meeting of dancers to discuss the foundation of the new group. When, sternly, he asked them what their credo was, the assembled friends chorused that they would do anything Balanchivadze wanted.

Some time during the first half of 1922, Georgi introduced an outsider into the rebel camp of State Theater dancers. This slight, pretty, ash-blond girl of fifteen named Tamara Zheverzheyeva, who had received her early training elsewhere, had been admitted to the State School for evening classes. (Her name was subsequently westernized as Gevergeyeva, then abbreviated to Geva.) She first caught sight of Georgi at a ballroom-dancing lesson. He had come in with Grigoriev, who told the teacher, "George has a dancing itch." Soon it was the young choreographer, not the teacher, who was "inventing combinations, correcting, shifting partners. . . . His whole presence projected the confidence of a leader. With his aquiline features and Byronic hair, he seemed a combination of poet and general."

Shortly afterward, he invited Tamara to dance with him in *La Nuit*. They were attracted to each other from the start, and quickly became friends.

To Grigoriev's annoyance, Georgi moved into the Zheverzheyev apartment. Realizing how delicate his health was, the Zheverzheyev family looked after him when he was ill. The deserted Grigoriev spitefully made a point of being rude about Tamara's dancing, even in the presence of Balanchivadze. But, Tamara recalled, "George would continue with the conversation as if nothing hurtful had been said"; he never stood up for her.

As soon as Maria Balanchivadze saw that her son was settled with Tamara, she realized that he would no longer be alone in the city and went to join her husband and Andrei in the Caucasus. Georgi never saw her again.

At the first performance of the Young Ballet, or Ballet of Youth, as it was to be called, Georgi staged Chopin's *Marche funèbre*. This took place on June 1, 1923, in the Alexandrovsky Hall, formerly the seat of the City Council. Subsequent performances of the Young Ballet were given in any club, arena or institute where space could be rented.

.   .   .

JUDGING from the brief surviving descriptions of Balanchivadze's youthful works, one or two of them seem to be more significant than others. In *Poème,* to the music of the Czech composer Fibich, Balanchivadze "lifted Danilova in classic arabesque and lowered her softly on pointe." At the end, "[He] carried Danilova off, lifting her high in an arabesque with his arms extended. . . ." The gentle lowering onto pointe and the soaring supported exit would occur again in later more famous works.

The *Marche funèbre* was planned to be seen in the round; the dancers entered through the audience. Slonimsky considered that in "the passage of dancers followed by light through the audience" and "the modeling of sculptural groups as if to generalize individual experience," Balanchivadze showed the influence of the experimental theater director Vsevolod Meyerhold. And indeed, in the first performance of Fokine's *Carnaval,* which was given in a St. Petersburg club before it was ever presented by Diaghilev at the Paris Opéra, dancers entered through the auditorium—and Pierrot was played by Meyerhold.

In *Enigma,* to the Arensky music used for the exit of Cleopatra from Fokine's ballet *Une Nuit d'Egypte,* which Diaghilev made the choreographer transform with the addition of music by other composers into the sensational *Cléopâtre,* Balanchivadze at one point turned the ballerina into a bridge, a movement he would repeat some years later in *Le Fils prodigue (The Prodigal Son),* his last ballet for Diaghilev.

Another example of Balanchivadze's "expressionism" was a duet for Ivanova and the choreographer himself called *Valse triste* and set to the piece of that name by Sibelius.

By the age of eighteen, Balanchivadze, trained in the classical discipline of Petipa and in the more poetic classicism of Ivanov, had been exposed to the influence of the sensuous, iconoclastic Goleizovsky, to Lopoukhov, who used to say that dance could express everything with the help of music alone and who had

dared to turn a Beethoven symphony into a ballet. and to Meyerhold.

.　.　.

DURING a trip to dance in Moscow, as a result of jealousy and the
fear of losing Tamara, Georgi suddenly realized he was in love with
her. His rival, tall, flamboyant, famous and irresistible—everything, in fact, that Georgi knew himself not to be—was the poet
Mayakovsky. He was a friend of Georgi's father, had been brought
up in Georgia, and coincidentally had been a pupil of Georgi's
uncle, Vassili Balanchivadze, the crooked-faced painter from
Kutaisi. Tamara described the episode. Only one room had been
provided, with a bed which Georgi and another dancer, Nicolas
Efimov, were meant to share, and a couch. When Mayakovsky
insisted on taking Tamara out to supper, she was haunted by the
unhappy look on Georgi's face. Everybody made a fuss about the
poet in the restaurant, but he realized something was wrong and
took Tamara home. She found Efimov asleep on the couch and
Balanchivadze seated on the bed, waiting for her. He held out his
arms.

In his old age, Balanchine was to say, "I heard a story going
around that it was Zheverzheyev's idea that Tamara and I get
married. Nothing of the kind. . . . [He] paid no attention to Tamara
and me . . . Tamara and I got married on our own."

They were married in the chapel of the Theater School. The
bridegroom had borrowed a set of tails from the theater wardrobe,
and he wore black eyeshadow. The marriage came as a great
surprise and shock to Georgi's colleagues at the theater and the
school. "All girls were rather upset," Alexandra Danilova told me.
"I was."

Tamara considered that her husband had "an impregnable
face." She was therefore surprised to observe one day when he
returned from rehearsal that he was "visibly annoyed."

"That Semenov is really a bastard," he said.

"Why?" . . .

"He came up to me . . . and in front of all the other people he said, 'Why did you marry that trollop?' "

. . . "And you? What did you do?"

"Nothing. . . . What could I do? I turned my back on him and walked away." . . .

"You didn't defend me—your wife?"

Balanchivadze "looked on helplessly" as Tamara wept. Next day, he came home from the State Theater "sickly pale," accompanied by his friend Mikhailov.

"What is the matter?" asked Tamara.

"I've been suspended for two weeks," he replied.

"Why?"

"I hit him."

"You hit who?"

Since Georgi remained silent, it was Mikhailov who explained. "He hit Semenov. . . . Right in the face. . . . He asked him to apologize for yesterday's remark, and when Semenov refused, he hit him so hard that he almost fell backward."

Tamara threw her arms around her husband's neck, but he stood "completely impassive."

The young couple moved into an unfurnished apartment on the Moika Canal. Tamara's mother allowed her to take away very little furniture apart from a bed, an armchair, a table and a chest of drawers, so it was rather bare and comfortless; but Georgi was impervious to his surroundings. "Even with me," wrote Tamara, "he took me as he found me, and though I'm sure he loved me, he never showed any curiosity about my life before we met, and consequently never knew much about it."

■   ■   ■

IN 1923, Balanchivadze was appointed ballet master of the Mikhailovsky Opera Theater. That September, he created a dance for the Queen of Shemakhan in Rimsky-Korsakov's opera *Le Coq d'or*, and arranged the elaborate processional march in the last act, as well as providing the choreography for Bernard Shaw's *Caesar and*

Cleopatra, performed by the Petrograd Drama Theater. In December, he staged a dramatically appealing scene in *Hinkemann* (*Eugene the Unfortunate*), Ernst Toller's expressionist tragedy. In Act III, Scene 1, the silhouettes of dancers foxtrotting behind the illuminated windows of a café were contrasted with the prostitutes and crippled war veterans in the street outside, who stretched out their arms in direct appeal to the audience.

Balanchine was renowned in later years for his ability to work at high speed and to carry on several jobs for different companies simultaneously. When he was nineteen, he already showed signs of the same talent.

News of the Diaghilev Ballet's productions in Western Europe had reached Georgi and his colleagues through Tamara Karsavina, who had escaped to the West and was in correspondence with the teacher Agrippina Vaganova. The latter read Tamara's letters aloud at the Theater School, and one of the things she wrote about was Igor Stravinsky's *Pulcinella.* As early as 1918, Balanchivadze had played a small part in Stravinsky's opera *Le Rossignol;* later he had got to know *The Firebird* and *Petrushka.* Still later, a piano score of *Pulcinella* somehow reached Petrograd. In January 1924, Balanchivadze asked Lopoukhov's permission to arrange a ballet to it, but was told this was impossible on the ground that they did not have the hard currency needed to purchase the score. The orchestral parts would have to be bought in Western Europe.

In 1921, when Lenin's New Economic Policy opened the Russian ports for commerce, Lunacharsky persuaded Lenin to send certain groups of artists abroad, especially those whose work was being hampered by the effects of malnutrition. Under this policy, Olga Spessivtseva, whose health was poor, had obtained leave and been engaged by Diaghilev to dance in *The Sleeping Princess*—as he called his production of *The Sleeping Beauty*—in London.

In 1922 or earlier, Balanchivadze had met Vladimir Pavlovich Dmitriev, a former singer who had become a croupier in a government-licensed gambling house. He was a solid man of about forty,

handsome in a rugged way but with alarming "sawn-off fingers."
As croupier, he was entitled to a percentage of the take, and he
had accumulated a considerable sum of money. He somehow
managed to obtain permission from the authorities to spend his
earnings on presenting a small troupe of artists abroad, ostensibly
with the intention of displaying the latest achievements of Soviet
culture to the Far East or to Western Europe. On April 4, 1924,
an agreement was drawn up and signed by V. A. Dranyshnikov,
a conductor at the State Theater, who would act as pianist; the
singer O. F. Mshanskaya, who was his girl friend; the dancers
Danilova, Zheverzheyeva, Ivanova, Efimov and Balanchivadze;
and the "management": Dmitriev, G. D. Neliubim and E. G.
Olkovsky:

We agree to participate in a concert tour to the Far East and abroad, the
itinerary to be decided in the future. . . . The tour is organized on the
basis of comradely relationship, the net profits to be divided in ten equal
shares. . . . Should the collective suffer a deficit the members will not
be held responsible. . . . The beginning of the tour is projected to start
on the day following the end of the season of the State Academic Theater
of Opera and Ballet, unless there is an opportunity to leave earlier.
. . . The tour will end on [?] September, 1924.

The document bore the official stamp of the State Theater, but
Balanchivadze's signature, with many grandiloquent flourishes,
looks like a cartoon by Saul Steinberg, as if he were making fun
of the pompous nature of the agreement.

Within the next few weeks, the Far East was forgotten, the
singer and pianist dispensed with, Neliubim and Olkovsky
dropped out and it was agreed that the dancers' tour should be
confined to Germany.

Before they left, they were faced with a tragedy. Lidia Ivanova
had friends who were high party officials, and somebody apparently decided that she knew too much about a certain political
matter. As Balanchine told the story:

One of Lida's admirers talked her into going for a motorboat ride on the Gulf of Finland. He was a big shot in the Cheka, the Bolshevik secret police, and he always . . . wined and dined us. . . . He used to kiss Lida's shoulders. . . . There were five of them in the boat. A big ship crashed into it. The motorboat split up and Lida drowned. I think it was all a set-up. . . . The ship had time to turn. And then, Lida was a marvelous swimmer . . . There wasn't an investigation. I had heard that Lida knew some big secret, and they didn't want to let her out to the West. They . . . decided to fake an accident.

Geva described how she, Balanchine and Efimov were in an open-air theater, waiting for Ivanova and Danilova to dance "their inevitable *Moment Musical*" in the second half of a performance; how Ivanova never turned up; how a sinister-looking man came to tell Danilova that there had been an accident and she need not wait; how the manager of the park theater drove them to Vassilievsky Island; how they split into pairs and searched the shoreline toward Kronstadt; how they found the smashed motorboat and questioned the captain of the double-decker Kronstadt ferry that had rammed her. Danilova confirmed to me that everything happened "exactly as Tamara described." In her memoirs, she provided the additional information that the man who had brought the news of Ivanova's death was the adjutant to the commissar of the State Theater.

Depressed as they were, the little group did not delay their departure. One or two may have thought they were lucky to escape from Russia alive, but Danilova at least expected to return for the fall season. She had been promised the leading role of Kitri in *Don Quixote.* They all sailed for Stettin sometime in the second half of June.

Chapter 2

··

IN WESTERN EUROPE:

SUMMER 1924 - WINTER 1933

THE undernourished Russians gloated incredulously over the baskets of white bread and abundance of butter on the dinner table of their German ship, and Tamara was amazed when a stewardess brought tea to her cabin on a tray; she thought this happened only in Pola Negri movies. They landed at Stettin and the next day went on to Berlin, which was full of White Russians. A Russian-language newspaper dutifully reported their arrival. Dmitriev spoke only halting German, but Tamara's was fluent, so she took the lead in hiring a hall and organizing a recital. Although it was the height of summer and audiences were small and unappreciative, Dmitriev somehow managed to arrange a Rhineland tour.

It was probably in Wiesbaden that they all agreed to defect—an idea that had doubtless been in Dmitriev's mind all along—for it was there that on September 6 he drew up a contract extending their agreement until November 1. They traveled to Vienna to hear Rachmaninoff play his own works, but when, backstage, Georgi suggested to the composer that he might make a ballet to his concerto, Rachmaninoff exclaimed, "A ballet! To my music! Are you crazy?" and threw them all out. Danilova later recalled that for the rest of his life, whenever the composer was mentioned, Balanchine would say, "Lousy music."

Although they had an undistinguished series of engagements in Germany, they received an invitation to appear in October at London's Empire music hall; they stayed for four weeks, in lodgings near the British Museum. Lydia Lopoukhova, who was not yet married to John Maynard Keynes, visited them at the theater to ask about her brother, Fyodor Lopoukhov. On November 3, Dmitriev drew up yet another contract, binding the dancers to him until April 3, 1925.

When their English work permits expired, they decided to try their luck in Paris. After a few days in a cheap hotel in the rue du Pont-Neuf, near Les Halles, when their money and hopes were running low, a telephone call came from Diaghilev. His company had been in Germany in September and October, and somehow or other he had heard of them. He was always anxious for new blood from Russia, and he had been trying to track them down.

He was in search of a choreographer as well as dancers. It had been Fokine's choreography more than anything else that had made the Russian ballets Diaghilev presented for the first time in Paris such a triumphant success. These ballets were of a new kind, quite unlike the traditional entertainments provided for the czars and their courts, although Diaghilev had hired dancers from the Imperial Theaters to perform them. Stimulated by the American Isadora Duncan's new free style of barefoot dancing, Fokine had initiated a "return to nature" involving dramatic realism, local color, the abolition of virtuosity for its own sake and the use of more symphonic music than was customary at the Maryinsky.

Nijinsky succeeded Fokine as Diaghilev's choreographer; his experiments in Debussy's *L'Après-midi d'un faune* (1912) and Igor Stravinsky's *Le Sacre du printemps* (1913) were even more radical than his predecessor's. Soon after Nijinsky's marriage to Romola de Pulszky in 1913 separated him from Diaghilev, the impresario adopted the young Léonide Massine as his protégé and made him into a choreographer by sheer willpower. Massine's ballets were "character" dances as opposed to classical—comedies of manners in a Russian, Italian or Spanish style. In 1921 he, too, parted from Diaghilev, who was finding it increasingly hard, after the war and the Russian Revolution, to enlist good dancers, although the music he commissioned from advanced composers, together with his dazzling décors—often by painters of the School of Paris—helped to camouflage the deficiencies of his troupe. At the time he contacted Balanchivadze and his colleagues, he was being assisted in devising new ballets by Boris Kochno, a young Russian who remained his closest friend and right-hand man to the end of his life.

The group of defectors was summoned to the Left Bank, to the studio of José-María Sert, whose wife, Misia, was Diaghilev's greatest woman friend. Here for the first time they met Diaghilev and Kochno. Georgi, partnering Zheverzheyeva, showed them his Scriabin pas de deux, and Danilova danced a few steps of *The Firebird*, which Lopoukhov had taught her. Since one of Diaghilev's commitments with the Opéra de Monte-Carlo was to supply dancers for its opera season between January and April, he asked Georgi, "Can you make ballets for operas?" "Yes," the tyro replied at once, not knowing whether he could or not. "Can you do them quickly?" "Yes."

Diaghilev was told that he must take all of the group or none. He replied that they would hear from him. This was in mid-November. Diaghilev returned to London on November 20, by which time the little group had run out of money and Georgi sold his best suit to provide funds for all of them. When Diaghilev telegraphed, Dmitriev evidently suggested certain stipulations, for on November 23, Diaghilev received the reply: *"Acceptons engage-*

ment. Attendez detailles [sic] *par lettre. Balantchivadze.* " (Accept the engagement. Letter follows with details.)

Since Diaghilev had no place for Dmitriev, the others agreed that each would give a fifth of his or her salary to their "manager," who had made it possible for them to leave Russia. The four set off for London a few days later. Telegrams from Russia were ignored. Georgi had made his choice; his vocation was in the West.

. . .

THE DIAGHILEV BALLET of 1924 was not the large, well-trained company of dancers that had dazzled Paris and London between 1909 and 1914. With courage and determination—and out of love for Massine—Diaghilev had held together a scratch troupe throughout the difficult wartime years, when most European countries were closed to him; he had embarked reluctantly on extensive tours of the United States and had faced starvation in Spain. But after creating several highly successful ballets, Massine had left the company to get married.

In 1921, Diaghilev had staged his grandiose revival of *The Sleeping Princess* at the Alhambra music hall in London. The moderate success of this with English balletomanes—too few at that time to fill a large theater for a long run—left him deeply in debt to the theater's owner, Sir Oswald Stoll, who had rescued him from Spain in 1918. Once more he faced bankruptcy and the dispersal of his company. Once more he was saved, this time by an arrangement that would allow him to give regular ballet seasons at the Opéra de Monte-Carlo and to provide dancers for its operas. Nijinsky's sister, Bronislava, who had fled from Russia in 1921, became his new choreographer, and to her fell the honor of staging Stravinsky's *Renard* and *Les Noces*. When Georgi and his friends joined the Diaghilev Ballet in London, the company was on its first visit to England since the calamitous *Sleeping Princess*. Diaghilev had been paying off his debt to Stoll, but his troupe was still not allowed a proper season: they were appearing as a single act on the bill of Stoll's other music hall, the Coliseum, dancing one ballet every afternoon, one every evening.

Georgi thought the company very poor: "I was *so* disappointed," he remembered later. He admired only the Englishman Anton Dolin and one or two soloists, former members of the Maryinsky company, such as Ludmilla Schollar and Felia Doubrovska, who were well trained. The Massine repertory had consisted entirely of character or demi-caractère dances, and Georgi was at first used solely in character roles. He danced one of the warriors in Fokine's *Polovtsian Dances* from *Prince Igor,* the King of Spades in Massine's *Boutique fantasque* and the polonaise for twelve couples in a selection of numbers from *The Sleeping Princess,* which Diaghilev called *Aurora's Wedding.* Shortly afterward he was a Buffoon in *The Midnight Sun* (*Soleil de nuit*) and a folk dancer in *Children's Tales* (*Contes russes*).

Anton Dolin had been a pupil of Serafina Astafieva, one of Diaghilev's former dancers, who had a school in an old house in the King's Road, Chelsea. On December 1 he persuaded Diaghilev to go with Nijinska and Grigoriev, the *régisseur,* to audition another of Astafieva's pupils, fourteen-year-old Alicia Marks, whose technique was prodigious. Nijinska put her through her paces, and Alicia astonished the Russians with her high jumps, light landings and multiple pirouettes. It was arranged that she should join the company and lodge in Monte Carlo with Nijinska, who had a daughter aged ten.

Diaghilev needed to see a more sustained example of Balanchivadze's choreography than he had in Sert's studio. One Sunday morning, about ten days after the new group's arrival, Georgi demonstrated his Chopin *Marche funèbre* to Diaghilev. The Anglo-Irish dancer Ninette Devalois (as Diaghilev at that time spelled her assumed name) recorded the occasion:

I was summoned to Astafieva's studio with about six other artists. Balanchine was there, young and anxious-looking. He had an engaging charm and a great sense of humor, which made him popular with us. . . . His dancing had proved rather less than indifferent, but we suspected in him some other form of distinctive talent. For two solid hours we learnt a choreographic conception of his. . . . I worked with a will, for I was as acutely aware as others of his gifts. Just about midday Diaghilev, Kochno and Grigoriev arrived, and we went through our choreographic patterns. On such occasions Diaghilev was an enigma. Face impassive, manner aloof . . . and there was no means of fathoming the impression made on our director. I knew that a rumor was circulating . . . that Nijinska was leaving us quite soon, and that the young Balanchine might become our new choreographer . . .

Nijinska was indignant at the idea that there should be a second choreographer in the company. Conscious of her exceptional position as the sister of a god, she had no intention of sharing her honors with a stripling of twenty. She announced her departure. This was a blow to Diaghilev, who needed a choreographer for two new ballets he had commissioned. He even gave his beloved new favorite Serge Lifar—a young dancer from Kiev with a beautiful figure, limited technique and unlimited ambition—a tryout, but this was a disaster. Since Balanchivadze was still a comparatively unknown quantity, Diaghilev made up his quarrel with Massine, who happened to be in London.

Nevertheless, over the weekend of December 21, "the unknown quantity" underwent an historic transformation. Diaghilev, who usually Russianized his English dancers' names, liked to simplify any Russian ones that Westerners might have trouble pronouncing—particularly when they were names he hoped would be on everyone's lips. Nizhinsky had become Nijinsky, Miassin had become Massine, Spessivtseva had become Spessiva. Before the programs were printed for the week beginning Monday, December 22, Georgi Balanchivadze had become George Balanchin. (An "e" would soon be appended for the benefit of the French.)

The Ballet arrived in Monte Carlo on January 12, 1925, and Balanchine and his fellow "freshmen" set eyes on the Mediterranean for the first time. Before the ballet season opened in April, Balanchine had made dances for nine operas. Devalois, who took part in them, had a very high opinion of his resources. "He charged these dreary experiences with a new life and interest, and no demands on him could curb his imaginative facility. . . ." She particularly admired the ballet in Massenet's *Hérodiade,* which Balanchine led himself.

Yet by far the most interesting work that came Balanchine's way in those early months of 1925 was to provide choreography for the world premiere of Maurice Ravel's opera—or "lyric fantasy" as he called it—*L'Enfant et les sortilèges (The Spellbound Child),* to a text by Colette. Danilova recalled later that the composer himself played the piano for the rehearsals.

When Massine arrived, he took no notice of Balanchine and gave orders that he should not be allowed to watch his rehearsals. Balanchine, however, played small parts in ballets by both Massine and Nijinska. He also appeared in Fokine's ballets.

. . .

ALTHOUGH only a few months earlier Balanchine had been the acknowledged leader of the Young Ballet in Russia, he had yet to find his feet in the strange world of the Diaghilev company. For the time being he was content to do whatever he was told and to remain in the background. The handsome Boris Kochno, librettist for many Diaghilev ballets in the 1920s, and almost exactly the same age as Balanchine, had acquired such sophistication since he left Russia four years earlier that he at first regarded the new arrival as a character so unremarkable as to be almost nonexistent. Kochno also noticed that Balanchine had a childish side and was amused by trifles. However, it was to Balanchine that Diaghilev had entrusted the new staging of *Le Chant du rossignol,* a ballet to music extracted from Stravinsky's opera *Le Rossignol* of 1914.

In London in December, Diaghilev had said to Balanchine, "I have an old ballet that has been arranged before. It is by Stravinsky. Could you manage it?"

"Yes."

Diaghilev looked at him. "You are very sure of yourself!"

Perhaps Diaghilev had already considered young Alicia Marks for the role of the Nightingale. In any case, he had taken Balanchine to Astafieva's studio in London and Alicia had demonstrated what she could do. After the audition with Balanchine, she remembered later, she felt she had been working for three-and-a-half hours. At a New Year's Eve party for the whole company that year she danced Rubinstein's *Valse Caprice,* while Balanchine strummed the piano; she ended the evening seated on the stool beside him. He spoke no English, and she spoke nothing else, but they were already friends; he never talked down to children. Diaghilev had then changed Alicia's name from Marks to Markova.

Diaghilev wanted to be able to use the costumes Henri Matisse had originally designed for *Le Chant du rossignol,* so he persuaded himself that Balanchine might be able to pull Massine's only partly successful work together. But Balanchine, who had played a small role in the complete opera in St. Petersburg, knew the music slightly and thought the flute in the ballet version was no substitute for the soprano voice.

The former teacher of Pavlova and Nijinsky, Maestro Enrico Cecchetti, had been lured from Milan to give classes for the company. This was Balanchine's first sight of the Italian style, which he called "small" in comparison with the "big" St. Petersburg style—speaking of it in later years, he held his hands in front of his chest like a rabbit—but it was in Cecchetti's classes that he observed the further potentialities of Markova. He planned that she should make her entrance as the Nightingale with two men holding her aloft by one leg. She then had to dive and be caught by two other men very close to the floor. Alicia thought that working with Balanchine was like a lesson in arithmetic. "Give me this leg, give me this hand"—and then suddenly the whole sum would come out right. According to Danilova, it was also in this ballet that "Balanchine introduced châiné turns with the arms open, then closed, then open again—no one had ever seen that before."

Kochno observed how Balanchine arrived at rehearsals with the air of someone who had just dropped in to say hello and casually improvised the dance as he went along. After he had invented a passage and stood back to see the dancer perform it, he seemed as surprised as if it had nothing to do with him.

Anton Dolin, who was partnering her, complained that Danilova needed a piano mover to lift her, and she asked Balanchine to watch her from out front. He told her, "You look terrible—you've gotten so fat. What's happened to you?" She bought diet pills from a pharmacy, took five and fainted. Balanchine threw the bottle out the window and gave her a lecture. She was to eat no chocolates and no desserts and to wear a high-necked sweater and woollen leggings in class. She lost weight and blossomed into a beauty. Her charming heart-shaped face, distinguished profile, big green eyes and Cupid's-bow mouth were to become world-famous, as were her perfect legs.

Diaghilev watched rehearsals closely and would sometimes correct tempi wrongly. Stravinsky, who was living with his family at Nice, half an hour's train journey along the coast, often stopped in at rehearsals. Before he arrived, Balanchine had always changed the tempi back again.

Diaghilev had given Stravinsky his first commission, *The Firebird*, in 1908. He had presented his *Petrushka, Rite of Spring, Nightingale, Renard, Noces*; now he had brought him together with Balanchine, with whom his destiny was to be so happily linked during the next half century.

The first night of *Rossignol* was attended not only by Georges Braque, who had designed the scenery and costumes for Massine's *Zéphyr et Flore,* but by Pablo Picasso and his wife, Olga, a former Diaghilev dancer, who came from Paris for the occasion. Balanchine was not particularly impressed to find himself among these great painters—or, for that matter, to be creating a ballet with décor by Matisse—because he had hardly heard of them. Of Vladimir Dukelsky's music for *Zéphyr,* which contained a pastiche of eighteenth-century compositions, he later said, "It had some nice music, but Dukelsky never really understood orchestration."

The company left for a two-week season in Barcelona on May 1. This was to be followed by more performances in the music-hall program at the London Coliseum, with a week in Paris sandwiched in between. In Barcelona, a Spanish marquis fell in love with Tamara Gevergeyeva (as Diaghilev spelled her name).

In London, Balanchine took over Vilzak's role as Nemchinova's partner in the grand pas de deux in *Aurora's Wedding.* At the Gaîté-Lyrique, he played the grotesque role of the Mechanical Nightingale in his own ballet. *Le Chant du rossignol* was well received, but the hit of the season was Massine's light-hearted *Les Matelots,* in which Serge Lifar first cast his spell over a Paris audience. Diaghilev's former favorite, Anton Dolin, left the company at the end of the Paris season. So did Tamara Gevergeyeva. She had some anxious weeks of unemployment in Paris, but Diaghilev took her back in time for the London winter season.

Balanchine was as eager as Diaghilev to improve the quality of the company by luring dancers from Russia. On September 15 he wrote to Diaghilev:

5 rue de Gavarni, Passy 16me

I invited Barash and asked Herzenberg to come from Riga. She got her own visa and I sent her 1,000 francs of my own money. I wrote to Vadimova asking her to give you her address. . . .

Both Barash and Vadimova joined the Diaghilev Ballet, but no more was heard of Herzenberg, or of other artists Balanchine recommended.

During his summer holiday in Venice, Diaghilev met a young Italian composer, Vittorio Rieti, from whom he commissioned a ballet-*cum-*cantata on a comic theme entitled *Barabau.* The completed score was given to Balanchine after the company had begun yet another of their two-ballets-a-day seasons at the London Coliseum.

If he had been offered the choice, a farce was probably the last kind of ballet with which Balanchine would have wished to establish his reputation; but he was amenable, he did not despise humor and he took what he was given. Rieti's music appealed to him. The most unusual feature of the work was a group of six black-clad singers who popped up several times from behind a wall to sing *a cappella* a melancholy ballad (based on a nursery rhyme): "Barabau, Barabau, why did you die?" Tamara Geva later reported: "It was the first ballet during which the audience laughed aloud and throughout."

In the less than four years left before Diaghilev's death, Balanchine devised dances for twenty-six more operas. He saw the staging of old works by Fokine and of old and new ones by Nijinska and Massine. Above all, he was given new ballets to create with scores by composers as different as Auric, Satie, Berners, Sauguet, Stravinsky, Handel, Rieti and Prokofiev. It was hard work and poorly paid, but it was a wonderful apprenticeship. The obligation to turn out at high speed ballets for opera—a polonaise for *Boris Godunov*, dances for Honegger's *Judith*, a Hindu number for *Lakmé*, a waltz and a pas de deux for *Les Contes d'Hoffmann*, "medieval" dances for Gounod's *Jeanne d'Arc*, to mention only works produced in February and March 1926—undoubtedly extended Balanchine's natural ease of invention and prepared him for the tasks ahead. The precarious stability of the Diaghilev Ballet's existence depended on its yearly winter sojourn of four to five months in Monte Carlo. Without Balanchine to make the opera ballets, these annual periods of creation and consolidation in an agreeable climate would not have been possible: he was the company's principal breadwinner. If Diaghilev was secretly grateful for the young choreographer's willingness and adaptability, we may be sure he was careful not to express his gratitude in words. He did not like anyone to feel indispensable.

Even with the partial security afforded by the patronage of the prince of Monaco, channeled through the Société des Bains de Mer (i.e., the Casino), the company was run on a shoestring. At last, however, Diaghilev paid off his debt to Stoll and could have proper seasons in London where and when he wished. Thinking of England as a source of steady income, he paid court in Monte Carlo to Lord Rothermere, proprietor of the *Daily Mail,* who he had decided was the most likely backer. As a result, 1926 was a somewhat "English" year.

The first sign of Englishness was the ballet *Romeo and Juliet* by the twenty-year-old Constant Lambert, which Bronislava Nijinska was to arrange and the Surrealists Max Ernst and Joan Miró to design. Tamara Karsavina, whom Balanchine had revered in his youth, but who was now over forty, appeared as a guest artist, and Lifar had to be taught how to support her properly. Balanchine liked Lambert's music, but later observed that "Miró and Ernst were everything"—in other words, the décor was more interesting than the choreography. Massine's *Pulcinella* he described as "a long, boring ballet," adding that "Stravinsky and Picasso were everything."

For *La Pastorale,* Balanchine's own new ballet to a score by Georges Auric, Kochno provided what the choreographer considered a "messy" libretto about a Telegraph Boy (Lifar) who falls asleep beside his bicycle and wakes to find a film company at work on location. He flirts with the Star (Doubrovska) but finally returns to his Young Lady (Gevergeyeva). There was a remarkable pas de deux, in the course of which Lifar, kneeling, had to turn Doubrovska in arabesque by holding her supporting leg by the knee. (Balanchine used this again in later ballets, including *Serenade.*)

Diaghilev liked *La Pastorale* enough to persevere in continual adjustments to it; and although the British, from Sir Thomas Beecham to the music critic Ernest Newman, disliked it intensely, he kept it in the repertory until 1929. Balanchine was unable to read English at the time, so he could not be too depressed by the critics' reactions. "I was living in a [fool's] paradise," he told me once. "If I had known at the time language I should have committed suicide. But I can judge for myself. If I don't like what I do, I throw it away."

Diaghilev celebrated the opening of his first real London season since *The Sleeping Princess* by giving Stravinsky's *Les Noces* on the first night at His Majesty's Theatre. Balanchine heard for the first time the amazing cantata that had been begun before the war and was finished a decade later only after various experiments in orchestration. He thought Nijinska's choreography, with its mass movements and pyramidal formations, amounted to little, "the music was so great and complete."

Thanks to the success of the season at His Majesty's, there was to be a second visit to London in the winter of 1926, and Diaghilev spent much of July racking his brains for a subject that would please Rothermere and his compatriots. His chosen accomplice was the writer Sacheverell Sitwell. Diaghilev commissioned Lord Berners to write a score. Sitwell's story for the ballet would be part Victorian pantomime, with fairies and transformation scenes; part harlequinade; and part science fiction in the style of Jules Verne. The décor was to be copied literally from the printed sheets of scenery used in toy theaters. It was called *The Triumph of Neptune.*

Since Sitwell's father had a castle near Florence and Berners had a flat in Rome, Balanchine was summoned by Diaghilev to spend the latter part of his holiday working on the ballet in Italy. Kochno thought there was also another reason for the invitation: Diaghilev loved to educate his choreographers and leading dancers. How could they exist without drawing energy from the masterpieces of Italian art? Balanchine arrived in Florence with Dukelsky on September 14, and had long discussions with Diaghilev, Sitwell and Berners. Then they moved on to Rome, where Diaghilev left Berners to struggle with his composition while he took Balanchine, Kochno and Lifar to Naples. He showed them Pompeii and Herculaneum, as he had shown Picasso and Massine in 1917. Balanchine returned to Rome when the others went to Capri.

The second London season took place at the Lyceum. Balanchine was Kastchei, the evil enchanter, in a revival of *The Firebird* with new designs by Gontcharova. *The Triumph of Neptune* was given on December 3. Cyril Beaumont, the bookseller and ballet historian, a warm adherent of Diaghilev's since 1911, had thought *Barabau* "vulgar and rather tedious"; and *La Pastorale*—"feeble in action, slight in dance invention"—had not dispelled his misgivings at the appointment of Balanchine. *Neptune* won him over. He praised Balanchine's own solo in the role of the Negro, Snowball, as "a dance full of subtly contrasted rhythms, strutting walks, mincing steps, and surging backward bendings of the body borrowed from the cake-walk . . . a paradoxical blend of pretended nervous apprehension and blustering confidence." This was Balanchine's first creation to show American influence. It was also his last display of virtuoso dancing, for he developed trouble with his knee, had a piece of cartilage removed and was never so agile again.

Danilova had noticed that Balanchine was "somber, pensive." One day, when she had a bad foot, he massaged it—then kissed it. When she asked him a few days later what was wrong, he replied, "Don't you know? I love you."

"What about Tamara?"

"Well, I don't love her."

She was shocked, and even considered going back to Russia to avoid breaking up a marriage, but Balanchine was persistent. He could not get a divorce because his marriage papers had been left in Russia; however, Danilova decided that she loved him enough to forgo marriage. She wrote, "I moved in with him, happy to be with him but crying because I had always dreamed of being a bride and walking down the aisle in a long white dress. . . ."

Diaghilev was not pleased. While the company was at Le Touquet in July 1926, he summoned Balanchine to his hotel and they had a two-hour talk. Danilova asked Balanchine several times what had been said, but he would not tell her.

. . .

AT MONTE CARLO, Balanchine and Danilova stayed at the Hôtel de
la Réserve, right on the beach; so did Vladimir Horowitz, whom
Balanchine was always to uphold as one of the greatest—if not the
greatest—of living pianists. He and Danilova were often awakened
by Horowitz playing Liszt's "Valse oubliée" through the wall.
When Danilova yearned to go to a nightclub and dance the tango
and Balanchine said, "Why do you want to sit in a noisy room full
of smoke?" it was Horowitz who took her.

In those days, Balanchine's "worldly" side was shown in his
interest in Danilova's hats. "That's awful," he would exclaim. "Go
and change it." Or, "How nice! It suits you."

Balanchine was free with the little money he had, and inveterate
gamblers among his friends, notably the dancer Léon Woizikovsky, took advantage of him. Faced with a hotel bill for four
hundred francs, Balanchine said to Danilova, "Let's go to the
Casino." He won six hundred francs. She snatched five hundred,
left him to play and went straight back to settle with the hotel.

. . .

THE year 1927 began with performances in Turin and at La Scala
in Milan. Diaghilev had succeeded in re-engaging Olga Spessivtseva (whom, of course, he had renamed Spessiva), and she danced
Swan Lake. The long mime "monologue" in Act II, during which
Odette explains to the Prince how she fell under the power of
Rothbart and was changed into a swan, was replaced by Balanchine with a passage of dancing, which is still extant in the repertory of several companies. Danilova later described Balanchine as
giving Odette "droopy hands and sloping shoulders, to show that
she was unhappy."

Apart from such revisions, there was the usual miscellany of
opera ballets to be produced in Monte Carlo. *La Traviata* was the
first Verdi opera Balanchine worked on (in 1929 he would arrange
court dances for *Rigoletto*). In an interview years later he made an

interesting disclosure: "From Verdi's way of dealing with the chorus I learned how to handle the corps de ballet, the ensemble, the soloists—how to make the soloists stand out against the corps de ballet and when to give them time to rest."

Balanchine's only new ballet in 1927 was *La Chatte,* with a score by Henri Sauguet. The marvelous Spessiva had failed in ballets by Fokine and Nijinska, so Diaghilev was determined to show her in a new work. Kochno's point of departure was an Aesop fable about a cat who was turned into a woman. Knowing how difficult and unreliable Spessiva was, Diaghilev warned Balanchine that if she liked his ballet, it would probably be no good. During rehearsals she evidently showed that she did not, for Diaghilev said to Balanchine, "Congratulations!" Spessiva danced *La Chatte* only in Monte Carlo, having developed a real or imagined leg injury before the Paris opening on May 26, and Balanchine thought her "wonderful," although she was unmusical and "didn't turn very well."

In her pas de deux, supported by Lifar, Balanchine had her pirouette slowly down to the ground, and Massine complained to Diaghilev that he had always wanted to use this movement. "If it is so easy to steal your thoughts," Diaghilev said, "please don't think."

Spessiva's was the only female role. Lifar, wearing a minimum of celluloid armor, was carried on by six companions, a hero among heroes. Although Alice Nikitina (who replaced Spessiva for the final Monte Carlo performances) paired with him perfectly, Lifar stole the show. What had been a desperate attempt to display Diaghilev's preferred ballerina turned out to be a milestone—a triumphal arch—on Lifar's road to stardom. Danilova, to whom Balanchine had wanted to give Spessiva's part on the morning of the Paris premiere—he had made the role on her, and she already knew it—commented that since Lifar was not a strong dancer, George had created a neoclassical style for him and made him into a star above the ballerinas, including herself. More than anyone—

perhaps even more than Lifar himself, though he worked hard—
Balanchine helped Diaghilev keep the promise he had made to the
young dancer in 1924.

In a letter to Diaghilev dated September 28, Balanchine announced, "Gevergeyeva will not be working this year. Because of
her stupid methods of losing weight she has reached a point where
her doctor has forbidden her to dance. She has joined [Nikita]
Balieff [the presenter of small-scale "artistic" revues] and will sing
in a gypsy chorus and clap her hands."

This was not exactly true. Before Gevergeyeva left with Balieff's
troupe, Les Chauve-Souris, for New York, Balanchine arranged
two solos for her, a dance called *Grotesque espagnole*, to the *Córdoba* of Albéniz, and *Sarcasm*, to Prokofiev's Op. 17. These numbers, in which the renamed Geva enjoyed a considerable success,
were the first Balanchine works to be seen in America.

In another (undated) letter to Diaghilev, Balanchine wrote, "My
leg is unfortunately recovering very slowly. I think I shall have to
take it easy at first."

. . .

BALANCHINE's knowledge of the music of Stravinsky was increasing
all the time. During the Paris summer season of 1927, Diaghilev
had given three performances of *Oedipus Rex*, presented as an
oratorio without scenery or costumes. Two weeks later, in London,
there was a Stravinsky evening, with *Petrushka, Pulcinella* and *The
Firebird*. On September 30, when Diaghilev was in Monte Carlo
renewing his contract, Stravinsky summoned him to Nice to hear
a new ballet. It had just been commissioned for performance at the
Library of Congress in Washington, D.C., but Diaghilev was to be
allowed to stage the first European production. It was called *Apollon Musagète*, later shortened to *Apollo*.

On January 23, 1928, Balanchine went with Diaghilev to hear
the score for the first time and began rehearsing it immediately,
working out movements on Danilova. In a short Belgian tour in

May, Massine's version of Stravinsky's *Rite of Spring* (*Sacre du printemps*) was revived. Balanchine thought Massine's *Sacre*—at least when given by only forty dancers—"almost a joke." There was one gesture endlessly repeated: the dancers reached down with both hands to the floor on their right, then extended their arms upward to their left. It was as if they were picking books off a pile to place on a shelf, and Balanchine called it "working in a library." His dislike of Massine's version may have been partly what put him off staging the historic score in later life, but in fact he often said the music was "undanceable." Its Dionysian character was not of a kind to attract him.

.   .   .

BALANCHINE'S circle of acquaintances was being steadily enlarged; he met not only Sergei Prokofiev, but also the young composer Nicolas Nabokov and the painter Pavel Tchelishchev (always thenceforth simplified as "Tchelitchev"), who were collaborating on *Ode.* Despite these encounters, and although Balanchine sometimes dined alone with Diaghilev to discuss projects, he played little part in the social life of his employer's intimate circle; his face was comparatively unknown to the *beau monde.*

.   .   .

Apollon Musagète was a landmark in Balanchine's career. Its first performance by the Diaghilev Ballet, with a simple décor by the naïve painter André Bauchant, was given at the Théâtre Sarah-Bernhardt on June 12, 1928. The composer conducted. A version with choreography by Adolph Bolm had been performed at the Library of Congress on April 27.

For the sake of theatrical lucidity Stravinsky reduced Apollo's nine Muses to three, and because his composition was a ballet, he gave the favored ballerina role to Terpsichore, Muse of Dance. *Apollon* was written for string orchestra. While Stravinsky's division of the ballet into numbers was traditional, his music, whatever echoes of the past there may be in it, was utterly personal, new and of the twentieth century, so Balanchine had to find an appropriate way of dancing it. His re-use of Goleizovsky's "sixth position," in which the toes and heels of the feet are touching, although "modern," held a suggestion of archaic Greek sculpture; there were syncopated movements and whole passages without a single classical ballet step. The thin thread of story running through the ten numbers tells how Apollo was born, then educated by the Muses; how he took command of them, chose among them, and, conscious of his growing powers, was summoned to lead them to Parnassus.

Each Muse, to whom the god has given an appropriate symbol, performs a solo, watched by the seated Apollo. Stravinsky had the fanciful notion of making Calliope, the Muse of Heroic Poetry, dance partly in alexandrines. During the caesuras, she scribbles on her scroll, then, after she has put it down, clutches her side to convey the pangs of inspiration and extends a hand from her open mouth toward the audience. Polyhymnia, the Muse of Mime, dances a brilliant nonstop allegro, one finger to her lips. Terpsichore's variation is playful, provocative and jazzy, and it is she who seduces Apollo with little runs and kicks, fluttering hands and a backbend.

In Apollo's second variation, Balanchine hit on a startling image to convey that the god is conscious of his divinity. Twice Apollo stands in fourth position, forward left leg bent, left arm behind his back with clenched fist visible to his right, and with the right arm extended upward, the fingers of the right hand splayed like rays of light. Then, as the right fist clenches, the fingers of the left splay out. On—off; on—off; on—off; on—off. Balanchine said this idea came to him from watching an electric sign in Piccadilly Circus. At the end, Apollo sinks to the ground, facing offstage but extending an arm with pointing forefinger behind him. Terpsichore advances to press his finger with her own. This echo of Michelangelo's Sistine ceiling could be regarded as another "electric" image. In the following pas de deux, a sublime adagio, Terpsichore is at one moment supported, reclining, on Apollo's shoulder, facing skyward. She is also lowered to the floor in a deep split and dragged on pointe in arabesque.

The mounting excitement of the Coda, preceding the calm of the Apotheosis, is like the chase in the last sequence of a film, which holds the spectator in suspense before the happy ending. As Apollo stands behind the line of Muses, they grasp his wrists, extending their free arms as they take an arabesque; to an urgent, cantering music, he drives them as of they were pulling a chariot around the stage. Finally the Muses walk away from Apollo, turn about, prance toward him on their heels, clap their hands on a pizzicato chord and extend their open palms, conjoined. On the final pianissimo chord, Apollo abruptly lays his head in their hands.

Of the opening chords of the Apotheosis, Balanchine said, "He hears his father calling." When the principal theme, first heard before the rise of the curtain, sounds again, there is a maze of revolving rings. Then the Muses appear to hang from Apollo, each on one leg, extending the other, so that the extended legs fan out at varying heights to form a sunburst behind him. The theme has been repeating and will continue to the end. Balanchine ignores it. A persistent tremolo is heard on the second violins and violas. As this intensifies, a steady stepping on the second cellos and basses begins. The choreographer disregards the former atmospheric effect, but sets his dancers pacing to the latter music. While the repetition of the theme gives the number its Olympian peace, the mysterious tremolo envelops it in a golden haze, and the stepping contributes solemnity. Led by Apollo, the Muses walk, hands to sides, to climb the slope of Parnassus.

Balanchine's new ballet was well received, but there is no evidence that anyone (except Gordon Craig, who thought it so beautiful that he left the theater immediately after it) recognized a new kind of musical and choreographic masterpiece. Since his early "Russian" period, Stravinsky's music had been regularly derided by French critics. When *Apollon* was given in London on June 25, the critic of the *Times* was to write: "It used to be said that the

Russian Ballet would not be much without Stravinsky: his latest production makes us fear that soon it will not be much with him."

Yet Balanchine's choreography for *Apollon* had extended the language of the classical dance. It related in a novel way—several ways—to a heavenly score. It held in it the seeds of many later works. The ballet looks forward to the new, the "neo"-classicism, which would be the choreographer's gift to America.

Balanchine had trouble with Terpsichore's variation, and after the first night Diaghilev wanted to cut it. "He told me that the choreography for Terpsichore was no good. I said 'The choreography's fine. It's the dancer who is no good.' " This was Nikitina, and from then on Danilova was to alternate with her in the role. According to Danilova, Balanchine made some changes, adding "some soft, light, quick sissonnes," and all turned out for the best.

Earlier in the year, as a compliment to Sir Thomas Beecham, who was a lover of Handel's music (and possibly to avoid staging a ballet by Delius, whom Beecham never ceased to promote), Diaghilev had invited the conductor to send a bundle of scores to Monte Carlo. A choice was made, Kochno devised a slight story "based on eighteenth-century pastoral allegories," and in the course of the London season Balanchine put together a ballet in no time at all. This makeshift work had a totally unexpected success. *The Gods Go A-Begging*, known outside England as *Les Dieux mendiants*, proved so popular that Danilova was prompted to say, "It became our bread and butter."

That summer Balanchine found himself a small apartment in Paris, just north of the Arc de Triomphe, and when he spent a few days in Venice with Diaghilev and Kochno he asked the former to lend him some money for the necessary down payment. But Diaghilev went off with Kochno to Poland in search of rare Russian books. Kochno was always a helpful intermediary in dealings with Diaghilev, and he and Balanchine had by this time become friends. Balanchine's letter asking Kochno to remind Diaghilev that the matter was urgent arrived in Berlin on October 12.

5 Passage Doisy

Paris 17e

11 October 1928

Dear Boris,

I expect you know about my request to Sergei Pavlovich for 4,000 francs by October 15. I'm afraid he may have forgotten about this; but I absolutely must have the money on the 15th for the renting of my apartment. Please remind him and keep him up to the mark. I promise to repay the money in England at the latest, perhaps some of it before. I thank you in advance and kiss you . . .

If you think I have forgotten you you are mistaken.

Yours,

Georges

The news is that Spessiva has just divorced Kniaseff.

On the day Kochno received this letter, Diaghilev cabled his *régisseur* Grigoriev, "Send Balanchine 4,000 [francs]."

Dmitriev moved in with Balanchine and Danilova, who still gave him part of their salaries. Balanchine, wanting to buy some furniture, tried to persuade Woizikovsky and the other gamblers to return the money he had lent them. In this he was unsuccessful. He was, however, steadily gaining the respect of his employer. When there was a question of what should appear on the posters for a British tour at the end of the year, Diaghilev telegraphed to Grigoriev, "*Maître de ballet* Balanchine. Don't put any other artists' names on poster."

· · ·

BALANCHINE'S two new ballets for 1929, both with libretti by Kochno, were as different from each other as it is possible to imagine. Prokofiev's *The Prodigal Son* was to be another vehicle for Lifar, while both Diaghilev and Kochno agreed that Anton Dolin, who had been asking to be taken back into the company, would be an ideal partner for Danilova in Rieti's *Le Bal*.

Lifar already felt apprehensive about his future, because Diaghilev had fallen in love with Igor Markevitch, a sixteen-year-old music student. In 1939, describing his talks with Diaghilev at the end of February 1929, Lifar wrote that Diaghilev did not wish to entrust any more ballets to Balanchine, saying, "I'll soon be sending him packing." When he wrote these words, Lifar had his reasons for disparaging Balanchine's talents. It may safely be assumed that these "talks" were fictitious. In 1977, when I asked Balanchine whether Diaghilev could possibly have been planning to fire him and replace him with Lifar, he replied calmly, "He wasn't such a fool."

For *Le Bal,* Diaghilev had ordered a set and costumes from Giorgio de Chirico; these greatly enhanced the mysterious masked ball, which Kochno had borrowed from a Russian story of the Romantic period. Balanchine devised angular poses, with bent elbows and knees, and Danilova recalls the steps being "very syncopated." The choreographer himself danced a Spanish pas de trois with Doubrovska and Woizikovsky. First given in Monte Carlo on May 7, *Le Bal* was performed in Paris and Berlin before being acclaimed in London as "the most successful novelty of the last few years." Yet this "most successful" work would never be revived.

An element appeared in *The Prodigal Son* that had been absent from Diaghilev's ballets since the days of Fokine and Nijinsky—drama. Lifar could not believe his ears when he heard Diaghilev, who had always been opposed to any hint of intensity in mime, urging him to put more feeling into his role, to dramatize it. For Balanchine, too, it was something new to handle a subject that, despite Kochno's editorial adjustments, was traceable to St. Luke's Gospel. Diaghilev had invited Georges Rouault, the only religious painter of the School of Paris, to design the ballet, and although his sketches for the two sets—the first a harbor with a tower and sailing ships, the second a tent—appear almost perfunctory, they also strike us, after more than half a century, as just right.

Prokofiev was disappointed with Diaghilev's production of his *Prodigal Son.* Toward the end of his life, Balanchine told Solomon Volkov that Prokofiev had hoped for "bearded men sitting and drinking real wine out of real goblets, the dancers dressed with '. . . historical accuracy.' In a word, somewhat like *Rigoletto.* . . . He was horrified by my staging. . . . And Diaghilev, naturally, yelled at Prokofiev that he didn't understand a thing about ballet. . . ." In Kochno's simple libretto, the Prodigal's self-righteous elder brother is replaced by two affectionate servants or sisters; the fatted calf is omitted; and as much as possible is made of the Prodigal's "wasting his substance in riotous living." When the libretto was complete, Prokofiev wrote his score. Then Balanchine was presented with a *fait accompli.*

Of the ten numbers, some are composed as storytelling, some as dancing, some are mixed. In the departure from home of the Prodigal, who is impatient with his reproachful Father and pleading Sisters (or Servants), there is dramatic conflict; and his abject return at the end is pure drama. The Prodigal's meeting with a gang of "boon companions" in a far country and his seduction by the Siren, though dramatic, are celebrated in dance. The scene in which he is robbed while drunk is mime; the dividing of the spoils is part mime, part dance; and the Prodigal's awakening and repentance is again entirely mime.

Prokofiev's music for the Siren is almost ecclesiastical, with an Old Testament solemnity. The composer obviously saw her as a kind of priestess who initiates men in the ritual of love. Balanchine went further and made her terrifying. The tall, long-legged Doubrovska, walking on pointe, wore a towering headdress. Many years later the choreographer stated that the idea of making the Prodigal's boon companions bald, like certain figures with shaven heads in Egyptian reliefs or like creatures from outer space, was his. He was thus obliged to show them from their first appearance as sinister and abnormal, instead of happy-go-lucky confidence men, charming on the surface, who would later be revealed as thieves. It seems possible that he took his cue from the eighth number, called "Pillage" or "The Despoiling," which is indeed alarming; the scampering scales of its clarinets suggest rats or spiders. Yet there was nothing particularly evil about Prokofiev's boastful, stamping march for the entry of the boon companions, so a discrepancy arose. Later in the ballet, Balanchine would have them link arms, back to back in twos, then scud crablike across the stage.

John Taras has described the pas de deux of the Prodigal and the Siren as "a manual of erotic combinations." At one point she wraps herself around his waist like a belt, her hands clasping her ankles. The man, turning as he carries her thus, lets her slide slowly down his widespread legs till she touches the floor: he then steps out of her as if undressing.

Among the production's ingenuities are the several uses to which a single piece of furniture is put. Beginning as the stockade fencing the Prodigal's home, it is turned upside down and becomes a banqueting table in the orgy scenes. Stood on end, it is transformed into a pillar against which the Prodigal is flung to be frisked. Then the gang reverses it to use as a boat in which they play at rowing off, with the Siren as figurehead, her train held aloft as a sail; and it is in position once more as a fence for the homecoming.

Balanchine had been worried about how to deal with the episode of the Prodigal's return, the big emotional scene. Danilova remembers him sitting on their hotel terrace on the beach at Monte Carlo: "I don't know what to do when the son comes home, crawling on his knees—there are six pages of music. . . . I thought maybe he could have a staff, the way shepherds have, and he can hang onto that." So he does, but when he sees his father, he drops the staff.

Then, folding his arms behind his back in penance, the Prodigal advances on his knees, to collapse at his father's feet. The flute sings sweetly of contrition and forgiveness. Slowly the son clutches his way up his father's body, to hang from his neck and nestle like a baby on his breast. The Father, head held high, covers him with his cloak in a protective embrace.

According to Lifar, who never minimized his triumphs, "Pandemonium broke loose. . . . People were crying." "It was Lifar, on his knees, that made the ballet," commented the generous Balanchine.

Royalties on *The Prodigal Son* were to be divided between Prokofiev as composer and Kochno as author. Kochno had to go to court to claim his share, and won his case. Balanchine, whom Diaghilev paid a very meager wage, and who was often hungry, asked the composer, "Couldn't I be included?" Prokofiev screamed at him, "Are you mad? Who are *you?* You are nobody! You are nothing! Leave me alone! Get out!" Balanchine said, "I'm sorry," and went away.

· · ·

THE LONDON season of 1929 was heralded by a long letter from Diaghilev to the *Times,* in which he teased the critics for continually misunderstanding his experiments and praised Balanchine.

Our century interests itself in *Mouvements mécaniques,* but whenever new *Mouvements artistiques* occur people seem to be more frightened of being run over by them than by a motor-car in the street. For 25 years I have endeavoured to find a new *Mouvement* in the theatre. . . . The new definitions of choreography are "Athletics" and "Acrobatics" . . . In the plastic efforts of Balanchine in *The Prodigal Son* there are far less acrobatics than in the final classical *pas de deux* in *Aurora's Wedding.* . . .

Prospects looked good for the future of the Ballet, for, as Diaghilev told the company when he said good-bye to them shortly before the end of the London season, they had bookings in Barcelona and the possibility of a North American and South American tour. Following *La Chatte,* which was a hit, and *Apollon,* which was a masterpiece, Balanchine had brought off two more ballets that were successful in very different ways. Many years later, considering that summer of 1929, I asked Balanchine if he had then felt on top of the world. "No, I never felt that way," he said. He meant never in his life.

While Diaghilev, against his doctor's orders, took the young Markevitch to the music festival in Baden-Baden, then to hear Wagner and Mozart in Munich and Bayreuth, the Ballet went on to dance for a week in Vichy before dispersing for the holidays. The last performance there on August 4—which was also to be the last performance of the Diaghilev Ballet—was an all-Massine program. Balanchine mimed the role of the Corregidor in *Le Tricorne.* He then traveled to London, where he was to arrange a Tatar ballet, *Jealousy,* to music from Mussorgsky's *Khovanshchina,* for the first full-length talking picture made in England, *Dark Red Roses.* This was a kind of Apache number for Lydia Lopoukhova, Anton Dolin and himself. The three dancers were in the garden of the film studio at Isleworth, waiting to be called, when Dolin bought an evening paper and saw a photograph of Diaghilev on the front page. He had died that morning in Venice. It was August 19, 1929.

In later years Balanchine used to express gratitude for what Diaghilev had done for him and the possibilities he had opened up. This was courteous and also what writers and journalists expected to hear. "The first time I realized how beautiful painting was, it was Italian. When Diaghilev took me to Florence . . ." and so on. Yet, it was *not* "because of Diaghilev" that Balanchine came to make his finest ballets in the way he made them, or that he made them acceptable without décor and with a minimum of costume. It was music, not painting, that filled his mind, guiding his brain and hands. Balanchine acknowledged his debt to the impresario, and acknowledged it with grace; but when asked by McNeil Lowry in 1979 what artists in any field had helped to shape his life, he reacted with a doubtful "Ummm."

．　　．　　．

FOR TWENTY years "ballet" had meant the Diaghilev Ballet. When everyone realized that the company was not to continue, it was a case of every man for himself. Outside Russia, what was there except the famous old Paris Opéra Ballet, which had become a joke, and the Royal Danish Ballet, which nobody knew anything about? It is true that Ida Rubinstein, who could not dance, had a troupe for which she commissioned ballets by Bronislava Nijinska, with scores by Ravel and Stravinsky. It was because Stravinsky had composed *Le Baiser de la fée* for her that he and the jealous Diaghilev were barely on speaking terms during the final months of Diaghilev's life.

The hope that Diaghilev's company might continue under Kochno was dashed by Lifar's insistence on being co-director. Lifar had been built up into a star, but although amiable and enthusiastic, he was vain, had little talent for choreography and few ideas beyond a passion for publicity. Without the curb of Diaghilev's criticism, his "personality" was soon out of control. The company refused to serve under him. On the other hand, Kochno's name was comparatively unknown to the general public. The two young men, former rivals for first place in Diaghilev's friendship and almost the same age—as was Balanchine—did not like each other. It looked as if the company, which could not continue under Lifar, was impossible without him.

At this point, in October 1929, Balanchine was asked by Jacques Rouché, director of the Paris Opéra, to make a new version of Beethoven's *Les Créatures de Prométhée.* Balanchine would almost certainly have remained there as ballet master had he not developed tuberculosis. He left the partly completed ballet in Lifar's hands. Danilova took him to a sanitarium in the Haute-Savoie, then returned to Paris.

The next months were a time of isolation and crisis for him. He was fighting for his life and steadfastly refused to have a lung removed, since he regretted having allowed surgery on his leg. He had cut himself off from his family; and his adopted family, the Ballets Russes, had ceased to exist. Who was left except Danilova, Kochno, Lifar and perhaps the former conductor of the Diaghilev Ballet, Roger Desormière? He wrote to his mother for the first time in years; and he hoped that some of his friends would visit him. To Kochno he wrote:

Grand Hôtel de Mont Blanc
Passy
Haute-Savoie
[*undated, but probably late
November or early December
1930*]

Dear Boris,

This is what I have to tell you. My life here is not gay and the
only good thing about it is my hope—that is my hope of seeing my
old friends around the 6th, when they come here for a rest. Obviously they are not going to find much gaiety waiting for them, but
rest they can. We sleep a lot, and the food comes out of our ears.
The view is very picturesque. It's pure Picasso. [At the foot of the
first page the writing-paper is printed with a view of the hotel.
Balanchine has drawn an arrow pointing to one of the arches in the
arcaded terrace surrounding the ground floor, and written: "Here
lies the body of Balanchine."]

I have had certain thoughts about future GIRLS. [The English
word is transcribed in Cyrillic characters.] I'll tell you all about this
around the 6th. Please bring with you the white ointment for my
lips. It was in the drawer of my night table. My lips are cracked,
and I am obliged to put butter on them.

Give my greetings to the kid [Lifar]. [Here Balanchine wrote five
bars of music.]

I kiss you,
G. B.

In fact, neither Kochno nor Lifar visited Balanchine in the
Haute-Savoie. The first night of the Beethoven ballet took place on
December 30, and Lifar was busy establishing himself as *maître
de ballet* at the Paris Opéra in Balanchine's place. When the latter
returned to Paris with his health improved, he found himself
barred from the office, the most prestigious in the world of ballet.
He and Danilova were turned away at the stagedoor by orders of
"the kid." Danilova later remarked to me that she could forgive
Lifar for this perfidy, but she could never forget it.

Meanwhile, Balanchine was invited to London to choreograph numbers for C. B. Cochran's *Cochran Revue* of 1930. Lady Cunard invited him to supper, and he met the Prince of Wales and "his brother George" (the Duke of Kent). He might have decided to remain in England, but even Maynard Keynes, the husband of Lopoukhova and the by-then-famous author of *The Economic Consequences of the Peace,* whom he visited, could not get his visa extended.

After a stay in France, Balanchine accepted an invitation to be guest ballet master at the Royal Theatre, Copenhagen. The work there was uncongenial to him; he was asked to fake new versions of Massine's *Le Tricorne* and *La Boutique fantasque,* and of Fokine's *Schéhérazade* and *Prince Igor.* He could not have enjoyed dancing Fokine's (presumably edited) *Le Spectre de la rose,* with Ulla Poulsen, for a Christmas charity performance, but there was another Balanchine Evening on January 18, 1931, and this time the choreography was genuine Balanchine. In *Apollon Musagète,* Leif Ørnberg (an uncle of Peter Martins) was the second man ever to dance the principal role. Harald Lander interpreted the comic lead in *Barabau,* which had originally been Woizikovsky's. The choreography of Richard Strauss's *Josefs Legende* (*La Légende de Joseph*) must also have been Balanchine's own invention, as he had never seen the Fokine version of 1914. He wrote to Kochno in Paris:

[undated, but, since Joseph was produced on January 18, 1931, presumably written at the end of that month]

Dear Boris,

Greetings for the New Year, and I wish you every kind of happiness. Forgive me for not answering your last letter at once—I have been very busy. The people here are shit. [The Russian phrase used is obscene.] Nobody understands anything. Their heads are empty unless they see something resembling a sandwich. All this is a new and unexpected experience for me. So as not to feel lonely I have bought myself a Willis Knight. It's delightful and has a marvelous engine. . . .

I wish you were here with me. We could have done a splendid *Joseph* together. What came out of me is not bad, it would be something to put on for Lifar at the Opéra. Then we might have worked on it together.

I wish you all the best, I kiss you. And I send you every good wish for future happiness.

Yours,
Georges

Best wishes to Bébé [Bérard].

Balanchine returned to Paris with his car and some earrings for Danilova. They were made of lapis lazuli. "In Russia," she wrote, "we didn't consider [that stone] precious—there it was a building material, like marble. . . . I had been expecting diamonds, so I threw the earrings in his face. 'But they are so pretty,' he said. . . . Mr. Dmitriev took me aside and said, 'You see. . . . He will never, never give you the security you are looking for.' And I thought, He doesn't love me. . . ."

By February, Balanchine was back in London, turning out numbers for Sir Oswald Stoll's variety shows at the Coliseum. He also worked on the *Cochran Revue* of 1931, which, like its predecessor, was tried out in Manchester. Stoll owned the Alhambra as well as the Coliseum, and after Balanchine had devised some little Mendelssohn, Chopin and Johann Strauss ballets for that theater, he wrote again to Kochno.

Elisabeth House
Devonshire Street
Portland Place
W.1
[*undated, but probably
April or May 1931*]

Dear Boris,

I'm writing to you from hospital. I'm laid up with a boil on my backside. Giordano [Diaghilev's former doctor] operated on me, and he comes back every day to change the dressings. Thank God, it's much better now, but it was very painful. Thank you for your note. It was very sweet, and I don't think many people are lucky enough to get letters like that. We shall meet in Paris, that's certain. The Alhambra is closing down in May forever. Fate has probably decided all this to help me, for I can't think how I could go on like this, and the closing of the Alhambra will let me out of a lot of [uncongenial] work.

But the one thing that cheers me up is the thought of that game of tennis with you. Give my affectionate greetings to sweet, pretty Bébé.

Looking forward to seeing you again.

Yours,
G. B.

Danilova had taken a job in a musical, *Waltzes from Vienna*. She wrote to Balanchine that she thought it would be better if they went their own ways, because "life was separating us." After a long delay a letter came saying that if she wanted to leave him, she should do exactly as she pleased.

• • •

IT WAS on his return to Paris that Balanchine discovered the three young dancers whom he was to make famous as the "baby ballerinas": Tatiana Riabouchinska, a pupil of Kchessinskaya, and Tamara Toumanova and Irina Baronova, two precocious fourteen-year-olds whom he found in the school of Olga Preobrajenska. That winter, René Blum invited him to work for the newly formed Ballets de Monte-Carlo. Thus the year 1932 began, as other years had begun in the days of Diaghilev, with Balanchine grinding out dances for the Monte Carlo opera productions. He worked on eighteen before the end of March—and Toumanova was in *Turandot.* April brought the ballet season, and Balanchine created, on libretti by Kochno, *Cotillon, La Concurrence* and *Le Bourgeois Gentilhomme.*

Unfortunately, the Blum company was gradually being taken over by the scheming Cossack Vassili Vosskrezensky, who called himself Colonel de Basil. Balanchine's contract expired on May 4, but his new ballets were so successful there was every reason to count on its being picked up. It was not, however. The following letter from Balanchine to Kochno, written from Monte Carlo during the summer holidays of 1932, throws some light on the situation:

*[undated, but probably
August or September 1932]*

Dear — you-who-hang-about-the-streets-of-Toulon-at-night-and-go-to-bullfights-instead-of-getting-to-work-creating-new-ballets-of-genius — Boris,

Firstly, secondly and thirdly, I proclaim to you as follows. According to rumors coming from Branitskaya [a member of the Ballets de Monte-Carlo] at Juan-les-Pins, which are confirmed by the total silence of Basil, there will be no choreographer [in the Ballets de Monte-Carlo] this year. This is what Vladimir Pavlovich [Dmitriev] and I had decided was certainly the case on the day before we had the news from Juan-les-Pins. Then Hilda Sokolova told me that Woizikovsky [her boyfriend] had signed a contract with Basil as *répétiteur.* That makes it clear that they won't need either you or me [because Woizikovsky was famous for his detailed memory of the old Diaghilev repertory, and it was obviously de

Basil's policy to revive old ballets]. In my opinion now is the moment to start work in earnest. Return to Paris as soon as possible, and I will follow you soon. I do not want to be in Paris right now, as it might look as if I were there hoping to be signed up by them. I have decided to arrive in Paris about the 5th. Then we'll start looking for work together.

Meanwhile, I kiss you,

Yours,

G. Balanchivadze

De Basil engaged not only Woizikovsky but Léonide Massine, who was more famous than Balanchine both as dancer and as choreographer.

Nevertheless, as soon as he was back in Paris, Balanchine began to work with Kochno to create a new repertory, ignoring the fact that they had no backer, company or theater. Their faith was rewarded. The Vicomtesse de Noailles produced a rich young Englishman, Edward James, and he hired the Théâtre des Champs-Elysées for the season. The "work in earnest" that Balanchine had urged in his letter to Kochno turned into a company called Les Ballets 1933. A condition of James's patronage was the inclusion in the company of his Viennese wife, Tilly Losch, the exponent of a fluid style of dance, who often appeared in trailing draperies to mask her limited technique. Balanchine took this in his stride. Besides, he had brought Tamara Toumanova with him from the Monte Carlo company and she was a sufficient source of inspiration to carry him forward.

Chapter 3

....

HOW KIRSTEIN BROUGHT

BALANCHINE TO AMERICA:

JUNE - DECEMBER 1933

O N June 2, 1933, a twenty-six-year-old American arrived in Paris on a curious quest. At a time when the United States was struggling to emerge from the Great Depression, Lincoln Kirstein had the incredible idea that his country could be regenerated by classical ballet. A democrat might well consider it the most effete—if not depraved—of all the arts, but Kirstein's prophetic soul discerned in ballet's order and ritual an ennobling discipline for his troubled republic. This self-appointed ambassador, six feet three inches tall, with a short-cropped bullet head, piercing eyes and jutting nose, hoped to import from the French capital a choreographer who would enlarge the scope of life in a continent where civilization was still, in some ways, immature.

Kirstein's German grandfather, a lens grinder in Jena, had fled with his wife to America after the Revolution of 1848. They were nonpracticing Jews and pre-Marxian atheists. Their son Louis became a traveling salesman who sold spectacles and married a rich girl, Rose Stein, whose family made its fortune mass-producing uniforms for the Union Army during the Civil War. The second child and first son of this couple, Lincoln Edward Kirstein, was born in Rochester on May 4, 1907. About five years later the Kirsteins moved to Boston, where Louis joined the Filene brothers and eventually became a partner in their department store, today the most famous in the city.

Starting in 1922, young Lincoln Kirstein visited London and Europe with his mother every summer. In 1927, after entering Harvard, he and several friends founded a quarterly journal, *The Hound & Horn;* and in the following year, with his classmates John Walker III and Edward Warburg, he started the Harvard Society for Contemporary Art, putting on exhibitions of not only Picasso, Braque, Matisse and Derain, but also the Americans Alexander Calder, Buckminster Fuller and Gaston Lachaise.

The three young men had already had endless discussions on whether there was any way to be a constructive art patron, since all three received constant requests for financial help from artist friends. Kirstein, who had become enamored of the Diaghilev company's performances on his annual trips to Europe, suggested that the answer might lie in ballet, where the dancer, the musician, the painter and the poet could create a coordinated artistic effort and share in the box-office receipts. Overlooking the obvious pitfalls—the cost of new productions and the complicated labor-union rules, which varied from state to state—they agreed that this was a promising solution to the patronage problem, and various undertakings were begun.

In the four years before his mission to Paris in 1933, Kirstein had contributed dance reviews to *The Hound & Horn.* The "modern" dance recitalist Mary Wigman called forth his derision, but, he wrote, "there is actually in this country a potential audience for dancers"; "Americans appreciate good dancing"; and "perhaps it is not too much to hope that next year [i.e., 1932] the League of Composers [who had presented, under Leopold Stokowski, an amateurish production of Prokofiev's ballet *Le Pas d'acier* with the Philadelphia Orchestra Association] will give us Stravinsky's 'Apollo, Leader of the Muses' in the wonderful choreography of Balanchine—a masterpiece of classical dancing brought up to date. . . ."

After graduating from Harvard in 1930, Kirstein and Warburg had continued with their plans to found an American ballet. They concluded that the first necessities were to establish a school and to persuade the best available Russian choreographer to come over and be its director. To broaden his understanding of the field, Kirstein got in touch with Michel Fokine, who, embittered but not impoverished, was living on Riverside Drive in New York City, and took ballet lessons from him. "I know Fokine thinks I'm ridiculous," he wrote in his diary. "I only want to learn the structure of his teaching, but he thinks I'm a sort of mad millionaire (like Ida Rubinstein) who dreams of dancing. Do I want to start an 'American ballet'? I do, but of course this sounds crazy."

Another acquaintance on whom Kirstein counted for an introduction to the mysterious world of ballet was Romola Nijinsky, who came to New York to raise funds for her husband's care in an insane asylum, or, she dared to hope, for his cure. Even before Kirstein entered Harvard, she had agreed to collaborate with him on a life of Nijinsky, and Kirstein tried (with his father's help) to keep her in a semblance of luxury. She was fascinating, unscrupulous and ungrateful.

When he arrived in Paris in 1933, Kirstein half expected to find Romola there, and hoped to continue work with her on their book; but she was in Holland, burying a dead girl friend. Her absence made it harder for him to "insert himself" into the ballet scene.

At that time, the demigods of Paris society were Jean Cocteau and Serge Lifar. Kirstein noticed that shop-window mannequins were modeled in their likenesses. *Le Tout-Paris* went to the ballet. As Dolly Wilde, the niece of Oscar, remarked to him, "It was where one most wanted to be."

Lifar was at the Opéra; the Ballets Russes de Monte-Carlo under Colonel de Basil and Massine was about to open at the Châtelet; Edward James's Ballets 1933 under Balanchine and Kochno would soon be playing at the Champs-Elysées. Like Paris, the Trojan prince, the young American would have the opportunity to sit in judgment and award his apple. His education progressed at lightning pace, his discernment growing sharper from day to day.

On June 2, at the Opéra, Kirstein watched Lifar in his own ballet *Jeunesse,* and although he found the work poor and "post-Balanchine," Lifar's dancing was "a great pleasure." On the seventh, "in a fever of excitement," he saw Les Ballets 1933 at the Champs-Elysées: "First *Mozartiana* with dull decor but nice costumes and very lovely choreography, witty and Mozartian, by Balanchine. . . . *The Seven Deadly Sins* by Kurt Weill to his familiar haunting delayed music. . . . *Songes* of Milhaud and Derain very dull and boring. . . . Too much choreography by one man for Balanchine to do perfectly. He's no Fokine. . . ."

On the ninth, Kirstein attended a morning rehearsal of *Errante* and *Fastes* at the Champs-Elysées. In the former, he thought Toumanova fine but disliked Tilly Losch's music-hall style of movement and found the work nothing more than an animated Tchelitchev painting (which was doubtless what the designer intended) with some "nice passages." He reflected on Balanchine's tragic ideas of the relation between men and women—"always broken up by someone jumping in between"—and watched the twenty-nine-year-old choreographer holding the arms of a little girl, teaching her a passage of mime and placing her correctly.

That evening Kirstein went to the Châtelet. He thought Massine's *Les Matelots* "nearly as charming as ever, except for the part once danced by Lifar, who sat in the front row." He next saw Massine's new *Présages* for the first time. This was the choreographer's daring attempt to arrange a ballet to a well-known symphony, Tchaikovsky's Fifth. The third ballet of the evening, *Le Beau Danube,* had been revived not only because Strauss waltzes were always popular, but because it provided Massine and Danilova with striking roles as the Hussar and the Street Dancer. *"Beau Danube,"* wrote Kirstein, "a continued enchantment. Massine's sly, steady grace, his lovely style . . . We all went up to Fouquet's on the Champs-Elysées . . . [and] drank to [Diaghilev's] immortal memory."

On June 14, at the Opéra, Kirstein watched Lifar in Nijinsky's great role in *Le Spectre de la rose.* Back at the Châtelet for another program by the Monte-Carlo Ballet on June 16, he saw Fokine's *Les Sylphides,* which he enjoyed "beyond anything." *Scuola di ballo,* a new Massine comedy of manners, had "moments of great charm." As for the year-old *Jeux d'enfants,* which Kochno had devised to Bizet's score, then invited Massine to arrange and Miró to design, Kirstein thought it one of the best ballets he had ever seen, with "wonderful turns" by Baronova.

These entries in his diary reveal that even after three weeks in Paris he had not made up his mind which choreographer or performer could best preach and teach the classical ballet to Americans. By the end of his first week, he had written of Balanchine: "He's no Fokine." Yet even if Fokine had created a perfect work in *Les Sylphides,* Kirstein must have known that he had done very little of interest for twenty years. If Kirstein had had unlimited means, which he did not—he was always worried about running short of cash in Paris—he might well have decided that Massine was the right man. But Massine was thirty-eight and apparently settled as the artistic director of a successful company. Balanchine's position seemed less secure, since Edward James was unaccountable.

Just as Kirstein's Paris ballet going drew to a close, and he decided that his only hope lay with Romola Nijinsky, who was still in Holland, he managed to talk to some of the characters in the ballet world. On June 21 he was taken to see Tchelitchev. On June 24 he called on Lifar, "and soon found he would be no use to me at all." Later that morning, he tracked down Boris Kochno. Kochno was leaving for London the next day, but wrote a letter of introduction to Diaghilev's old colleague Walter Nouvel, who warned Kirstein against Romola Nijinsky and gave him the address of Alexandre Benois. He went again to call on Tchelitchev, who made him wince by saying "toe-dancing was over," but who confirmed that Balanchine was a great man.

Kirstein stayed three nights in Holland. Romola Nijinsky was preoccupied with the tomb of her girl friend, but she had done some work on the biography of Nijinsky. Kirstein went on to England with the understanding that she would follow shortly. The oddest thing about his stay in Holland—to judge from his diary— is that he agreed with a "tall, attractive Russian boy, Igor Schwezoff," whom he met in a dance school, that "Balanchine was much less serious than Massine."

In London, the balletomane and critic Arnold Haskell entertained Tamara Toumanova, her mother and Kirstein at a Soho restaurant. Tamara adored Balanchine, and perhaps it was something she said that finally convinced Kirstein of Balanchine's exceptional qualities as a choreographer and as a man.

After telegraphing twice for money, Romola Nijinsky arrived in London on July 7. When, on the following day, Kirstein took her to see Les Ballets 1933 perform *Mozartiana*, *Songes* and *Errante*, he was on tenterhooks that she might not enjoy Balanchine's ballets as much as he did. That night, because Roman Jasinsky had a splinter in his knee, Balanchine danced *Songes* in his place. According to Jasinsky, he jumped high, turned in the air and landed like a cat. After the ballet, Romola sent a note to the choreographer, and he came out to speak to her. At the Savoy Theatre, Lincoln Kirstein was introduced to George Balanchine at last.

Four days later, at the house in Chelsea that Kirk Askew, the New York art dealer, had taken for the summer, he met him again. Kirstein wrote in his diary, "Balanchine was wholly charming, and I had a long and satisfactory talk with him. . . ."

In their first conversation, thanks to Kirstein's probing questions and Balanchine's apparent eagerness to impart his views, they covered a lot of ground. By rearranging the order of Kirstein's notes, it is possible to see Balanchine's survey of the state of ballet over the past century. The Romantic period? "Taglioni would be an inferior technician to any well-trained modern dancer—always on demi-pointes." Technique had not been developed in her day; and "the music then was all tinkly with small intervals." "The conventions of Petipa" would be "intolerable for the present" and "should be restudied." Mime, the old style of gesture language, was antiquated. "Fokine can no longer compose [ballets]. He can teach, sitting down, but no one can compose long after they forget the actual movement . . . in their own bodies."

Of Massine, Balanchine observed that he had been trained, when choreographing *Le Tricorne*, by Felix, a Spanish dancer, and "the Spanish style had left its strong imprint on him." He added, "He is unmusical. The Fifth Symphony of Tchaikovsky explains itself; it needs no accompaniment in dancing. It is, to start with, a masterpiece."

Lifar had once been modest, now "you couldn't tell him a thing"; he hated competition, and even tried to reduce Spessiva's role in *Giselle*.

Were systems of notation useful? Not really. It was all a question of memory. "Nijinsky notated *Le Sacre du printemps*, but couldn't remember it the next week." Balanchine had learned a notation system in school, but he could compose only with flesh and blood before him, like a sculptor with clay, "putting off here, taking on there." Ballets were like butterflies—"a breath, a memory, then gone. One must never revive anything."

A cynical historian, reading Kirstein's report in his diary, might judge that Balanchine saw in the American, three years younger than himself, a possible savior, and that he was at some pains to discredit rival choreographers. Yet Balanchine was neither calculating nor particularly malicious: confident of his own musical and choreographic powers, he was never shy about expressing in private his views on the limitations of others, and he was convinced that the whole history of ballet was a process of evolution of which he was the most advanced specimen. Luckily, Kirstein's instinct told him that this might well be true.

At the end of their conversation, Balanchine said that he wanted to go to America. He told Kirstein that "with twenty girls and five men he could do wonders; particularly in the classical style or his adaptation of it." Kirstein found Balanchine "intense, convinced, not desperate but without hope." That night he dreamed about him.

During the next ten days there were three more conversations with him; these took place against a background of fantastic scandals and intrigues. Balanchine had to cope with the vagaries of Edward James, the temperament of Lifar, the rivalry between Toumanova and Tilly Losch and rows over money, programs and casting. Edward James had undertaken to back Les Ballets 1933 largely in the hope of making his difficult wife, Tilly, love him more. But she snubbed him, took possession of one of his London houses (while he stayed at the Ritz) and went about telling everybody that he was homosexual. Although the company had been a magnet for *Le Tout-Paris,* Les Ballets 1933 enjoyed no such fashionable triumph in London. Then Lifar and James sued each other. Arnold Haskell, who adored Toumanova, thought she should be with de Basil at the Alhambra, but she would work only for Balanchine.

On July 16, Balanchine had luncheon with Kirstein and Romola Nijinsky. His simple, well-cut English clothes, had he but known it, were bound to prejudice Kirstein in his favor.

Balanchine was charming in a fresh grey flannel suit. . . . We talked in detail about the possibility of an American Ballet. . . . He wants to bring Jasinsky and Toumanova with him; and with little Tamara, Maman has to come. We got frightfully excited about it all. . . . Romola and I could give lectures with the dancers demonstrating. Balanchine says it has always been his dream. He would give up everything to come. Madame

Toumanova could cook for them. . . . Romola will give us all the rights to Vaslav's ballets: systems of notation and education . . .

Kirstein's college friend A. Everett Austin, Jr., known as Chick, was the director of the Wadsworth Atheneum, in Hartford, Connecticut, and was just completing a new wing for that museum which included a theater. Kirstein had envisaged this home of the Muses, within a hundred miles of New York City, as a base for his enterprise. There Balanchine could train young Americans and, when they were ready, present them in the theater. That afternoon he wrote a long letter to Austin, beginning, "This will be the most important letter I will ever write to you. . . . My pen burns my hand as I write. . . . We have a real chance to have an American ballet within 3 years time. . . ." He set out his ideas in some detail, and concluded, "I won't be able to hear from you for a week—but I won't sleep till I do. Just say *Proceed* or *Impossible*. . . . We have the future in our hands."

By July 19, Balanchine's situation in London had become worse than ever, but he spent from three in the afternoon till seven with Kirstein and Romola, "talking about the American project." He said he wanted to stage *Apollon* at once, and proposed starting a class for *maîtres de ballet*. He was frank about his state of health, acknowledged that he had suffered from tuberculosis in the thigh, and said that one of his lungs was all right, the other not. Two days later, he left for Paris on his way to take a holiday in southwestern France.

On July 26, Kirstein received an enthusiastic cable from Chick Austin, and on August 6 a second with the promise of $3,000 from Paul Cooley, James Thrall Soby, Philip Johnson, Edward Warburg and himself. On the eighth, Austin cabled again: "Go ahead, iron-clad contract necessary, beginning October 15. What about entry permits? Can you settle as much as possible before leaving? Bring photos, publicity. Museum willing. Can't wait."

On August 9, Kirstein left for Paris and found that Balanchine would be driving back from the south in two days' time. Austin cabled: "Guaranteed living expenses up to $6,000." Still Kirstein worried. Perhaps Toumanova and Jasinsky would not want to come. Or Toumanova's mother might object. And what should be done about Balanchine's friend Dmitriev? In the program of Les Ballets 1933, Dmitriev had been credited with the *"Direction Administrative."* Balanchine had arranged that any profits that accrued from the James enterprise should be divided in three parts among Kochno, Dmitriev and himself; but, of course, there were none.

When, on August 11, Kirstein met Balanchine and Dmitriev in Paris, it became clear that the choreographer took Dmitriev's advice on all matters of business, which bored him, and that it was with Dmitriev that agreements must be made. Kirstein recorded in his diary their first conversation:

[Dmitriev] at once began to make stipulations about money and the control of the future company. He rejected the suggestion that Balanchine go alone to New York to sum up the situation, insisting that the choreographer must arrive with his dancers to demonstrate his work. Balanchine had had other offers, but after the Edward James catastrophe he could accept nothing without proper guarantees; and he needed a longer rest.

After the three men had picked up Dmitriev's girl friend, the dancer Kyra Blanc, they continued the conversation at a restaurant in Montparnasse. Balanchine was apprehensive that an American tour of de Basil's Monte Carlo Ballet, if unsuccessful, would ruin their chances. De Basil was suing Balanchine for taking Toumanova away from the Ballets Russes, while still presenting two of his ballets, but Toumanova and Jasinsky, who usually demanded large salaries, would give up anything to be with him. Dmitriev inquired about the cost of living in the United States.

On the next day, Dmitriev laid down a principle that determined the future of ballet in the United States of America: *"The whole project fell into two basic parts: a school and a ballet company."* Kirstein wrote in his diary:

Dmitriev said not even to talk about ballets produced for three or four months after starting. They need $3,000 to guarantee passage back and forth for five of them, and let Toumanova's taxi-driver father have a little money to live on. They can all live for $1,000 a month in Hartford. I should hope they could. . . . I told them that the tragic style and *le style noble* were unknown in America. Dmitriev said anything was possible in mixing strains, that the pure Kentucky horse crossed with a Russian strain was better than either virgin breed. They agreed that what was needed more than anything was the insistence on a school. . . . [Piotr] Vladimirov, a miraculous technician, could be brought over to teach the perfection class. Preobrajenska to teach women and children. Even to import Baronova and other dancers. . . . We parted amiably, shaking hands, hoping to see each other in America.

Kirstein was told at the American consulate that the granting of emigration passports to the Russians was entirely a question of money to guarantee their livelihood. If he could get $10,000, it would be easy. He wrote to Balanchine, who had gone to Monte Carlo, "asking him as nicely as possible what the hell Dmitriev did, anyway; was he . . . necessary?"

Kirstein's first visits on his return to America were to Hartford and to Edward Warburg. On September 8, the latter promised Kirstein $5,000 a year for the ballet.

A series of cables went back and forth:

Balanchine in Monte Carlo to Kirstein in New York
29 AUGUST 1933
AWAIT YOUR DECISION   PRESENCE DMITRIEW IS NECESSARY

Kirstein in New York to Balanchine in Monte Carlo
29 AUGUST 1933
LANDED ONLY YESTERDAY   SURE COMPLETE SUCCESS   MINOR DIF-
FICULTIES CLEARED BY SEPTEMBER FIFTEENTH   WILL TRY SEND MONEY
LLOYDS BEFORE   HARTFORD SUPERB EQUIPMENT   GREAT ENTHU-
SIASM

Kirstein in New York to Balanchine in Monte Carlo
30 AUGUST 1933

WOULD YOU OBJECT USE NAME FOKINE STOKOWSKI SPONSORING? . . .

Balanchine in Monte Carlo to Kirstein in New York
1 SEPTEMBER 1933

MUST USE NEW NAME   AWAIT MY ARRIVAL   WAITING UNTIL FIF-
TEENTH VISAS AND MONEY   WILL SAIL IMMEDIATELY

Kirstein in New York to Balanchine in Monte Carlo
5 SEPTEMBER 1933

LETTERS MONEY SENT PARIS TODAY ARRIVE THIRTEENTH

Kirstein in New York to Balanchine in Paris
13[?] SEPTEMBER 1933

WORRIED BY NOT HEARING FROM YOU   PLEASE UNDERSTAND YOUR
PRESENCE WITH DMITRIEW IS OUR ONLY INTEREST   ALL OTHER CONSID-
ERATIONS SECONDARY . . .

Balanchine in Paris to Kirstein in New York
14 SEPTEMBER 1933 [*delivered on the 15th*]

LETTER AND THREE THOUSAND DOLLARS RECEIVED   OWING NECESSITY
DISCUSSING ON THE SPOT ALL ARRANGEMENTS TO BE MADE AND PRESENCE
JASINSKY AND TOUMANOVA NOT INDISPENSABLE PRESENTLY [*at present*]
DECIDED SAIL ALONE WITH MY ASSISTANT DMITRIEW   CABLE AGREE-
MENT

Kirstein in New York to Balanchine in Paris
15 SEPTEMBER 1933

TOUMANOVA JASINSKY ABSOLUTELY NECESSARY TO DEMONSTRATE WHAT
YOU HAVE DONE   MONEY RAISED ON THAT UNDERSTANDING   THEY
CAN FOLLOW LATER IF NECESSARY BUT PREFER ARRIVAL TOGETHER WITH
YOU   SAIL AT ONCE BUT PLEASE UNDERSTAND I AM RESPONSIBLE TO
CITY OF HARTFORD FOR PRESENCE OF ALL FIVE WHO ARE EAGERLY
AWAITED

Balanchine in Paris to Kirstein in New York
15 SEPTEMBER 1933 [*delivered on the 16th*]
[*in French*] CABLE RECEIVED   PRESENCE NOW TOUMANOVA JASINSKY
ABSOLUTELY UNNECESSARY SINCE AMERICAN DANCERS WILL NOT BE
READY FOR THE BALLETS TO BE CREATED IN YOUR SCHOOL   PREFER
SAVE EXPENSE JASINSKY TOUMANOVA AND MOTHER AND REPLACE THEM
BY FIRST CLASS TEACHER LIKE VLADIMIROV   I UNDERSTOOD THERE WAS
A PLACE TO START SCHOOL AND PREPARE AMERICAN DANCERS   I SUG-
GEST VLADIMIROV DMITRIEW AND I LEAVE IMMEDIATELY   IF YOU PRE-
FER SUGGEST YOU COME IMMEDIATELY TO PARIS OR THAT I LEAVE ALONE
FOR NEW YORK TO SORT EVERYTHING OUT   PLEASE REASSURE YOUR
FRIENDS THREE THOUSAND DOLLARS HELD IN TRUST PENDING YOUR
DECISION

Kirstein in New York to Balanchine in Paris
16 SEPTEMBER 1933
EXTREMELY DIFFICULT TO EXPLAIN BY CABLE   PREFER YOU WOULD
SAIL ALONE AT ONCE   WHEN YOU HAVE TALKED TO ME YOU ARE AT
PERFECT LIBERTY TO SEND FOR VLADIMIROV DMITRIEW   YOUR PRES-
ENCE WHOLLY NECESSARY TO UNDERSTAND AMERICAN SITUATION
HAVE PERFECT CONFIDENCE IN ALL YOU DO

Balanchine in Paris to Kirstein in New York
18 SEPTEMBER 1933 [*received on the 19th*]
DMITRIEW LEAVING WITH ME   I WILL PAY HIS EXPENSES   PLEASE ASK
AMERICAN CONSUL PARIS PERMANENT VISAS AS WITH TEMPORARY VISAS
WILL EXPERIENCE GREAT INCONVENIENCE   CABLE

Kirstein in New York to Balanchine in Paris
25 SEPTEMBER 1933
HAVE SENT CONSUL ONE YEAR CONTRACT AS REQUIRED . . . IN CONTRACT
WE STATE YOU AND DMITRIEW ALONE PAID FIVE HUNDRED DOLLARS PER
MONTH BUT WE HAVE ALSO MONEY FOR OTHERS   HOPE YOU UNDER-
STAND THIS DOES NOT PREVENT OBTAINING VLADIMIROV TOUMANOVA
LATER . . .

Kirstein in New York to Balanchine in Paris

27 SEPTEMBER 1933

MONTE CARLO BALLET DEFINITELY IN NEW YORK NOVEMBER FIF-
TEENTH   DO YOU CONSIDER IT DESIRABLE TO OBTAIN TOUMANOVA FOR
YOUR SCHOOL AFTER SHE FULFILS PRESENT ENGAGEMENTS WITH BASIL?

Dmitriev and Balanchine in Paris to Kirstein in New York

10 OCTOBER 1933

SAILING OLYMPIC   WOULD BE VERY MUCH OBLIGED IF COMMUNICATE
TAMARA GEVA OUR ARRIVAL

The most startling of these cables is that of September 14, in
which Balanchine declared that Toumanova and Jasinsky were
"not indispensable." This change of heart threw Kirstein into
despair. He had felt all along that he must have something to *show*
Austin and his confederates in Hartford, not to mention Warburg
and other potential backers. What more perfect exhibit than the
beautiful Toumanova, marvelous technician that she was, executing, with her partner, Balanchine's choreography? She was to
inspire the youth of America and attract them to the new school
and the new company. Kirstein felt he had been let down, and that
he was responsible for $3,000 being sent under false pretenses.
But the situation was more difficult than he realized.

After the disastrous winding-up of Les Ballets 1933 in London,
Tamara Toumanova had gone to Normandy, leaving her parents
in Paris. Balanchine had told her she would be going with him to
America, and Dmitriev, whom neither she nor her mother liked,
instructed her to do nothing without consulting him. She was aware
that Balanchine allowed himself to be led by Dmitriev: "He hated
scandals and said yes to everything." When she returned to Paris,
she took classes with Preobrajenska and waited for something to
happen. All this time—indeed, since July 4—the Ballets Russes
de Monte-Carlo had been playing at the Alhambra in London; their
success was so great that their season was continually being extended (and eventually lasted until November 4). In Paris

Toumanova received a telephone call from de Basil: he said he was just back from Monte Carlo, where he had seen Balanchine, who had sent her a message. The last time Tamara had set eyes on de Basil was in a French courtroom, just before the Paris opening of Les Ballets 1933, when he had sued her for leaving his company along with Balanchine. With the consent of her parents, she called on de Basil, who embraced her as if nothing had happened. He told her that Balanchine wished her to rejoin the Ballets de Monte-Carlo in London. He would see her there, as he was returning to de Basil's company himself. The only true word in all this was that Balanchine was indeed in Monte Carlo. Tamara packed in a hurry. She and her mother crossed the Channel next day. At the Redcourt Hotel, they met Nina Verchinina and her sister, Olga Morosova, and asked, "Has Balanchine arrived?" As Nina exchanged glances with Olga, Tamara realized in a flash that she had been tricked. So Toumanova rejoined de Basil's company "with" as she said in an interview, "a stone in my heart." She danced in Balanchine's ballet *La Concurrence* on September 13.

Balanchine and Dmitriev had heard in Monte Carlo that Toumanova was back in London. No doubt they thought she had betrayed them. For several days they could not decide how to break the news to Kirstein. Without Toumanova, the whole deal might be off! Sometime between the ninth and the fourteenth of September they returned to Paris. When Kirstein cabled that he was worried by their silence, they felt obliged to reply; but they were not frank with him. Instead of saying, "Toumanova has let us down," they cabled that she and Jasinsky were "not indispensable." Poor Jasinsky had placed high hopes on his future in America. In London, Dmitriev had withheld half his weekly salary; when James offered him a year's contract for a new company he hoped to form around Tilly Losch, he refused out of loyalty to Balanchine and faith in Kirstein's project. He had spent all his savings in Monte Carlo, and now he was callously abandoned. Dmitriev said he could spare him only two hundred francs. (Jasinsky was saved from starvation by Lifar two months later.)

.　.　.

ALTHOUGH many Europeans thought of America as El Dorado, it is surprising that both Balanchine and Dmitriev saw in the inexperienced twenty-six-year-old Kirstein the fulfillment of their hopes. Even if Balanchine had long nursed romantic dreams about America and its possibilities, even if he loved American movies, jazz and the challenge of Western frontiers, Dmitriev might easily have put him off Kirstein's plan. He could well have objected that Kirstein had no company to dance Balanchine's ballets; that although he must have rich friends, he seemed to have little money of his own; that while Balanchine had solid offers from Denmark and from Ida Rubinstein, it was ten-to-one that Kirstein's Hartford project would founder (and in fact *did* founder), so that they would find themselves stranded in a far land where the name of Balanchine carried no weight. Dmitriev might have said all this and more; but he did not. It is clear that both he and Balanchine trusted Kirstein and were convinced that he offered a new beginning. Dmitriev saw himself, rightly, as it turned out, as an essential part of the perilous American venture, an agent and bodyguard to Balanchine, a mentor to Kirstein—quite aside from the fact that he needed to earn a living.

On September 16, the day Balanchine's next telegram arrived, Kirstein reconciled himself to using only American dancers from the very start of his enterprise. It was not till September 27 that he learned from an article in the *New English Weekly* that Toumanova had rejoined de Basil. Perhaps it was to show that he knew Balanchine and Dmitriev had concealed this from him that he fired off the cable asking if they should not take steps to secure Toumanova's services "after she fulfils present engagements."

On October 1, the scaffolding was down in the new theater at Hartford, and Austin had a congressman working on Balanchine's and Dmitriev's visas. On the fourth, Kirstein had lunch with John Martin, dance critic of *The New York Times*, and asked him what he thought were the prospects for the school; Martin prophesied it would be "swamped with applicants." On the thirteenth, he spent an evening with Fokine, who "expressed contempt for Balanchivadze and Miassin, saying it was his innovation that had made them possible, but they themselves were no good."

. . .

KIRSTEIN longed for Balanchine to fall in love with New York at first sight. He had booked a suite with two bedrooms at the Barbizon Plaza, overlooking Central Park from the south. On October 17, he wrote:

Lunch with Mrs. Murray [of the *Hartford Times*], who failed to sell any ballet story to A.P. [Associated Press], and the Austins. . . . Afternoon pouring with rain. . . . Called up the White Star Line: *Olympic* docks at 5:30–6. When we got down to the dock, Eddie Warburg was very professional about what a damn bad landing they were making. The tide had swung the boat around. Finally, it was nosed in, and for the longest time I could find no friendly face on that boat. Had they come First Class or Third? I spotted Balanchine in Tourist, with Dmitriev. Amid the roar of unloading he told me they couldn't land; had to go to Ellis Island in the morning; must stay on the boat all night. I told Eddie, who disappeared. . . . Some months [*sic*] later Eddie emerged saying it was O.K. Use of Felix Warburg's magic name. They had only a six-months' visa with a year's contract. Hence the delay, plus a lousy Immigration Officer. When Balanchine was at the top of the gangway he had misplaced his landing-card. Eddie had a dinner date but waited for a picture, and he snapped one of all of us and left. . . . I took Balanchine and Dmitriev to the duplex apartment, $12 a day, at the Barbizon Plaza, 34th floor. They gasped at the view. . . .

Balanchine, not yet thirty, had been a subject of the czar; he had starved and frozen in revolutionary Russia; he had enjoyed the fleshpots of Western Europe. Now he had stepped, as it were, through the silver screen into a world he had known before only in movies—and was delighted to find himself there. None of the big steps of his life had been taken on his own initiative. He had entered the Ballet School at the suggestion of a stranger; Dmitriev had arranged his departure from Russia; Diaghilev had sought him out; Kirstein had lured him to America.

Other Russians had opened schools of classical ballet in the United States before him. Mikhail Mordkin (1881–1944), a one-time partner of Pavlova's, after touring in America before the war, settled in New York for good in 1924. Adolph Bolm (1884–1951), the original Chief Warrior in Fokine's *Polovtsian Dances*, had remained in America after the second tour of the Diaghilev Ballet in 1917 and founded a school in Chicago. Fokine had lived in New York since 1923. Louis Chalif (1876–1948), from Odessa, had the biggest school in New York, founded in 1907. He was the only one Kirstein and John Martin regarded as a possible rival.

During dinner at the hotel, and later at the Askews', where Kirstein had taken them in hopes of whiskey—for Prohibition was still in force—Dmitriev and Balanchine tried to put off talking business while Austin was present. Kirstein walked them down Park Avenue, through the Waldorf-Astoria, around Rockefeller Center, to Broadway. Back at the Barbizon Plaza, the three men talked till 2:00 A.M. As the two Russians gradually revealed that Copenhagen had asked for a Balanchine ballet, that Blum intended separating from de Basil and hoped Balanchine would join him, that Ida Rubinstein wanted Balanchine for two ballets, that he had been offered a teaching job at The Juilliard School and a show at Radio City Music Hall, Kirstein thought that Dmitriev was holding out for more money. Somewhat chilled, he said he knew "Balanchine's works and services were not to be named in mere figures, but if it was money he wanted he wouldn't be here."

Kirstein suggested that it might be a good idea to accept the Music Hall job, for Balanchine to see what it would be like and also to keep his hand in. But Balanchine said he was not interested; he would have to work nine hours a day at the school. They did not want to start in too small a way; they must plan many years ahead. An American dancer in France had told him that if he were working professionally in the United States he should get not less than $1,000 a week. Finally, the three "agreed to agree in principle, and try to find a form that was satisfactory upon which to proceed." It was an anticlimactic evening for the expectant Kirstein.

Next morning, Kirstein found Warburg getting on well with the new arrivals. When Warburg left, Balanchine remarked, "He is one swell guy." Kirstein took the two Russians to Tamara Geva's, then picked up John Martin, who was to interview Balanchine.

Geva and Balanchine had not met or corresponded for six years. She was now married to another expatriate Russian, Kapa Davidov, whose former wife, Lucia, was soon to become a close friend of Balanchine's. But Dmitriev referred to Tamara as his best friend and obviously adored her. Kirstein was struck by the awful thought that she might lure Balanchine to Broadway. Luckily neither Dmitriev nor Balanchine approved of her suggestion that they hire twenty chorus girls at twenty dollars a week, rehearse them for three months and then put on a sample show. That night Warburg and Kirstein took the two Russians to Radio City Music Hall, and Balanchine decided he could do nothing interesting on its stage. Standing on the top of the R.C.A. building, and looking across at the lighted tower of the General Electric building, he exclaimed in French "My God, they have ruins here already!"

On October 19, the three men drove to Hartford, where they found all the local dance teachers protesting against the importation of Russians. Balanchine and Dmitriev were, Kirstein reported, "well satisfied with the space for the practice halls . . . but when we came to the theater it was a big disappointment; there is no height; they couldn't use any scenery in it; the floor is too hard for dancing; the whole place is much too small." Dmitriev said it might do for school performances. Next day, after a meeting of indignant dance teachers had been faced, there was more talk of budgets. The three drove to Kirstein's parents' home in Springfield; and it was there that the realism of Dmitriev and the quick understanding of Kirstein carried the Grand Design a step nearer to its destined form:

Discussed the possibility of opening in New York . . . without the
Hartford preliminaries, perhaps under the auspices of the Museum of
Modern Art, which we thought Warburg could arrange, as [his family]
had just given them $100,000. . . . As we talked it seemed better and
better. Hartford faded into the background. Balanchine, silent, interested, played Negro spirituals . . . and Gilbert and Sullivan, never having
heard of them before.

The birch trees, the dogs, the Kirsteins' white *dacha* made
Dmitriev homesick. After talking to him at length, Mina Curtiss,
Lincoln's sister, said she was sure the Russians could never work
with Austin. Yet the three had to drive back to Hartford and face
the man they were to disappoint. Because of their reluctance to
prolong discussions, Austin became suspicious.

Within a week of Balanchine and Dmitriev's arrival in the
United States, the whole Hartford project had been scrapped. It
still remained to sort out the money question and to make peace
with Austin, who was justifiably bitter. Meanwhile, a rumor that
Kirstein's plans were "all washed-up" had spread around Manhattan. When Kirstein tried to introduce Balanchine to Philip Johnson
at the Museum of Modern Art, Johnson fled: "The smell of failure
terrified him." The idea of attaching the new School to the museum
lasted no more than two days. Balanchine was filling in time by
"freshening up on counterpoint and harmony with Nicolas Nabokov." Kirstein discovered for the first time his childish sense of
humor: when he called Nabokov on the telephone Balanchine said,
" 'Allo, this is President Roosevelt."

Convinced at last that the three of them would be better on their
own, possibly with financial help from Warburg only—luckily
Balanchine and Warburg liked each other at once—Kirstein began
to draw up a prospectus for the ballet school and to look for
premises.

When two dance companies from Europe appeared in New
York, there was the danger that, if they were too good, they might
diminish the prospects of Kirstein's enterprise, or, if they were

terrible, give ballet a bad name. But Kirstein found the Ballet Jooss from Germany "without the slightest interest whatever" except for two or three good ideas in *The Green Table.* A troupe Serge Lifar brought to the Forrest Theater (which included Jasinsky) was a more serious threat because it was presenting Balanchine's *La Chatte,* and presenting it very badly. Balanchine was furious and said that Lifar could never use his ballets again.

The next day, Kirstein and Dmitriev found the right site for the School, at 637 Madison Avenue. They also signed papers to establish The American Ballet Incorporated, for which they hoped the School would one day provide dancers. The School and the company were to be two separate entities: students would pay to work under Balanchine in the former, but they would presumably have contracts and salaries to dance with the latter.

That autumn and winter the United States conditionally recognized Stalin's regime; Prohibition was abolished; and Fiorello La Guardia was elected mayor of New York City.

On November 10, Balanchine returned with a fever from Philadelphia, where he had been looking over Dorothie Littlefield's dance school. Kirstein escorted him to a doctor, then to be X-rayed. Back in their hotel room, Dmitriev took his temperature continually. Next day the fever was higher. Balanchine was ordered to the hospital and refused to go. The doctor said he should rest for six months and could not live more than ten years. Balanchine, looking green, announced he was going to die. On November 21 he was admitted to Presbyterian Hospital. When he was discharged, he went to stay with Mina Curtiss in Massachusetts, to rest and be fattened up, and he remained there for nearly a month. No clear diagnosis of his illness was ever offered, but Lucia Davidova has always been convinced that Mina Curtiss saved Balanchine's life.

During this anxious period, Balanchine was sometimes resentful of Dmitriev, who complained about him constantly to Kirstein. He told Kirstein that nine days after Balanchine had said he was going to live with Danilova, he went off to Italy with Diaghilev and never wrote her a line. He was "Georgian, heartless"; he had treated Geva and Danilova abominably and would think nothing of screwing his best friend's wife. Once, in 1931, he had telegraphed from London that he was ill and would arrive in Paris by car. He was twelve hours late. Danilova became hysterical, and Dmitriev went to the police. Balanchine walked in gaily at one in the morning. It had never occurred to him to send a telegram.

■　■　■

EVEN in Balanchine's absence, plans for the School were moving ahead. Dancers showed up to inquire about it. Pierre Vladimirov, who had come over with Lifar, agreed to stay and teach for six months at least. Balanchine, much restored, returned from the country on December 21. On December 22, the School of American Ballet opened.

The same night de Basil's Ballets Russes de Monte-Carlo, presented by Sol Hurok, opened at the St. James Theater. Toumanova danced in *La Concurrence,* and Balanchine, who had never before watched his ballet from the front of the house, loved Derain's costumes but said he was "through forever with that kind of stuff" and had lots of new ideas.

Dmitriev considered that a state of war existed between the new School and the Ballets Russes de Monte-Carlo. He condemned Kirstein for having lunched with Haskell, and Warburg for having gone to Hurok's party on the previous evening; when Balanchine ran into some Monte Carlo dancers in the street, Dmitriev quickly separated him from them. Some, however, came to the School and were impressed. Meanwhile, more students were registering. By the end of the month, there were about twenty-two enrolled.

There was to be an impromptu party at the School on New Year's Eve. Eddie Warburg sent over a case of champagne and Kirstein borrowed some of his Persian rugs to make the place look "more inhabited." ". . . The boys brought fruit and nuts. Tilly Losch came early, and we all dressed up. There was plenty to drink and Balanchine banging on the piano. . . . Tamara Geva, George

Kirstein [Lincoln's younger brother] . . . and later Danilova and Jasinsky came in from the ballet." Dmitriev grew almost sentimental.

In that loft on Madison Avenue, at which Kirstein had arrived by such painful stages over the past seven months, four out of the five Russians who had left Leningrad for Germany nearly ten years before were present.

Chapter 4

··

THE SCHOOL ESTABLISHED:

FIRST SKETCH FOR A COMPANY,

JANUARY 1934 - APRIL 1937

I N 1934, the School of American Ballet depended for its existence on six people: Balanchine, Dmitriev, Warburg, Vladimirov, Dorothie Littlefield, whom Balanchine had enticed away from Philadelphia, and Lincoln Kirstein. Balanchine was, of course, the raison d'être of the whole enterprise; Dmitriev was the lawgiver, determined to put the School on a businesslike basis; Warburg was almost entirely responsible for finances until the School could pay its way; Vladimirov and Littlefield did most of the teaching; Kirstein concentrated on propaganda and public relations. A discovery of Dmitriev's, Eugenie Ouroussow, a Russian aristocrat in exile, was the secretary.

Nobody liked Dmitriev. He goaded Balanchine, Warburg and Kirstein, complained of each man behind his back to the other two, and staged appalling scenes. He kept meticulous accounts, and he had spy holes made in his office walls so that he could see that classes were being properly conducted. Yet Balanchine continued to tolerate him; and Kirstein, often rebellious, recognized the value—even the necessity—of Dmitriev's contribution. Either Dmitriev's bullying or Kirstein's persistence led Warburg to increase his subsidy; and when Lincoln's father, Louis Kirstein, eventually forked out, it was partly because of the impression Dmitriev had made on him.

Balanchine, with his Oriental patience, worked hard, but he also enjoyed life in his quiet way; Dmitriev brooded and planned; Warburg, who had many demands on his purse, blew hot and cold; Kirstein encouraged and educated the brighter students, lectured on the history of the dance, wrote articles and badgered his richer friends to give scholarships. During the first half of 1934 hope alternated with fear.

The curriculum of the School was rearranged so as to get more out of Vladimirov. After a long and nervous delay, Kirstein brought himself to ask his father for money and obtained $4,000. Dorothie Littlefield had brought with her from Philadelphia five students whose previous training Balanchine appreciated, and gradually others trickled in. In October 1933, Erick Hawkins, the first of the boys, had turned up. Colorado-born and Harvard-educated, he had studied under the expressionist "modern" dancer Harald Kreutzberg. On January 2, 1934, came Leda Anchutina, who was working at Radio City Music Hall. She had astonishing strength and technique, but she was tiny. Even when exercising at the barre, she used to rise on pointe as soon as Balanchine appeared, because of his known preference for tall dancers. Marie-Jeanne Pelus (who soon dropped her surname because no one could pronounce it correctly) enrolled on the following day. She was the only child of Italian and French immigrants, and although she was only fourteen, she had already tap-danced in public. January 4 brought William Dollar, a native of St. Louis, "the prize pupil of Fokine and Mordkin." Balanchine, who was proud of his newly acquired American slang, seemed delighted by his name: "William Dollar, Dollar Bill. Don't you get it? Isn't it perfect?" Gisella Caccialanza, born in San Diego, enrolled on January 14. She was a pupil of the great Italian teacher Enrico Cecchetti. Charles Laskey, Paul Haakon and Annabelle Lyon also registered at the School in January. In February, the two Christensen brothers arrived. Harold and Lewellyn Christensen, born in Brigham City, Utah, were of Danish ancestry and had been performing for years in vaudeville. Brooklyn-born Ruthanna Boris, trained at the Metropolitan Opera School by Rosina Galli, came in May. Elise Reiman, born of German parents in Terre Haute, Indiana, was studying dancing in California when her sister sent her an article about Balanchine by Kirstein that had appeared in *Vogue.* She headed straight for the School of American Ballet. Thus, from its earliest days, the School attracted pupils of various backgrounds, from various states, representative of many of the racial strains that have enriched the American heritage.

Sixteen-year-old Ruthanna Boris, whose father had been brought from the Caucasus as a baby and whose mother was Viennese, always remembered her first sight of Balanchine and Vladimirov. At the Metropolitan Opera School the girls wore pink tunics to below the knee, with little bows tied so their brassiere straps wouldn't show; and that is how she was dressed.

These two men came into the room. I thought one of them was Chinese. That was Mr. Balanchine. He sat down, and the other man, who had blue eyes and a towel over his shoulder, gave me a full barre. After we had done some center work, Balanchine got up and said, "Corner." He gave me a piqué arabesque, quatrième, two pirouettes, finish in quatrième. Now at the Metropolitan you didn't do two pirouettes till they thought you were ready. I could do one beautiful one. I said, "I don't do two." He said, "But you will, you see. You do, and you'll do two." I did piqué, quatrième, and he gave me a little pat on the behind, and I went round twice and fell down. He laughed and said, "You see? Two!" . . . I could pirouette from then on. Balanchine told me later, "You were so old-fashioned, so cute, so Italian, if you could not dance at all I would have taken you. I wanted to bite your knees."

Sooner or later these professionals and students would have to dance Balanchine's ballets in Balanchine's way, so he had begun from the start to teach them works he had done for Les Ballets 1933. The first was *Errante,* which made no severe technical demands. On the January day that Kirstein saw Balanchine actually rehearsing one of his creations in America, he was moved. A week later the more classical *Mozartiana,* to Tchaikovsky's Suite No. 4, had its first rehearsal.

On March 14, Balanchine began sketching out a ballet to Tchaikovsky's Serenade in C for string orchestra, op. 48. Kirstein has described how *Serenade* took shape:

Balanchine commenced by lining up as many girl students as chanced to be in class. . . . On that day there were seventeen. These he placed in military order according to height. One more, a tiny but brilliant dancer, Leda Anchutina, slipped into the studio late. . . . Her tardy entrance was incorporated. . . . At the next rehearsal only nine girls appeared; at another, only three. For them he arranged other portions of action, exactly as if they had been especially summoned and scheduled. The ballet was structured piecemeal, with no time wasted. . . . At the start no boys were available; when five eventually appeared, three were used.

All the same, Balanchine had his difficulties with the undisciplined American girls. Probably because of the delicate state of his lungs, he disliked raising his voice and had trained himself not to. One day, at a rehearsal of *Serenade* the dancers would not stop talking. He stood on a bench, clapped his hands, obtained silence and said, "If you don't care, why should I?" Then he went to the dressing room. An anxious deputation followed him to apologize.

In mid-May, Warburg's impatience to see the curtain go up overcame Balanchine's reluctance to show raw students performing in front of an audience. It was agreed that a private tryout should take place outdoors, on the Warburg estate at White Plains. Edward Warburg later wrote: "I convinced my long-suffering parents that what I wanted most for my twenty-sixth birthday on June 5, 1934 was to have these ballets performed in the garden of our family place." The program was *Mozartiana, Dreams* (*Songes*), in remade Derain costumes with new music by George Antheil, and *Serenade.* Because the noted stage designer Jo Mielziner had made some designs for this that were unsatisfactory, the new work was to be danced in an approximation of practice costume: white tarlatan skirts for the girls, and for the boys, shirts from a department store. Instead of an orchestra, there was an upright piano in the bushes.

On June 8, the day of the dress rehearsal, the dancers left in a bus at three. According to Kirstein, "It got dark about nine and *Mozartiana* looked heavenly. Very brilliant and the kids superb. Vladimirov was in all of his states. When he saw Marie-Jeanne Pelus in the [*Mozartiana*] Ave Verum, he said he was reminded of the debut of Pavlova."

The weather was a problem on the next two evenings. On the ninth, a drizzle wasted an hour and a half of rehearsal time. Balanchine drove himself into town. When the sun came out, Dmitriev looked in vain for him to rehearse *Mozartiana.* It started to rain again. When Balanchine finally got back, he merely glanced at the weather and said, "God's will be done." Guests began to arrive. At 8:40 it was decided to give as much of the performance as possible. And so, on June 10, the first version of *Serenade,* a ballet that would become beloved throughout the world, was, somehow or other, performed at last. According to Warburg, the lawn where Dmitriev's stage had been erected "never recovered from the shock."

The School closed for the summer on July 6. The immediate future had been taken care of. Warburg, who had already given thousands, paid $6,000 more, two quarters' subsidy in advance, plus $8,000 for costumes and scenery for future ballets. The arrival of Doubrovska ensured that her husband, Vladimirov, would not run off to France.

Kirstein was still searching for American themes, musicians and painters "that would make the company more 'Buckeye' and less Russian." He explored the possibility of material in the early minstrel shows and even looked at the text of *Uncle Tom's Cabin* and various Western sagas. Not to be outdone, Warburg came up with a proposal for a ballet relating to college football life, "in the wonderful tradition of team photographs with the players posed like river gods on Greek pediments or posturing against the goal-posts." The popular cartoonist John Held Jr. agreed to design the costumes and even managed to include Warburg's old hand-me-down raccoon coat. Kay Swift wrote the score. But Warburg always felt that the ballet was not as successful as it should have been because of Balanchine's steadfast refusal to see a real football game. "Look, Eddie," he protested, "I know already what those games are. I don't need to go. The main thing is that Kay Swift's music is excellent. It will be wonderful ballet." When *Alma Mater* finally premiered, it received mixed reviews, and in Warburg's opinion the weak spot was Balanchine's lack of understanding of the material.

So absolutely were Balanchine and Kirstein under the spell of Diaghilev's inspired window-dressing that it had not yet occurred to either of them that ballets might be presented without the aid of painters or stage designers. When Pavel Tchelitchev moved to America in the summer of 1934—Balanchine had already cabled him in Paris that he was looking forward to working with him—the painter announced in his Delphic way that ballet as they had known it was finished: the time had come to invent a new theatrical form. This is exactly what Balanchine would do; but in the ballets of his new era, painters were to play a negligible part.

.   .   .

A DOCTOR had told Balanchine that his state of health would permit him to make love, but that he should not kiss girls for fear of passing on tubercular germs. This injunction was presumably soon forgotten. There had been talk earlier in the year of an ash-blond "fiancée" called Miss Elmore. Then there were Heidi Vosseler and Holly Howard, who had come with Dorothie Littlefield from Philadelphia. All the girls in the School adored Balanchine. Ruthanna Boris could not resist following him around. One day he felt obliged to tell her, "I'm not a god. When I pull the chain in the toilet, I do it for same reason as you."

Balanchine apparently never felt the need for close friendship with another man. He enjoyed company at the dinner table and liked conversation in small doses, but nothing deeper. Diaghilev's former rehearsal pianist, the plump, charming and amusing Nicolas ("Kolya") Kopeikine, was always on call to keep him company, and several other slaves attached themselves to him in the course of time. But both Dmitriev and Kirstein, who saw him daily for years on end, disclaimed the title of intimate friend. If he took a pretty girl out to dinner, it was unusual if he did not try to make love to her. Nevertheless, he had at least one close woman friend, apart from his professional colleagues. Lucia Davidova, the former wife of Tamara Geva's husband, was small and dark, with classical features; she was also extremely intelligent, loved music and flew airplanes. Balanchine confided in Lucia about all his love affairs, and they remained friends until his death. Another woman friend in the early American years was Nicolas Nabokov's first wife, born Princess Natalie (Natasha) Shakhovskoy. Although he confessed to her, too, the hopes and disappointments of his affairs, she later said she "never thought of him as a man."

On July 12, during the School vacation, while Kirstein was driving him to visit friends in Connecticut, Balanchine had something like an epileptic fit. He grew rigid, then violent and had to be restrained and taken to the hospital. Doctors spoke of meningitis or a brain tumor; and Kirstein foresaw the end of all his hopes. But since no one could agree on a diagnosis, no action was taken. Kirstein drove him back to New York, showed him the enlarged school, with which he was delighted, and took him to hear *Faust.*

After a few days in the country he returned, looking well and happy, for the reopening of the School on August 27. The mystery of the seizure was never solved.

.   .   .

THE SCHOOL'S new term began in an atmosphere of bitterness and bickering. Nothing Warburg, Kirstein or Balanchine did seemed right to Dmitriev, although he depended on them for his livelihood. At a dinner given by Kirstein's father, it was decided to form a separate production company, which would constitute no threat to the School's bank account. When this came into being, Warburg, who had put up the capital, was elected president. There was a row because Vladimirov had dismissed an adagio class half an hour early. Dorothie Littlefield decided to stop teaching because, she said, she wanted only to dance; but her pupils thought it was really because Balanchine did not return her love. Kirstein began to worry about who might one day succeed Balanchine, a problem that would occupy him for the next fifty years.

.   .   .

ONCE when Balanchine conducted the beginners' class, which he hated doing, he spent an hour teaching a boy of fourteen, who took only one lesson a week, how to do a glissade. Elise Reiman had been badly taught by Bolm and realized that she had "sickle feet," which Balanchine, who admired her, was determined to correct by improving her whole placement. When, as sometimes happened, he reduced a girl to tears, his insistence looked to Kirstein like sadism. Ruthanna Boris, however, was fascinated by Balanchine's patient, endless explorations of every possible way to do emboîtés or tendu, and she accepted them as a lesson in choreography.

Balanchine thought the Littlefield pupils from Philadelphia had good feet, but no speed. That, he told dancer Georgia Hiden some years later, was why he made *Serenade*. Lew Christensen, who had been a professional for seven years, thought he "really only learned how to dance from Balanchine and Vladimirov." "I did damn good tricks, nothing else. I knew the steps but not how to put them together."

Balanchine began to sketch out a "Valse romantique" for eighteen girls and three boys to the music of Glinka (which he used in a ballet many years later). The question arose of devising a new dramatic work to give variety to the nascent repertory, and Balanchine wanted to do something Hungarian about the lives of great virtuosi like Liszt or Paganini. Kirstein was allowed to think up the story of a ballet, which became *Transcendence*.

Chick Austin had offered to let the company give a performance at the Avery Memorial Theater in Hartford, and on the eve of the opening the situation was chaotic. The costumes for *Serenade* were awful; those for the principal girls had to be scrapped. Kirstein was pleased with John Held Jr.'s costumes for *Alma Mater* and Franklin Watkins's for *Transcendence*, but Tchelitchev, who had just arrived, described the latter as *"merde."* Two new pianists played so badly that Balanchine was driven to ask desperately, "What is the use of choreography, or costumes, etcetera? The music is the most important thing."

At Hartford, the new company was billed for the first time as "The American Ballet." Unfortunately the Avery Memorial Theater proved unsuitable from every point of view. The stagehands were volunteer Trinity students, and the chief electrician had to keep darting back to the campus to give lectures. On the night of December 5, Kirstein and Austin helped Franklin Watkins paint the scenery.

On the morning of the sixth, there was a dress rehearsal and photo call. The house was not sold out. In the evening, the stage seemed to be on top of the fashionably dressed audience—which included George Gershwin and Salvador Dali; the dancers could be heard breathing, and their shoes squeaked. Because Austin had not unionized the theater, there were two pickets at the door throughout.

At the dress rehearsal of *Serenade* on December 7, the smallness of the stage became more evident than ever. The primitive lighting and the proximity of the stage to the audience cannot have flattered the ballet. In the evening, Warburg stood at the back and started the applause.

Hartford nevertheless gave Warburg the confidence to show the young troupe to a larger public. Through Alexander Merovitch, president of the Musical Art Management Corporation, the American Ballet was given a week's season at the Adelphi Theater in New York City. The orchestra would be conducted by Sandor Harmati, and Tamara Geva would appear as guest artist in *Errante.* But one more "closing ballet" was needed. *Transcendence,* with its hypnotic Monk (the Devil), its Witches and its final mazurkas, was a strong dramatic piece; *Errante* and *Serenade* were romantic in their different ways; *Mozartiana* was classical. The new ballet, *Reminiscence,* to music by Benjamin Godard, was therefore to be a brilliant divertissement, set in a ballroom.

While Warburg and Kirstein were happy to be able to show their young company on Broadway and to prove that their investments of time, trouble and money had produced dividends, Balanchine regarded the Adelphi season less as a triumphant demonstration than as a valuable experience for his dancers. He knew very well that the few polished artists in whom he took an interest were mixed with others less talented.

The opening program was *Serenade, Alma Mater, Errante* and *Reminiscence.* Balanchine had arranged only three movements of Tchaikovsky's Op. 48 for *Serenade*. (The Tema Russo finale would be added in 1941.) New costumes had been ordered from the French painter Jean Lurçat, and in a photograph they look fussy and hideous. Even apart from the missing movement, the ballet was not yet the wonderful work it became later. (There was, for instance, no man in the Waltz.) Perhaps only the opening Sonatina and the final Elegy were almost as we see them today.

Alma Mater went down well with the audience. They recognized that certain stock American characters had been absorbed for the first time into the exotic medium of ballet. *Errante* was, of course, more a painter's than a choreographer's ballet: the realization of one of Tchelitchev's visions, with fantastic lighting effects. *Reminiscence* was explained, or perhaps excused, in a long program note. The Balanchine who did not give a damn for what anyone thought had an alter ego who was expert at providing the public with what it was supposed to want. His occasional showy, childish or cloyingly sweet ballets were often to music of an obvious kind, which he professed to enjoy. Godard was not a composer to alarm a new public. Kirstein, who recognized *Reminiscence* for what it was, a venial sin more appropriate to de Basil's company than his own, felt all the more furious when John Martin of *The New York Times* wrote that while *Serenade* was "serviceable rather than inspired," *Reminiscence* was "the real hit of the evening." Samuel Chotzinoff in the *Post* wrote, "I liked this number best because I did not have to understand anything." *Serenade* was the least popular work. However, the acclaim the company had received persuaded Warburg to extend the week's season through March 15.

．　．　．

THE EXCURSION of the young dancers from the School on Madison Avenue into the harsh realities of performance on Broadway had an unexpected result. Edward Johnson, a former tenor and the new general manager of the Metropolitan Opera House, asked Balanchine to renovate the dance passages in their operas.

Lew Christensen, who was taking classes at the School, remembered how he heard the news. "Harold and I were out buying tickets at the Adelphi box office, and Lincoln and Balanchine came by and said, 'Would you like to join the company?' Balanchine said, 'I think I'm going to be ballet master at the Met. When that time happens we'd like to have you in the company.' " Christensen went back to vaudeville for a while "to get enough to eat." Then he, his brother Harold and Ruby Asquith, Harold's wife, decided they were finished with vaudeville forever, and Lew joined Balanchine.

There were changes at the School. Vladimirov had been replaced by Anatole Vilzak and his wife Ludmilla Schollar, both former dancers in the Maryinsky and Diaghilev companies. Marie-Jeanne later described how the students adored "the handsome and dashing" Vilzak, but resented his wife, who was ten years his senior and "jealous of him looking at his girls." Yet Schollar was the better teacher. The faculty had also been increased by Muriel Stuart, a former member of Pavlova's mainly British company, who had run a school in San Francisco and worked with modern dancers. She came to Kirstein with an introduction from Martha Graham, proved invaluable and remained with the School longer than any other teacher, finally retiring in 1984.

The Metropolitan Opera's engagement of the American Ballet was announced in the press on August 8, 1935. The first voice to be raised in opposition was John Martin's: "It is deeply to be regretted that once again American artists have been passed by for a high artistic post for which at least half a dozen of them are eminently fitted." He granted that Balanchine was "unusually inventive" and would "grace his new position," but the American Ballet was "still an apprentice group," and Lincoln Kirstein should "get to work starting an American Ballet [*sic*]."

Since the Metropolitan season did not begin until the autumn, the enthusiastic Merovitch had booked the American Ballet for a tour to be preceded by outdoor appearances at Lewisohn Stadium in New York and Robin Hood Dell in Philadelphia. The tour, which was supposed to cover sixty towns in ninety-eight days, opened on October 14 with two performances at the Greenwich High School, Greenwich, Connecticut, followed by one-night stands at Bridgeport and New Haven in Connecticut, Princeton, New Jersey, and Harrisburg and Scranton, Pennsylvania. At Scranton, Merovitch's road manager vanished. Warburg was summoned from New York. According to Anatole Chujoy, there had been no money to pay the orchestra, which, unlike the dancers at that time, was unionized; so the musicians walked out. Ruthanna Boris recalls that the company was summoned to a meeting in the Jermyn Hotel, Scranton, where Balanchine announced, "Dancers.

We have manager. We gave him sixty thousand dollars. He has gone and sixty thousand dollars with him. And you know that list you have, tour: we don't have. And bus is outside. Will you please go in bus to New York. Come to class tomorrow, and we will think what to do."

It was during this tour that Elise Reiman first noticed Balanchine's extraordinary calm in the face of disaster. "I remember a performance of *Reminiscence* . . . when I was in the wings waiting to go on in my part with Holly Howard, the Pas de Trois with Bill Dollar. The floor was like glass. Two people had already fallen, and a third fell right in front of Balanchine and me. Instead of getting furious, he leaned his elbow on the wall and said, 'They fall like snow.' He never got mad."

■   ■   ■

KIRSTEIN was happy to find himself and his company established at the Metropolitan Opera House in November, but Balanchine, who had worked in many European opera houses, was less impressed. Also, he clearly started off on the wrong foot with the opera company, or perhaps vice versa. Looking at the hereditary costumes for his first opera ballets, heavy with dust and history, he demanded that they be cleaned. His request was refused. A slur on the dignity of his dancers was the kind of thing that ruffled his serenity, for he knew that a girl must feel right in order to look right. It was the first hint of the antagonism of the Metropolitan's permanent staff. "They absolutely loathed us," Elise Reiman recalled.

Indeed, as long as the ballet was at the Metropolitan, the dancers' costumes were always the last to be made—and sometimes weren't finished. Edward Warburg remembers that one evening the girl who was to dance in *Carmen* found that she couldn't move in the costume provided for her. "Balanchine said, 'Eddie, go in your car up to the School and get any costume that was made for her and bring it back here. It doesn't make any difference if it is right for the occasion or not.' And so I did, and when I came back, the stage doorman said, 'Hello, Mr. Warburg. What are you doing with that dress?' I said, 'It's the costume of the girl who's got to go on in the ballet twenty minutes from now. They can't use the one that was made, so I brought this from the School.' And he said, 'O.K., Mr. Warburg, but put it under your coat. You have to have a union truck to bring that into this place.' "

The opera season opened with *La Traviata* on December 16, 1935, and before it closed in June 1936 Balanchine had made dances for thirteen operas. Thus began what Reiman has described as "the three most hilarious years" of her life. She and the other young people were astounded at what happened on the vast stage of the opera house. To begin with, there was an overpowering smell of garlic. Then, the noise was appalling. The prompter and the chorus master were shouting above the music. The principal singers used to walk to the back of the stage when they were not singing, clear their throats and spit. Most newspapers relied on their music critics to cover such dancing as they thought worthy of comment, and these gentlemen tended to resent Balanchine's small innovations.

In *Aida* he inserted "genuine" Egyptian belly dances—and also "genuine" Egyptian suntan, which the dancers had trouble washing off because their dressing room was on the floor above that of the chorus, and the water "didn't get up to their tubs." In desperation the boys turned on the fire hose; the water overflowed into the costume department, and Balanchine had a lot of explaining to do.

His Venusberg dances in *Tannhäuser* were inspired by Isadora Duncan in her erotic vein. Even when one of his arrangements scored a success with the public, it did not necessarily please the authorities at the Met. Ruthanna Boris's solo in *Carmen* was much applauded, and the dances in *Aida* stopped the show, but both brought a reproof from Johnson's deputy Edward Ziegler. Opera was singing, and the ballet should not have drawn attention to itself. For Lew Christensen, who had to flirt with Rosa Ponselle, the prima donna, in the tavern of Lillas Pastia, *Carmen* was an ordeal. According to Kirstein, the great lady "refused to rehearse;

she was saving her voice. She sent her own dancing teacher to arrange her stage business with Lew; she would learn it all, somehow, 'later.' When they met for the first time onstage and commenced their routine, she seized a goblet of wine (grapefruit juice), quaffed a gulp, and tossed the rest in his face. Then she pulled down his head and smacked him full on the mouth. For six seconds they were locked. It seemed sincere. In the intermission he said: 'I thought she was trying to make me in front of God and everybody.' "

Among Balanchine's few supporters was Dorothy Kilgallen, the celebrated columnist of the *New York Evening Journal*. Miss Kilgallen wrote: "Mr. George Balanchine is the daring young man who lifted the Metropolitan Ballet out of its petticoats, gave it snake-hips, a dash of hi-di-hi. . . . He put a reptilian wiggle into the torsos of the 'Aida' chorus until the dowagers couldn't believe their lorgnettes." She quoted him as saying, "The critics don't know anything about dancing. . . . They like prima donnas. . . . They are like prima donnas."

Elise Reiman considered that Balanchine "gave the dancers things beyond their technical ability" so as to extend their powers. These dancers could also be grateful that they were earning a small salary for six months of the year. They were not paid during the recess from June to October.

During the first 1935–36 season at the Met, either *Reminiscence, Serenade, Mozartiana* or *Errante* was occasionally given on the same bill as *Hansel and Gretel* or *Cavalleria Rusticana* and *Pagliacci* or in "mixed concerts" of opera extracts and ballets. Then, because the Metropolitan's orchestra knew the music, Kirstein devised and Balanchine arranged dances to extracts from *Die Fledermaus* for a ballet called *The Bat,* which proved to be popular and was danced as a curtain raiser to operas.

In February 1936, Chick Austin commissioned Balanchine to do a ballet for the Hartford Festival. This was a *Serenata*—called *Magic* in honor of Austin, who was an accomplished magician—to an unidentified Mozart composition for eight instruments, with sets

by Tchelitchev. In it, Felia Doubrovska gave her last public performance. The Festival culminated in the Paper Ball on the last
night, in which, in costumes by Tchelitchev and to music by
Nicolas Nabokov, the three heads of the American Ballet—Balanchine, Kirstein and Warburg—appeared as beggars. The role obviously appealed to Balanchine, since almost forty years later he
again played one, this time with Jerome Robbins, in the Stravinsky
Festival of 1972.

Another interruption to Balanchine's work on operas—*Mignon,
Manon, La Juive* and *La Rondine*—in the early days of the year,
Die Meistersinger in February—was the invention of dances for the
Ziegfeld Follies, which had its premiere on January 30. The music
of the *Follies* was composed by Vernon Duke, who, under his
original name of Vladimir Dukelsky, had written *Zéphyr et Flore*
for Diaghilev in 1925; and the lyrics were by Ira Gershwin.

Even more interesting was the musical comedy *On Your Toes,*
which, after an out-of-town preview at the Shubert Theater in
Boston, opened in New York on April 11, 1936. This was Balanchine's first collaboration with Richard Rodgers and Lorenz Hart,
and with the producer Dwight Deere Wiman. The Eakins Press
Choreography describes it as "the first Broadway musical to credit
staged dances as choreography (a practice already customary in
Europe), as well as being the first musical in which the dances were
integrated into the plot, performed by dancers who were also
dramatic characters." The subject was the life of a Russian ballet
company. Monty Woolley played a caricature Diaghilev, and there
was a scene in which all the girl dancers, after taking class, went
up to kiss him. Balanchine suggested that the boys should kiss
him, too.

There was a spoof Oriental "Princess Zenobia Ballet" in the
style of Fokine's *Schéhérazade,* of which Brooks Atkinson, drama
critic of *The New York Times,* wrote: "Tamara Geva, who plays the
wicked ballerina, is so magnificent a mistress of the dance that she
can burlesque it with the authority of an artist on holiday." Geva
noticed that "the balcony caught on before the orchestra [stalls]."

"Slaughter on Tenth Avenue," a sensational number that occurred in Act II, Scene 4, was epoch-making. William Dollar assisted Balanchine in working it out, and Herbert Harper helped him with the tap dancing. Ray Bolger gave an unforgettable performance. Geva, in an interview with Nancy Reynolds, declared: "You bet it was a pretty good musical, a milestone. . . . 'Slaughter' . . . started off as a takeoff of Gypsy Rose Lee. I did a strip. . . . There was one moment when Ray Bolger and I were discovered at the bar. Then we started this love duet, and we had a bottle with us. The bottle passed from one hand to the other while we were dancing in such a way that [nobody] knew where the bottle was going. . . . George was a master of things like this."

After Geva was shot by the jealous Big Boss, a waiter passed a message to Ray Bolger that he, too, would be shot at the moment his dance finished. Then came Bolger's brilliantly frantic tap dance over tables and chairs, which, just as it seemed to be coming to an end, would be repeated "one more time" until the police arrived.

After the New York premiere, Balanchine was introduced at a Russian Easter party to a strikingly pretty blond nineteen-year-old who was a member of the Ballets Russes and had been given the name of Vera Zorina. She congratulated him, and her recollection of that first meeting was, "*He* was very nice, *I* was very nice, *it* was very nice."

．　　．　　．

THAT SPRING, Kirstein, as well as Balanchine, launched out on a new line of his own. He decided to form a group of dancers called Ballet Caravan to tour during the summer recess. This would not only enable members of the American Ballet to earn a small living during the time the Metropolitan was closed; it would also give some of them an opportunity to try their hands at choreography.

The previous December, Tchelitchev had told Kirstein that he was prepared to design a production at the Metropolitan with Balanchine and the American Ballet. The work, on which Balanchine was happy to collaborate, and which the Metropolitan consented to stage as a curtain raiser to *Cavalleria Rusticana,* was Gluck's *Orpheus and Eurydice,* sung by singers in the pit and performed by dancers on the stage. At a house dedicated to "grand" opera, to revive *Orpheus* at all was almost an eccentricity: staging it *à la* Tchelitchev was asking for trouble. To ensure the cooperation of the Met, and so that the painter so admired by Balanchine, Kirstein and Warburg should have a free hand, Warburg undertook to pay for the production, which Kirstein was always to remember as a shining landmark in his life. Orpheus was danced by Lew Christensen, Eurydice by Daphne Vane and Amor by William Dollar.

"ORFEO BACK AT THE MET, BUT PROVES TRAVESTY" proclaimed the *New York World Telegram* the next day. The powerful Olin Downes found the production "absurd"; and in a summary of Balanchine's recent activities a few days later, he wrote, "Of the American Ballet as an element of operatic performance he [the critic] is obliged to speak in terms of great disappointment. In hardly a single instance have the ballets coincided with the operas of which they are a part." "The public liked it," Christensen explained, "but the critics thought it was awful. Of course, they thought everything Balanchine did was awful. . . . He had a hard time, a very hard time." The opera-ballet had only two performances.

In the winter of 1935–36, Stravinsky paid his second visit to the United States, conducting concerts and giving recitals with the violinist Samuel Dushkin. It was probably at the end of this tour, just before his return to France in April 1936, that he dined with Balanchine at his apartment. Lucia Davidova remembers the choreographer describing how he had cooked a delicious dinner and taken particular trouble to obtain two bottles of vintage claret, but Stravinsky arrived with two other bottles under his arm, saying that he had no faith in American wine and had brought his own.

Balanchine's admiration for Stravinsky was unbounded. Robert Craft wrote to me after the choreographer's death: "Igor Stravinsky was really a father figure to George, who several times took the trouble to fly to California to see Stravinsky, sometimes to weep on his shoulder." Stravinsky, for his part, appreciated Balanchine's musical understanding.

Either during the dinner or shortly afterward, Balanchine, Kirstein and Warburg decided to plan a "Stravinsky festival" at the Metropolitan, which would consist of a single program of three ballets by the master. A new work was to be commissioned, and the other two would be *Apollon* and *Le Baiser de la fée*. Balanchine asked merely for "a classical ballet," and on June 30, 1936, on his return to France from a South American tour, Stravinsky wrote to complain that he had not been given exact requirements. According to Kirstein, Malaieff, a friend of Stravinsky's son, came up with the idea of a poker game. The drama, such as it was, would depend on the Joker's ability to represent any card in the pack; but he would be defeated by a royal flush at the end.

In December 1936, the score of *The Card Party* (*Jeu de cartes*) was delivered to New York. Balanchine was fascinated by its rhythms as he tried out an adaptation of the score for the piano and spotted quotations from Rossini's *Barber of Seville,* as well as echoes of other composers. Stravinsky agreed to conduct the two-day, one-program "festival" in April, and Warburg decided to hire the New York Philharmonic, rather than use the Metropolitan's orchestra.

When Stravinsky arrived in New York at the end of March 1937, his busy choreographer was working on his third musical, *Babes in Arms,* again a Dwight Deere Wiman production with music and lyrics by Rodgers and Hart. "Peter's Journey," the Act II ballet in this, was a dream sequence, the first, it is said, to be included in a Broadway musical, so Balanchine had once again broken fresh ground.

Warburg had commissioned *The Card Party,* and he was beseiged by requests from friends to see the first rehearsal, at which Balanchine would set the choreography, so the rehearsal room at 637 Madison Avenue was jammed when Stravinsky came in, smiling and bowing to everyone. Warburg recalls that "he sat down at the piano and ran through a few little runs, and Balanchine came in looking like a dormouse and spoke to him in Russian. After a few exchanges, Balanchine sat down with his back to the mirrors, looked at the kids who were waiting for the great moment when all this would start, stared into space and finally said, 'You,' pointing to a tall girl. Then he pointed to the man who was usually her partner. 'You . . . arabesque.' So they both did an arabesque, and he had them facing each other—like bookends. After studying this carefully, he suddenly turned to them both and said, 'Scram.' The whole thing had been a false start."

Irene Sharaff had used the tarot pack of cards for her costume designs, but Stravinsky objected violently to them. Since his three "deals" were played as a possible real poker game, he wanted them to be easily recognizable to card players in the audience, and he insisted that the dancers resemble modern playing cards. Kirstein noticed that he also curbed Balanchine's prodigality of invention. "At the end of the first deal, where Balanchine had worked out a display of the dancers in a fan-like pattern to simulate cards held in the hand, Stravinsky decided . . . [that] instead of so much variety in the pictures he preferred a repetition of the most effective groupings. . . . On another occasion he composed some additional music to allow for a further development in the choreography."

In the days before music could be taped, the piano reductions to which dancers rehearsed and worked out their counts—which differed from the composer's counts—were often misleading. When a company rehearsed for the first time with an orchestra, usually on the day before the first performance, they were frequently baffled by unsuspected sonorities. Balanchine liked to make his own piano reductions, and as he worked on them he already had the sound of the full orchestra in his ears.

. . .

THERE had not been such a "Stravinsky evening" in the theater since the death of Diaghilev. Lew Christensen found that with

Balanchine's ballets "the character came out as the choreography developed, and a lot happened between the steps"—perhaps the most important things. "You don't just do a couple of pirouettes and walk off and spit on your hands. You work your way into it and work your way out of it." Although only one ballet was totally new, another had never been choreographed by Balanchine before, and, of course, his version of *Apollon* (as opposed to that of Bolm) had never been seen in America. The first American production of *Apollon Musagète*—as it was still called—was more of a landmark than either of the new ballets; and in the modest Christensen the role of Apollo had a great interpreter.

Memories of the Diaghilev production were still vivid in the minds of those who had admired Lifar's Apollo in Paris or London in 1928. Christensen was a totally different type of dancer both physically and temperamentally, and Balanchine took endless pains teaching him the role. Because the hero is onstage throughout and can rest only when he sits to watch the Muses' variations, Christensen found *Apollon* "a very difficult ballet." The coda was "so damned hard. It's like you're driving a team of horses, but you're in a plié with them dragging you back. . . . We used to get through it, but by that time your legs are tired and aching. And when finally . . . you have to climb this cliff . . . it's such a relief that it's like going to Heaven." Christensen discovered that Balanchine did not tell him much about his role. He was merely expected to learn the steps correctly; and the process of learning was a revelation.

He went through each detail with me, *over* and *over* and *over* again. That's how I learned how to do Balanchine technique. That's the reason I could do it kind of well, because he *really* worked on me. . . . I really got his style, his way of thinking. . . . Lifar didn't dance like I did. He danced more—easy. I danced hard, fast, sharp, quick. That's what Balanchine liked about it. I was wondering if he changed it for that one reason—if there was a change. I really don't know. He didn't say anything about it. There were some very fast pirouettes in it—which I'm sure Lifar didn't do . . . that was the hardest damn thing. I practiced that by the hour.

By a curious chance, Elise Reiman, who was to dance Terpsichore, had appeared, when hardly more than a child, in Adolph Bolm's version of *Apollon* at the Library of Congress in 1928. She remembered the old production as "stilted," and found Balanchine's a very different affair. She thought Christensen "stunning and beautiful" in his difficult variation.

Le Baiser de la fée, commissioned by Ida Rubinstein in 1928, was Stravinsky's homage to Tchaikovsky. Musical themes were taken from his piano pieces and songs, notably "None but the Lonely Heart," and Stravinsky read the theme of the composer and his Muse into Hans Christian Andersen's story of the Snow Maiden, whose kiss obliges the young man to leave his mortal bride on the eve of their marriage. Stravinsky, in *Expositions and Developments,* commented: "The fairy's kiss on the heel of the child is also the muse marking Tchaikovsky at his birth—though the muse did not claim Tchaikovsky at his wedding, as she did the young man in the ballet, but at the height of his powers."

Balanchine and his troupe came off better than Stravinsky with the critics, who were invited to the first performance on April 27, 1937. John Martin wrote, "The American Ballet covered itself with honor last night. . . . Balanchine has begun to depart from his previous absorption in seeking for strangeness and novelty. . . . *Apollon* . . . was produced for the Diaghileff Company in 1928, and it bears the strong impress of that period of artiness and affectation. . . . *The Card Party* has humorous episodes. . . . When it has been polished . . . it will be cute if nothing more. . . . *Le Baiser de la fée* is far and away the best work on the bill. . . . It is difficult to remember that the composer of these distinctly minor ballets is also the composer of *Petrushka* and *Les Noces.*"

Samuel Chotzinoff in the *New York Evening Post* found that

"*Appolon* [*sic*] *Musagète* did not sound any better than when I heard it in Washington. Illustrating a dull scenario . . . it shows the celebrated composer in one of his numerous transition periods. . . . The choreography [of *Le Baiser de la fée*] . . . would do just as well for a drama by O'Neill or a tale by Kipling. . . . I suppose The American Ballet acquitted itself splendidly."

If the critics didn't like the music of Stravinsky, the Metropolitan Opera didn't like Balanchine; and Balanchine didn't like either the critics or the Met. It looked for a moment as if his future were to be on Broadway and Kirstein's on the road with Ballet Caravan.

Chapter 5

....

DIVERGING PATHS:

APRIL 1937 - MAY 1941

LTHOUGH the American Ballet and the Metropolitan Opera did not part company until the end of the spring season in 1938, Balanchine and Kirstein had launched out in very different directions two months earlier.

Shortly after the Stravinsky Festival, Balanchine went to Hollywood at the invitation of Sam Goldwyn to make dances for a musical-comedy film, and he insisted that the dancers be recruited from the School of American Ballet. This led to a certain rivalry with Kirstein's Ballet Caravan. William Dollar, Gisella Caccialanza and Annabelle Lyon went with Balanchine, but Lew Christensen, Marie-Jeanne and Ruthanna Boris stayed with Kirstein. According to Christensen, who became ballet master of the touring company, "I stole some of Balanchine's leading dancers, so he refused to

choreograph for us." Yet in private life Balanchine and Christensen got on very well: they both liked cowboy films and used to
go off together to cheap movie houses on Forty-second Street.
Years later, Christensen reflected, "Balanchine was a strange guy.
A guy with his intellect, and he was in love with cowboy movies."

By mid-August 1937, Ballet Caravan had bookings into February 1938. This meant they could not fulfill commitments with the
Metropolitan Opera, so they decided to divide themselves into two
companies. Lincoln Kirstein also resigned from the board of the
American Ballet that May, and both Balanchine and Warburg
resigned from the board of the School.

Meanwhile, Balanchine was basking in the California sunshine.
In May he and Kolya Kopeikine had traveled by train across the
United States for the first time. When they arrived at the Los
Angeles railroad station, they were met by reporters and photogra-
phers. Balanchine refused to smile because it was too early in the
morning.

"But everyone smiles!"

"I am not everyone. I am myself. Only one person."

He and Kopeikine took a house together, and George Volodine,
a dancer who was devoted to Balanchine, came to manage it for
them.

According to Garson Kanin, who was working for Goldwyn at
the time, Balanchine made an unprecedented impression on Hollywood, the press, the studio and Goldwyn himself. The producer
was jealous of the fame of Flo Ziegfeld, the Broadway impresario,
so he had hired George Gershwin, the scriptwriter Ben Hecht,
Balanchine and his American Ballet to give the film *Goldwyn
Follies* a touch of class. Kanin thought the last group "made
Hollywood history." Their requirements and demands were unheard of. Kanin recalled:

Goldwyn cheerfully ordered a new building—a dance studio to be constructed on a faraway part of the lot. . . . He sensed . . . that he was
somehow entertaining royalty. The American ballet had brought its own

rehearsal musicians, wardrobe attendants, makeup artists. . . . No one except members of the company were allowed inside at any time, including Samuel Goldwyn.

For Balanchine, the lure of Goldwyn's film was its composer, George Gershwin, who unfortunately fell ill shortly after the choreographer arrived. Both Georges had hoped they might use the symphonic poem *An American in Paris.*

With his still somewhat limited English, Balanchine had trouble explaining his ideas to Goldwyn and the studio staff and understanding what they wanted from him. He therefore telegraphed to Natasha Nabokov, "Help me! Come!" Nicolas Nabokov was teaching at Worth University in upstate New York, and she was free. She came at once, accompanied by her small son.

During the first weeks in Hollywood, a period of discussions and experiments, Balanchine had time to make new acquaintances, and Mme. Nabokov witnessed several odd encounters. Balanchine had long been a fan of Fred Astaire and Ginger Rogers, and admired the latter's beauty. Muriel King, the Chanel of Hollywood, who dressed Ginger Rogers and Katharine Hepburn, doted on Balanchine and decided to stage a surprise meeting. She asked him to dinner. Balanchine told Natasha Nabokov, who was in on the secret, that he didn't want to go. She tried at once to persuade him. "I'm shy," he insisted. "You know I don't like parties." "But there's going to be a wonderful dessert!" At last he agreed. Before dinner Muriel King took him by the arm and led him into another room. "There's somebody who wants to meet you."

"Who, me?" he asked. (He could never imagine why anyone might want to meet him.)

Ginger Rogers sat waiting. Balanchine was speechless, but after she put him at his ease, they got on well. Later he went to visit her at the studio and found her on the set, reading a book. "What are you reading about?" he asked. "Christian Science." That was the end.

The composer George Antheil was in Hollywood and had established an intimate relationship with a young lady whom Balanchine also found attractive. "I'll introduce you," said Antheil. "But she's your friend—" "Take her," said Antheil generously. The girl came to supper, and Balanchine asked her what she would like to drink. "Vodka? Whiskey? Champagne?" "Do you have any beer?" she asked. Balanchine was startled. "Why do you like beer?" "Because it makes me belch so nicely."

Once again, it was the end.

According to Garson Kanin, for an entire month Balanchine refused to let Goldwyn know what was going on behind the closed doors of his ballet studio. Rumors spread. But Goldwyn admired Balanchine and persuaded himself that all the doubts and stories reported by the press were "free publicity." Nobody pointed out to him that the free publicity was costing about $15,000 a day.

· · ·

GOLDWYN had engaged as ballerina for his film the dancer Vera Zorina, whose real name was Brigitta Hartwig. She had been born in Berlin of a German father and a Norwegian mother, and had studied ballet in Berlin and London. When Dolin engaged her to act and dance in a play, her good looks made such an impression on Massine that he invited her to join the de Basil company. During the two years she remained with them, she danced leading roles in several ballets by Massine, with whom she had an unhappy romance. When he first made advances to her, she was sexually innocent, and she fell in love with him. Massine treated her abominably.

A London production of *On Your Toes* was scheduled, and her agent sent her to audition for Tamara Geva's role; she got it. Although both she and Jack Whiting were acclaimed in the leads, and although her personal success was such that she aroused the interest of the great British film producer Alexander Korda, the UFA studios in Berlin and a number of Hollywood scouts, *On Your Toes* was not a success in England. Her agent then arranged for her to make a screen test for Samuel Goldwyn's movie, and the movie magnate was delighted with the result. Zorina was dazzled by her prospects, but she was more interested in a stage career than in films, and she made conditions. Dwight Deere Wiman had spoken to her about a new musical, and she delayed signing with Goldwyn until she was certain that Balanchine, whose ballets she admired though she had met him only once, would be working on *Goldwyn Follies.* Then she agreed to a seven-year contract.

When he was told of Goldwyn's choice, Balanchine cabled Zorina at once, suggesting that she come to Hollywood to discuss their work even before her contract stipulated, promising that they would "have much fun."

On July 10, the day after Zorina's arrival, George Gershwin died of a brain tumor, aged thirty-eight. He had composed five songs for the movie, but no ballet music.

Production could not be held up. Balanchine suggested that Vernon Duke be hired to complete the score, and he was summoned from New York. Meanwhile, talks continued with Ira Gershwin, the composer's brother and librettist, about using *An American in Paris* for a ballet sequence. A week passed before Balanchine visited Zorina. During this time she was being scrutinized by Goldwyn's makeup department and hairdressers, who removed moles, filed and capped her teeth and tried to make her as close as possible to the Hollywood ideal. She also had driving lessons, while her mother went house-hunting in Beverly Hills. Eventually Balanchine called to ask her to dinner.

Zorina, whom nobody ever called anything but Brigitta to her face, now found herself plunged into a Russian "family," as she had been when she joined the Ballets Russes three years before. Although, as she wrote later, "Russians tend to be clannish, this group did not make me feel like an outsider but surrounded me with affection—mostly due to Balanchine, who was kind, gentle, and a marvelous host." Brigitta was soon learning from Balanchine in class as well as rehearsing the ballet he had prepared.

I could see [she wrote] how differently from Massine Balanchine approached choreography. His impulse was always music. . . . He played a piece over and over again on the piano until it was entirely in his head. He had no . . . diagrams with choreographic notes, but would begin choreographing by lightly touching a dancer's hand and telling him or her how or where to move. He was certain what he wanted but sometimes stood still as if listening to inner music. . . . There was no sign of rapid re-creation of preconceived ideas, but the unfolding of steps and patterns born at that moment. . . . For an inexperienced choreographer, it is a nightmare to have dancers standing around waiting to be told what the next step is. Or worse, trying choreographic sequences which do not work out. The dancers . . . sense very quickly whether a choreographer is in command or not. George's "silences" were always pregnant with ideas ready to emerge into action—with him it was merely a process of selection.

She was also impressed by Balanchine's instinctive understanding of how to make dance effective on the screen. Although he respected the technical expertise of the cameramen, sound men and cutters, he would quietly and "conspiratorially" point out the solution to a problem, never causing offense but rather a sense of relief. It was therefore galling that Goldwyn failed to appreciate the thought Balanchine had put into *An American in Paris.* The action was to take place in an International Exhibition. Sets representing the pavilions of different nations were erected all over a vast sound stage, and Balanchine timed every sequence with a stopwatch. When Goldwyn was shown the ballet, it annoyed him to find that he and his entourage were obliged, every few minutes, to have their chairs moved and walk to another set. He left in a huff and canceled the ballet, wasting four weeks of work.

Balanchine was disgusted and felt that drastic action was called for. Natasha Nabokov advised him to disappear for a few days; she would inform the studio that he had left for New York. He took a small apartment over a shop. The art director Richard Day came to North Fairfax Avenue to look for him. Natasha said he had gone

THE FAMILY: *1. Andrei, Georgi and Tamara Balanchivadze;
2. Maria Nicolaievna von Almedingen, called Vassilieva after her mother; 3. Meliton
Antonovich Balanchivadze, drawn by his daughter, Tamara.*

4

5

4. Andrei, Tamara and Georgi at a fair; 5. Maria Balanchivadze, Georgi and Tamara at the dacha *in Finland, with a student friend and Andrei in the background.*

6

6. *Georgi in Finland, aged about ten; his cropped hair suggests that he had already been accepted at the Maryinsky Ballet School.*

APOLLO: 7. *Serge Lifar and Alexandra Danilova in the original Diaghilev production of* Apollon Musagète *(1928)*. 8. *Edward Villella as Apollo (1950s)*. 9. *Lew Christensen in the first American production (1937)*.

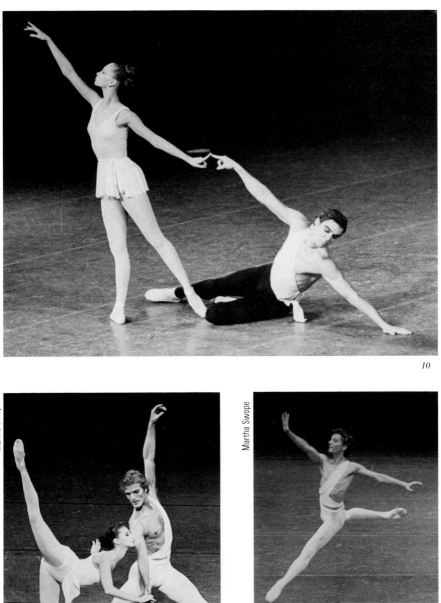

*10. Jacques d'Amboise and Suzanne Farrell (1960s). 11. Peter Martins
and Suzanne Farrell (1970s). 12. Ib Andersen (1980s).*

13

14

15

13. *Balanchine and Vera Nemchinova in the pas de deux from* Aurora's Wedding *(1925).*
14. *Tamara Geva in* Errante *(1935).* 15. *Tamara Toumanova in* Cotillon *(1936).*

16

17

16. Balanchine's first American ballet, Serenade, *shown
here in a later production. 17. Vera Zorina rehearsing with Balanchine
for the movie of* On Your Toes *(1939).*

18

19

20

18. Concerto Barocco *(1941): Marie-Jeanne, William Dollar and*
Mary Jane Shea. 19. Todd Bolender as Phlegmatic in The Four Temperaments *(1948).*
20. Maria Tallchief and Francisco Moncion in The Firebird *(1949).*

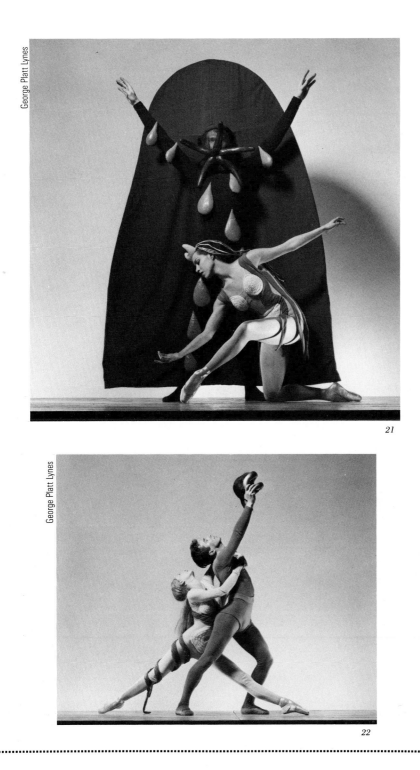

21

22

ORPHEUS: *21. Maria Tallchief and Edward Bigelow;*
22. Tanaquil Le Clercq and Nicholas Magallanes.

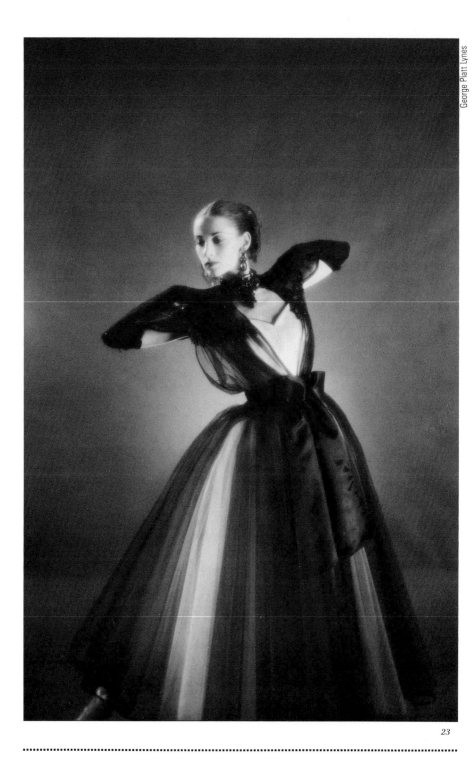

23. *Tanaquil Le Clercq in* La Valse *(1951).*

Martha Swope

24

Martha Swope

25

24. *Edward Villella and Karin von Aroldingen in* The Prodigal Son *(1960s).*
25. *Maria Tallchief and Jerome Robbins rehearsing for the first revival of* The Prodigal Son *(1950).*

Martha Swope

26

Martha Swope

27

THE NUTCRACKER: *26. The Dance of the Snowflakes (1982); 27. Maria Tallchief as the Sugar Plum Fairy (1954).*

Martha Swope

Martha Swope

28

29

28. Edward Villella as Candy Cane (1960s); 29. Suzanne Farrell and Peter Martins as the Sugar Plum Fairy and her Cavalier (1970s).

AGON: *(1957): 30. Balanchine and Stravinsky at a rehearsal.*

Martha Swope

Martha Swope

Martha Swope

31

32

33

31, 32, 33. Diana Adams and Arthur Mitchell.

34

35

LIEBSLIEDER WALZER (1960): 34. Jillana and Conrad Ludlow,
Violette Verdy and Nicholas Magallanes, Melissa Hayden and Jonathan Watts,
Diana Adams and William Carter; 35. Violette Verdy and Nicholas Magallanes,
with Robert Irving and Louise Sherman at the piano.

away. Day asked permission to search the house. It was given, but there was no sign of the missing choreographer.

Balanchine decided to disappear even farther from the studio; he, Brigitta, Mrs. Hartwig, Natasha, her son Ivan and Kopeikine set off in two cars for Lake Arrowhead in the San Bernardino Mountains. Brigitta's driving in the Los Angeles traffic made Balanchine nervous, and when it came to the hairpin bends of the climb he asked if he might take the wheel to try out her new car. The party arrived at dusk, and after dinner, Brigitta wrote, "George and I went for a long walk. It was a beautiful night, with the lake looking mysterious in the dark and huge pines silhouetted against the starlit sky."

Although Brigitta was spectacularly beautiful, with her wide-apart blue-gray eyes, delicate nose, wide, well-formed mouth, good complexion and golden hair, Balanchine had not fallen in love with her at first sight. It was Lake Arrowhead that cast the spell from which there would be no escape for the next decade.

In spite of the thirteen-year difference in age between them, Balanchine and Brigitta had their European backgrounds in common. He had spent part of his childhood in Finland, and she had been brought up by her Norwegian mother. Both had known the snow and darkness of northern winters; it was a bond between them in California. He told her about his training at the Imperial School; and she told him about her disastrous relationship with Massine. This experience had left her, as she confessed, "incapable of trusting and giving myself in love to another human being." Yet, she wrote "I knew George was good, and I felt safe and protected when we were together. He had something trustworthy and priestlike about him. . . . I called him my mystical Prince Myshkin and became utterly, completely, and totally devoted to him." But Brigitta could not respond to the intensity of George's love; and "he accepted that it would take time."

The quarrel with Goldwyn was patched up. The boss had learned his lesson and did not interfere again. What had been planned as the second ballet was rehearsed and filmed first. It had a *Romeo and Juliet* theme, with classical-dancing Montagues and tap-dancing Capulets in a battle of ballet versus modern. Goldwyn got a shock when he saw the laundry strung across the Italian street scene (a brilliant touch of Balanchine's), but when this was whisked away he enjoyed the "dance war" and admired the pas de deux of Zorina and William Dollar.

Balanchine's idea for the other new ballet was startling in 1937. The setting was a circular stage surrounded by columns with a pool in the middle and, at the back, the statue of a rearing white horse (suggested by Chirico's décor for *Le Bal*). As a poet stands musing, a water nymph rises slowly from the pool and dances on the water. Girls in ball gowns appear to dress her for the waltz. A storm interrupts the dancing, and the nymph is seen seated on the white horse, her draperies floating and gradually blown away by the wind. Finally she returns to the pool. As Balanchine described it to Brigitta, "Her body disappears . . . until only her head is visible, and then she puts her cheek on the water like pillow and she is gone like sun disappearing in ocean."

Brigitta was amazed. Even though she would emerge from the pool looking, as Balanchine said, *"very* sexy" with wet golden material clinging to her body, she knew she would have to hold her breath underwater; and the water would have to become glass for her to dance on it. Gregg Toland, the cameraman, was enthusiastic about Balanchine's idea of sinking the camera into a trough at floor level so as to make the dancers look taller. Many technical difficulties had to be overcome, but the ballet made film history.

In the course of the filming, Balanchine paid Goldwyn back for his rejection of *An American in Paris.* During one take, after Zorina had disappeared into the pool, Dollar, as the poet, ran to the brink to stare after her, lost his balance and fell in. When Goldwyn came to see the cut and edited ballet, Balanchine left the big splash tacked on at the end. Goldwyn loved the ballet, but "when the lights went up he remained silent, true to his promise of non-interference. . . . He could not afford to have his 'mad' choreographer walk off again in the middle of the production. He was greatly relieved when George confessed his joke and ran the real ending."

On September 1 Balanchine and Brigitta had a quarrel because he confessed to her about his girl friends. Next day he called her "as if nothing had happened" and took her to try on wigs. His work on *Goldwyn Follies* was completed on schedule, but he lingered a few days longer. Brigitta had to remain in Hollywood to film the "acting" part of her role. Some of this was shot at Lake Arrowhead, and Balanchine drove there with her. One night they cooked dinner together—"as if we were married," wrote Zorina, "and ate by candlelight." On October 10 it was "a very sad goodbye from George." Roses came with the message "I love you" in Norwegian. It was the title of Grieg's most sentimental song.

After Balanchine had gone, Brigitta did not lack admirers. Goldwyn himself had a crush on her. More important to Brigitta, however, was the question: Would Goldwyn allow her to make the Dwight Deere Wiman musical *I Married an Angel,* with music and lyrics by Rodgers and Hart?

■   ■   ■

DURING the summer of 1937, Felix Warburg died, leaving an immense fund that his son Edward was to administer for charitable purposes. Edward, who had already resigned from the School, felt compelled to resign from the board of the American Ballet. He gave all the company's properties to Balanchine, who, since Kirstein was working with Ballet Caravan, found himself sole director of the American Ballet. Back from Hollywood with his dancers, he prepared to rehearse for the Metropolitan's 1937–38 season.

Toward the end of 1937 or early in 1938, *The New Yorker* magazine sent a reporter named Richard O. Boyer to the School to interview Lincoln Kirstein. He watched Vilzak holding a class and Balanchine conducting a rehearsal. When he settled down to write his piece, which was entitled "Americans Dance, Too," he had to decide on "an angle," and the line he took was to emphasize the utter strangeness of it all. It was extraordinary to him that a hairy man in a bathing suit could "flap his arms daintily in a gesture of flight." Balanchine was portrayed as exotic; and Kirstein, in a far from sunny mood, appeared about as optimistic as an Old Testament prophet.

"I have learned not to hope," Kirstein told him. "Transplanting ballet in this country is like trying to raise a palm tree in Dakota." He insisted that American ballet dancers were not inferior to European talent, but "the men especially are an unhappy crew, since most Americans become skittish at the mention of a male ballet dancer. . . . In short, there is something sinister about the whole business."

"Sinister" was the word of the afternoon. No need to ask against whom the following crack was directed: "Some choreographers fall in love with a ballerina and write ballets to bring out her best points. They're nothing but memorials to his private passion. It's really rather sinister." When Kirstein introduced him to Balanchine, Boyer noticed "the redness of his lips, his brown eyes, the sweep of his black hair. His voice was sleek, like a cat's purr." But, Boyer continued, "Kirstein drew me aside. 'He's Georgian,' " he whispered admiringly. 'Stalin's type. He seems as soft as silk, but he's like steel. He's really rather sinister.' "

Balanchine had another appointment, and the reporter watched Dollar rehearse *Apollon.* Then Holly Howard complained to him about the price of ballet shoes—four dollars a pair; and Christensen had a go at "goddam foreigners." "They make a couple of spins, and American audiences think they're wonderful." He alleged that foreign choreographers never explained to the dancer what their ballets were supposed to be about. This can only have been a dig at Balanchine.

· · ·

BRIGITTA arrived back in New York with her mother on Christmas Eve, and Balanchine gave her earrings from Cartier. Three days later he took her to *Tannhäuser* at the Metropolitan Opera.

In later years Brigitta grew angry at all the talk about Balanchine's unrequited love. "I loved George, and I love him to this day," she kept insisting. But there are different ways of loving, and she acknowledged in her autobiography that although Balanchine became increasingly important to her "as teacher, guide, mentor, and closest intimate friend" she could not "match" his love. Balanchine's soul was clearly no longer his own: his obsession was like that of the Scotsman for the Sylphide in the old ballet. He was almost bound to be dissatisfied. The mere fact that there are moments in such a relationship when the loved one's feelings do not coincide in perfect harmony with those of her lover gives him a sense of the impossibility of their union. He wants nothing less than everything; and his tragic intensity does not make him more attractive. Indeed, to be loved too much can be very annoying to the object of devotion. Brigitta confessed as much.

In the early days of 1938 Balanchine asked her to marry him, but she said, "Let's wait." This made him "depressed, jealous, withdrawn." They went together to see Thomas Dekker's *Shoe-maker's Holiday* at the Mercury Theater, and the twenty-three-year-old Orson Welles, one of the new repertory company's founders, directors and actors, fell in love with Brigitta.

On February 18, after dining with Balanchine, Brigitta wrote in her diary, "George is *so* tragic, it is almost unbearable." On the nineteenth, *Goldwyn Follies* opened in New York to considerable acclaim. On the twentieth, the American Ballet danced *Serenade* at the Met, and Brigitta thought it was the best ballet she had ever seen. On the twenty-fifth, she wrote in her diary: "Dinner with Orson Welles. I have never enjoyed anything more. . . . How we talked and understood each other. He is wonderful and for the first time since Léonide [Massine] I felt my heart pounding and hands trembling."

Edward Johnson had decided to dispense with the services of the American Ballet, and he wrote on March 19, 1938, to inform Balanchine of the fact. On April 12, the day before *I Married an Angel* opened in New Haven, Balanchine gave his views on the subject to a journalist. "I try to adapt myself to the Metropolitan

. . . but no use. The tradition of the Metropolitan is bad ballet. I cannot do bad ballet . . . [Mr. Johnson] is an artist, and he could do fine things, but he has no wings. . . . These people [the rich box-holders] have been buying tickets . . . for many years and they have never seen the first act of any opera. If the Met wants new operas, let it take all the first acts and put them together in threes. . . ."

Happy to be back on the stage, Brigitta had enjoyed the rehearsals of *Angel* and considered her "dream part" of the angel married to a human "practically foolproof." Balanchine had thrown himself with childish enthusiasm into planning the winter "Honeymoon Ballet" for Brigitta, as if it were a fairy-tale honeymoon he himself was going to enjoy with her, or an excursion into their youth in the frozen north. The happy couple left in a sled "drawn by real huskies." Brigitta felt that George's love for her "spilled over" into this dance. Even so, there was at least one alarming stunt. Balanchine made her enter poised in arabesque on the boot of a roller skater, and the young man had difficulty in stopping dead at the footlights on cue. "George tried to reassure me. 'You see, will be okay. Looks fantastic—just like ice skating in St. Moritz.' " But when the roller-skating boy fell on top of Brigitta on the second night in New Haven, Balanchine decided to cut him out.

There was torrential rain on opening night in New York, but Brigitta received "thunderous applause." Balanchine himself had repainted her dressing room as a surprise.

During the post-opening supper party at Sardi's, Zorina's crowds of admirers made Balanchine jealous and miserable, and he talked nonsense. He was incapable of competition in a worldly milieu. Even before he came to America he had loved movies and been a fan of certain stars. Now he had created a movie star of his own, and this was the result.

Brooks Atkinson called the "Honeymoon Ballet" "the most entrancing ballet the musical comedy has staged for some time"; John Martin found that "George Balanchine has clinched his right to the title of the first choreographer of Broadway." *Angel* ran throughout the year and into 1939.

The American Ballet now existed only on paper, but Balanchine had employed some of its dancers in *Angel,* and he would use more in subsequent musicals. Still, if Zorina had not put everything else out of his mind, he might have been tempted by a gypsy life with Kirstein's touring troupe. Indeed, Ballet Caravan was getting more bookings, embarking on longer tours and enjoying greater success than ever before. In Chicago it launched the most popular of all its creations, Eugene Loring's *Billy the Kid,* with music by Aaron Copland. It was ballet's first Western.

On October 12, the Ballet Russe de Monte-Carlo opened in New York at the Metropolitan Opera House. This was not the de Basil company, but one directed by Massine and backed by Sergei Den-ham, which had split away from it. Its title, Ballet Russe in the singular, was a way of distinguishing it from the companies run by de Basil and Blum. Sol Hurok, who had sponsored six seasons of the de Basil Ballet and was now presenting Massine's troupe, had acquired almost a monopoly on ballet in America. The critics who had slighted Balanchine's young Americans were more favorable to the foreigners. Martin wrote of their "freshness."

Balanchine continued to work for Broadway. He arranged dances for *The Boys from Syracuse* (a musical version of Shakespeare's *Comedy of Errors*), which ran for 235 performances, and for *Great Lady,* with music by Frederick Loewe, which opened a week later and ran for only twenty. Since *I Married an Angel* was still playing, he could almost claim—not that he was given to claiming—that he had three shows running on Broadway simultaneously.

· · ·

MRS. HARTWIG and Brigitta were living in an apartment at the Ritz Towers: thither Natasha Nabokov, Nicolas Kopeikine and George Volodine were bidden to a late Christmas Eve supper, which would take place after Brigitta had finished her second performance that day—for it was a Saturday. At midnight there was still no sign of her or of Balanchine; everyone waited, while Kopeikine played the piano. Charles Laskey, Brigitta's partner, lived on Staten Island, and he had arranged for Balanchine and Brigitta to be married there at the Borough Hall in St. George that morning. When the happy couple at last arrived at the Ritz Towers, no explanation was given. There was a distribution of Christmas presents. Balanchine's present to his beloved was an ermine coat, for which he had personally chosen every skin. Natasha was expecting Balanchine, who lived near her, to drive her home, but as the hours went by and he showed no sign of leaving the apartment, she fell back, mystified, on Kopeikine, who lived in quite a different direction. No announcement was made that night.

Balanchine's father had died in November 1937, so it was to his mother that he wrote, telling her of his marriage. The letter is undated.

11 East 77th Street
New York

Dear Mamoushka,

I want to give you the pleasure of a good piece of news. I got married a few days ago and am asking for your parental blessing. My wife is called Brigitta. She is of Norwegian origin. I enclose her photo.

She and I were making a film in Hollywood. She is a splendid dancer and actress. I talk to her in English and French, and at the moment she understands about two words of Russian. I shall gradually be sending you photographs of various theater and film productions.

The last film which I made in Hollywood with Brigitta was called "Goldwyn Follies." In it I made use of an entirely new principle of dancing on the screen. This summer I am again going to Hollywood to produce a new film. I do not think our films reach you in the Caucasus.

Mamoushka, ask Andryusha to have his ballet copied out, I shall send him whatever money is needed. And also send me Georgian herbs which are used in making *kharsho* [meat soup] and other dishes. And send me the recipe for making *satsivi* [cold chicken with walnuts]. I love cooking myself. And also I would like to have a black *boorka* [felt coat], write and tell me how much it will be and I shall send you the money.

Brigitta and I send our love to all of you and wish you health and happiness.

Your loving Georgi

Balanchine went to Florida after Christmas—Brigitta could not, of course, leave New York—and the press was not informed of their marriage until after his return in the middle of January 1939. A picture of Brigitta and Balanchine dancing at the Stork Club was captioned "Angel on Earth." Lucia Davidova had rented the Balanchines a self-contained duplex apartment with its own entrance on East Seventy-seventh Street. They left most of the furnishing to Mrs. Hartwig. Balanchine had his piano in the dining room. When a small fire broke out on February 23, the *New York Daily News* published a picture of the newly married pair, with the caption "Angel Fights Fire. Smoke got in her eyes. Vera Zorina, star of *I Married an Angel,* and husband George Balanchine examine damage. . . . The Angel helped firemen put out the blaze." To the press, Balanchine had become "Zorina's husband."

In February 1939, *I Married an Angel* closed in New York and went on a nationwide tour. It played six weeks in Chicago, and there Balanchine joined his wife for Russian Easter and spent three days cooking *pashka, kulich* and other delicacies in the small kitchen of a suite at the Ambassador Hotel. He and Brigitta also tried in vain to have their marriage ratified in a Catholic Church. There were obstacles. Brigitta, though a Catholic, was not yet an American citizen; George had been married in the Russian Orthodox Church under a Soviet régime but could produce no evidence that he was divorced. The priest waved them aside. They were too depressed ever again to attempt marriage in church. Besides, Balanchine did not want to create complications for Tamara Geva, who had married in America even before his arrival.

In May 1939, Balanchine and Brigitta set off for Hollywood to make a film of *On Your Toes* for Warner Brothers. Eddie Albert was Brigitta's partner in "Slaughter on Tenth Avenue," but since he could not tap, Balanchine "found a superb black tap dancer and cut back and forth from Eddie Albert's face and torso to the tap dancer's legs and feet [and] it worked perfectly." As soon as the film was completed, Goldwyn lent Zorina to Twentieth Century–Fox for another. *I Was an Adventuress* also needed a ballet, and in this Balanchine realized his ambition to conduct a symphony orchestra.

By the end of the year, Balanchine was working on a new musical, *Keep Off the Grass,* and Brigitta had signed up to appear in *Louisiana Purchase,* but the only new work of Balanchine's seen by the public in 1939 was the film of *On Your Toes.*

In November 1939, Massine's Ballet Russe de Monte-Carlo, which had been obliged to cancel its London summer date because of the outbreak of war, opened at the Metropolitan and broke all box-office records for ballet at the opera house.

Since 1938, plans had been afoot for the formation of a new American dance company, which was eventually to be called Ballet Theatre; during 1939 the planners were busier than ever. The organization started as an offshoot of the Mordkin Ballet, which had enjoyed an intermittent life since the 1920s. One of Mordkin's most talented pupils was Lucia Chase. Ballet Theatre came into being through the efforts of Mordkin; Rudolf Orthwine, a businessman; Richard Pleasant, an entrepreneur; and Lucia Chase. The fact that Chase had inherited a million dollars from her short-lived husband, Robert Ewing, was relevant. The temperamental Mordkin was an undistinguished choreographer, but Pleasant and Chase had grandiose ideas: they wanted the best of everything, whether it was Russian, English or American. Balanchine was asked to work for Ballet Theatre, but refused.

When "America's first Ballet Theatre," "the greatest ballets of all times, staged by Greatest Collaboration in Ballet History" opened at the Center Theater on January 11, 1940, William Dollar was in the first ballet, Fokine's *Les Sylphides,* and the second was *The Great American Goof* by Eugene Loring, who had been offered a higher salary than Ballet Caravan could afford to pay him. It cannot have been a happy moment for Kirstein. At the same time, he must have realized what such an assemblage of talent and famous names was costing someone—presumably Lucia Chase. (In fact, the three-week season, though moderately successful in such a huge theater, showed a loss of $200,000.) The *Herald Tribune* exulted: "Here at last is a solidly American organization."

Members of Ballet Caravan did manage to appear in the Ford Motor Company's five-hundred-seat theater at the New York World's Fair. "The pretext for our dancing [wrote Kirstein] was the fate of the horse in the path of the automobile. . . . We never knew whether or not it sold a dozen automobiles, but for six months it provided food and rent for forty dancers in . . . an eighteen-minute ballet entitled *A Thousand Times Neigh!* every hour on the hour, twelve times a day. . . ."

William Dollar did the choreography for this farcical ballet, and the company was divided into two groups led by Marie-Jeanne and Leda Anchutina. In September, Marie-Jeanne left to appear with the Ballet Russe. Balanchine, who had already staged his *Baiser de la fée* for that company during their March season, was going to revive three more of his old ballets in October, and he wanted Marie-Jeanne for *Serenade.*

The Tema Russo, which Balanchine now decided to add to *Serenade,* was written by Tchaikovsky as a lively finale, but the choreographer placed it third, so as to retain the Elegy as a dramatic ending. Like the much-worked plate of an etcher, Balanchine's first ballet conceived for American dancers, begun six years before, at last arrived at its more or less final "state," and "prints" could be made and sent throughout the world.

Although there are slow sculptural episodes in *Serenade*—the opening ritual, for example, where the strange band of women are aligned, as it appears, to salute the moon, and the beginning and end of the Elegy—the most novel and wonderful element of the work is the surge of Balanchine's corps de ballet. The unprecedented speed, first seen in the central allegro section of the Sonatina, with which the girls sweep across and twirl around is a quality that has been associated ever since with Balanchine and America. It necessitated a new kind of partnering—a pulling-apart or a brief "interlocking of horns." The girls rush at the boy, either to fling themselves away or to be thrown aside, or, after a series of wild twists, to collapse on the floor. Nowhere in the ballet is there a touch of sentiment, and the absence of a smile during the whole work is never noticed.

In the Ballet Russe *Serenade,* Marie-Jeanne danced all the ballerina roles, which in the past had been shared by two, three or more dancers, and in later years would be thus distributed again. Her appearance with the Ballet Russe was hailed by the press not as a defection from Kirstein's American company but as an accolade bestowed on a humble twenty-year-old native dancer by the illustrious Russians. In 1941 she was invited to judge a scholarship contest at the School of American Ballet. There were more than a hundred entrants; among the three successful ones was an eleven-year-old named Tanaquil Le Clercq.

.   .   .

HUROK booked Colonel de Basil's company, now known as the Original Ballet Russe, which had been touring Australia since the outbreak of war in Europe, to appear at the Fifty-first Street Theatre immediately after their rivals, the Ballet Russe de Monte-Carlo. Whether or not the public was confused as to which "Russian Ballet" they were seeing, they flocked in. Hurok therefore had two exotic troupes on his books. The Original Ballet Russe beat even the record run of its predecessors and did not close until January 12, 1941.

During this "bad time," Kirstein poured out articles denouncing Slav kitsch and exalting the classical tradition of which Balanchine—he hoped against hope—was the greatest exponent. And Balanchine continued to choreograph musical comedies.

In 1940, the year Balanchine became an American citizen, Balanchine built a house at Fort Salonga, near Northport, Long Island, as a surprise for Brigitta, and would not let her see it till it was finished. Someone gave it the awkward name of "Balarina," incorporating the first syllable of his surname with the last two of hers, but they never used it. Their first night there, the house was blessed in the Russian way with bread and salt. Brigitta drove herself home every night after the performance, but this did little to mitigate Balanchine's sense of the impossibility of love. He lost his self-possession and cried when he had dinner with friends. Natasha Nabokov scolded him. "You are even getting uglier," she said.

Only work could provide a temporary consolation. Stravinsky had moved to America in 1939; his first wife was dead, and he was married to Vera Sudeikina. In default of a new ballet score, there were several of his compositions not written expressly for dancing that Balanchine considered danceable. What ballerina could do justice to a new Stravinsky ballet?

Toumanova was back in New York with the de Basil company. One night, after she had danced *Swan Lake,* Balanchine brought Stravinsky and Tchelitchev to her dressing room. "We want to give you a present—a diamond necklace," he said. This was a figure of speech for a ballet to Stravinsky's Concerto in D for violin and orchestra. The dancers were to be only partly visible, like apparitions, dreams, insectlike or vegetable creatures appearing out of a dark night.

"Will people understand?" asked Balanchine.

Balustrade opened on January 22, 1941, with the composer conducting. To judge from old and rather bad photographs, the lovely designs of the genius Tchelitchev, not for the first time, ruined a ballet. Brigitta thought so. In retrospect, she wondered if it might have been while watching *Balustrade* that Balanchine first realized how much his ballets would benefit if costumes were reduced to the minimum. There were only three performances: presumably "people," including Hurok and Colonel de Basil, had *not* "understood."

John Martin wrote regretting that Russians, like Stravinsky, Tchelitchev and Balanchine, were replacing American artists. Brigitta was furious about this comment, but her husband told her never to give a critic the satisfaction of showing that he had hurt your feelings: "On the contrary, if you meet one, say, 'Ah, good evening! Nice to see you. Are you in New York?' " "People said he was indifferent," she wrote. "He was not. He simply hid his disappointment better than anyone I know."

．　．　．

BALANCHINE'S appearances at the School of American Ballet had been infrequent for several years, but the School was flourishing. Natalie Molostwoff, a beautiful Russian girl of Armenian descent, who was engaged in 1938 as assistant to Eugenie Ouroussow (and who was still with the School in 1987), witnessed the period of transition between 1938 and 1940. She found the tyranny of Dmitriev insupportable: "Everyone was happy till he arrived about midday, then the temperature dropped." In 1939, Kirstein had started negotiations to buy Dmitriev's shares; and, in 1940, the sad, unloved Russian was able to retire in comfortable circumstances and spend his winters in Florida. He was so sure that the School would collapse when he ceased to rule it that he gave Eugenie and Natalie letters of recommendation to serve as references when they looked for other jobs. Yet he continued loyal to the institution he had helped to found and of which he had been president. When Anatole Oboukhov arrived in New York with the de Basil Company in 1940, Dmitriev advised Kirstein to engage him because he was an excellent teacher. His advice was taken, and Oboukhov remained with the School until his death in 1962.

On March 30, 1941, a fire started in the upper story of the School. Balanchine, who was present, noticed the smell of burning at about six in the evening, then he, Muriel Stuart and Oboukhov saw smoke. He sent the students down into the street in their rehearsal clothes and called the Fire Department. Within an hour the blaze had been extinguished. When the scare was over, Balanchine said to Natalie Molostwoff, "I wouldn't have cared if it destroyed me."

Chapter 6

SOUTH AMERICAN ADVENTURE:

MAY - DECEMBER 1941

N 1940, with a strong likelihood of America's being involved in a world war, the prospects of Balanchine's establishing a great American ballet company seemed more remote than ever. If he took stock after his first seven years in America, he must have admitted to himself that his achievement had not been impressive. *Serenade,* begun in 1934, had only recently achieved its final form—in a production for Massine's company. Neither *The Card Game* nor *Le Baiser de la fée* was of prime importance. *Balustrade* had not been liked. More and more young dancers were being well trained at the School he had founded, but he had no company of his own. Suddenly, in the early months of 1941, he had one.

Franklin D. Roosevelt, re-elected for a third term in November 1940, had appointed Kirstein's friend Nelson Rockefeller Coordi-

nator of Inter-American Affairs, charged with facilitating commercial and cultural relations between the United States and other
American republics. Thus it came about that Kirstein and Balanchine were given a subsidy to take a ballet company on tour in
South America. The main advantage of the composite troupe,
hurriedly assembled from the dancers of Ballet Caravan and former members of the American Ballet, was that, unlike the Ballet
Russe de Monte-Carlo, with which Balanchine had lately been
working, most of its artists—and certainly all its principals—had
been students of the School on Madison Avenue. In this sense it
was a "Balanchine company." The stars were Marie-Jeanne,
Gisella Caccialanza, Lew Christensen and William Dollar. Spurred
into action, Balanchine turned out two masterpieces to the music
of Bach and Tchaikovsky—*Concerto Barocco* and *Ballet Imperial*—in no time at all.

Kirstein knew a good ballet when he saw one, and Balanchine's
choreography for the Bach Double Violin Concerto in D minor and
for Tchaikovsky's comparatively little-known Piano Concerto No.
2 in G major must have consoled him for the years of disappointment and separation.

The Tchaikovsky was the result of Balanchine and Kirstein's
feeling that they should show a purely classical ballet in South
America, if only to make clear that native North Americans were
capable of dancing one. On consideration, the choreographer had
decided not to revive *Giselle* or *Swan Lake,* but to invent a new
display piece, using the vocabulary of Petipa. He would make a
ballet without a story, thus allowing more time for dancing than
in any one act of any long Petipa ballet. And although he chose
a composition by Tchaikovsky, with whom Petipa worked, it was
music of a kind to which Petipa never arranged dances—symphonic rather than divided into numbers. He would avoid all the
"eccentricities" of his earlier works. Although only academic steps
were to be employed, the corps de ballet, which in Petipa's day had
merely formed a background to the soloists, would be an active
participant, sharing the dances and technical demands made upon

the principals. Balanchine's choreography proved to be more challenging than any ever before devised for a corps de ballet.

Because no ballerina, with or without her partner, could dance all the cadenzas in Tchaikovsky's concerto as well as join in the ensembles, there would be a second ballerina, with two men to support her, and two female demi-soloists, in addition to the corps of sixteen girls and eight boys (including the two supporters). Mstislav Dobouzhinsky, a former colleague of Diaghilev, designed a grandiose setting. Columns and rich hangings in Maryinsky blue and gold surmounted by an Imperial eagle framed a vista of the Neva and the distant fortress of Peter and Paul.

One of the marvels of *Ballet Imperial*'s long and brilliant first movement is the way in which the corps changes from formation to formation; another is the impetuous dash of the two ballerinas' entries. The second movement contains one of Balanchine's most beautiful inventions. The boy partners ten girls, who extend behind him like two wings. As he lunges first to one side, then to the other, the girls, who seem attached to his shoulders, swing to and fro. Then, as he rushes first to the downstage right corner, then downstage left, he is pulled back by all ten, who seem less like his fellow human beings than like symptoms of some inner trouble that assails him in waves. The third movement is festive, folk accents echoing hints of a typical Russian dance in the music. In its finale, all repeat the folk step ever faster, traveling from side to side, and end suddenly kneeling.

■   ■   ■

WHILE Balanchine and his dancers traveled south, Brigitta set off once more for Hollywood. It was five months before her husband saw her again.

In the course of the South American tour, one of the dancers—Georgia Hiden, an attractive and intelligent Virginian—struck up a friendship with Balanchine and found him "great fun to be with." She remembered many little details about him. For example, he had a habit of saying at the beginning of rehearsals, "Soon as we start, soon as we finish!" A Cuban girl, Olga Suárez, corrected him: "That's not right. You should say, 'The sooner we start, the sooner we'll finish.' " Next day, however, Balanchine repeated, "Soon as we start—" and Olga exclaimed, "You'll *never* learn!"

The food in Rio was so good that after two days Balanchine issued an edict that the girls must skip a meal every now and then.

On June 25, the curtain went up on the first South American performance of the American Ballet, and *Serenade* was seen for the first time outside the United States. There stood the seventeen girls, eyes and right arms raised to the spotlights high up in the flies to stage right. Then came *Ballet Imperial*, performed for the first time in a real theater; it received eighteen curtain calls. Looking back more than forty years later, John Taras, by then a ballet master at the New York City Ballet, who had seen *Ballet Imperial* performed by many dancers in many companies, thought that no dancer in the role of the first ballerina ever possessed the explosive brilliance of Marie-Jeanne, who created it. Balanchine brought out and used all her strength, tension, elegance and authority. Subsequent dancers may have been her equals in technique, but none possessed her fiery, indomitable impatience, so that the original shock of her performances, which were acclaimed throughout South America, never recurred.

The second ballerina was Gisella Caccialanza, who had married Lew Christensen in May. During rehearsals with Balanchine, she thought, "How can he do this to me?" and she protested at all the running that was expected of her before she even started a variation. "What are you complaining about?" asked Balanchine. "Before your variation you're just resting." "Where?" "You're just running." It had been the same with *Le Baiser de la fée* at the Metropolitan, when he pushed her onstage to make her entrance with a series of pas de bourrée, which always hurt her feet. "He called them 'rest steps,' " Lew Christensen said.

The second performance, on June 27, opened with *Errante*. The first showing of *Pastorela*, choreographed by Lew Christensen and

José Fernandez, followed. Then came *Concerto Barocco.* Bach's Concerto in D Minor was one of the few masterpieces of old music that Balanchine ever trusted himself to turn into a ballet. He could never lay hands, as Massine had done, on a Beethoven symphony, or on a Mozart piano concerto or a Schubert quartet. Yet he dared the Bach—and brought it off.

The corps of eight girls was onstage throughout, and the first ballerina left the stage for only a few seconds. The single boy, William Dollar, appeared only in the second movement, from which the second ballerina, Mary Jane Shea, was omitted. The two principals, representing for the most part the two violins, responded to each other with extraordinary delicacy in the opening Vivace and wove intricate mazes with the eight other girls. In the Largo, the lifting of Marie-Jeanne, the first ballerina, in huge but diminishing arcs was wonderful in the way it complemented the music's climax of emotion without following the notes. Twice in the final Allegro there was an unpredictable but delightful jazzy element of syncopation when, to reiterated passages on the solo violins, the corps drummed out the rhythm on their pointes while their arms moved *against* the music from one classical pose to another.

For all its apparent simplicity, Marie-Jeanne thought the Bach a greater work than *Ballet Imperial*—an opinion that has found numerous adherents since—and her role, which called for so many contrasting qualities, the most demanding Balanchine ever made on her.

The final ballet was *Divertimento,* to piano music of Rossini orchestrated by Benjamin Britten, which proved to be one of the most popular ballets on the entire tour. It took place at a costume ball where a guest dressed as a rat scares the other guests, who are provoked to attack him. The rat is unmasked and revealed as an acrobat in disguise. Nicholas Magallanes played this part, and Marjorie Moore, who was in love with him, used to stand in the wings, murmuring encouragement and blowing kisses. One night in the course of the tour Balanchine decided to fool Marjorie and the company. Warning only the Christensens and, of course, Magallanes, he put on the rat costume and danced. He submitted to the kicks and blows of the other dancers, but when Marjorie Moore blew him a kiss he did a double turn in the air, and she got a shock. When Balanchine removed his headdress, the company fell apart with laughter.

For Kirstein, *Apollo,* which was performed on the third night, was an "unforeseen success."

Maybe the name of Stravinsky had something to do with it. Certainly Lew Christensen's inspired rendition of a cruelly difficult technical role had a great deal. He was very nervous the first night. He could even barely let his newly acquired wife . . . sew on his gilt leggings. But his turns exploded and his beats fairly crackled. The ovation at the end was something to live for. And the little pupils of the local dancing academy presented Balanchine with a wreath of bays, which he gave to Lew who didn't know what to do with it, while everyone took pictures.

At press conferences, Balanchine had his own way of being amusing. He could not take anything official seriously and talked nonsense about himself and ballet in general. In São Paulo, he surprised his interrogators by saying, "Tiller Girls [a troupe of precision dancers of the 1920s] are for older people like our grandparents. Nowadays we do different—more modern. I call it 'organized chaos.' "

When, as he liked to do, he watched *Ballet Imperial* from the wings, he made everyone nervous. One night, as he stood talking to Olga Suárez while she waited to make her entrance, he remarked, "Once you fall on stage you can never build up again. You have to fight hard to make audience forget you fall." He described how it had once happened to Olga Spessiva in the days of Diaghilev, and how she ruined her performance in *Swan Lake.* "Dancers must never fall," he concluded. Olga nodded in agreement, ran onstage and immediately fell flat.

Because of the war, there seemed to be no way to get the

company to Buenos Aires, but the American vice-consul moved heaven and earth and produced a boat. The whole company traveled first class on *El Cabo de Buena Esperanza,* which had been built to hold eight hundred and now had twelve hundred people on board. Balanchine, who shared a cabin with Dollar and Fred Danieli, complained that girls were always scratching on the door asking for Dollar.

In Argentina, a law had just been passed raising the age when young people attained majority from eighteen to twenty-one. No sooner had the crowded ship docked at Buenos Aires on July 16 than all the minors in the company—Magallanes as well as the girls—were taken off the boat and held in jail from six-thirty in the morning until five that evening. It was suggested that white slave traffic was involved. Marie-Jeanne became hysterical, and Balanchine tried to get himself arrested, too. The jail was freezing, for this was the Argentinean winter. Nevertheless, everyone was summoned to attend class by Balanchine at two the following afternoon.

Again, the opening was a success, with an ovation for *Concerto Barocco* and rave reviews the following day. Balanchine and Kirstein were soon planning an Argentinean ballet with the young composer Alberto Ginastera.

■　■　■

THE AMERICAN BALLET gave nineteen performances during their sixteen-day stay in Buenos Aires, then, on August 1, crossed the Río de la Plata to give several more in Montevideo, the Uruguayan capital. On August 5 they returned to Buenos Aires to take an evening train inland to Rosario, the first of three provincial cities they were to visit.

The company's two-day stay in Córdoba was the occasion for a historic encounter. Manuel de Falla, the greatest Spanish composer of the twentieth century, whose *Tricorne* had been commissioned by Diaghilev, was living in Alta Gracia, a little town a few miles away, and Balanchine drove out to visit him. In 1939, Falla had come from Spain to conduct four concerts of Spanish music in Buenos Aires. After the concerts, he and his niece had settled at Alta Gracia.

The company interpreter, John Graham Luhan, went in to interpret between Falla and Balanchine, while Georgia Hiden waited outside in the car. How one would like to know what they talked about, the two men of genius. Luckily, *Tricorne* was the one ballet of Massine's that Balanchine could praise wholeheartedly. Falla was currently working on his "Atlántida" (Atlantis), which he left unfinished at his death there five years later. Georgia Hiden remembers Balanchine coming away well pleased with the promise that Falla would allow him to produce "Atlántida" on the stage.

The dancers went on to Mendoza to give a performance, and were supposed to take the train from there to Santiago, Chile, which was only about a hundred and forty miles away. Unfortunately the two cities were separated by the highest peaks in the Andes, and there had been the worst winter storms in years. The railroad was broken, mountain villages had been submerged by snow and the highway was blocked. There was a period of anxious waiting before Kirstein eventually succeeded in borrowing a Boeing transport plane to ferry the fifty-one members of the company in two trips through—not over—the Andes. No one was allowed more than twenty-five pounds of luggage. Luhan had to take the rest—which consisted of hundreds of trunks and suitcases— through Bolivia to await the company in Lima, Peru. Most of the dancers had never flown before, and none had flown under such conditions; they were all scared stiff. Todd Bolender recalled his relief as the plane emerged from the mountains: "Everything began to turn green, and we saw the sea. The land came up at us. We landed on a shelf of green."

In Chile, Balanchine put together and presented *Fantasia Brasileira*, commissioned in Rio from Francisco Mignone two months before. It took him only one week to arrange the choreography. Although, as Kirstein observed, *Brasileira* was about as Brazilian as *Prince Igor* was early Russian, it was a successful closing number; but like others in the repertory, it would never be seen in North America.

Kirstein was obliged to fly back to the United States. The company understood that he was trying to get the male dancers excused from the draft "for six months or so." There were, however, other problems to be dealt with, and these he did not discuss with them. He had to account for the money the tour had cost Nelson Rockefeller's agency. Successful as it had been, box-office receipts had not, of course, covered expenses. In Washington, Kirstein dealt with his old friend Wallace Harrison, the architect, who represented Rockefeller. The tour was allowed to continue.

From Valparaiso, the company took a cattle boat up the west coast to Peru. They were the only passengers, apart from the smelly beasts in the hold, and the food was awful. Balanchine, who never complained, urged everyone to stick to pancakes with fresh lime juice and sugar. There was nothing to do on board but sunbathe, play games and act charades, but nearly every day the boat put in at a little port. One day when Georgia Hiden was going ashore with Balanchine and a few other dancers, he pointed out a high building in the town for which they were headed. It might have been the customs house, a government office or the jail, but Balanchine said, "That is hotel, and it's called Pacífico." It turned out that he was right, although none of them could figure out how he knew. Another day, at another small harbor town, he and his friends hired a taxi to take them inland to see some bleak nitrate hills devoid of vegetation, where there was no animal life, not even ants. The group became uneasy as they sensed that their driver was steering them in the wrong direction. "He wants to tell his wife something," said Balanchine. Sure enough, as they drove down a street in the poor quarter, a woman came running from a house to speak to the driver. Georgia decided that Balanchine must have second sight.

In Lima, they found that Aaron Copland was staying at the Bolívar Hotel. He agreed to conduct his own *Billy,* which seemed to galvanize the orchestra. The first performance, on September

10, was attended by the president of Peru, his wife and family, the head of the army and all the foreign ambassadors and ministers—except the German, Italian and Japanese—all wearing white tie. The company received the greatest ovation of the tour.

When the scheduled season ended, Balanchine, the *chef d'orchestre* Balaban and the Christensens went by air to Cuzco and Machu Picchu to see the ruins of the old Inca capital. In the (unpressurized) plane, flying at 14,000 feet, Lew and Gisella watched Balanchine grow whiter and whiter. Lew thought he "damn near died." But the excursion was worth it, and everyone, including Balanchine, took photographs. Because Peru was at war with Ecuador, the performances planned for Quito were canceled. To fill the gap, the United States Embassy in Lima arranged for extra performances there.

Balanchine left for the United States the day before the company's last appearance in Peru. Three days later, the company sailed for Colombia. By the time they returned, they had given more than a hundred performances in six countries over five months. On their arrival home, they were disbanded. Looking back on the tour, Lincoln Kirstein wrote:

I never failed to be amazed by Balanchine. He has always had a remarkable disposition for work, quiet, patient, undemanding, yet perfectly firm. But on this fantastic tour, the difficulties of which can never be appreciated by anybody but the dancers themselves, . . . he loved every inch of the journey and his own personal prestige became enormous. Long after we left Buenos Aires came insistent offers to return to the Colón.

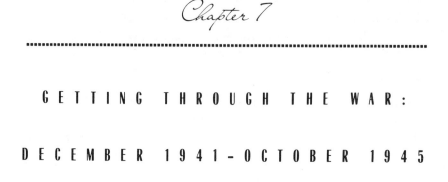

Chapter 7

GETTING THROUGH THE WAR:

DECEMBER 1941-OCTOBER 1945

O N December 8, 1941, the United States declared war on Japan. By December 11, it was also at war with Germany and Italy. Sooner or later the draft would diminish the number of available male dancers, but because of his fragile physical condition there was no question of Balanchine's being drafted. Kirstein, however, was.

In June 1938, in an article in *Dance Magazine,* Kirstein had made certain predictions about world politics and the future of ballet in America. He took for granted—as most of the British and French did not—that war in Europe was inevitable, and he accurately dated "the closing of international frontiers" as 1939–40. The result would be that what he called "the Slavo-International company" would be restricted to appearing in the

United States with a decreasing number of foreign stars and an increasingly American—and far better—corps de ballet. Kirstein did not mention the Japanese threat, which had not loomed, but he foresaw the American entry into the war against Hitler and the alliance with Russia. Although the all-powerful Sol Hurok, fearful of being saddled with Colonel de Basil's debts, was to banish the de Basil company to South America, he would indeed present Massine's Ballet Russe and Lucia Chase's Ballet Theatre in the course of one New York season; and the Ballet Russe de Monte-Carlo, even when led by a Russian-born director other than Massine, would tour the States with an increasingly American company for twenty-two years.

Balanchine, who had to earn a living, took any work that was offered him. If Hurok had been perceptive enough to realize that Balanchine was the greatest living choreographer, and if he had supported and enlarged the American Ballet to give him the scope to create a new repertory of masterworks, how different history might have been! But it is inconceivable that the two men could have worked together steadily, for Balanchine would never have submitted for long to the tyranny of the box office. Nor could Hurok, in spite of all his influence and know-how, ever have created for Balanchine, as Kirstein was to do, a climate in which his genius could flower with the profusion it did in the postwar years.

Of all Balanchine's wartime jobs, none was odder than the *Circus Polka.* At the end of 1941, Ringling Brothers and Barnum & Bailey Circus had suggested that he do some choreography for their elephants. He agreed, on condition that Stravinsky write the music, probably realizing that the composer needed money. Balanchine telephoned Stravinsky in Hollywood on November 12; in January the composer made some notes in preparation for another talk with his choreographer: "How many minutes?" "The less the best." Balanchine went to the circus's winter quarters in Sarasota, Florida, to rehearse the elephants, and enjoyed himself tremendously. Brigitta appeared in the first performance, in New York

City's Madison Square Garden on April 9, 1942, which was a benefit for a war charity. At the end, Balanchine had both the star elephant, Modoc, and Zorina kneel in salutation to each other, touching foreheads in the sawdust.

During this period, Balanchine used to hold musical evenings in his apartment, with Kopeikine at the piano and Nathan Milstein playing the violin. He even bought a violin himself, and said to Georgia Hiden, "You must learn the piano, Dottie Littlefield can learn the viola, and then we will play very slow, very loud, everything that Mozart ever wrote!"

■　■　■

THE WAR brought a wave of prosperity to the United States; and, equally ironically, ballet grew more popular than ever.

By the beginning of 1942, de Basil was in Mexico City with his company—or what remained of it—preparing to embark on a long tour of South America. It would be four years before they were seen again in the United States. Meantime, Hurok resolved to present both the other rival companies in New York. Ballet Theatre had a week at the Metropolitan Opera House, followed immediately by the Ballet Russe; then there was a week in which the two companies alternated. In spite of Ballet Theatre's ambition to be eclectic and to produce new and/or American works, both were as Russian in color and magnificence as Hurok could make them. In fact, he had shamelessly advertised Ballet Theatre as "the greatest in Russian Ballet."

■　■　■

BRIGITTA had cropped her hair to be tested for the role of Maria in *For Whom the Bell Tolls,* a part she regarded as the chance of a lifetime. Believing she had got it, she sent a triumphant telegram to her husband, who was working at the Colón in Buenos Aires. After that, he wrote her regularly. He thanked her for the lock of her shorn "dark gold" hair, and wanted her to return with him to Argentina the next year; he thought Mozart would be "rather pleased" with his ballet to the Violin Concerto in A major; without her, when something funny happened, he had to "laugh alone"; he was counting the days till he saw her again. But Brigitta lost the part to Ingrid Bergman and became distraught.

Marie-Jeanne was living in Buenos Aires with her husband, the impresario Quesada, whom she had met on the tour, and Balanchine asked her to dance in the revival of *Apollon* and in *Concierto.* But she was trying to get pregnant and refused. "Balanchine didn't like that," she remembers, "and I wasn't very diplomatic. . . . I had never taken him seriously, because he had so many girlfriends. With me it was short-lived. I was one of a hundred and didn't fall madly in love with him. . . . I loved him as an artistic genius." In Balanchine's eyes, for a ballerina to have babies was a form of treachery to himself and to the Muse. Although his admiration for Marie-Jeanne's exceptional qualities never flowered into a more intimate passion, he continued to work with her and on her. She was rather self-indulgent, and he was known to give her money for steaks, to discourage her from putting on weight.

On his return from South America, Balanchine helped to direct and made dances for a version of *Die Fledermaus* called *Rosalinda,* which was presented by the recently formed New Opera Company. Lacking Marie-Jeanne, he cast a young dancer named Mary Ellen Moylan, who had been at the School only since 1940, as the ballerina.

The New Opera Company was also presenting Mussorgsky's *The Fair at Sorochinsk,* which opened six days after *Rosalinda.* Because of the failure of a short opera by Walter Damrosch, included as a curtain raiser, Balanchine's *Ballet Imperial* was hastily substituted. A company was assembled from former dancers of the American Ballet and from the School. Moylan recalls Nicholas Magallanes coming to her and saying, "Let's learn the pas de deux. You're going to be doing Marie-Jeanne's part." She nearly fainted. As she and Todd Bolender appeared only in the second act of *Rosalinda,* they were bustled into taxis after dancing *Ballet Imperial* and driven to the theater where *Rosalinda* was playing. "Can you imagine what it was like to be seventeen and doing both those shows every night?" Moylan said later. "It was awesome just being on the stage in New York City."

Among the seven men in *Rosalinda* were two, soon to be drafted, who became closely associated with Balanchine after the war. Both had started at the School the previous year and were appearing professionally for the first time. Edward Bigelow, a New Englander, was to prove the staunchest of friends. Francisco Moncion, a native of the Dominican Republic, would become one of Balanchine's most reliable dancers. When he arrived at the School, he already thought of Balanchine as *The Man.* "Although Balanchine was an odd mixture of glamour and mousiness, he had an aura about him. I really got a crush on the man, a real crush."

Balanchine tried to help old colleagues who had been drafted find congenial work in the armed services. Irving Berlin was organizing a show to entertain the troops, and Balanchine wrote to him about Zachary Solov, who had been with the American Ballet in South America: "I would be grateful if you could keep him in mind in case of a vacancy in *This Is the Army.*"

When *Rosalinda* finished its run, Mary Ellen Moylan had the option of joining Ballet Theatre or the Ballet Russe. At eighteen, she felt she was "getting on in years." Sergei Denham of the Ballet Russe came to watch her in class and offered her a job. When she asked Balanchine what he thought she should do, he "wasn't too enthusiastic." Finally he said, "Go ahead to Ballet Russe, but I will give you a piece of advice. Don't sign a two-year contract." It was excellent counsel. Within a year her salary was doubled.

In the spring of 1943, Hurok needed another ballerina for Ballet Theatre and was delighted to find that the celebrated Vera Zorina was available. Balanchine undertook to revive two of his ballets for her. His first task for Ballet Theatre, however, was the comparatively menial one of pulling together a ballet which was already in the company's repertory. *Helen of Troy* was a farce to Offenbach's music that Fokine had arranged shortly before his death the previous August. Although it had been danced in Mexico City, it was considered unsatisfactory, and David Lichine had made a new version in the fall. Now Balanchine collaborated with Lichine in devising an ending that would show his own wife off to the best possible advantage.

Three weeks later, on April 25, 1943, *Apollon*—called *Apollo* at last—was performed once more at the Metropolitan, with Stravinsky conducting. André Eglevsky danced the title role and Zorina was Terpsichore.

.   .   .

Time magazine was so pleased with a would-be learned article on Ballet Theatre's season, which was to appear on May 17, that they sent Balanchine an advance proof, asking for comment. They got more than they bargained for. The critic, in a mistaken display of expertise, had made invidious distinctions between Markova, Baronova and Zorina, calling the first a *"danseuse noble,"* whom *"*only the cautious conservatism of ballet's experts keeps from being hailed unreservedly as a *ballerina assoluta,"* placing the second in a lower category with the novel designation of *"mime dansante,"* and dismissing the third as a *"soubrette."* Without naming his wife, Balanchine sprang to her defense:

May 14, 1943

Gentlemen:

Thank you for sending me the article entitled "Danseuse Noble. . . ."

Most professionals of the dance have long ago given up wondering at the strange writings of the dance critics in the daily papers because they have finally realized that many of them simply don't know their subject. However, it seems a pity that when a magazine as important as *Time* devotes an entire page to the ballet, it is unable to come closer to the truth.

The author of your article juggles with magic-sounding words: *ballerina assoluta, danseuse noble, mime dansante,* without apparently realizing that the first one denotes an official rank in the theater (such as a colonel or general in the army), while the second one describes a quality and the third one a style of dancing. To say that the *danseuse noble* Markova "is well above a *mime dansante* (like Irina Baronova)" is equal to saying that Caruso was less great than Chaliapin because he was just a tenor while Chaliapin was a basso. As to the word *soubrette,* this is the first time I have heard it mentioned in connection with dancing and have associated it, until today, with the unfortunate maid in comic plays who brings in the breakfast tray and upsets it upon finding the *ingénue* in bed with the *jeune premier.*

Most professional dancers and choreographers consider Markova as one of a few great contemporary ballerinas, but they refrain from making comparisons between dancers because they know that each is outstanding in her own way and has qualities completely different from the others. It is your right to praise the ballerina you prefer, but I do not think it wise to do so by disparaging other prominent artists who may in their turn become the critic's and the public's favorite.

Sincerely yours,
George Balanchine

Neither Markova nor Baronova took part in Ballet Theatre's long cross-country tour which followed, so Hurok was at liberty to announce his "internationally famous dance stars" in "the greatest in Russian Ballet," while naming only "Zorina," "glamorous dancing star" in bold capitals three times the size of those in which the words "Ballet Theatre" were printed. During this tour, Brigitta was sometimes visited by a new admirer, Goddard Lieberson, who worked for Columbia Records. When the tour was over, she left Ballet Theatre.

In the winter of 1943, Balanchine had made dances for the musical *What's Up?*, the first collaboration of Alan Jay Lerner and Frederick Loewe, who went on to write *My Fair Lady* and *Camelot*, among others. In the spring of 1944, just about the time Private Lincoln Kirstein arrived in London, he was working on *Dream with Music*, in which Zorina starred. It was while the latter was being tried out in Boston that Georgia Hiden heard the unusual sound of Balanchine's voice raised in anger—at the stage manager. She later remarked, "That's the only time I heard you yell." Balanchine said, "It's only the second time since I came to America. I wouldn't yell at a dancer. I'd yell at Hurok."

Another musical show—operetta, rather—led to Balanchine's two-year association with the Ballet Russe de Monte-Carlo, for which he had staged four productions in 1939. Dancers were often laid off during the summer, and in 1944 Frederic Franklin asked Denham's permission to appear in an operetta based on the life of Grieg that his friends Robert Wright and George Forrest had put together in California. Denham lent the whole Ballet Russe. Danilova urged the authors to employ Balanchine as their choreographer, and they agreed. He made several dances, folk, comic and classical, using Grieg's incidental music for *Peer Gynt* and other compositions, and wrote to Brigitta, "Why don't you come out and be wife of poor choreographer?" But Brigitta was already in love with Goddard Lieberson.

Song of Norway was rehearsed in San Francisco, and Balanchine shared a hotel room with Franklin, the English *premier danseur* who was the partner of Alexandra Danilova. They had been friends since 1940, when Balanchine had produced *Serenade* and *Jeu de cartes* for the Ballet Russe, and Franklin had danced Dollar's old role of the Joker. Balanchine liked the fair-haired, cheerful young man from Liverpool and evidently saw some latent gift in him, besides his ability to dance, to partner and to please. Before he left for South America he told Denham, "When I go, this ballet has got to be rehearsed by Franklin." After Balanchine and Franklin became roommates at the Clift Hotel in San Francisco, the latter noticed that "everything was choreographed": "When we got up, the meal was ordered from downstairs, we each had so long in the bathroom, we went to rehearsals and came home on time." Then Balanchine took the opportunity to do his roommate a good turn. According to Franklin:

I was quite close to him then. One day in San Francisco I said, "There must be something else in life besides going on stage every night, dancing all the lovely ballets, having all the lovely applause. . . ." He looked at me and said, "You'd like to be doing something else?" I said yes. On the opening night of *Song of Norway* in Los Angeles, it was my birthday, 12 June. There was a cake on the stage; everyone was there; Mr. Denham made a speech. He announced, "From now on Frederic Franklin will no longer be *only* my *premier danseur,* he's going to be my *maître de ballet.* " Balanchine looked at me, wagged his finger and smiled. . . . And Danilova said, "So, young man, you are going to be my boss." I had no idea this had been arranged. . . .

Balanchine told Franklin, "You know, it's not fun being *maître de ballet,* Freddie. From now on you're going to get up every morning and stand in front of people and give and give and give. It's going to be for the rest of your life, because now you will only be giving."

One night Balanchine asked him, "Have you read *War and Peace?*" The answer was no. Another night it was, "Have you read the Sermon on the Mount?" "I suppose I must have. I really don't remember, Mr. B." "Call me George." "I can't, Mr. B." "Well, go home and read it." Franklin said later, "It was a sort of education being with him. He was very dear to me indeed."

In Hollywood, Balanchine was reunited with the Stravinskys, who were living in Beverly Hills, and it was agreed that he would make a ballet to Stravinsky's *Danses concertantes,* composed two and a half years earlier. On the morning of June 16, Stravinsky discussed with Anton Dolin the scenario of a ballet to be included in Billy Rose's revue *The Seven Lively Arts,* which was to be arranged by Dolin and danced by Markova and himself. On the same afternoon he talked to Balanchine about *Danses concertantes.* Denham, Balanchine and Eugene Berman were summoned to Stravinsky's house to decide on the costumes; then Balanchine said to Franklin, "We're all Russians. You had better come, too." When

Berman produced a piece of black velvet and a swatch of colors, an argument broke out. Finally, Balanchine told Franklin to choose. The new ballet master first picked out a vivid yellow, then some other colors, and Stravinsky's eyes lit up. During the San Francisco run of *Song of Norway,* Balanchine signed an agreement with Denham to arrange not only *Danses concertantes* but Strauss's *Le Bourgeois Gentilhomme* for "a flat amount of two thousand dollars."

Song of Norway did well at the Philharmonic Auditorium in Los Angeles, and even better when it opened in San Francisco on July 1. It was a smash hit at the Imperial in New York, so successful that a replacement cast—led by Dorothie Littlefield and Olga Suárez— had to be found to allow the principals to take part in the fall ballet season at City Center.

While Balanchine had been rehearsing *Song of Norway* in California with members of the Ballet Russe, the rival company, Ballet Theatre, happened to be there, and he undertook to make a new ballet for them, too—*Waltz Academy,* to music by Vittorio Rieti, his old collaborator on *Barabau* and *Le Bal.* Rehearsals were begun at once.

The period from summer 1944 until summer 1945, which saw the defeat of Nazi Germany and Japan, was one of frantic activity for Balanchine. His work for several different organizations necessitated constant travel around the United States. It almost seemed as if he accepted any job that would distract him from unhappy thoughts of Brigitta.

Danses concertantes was given by the Ballet Russe on the opening night of the season. There was a parade of dancers in Berman's costumes "looking as brilliant as scarabs," and when an inner curtain rose to reveal a black background, they shone more brightly still. Four pas de trois were followed by a pas de deux for Danilova and Franklin and a finale for the whole cast of fourteen. The fourth variation was danced by Mary Ellen Moylan, Nicholas Magallanes and a new dancer named Maria Tallchief.

Born in 1925, Maria was of American Indian descent on her father's side and Scottish, Irish and Dutch on her mother's. Her grandmother Tallchief had lived in a tent and carried Maria's father on her back. But since her father, like other Osage Indians, received substantial royalties from oil wells, he made his home in Hollywood, played golf and, as Maria said, "that was about it." Maria, a striking-looking girl with black hair and high cheekbones, was brought up by her mother, who was a devout Catholic. She learned music and had perfect pitch. She took ballet lessons with Bronislava Nijinska and joined the Ballet Russe in 1942. When Balanchine came to stage *Song of Norway,* Maria had seen no other work of his except *Serenade,* but the inventiveness and musical sense displayed in that had been enough to amaze her. Besides dancing in the corps in the Grieg operetta, she understudied Danilova in Anitra's dance. As she worked with Balanchine, she realized at once how much she had to learn, and she wondered at his infinite patience: "He never said, 'You're this or that, but you're not something else.' What he did say was 'If you can do a perfect battement tendu, you can do anything.' " When the second cast was being assembled so that *Song of Norway* could extend its run after Danilova, Franklin and the others had left, Maria was offered the leading role. She refused in order to continue studying with Balanchine.

· · ·

THROUGHOUT the war years, John Martin did not cease to disparage Balanchine's ballets in the pages of *The New York Times,* although he was sometimes able to find words of praise for his work in Broadway musicals. When Walter Terry of the *Herald Tribune* was drafted in 1942, his place was taken by Edwin Denby, who became Balanchine's most impassioned and eloquent admirer. Denby, a Harvard graduate who had studied dancing in Germany, was a poet, better equipped than most to assess Balanchine's exceptional quality and originality. It is amusing to compare his verdicts with those of Martin.

On *Danses concertantes:*

MARTIN   Mr. Balanchine has done a clever, somewhat mathematical, job
of choreography, almost totally devoid of dancing.
DENBY   The shift of the figures and the order of the steps is miraculously
logical and light, and so even fitful changes have a grace and a
spontaneous impetus. . . . The dance is like a conversation in Henry
James.

On *Le Bourgeois Gentilhomme:*

MARTIN   Mr. Balanchine has paid little or no attention to the style of the
theater or the dancing of the seventeenth century.
DENBY   After thirty years of stress on detail at the expense of flow, *Le
Bourgeois* marks a complete turnabout in dance style. . . . It shows off
the dancer, not the choreographer. . . .

When Claudia Cassidy, the critic of the *Chicago Tribune* and a
warm adherent of Balanchine, suggested to him that "an older,
more experienced troupe, say of Diaghileff vintage" might dance
so sophisticated a work as *Danses concertantes* better than the
Ballet Russe, the choreographer burst out with, "Why do Americans hate Americans?" He told her that the Diaghilev corps
"couldn't have achieved the pinpoint brilliance of *Danses concertantes* in a million years."

Danilova was always telling Balanchine that the company
should revive Petipa's *Paquita.* He invariably replied, "No,
Paquita's awful ballet, awful!" Ruthanna Boris asked him one day,
"What's so bad about *Paquita?*" Balanchine replied, "Nothing.
It's very very good." "Then *why* do you not want to do it?"
"Because if we do *Paquita* everybody will see what I stole for
Ballet Imperial."

Balanchine's next production for the Ballet Russe was, in fact,
a revival of *Ballet Imperial.* The great ballet was taught to the
company during the autumn tour and even rehearsed after evening
performances in Chicago—which was against union rules. The
reason for this was that Ballet Theatre was expecting Balanchine

to put the finishing touches on *Waltz Academy* in Montreal. It had
to be ready for its premiere in Boston on October 5. As the Chicago
premiere of *Imperial* was on the fourth, Balanchine could not stay
to see it. On the afternoon of the fifth, after the dress rehearsal of
Waltz Academy, he went for a walk with Rieti and discussed
another project. Some years before, Rieti had written the scenario
of a melodramatic ballet set in the Romantic 1830s that wove
melodies from some of Bellini's operas into a strikingly theatrical
series of numbers. He had not been able to interest either Dolin
or Nijinska in the project, but Balanchine was quick to see its
possibilities. Suddenly Rieti exclaimed, "What are we doing—
talking about *Night Shadow*? In an hour or two we are going to
see *Waltz Academy* on the stage!" "*That* old ballet!" said Balanchine.

By November, Balanchine was back with the Ballet Russe, rehearsing *Mozartiana* and *Concerto Barocco* in Houston. All the
dancers hoped he would become the company's artistic director,
for he had put new life into the battered troupe, but he did not like
Denham, and Denham did not want to relinquish his artistic authority. Nevertheless, he wrote to a friend that *Danses concertantes*
was one of the ballets most in demand: "Balanchine became a sort
of adopted son and travels with us, sharing our hardships, fun,
glory and drinks."

When Balanchine was on tour with the Ballet Russe, whether
by train or bus, he sat alone in the front, writing in a book.
Sometimes he looked out the window, as if searching for a word,
then continued writing. Eventually he presented each dancer with
a four-line poem, describing what he or she might be like in bed.
Ruthanna Boris, he wrote, would have no room for another person
because she always took her toe shoes to bed with her.

During the Ballet Russe's spring season at City Center, which
opened as early as February to avoid competition with Ballet
Theatre, Denham offered two "Balanchine Festivals"—programs
made up entirely of Balanchine's own ballets. The pretext was that

1945 was Balanchine's twenty-fifth year as a choreographer. After the first festival, Denham came onstage to present him with a gold cigarette case. The program was *Mozartiana, Le Bourgeois Gentil-homme* and *Ballet Imperial.*

Ruthanna Boris, who had adored Balanchine since she first arrived at the School of American Ballet in 1934 wearing a pink tunic, danced in all his new productions for the Ballet Russe, as well as in the revivals of older ballets. He once told her, "I envy you because you are a Jew. You have something warm here [touching his heart] like the sun. And I have here a little dagger." She thought a lot about his character and decided that he had been deeply hurt early in life. "He was a dear, loving, anguished man," she said, but he was too proud to share his sorrow.

Ruthanna had been present when Balanchine created the first version of *Serenade;* she remembered how Heidi Vosseler had fallen down, and he had said, "Stay." Then he put Kathryn Mullowny behind Charles Laskey, who was nearsighted. And Kathryn had to propel him forward to the fallen Heidi, holding her hand over his eyes—"He can't see anyway," said Balanchine; and the adagio grew from that. *Serenade* was "a lot of little parts"; and after Ruthanna joined the Ballet Russe in 1943 she danced most of them.

One night, when they picked me up at the end to carry me off to Heaven, I thought: This is Balanchine's theory about his life. In a way it almost *is* his life, because the dancer who brings in the theme introduces it and the group picks it up—and so on. In some subconscious way, in his first American ballet, made with his children who loved him, he had poured himself out. Well, I thought, we're older now. I wonder if he would mind. And I told him, "I love dancing *Serenade,* and I find that, when I've put it all together in my mind, I know what it's about." The mask came down. [As she described this, Ruthanna made the gesture of passing her hand downward in front of her face, which in the old mime language of Russian ballet signifies darkness, secrecy, night.] "You do?" said Balanchine, with a cold stare. "That's very nice." Then he walked away.

In the first postwar period, Balanchine, who loved good food, did not forget that friends in Europe were sadly short of it.

Balanchine to The Tolstoi Foundation Inc., 289 Fourth Avenue, New York City

21 May 1945

Gentlemen,

I enclose herewith a check for $100.00 as my contribution for parcels sent to Russians in France.

I would like to put three of my friends in Paris on your list of persons entitled to receive food parcels. They are: Mr Alexandre Benois . . . Mme L. Egorova-Troubetzkaia . . . Mme Olga Preobrajenskaia . . . [He gave their addresses.]

If it is possible I would like you to use $50.00 of the amount I am sending you as a fund to assure monthly parcels for the above mentioned persons. The balance of my contribution to be used by you for any Russians in Paris that need assistance.

At the end of May 1945, shortly after the defeat of Hitler, Balanchine accepted an engagement with the Opera Nacional of Mexico to arrange ballets for operas and to stage some of his own works. His small troupe—William Dollar, Marie-Jeanne, Yvonne Patterson, Nicholas Magallanes and twelve girls, including Patricia White, who later became Patricia Wilde, and Georgia Hiden— went ahead of him by boat. As some of the others were still students at the School, Natalie Molostwoff accompanied them as chaperone. Balanchine followed by air a few days later. Georgia Hiden had stayed with him and Brigitta on Long Island, where they kept several pets—a German shepherd; Mrs. Hartwig's Pekingese, Boogie; a Yorkshire terrier called Mr. Chips; and a chicken named Joey. When Georgia asked, "How is Joey?" and Balanchine replied, "I don't know," she realized things were going badly between him and Brigitta. In fact, Brigitta had already told George, "I think we had better plan on getting a divorce."

. . .

BALANCHINE could almost, after all these years, have arranged the dances for *Aida, Faust* and *Samson et Dalila* in his sleep. In Mexico he also staged *Concerto Barocco, Apollo*—in which Magallanes appeared for the first time—and Fokine's *Les Sylphides.* He did not forget Stravinsky's birthday, and on July 18 he telegraphed to his revered Igor Fyodorovich:

IF APOLLO'S MOTHER WAS LETO THEN CERTAINLY HIS FATHER WAS FYODOR

It was in Mexico that Natalie Molostwoff, who had never lived at such close quarters with Balanchine before, realized that, as she put it, "there was nothing he could not do." When he discovered that the costumes provided by the theater for *Aida* were dirty and unusable, he said, "Okay. We'll make the costumes." Natalie, who was not good with her needle, nearly packed up and went home. "Why don't we buy a lot of bras and cover them with orange silk?" he suggested. This was done, and he got busy with a box of pins. Natalie observed that "the girls seemed to enjoy the fittings."

He flew back ahead of his troupe to arrange dances for *Mr. Strauss Goes to Boston,* which had its first out-of-town preview at the Shubert Theatre in Boston on August 13. The atomic bombs had been dropped a few days before.

That summer and fall, Balanchine encouraged two young choreographers. For the summer dance festival at Jacob's Pillow near Lee, Massachusetts, Todd Bolender had made a ballet to Stravinsky's *Pulcinella* suite, which he called *Musical Chairs.* Balanchine loved it, and asked, "Has Denham seen this?" He had not, and Balanchine brought him along to view it with "the whole Ballet Russe." Denham accepted the work and paid five hundred dollars for it, but insisted on changing its name to *Comedia Balletica.*

John Taras's first ballet, *Graziana,* to Mozart's Violin Concerto in G major (K.216) was given on the second night of Ballet

Theatre's season. A few days later, Todd Bolender ran into Taras outside the Russian Tea Room on Fifty-seventh Street and asked, "Have you seen George?" "No," said Taras, who never in his life called "George" anything but "Mr. Balanchine." "I haven't seen him for ages." "He has seen your ballet, and he just loves it. He wants to talk to you." Taras was incredulous, but he and Balanchine got together. Both Bolender and Taras later found out separately that when Balanchine had taken each of them to supper at Tony's, a former speak-easy, he had wept as he spoke of his troubles.

Balanchine's divorce from Zorina came through in January 1946. Todd Bolender believed he had intimate talks with Balanchine only when he was not married, that is to say, between grand passions.

Then he always turned to one. I would be upstairs at the School, having had a class, and he would say, "What are you doing? Let's have some dinner."

He was lonely, and he talked for *hours.* And it was fascinating. That was the first time I really got to know him. We went not only to Tony's but to Sammy's delicatessen on Madison, directly under the School. They had a "George Balanchine sandwich" there—smoked salmon with chopped onions.

Although he admired *Lilac Garden,* he was always using Tudor as an example of what not to do. "Don't make complicated stories in which you have aunts and uncles and mothers-in-law. The audience shouldn't have to read a program." He made fun of some of the old dancers—Pavlova, for example, people who were sacred figures. Of Isadora he said, "She's a *pig.* " He spoke *endlessly* of Spessiva. "She was so exquisitely made." He always spoke of her feet being like hands. He said, "I steal a lot from Petipa."

Though Balanchine may not have realized it at the time, he was indeed "between marriages." During Ballet Theatre's summer tour of 1945, Bolender noticed that he was interested in Maria Tallchief. The Catholic Maria had no intention of having premarital relations, however, even with Balanchine. Confessing that he was extremely attracted to her, the choreographer asked Natasha Nabokov's advice. Natasha, after talking to Maria alone, gave her opinion that matrimony was the only solution.

One day Tallchief said to Vida Brown, another dancer friend, "What would you think if I married George?" Vida asked, "George who?"

Chapter 8

NEW BEGINNINGS:

NOVEMBER 1945-APRIL 1948

D URING the winter of 1945–46, the clouds began to lift for
Balanchine. The war was over, there was Maria, and Kirstein would soon be getting out of the army. On January 16,
1946, the day before Balanchine's divorce from Zorina came
through, he and Stravinsky dined together at Tony's. When the
Ballet Russe opened its season at City Center the same day with
a revival of *Le Baiser de la fée,* the role of the Fairy was taken by
Maria Tallchief.

Maria was still very conscious of how much she had to learn
from Balanchine. Nijinska had taught her breathing, but it was he
who remodeled her body from the hips down. She had to be given
correct placement and turnout; once she had laboriously acquired
this, her legs, feet, strength and line would improve. Her eagerness

as well as her musical gifts were a thrilling encouragement to Balanchine. In spite of her beautiful bone structure, Maria had a rather big head, and she was not tall. But she believed Balanchine had the skill to devise dances that would make her head look small. He had a gift for seeing the potential in an unskilled dancer. He *knew* what she would be capable of in his hands.

Maria created the role of the Coquette in *Night Shadow,* the ballet Balanchine and Rieti had discussed in 1944, which was first performed in February 1946; the Sleepwalker's part was danced by Danilova.

Night Shadow has as Gothic and improbable a story as *Giselle,* but in its way it is just as effective. A Poet at a masked ball is attracted first by the mistress of his Host, the Baron, then by the Host's sleepwalking wife. There is a polonaise danced by the other guests, and a fantastic divertissement performed to amuse them, but the ballet's remarkable inventions are two contrasting pas de deux. That of the Poet with the Coquette is an ingenious display of enticing, escaping and entrapping movements. The second, danced by the Poet and the Sleepwalker, is even more extraordinary.

The Poet is left alone after the other guests have gone to supper, and the Sleepwalker appears in her nightgown, with flowing hair, holding a candle. The fact that she is aware of him only in her dream gives her the unattainable quality of a *princesse lointaine.* The Poet first flattens himself against a wall to watch this tiptoeing woman cross and recross the stage, only to halt abruptly just as she seems about to step over the footlights. Not until he has knelt to interrupt her progress and bowed without evoking any response does he pass his hand over her eyes and realize her condition. Like a choreographer devising a sequence—like Balanchine himself molding a dancer at rehearsal—he grasps her lit candle to raise her on pointe, lifts one of her legs, promenades her. When he runs round to embrace her, she evades him; when he makes his arm into a barrier, she dips under it; when he interposes his whole body, she swerves and glides past him; when he extends a leg, she steps over it. He tries lying full-length on the floor, but this too fails. In a singularly touching movement, he sinks to his knees in a deep backbend and stretches both his arms to encircle her. Still she continues on her way. He catches her by the shoulders and kisses her before sending her through the arch into the castle. Looking around cautiously, he follows her. This episode unfolds to variations on what Lord Harewood called "a melody of infinite pathos and beauty," namely "*Qui la voce,*" developed and embroidered by Rieti—the aria of Elvira's mad scene in *I Puritani.*

The Coquette has spied and seen the parting kiss; she fetches the Baron and directs him to the castle door. As the guests return, she sweeps with them into a formal dance, while the Host draws a dagger and runs into the castle. A sudden halt in the music, which brings the party to a standstill, signals the Poet's death wound, and he staggers in to die. The performers of the divertissement, acknowledging their kinship with a fellow artist, raise his body aloft; but before they can carry it away, the Sleepwalker appears, takes it in her arms and walks backward with it into the castle. As we see the light of her candle shine from successive windows of the spiral staircase up the tower, we imagine her bearing him to some cold consummation of their union in an upper chamber.

This is real Romantic melodrama, but we accept it because of the beauty of Bellini's melodies, the skill with which Rieti has interwoven them and the marvelous originality of Balanchine's dance of the Poet with the Sleepwalker.

Night Shadow (later renamed *La Sonnambula*) was to become a popular work in many countries. The wonder is that Dorothea Tanning's surrealist headdresses for the ball guests in the original production did not kill it from the start. Both Martin and Terry scorned it. Denby, however, did not miss the point: "Its effect when it is over is powerful and exact. It gives you a sense—as Poe does—of losing your bearings, the feeling of an elastic sort of time and a heaving floor." In fact, Balanchine, the archclassicist, could out-Byron Byron and out-Hoffmann Gautier.

．　．　．

IN 1946, Lincoln Kirstein returned from active service with the U.S. Army in Europe. Before the war he had succeeded in bringing Balanchine to America and founding a school—which was now better than ever—but he and Balanchine had failed to sustain their own troupe of dancers. Throughout the first postwar spring they plotted and planned. They were not yet ready to compete with the elaborate organizations of the Ballet Russe, Ballet Theatre or de Basil, but as early as March 1938, Kirstein had considered a project of staging nonprofit Sunday performances. Could a group similar to Marie Rambert's prewar Ballet Club now be formed? Plans were made, but nothing was to be announced before the fall. Kirstein asked Balanchine to discuss with Stravinsky the possibility of his composing a new ballet. Balanchine went to Hollywood for talks with the composer. On April 4 and 5 they completed the scenario of *Orpheus* and celebrated Russian Easter together.

．　．　．

IN SPITE of the strong opposition of Mrs. Tallchief, who objected to Balanchine on the grounds that he was "foreign," divorced, not Catholic and twice the age of her twenty-one-year-old daughter, Maria and Balanchine were married at New York's City Hall on August 16, 1946. Their first home was the apartment Balanchine had been renting for several years, but they spent a weekend honeymooning at costume designer Barbara Karinska's house in Massachusetts. Maria had to go on tour with the Ballet Russe almost immediately, and for the last time Balanchine traveled with Denham's company. When Maria was dancing in St. Louis, they drove together to visit her Indian relatives in Fairfax, Oklahoma, where her brothers were cowboys. Maria's cousin Helen, who lived on the Osage reservation, gave Balanchine a turquoise bracelet that he always treasured. He felt he had married America. It was at this time that he began to wear Western plaid shirts and string ties.

. . .

THE NEW Kirstein-Balanchine project was to be called Ballet Society. A handsome twelve-page announcement was sent out in October.

The most incredible and audacious decision was to sell no tickets to the general public. The only way to see a performance was to become a member. An Associate Member, in exchange for fifty dollars a year, received two seats for every performance, admission to special events, a subscription to *Dance Index* and various other publications and the chance to attend dress rehearsals. A Participating Member paid fifteen dollars a year and received one seat per performance, *Dance Index* and the Ballet Society Year Book.

Another gesture of bravado—of defiance, even—was the abolition of press tickets. If newspapers wanted to send their critics, they had to subscribe for them. This was unheard of, but newspapers toed the line. The "announcement" attracted about eight hundred subscribers.

The first program brought a regular gathering of the clans. Lew Christensen, out of the army, and Fred Danieli, out of *This Is the Army*, were together again, along with several other South American adventurers of 1941: Gisella Caccialanza, who had been dancing with her brother-in-law William Christensen's San Francisco Ballet; William Dollar, who, since Ballet International—a short-lived company under the direction of the Marquis de Cuevas—and the Mexican excursion, had worked in musicals and formed his own group; Georgia Hiden, who had been with Ballet Theatre; Beatrice Tompkins, who had been briefly with the Ballet Russe; Todd Bolender, who had danced with both Ballet Theatre and the Ballet Russe and begun to be a choreographer; John Taras, who, after four years with Ballet Theatre, had just made *Camille* on Dolin and Markova for de Basil's Original Ballet Russe. In addition to these, there were Elise Reiman, who had not worked with Balanchine since the days at the Metropolitan, and Mary Ellen Moylan, who had spent two years with the Ballet Russe and tried to sing as well as dance in a musical. There was also sixteen-year-old Tanaquil Le Clercq, whose only public appearances had been in two student performances given by the School of American Ballet.

The opening took place on November 20, 1946, at the auditorium of the Central High School of Needle Trades. Anatole Chujoy, the editor of the monthly *Dance News,* thought it was "as unlikely and unsuitable a place to present ballet as one can find in New York. A huge, barn-like hall, cold and uninviting, it is as impersonal as a railroad station. . . . It has hard, uncomfortable chairs and a stage devoid of any facilities." The instruments of the fifty-odd musicians of Leon Barzin's National Orchestra Society obstructed the public's view. For half an hour the audience sat listening to hammering and excited voices. "Then the curtain went up. The long wait, the uncomfortable seats . . . were immediately forgotten, for there was magic on the stage."

From the Hurok point of view, the first program contained all the seeds of unpopularity. But the subscribers were obviously devotees of Balanchine, old faithfuls, so that a little opera with dancing, which was new to New York, and a brand-new ballet by Hindemith were not going to put them off. The former was Ravel's *L'Enfant et les sortilèges* (translated by Kirstein and Jane Barzin, the conductor's wife, as *The Spellbound Child*), whose first performance Balanchine had staged with artists of the Diaghilev Ballet for the Opéra de Monte Carlo in 1925. The second was a new ballet, *The Four Temperaments.*

In both his productions of *The Spellbound Child,* Balanchine used two casts, with each role doubled by an offstage singer and an onstage dancer; but the Child, intended for a mezzo-soprano, was both sung and danced in the Ballet Society production by the young Joseph Connolly. The large cast was one complication—and expense. Another lay in the very nature of Colette's idea, for the Child is assailed by animals and inanimate objects—Cup, Tea Pot, Fire, Squirrel, Shepherds and Shepherdesses from the wallpaper, Princess from a book of fairy tales, Bat, Cats, Tree, *et al.,* and some of these characters converse in a mixture of English nonsense and pseudo-Oriental gibberish. No work could be more difficult to produce, especially on such a shallow stage. Todd Bolender, watching rehearsals, thought, "There's nothing you can do with it!" And most of the critics concurred.

The Four Temperaments had a long history. When Balanchine was in Hollywood in 1937, he had felt sufficiently affluent and optimistic to ask Hindemith for a ballet. Hindemith had been "willing," but he was busy. By 1940 he was a refugee, teaching composition at Yale; his financial expectations had decreased, and he made Balanchine an offer of "a danceable, nameless suite for $250." Balanchine personally paid for the score that was to become *The Four Temperaments.* But when Tchelitchev was called in, his designs and demands were so extravagant that the ballet was set aside.

When Balanchine began to make new choreography for the score, he retained Tchelitchev's idea of the four "cardinal humors" or "temperaments," the preponderance of any one of which, according to medieval lore, was said to determine a person's character. Although Tchelitchev was no longer working on the production, Balanchine accepted his recommendation of the painter Kurt Seligmann. His designs proved as disastrous as Tchelitchev's earlier ones; yet the marvels of movement were not entirely invisible beneath the dancers' cumbersome trappings.

Hindemith's scheme for *The Four Temperaments* is complicated. Three themes are stated. In Balanchine's ballet, the interpreters of the four temperaments—Melancholic, Sanguinic, Phlegmatic and Choleric—dance variations on all three. Because the pace had to be varied, Balanchine could not keep Melancholic drooping sadly throughout his scene, or Phlegmatic sagging lazily in his; each had a lively dance with partners. Inconsistencies do not matter in the light of the choreographer's blazing invention. At the premiere, Taras thought that in the final dance, "Tanaquil Le Clercq [as Choleric] appeared like a flash of lightning, searing the eyes of the audience." In this work, Balanchine crossed a new frontier and extended the possibilities of ordered movement. Chujoy wrote later that "there were requests for a repeat performance, but Kirstein and Balanchine held to their intention of performing only for subscribers. As a result there was a new spurt of subscriptions: the plan caught on." Nearly four years later, Balanchine discarded the grotesque costumes, and *The Four Temperaments* was henceforth performed in practice clothes. It is now one of Balanchine's most popular ballets all over the world.

．　．　．

SOON AFTER the end of the Japanese war, the directors of the Paris Opéra had begun writing to Balanchine. Lifar, accused of collaboration, had been "purged," and the theater needed a choreographer. In 1946, Balanchine reached an agreement with the administrator, Georges Hirsch. An attraction for him was that his old friend Roger Desormière would be conducting the Opéra's orchestra. It was understood that Toumanova would accompany Balanchine to Paris as a guest artist. On September 11, he wrote to his *"cher* Deso" about the possibility of staging *Firebird* with new choreography and getting away from the "Russian restaurant style," and about *Apollo, Symphonie concertante,* even *The Sleeping Beauty* and *Casse-Noisette.* Of these projects only *Apollo* was realized. He concluded: "I should also like to bring an American dancer . . . Maria Tallchief, who has become my wife. . . . You may be sure I should not have married a dancer who was no good. . . ."

Balanchine had not been in Paris since he had left it with Dmitriev to join Kirstein in 1933. And he had never, even in the days of Diaghilev, had so large a company as the Opéra's at his disposal. He was amazed that the Opéra dancers were so well trained, although they had been given second-rate ballets to perform in recent years, and he watched the classes of Carlotta Zambelli to discover the secret. Many of these dancers were warm adherents of Lifar, so they might well have been expected to resent Balanchine's presence, but at first he met no opposition inside the company. With all his mastery, he was so simple and natural that he inspired affection as well as respect. Only when he began to bring forward and give roles to talented girls from the school, whom the French dancers called "*les petits rats,*" and to junior members of the corps de ballet, did he provide senior dancers with a pretext for indignation. Balanchine was indeed frustrated working with *fonctionnaires* (as opposed to *employés*) who could not be dismissed; he complained bitterly to Maria that the dancers' union allowed them two hours for lunch—in the course of which they drank wine.

Mina Curtiss was in Paris working on an edition of Proust's letters, and she is our evidence that by early April the choreographer had less cause for optimism than he had had on his arrival five weeks before. In her diary for April 5 she wrote:

I had a very congenial dinner with George Balanchine last night. He is suffering the same kind of frustration I am at French laziness and inefficiency. I've got more or less used to a four-day week, a four-hour day. . . . George swears that he has at most a two-hour working day twice a week. The *corps de ballet* has only one full rehearsal a week and this week they're not having any because of the holidays. The *régisseur* [probably Hirsch, the administrator], like the director of the library, is never available without an appointment and George can't get any scores at all to plan ballets, not even some Bizet he wanted. Then Lifar has left a corps of saboteurs and he [Balanchine] doubts whether he will get even two ballets done in the six months [*sic*] he is here. However, they are making beautiful new costumes for *Sérénade.* . . .

Maria, who had had to complete the Ballet Russe tour before coming, had injured her foot in Chicago, and it was still swollen when she arrived in Paris. At twenty-one, she had never been abroad before. She was overawed by Toumanova, the inspiration of her childhood. Because George paid so much attention to his old Russian colleague and because most of the press photographs were of him with Tamara, Maria felt slightly left out of things. She had never danced on a raked stage before. When she looked down the slope of the Opéra stage toward the footlights she was scared to death.

Although Balanchine never gave class to the company, he taught Toumanova and Maria in private. He delighted in showing Paris to Maria and introducing her to people. They visited "Deso," who was to conduct Balanchine's ballets, and his wife in the country. They lunched with Matilda Kchessinskaya and her husband, the Grand Duke Andrei, and it was at "the Princess's" that Maria first met Margot Fonteyn, who was taking a holiday from the Sadler's Wells Ballet. Old friends like Nicolas Nabokov and Nathan Milstein were also in Paris.

Serenade was danced for the first time in Europe on April 30. At the suggestion of Tchelitchev, Balanchine had invited André Delfau to design the setting, which consisted mostly of white draperies. In *Apollon Musagète,* Michel Renault and Maria Tallchief were Apollo and Terpsichore. On July 2, Maria danced the Fairy in *Le Baiser de la fée,* with Alexandre Kalioujny and Toumanova as the Bridegroom and the Bride and was much praised.

Balanchine's final work for the Opéra was entirely new. Bizet's Symphony in C Major, written when the composer was seventeen, had never been performed in his lifetime; it was, in fact, not discovered and played until 1935. An exhilarating piece, with a romantic slow movement, it is ideal dance music. A complicated synopsis for a ballet, with a Ruby Priestess, a Sapphire Spirit, an Emerald Spirit and a Crystal Spirit in a Palace of Diamonds, has survived. Whoever concocted this—possibly the designer—Balanchine soon discarded it; he retained only the idea of using red costumes in the first movement, blue in the second, green in the third and white with diamonds in the fourth. He called the work *Palais de cristal.* It was the most spectacular choreography he had made since *Ballet Imperial,* and he arranged it for more dancers than he had ever before been able to muster simultaneously on a stage—forty-eight in all. Leonor Fini created a handsome grotto, and the stage was full of color and glitter.

This was to become one of the choreographer's most acclaimed and most popular ballets, yet it was created under enormous difficulties. It had been hard for Balanchine to get at the music because the archives were always shut, and hard to assemble his dancers for rehearsal. He also suffered the antipathy of Lifar's adherents. It was a real test of endurance.

Before the end of Balanchine's stay in Paris, there was a gala performance at Les Ambassadeurs restaurant in the gardens of the Champs-Elysées. Various stars were to perform, and Balanchine asked his dear Tamarochka if she would like him to arrange a number for her. *Would* she! He had found a Russian dance for solo violin by Tchaikovsky; he and Mama Toumanova discovered an old traditional costume with *kokoshnik* (beaded headdress) in the wardrobe of the Opéra. Toumanova thought that the dance was like a Fabergé jewel, but Balanchine's name did not even appear on the program. It was the last choreography he made on her.

·   ·   ·

THE DANCERS of the Opéra petitioned the directorate to give them a permanent *maître de ballet.* (Lifar would be allowed back in September, but not as a dancer, and his return caused a stage-hands' strike.) But Balanchine had never intended to stay longer than five months in Paris, because, as he told Maria, he felt that something was really starting in New York at last.

The Marquis de Cuevas had taken over the Nouveau Ballet de Monte Carlo from Lifar, and Maria's younger sister, Marjorie, had joined it. So had the tall, romantic-looking, Russian-born George Skibine; and during the Cuevas company's visit to Vichy that August he and Marjorie were married. Maria and Balanchine attended their wedding, as did Maria's former teacher, Bronislava Nijinska. Balanchine respected Mme. Nijinska, though he did not like her choreography. When she attacked him with the words, "I always thought you were such a gentleman. How could you do *Le*

Baiser de la fée when you knew I had done it?" Balanchine replied, "I *am* a gentleman. I let you do it first."

Balanchine and Maria arrived back in New York on August 14. After a weekend on Fire Island with Natalie Molostwoff, Balanchine took the train to Los Angeles. He arrived at 7:30 A.M. on August 21, spent most of every day with the Stravinskys and left on the twenty-sixth. Vera Stravinsky wrote in a letter to a friend: "Balanchine, returning from Paris, told how difficult it was for him to struggle against all the intrigues of the Opéra and the cost of living. He returned without a penny and as thin as a wick, and came here for a week [*sic*] for the sole reason of telling us in detail about his life there and how much he suffered." But surely Balanchine must also have been longing to hear how *Orpheus* was coming along, and Stravinsky must have played him some of it, even though he had not finished the orchestration.

Shortly after he got back from California, Balanchine abandoned his dancers to rehearse a new work for Ballet Theatre. He may have needed the money, but he also liked what he had been asked to do. Lucia Chase and Oliver Smith wanted a ballet to show off the technique of Igor Youskevitch, whom Balanchine had proposed taking with him to the Paris Opéra and who did not fit into Ballet Theatre's modern repertory. Charles Payne describes how Balanchine was asked if he could make a ballet to the fourth movement of Tchaikovsky's Suite No. 3 in G Major:

Balanchine took the score and returned shortly with the answer, "But of course." Four days before the company departed on tour, he auditioned and chose the female soloists and corps de ballet. In the next three days he set the first movement [*sic*] in seven hours of rehearsal. While the company was on tour, Nora Kaye conducted three one-hour rehearsals to keep the choreography fresh in the dancers' minds. Balanchine rejoined the company in Wilmington, Delaware, and continued rehearsing during the next few weeks until the opening at the New York City Center on November 11, 1947. [The premiere had in fact taken place in September in Richmond, Virginia.] In all, he had taken thirty-nine hours to create a thirty-two-minute ballet. . . . The ballet . . . was formally named *Theme and Variations* and opened on schedule. It not only provided Youskevitch with a stellar role, but it became, and has remained, one of the undimming gems in the Ballet Theatre repertory. It is safe to say that additional hours expended on its creation would not have improved this work of genius.

Before *Theme and Variations* was shown to New Yorkers, the opening performances of Ballet Society's second "season"—or, rather, second year of intermittent performances—had taken place at City Center, where future seasons were to be held. Balanchine's contribution was the Mozart *Symphonie concertante,* which was given a backcloth copied in gold monochrome from an architectural décor by one of the Bibiena family; the women dancers were dressed in the plainest white ballet costumes with the briefest of tutus; and the two *concertante* instruments, violin and viola, were represented by Tanaquil Le Clercq and Maria Tallchief—the latter appearing with Ballet Society for the first time.

Because Balanchine submitted himself completely to the subtle measures of Mozart's music, *Symphonie concertante* is probably the least theatrical ballet he ever made. It lacks even the implied man-woman relationship that classical pas de deux can hardly escape, for the single man is used for support only in the slow movement, while in the first and third movements the two women respond to each other. The music in the Andante is irresistible, but the opening Allegro maestoso and the closing Presto might seem mathematical to the inexperienced listener. The marvel of the music is the interplay between the two solo instruments and their relationship to the orchestra; and this correspondence is echoed in the choreography. Counterpoint is, after all, the most intellectual of aesthetic pleasures.

. . .

THAT AUTUMN, a handsome and intelligent girl from Buffalo named Betty Cage telephoned the Ballet Society office to ask for a secretarial job. She had been working for an avant-garde art magazine, *View,* and Tchelitchev told Kirstein she would be useful. She was hired as assistant to Frances Hawkins, the business manager, and when Hawkins left in 1948, Betty, aged thirty, was on her own. Balanchine and Kirstein came to rely on her more and more, first as a sort of personnel manager and eventually as general administrator. She held her position, which became of ever-increasing importance, for thirty-eight years.

．　．　．

ON MAY 20, 1947, Kirstein wrote to Stravinsky that he wanted to have a two-week season in New York, that he hoped the composer would score *Orpheus* for a small orchestra, and that he would like to give *Apollo* on the same program. Stravinsky telephoned back that *Orpheus* required only forty-three musicians, twenty-four of whom would be strings, but *Apollo* would need thirty-six strings. On September 23, Stravinsky finished orchestrating the ballet. On October 16, when Balanchine and Kirstein received copies, Balanchine sat straight down at the piano and began to play it.

Because Stravinsky knew that Balanchine understood his music, he accepted suggestions from him. It had been agreed that at the climax of the pas de deux, when Orpheus, against the orders of Pluto, tears off his blindfold and looks at Eurydice, there should be a moment of silence in the music. "How long will it take you to die, Maria?" Stravinsky asked. It took her one measure, and this was written into the score. Balanchine then proposed that the string music in F major should return at this point, and his idea was adopted.

In December Maria was in Hollywood with her family, and Balanchine planned to join her for Christmas and spend some time with Stravinsky. He arranged to travel with Nicolas Nabokov, who had been invited by the composer. Christmas dinner was at the Stravinsky house. "There were," wrote Nabokov, "Stravinsky's daughter and her French husband, the two Bolms . . . Eugene Berman and Stravinsky's physician, Dr. Edel, . . . and, finally the two Balanchines. . . . (Balanchine and I had silver goblets for drinking vodka.) . . . Conversation, out of deference to Maria Balanchine, lingered in a kind of pigeon [*sic*] English, but after dinner and late into the night the linguistic wind blew stronger and stronger in the Russian direction. . . ."

Tchelitchev had bowed out of doing the décor for *Orpheus,* so Kirstein, who had spoken to Balanchine on the telephone, wrote to Stravinsky proposing Isamu Noguchi, an American of Japanese parentage who was famous for his fine pottery fired in Japan, for his carvings and perhaps most of all for his globular lampshades of waxed paper stretched over wire frames. His work was startling, but fortunately both the Stravinskys, who came to New York to attend rehearsals, loved the scale models they were shown.

On the evening after their visit to Noguchi's studio, the Stravinskys were to dine with the Balanchines. That afternoon George had a rehearsal, and he left a note for "dear Mashka" asking her to keep an eye on the meat in the oven and to pour two spoonfuls of wine over it; he signed himself "General Coock," with a little self-portrait wearing a chef's hat. When Stravinsky rang the bell and burst into the apartment Maria dropped the potatoes. She was upset, but he said, "Oh, Maria, they'll taste much better now."

The poet W. H. Auden, who was writing the libretto of Stravinsky's opera *The Rake's Progress,* also came—and drank a whole bottle of Cointreau after dinner. Robert Craft has recorded that Stravinsky often found it hard to make out Auden's English—and, for that matter, his French and German. Balanchine could not understand a single word he said.

Rehearsals for *Orpheus* were spread over several months. Meanwhile, two more new ballets were presented by Ballet Society. The idea for *The Triumph of Bacchus and Ariadne* came from its designer, Corrado Cagli. His fellow Italian Vittorio Rieti took a carnival song written by Lorenzo de' Medici as the starting point of a masque "celebrating Youth and Age, sacred and profane love: of a kind that might have been performed at the Florentine "court." These masques were, in fact, the predecessors of classical ballet.

Nicholas Magallanes thought that the pas de deux he danced with Tanaquil Le Clercq was a "very pretty, leaves-in-the-hair, nude-looking, drapery kind of thing." Marie-Jeanne, who had recently rejoined the company, danced a Nymph; she considered her wild solo one of the most effective of her career. Francisco Moncion played Midas, who in his greed for gold had to grovel on the ground, scratching the stage with his nails. "Make more noise," said Balanchine. "More noise! Like chalk on blackboard!"

For the next program, Balanchine staged a simplified version of the Bizet ballet he had devised for the Paris Opéra, renaming it *Symphony in C.* Since Ballet Society could provide only thirty-eight dancers, as opposed to the forty-eight he had used in Paris, every member of the corps, instead of appearing in only one movement and then the finale, had to dance in all five, so there was no question of dressing them in different colors. All the women were in white and the men in black tights with white socks and slippers.

Like the French, most New Yorkers found the ballet irresistible. "If there ever was any doubt that Balanchine was the greatest choreographer of our time," wrote Chujoy, "this doubt was dispelled when the curtain came down on his *Symphony in C.*" But John Martin was still unpersuaded: "Balanchine has once again given us that ballet of his, this time for some inscrutable reason to the Bizet symphony. Up to the middle of the third movement [when Martin left the theater to write his piece], he had used virtually all of his familiar tricks. . . . "

Nicholas Magallanes was to create the role of Orpheus, but Balanchine had begun to work out his choreography at the very beginning of 1948, before Magallanes became available, and Francisco Moncion, who would dance the Dark Angel, had not only to learn his own part but to stand in for Orpheus. Moncion found, as he had with *The Four Temperaments,* that to work on a ballet with Balanchine from the very start was intensely stimulating. "Nobody showed how to perform a movement, whether for man or woman, more wonderfully than Balanchine," Moncion explained. "His limbs expressed his mind." He took such pains that Moncion thought working with him was like a million dollars' worth of training. One day at the School, Maria came in after a class to find the two men tied together in an extraordinary knot. "Take your hands off my husband!" she exclaimed; then, after asking George if he would like chicken for dinner, she departed with a good exit line: "I'll leave you boys together."

Maria was, of course, to dance Eurydice; and the Bacchantes, who tore Orpheus to pieces after his return to a second mourning on earth, were led by Tanaquil Le Clercq, the first ballerina to be completely a product of the School of American Ballet.

Three years after she won a scholarship in 1941, she was given a fellowship. Since then, Balanchine had entrusted her with Choleric in *The Four Temperaments;* she had been singled out by the critics in Taras's *Minotaur;* she had danced with Magallanes in Merce Cunningham's *The Seasons,* with Maria Tallchief in *Symphonie concertante,* and in the second movement of Bizet's *Symphony in C.* Her father was of French origin, and her mother came from a well-to-do St. Louis family. Tanaquil, who was born in Paris, was witty, intellectual, impulsive, tall and thin, with long, Alice-in-Wonderland hair. Her mocking eyes seemed to indicate that she was cut out for comedy, but the very different roles listed above indicate how versatile she became. In 1948 she was eighteen.

None of Balanchine's dancers, who worked so hard in these months to make possible the sparse performances of Ballet Society, had any notion that he or she was in at the beginning of a great venture. None had any other employment in the theater. They rehearsed unpaid, knowing that they would receive eighteen dollars a show. They were grateful for a chance to perform, and as the date of the next program drew near, they went on diets. Maria, of course, lived with Balanchine, but he had very little money at the time, and he never took a penny from Ballet Society. Tanaquil lived with her mother. Magallanes roomed with a friend. Moncion worked as a model in an art school before going off to take class. But all of them were to look back later in wonder on these "great days" when Balanchine and Stravinsky made each one of them a star.

Kirstein thought the collaboration of composer and choreographer on *Orpheus* must have been the closest since that of Tchaikovsky and Petipa. Balanchine had told Stravinsky that the pas de deux should take "about two and a half minutes," but Stravinsky scolded him. "Don't tell me 'about.' . . . It's either two minutes and twenty, thirty or forty seconds; no more, no less."

An important part of the décor was a "translucent curtain of China silk" similar to that which had fallen from the flies to cover the heroine of *Errante*. According to Kirstein:

The silk for this curtain cost over a thousand dollars. Having it sewed and delivered to the theater cost even more, and . . . we had no cash to pay for it two days before a dress rehearsal. . . . We had spent what there was and could borrow no more. . . . Noguchi was a model of patient despair, having been refused further credit from one scenery shop because previous bills were unpaid . . . We did not notice that Balanchine had disappeared from rehearsal. Suddenly he reappeared with five hundred dollars in cash in each hand and tossed the money to Frances Hawkins. We begged to know where he'd found it; he would say nothing except that he hadn't robbed a bank.

John Taras has said of *Orpheus*:

The choreography for Magallanes was unlike anything Balanchine had done before. There were very few steps and no conventional ones. The movement was more like the miming of a song than the execution of a dance. It implied a vocal origin. The long, sustained phrases of Eurydice, as she yearned for a reaction from Orpheus, were beautifully interpreted by Tallchief. The [Dark] Angel and Apollo mimed rather than danced, as Balanchine played down the cool emotions of the score. Only the Furies and the Bacchantes really danced, and with his arrangement for the former, Balanchine was never completely satisfied. But the Bacchantes were given an extraordinary exultant choreography, in which the terrifying Le Clercq, wearing a long red wig, clawed, pounced and stamped on Orpheus, finally destroying him; and this was the passage that Balanchine most loved to rehearse at subsequent revivals.

That Stravinsky himself was to conduct the first performance of his new ballet made April 28, 1948, a doubly special occasion for the members of Ballet Society. When the ballet was over, Chujoy reported, "there was a seemingly unending ovation for the dancers, for Balanchine, for Stravinsky, for Noguchi. The audience applauded, stamped, shouted. Everyone . . . was very happy." There were four more performances by Ballet Society on the three following days, each including *Orpheus.* To these the nonsubscribing public was admitted. Yet with all its success, Ballet Society still could not count the New York City Center of Music and Drama as its home.

Shortly before the first night of *Orpheus,* Kirstein had been summoned to Nelson Rockefeller's office in Rockefeller Center to meet the latter's first cousin by marriage, George de Cuevas. The marquis offered him the Cosmopolitan Theater at Columbus Circle, which W. R. Hearst had built for Marion Davies and which de Cuevas had renovated. He announced that he and the new company he planned to found would share it with Ballet Society, and that for the latter it would be rent free. "Too good to be true," wrote Kirstein; and "too good to be true" it was. The marquis returned to Europe, and nothing more was heard of the plan. When, therefore, Kirstein was asked to pay a visit to the office of the managing director of City Center, Morton Baum, to discuss a new proposition, he was "short and irritable." Hadn't he heard it all before—from Edward Johnson at the Metropolitan, from Cuevas?

On the previous evening, Baum, lawyer, tax counsel to the city and amateur musician, had seen *Orpheus* and had fallen in love with it. By his own account:

It was the strangest meeting. Kirstein was belligerent, almost hostile to me, vituperative against the entire ballet field, its policies, managers, repertoire. He seemed not to believe in the sincerity of my call and was suspicious of everything I said. He told me that the funds of Ballet Society were exhausted and that it might have to fold, but that he would carry on his struggle to create an American ballet.

There was already a New York City drama company and a New York City Opera that held seasons at the City Center at popular prices. Baum asked Kirstein if he would like Ballet Society to participate in the opera seasons, as well as giving regular performances of its own. He emphasized that he was only one of the board of directors and that the others might not approve the idea. He explained that the drama company, with its lower costs, brought in revenue, while the opera company ran at a loss. There would be no question of diverting funds to subsidize the ballet. The ballet company would, for the time being, have to cover its own deficit, but with the amalgamation this would surely be smaller than before.

Finally he asked, "Mr. Kirstein, how would you like the idea of Ballet Society becoming the New York City Ballet?"

After a moment of stunned silence, Lincoln Kirstein exclaimed, "If you do that for us I will give you in three years the finest ballet company in America."

He ran all the way to Madison Avenue to tell Balanchine.

Chapter 9

IN SEARCH OF A FORMULA:

1 9 4 8 - 1 9 5 7

UNA KAI, a dancer in the company who later became a ballet mistress, remembers what a thrilling moment it was for the dancers of Ballet Society when Lincoln Kirstein came backstage and told them they were to become the New York City Ballet. Some of them, who had given up much to work for Balanchine, saw for the first time the prospect of financial security.

The security was, however, of a very limited kind. The final season of Ballet Society had lasted from April 28 to May 1, 1948— four days. The new company's first season would begin October 11. Until rehearsals started, the dancers would live on unemployment insurance, and Balanchine himself would be working in Europe for the Marquis de Cuevas's Grand Ballet de Monte-Carlo. During the fall, he would be back at the old grind of devising dances for operas—this time for the New York City Opera.

For the next few years, Kirstein and Balanchine were uncertain up to the last moment when their New York seasons would be—or if they would be at all. Morton Baum made money for City Center by renting it out to visiting attractions, and the new ballet company had to be fitted in when there was a gap. Once they had resigned themselves to the fact that they would never enjoy a federal sub-sidy—for what did Louisiana or North Dakota care about subsidiz-ing a New York company?—and once Balanchine had firmly declined to embark on tours with Hurok, which would have meant one-night stands and a reduced orchestra, it was necessary to find other opportunities to keep the dancers dancing. At first, foreign tours were the only solution, then gradually it became possible to count on summer dates on the West Coast and in Chicago.

During all the years at City Center, Balanchine never accepted a salary. He was paid to stage ballets for other companies and occasionally to arrange dances for a musical.

When one realizes how difficult it was to hold a short New York season once, twice or three times a year; to plan tours and over-come the incessant problems that cropped up in the course of them; to meet deficits, raise money for production costs and pay dancers a meager wage, the actual making of ballets by Balanchine— several new ones every year—appears almost incidental. Yet it was for the creation of these ballets that the School and the company had come into existence; and it was to facilitate their performance under the best possible conditions that Kirstein, Cage and produc-tion manager/stage director Edward Bigelow devoted their lives.

On October 11, the first performance of the New York City Ballet (apart from the company's participation in *Carmen* the previ-ous day) took place. The program was *Concerto Barocco*, *Orpheus* and *Symphony in C*—three marvels, but chosen because there was no money for a new work.

That fall Marie-Jeanne danced in *Serenade;* and since the Cuevas company had temporarily fallen apart, André Eglevsky was free to make guest appearances in *Symphony in C.* On November 8, Balanchine surprised everyone by taking Barzin's place on the podium to conduct the Bizet. At the end the orchestra stood to applaud him.

This first season, which ended on November 23, the company played to little more than fifty percent of capacity. According to Chujoy, Kirstein, who himself had made up the $47,000 deficit, was deeply discouraged. Balanchine, however, argued that "the company simply had not had a fair chance," since the seasons of the Ballet Russe and the Paris Opéra company had emptied the purses of the ballet-going public; and Baum agreed with him. His admiration for the company had increased. He proposed that in the future the New York City Ballet be independent of the Opera, and City Center would take over from Ballet Society the financial responsibility for its running expenses, leaving the Society simply to raise money for new productions.

Jerome Robbins, whose ballet *Fancy Free* had been the basis for a successful musical, *On the Town,* and who was much in demand for devising dances on Broadway, felt irresistibly drawn to become part of the noble enterprise, and offered his services as a choreographer. He was made welcome and began work on *The Guests,* to a score by Marc Blitzstein. Balanchine also asked Antony Tudor to revive his *Time Table,* which had been performed only in South America. Its music by Copland added another American component to the repertoire.

In July 1948, Balanchine and Maria left for Monte Carlo, where Balanchine was to rehearse two ballets with the Grand Ballet de Monte-Carlo. When the company traveled to London for a season at Covent Garden, *Concerto Barocco* was given on opening night. It was the first time the work had been performed outside the Americas: but by the time *Night Shadow* was given and acclaimed at the end of August, the Balanchines had returned to the States.

In the fall, not only did all the principal dancers of the New York City Ballet—except Marie-Jeanne—return to the fold for the

November season, but little red-headed Janet Reed and dark, imposing Melissa Hayden came from Ballet Theatre to join the company. Jerome Robbins signed on as a dancer as well as a choreographer. Balanchine made him associate artistic director of the company.

. . .

AT THE end of Janaury 1949, NYCB dancers were faced with a nine-month layoff. No one could blame them if they sought employment with other companies. Balanchine was concerned that Maria, who was becoming a better dancer than ever under his guidance, keep dancing. The resuscitation of Ballet Theatre provided her with an opportunity, and she went on tour with them. Her husband rehearsed her in the "Bluebird" pas de deux from *The Sleeping Beauty*, which she danced with Youskevitch, and also in *Apollo*, *Theme and Variations* and Antony Tudor's *Jardin aux lilas.*

While Maria was with Ballet Theatre, Balanchine did his first work for television, a version of *Cinderella* to the music of Tchaikovsky, with Tanaquil Le Clercq and Herbert Bliss as Cinderella and the Prince.

One evening in the spring, when both the Balanchines were in New York together, Sol Hurok asked them to dine at the Russian Tea Room. His question to Balanchine came as a surprise: "Don't you want your wife to dance the Firebird?" Maria, with "visions of Karsavina in her mind," nearly fainted. Balanchine, who seldom showed surprise, sniffed, made his customary "mmm" noise and murmured, "Oh? Well . . . perhaps." As it turned out, this friendly suggestion from his old enemy Hurok was not entirely disinterested. Since Hurok had ceased to present Ballet Theatre, he had been paying storage fees for Chagall's *Firebird* sets and costumes. Balanchine, like the composer himself, was less fond of Stravinsky's early "Russian-export" style than of his later work, but he recognized that the Firebird would be an ideal role for Maria. A bargain was struck: New York City Ballet bought the Chagall production for $2,500, and during a summer holiday with Maria in California, Balanchine discussed with Stravinsky the form his new version, which was to be a suite from the original score, would take.

Meanwhile, the fame of *Orpheus* had crossed the Atlantic. David Webster, the general administrator of London's Royal Opera House, coveted it for the Sadler's Wells Ballet—which, incidentally, Hurok was planning to present at the Metropolitan Opera House in the fall of 1949. The company had been founded—and was directed—by Balanchine's old colleague Ninette de Valois. David Webster cabled Balanchine asking if he would produce *Orpheus* for the English company while they were in New York. Betty Cage forwarded the cable to California, asking him, "Why not tell him we'd be glad to take our company over and perform *Orpheus* for them?" This is the first known suggestion of a London season for the New York City Ballet—or of any season outside the United States. Balanchine answered that he would be busy with his own company at the time of the Sadler's Wells visit, but that he and Webster could at least discuss matters then.

The Sadler's Wells Ballet opened at the Metropolitan Opera House on October 9 with *The Sleeping Beauty;* Margot Fonteyn was Aurora and Constant Lambert conducted. New York had never seen a full-length classical ballet presented with such magnificence, and the show was a sensation. Kirstein and Balanchine, whose favorite ballet this was, witnessed the ovation, attended Mayor O'Dwyer's party for the visitors at Gracie Mansion and read the laudatory notices with mixed feelings. They could never hope for a federal subsidy such as Sadler's Wells received through the Arts Council from the British Treasury. Whatever reservations they might have about some of the British dancers and their training, there was much for them to admire—and envy.

I had written from London to ask Kirstein, whom I had never met, to write an article on the American debut of Sadler's Wells for my magazine, *Ballet.* Since Kirstein was hoping to take the New York City Ballet, sooner or later, to London, this was something he could not provide, but he wrote me his opinion very frankly, and a correspondence began which continued intermittently for over thirty years. He ended his first letter with a statement of the credo that had guided and would continue to guide his life: "Balanchine is simply the only genius of the dance since Petipa. . . . This is hard to swallow, as you know; and to dance the hard works you need a kind of heartless, soulless, angelic type of dancer, which he has invented from our school."

.   .   .

Firebird, whether choreographed by Fokine, Balanchine, Cranko or Taras, is an unusual ballet in that the ballerina's big solo comes right at the beginning and is followed by the *pas d'action* of her capture by the Prince. Maria Tallchief described how Balanchine's choreography took shape:

After the opening variation, you immediately go into the pas de deux. Breathwise and musclewise it was very demanding. [Balanchine] did the variation first and then the pas de deux; we didn't really do it all in one stretch. It was only when it was all together and I finally went through it without stopping that I realized it was practically impossible. The variation contained many low, fast jumps, near the floor, lots of quick footwork, sudden changes of direction, off-balance turns, turns from pointe to pointe, turned-in, turned-out positions, one after another. It was another way of moving. . . . There was no time.

Moncion, who danced the Prince, has said, "The ballet was made for Maria, and she went after it like a demon, with ferocity, as if possessed."

When the pas de deux, rehearsed in private, was shown for the first time to the company, they burst into applause. Even so, the ballet's overwhelming success with the public took everyone by surprise. "It was like a football stadium." Indeed, *Time* magazine wrote, "The flashing first-scene duet brought a touchdown roar from the audience." Next morning, as the Balanchines were out walking, George took Maria into Tiffany's and ordered her a gold compact with a firebird on it.

Four days afterward, Balanchine presented a new ballet, *Bourrée fantasque.* It had four movements, and Una Kai said he arranged one a day. The music was by Emmanuel Chabrier. Barbara Karinska, the celebrated theatrical dressmaker, who had worked in London and Paris before the war, arriving from triumphs in Hollywood to begin what was to be a long association with the New York City Ballet, made an extraordinarily generous gesture: she gave Balanchine the costumes for *Bourrée fantasque* for the price of the materials.

Balanchine also staged *The Prodigal Son* for the first time since the death of Diaghilev, and took endless pains rehearsing Robbins and Maria in the two main roles. Apart from his *Petrushka* for Ballet Theatre, Robbins had never been seen in a great tragic role before—and of course he had never seen Lifar in 1929. Vera Stravinsky *had,* and toward the end of her life she said there had never been a Prodigal as good as Robbins.

Balanchine left New York before the end of the season, arriving in London on March 18 to teach *Ballet Imperial* to the Sadler's Wells Ballet. Margot Fonetyn and Michael Somes, the two principals, were so used to dancing Ashton's choreography that Balanchine's demands were a shock to them. Nevertheless, Somes was thrilled by the arrangement of the piano cadenzas in *Ballet Imperial,* and always remembered how Balanchine liked "long leaps, high arabesques and little or no demi-plié, also most things done at double speed!" Later Somes became exasperated at always being congratulated on his noble manner as he walked on and off the stage in the second movement—from which Balanchine had cut all the pantomime.

Beryl Grey was happy to be chosen as the second ballerina, and was determined to learn all she could during the "wonderful classes" Balanchine gave before rehearsals. She was "amazed when he taught not to put the heel down when landing from a *grand jeté en tournant.* " Beryl became engaged to be married that spring and rushed to announce the good news to Balanchine. To her disappointment "he showed much displeasure and said a ballerina could not spare time for the luxury of being married." Still, she recognized that "he was a great man who demanded everything from his dancers and knew how to extract it."

On the evening after Balanchine's arrival, he, Kirstein, Ashton and I dined with Lydia Lopoukhova (Lady Keynes) in Gordon Square, Bloomsbury. This was very near to where Balanchine and his colleagues from Russia had taken lodgings in 1924. It was long after midnight when we started home, so the square where Vanessa Bell and Virginia Woolf had held court was silent and empty of traffic. A solitary black cat lingered near the big Victorian church at the corner; when I called "pooza-pooza!" to it in the wheedling voice I always use for addressing cats, it crossed the road to be patted. Balanchine, whose love of cats became legendary, was intrigued. Many years later, he interrupted a class he was giving in New York to inquire, when he saw me enter the room, "How are the poozas of Bloomsbury?" And during one of the last rehearsals for the Stravinsky Festival of 1972, when Kay Mazzo appeared with a very small kitten in her arms, Balanchine instantly dropped everything and went to it, crooning, "Kitty, kittteee. . . . "

. . .

KIRSTEIN was hoping to sign a contract with David Webster for a NYCB season at Covent Garden, but he found him hard to deal with; so Frances Hawkins flew over to see what she could do. She was no more successful than Kirstein and decided to leave on April 6, the day after the first night of *Ballet Imperial.*

That ballet's triumph changed everything. There were seventeen curtain calls, and the company gave its guest choreographer a wreath. Balanchine wrote to Maria that the "cold" London audience "was wild almost like New York." At a party afterward, Frances Hawkins went up to Webster to say good-bye. "Webster,

all smiles, stopped her farewells; she must not leave London until
he had signed our contract," wrote Kirstein. Would Miss Hawkins
be at his office at eleven next morning? She would. Covent Garden
agreed to pay the New York City Ballet £2,000 a week during their
six-week season, and half their transportation costs. A provincial
tour was also planned.

To make the London season possible, all the dancers took a cut
of ten dollars a week, because living in England was said to be
cheaper. The night of July 10, 1950, when the company opened
their first season abroad, at Covent Garden, was as momentous an
occasion for them as the opening night at the Metropolitan Opera
had been for Sadler's Wells. If they failed, they might have to close
for good.

Although Londoners, accustomed to spectacular classics, were
slightly chilled by NYCB's sparsity of décor, they responded on the
whole with enthusiasm to Balanchine's inventiveness and to the
special quality of his dancers. The theater was sold to about 75
percent capacity throughout the season. Most of the critics, however, were both disappointed and disappointing. Cyril Beaumont,
in the *Sunday Times,* wrote of the "cold, impersonal quality" of
Balanchine's ballets, which strongly piqued Balanchine. Even a
quarter of a century later, when he watched a dancer moving too
carefully or "correctly" in class, he would exclaim, "Beaumont,
Beaumont!" James Monahan in the *Guardian* called *Orpheus* "a
mild, undramatic account of a legend which itself is far from
undramatic or mild." The critics' reaction to *Firebird* was the
biggest disappointment of all. The Fokine version, with its much
longer score, was clearly considered sacred. But my life was
changed by the revelation of Balanchine's varied genius.

The company had a week's layoff without pay, and because
living in London had indeed proved cheaper than New York, some
dancers, including Maria Tallchief, could afford a trip to Paris.
They returned to embark with the company on an unsuccessful
provincial tour of Manchester, Liverpool and Croydon.

When Balanchine and I dined alone at Venezia in Soho, I asked innumerable questions but was too scatterbrained to record most of the answers. I can remember only a few fragments. "Do you think history goes in circles, repeating itself at regular intervals?" "No, it goes in spirals." "Who is your favorite heroine in fiction?" "Natasha in *War and Peace.* " "Which is your favorite opera?" "*Don Giovanni.* " We also discussed food and cooking. Balanchine said that if he ever retired, he would like to open a restaurant— "quite a small one, just six or seven tables." He had taken a furnished flat near the Wallace Collection. It was here, at supper with Maria and Tanaquil Le Clercq, that he quoted my review of the Weber *Pas de deux romantique,* which had appeared that morning, saying I had "understood exactly" the demi-caractère, slightly tongue-in-cheek quality he had introduced into the classical pas de deux. This would hardly be worth mentioning if it were not for the fact that even admirers such as Chujoy missed the point of the duet, calling it "plain bad." It was also in Balanchine's apartment, on the Sunday night after the season finished, that Lucian Freud began a drawing of Balanchine, which he never completed. The only paper available was a sheet of foolscap ruled for the keeping of accounts.

The New York City Ballet would give only three more seasons in London before Balanchine's death thirty-three years later. In spite of this, the number of his British admirers steadily increased, and several British companies asked him to produce—or send one of his assistants to produce—some of his most popular works for them.

.   .   .

To SAY that Balanchine was not cut out for matrimony—at least for matrimony American-style—is an understatement. Although in the ballet classroom it was all blood, sweat and tears for the girls he schooled and loved, "making the beautiful more beautiful" (his own expression), in the home he expected them to recline in a perfumed paradise, fanned by eunuchs. It is paradoxical that he, who liked to do his own ironing—not only because he found the whole procedure relaxing, but because of the unpleasant smell shirts had when they came back from the laundry—should be irritated when Maria scrubbed the floor and asked him to walk on newspaper. Maria had a very strong character and was not prepared to stand for any nonsense. She also liked to play poker—which Balanchine did not—and on free evenings Magallanes and a few other dancers were glad to have a game with her. Friends noticed that Balanchine and Maria were seldom alone together.

Byron once confessed, "My heart always alights on the nearest perch." With Balanchine it was natural that the nearest perch should be the latest young dancer he was training and creating roles for, the up-and-coming ballerina, the rising star. In London, he and Maria had "more or less agreed to separate." Tanaquil Le Clercq was sharing their apartment. "I was very close to Tanny," Maria said later. "I had no idea there was a romance going on. I thought she liked Lew." It was when Maria returned from her visit to France between the end of the London season and the opening of the tour in Manchester that she became aware of the situation. Her response was to move out.

. . .

BALANCHINE had always loved the music of Ravel, which musicologists tended to rate as of lesser importance, because less revolutionary, than that of Debussy. Diaghilev had refused Ravel's *La Valse,* written for him in 1920, because he found it untheatrical; Ravel never forgave him. In 1951, Balanchine decided to make a ballet to it, but since it was short, he decided to preface it with the composer's earlier *Valses nobles et sentimentales.*

When Ravel composed *La Valse* in the 1920s, the theme of what Ravel, quoting Comte de Salvandy, had called "dancing on the edge of a volcano" was associated in his mind with 1914; to us it may suggest 1939. It was a Romantic or Gothic theme that recalls Poe's "Masque of the Red Death." When Balanchine decided to link the two compositions, the first part of his ballet took on a quality that, without having any specific period, was essentially French. By some marvel of intuition, the choreographer, who never went out in society because it tired and bored him, saw into the heart of sophisticated Paris. Here was a *beau monde* which, despite the thunder and sunsets of the Romantic movement, had never outlived the rococo period, when love was a game or an applied art, like cabinetmaking or *haute cuisine.*

The costumes for such a ballet had to attain the very height of elegance, which in France implied simplicity and understatement. Karinska had, after all, worked in Paris—and made Bérard's costumes for *Cotillon*—before she came to America. Her full-skirted ball gowns had steel-gray satin bodices, and beneath the layers of gray tulle overskirt, crimson or vermilion petticoats flashed through. These dresses, as well as the women's long white gloves, appeared at moments almost to have dictated the choreography. A characteristic gesture of the feckless girls would be a coquettish fluffing-up of their skirts. The men wore stylized evening dress, black and white.

The first of the eight waltzes in the opening section is played as an overture. The second reveals three ladies, who stand in a row facing the audience, holding up their arms affectedly in a way that appears to proclaim their charming but sinister authority. They are society's witches, who console themselves for the loss of youth by the exercise of power. As they dance, their hands make absurd, coy, mannered gestures, which seem traditional signals, like the language of an eighteenth-century fan.

The tripping third waltz, in which two lovers dance slowly, acquires an almost pastoral quality from the oboe. The fourth, for another couple, is more ecstatic. In the fifth there are plaintive clarinets. The quicker sixth is a solo for a girl. As she dips and circles, she seems to sweep the floor with her skirt. Her lover comes to rejoin her in the seventh, but is intercepted by the three affected, dangerous ladies, and the girl runs off.

A climactic phrase of music foretells the coming nightmare of *La Valse.* This may have been what gave Balanchine the idea of linking Ravel's two compositions; certainly it allows us to recognize the three ladies as harbingers of doom. The eighth waltz brings on a hesitant girl in white. (Tanaquil La Clercq later described how she enjoyed watching the earlier waltzes from the wings. When she made her entrance it was "like going to a party.") Her arms mime the music. A man comes toward her. They do backbends and at first seem not to know each other. They dance with a ceremonial and slightly depraved elegance. Dark-blue gauze curtains—which have hitherto reduced the depth of the stage— part as the music of *La Valse* begins, revealing black-draped chandeliers glimmering in the shadows; the decks are cleared for some disastrous event. Low bass rumblings are followed by eerie glissandos on the woodwinds and deceptive showers of golden rain on the harp. Lit by spotlights, dancers pursue each other in a desperate search. We have a glimpse of three ladies hiding their faces—are they the ominous trio of the preceding scene? The lights go up. The girl in white is the leader of the ball. But she is doomed. A sinister black-clad man stalks on, followed by a servant bearing gifts. At first the girl turns away in horror, then she becomes fascinated and accepts the jet necklace, the transparent black dress to be fastened on over her white one, the long black gloves. Balanchine gave Le Clercq no indications of how to act or react. The dramatic mood grew completely out of the steps. Denby paid tribute to her extraordinary interpretation when she accepted the black ornaments. "The way I remember Tanny's marvelous gesture of putting on the gloves was that when she put her hand into the glove she threw up her head at the same time, so that it was a kind of immolation, you felt, like diving to destruction." Moncion, the man in black, steers her into a frenzied dance. When at last she falls dead, she is lifted by a group of men as the crowd continues its heedless whirling.

Balanchine had found an admirable way of making a plotless, all-dancing ballet into something intensely dramatic that was also a delight to the eye. And he had done this, as always, by remaining faithful to the spirit of the music.

. . .

FROM the time of their return from England in the fall of 1950 until April 1952, when they went abroad again, the New York City Ballet came to accumulate the kind of eclectic repertory at which Lucia Chase had aimed when she founded Ballet Theatre just over ten years before. The ballets of Jerome Robbins had already added diversity to the repertory (and, God knows, Balanchine's works were diverse enough, whatever the English might think). Now Antony Tudor joined the company, bringing with him Hugh Laing, who had been his friend and the protagonist of nearly all his works, and Laing's wife, Diana Adams, from Virginia, as well as Nora Kaye, who specialized in dramatic roles. Then there was Eglevsky, who joined the company not exactly as a guest artist but as a glamorous Russian outsider. Special pas de deux were included in the programs to display his exceptional technique, which was matched by that of Tallchief. Balanchine even made a one-act version of *Swan Lake* for them, with a soaring pas de trois in which Patricia Wilde was given a chance to show her almost masculine power of beating and jumping. This *Swan Lake* shocked many of the dancers, who considered it a betrayal of the company's avant-garde tradition.

Balanchine revived *Card Party* (as it was now called) for Bolender and *Apollo* for Eglevsky. He created a comic role for Robbins in *Tyl Ulenspiegel*, and he made an American ballet, *Bayou* (about the Acadians of the Southern swamps), to please Kirstein, who wanted to use Virgil Thomson's music from the film *Louisiana Story*.

Although NYCB would always need "novelties," which, in fact, Balanchine was quite capable of turning out without help from others, there would never again be such a panicky period in the company's history. Antony Tudor did not stay for more than a year, but when he, Laing and Kaye left, Diana Adams remained behind and became a great ballerina.

In the middle of this orgy of eclecticism, Balanchine produced a ballet in his most limpid classical manner. At dinner with Lucia Davidova one evening, the music lover and balletomane Bob Sandbach drew Balanchine's attention to a Mozart divertimento (No. 15 in B-flat major, K. 287) which Toscanini had performed and recorded in 1947, and Balanchine fell in love with the music at once and forever. After he had decided to omit the second of the two Minuets and the Andante opening of the sixth and last movement, he was left with an opening Allegro, a Theme and six Variations, a Minuet and an Allegro finale. Bérard's old costumes for *Mozartiana* were used. There were five wonderful ballerinas, Adams, Hayden, Le Clercq, Tallchief and Wilde; three distinguished male dancers, Eglevsky, Magallanes and Robbins; and a corps of eight girls. "A heavenly piece," wrote Denby, "and everyone knows it immediately." It was called *Caracole*. (Balanchine's later *Divertimento No. 15* is an almost completely different ballet to the same music.)

. . .

NINETEEN FIFTY-TWO saw the first of the grand tours of Europe, which would be repeated with variations in 1953, 1955 and 1956. These tours were organized by the Paris agency of Léon Leonidoff, who was as fervent an admirer of Balanchine the choreographer as he was devoted to Balanchine the man. Betty Cage also traveled with the company, and soon found that there were unforeseen difficulties to contend with every day. Details of program planning and casting for the tours often had to be carried out while Balanchine was away staging ballets for European companies.

In 1952, he left for La Scala, Milan, before the end of the February–March season in New York, so Betty Cage had to plan the European tour with him while he was over three thousand miles away. She had wrung a salary of $10,000 a year for him from Morton Baum. But Balanchine wrote, "I don't want any contract with City Center. . . . I don't want any ten thousand dollars from Baum, and that's definite." Meanwhile, Antonio Ghiringhelli, Intendant of La Scala, had become a devotee of Balanchine, whose professionalism in teaching a difficult ballet to a strange troupe in the shortest possible time impressed him enormously.

Balanchine joined his company in Barcelona. Kirstein stayed at home because his mother was dying. There were fears that the more elegant Catalonians would have gone to their country houses, which was usual during Holy Week, but all turned out well, except that the box holders tended to arrive only after the first intermission. Barcelona's farewell to the company was sensational. As the final ballet, *Symphony in C,* closed, rose petals and laurel leaves fell from the upper tier of the Liceo, attendants brought on so many baskets of flowers that the stage became a garden, and a flock of doves was released.

In Paris, the Ballet was to open with one performance at the Opéra, then move to the Théâtre des Champs-Elysées for four more nights. But the Opéra staff hated them and dropped and broke their scenery. At the Champs-Elysées, stagehands sat in the flies and fired water pistols at one another during performances. It was a period when Europeans had begun to resent the "taking over" of Europe by rich Americans. But although people spoke of "Coca-Colonization" and wrote "Yankee go home" on walls, the company was booked to return to Paris in June.

Kirstein insisted that his tired troupe oblige the State Department by dancing in Berlin after the Edinburgh Festival. "We are really working for the Government now," he explained, "and very big stakes are involved. If we have official State Dept. support this time it is a very valuable precedent to establish. . . . It will also help us with the Ford Foundation, with whom I am talking. . . ."

This was the first mention of the great foundation that would play so vital a part in the later years of the New York City Ballet.

．　．　．

BALANCHINE used to keep up the spirits of his company when he traveled with them by train or plane by devising limericks. These were invariably scandalous, though they did not always scan. Edward Bigelow remembered a few. One concerned "red-headed Michael Maule/About whom all the girls seemed to fall"; then "There was a young lady from the West/Whose control was not of the best./In the paper we read/Ballerina pee-ed/While doing a third arabesque."

The choreographer's English was becoming more vivid and expressive. At about this time he wrote to Betty of a fellow artist: "[Name suppressed] is a nice chappie, but I don't like his tail of disciples, extras, connoisseurs, snobs, parasites, idiots, megalomaniacs, carnivorous lizards, etc." Of an ill-matched dance partnership he said, "It's like a lobster screwing a steak."

The company appeared for a week in The Hague before settling down for six weeks in London, where Balanchine and Tanaquil rented a small house with a garden and shared it with Nicholas Magallanes and Roy Tobias. When Roy retired for the night, he used to see, through an open door, Balanchine in bed, wearing his spectacles to read a musical score. I lived nearby, and often went there for dinner. One morning as I was arriving to keep an appointment with Balanchine, Roy told me, "He's gone to the laundry with Nick." I was astounded: *"George Balanchine* has taken the *laundry!"* Roy confessed later, "It was the first time I saw Balanchine with different eyes. He had always been just one of the family, and now I realized that people outside might look on him as something sacred."

▪ ▪ ▪

FROM London, Balanchine wrote a serious letter to Kirstein:

4 August 1952

Dear Lincoln:

I am very sorry to hear about your mother's death. I am so touched that she remembered me. She was always so nice to me. If it wouldn't be for her I don't think we would have a company

now. But I believe that she's going to help us still, because I believe
in that.

I don't think you should make any decisions now. And certainly don't put more money into the City Center. It is a bottomless
pit. About your taking Baum's place, I am not very much in
favor of it. It is not your nature to be involved in money and
commercial things. You could be an official adviser or something
like that. . . .

It would be better to think about my idea of free performances
for children. Not only ballet, but drama (maybe Midsummers
Nights Dream) and opera. It's the only thing for the future and the
only reason for keeping a theatre in New York. I would say that
if we eventually get people to help us financially it will be through
this idea. There could be a committee of rich people to raise money
for free performances for children. There is no progress in just
inventing new small ballets every season just to exist. Until now,
somehow we have created new ideas and we were progressive and
now the company is established and can perform as well as the
other famous companies. But that is not enough. If we continue in
the same way we will become standardized, just like the others. We
shouldn't do millions of little hors d'oeuvres. It is no longer progressive. And it is impossible to do new things so fast. It must be
a process of evolution. But if we create a purpose for the company
and for the theatre, we can afford to fill in with little things now
and then, but really have time to do something interesting. The new
generation which would come to the performances will be the
future citizens of the United States, some poets, some musicians.
We have to do something for their souls and minds. Nobody is
doing anything at all except the police department.

It's true that in the beginning there will be a loss. But we would
have a loss anyway, and this idea eventually will help us. The
nation that develops from this public will be the reason for asking
people for money. Then people will give with pleasure. Maybe the
Mayor will be interested, and all the rich people. But they are not
interested in giving us money to pay [so-and-so's] salary.

We would still have one matinee a week to sell tickets for,

and it will probably bring in as much money as two would. Please, Lincoln, think about this. It's not as stupid as it sounds at first. . . .

Don't worry about anything, Lincoln. Everything is all right.

Love
George

"We shouldn't do millions of little hors d'oeuvres." Balanchine had come to the conclusion that, in a desperate attempt to please, Kirstein was in danger of turning his repertory into a hodgepodge like that of Ballet Theatre.

Kirstein went to see the mayor about the free matinees and wrote to Betty Cage, "He is very agreeable and will help us. . . . He is calling a meeting." The first free matinee would be in 1960.

Meanwhile Balanchine came up with a delightful new idea for a ballet, as a result, surprisingly, of attending the Edinburgh Festival's Searchlight Tattoo, performed on the Castle Esplanade almost nightly during the three-week festival, and perennially popular. It was organized by the army and carried out with military magnificence and precision. Watching the marching and counter-marching of massed bands of pipers and drummers in their swinging tartan kilts, and the dancing of reels, Balanchine, seated in the front row with Tallchief, Le Clercq and other principals of his company, felt the fascination of Scotland's music and history. Through Walter Scott, the country had become one of the chief sources of inspiration for the Romantic movement. James Macpherson's forged poems of Ossian, the legendary Gaelic bard, were translated into several European languages. In 1829, Mendelssohn had been irresistibly drawn to visit Scotland, and his journey inspired him to compose the "Scotch" Symphony (No. 3 in A minor, Op. 56, dedicated to Queen Victoria). How delightful that the Russian-born choreographer, one hundred and twenty-three years later, should feel the same Romantic impulse and decide to make a ballet to the music of this composition!

. . .

Two Silver City cargo planes were provided for the transportation of the New York City Ballet from Edinburgh to Berlin. One was much more primitive than the other. There was a muddle at the airport, and the corps de ballet traveled on the better plane; Balanchine, the principal dancers and staff on the worse. Tallchief found that when she went to the toilet she could see the ground below through the cracks in the floor. Returning to her seat, she noticed Balanchine sitting impassively as rain fell on his head. He was, in fact, exhausted by the tour.

Yet Europe's reaction to the New York City Ballet left no doubt that the tour was a triumphal progress. The acclamations in Barcelona were unprecedented. There were twenty-nine calls at the Paris Opéra. The 4,500 seats of the Teatro Comunale in Florence were sold out. A Milan editor, whose critic saw the company there, announced "The revolutionaries of the dance have arrived from New York." The 2,100-seat theater in The Hague was sold out for a week. During the six weeks in London, as Chujoy recorded, choreographers and dancers from "at least a dozen" European countries came to see them. Their appearance at the Edinburgh Festival was well received. They were warmly applauded in Berlin. The Florentines invited the company to make their city its permanent base. Betty Cage, exasperated with the difficulties at City Center, had considered this seriously. What is more, so had Balanchine. New York City actually ran the risk, in 1952, of losing its ballet company to Europe—over Lincoln Kirstein's dead body!

. . .

BALANCHINE'S dislike of communism made him vote Republican. Like many Russian émigrés, he could not help admiring what he considered the boundless political cunning of the Soviet leaders, and he believed Americans were naïve by comparison. Doubtless he thought Roosevelt had been sold down the river at Yalta. During the election campaign of 1952 it was, therefore, to General Eisenhower that he wrote, pledging his support in return for encouragement to the arts.

1 October, 1952

My Dear General:

May I first take the liberty of introducing myself: I am Artistic Director of the New York City Ballet, my name is George Balanchine. I left Russia, my country of birth, as a boy of nineteen [*sic*] because I wanted artistic freedom more than anything else, and I have found it here. I have been an American citizen for fourteen years and I am convinced that you are the man to lead this country in its fight against communism.

This letter is written in the hope that the suggestion it humbly submits may bring more votes to our future President. There is a vital section of this country's population which, so far as I know, is never mentioned in campaign speeches. —They are the artists of America: writers, poets, painters, sculptors, composers, musicians, actors, dancers. The artists and their creative efforts are an integral part of American life and an increasingly important one, with a vital influence on public opinion at home and abroad. In fact as an instrument of the "propaganda of truth" which you advocate it is unsurpassable. I am sure that you are aware of the success in this respect of American theatrical, dance, and music productions, and art exhibits abroad since World War II. I have just returned with the New York City Ballet from an extensive tour of Europe, ending in Berlin where we went at the request of the State Department. In every country people came to me to express their surprise that a native American company should achieve such a standard of excellence, for Europe is only beginning to realize that America can produce great art.

This is hardly surprising for art and artists are never mentioned by our statesmen. . . . The materialistic part of life is the only one that is talked about. But there is another part which is the spiritual life of the nation, its culture. I know that you are deeply concerned with that life as you have proved during your presidency of Columbia University. It would be wonderful if you would reaffirm that interest now. . . .

I ask you to recognize the American artists in one of your speeches and to appeal to them and you will get a million votes! I cannot presume to ask you to promise them government support, although in many respects this is sorely needed, but the assurance of your moral support would already be invaluable.

With all my good wishes and hope for the success of your campaign,

> Respectfully yours,
> George Balanchine
> Artistic Director
> New York City Ballet

Eisenhower's answer—if, indeed, he did answer—has not survived.

Having got that off his chest, Balanchine was free to rehearse two new ballets, which were ready for the winter season at City Center. This season, opening on November 5, continued for nearly three months and was the longest the company had ever had.

.   .   .

AT ABOUT this time, Balanchine's marriage to Maria Tallchief was annulled on the ground that Balanchine refused to let her have a child. It was stated in the newspapers that she had asked for no alimony as she was a dancer and could earn her own living. This was honorable, but her mother was "not too pleased." Balanchine had helped her move into a new apartment, which she was to share with Vida Brown. He made suggestions about the decoration and hung mirrors. She had a sudden pang and said, "I won't leave you if you'd rather I didn't." "No, no," said Balanchine, "go ahead. It's O.K." Balanchine never completely severed contact with his ex-wives. When Brigitta gave birth to her first son, he telephoned the next morning, proposing to visit her in the hospital and see the baby. Goddard Lieberson, however, thought it would be better "to wait a little." Maria remained in the company, working side by side with Tanaquil Le Clercq. In November 1952, Balanchine made *Scotch Symphony* for her and Hindemith's *Metamorphoses* for Tanaquil.

Balanchine cut Mendelssohn's somewhat portentous first movement, so that *Scotch Symphony* begins with some spirited Scottish steps by a girl and eight boys, all dressed in kilts. The Andante brings on the lovelorn, questing man in search of an evasive sylph, with whom, nevertheless, he performs a long and dreamlike pas de deux. Tallchief was associated with dazzle rather than romance, but critics acclaimed her "newfound gentle radiance" in this duet. *Scotch Symphony* is one of those Balanchine ballets—the Weber *Pas de deux romantique* is another—that hover between romance and comedy or pastiche. Like Mozart, Balanchine had an infinitely subtle way of striking a balance, and he was sometimes too subtle for his critics.

Metamorphoses, to Hindemith's *Symphonic Metamorphoses on Themes of Carl Maria von Weber* enabled Tanaquil Le Clercq to show her rare qualities of fantasy and style—but, actually, there has never been anyone like her in *any* of her roles. The economical but ingenious décor was formed by cascades of metal coat hangers, which glittered as they caught Jean Rosenthal's golden light. Karinska's costumes were weird. In the Allegro first movement, the dancers were acrobats in form-fitting leotards of a new elastic material. For the second movement, based on a Chinese theme Weber had discovered and Hindemith had transformed into what he called a "Turandot Scherzo," Le Clercq wore a "Balinese" bra, a minimal tutu, wings, a mask and a headdress with quivering antennae, thus becoming the most elegant Oriental dragonfly. She was supported by Todd Bolender, dressed as a beetle or turtle, who never rose from his knees. Balanchine deliberately set himself a new and almost impossible task—who had ever heard of a pas de deux in which the ballerina was partnered by a kneeling cavalier? Yet the passage was reminiscent of his favorite theme—his basic theme, Bolender thought—of unlucky love. Todd was told to be "very passionate." "I was the rejected lover, the ugly little man who was always just missing her, yearning but repulsed." It turned out to be a wonderful dance. For the final March everyone acquired huge wings, Magallanes "flapped on . . . to chase the beetle" and the corps made Busby Berkeley-ish patterns.

Rehearsals at City Center were held either in a sixth-floor room at the back, or on the stage when it was free. Betty Cage knew that when Balanchine was working out a new ballet he lost all sense of everything else, and as there was no money to pay overtime, whenever she thought he had reached the limit she used to leave her office on the eighth floor, go down and simply stare at him.

． ． ．

BALANCHINE and Tanaquil Le Clercq were married on the last day of 1952. "At midnight we all foregathered," Kirstein wrote me. "As the Russians and Russians continued to troop in, Tanny said to me: 'Oh, my God, what Have I Let Myself IN FOR?' "

At this time Kirstein was producing Shakespeare plays for City Center, and Balanchine was directing Stravinsky's opera *The Rake's Progress* at the Metropolitan Opera House. It had already been given in Venice, Zurich and Milan. Balanchine thought the Met was far too big for it. He was obliged to have crowd scenes, which were not called for in the libretto or the score; the production was too naturalistic; the harpsichord continuo was inaudible; and he disliked the conductor, Fritz Reiner, who kept pointing out "errors" in the orchestration. He loved the opera and hated the whole business.

In February 1953, after its long season at City Center, NYCB danced for the first time in Baltimore and Washington. In March, Balanchine and Tanaquil were in Milan. In July, when Betty Cage, on tour with the company, heard from Kirstein that the New York winter season might be canceled, she reported from Los Angeles that Balanchine was threatening to resign. But there was no season at City Center that fall; the company set off on another European tour instead. In October she wrote from Naples that she, too, was thinking of resigning. She complained that the State Department was paying all expenses in Germany for Ballet Theatre, and that Lucia Chase's troupe opened every program with Balanchine's *Theme and Variations* and Robbins's *Fancy Free,* giving the impression that they were the *only* American company. It was time Baum realized that the New York City Ballet was *not* a touring company. They should be sure of four New York seasons a year.

Because Sadler's Wells Ballet had broken its own record at the Metropolitan Opera House with a repertory including not only the ever-popular *Sleeping Beauty* but a new full-length *Swan Lake* and Ashton's new version of Delibes's *Sylvia* in three acts, both Baum and Kirstein were convinced that the New York City Ballet should put on a ballet lasting all evening. Balanchine suggested *Casse-Noisette (The Nutcracker).* Kirstein liked the idea. He thought it would cost $50,000, of which he allotted $20,000 to the scene builders and prop makers and $30,000 to Karinska for costumes. "Please let me hear from you about *Nutcracker,*" he wrote to Betty and Balanchine. "I am very nervous that you will want to junk it. . . ."

But Balanchine was pleased to be staging the old ballet in which he had danced as a child. From the start, his aim was to create magic: the kind that holds children spellbound and makes older people feel hopeful and young again. In *Nutcracker* he relived the Christmases of his childhood.

One of the "miracles" in the ballet is the growing of the Christmas tree. Beginning no bigger than a real tree, during Marie's dream it grows and grows, until she herself, like Alice in Wonderland, is reduced to the scale of the mice and toy soldiers who battle around her. There was no trapdoor in the City Center stage, and Balanchine insisted on a three-dimensional—as opposed to a painted—tree. Jean Rosenthal, the lighting wizard, devised a model of "umbrella-like spokes" which lay flat in a heap, hidden by piles of presents, until they were pulled upward. The estimate for making this was between five and ten thousand dollars, and Kirstein was afraid to tell Baum. When expense was discussed, Balanchine always said, "Tell Baum it will only be half as much. The production will get back the money, and he will be happy."

Given the limitations of City Center, it was extremely difficult to accommodate and control the number of children from the School who were needed for the Christmas party scene in Act I: and the ingenuity of Edward Bigelow, the stage manager, was taxed to the limit. Numbers of children playing mice or soldiers had to be crowded along stairways and in the wings, and controlled by signals. There was also a choir of forty boys from St. Thomas's Episcopal Church, who had to hum during the Snowflakes scene.

Jerome Robbins arranged the battle between the Toy Soldiers and the Mice. Balanchine stuck, when it suited him, to what he remembered of the Ivanov version, but sometimes he elaborated. He also invented a brand-new character, Dewdrop, to lead the Waltz of the Flowers in the second act. This virtuoso role—with continual entrances and exits, dazzling aerial ronds de jambes and arabesques voyagées along the line of girls, and, at one exit, a breathtaking balance—was danced to perfection in the first performance by Tanaquil Le Clercq.

The Ivanov-Balanchine pas de deux of the Sugar Plum Fairy and her Cavalier, danced at the opening on February 2, 1954, by Maria Tallchief and Nicholas Magallanes, is one of the most dazzling and at the same time moving in the history of ballet. Alexandre Benois, who attended the very first night of the ballet in 1892, felt that Tchaikovsky had invested the music for this dance, written a year before the Sixth *(Pathétique)* Symphony, with a tragic character. Indeed, each time the cymbals clash and a descending motive is repeated, there is a splendor of desperate passion about the way the ballerina hurls herself at her partner, as if risking life itself.

A week before the premiere of *The Nutcracker, Time* magazine put Balanchine on its cover. The accompanying article gave an outline of his career and quoted a few of his typical remarks: " 'When you get older,' says George Balanchine, who is 50 this week, 'you eliminate things, you want to see things pure and clear' "; and " 'Central theme of *Nutcracker:* food.' "

John Martin, who had for so long resisted the appeal of Balanchine's talent but had recently been converted, wrote in his unappreciation of *Nutcracker* for *The New York Times:* "It denies the very basis of the 'Balanchine revolution,' which has changed the entire art of the ballet by showing it to be an art of dancing—not of miming, spectacle or story-telling." He might have been surprised to be told that *The Nutcracker*—which has enjoyed an uninterrupted season at NYCB every Christmas for about a month from the winter of 1954 on—would become as regular an American habit as turkey at Thanksgiving.

.   .   .

IN 1954, when I was arranging an exhibition for the Edinburgh Festival to mark the twenty-fifth anniversary of Diaghilev's death, I wrote to Balanchine asking if he had any designs for ballets or portraits of himself dating from the Diaghilev period. Balanchine replied that unlike certain people—a snide reference to one or two acquisitive friends—he had no relics of his time with Diaghilev except "some pornographic drawings I made for him." I responded, "I quite understand that you are not clever like Massine and Lifar . . . but I think it is extraordinarily lazy of you never to have sat to a good artist, whose portrait of you we could include in our Exhibition. After all, anyone can keep making up ballets, but it is the people who have their portraits painted by Tchelitchev who are remembered by posterity. . . . I have just got your *Complete Book of Great Ballets* [*sic*] from Francis Mason. My word, you have been busy. . . ."

He responded:

March 9, 1954

Dear Dicky,

I did sit for Tchelitchev when he asked me, but I was extremely difficult, and he didn't have the inspiration to finish it. Nobody wants to paint me. I admit I'm not very pretty. . . .

George

The reference to drawings was not entirely, as I had thought, a joke. Years later Boris Kochno showed me several drawings, somewhat surrealist and not unskilled, that Balanchine had made when the two young men were on holiday with Diaghilev in Venice. And a strange pencil sketch of Lifar in *The Prodigal Son,* pregnant, and crawling with truncated legs, was sold in the Lifar sale at Sotheby's in 1984 for £3,000. Then I discovered that Balanchine had given caricatures of himself to several American friends.

. . .

DURING the second of the three 1954 New York seasons, Balanchine produced a piece of Americana that surprised even Lincoln Kirstein. It was said that the idea came to him during a stay in Wyoming. The composer Hershy Kay recalled that Balanchine turned down his early sketches for what became *Western Symphony*—the first because it was "too much like Copland," the second because it was "too complicated." The third time he was lucky: "simple tunes with skeletal, guitarlike accompaniments" were combined in the form of a classical four-movement symphony. These tunes were mainly cowboy songs, with "Red River Valley" as the unifying theme.

Although there was no money for costumes until a year after its first performance, Balanchine contrived to give his strictly classical choreography a Western slant: there were suggestions of "the intertwinings of square-dance figures," one man strummed an imaginary guitar and another fanned himself with a hat. In the opening Allegro there were many lifts for Diana Adams and Herbert Bliss. Magallanes partnered Janet Reed in the sentimental

Adagio, and she had to hurl herself halfway across the stage into his arms. It was in the final Rondo, however, that Tanaquil Le Clercq, supported by the bouncing, grinning Jacques d'Amboise, set the house on fire with her chic, her fouettés and her provocative smiles. *Western Symphony* is one of Balanchine's "closing ballets" that has given the most joy—and has lasted.

Although in 1955 Betty Cage had sworn never to go on another European tour, she dutifully embarked on a fourth odyssey in 1956. Preoccupied as she was by moving the company from city to city in eight different countries, she still wrote to Kirstein about plans for the next two years. Should the company go to Japan under the aegis of the State Department? Should they go to South America? The State Department was beginning to regard ballet as a means of making friends and influencing people. Should they go to Russia?

Balanchine did not want to go to Russia. Could the company go without him? Ballet Theatre was longing to get there first (and in the end succeeded in doing so). City Center was in a deplorable situation, thousands of dollars in debt.

Nevertheless, there was stirring news from home. Kirstein reported, "Mayor Wagner has pushed the Lincoln Square plan [for a new complex of buildings for concerts, opera and ballet] through the Board of Estimates. . . . The City turned over the land, and the Rockefeller Foundation is close behind, and I think it is only a question of WHEN, no longer IF."

On tour, Balanchine rarely had cause to complain of an unresponsive audience. In Vienna, it is true, the public showed little enthusiasm for *La Valse,* which Ravel had intended partly as a kind of apotheosis of the Viennese waltz, and the choreographer was bitterly disappointed. "Here in Vienna at least I thought they'd understand," he said to Roy Tobias. On the whole, though, reactions in Salzburg, Berlin, Brussels and Copenhagen were enthusiastic. But it was in Copenhagen that tragedy struck.

Tanaquil Le Clercq was taken ill and did not dance on the last night. At first the doctors were uncertain of their diagnosis, but by the time the company traveled on to Stockholm—which was luckily the last stop on the tour—leaving behind Balanchine and Tanaquil's mother, Edith, who had gone along with the company for fun, it was known that Tanaquil had polio. The train from Malmö was met by Swedish health authorities in case other dancers had succumbed to the disease. Tanaquil was racked by a high fever, and Balanchine, too, grew feverish. When the news reached New York, consternation was widespread. Lincoln Kirstein wrote to Betty Cage:

Everyone has rallied around with the most extraordinary rush. John [Rockefeller] III asked if he could do anything through the Institute here. . . . Jerry Robbins, in tears, called from Boston twice and will do anything we ask him. . . . Jacques [d'Amboise] was absolutely destroyed; Carolyn [his wife] cried all day long . . . and Minnie Astor and John Martin and everyone you can think of. . . .

The programs for the New York season, opening on December 18, still had to be discussed with Kirstein, and Betty suggested that "it might be better not to do *La Valse* because George thinks of it as Tanny's and it might be painful for him."

. . .

WHEN the company returned to America, Balanchine remained behind in Copenhagen. Edith Le Clercq sent regular bulletins of her daughter's ups and downs, of her own and George's hopes and fears. Nursing Tanaquil kept her so busy that she had little time to dwell on the tragedy. Balanchine had moved into a cheap room at the top of the Hôtel d'Angleterre. During the day, he cooked special meals for Tanaquil at Vera Volkova's apartment.

It was at the suggestion of Volkova that Balanchine agreed to work once more with the Royal Danish Ballet. She thought it would distract him. Henning Kronstam, who was to dance Apollo, found the choreographer "very precise at rehearsals, absent-minded at other times. To us he was kind, very firm about what he wanted. We didn't get too many corrections. He said, 'Can you do this?' " Yet Balanchine could not concentrate long on these rehearsals, or spare much time from his cooking and his encouragement of Tanaquil. When he showed Kronstam Apollo's first variation, he did it very quickly, then said, "Here's the pianist. Here's the score. You have three hours. See what you can do." Then he went off.

Kirstein, who had presented the young Gian Carlo Menotti's immensely successful operas *The Telephone* and *The Medium* in the early days of Ballet Society, had recently agreed to put on his ballet *The Unicorn, the Gorgon, and the Manticore,* with choreography by John Butler; Butler wanted to use one of his own dancers in it. This was reported in detail to Balanchine on November 30. He wrote to Betty Cage:

[*Dictated to Edith Le Clercq, in whose hand it is*]

Hôtel d'Angleterre
Copenhagen
Tuesday? 2 or 9 December

Dear Betty,

First I want to thank you very much for your kind words of encouragement and for the cigarettes that makes us feel back home. . . .

Now about Butler: he should be very grateful to do this choreography for us without dictating his terms. If he is not satisfied with our dancers then we don't want him either. (Who the Hell he thinks he is?)

Please no "Sebastian." It is the most dreadful ballet, lousy music, stinking story—better nothing than that. I don't like Cranko idea either. Don't spend money on that junk. Let Todd do his Poulenc ballet. . . .

Tanny is getting along slowly. God will help us I believe. . . .

Love
George

Diana Adams wrote daily to Tanaquil, and Balanchine read her letters aloud. He later told her, "You're very *funny!*" He talked to his wife by the hour to keep her from brooding on her condition. (Both legs were paralyzed.) It was a huge effort of will. Every night he played solitaire, sitting with his mother-in-law in the hotel bedroom. Kirstein arranged that Natalie Molostwoff should fly over to spend Christmas with the stranded family.

Balanchine in Copenhagen to Kirstein in New York
[Dictated to Edith Le Clercq, in whose hand it is]

> Hôtel d'Angleterre
> Copenhagen
> Tuesday [*probably December 18*]

Dear Lincoln,

Thanks very much for your letter and clippings. Please send all clippings to me at hotel. . . . Could you write [Tanny] a cute letter?

I have already written Betty about Butler. Our company is good enough for me—should be good enough for him. . . .

Tanny is very grateful to you for the Christmas present you are giving her—Natasha [Natalie].

Edith and I are trying to be cheerful. We are hoping and hoping and hoping and waiting.

> George

Natalie Molostwoff's calm, good sense and humor brightened their Christmas. She helped to alleviate the strain under which all three exiles were living, giving them a better sense of perspective; and Balanchine had a friend to keep him company until he went to the hospital at four each afternoon.

At the Royal Theater, Copenhagen, Balanchine presented *Apollo* on January 9, 1957, and *Serenade* two days later. The New York City Ballet gave the Menotti-Butler work on the eighteenth. Betty Cage reported to Balanchine about it and he sent a handwritten letter back to her:

[End of January]

Dear Betty—Your letter just arrived. I hope that in spite of all this bedlam you have fun and your box office is plenty.

. . . Soon, it will be three months since Tanny became ill. She is some how happier in her room and we are trying to make her feel as if she were at home. I am cooking every day in Volkova's apartment and take food to the hospital.

I hear you have two pretenders on "poor swan lake." I highly disapprove of this two girls dancing it. Certainly I am not going to see them in swan when I return. (Not everybody should dance everything as president Lincoln said.) . . .

With my love to you.
Your
G.

Balanchine's single aim was to restore his wife's will to live: he was so exhausted that although he went to bed early he could not sleep. When Tanaquil got back her appetite, he took a day or two off to visit an old friend in Jutland.

The National Polio Foundation undertook to pay all expenses for the family's return journey to New York. At Lenox Hill Hospital, Tanaquil would be under the care of Dr. Jordan, an orthopedic surgeon Balanchine had found helpful to his dancers. The American Embassy made the arrangements. Nobody in New York—except Kirstein, Betty, Natalie and Edward Bigelow—was to know anything about the homecoming until Tanaquil was safely installed. The little party set off on March 13, 1957; their nonstop flight got in at 6:00 A.M.

Chapter 10

···

NEW BALLETS

FOR NEW DANCERS:

1957 - 1964

THE first eight months of 1957 were an interlude in Balanchine's career. He set his work aside to look after Tanaquil. When she left the hospital, he took her for treatment to Warm Springs, Georgia. His devotion was extraordinary, but his company felt bereft. During the summer he grew roses at their house in Connecticut. In the winter, however, he made a dazzling comeback. Between November 1957 and mid-January 1958, he created four ballets so fantastically different from one another, and each so successful in its own way, that there is no word for his New York winter season but miraculous.

Who but Balanchine would have related, as he did in *Square Dance*, ancient formal dances and classical steps to the American square dances surviving from the nineteenth century, or dared to combine the music of Vivaldi and Corelli, played onstage by a string band, with the patter of a professional "caller," standing in a corner and tossing his rhymes to individual dancers: "Down the center, lonesome gal/Now she's waiting for her pal/All alone, swing and whirl/Down the center in a butterfly twirl"? Kirstein later wanted to eliminate the caller, but Balanchine said, "Remove the caller, and it's just an inferior *Barocco.*" Eventually, however, the caller was dropped, and the ballet continued to be popular.

Who but Balanchine would have hit upon Gounod's little-known Symphony No. 1 in D major and made for two principal dancers and a corps of twenty girls and ten boys a ballet *(Gounod Symphony)* so gentle, so sweet, so unspectacular and so essentially French that one sees it as exactly the kind of work the Paris Opéra should have presented in the 1880s—but probably never did?

Who but Balanchine could have conceived the semicomic, totally flamboyant *Stars and Stripes*? After the strutting, high-stepping Rockette drum majorettes, the cabrioling soldiers saluting in midair, the pas de deux that has been called a "delightfully witty soldier's-sweetheart duet"—but which nevertheless contains difficult classical steps—the whole company swarms on for a blazing finale, and, at the very end, the music is reined in to a steady slow march (to the tune that gives the ballet its name), and the largest Old Glory ever seen in comparative closeup is unfurled to form a background. "Calculated vulgarity is a useful ingredient," Balanchine once observed, and confessed to being an old hand at working what he called "the applause machine."

The fourth major ballet of winter 1957–58, actually the second chronologically and the most memorable of all, was *Agon.* In 1954, a Rockefeller Foundation grant had enabled Kirstein and Balanchine to commission the longed-for Stravinsky ballet that would form a trilogy with *Apollo* and *Orpheus.* Its title, *Agon,* means contest or struggle.

Stravinsky interrupted his work on the score to write two other compositions, and *Agon* was not completed until April 27, 1957. Its point of departure was a French Baroque dance manual, the

1623 *Apologie de la danse* by de Lauze, with accompanying musical examples by Mersenne. Traces of this influence are evident in
the names of certain old dances—saraband, galliard and bransle
(although Stravinsky's versions bear little metrical resemblance to
their models)—and in the tone color, reminiscent of Baroque
sonority. But, encouraged by Robert Craft, Stravinsky had been
employing serial techniques in his works since 1952, and they are
the basis of approximately half the composition.

A document survives from Balanchine and Stravinsky's consul-
tations over this mathematically organized ballet—a scheme of
Agon in the composer's hand. It is written on sheets of ruled paper
taped and stapled together to form one long page. For each number, Stravinsky indicated the projected timing in minutes and
seconds and—by drawing stick figures, some with skirts—how
many male and/or female dancers were to perform it. In its final
form, *Agon* has twelve movements that are grouped into four parts
punctuated by the recurring prelude (the prelude's two subsequent
repetitions are called "interludes," but these three passages are
essentially the same); and at the very end the twelve dancers
regroup from four trios to three quartets for a coda "in imitation."

Stravinsky made a few choreographic suggestions. Balanchine
said the plan of using twelve dancers was his own, but that their
division into eight girls and four boys was Stravinsky's.

Diana Adams remembered the first day that a call for *Agon* was
posted on the board at City Center. "I had something terribly
important to do that day. . . . I had to nerve myself up to ask him,
'Could you start with someone else?' But he said, 'No, pas de deux
is where I start. I have to do first.' Of course I was there."

In Arthur Mitchell, a student of the School who had danced for
Balanchine in the musical *House of Flowers* in 1954 and joined the
company two years later, the choreographer had found, after all
these years, his first black *danseur noble.* Mitchell, with his good
looks, heroic bearing and radiant personality, was chosen to dance
the climactic pas de deux in *Agon* with Adams. He was not yet even
a soloist, let alone a principal.

"Nothing stopped [Balanchine] when he was ready to go," Adams recalled about the rehearsals for the pas de deux. "I told him that my [left] foot was not really healed. He said, 'That's all right. I'll do everything on right foot.' "

Balanchine's choreography has next to nothing to do with the court dances after which some of the numbers were named—*next* to nothing because the roots of ballet are imbedded in the French Baroque, and the choreography naturally has a balletic basis, although in *Agon* Balanchine extended the idiom with movements that had never been seen before. Near the beginning of the pas de deux, Adams revolved into a pose in which she abruptly wrapped a leg around Mitchell's neck. Later, with one arm round her waist, he took the foot of her bent leg raised behind her in attitude; as she arched backward, he touched it to her head. Another feat called for her to balance in arabesque while he first supported her at arm's length, then stretched himself suddenly flat on the floor without having relinquished contact with her forward hand; she was to retain her pose as if unconscious of his reversal.

The time came when Balanchine wanted to show Stravinsky what he had worked out. Lucia Davidova was asked to bring him to a rehearsal. When they arrived at the School—which had moved from Madison Avenue to the Upper West Side in the previous year—Martha Swope was there to take photographs (it was her first professional assignment), along with Bernard Taper, Balanchine's future biographer. Roy Tobias remembered the scene:

Balanchine was so happy when Stravinsky came downstairs. Everyone was "at attention." Stravinsky went to the piano, took off his coat and scarf and said, "George, to work! To work!" Hitherto, in the opening pas de quatre the four boys had faced the audience. The composer suggested that they should turn their backs. This was agreed. In Melissa's variation [the Bransle gay, central section of the second pas de trois] Balanchine made me beat on the stair rail with a stick to represent the castanets. While we were working on the Bransle double [which follows], Balanchine was called to the telephone. On his return he made the boys enter together rather than in canon. During the pas de deux, Kopeikine, at the piano, said, "I'm terribly sorry. There are parts of this music I don't understand." Stravinsky said, "It's perfectly all right. I don't understand them either!"

At the end of the Bransle double, according to Taper (when Tobias threw Hayden to be caught in mid-air by Watts, while he himself sank neatly to one knee), Stravinsky exclaimed, *"Horosha!"* [Good!]. After the pas de deux, he clapped and cried, "Wonderful!"

Agon had its premiere on December 1, 1957, and from the start was recognized as a masterpiece. Programs were arranged to include six extra performances. It has since been acclaimed in many countries. After nearly thirty years, we are still rediscovering, each time we see it performed, some breathtaking wonder that we had forgotten. Although the ballet ends as it begins, we are not left with a sense of QED—nothing has been proved—but of "Here we are again, back where we started and none the wiser." It has been "pure entertainment." A contest? Yes—a kind of tournament of dance introduced and terminated by fanfares, though not for a stadium packed with applauding crowds. It is as if the dancers' infinite skills and throwaway insouciance are to be taken for granted by a small audience of their peers: they are to be appraised less for the difficulty of the feats they perform than for the cool manner and sure timing with which they ignore difficulty. This is the way bullfighters are judged.

. . .

WITHIN two months of the end of the 1957–58 winter season, the company was in Japan with Kirstein. Balanchine, who had moved with Tanaquil into an apartment on West End Avenue, stayed home, but he thought deeply about the future and came to some surprising conclusions. When Kirstein returned, leaving Betty Cage to take the dancers on to Australia, Balanchine confronted him with his ideas, and Kirstein wrote to Betty:

Balanchine wants to get through the winter as well as possible, and in the summer start from scratch with a small company and six new ballets, à la Ballet Caravan, which we feel we can book, and then enlarge the group to a company like 1947 at the Center, but there will be the difference of a repertory and ten years of work.

Betty responded with great restraint: "I am sorry Balanchine feels as he does about the company. . . . I hope he changes his mind after we get home." After some argument and persuasion, he did.

Later that year, Leon Barzin, who had conducted for NYCB since its foundation, decided to retire. He had for some years shared his labors with the former violinist Hugo Fiorato, but Balanchine and Kirstein considered it necessary to employ another *chef d'orchestre*. Balanchine's choice fell on an Englishman, the Sadler's Wells conductor Robert Irving, and their partnership led to the creation of the world's most distinguished ballet orchestra.

Another musician who joined Balanchine's team shortly afterward was the Californian Gordon Boelzner. While he was studying at the Manhattan School of Music, he learned from a girl friend that the New York City Ballet needed a pianist. Boelzner was not interested in ballet, but he applied and was engaged. It was his first job—and he was still with the company in 1987. Balanchine, who began by handing him his own piano reduction of *Orpheus*, appreciated his quickness in reading an unfamiliar score. Boelzner for his part was soon hooked by Balanchine's personality. He became the company's pianist in performance as well as at rehearsal, and finally assistant conductor.

Soon after the company's return from the Far East, Balanchine began work on a new production of *The Seven Deadly Sins*. W. H. Auden and Chester Kallman made a translation from the original German, and Lotte Lenya came from Germany to stalk the stage and harangue in her rasping voice her dancing "double," the ethereal young Allegra Kent.

In March 1959, Balanchine received the news from Tbilisi that his mother was dead. The extent to which he had been cut off from his family may be measured by the fact that his brother Andrei's cable was addressed to the Metropolitan Opera House. Lucia Davidova, on the point of leaving for Europe, was aware of Balanchine's reluctance to put pen to paper, so she begged him, "Be sure to write a nice letter to your brother." When she returned to New York some weeks later, she asked, "Did you write to your brother?" Balanchine said, "No. I just could not bring myself to write." The kind of letter in which there is "so much to say" was even harder for him than the ordinary kind.

.   .   .

EXCEPT for Robert Craft, Stravinsky had no more ardent devotee than Balanchine, who was cool toward most other great contemporary composers, notably Bartók. He turned to Anton Webern in the 1950s because of Stravinsky's interest in the Austrian composer. Like his teacher Schoenberg, Webern wrote twelve-tone music, but his personal style is characterized by modesty of scale and a sense of fragmentation derived from the breakup of musical lines into tiny pieces by means of frequent silences and shifts from intrument to instrument, with consequent changes of tone color. Balanchine once told Francis Mason that as soon as he heard Webern's music he knew it could be danced to, like that of Mozart and Stravinsky.

He had made at least two plans for Webern ballets before the idea came to him, in 1959, of staging all seven of his orchestral works, which would come to less than an hour of music. Kirstein made a most unexpected suggestion: that Martha Graham contribute some of the choreography. Graham consented, and agreed to do a dance-drama about the death of Mary, Queen of Scots, to Webern's *Passacaglia*. The notion that Graham should work entirely with New York City Ballet dancers was soon discarded. Balanchine would use his own artists and make a solo for one of Graham's. Later, when Graham found she needed more music, Balanchine, who had already begun to work on the *Six Pieces* with

Adams and d'Amboise, cheerfully relinquished the music to her. Graham's part was to be called *Episodes I*; Balanchine's, *Episodes II.*

In Martha Graham's condensed mini-drama, the Scottish queen, about to die on the scaffold, relives episodes of her past life. The Graham dancers, a powerful group, interpreted Mary's ladies-in-waiting, husbands and lovers, but perhaps as a gesture of solidarity, Sallie Wilson, an NYCB dancer, represented Elizabeth of England, with whom Mary dueled in a symbolic game of tennis. The tragic presence of Graham, the way she stepped out of the monumental dress she had devised, as if escaping from a cage, and the simple device of turning a red light on this abandoned structure to mark the moment of decapitation, have remained in the spectators' memories.

In choreographing *Episodes II,* Balanchine later told an interviewer he "had to try to paint or design time with bodies in order to create a resemblance between the dance and what was going on in sound." Academic steps could have looked ludicrous accompanied by Webern's music; that Balanchine was able to find movements based on these that did not appear incongruous is proof of his unlimited invention. There were five numbers. *Symphony* (Op. 21) was for two principals and three couples. Toward the end, Balanchine, tongue in cheek, made the men invert the women to coincide with an inversion of Webern's tone row; thus upended, the women beat their legs in upside-down entrechats. *Five Pieces* (Op. 10), a pas de deux, ends with a magic trick: the girl flops over the man's right arm, head down, both hands on the floor, her right pointe resting on the stage, her left leg, bent, raised behind her; the man, who appears to be "supporting" her in this unclassical pose, looks not *at* her, but away from her, his left arm extended. His "support" proves illusory, for when he withdraws his right arm and walks away, she remains in position. Balanchine was rather annoyed that some people found this funny. *Concerto* (Op. 24) was for two principals and five women. Balanchine quoted Robert Craft's comment on the music: "At first the listener might be reminded of a switchboard sporadically lighting up, but the plot of wires between the lights is what must be illuminated"; and he confirmed that this was what he tried to do.

The *Variations* (Op. 30) were arranged as a solo for Paul Taylor of Martha Graham's company, who later became a highly inventive choreographer with a troupe of his own. The white-clad dancer was called upon to clutch himself, wrap himself up and tie himself into such perverse knots that his number seemed almost a defiant demonstration by Balanchine that he could be as crazy as any "modern" choreographer or dancer in existence. Finally, after all these perilous explorations, came the *Ricercata* (in six voices, from Bach's *Musical Offering*), danced by two principals and a corps of thirteen girls, so that the breathless spectator felt he had reached a more familiar paradise, perhaps even "come home."

. . .

AFTER a long spell in Europe as ballet master to the Cuevas company, John Taras was back in New York. He was sitting in the hallway of the School when Balanchine walked in and asked him, "What are you doing these days?" "Nothing." "Then why don't you come and starve with the rest of us?" So Taras rejoined NYCB. Balanchine valued Taras's good memory of certain ballets that he himself recalled only imperfectly. Taras would also make new ones of his own. His return to the fold was especially timely because in 1958 Jerome Robbins had withdrawn to found a group called Ballets U.S.A., which appeared at the Spoleto Festival in Italy and toured Europe with outstanding success.

Robbins's highly involving work on two musicals, *West Side Story* and *Fiddler on the Roof,* both of which became famous, plus other work on and off Broadway, prevented him from devising any new ballets for Balanchine's company until 1968. Taras was soon rehearsing *Apollo* and restaging *Night Shadow,* now called *La Sonnambula,* which its creator had completely forgotten.

In the Bellini/Rieti ballet, the Poet was Erik Bruhn, a world-renowned Danish dancer who was engaged as a guest artist for the 1959–60 season, and again in 1963–64. He was not only a first-rate *danseur noble* but strikingly handsome; and perhaps Balanchine revived his "Romantic" ballet because he considered it a work in which Bruhn and the wistful, fey Allegra Kent, whom he cast as the Sleepwalker, were bound to make a strong impression. This they did. The ballet that had been scorned by all the American critics except Denby when it was first given in 1946, and which had then been admired throughout Europe, was at last accepted in New York.

One reason Bruhn had joined the company was that he hoped to dance *Apollo*, which had been revived for Jacques d'Amboise—danced in practice costume, without scenery—in 1957. He never did. Choreographically speaking, Balanchine's Apollo had a coltish side, and Bruhn may have struck Balanchine as too beautiful.

When Balanchine decided to revive *The Prodigal Son* for Edward Villella, a highly talented dancer who had studied at the School as a child, left to go to college and later returned, Villella had the impression that it rather bored him to restage his thirty-three-year-old ballet. "He did the opening and closing scenes in twenty minutes each. He did the pas de deux for Diana [Adams] and me in half an hour. I didn't have any in-depth coaching. In addition, the ballet had been forgotten, and they had to bring in Vida Brown, who had retired. I was literally learning the ballet as I was dancing it."

Nevertheless, Balanchine gave his two principals an illuminating clue to the style needed in their weird duet. Villella explained:

At the beginning of the pas de deux the Siren and the Prodigal are standing at opposite ends of the stage; then they begin to raise their hands, then their elbows, holding their hands out flat. Then they lean and fall toward each other. As we began, Balanchine said, "You know, dear, like icons." Then he walked away. That simple idea was enough. I went and got some books. Then I could realize the role.

Balanchine made Brahms's *Liebeslieder Walzer* into a ballet in 1960 to please Morton Baum, who had been begging him to use them for several years. Artists do not often welcome such "commissions," and the choreographer probably considered the two song cycles complete in themselves. Yet things turned out better than he had expected. The ballet has pleased many people apart from the benevolent Baum.

When the curtain rises, two pianists are seated side by side at a piano, with two male and two female singers standing nearby. There are four pairs of dancers—the girls in pink satin dresses sitting demurely on chairs, their partners behind them. As waltz follows waltz, revealing different relationships between the couples, the songs and dances cast a kind of spell, and the audience loses itself in a dream. But there is a surprise in store. After the curtain falls at the end of Part I, there is a short pause. When it rises again, the ballroom has become transparent to the stars; the girls are in ballet dresses and pointe shoes—no longer women, but ideal creatures. For the final waltz, however, they become well-brought-up, satin-clad ladies once more, seated on their chairs to applaud the music and song.

.　.　.

WHEN, in 1960, Balanchine held the first of his American Ballet Seminars for regional teachers from all over the United States, he spent half an hour analyzing the tendu and devoted a whole two-hour class to port de bras. This may have given him the idea of voluntary classes for his own dancers in the afternoons, for they started soon afterward. Rosemary Dunleavy, who joined the company in 1961 and is now a ballet mistress, remembers that they were held mostly during layoff periods. "You could take regular class at the School from 10:30 to 12:00, then be warm enough for Balanchine's special class from 12:00 to 2:00." Rosemary felt that Balanchine wanted to "spread his ideas across the nation"; as she "really began to learn what he was talking about," she used to go home and write it all down. She was afraid the precious knowledge might be lost. For his part, as he told Natalie Molostwoff, Balanchine spotted Rosemary early on as someone with an analytical mind and a good memory who would one day be able to reproduce his ballets—which indeed she has done.

He also believed that dancers learned from teaching. He told lively little Suki Schorer, who joined the company in 1959, that she should get a notebook and write down his corrections, which she did. In 1961, Balanchine asked her to give a class for children at the School. It happened that he came in with Kirstein at a moment when she was kneeling to mold a girl's feet into a correct position, and she overheard him say, "You see, I told you she'd be down on her hands and knees."

. . .

IN 1962, Balanchine created one of his greatest masterpieces. He had been familiar with Shakespeare's *A Midsummer Night's Dream* since his youth; he had both danced and acted in it, and he claimed to know it—or most of it—by heart in Russian. He had a particular affection for the work, and he also loved Mendelssohn's Overture and incidental music. Mendelssohn as much as Shakespeare would guide him. Yet because he intended to make a full-length ballet, and the Mendelssohn score lasted in all no more than an hour, it would have to be augmented with additional music by the composer. Balanchine claimed that it took him twenty years to put together the score. It was the nearest he ever came to composing the music for a whole ballet himself.

The curtain rises when about one-third of Mendelssohn's Overture has been played. What remains serves as a perfect exposition, in which all the elements of the play can be presented in rapid succession. Once this is done, Balanchine is free to allot what time he chooses to dancing or to storytelling.

Shakespeare begins his comedy with the court of Athens, then goes on to Bottom and his companions. Yet the wood is the dominant presence of the play; and Mendelssohn judged it proper to begin his Overture with its changing moods and lights and tripping fairies before introducing the theme of the clowns, or the court's hunting horns, or the lovesick Helena.

Balanchine makes masterly use of the score in the first episode. The creation of a fairy court of insects played by children, whose diminutive size is accentuated by a corps de ballet of butterflies played by adult girls, wins the audience's heart from the start. Puck is established as a comic—as well as nimble—figure, who takes the public into his confidence. Special marvels are the confrontation of glittering Oberon and beautiful Titania, who struggle over the little Indian boy; the slow crossing of the stage by mourning Helena, who listlessly plucks a leaf from a tree, which is in fact the (to her) invisible Puck; and the relentless attitudes of the four courtiers, who stand like medieval carvings of (family) pride behind the amiable Theseus.

After these lightning introductions, it is time to dance. In Mendelssohn's Overture to Racine's *Athalie,* Balanchine found music for strings of extraordinary sweetness to which Titania may dance with her Cavalier, alternating with more dramatic warnings and scurries during which Puck makes unsuccessful attempts to steal the Indian boy for Oberon—only to be driven away by fairies with switches. The famous Scherzo is danced by Oberon and his followers. While Oberon gets his breath back between outbursts of beating and turning steps, the bugs and butterflies disport.

To some short passages from the incidental music (written seventeen years after Mendelssohn's youthful Overture), which Balanchine and Robert Irving patched together, Oberon tells Puck about "a little western flower," and sends him girdling round the earth in an abbreviated "forty minutes."

Without a pause, the warbling clarinets of Mendelssohn's Concert overture, *Die schöne Melusine,* have stolen upon us. These alternate with agitato passages on the strings, a rising figure that signifies despair and great sighs on the cellos, till all are finally intermingled. Thus the billing and cooing of Hermia and Lysander in their "troubadour"-style costumes, the scorn of Demetrius for Helena, the sudden love of Lysander—whose eyes have by now been anointed by Puck—for Helena, and all the consequent confusions are woven by Balanchine into a tissue of movement and action. By allowing the music to dictate his scene's artistic shape, he avoids the pitfalls of storytelling, always so tedious in ballets based on novels or plays.

An imperceptible scene change to another part of the wood brings us to Titania's bower. The Fairies' march is followed by the song "You spotted snakes," for soprano and mezzo, in which the chorus joins so sweetly with the refrain "Philomel, with melody"; and in her pink scallop shell Titania is lulled to sleep. The first part of Mendelssohn's Intermezzo provides a most effective solo for the distraught and unloved Hermia; the second part allows the briefest possible rehearsal for the clowns before Puck places the ass's head on Bottom, causing his companions to disperse in terror.

The pas de deux of Titania with Bottom in his ass's head is (to me, at least) the jewel at the heart of the ballet. It is Balanchine's triumph, not just as a choreographer—for the dance steps are very traditional—but as a man of the theater—a dramatist, even—and as a commentator on human absurdity. Like Shakespeare, Balanchine knew that the infatuated of either sex discerns qualities in the loved one which do not exist; that love is blind; that we love monsters and become monsters of jealousy when loving; that anyone can get carried away by fantastic hope on a Saturday night and wake to a nasty shock on Sunday morning. If Mendelssohn might well have been surprised to find Bottom moving to the heavenly music of his Nocturne, Shakespeare would certainly have seen the point. In comic ballets, the jokes about the awkward partner who gets on the wrong side of his ballerina or misjudges distance are all too frequent and vulgar: this is matter of finer quality. Titania goes through her motions with devout seriousness: Balanchine knows that while she seems to show Bottom tenderly how to partner her—just as a woman, without giving a lecture, might initiate an awkward boy into the mysteries of lovemaking—the clown, supporting the fairy queen in an arabesque penchée, has only to turn his grotesque head a very little and look wistfully over his shoulder at an imagined thistle to prick us with laughter. Yet even as we laugh we experience a pang of sadness. The comedy is in the pity; and it is comedy of the very highest kind, such as we recognize when Congreve's Millamant reveals the heart behind her fashionable patter, and, indeed, such as Shakespeare gives us in Titania's admiring observation to Bottom, "Thou art as wise as thou art beautiful."

Roland Vazquez, who had come to the New York City Ballet from the Christensen's San Francisco Ballet, was the first Bottom. He thought of Balanchine as someone he did not want to disappoint. "The man was so great. . . . There are no words to describe it. He was perfect. In my eyes he couldn't do wrong. He demonstrated every step, every gesture. He was different with everyone. He knew exactly what you thought and felt, what you could do—a sort of clairvoyance."

After these marvels, the act has to conclude with something more down-to-earth. Balanchine decided to bring on the Amazon Hippolyta with a pack of hounds; and he found in the Overture to Mendelssohn's cantata *Die erste Walpurgisnacht* some galloping music. He also conjured up, with the aid of Ronald Bates, the new stage manager, a "drooping fog as black as Acheron," in which the two confused pairs of lovers can quarrel and get lost, in which Puck can fence with Lysander and Demetrius in turn, impersonating the one while he abuses the other, in which all four Athenians can at last be put to sleep, then dragged into appropriate pairs. Alternating with the entries of hounds, which have horses' tails, come the reconciliation of Oberon and Titania and a series of fouettés by Hippolyta. The act ends with a rousing chorus, like a national anthem, from the same cantata, to the music of which Theseus approves the marriages and names the day.

Throughout the first busy act of this Greek-English-German fantasia there have been recognizably American gestures. Puck has kicked backsides, wiped the sweat from his forehead, then flicked his hand; Demetrius has done a downward flap of the hand, signifying "Get lost!" to the rejected Helena. To the final chords, before they follow the court back to Athens, the rival lovers shake hands and trail off with their arms round their girl friends' waists, resting their rapiers on their shoulders like baseball bats.

The drama of the ballet is now pretty well over, and the much shorter second act, like the much longer last act of *The Sleeping Beauty,* will be mainly a divertissement. Some of the choreographer's warmest admirers complained about this in 1962. In 1987, it is hard to see why.

The second act begins with the Wedding March, in which Theseus and his court process grandly in and out. For his celebratory dances Balanchine unearthed a piece of Mendelssohn's juvenilia, the Symphony No. 9 for strings. The first (allegro) movement of this, with its wistful tune, is danced by two principals and eight couples; the second (slow) movement is a pas de deux. To the third movement of this symphony, Balanchine tried to "do something for the boys." This passage, soon cut, may have justified Denby in finding the effect of the divertissement—except for the pas de deux—monotonous.

The Overture Mendelssohn wrote for his *liederspiel, "Die Heim-kehr aus der Fremde,"* with its sentimental melody on the strings, brings on the court once more for a formal finale. Then we are back in the wood. The chorus sings "Through the house give glimmering light," the bugs and fairies dance, Oberon and Titania celebrate their truce, and when Puck comes "to sweep the dust behind the door," he is whisked on a wire skyward. To me, an act that begins with the grand patterns of the Wedding March, continues with such pretty music—admittedly gentle and unspectacular—contains so exquisite a pas de deux, and ends with fairy song, dance and a joke is entirely satisfactory.

At first Villella did not know how to cope with the role of Oberon. It had much more mime than was usual in Balanchine ballets, and Villella was completely ignorant of mime. At rehearsals, Balanchine tended to postpone certain passages, saying, "Well, you have an entrance here. We'll do that later. Don't worry." He even arranged the brilliant Scherzo in bits and pieces, and always took the children first. Villella began to think, "He doesn't like me," and wondered if he had a role at all. Since 1960 he had been taking class with the Dane Stanley Williams, who was a guest teacher at the School. Stanley's forty-minute barre was beneficial to a young man whose training had been interrupted between the ages of sixteen and twenty. (Villella had explained to Balanchine why he took class with Williams, and Balanchine said he understood, but Eddie felt he was offended nonetheless.) When Stanley Williams asked him about his role in *A Midsummer Night's Dream,* he complained, "I've got nothing to do; and to top it all I'm dancing with a bunch of kids." Finally, when Balanchine had "knocked off the Scherzo and put it together," Villella got "a totally different idea." With its bounding jumps and rapid changes of direction, the Scherzo was revealed as one of the greatest variations ever created for a male dancer. Yet it was only three or four days until the premiere, and Balanchine had not shown Villella the mime. Kirstein went to Williams and said, "Eddie has a pivotal role, and he's going to ruin the production. What can you do?" Stanley took Eddie in hand, and for two days they worked on the mime.

Villella recalled:

Opening night came. I did the performance. I was exhilarated. The ballet had a wonderful success. I was received very well. Next morning I was onstage, warming up at ten, waiting for rehearsal, sore and tired, in the gloom of the working lights. Balanchine came walking by, in his trench-coat, with a newspaper under his arm. He walked past me, then stopped, turned around and came back. He said, "You know, you danced *excellent* last night, *excellent*." He put his arm round me, then turned and walked away. That is probably the single biggest compliment I have ever gotten in my life. But *in addition* he put his arm around me. Our major goal in life was to please this man. It was an extraordinary moment.

Diana Adams, who had been intended for Titania but who because of injury was replaced by Melissa Hayden, remembered other moments with Balanchine. She first worked with him during the war as a member of Ballet Theatre, and he had liked her appearance, her height and her "nice long legs," but he was determined to make her move faster. She had been dancing Tudor ballets, which were not technically demanding, and she was afraid of pirouettes. Balanchine arranged *Aurora's Wedding*, took the Lilac Fairy's slow variation away from her and gave her the faster "finger" variation. At first she thought he was mad, but in time she came to realize that she was "more interesting" in the latter.

When she joined the New York City Ballet, she was taught *Symphonie concertante*, which gave her blisters; but Balanchine disregarded the blood on her shoes:

There was not an instant of sympathy. Mr. B. would look and say, "Third movement!" In Ballet Theatre I never used to rehearse on pointe—and I thought I was going to die. He'd say, "I think if you are going to do this, you should do it from a real fifth." I thought I *was* in fifth. It was from that ballet I realized I was only about half trained. At the same time I was learning *Serenade.* I was the one who came running in at the end of the first movement. I didn't think I had the endurance: but the fast part was still to come. That was the first ballet I danced with the company. He came backstage afterward and clasped me by both hands and said, "That was *wonderful!*" and I was so happy. But he was sometimes implacable.

Balanchine may have been implacable, but Diana Adams could inadvertently hurt his feelings. She had danced in the first performance of *La Valse*, and Balanchine arranged the fast fifth waltz for her and Herbert Bliss. Some nights later, since *La Valse* was the only ballet she was down for and it came last on the program, she asked if another girl could stand in for her, so that she could have the evening off. "His face crumpled, and he said, 'But it's very *nice* what I did for you!' It was very callous of me. He had worked out my role with great care. He always made a dance with one person in mind, and if another person was to dance it, he would change the steps. He never tried to make you look like someone else."

Diana thought she would never be strong enough to be a "classical ballerina," and preferred modern roles. "So I was always pulling back. There was a tug-of-war. After a performance of *Swan Lake* he would say, 'Why are you so *boring*? Why don't you do something? I don't care what steps you do, but do *something*.' He used to give me a real hard time. But I found that when I let myself go it was twice as easy." In the end she decided she was acceptable in *Swan Lake*: "odd but interesting."

·　·　·

RECOGNITION of Balanchine's company and of his fame as a choreographer was increasing throughout New York State, throughout the country and, indeed, all over the world. In 1959, the New York City Ballet had danced in Albany for Governor Rockefeller's inauguration. In 1963, it would appear in Washington at the second anniversary of Kennedy's presidency. In 1960, Balanchine's dream of free matinees for children came true. Three thousand of them, chosen from all over greater New York, poured in, gasped, cheered and asked for more. When he made his ballets available, free, to regional companies in the United States, the Atlanta Civic Ballet was the first to stage one—*Serenade*—in 1961. In 1962, the New York State Council on the Arts sent the company on its first upstate tour, and Balanchine gave lecture-demonstrations in twelve cities. In 1963 they were to begin in New York schools. By 1964, the company had had seasons in Chicago, Los Angeles, Ravinia, Washington D.C., and San Francisco, besides dancing in Baltimore, Seattle, Philadelphia and a number of smaller cities. Its members had danced in nearly every European country, in Russia, Israel, Japan, Australia and the Philippines. And Balanchine's ballets were known worldwide. Ballet Theatre gave *Theme and Variations* in Russia two years before the New York City Ballet appeared there. In the same year, *Symphony in C* and *The Four*

Temperaments were danced by the Royal Swedish Ballet in China. In 1962, Balanchine would take his company to Hamburg to celebrate Stravinsky's eightieth birthday by dancing *Agon, Orpheus* and *Apollo*. In 1963, he would work for the third time with the Paris Opéra Ballet, staging *Concerto Barocco, Scotch Symphony, The Four Temperaments* and *Bourrée fantasque*. And during these last years at City Center, his choreography began to reach an even wider public than the theatergoing one, because of his experiments—which did not satisfy him—in television.

It was also in 1963, at the very end of NYCB's City Center period, that Balanchine made one of his most unpredictable works, *Bugaku,* with music commissioned from the Japanese composer Toshiro Mayuzumi, but written for a Western orchestra. The whining, feline glissandi lead the audience to a vermilion-railed platform simulating a Japanese stage, on which the rites of marriage take place between a samurai warrior and a woman treading delicately on pointe. Although in the first and third movements the hero and heroine wear diaphanous white garments and trains held by attendants, for the central pas de deux she wears a white bikini decorated with flowers, and white tights, and he, a white leotard. Their dance is the most erotic Balanchine ever invented, and almost appears to be the fulfillment of a personal fantasy. In the first performance, the highly masculine Edward Villella remained impassive and the flowerlike Allegra Kent kept her eyes downcast, both retaining perfect manners even in the throes of stylized orgasm. (Balanchine's old friend Lucia Davidova had always told him that if people could see into his mind, he would be in prison.)

. . .

THOUGH Balanchine had choreographed Stravinsky's Violin Concerto and *Danses concertantes* in the forties, Stravinsky was wary of having his concert music appropriated for the ballet stage. Balanchine, however, successfully arranged two more ballets to Stravinsky's music never intended for the theater. These short works, *Monumentum pro Gesualdo* (1960) and *Movements for Piano and Orchestra* (1963), were, from 1966 onward, always performed together.

Monumentum pro Gesualdo di Venosa ad CD Annum, to give the piece its full title, is Stravinsky's quatercentenary tribute to a forgotten Renaissance composer; he "recomposed for instruments" three of Gesualdo's madrigals. Balanchine seized upon the score, and his ballet had its premiere less than two months after the music's first performance in Venice. Without recourse to period costumes or accessories, Balanchine made a serene evocation of the High Renaissance: the dancers embody the aristocratic, effortless elegance about which Baldassare Castiglione wrote in *The Courtier.* It must be one of the very few ballets in which none of the men jumps.

Movements was arranged for a principal couple and an ensemble of six girls. The small corps, which alone moves during the terse intermediate sections connecting the five movements, and which backs up the principals in the remainder of the ballet, is often divided into two groups of three; and these assume an extraordinary variety of poses, like eccentric modern versions of the Three Graces.

Sometimes, for instance, the middle girl of each trio will stand upright, legs apart and arms hanging, while her two comrades, facing away from her, adopt a Degas pose as they adjust their shoe ribbons; or three girls, back to back in a triangle, bend forward with extended arms; or they all take a haranguing *Lysistrata* stance, one arm raised in exhortation; or they bend forward in fourth position, hands to shoulders with jutting elbows. While the corps sustains this last pose, the man crouches like a hunter, as if holding out an invisible net to catch his ballerina, watching her turn, kick and perform arabesques before she falls backward into his arms, legs and arms wide open but with one knee bent. While the couple embrace, the two trios face outward and adopt a striding pose like marching guardsmen.

The music, for piano and orchestra, is sure to baffle, if not irritate, an audience. To stage it at all was an act of conviction and courage. Hugo Fiorato once remarked candidly, "Who . . . would listen to *Movements* of Stravinsky by itself? . . . I don't think I would. But when you hear *Movements* and you see *Movements* through Balanchine's eyes and what he has added to the score, it suddenly becomes an amazingly exciting work."

Stravinsky was well aware of what Balanchine had done to popularize his music; and he wrote that watching *Movements* "was like a tour of a building for which I had drawn the plans but never explored the result."

Movements was made on Diana Adams, who had been married for several years to Ronald Bates. Shortly before opening night, her doctor told her she was pregnant. "You'll have to lie down *today,*" he added. She went back to City Center, where she happened to run into Balanchine downstairs. "He knew. He walked right past me." To Balanchine, the pregnancy was a betrayal of the Stravinsky ballet. He told John Taras, "I don't want to hear anything more about *Movements.*" Taras protested, "But the ballet's all finished." "If *you* want to do it, do it," was the only reply. So John Taras rehearsed the six girls, and Jacques d'Amboise, the male lead, took a seventeen-year-old soloist in the company named Suzanne Farrell to Diana's apartment to be taught her role by the recumbent dancer. Luckily, this girl, who was destined to become the most celebrated of all Balanchine's ballerinas, was a quick learner.

Chapter 11

....

TO RUSSIA :

OCTOBER - NOVEMBER 1962

S HORTLY after the staging of *A Midsummer Night's Dream,*
Balanchine went to West Germany to direct Tchaikovsky's
Eugene Onegin for the Hamburg Opera. Betty Cage was
amazed to receive in rapid succession four handwritten letters from
him, one of which concerned the engagement of a dancer who, at
the end of his life, was to become his closest friend: "I saw KARIN
VON AROLDINGEN dance in Frankfurt, which Lotte [Lenya]
recommended. I think we could take her, not as solo but regular."
In another letter, he asked Betty to deal with a request from Walter
Terry for permission to write his biography. "I did not want to
write to him a letter of explanation. Because it would be sort of
letter for posterity, like second-rate correspondence between famous choreographer and Voltaire. . . . Please call him and say that

my personal life is not very interesting and that Taper's book is coming out soon with everything that one can possibly find out about me, which is not very much. If Terry want to bother writing about my work . . . then he can do this without my permission . . . but I don't want to participate in it. If Terry wants to know about my inspiration or who is my Muse then he will never know that. Because I won't tell him, and it is not going to be written anywhere, for anybody to know. Don't tell him this. . . ."

In the former letter he wrote, "I agree with you about not going to Russia now, there is no reason why we should rush. . . ." Yet that very fall, in October 1962, at the end of an arduous European tour that began in Hamburg and included not only German towns but engagements in Switzerland and Austria as well, the New York City Ballet paid its first visit to Russia, and Balanchine saw the land of his birth after an absence of thirty-eight years. While the Americans were in Russia, the Bolshoi Ballet appeared in New York. It was a "cultural exchange" agreed upon by the two governments.

In addition to Balanchine and Natalie Molostwoff—who took a holiday from her duties at the School to revisit the union of republics she had left even earlier than he—there were several others who spoke a little Russian. Kevin Tyler, assistant stage manager under Ronald Bates, had been born a Russian subject; his name was originally Arkady Tkatchenko. Naturally he was given the job of traveling ahead of the company to bring the scenery and costumes from Vienna to Moscow. Attempts were made to delay him at both the Czech and Polish frontiers, since the Czechs and Poles hated Americans and Russians equally. The company arrived by air before Kevin, and everyone feared that he was lost. But the stage was set in time.

One of the dancers, Robert Maiorano, reported that the New York City Ballet was met at Moscow airport by "floodlights and interviewers, cultural-affairs officials, interpreters and State Department delegates." Kirstein thought Balanchine behaved as if he only remembered Russia before the Revolution. When he was bade

"Welcome to Russia, home of the classical ballet," he replied, "Thank you, but America is now home of the classical ballet. Russia is home of the old romantic ballet."

Andrei Balanchivadze had come from Georgia to greet his brother. The next day's *New York Times* described their reunion: " 'Andryusha, it's you,' the slender 58-year-old balletmaster exclaimed as he embraced his brother. Cameramen and photographers recorded the scene in the brightness of truck-mounted floodlights." But Patricia Neary observed that the moment Balanchine produced his American passport to make clear that he was not coming *home,* the cameras disappeared.

It cannot have been easy for the two brothers, who had not seen each other since 1918. George was now world-famous; Andrei, a respected composer, was a hero in Georgia and known throughout the USSR. His elder son, Amiran, was a physicist; his daughter, a dancer at the Tbilisi Opera and Ballet Theater; his second son, Georgi, a pianist, studying under the great champion of Stravinsky's music Maria Yudina, as Andrei himself had done. She, Balanchine, Andrei and young Georgi posed for a photograph together.

NYCB's opening performance in Russia was given two days later in the famous old Bolshoi Theater. No American company had ever appeared there until Balanchine's. Ballet Theatre, on its 1960 Russian tour, had danced at the Stanislavsky Theater and the Lenin Palace of Sports.

The occupants of the packed crimson-and-gold auditorium were taken aback by *Serenade.* In his report, printed in New York the next morning, John Martin, whom Kirstein had invited to travel with the company, tried to soften the blow:

The Russian audience is an altogether honest one. It applauds furiously when it is moved to do so, and it sits in absolute silence when it is not so moved. The evening opened in the latter mood. The first ballet was . . . *Serenade,* beautifully danced. . . . But the response was a perplexed and fairly indifferent one.

The atmosphere began to warm with the Robbins-Gould *Interplay*. . . . Then followed *Agon* . . . which is not easy for any audience to take at first seeing. But the pas de deux by Miss [Allegra] Kent and Arthur Mitchell brought forth the first sign of genuine enthusiasm. When the curtain rose on . . . *Western Symphony* and revealed a painted backdrop, there was a wave of heartfelt relief. . . . From then on, the temperature was high. . . . At the final curtain Mr. Balanchine was the center of the greatest ovation. . . .

Stravinsky himself was in Leningrad when Balanchine's company opened in Moscow. His return to Russia had preceded that of his friend by two weeks. Under Hurok's auspices he had conducted concerts of his own music in Moscow and Leningrad. He was back in the capital in time to be received by Khrushchev on October 11, and Balanchine managed to visit him that afternoon.

After one performance at the Bolshoi, NYCB moved to the 6,000-seat Palace of Congresses within the walls of the Kremlin, a recently completed and luxurious hall, the main use of which—as its name suggests—was not theatrical. It was so vast that the dancers had difficulty putting themselves across, and applause, however warm, tended to get lost. Applause there was, but it was confined mostly to the end of a program. The reason for this was the excellent buffet on the top floor of the palace. After the first and second ballets, the spectators made a dash for the fast-traveling escalators in order to gorge on caviar, hot blinis and sausages, which were unobtainable in restaurants and stores. After two repetitions of the first program shown at the Bolshoi, the second program opened on October 12; and its final ballet, *Symphony in C*, was considered by Martin to be the turning point of the company's reception.

The Bizet work brought forth not only applause throughout and repeated curtain calls at the end but also rhythmic cries of "Bal-an-chine" until the choreographer was forced to come forward and bow his acknowledgment.

At a later performance of *Agon*, Arthur Mitchell was greeted by cries of "Meet-shell! Meet-shell!" and Villella had to repeat his number in *Donizetti Variations*. Webern's *Episodes* was received with "tumultuous favor," which astounded John Martin.

The members of the company were segregated from other clients of the hotel, with their own dining room and their own bus to take them to and from the theater. Balanchine usually ate in restaurants, and very shortly after his arrival he asked his brother to recommend the best. Andrei took him to a Caucasian restaurant near the Kremlin. There was an enormous bill of fare, but one thing after another that Balanchine chose was unobtainable. He ended by eating chicken with coriander sauce; it was all there was. Usually the two brothers lunched and dined alone together, but sometimes Natalie Molostwoff accompanied them. On one of the latter occasions, all three were struck by the good manners and assiduous attention of the young man who was serving them. He seemed a phenomenon in a country where service was not on a high level. Balanchine immediately said, "He's an out-of-work actor playing the part of a waiter." This turned out to be the case.

Soon after the opening of the Moscow season, there was an enormous party at the American embassy, and Kirstein had a further opportunity to observe Balanchine enacting what seemed to be a deliberately chosen role. When Khrushchev's son-in-law, the newspaper publisher Adzhubei, came up to talk to the choreographer, he appeared to be too absorbed in his conversation with some young dancers to notice him. What Kirstein did not include in his printed account was that Adzhubei was Ukrainian, and the Ukraine was at that time a disaffected republic; Adzhubei was involved in the disaffection, and Balanchine knew perfectly well that he was a hot potato.

At the beginning of the company's second week in Moscow, President Kennedy learned from aerial photographs that the Russians were building missile sites in Cuba. On October 18—the day Edward Villella's solo in *Donizetti Variations* was encored in the Kremlin—Andrei Gromyko, the Soviet foreign minister, who was on a visit to Washington, denied that there were any such sites. It was in the bus, returning from an evening performance, that Balanchine's dancers first heard there was a possibility of war. During supper in the hotel, the waitresses, noticing their downcast looks, asked Natalie Molostwoff what the matter was. When she told them, they said, "You are artists. We don't associate you with your government."

During the following days, messages from the embassy kept the company informed of the course of events. Kirstein devised Plan A and Plan B in case of an emergency, but the cultural attaché told him, "*You* don't have plans. You leave when they tell you to leave. The first thing we will know at the embassy is that the phone will be cut off."

At best, members of the company thought, they would be sent straight home. The fact that the Bolshoi Ballet was appearing in the United States gave them hope that they would not be interned even if there was war. Balanchine said, "I've never been to Siberia."

Dancers were able to get hamburgers and bottles of Scotch from the American embassy. Returning for lunch at the hotel, they saw a mob outside the embassy preparing to throw stones. Betty Cage gave the order to drive on. As it turned out, the light was bad for the television cameras, so the "spontaneous" demonstration was postponed.

The dancers were naturally worried about the kind of reception they would get from their audience that evening. As the curtains parted, Robert Maiorano observed, "Robert Irving cautiously raised his baton. Suddenly the entire audience of six thousand rose, then cheered." Nothing could have been more heartwarming to the dancers. When they returned to the Ukrainia Hotel, they found that the waitresses had put flowers on all the tables.

On October 20, President Kennedy decided to "quarantine" Cuba. Ships were deployed in the Caribbean. On the twenty-second, the president had a difficult session with leaders of Congress, some of whom were impatiently belligerent. At seven that evening he appeared on television to inform the nation that Soviet engineers had installed in Cuba sites for medium-range missiles capable of reaching Washington, D.C., the Panama Canal, Cape Canaveral, Mexico City and any city in the southeastern part of the United States. He had therefore ordered that "all ships . . . bound for Cuba . . . if found to contain cargoes of offensive weapons, be turned back." Russian ships continued to sail toward Cuba; but on Wednesday, twenty stopped or began to make for home. On Friday, Khrushchev admitted that the missiles were already in Cuba. On Saturday, Kennedy told him they must go. On Sunday, October 28, Khrushchev complied with the president's demands; and the world breathed again.

Kirstein wrote: "Through it all, Betty Cage and Balanchine cushioned the brunt of unimaginable possibilities with such tact and skill that the danger of our situation hardly percolated down to the dancers, who, night after night within the Kremlin's walls, heard six thousand voices yell for fifteen minutes after every performance: 'Bal-an-chin, Bal-an-chin!' "

Principal dancer Violette Verdy later admitted that she and most of her colleagues were too concerned with their work to think much about politics; perhaps the men worried more. Protocol was strict, and every member of the company had to produce an identity card to gain admittance to the Kremlin. One night Balanchine found he had left his at the hotel. Although interviewers were waiting for him, and although the guards knew very well who he was, he was not allowed in. He went back to the hotel, quite pleased to have missed the journalists and to have proved how foolish the regulations were.

Programs for the Russian tour had been agreed on in advance in New York. Russian objections to *The Prodigal Son* because of its biblical theme were quashed. The only attempt made by any Russian to change the planned program took place backstage at the Palace of Congresses after the first performance of *Episodes* during the third week in Moscow. Following the tremendous ovation, which astonished the whole company, Balanchine was approached by an official who told him that Russians did not really understand this type of ballet. "What do you mean?" asked the choreographer. "Didn't you hear? They loved it." The official argued that the Webern ballet was an example of decadent modernism, unsuited to a democratic audience, and he begged that they drop this dangerous and corrupting work from the repertory. Balanchine refused.

.　■　.

MOST mornings Balanchine taught class, and Soviet dancers and teachers came to watch. Elizaveta Gerdt—daughter of the famous Pavel Gerdt and the idol of Balanchine's student years—now seventy years old, was a teacher at the Bolshoi School. Balanchine arranged that she should give his company a class.

When the Bolshoi directors invited members of the New York City Ballet to watch one of their own classes, they put on a show. Everybody, from the principals down, went through a demonstration that lasted two hours. But Balanchine had secretly told Suki Schorer, Gloria Govrin, Patricia Neary and Suzanne Farrell to bring their practice clothes, and it needed only a few minutes of their haphazard tendus and battements at the barre to make clear that Balanchine had given them a speed the Russians had never acquired. This was not an exhibition, but it was a proof.

At one point, Andrei asked his brother the difference between the Russian style of dancing and George's new American style. Balanchine replied, "The Russians divide the dancer's body horizontally—heads, bodies and legs. I divide it vertically." He made a slicing movement down his face to his crotch.

The Russian critics, rather like the majority of English ones twelve years before, found that the Americans had no "soul." After the first night, the former ballerina Olga Lepeshinskaya had told the news agency Tass, "Of course, we cannot accept everything we saw." The composer Aram Khachaturian said, "The only shortcoming of the American ballet troupe is the absence of a story line."

On Friday, October 26, when the company returned to the Bolshoi for their last four days in Moscow—the day when Khrushchev admitted to President Kennedy that the missiles were already installed—Balanchine was, according to *The New York Times,* "mobbed at the stage door by enthusiastic balletomanes who told him emotionally and in extravagant terms that this was the greatest thing that had ever happened in the ballet here." Although many seats had been reserved for officials or given in blocks to unions or factories, there was a group of about a hundred fans who had not missed a performance and knew even members of the corps de ballet by name.

The last performance in Moscow was recorded by television cameras. "It was a gala evening in every respect," wrote Martin, "with almost continual applause . . . and cheering and countless curtain calls at the conclusion. There is no knowing how long the demonstration would have gone on if George Balanchine had not stepped forward and made a short speech in Russian in which he invited those who wished to see more to follow the company to Leningrad." The theater staff declared that the applause throughout the season had been "unprecedented." As Balanchine joined his dancers in the bus to return to the hotel, the crowds called after him, "Come back! Come back! Come back!"

. . .

LENINGRAD was, of course, magnificent, and the whole company was housed at the comfortable, old-fashioned Astoria Hotel. The moment after he had checked in, Balanchine grabbed Natalie Molostwoff by the hand and rushed out to show her his old home in Bolshoya Moskovskaya, which was not far away. He was very emotional.

In Moscow, the audience had taken some winning over. In the former capital of Imperial Russia, the public was more sophisticated. As Kirstein recorded, *Serenade* had five curtain calls; *Agon* "carried the house along with it"; during *Western Symphony,* "spirits were high, and the demonstration for Balanchine himself fairly tore the house down. There were many flowers." The only pity was that after two performances the company had to move from the Kirov Theater to the shabby old Lensoviet Palace of Culture, which held twice as many spectators.

It was inevitable that the anxieties of the tour and its crescendo of acclaim, the fears aroused by the Cuban missile crisis and the need to maintain a calm front, took their toll on those in command. On the fourth day, Balanchine decided to skip his company's week in Kiev, fly back to New York, then rejoin them in Tbilisi. John Taras was not the only one to observe that he was unusually depressed and longing to get out of Russia. He told Patricia Neary that he felt he was being spied on; he was certain his room and perhaps even his clothes were bugged; and he complained that his telephone rang and woke him all night long. He had lost weight. He also had a faint suspicion that if he were to travel alone without the company he might not be allowed to leave; perhaps he wanted to discover if this was so.

Kirstein wrote: "Balanchine leaves after tomorrow for a well-earned rest. . . . His return to his early youth has been touching in the extreme and historic in Terpsichorean annals. We went to the school and were shown his class-portraits, etc. And they made him an honorary member of the Conservatory. The reception beggars description. He has to go out and send them home. . . ."

Because of the Russian way of allotting theater tickets, and because the theater was always full, Balanchine discovered that many young dancers and musicians, as well as some of his old colleagues at the School and Conservatory, had been unable to see the New York City Ballet. Before flying to America he arranged an extra matinee for artists, to which admission would be free.

At the end of this performance a deputation presented him with a silver samovar full of roses, and Konstantin Sergueyev, director of the Kirov Ballet, made a speech. Balanchine looked at the floor for what Kirstein called "a long half minute" while the audience applauded. A woman from The Hermitage, sitting with Kirstein, translated the Russian words, which were received in breathless silence. "It was rather sad," she said. "It was simply, 'Thank you. In troubling times which we may share in time to come, try to think of us as we are tonight; we'll try to think of you as you are tonight.' "

Martin thought that perhaps the most important event of the tour was a talk on the principles of his choreography that Balanchine gave to the choreographers of Leningrad and twelve student choreographers. This took place around a table in the room adjoining the little museum on the top floor of the Ballet School on Theater Street. "The response varied from something like despair to starry-eyed eagerness. The students requested a second session, which was duly held in a corner of the theater itself."

Back in New York, Balanchine went to see the Stravinskys, whose reaction to Russia had been very different from his. Balanchine had not been received by Khrushchev—which is the last thing he would have wanted—but he, too, had been made much of by the dignitaries of the Soviet Union, by the minister of culture, Mme. Furtseva, and by the leading composers, ballet masters and dancers. He had been welcomed by his brother, by Elizaveta Gerdt, by Gusev and Mungalova, who had danced some of his earliest choreography, and by other old friends. Stravinsky's reaction had been euphoria; Balanchine's, even when he was received with acclaim in his native Leningrad, was a kind of panic. The ballet master to whom all turned for assurance had followed a sudden impulse and fled.

The Leningrad visit was much shorter than the Moscow one. *Apollo* was danced twice there, but nowhere else in Russia. Balanchine rejoined the company in Georgia. He was met at Tbilisi airport by his brother, sister-in-law, elder nephew, Amiran, and niece, Tamara. A mass was sung in the cathedral for the success of the New York City Ballet and the former Georgi Melitonovich Balanchivadze. The prayers were granted. After the first performance, at the end of an incredible ovation, Balanchine took a curtain call alone in the old Moorish-style opera house, and the audience rose to its feet in homage to the man they regarded as a compatriot.

The appearance of the American dancers in the streets of Tbilisi almost brought traffic to a halt. The fair-haired girls in particular caused a sensation. Violette Verdy, noticing how Georgian men looked at women, how eager they were to make contact with them, talk to them, touch them or escort them home, thought she had found a clue to Balanchine's adoration of the female sex.

A mountaintop picnic was given for the whole company, and the daredevil Georgians, who liked to show their contempt for danger, took the hairpin bends on the way up at high speed. "Wild Caucasian dances were performed in our honor," wrote Robert Maiorano. "A bottle of wine later, I joined in, along with Arthur Mitchell. Soon everyone was drunk with happiness. Mr. B. was toasted as everyone's brother."

Taking Natalie with him, Balanchine traveled to Kutaisi, the small provincial town where his elder half-brother Apolon lived and where his father was buried. It was a night's journey away, and since he and Natalie were tired at the end of the day's work, they hoped for sleep. This proved to be out of the question; the Georgians who accompanied them were determined to drink and sing all night long. Andrei and his son Amiran were of the party. When the honored guests got off the train early in the morning, they were driven at once to a big banquet that had been prepared at Apolon's house. They were expected to sit without eating or drinking while speeches were made in their honor. Then the toasts began. There were two other banquets that day, during one of which a group sang Georgian folk songs in Balanchine's honor; then they were driven at mad speed up more hairpin bends to a castle. However, the hospitable Georgians neglected certain courtesies: never once was Natalie shown a ladies' room. She could not think how she survived, and from then on Balanchine called her "the camel."

By the time the company reached Baku, on the Caspian Sea—a city of oil wells and caviar—and the final date of their tour, the dancers were in a state of exhaustion. A huge party was given in the hotel ballroom on the night before they left, and everybody got drunk. Shaun O'Brien put on his new Russian musquash hat and removed his pants. When the party broke up, dancers began to visit one another's rooms. Shaun called on Betty and Natalie, to find the latter ready for the morning flight, fully dressed and wearing her earrings, but fast asleep on top of her bed. Then Balanchine came in and sat down. He said, "Well, I suppose now the tour is over everybody's little love affairs will be over too. All except mine—I never had any." Shaun remarked, "You could have, if you wanted to." "No," said Balanchine, "nobody loves me." Then Shaun did something he would never have dared do if he were sober; he ran to Balanchine, sat on the arm of his chair, patted him and exclaimed, "But we *all* love you!" Balanchine looked him in the eye without expression and said, "Where are your pants?"

Chapter 12

· ·

P R O B L E M S   I N   P A R A D I S E :

1 9 6 4 - 1 9 7 2

W HEN Lincoln Center, a complex of buildings dedicated to the performing arts, was built in the early sixties, the New York State Theater, designed by Philip Johnson, was planned as a shrine for the works of Balanchine, but only in the nick of time did he manage to avert a potentially fatal mistake. The orchestra pit had been constructed to accommodate only thirty-five musicians, the usual number for a Broadway musical. According to Kirstein:

Concrete had been poured, but early one morning Balanchine chanced into the auditorium, crowded with forests of scaffolding, to stage one of the most moving and effective solos of his career. After his immediate threat to withdraw our company from further tenancy if the orchestra pit remained straitjacketed, power drills were brought to double the space, so that it can now, with discomfort, hold some seventy men. . . . By this time it was apparent that the State Theater would be shared by the New York City Opera. . . .

Balanchine's preoccupation, apart from space for the musicians, was the need for the most perfect dance floor possible to lessen the pains and hazards of performance. For several years he had been discussing the problem with Ronald Bates, who, after war service in the navy, had done many jobs before he became associate stage manager of NYCB in 1957.

During weekends in Connecticut, Balanchine and Bates experimented. As Don McDonagh, a dance critic for *The New York Times*, described it later, "Clearing the kitchen table, the two set to work hammering together models of a floor that incorporated a 'basketweave' principle that would be firm and also have the right degree of elasticity to minimize injury." A linoleum covering—which traveled to other stages on tour—would always be rolled out over the wooden surface.

In December 1963, *The New York Times* announced that the Ford Foundation would give $7,756,000 to ballet in America, the money to be divided between schools and companies. The director of the Foundation's humanities and arts programs, W. McNeil Lowry, was a keen supporter of Balanchine. Seven companies received grants. The New York City Ballet was guaranteed $200,000 a year for ten years, and the School of American Ballet would receive $242,500 a year, which meant that almost every student would be on scholarship and the School could afford to accept only the most talented. It was just thirty years since SAB had opened.

The Ford Foundation made it a condition of its grants that Balanchine be paid a salary. He had never accepted one before as director of either the company or the School; now he was to be remunerated in both capacities. He asked Lowry, "Do you think I might spend some of the money on a secretary?"

In 1953 Betty Cage had hired a twenty-year-old assistant named Barbara Horgan, who was then a student at Columbia University with thoughts of becoming an actress. She resigned ten years later, just before her thirtieth birthday, because she felt she was getting nowhere. At the time Balanchine took her out for a drink and asked why she was leaving. When she explained, he said, "You'll be back." Now, a year later, she was working for a photographer. Balanchine walked straight to her office and hired her. He also made over to her the $10,000 a year Ford was giving him as director of the School, but she did not discover this for ten years.

. . .

THE winter season of 1963–64 was NYCB's final one at City Center. The last new work Balanchine staged in the old theater was *Tarantella,* a high-speed pas de deux to music by Gottschalk, designed to exploit the special talents of Patricia McBride and Edward Villella. The first work he arranged for his company at New York State Theater was *Clarinade* to Morton Gould's *Derivations for Clarinet and Jazz Band,* with Benny Goodman playing the solo instrument; he also revived *Ballet Imperial,* using a larger corps to fill the bigger stage.

Productions of *A Midsummer Night's Dream* and *The Nutcracker* were also revised and expanded; Rouben Ter-Arutunian's sumptuously redesigned *Nutcracker* sets, with their snow-heavy fir trees in the forest scene and fantastic rococo confectionery architecture in the Kingdom of Sweets, were to stir the imaginations of children for years to come. Another "spectacular" was Balanchine's *Harlequinade,* based on Petipa's *Les Millions d'Arlequin* and set to the tinkling music of Drigo—a ballet Balanchine himself had danced in as a child.

The French-born Petipa's old Russian ballet had imitated the still-older Italian commedia dell'arte, so there were opportunities for mime. Villella, who knew little about the commedia dell'arte style, later recalled how Balanchine had showed him the proper way to perform his role:

I was doing it rough and gruff in a—I thought—comical manner. But he said, "No, dear, it's commedia dell'arte, but it's French, not Italian." I still didn't understand. Then he turned around and said, "Harlequin is *premier danseur,*" and walked away. There was this elegant confidence this rogue of a Harlequin has. Harlequin is very pulled-up, not crouching. It was a point of departure.

In 1964, Balanchine took time off from the ballet to collaborate with Tanaquil Le Clercq and their cat, Mourka, on a book. He had trained the huge orange-and-white cat to jump, and a photograph by Martha Swope of the choreographer crouching to observe Mourka executing a side cabriole in midair had been published in *Life* magazine. This spurred the idea of the cat's autobiography—a very funny book describing Mourka's ancestry, ballet training in the Petipaw method, fame, friendship with Purr Mesta, lecture tour, love and excursion into space to inaugurate a Cat Star. Mourka's adventures were illustrated with photographs by Martha Swope, and the book was a success.

．　．　．

THE NEW YORK CITY BALLET now entered what came to be known as "The Farrell Years." Diana Adams, from whom Suzanne Farrell took over *Movements,* had been the one to discover her, on a scouting trip to Cincinnati in 1960. At fourteen, Suzanne already showed unusual grace, flow and musical sense but had not developed much strength. Diana hesitated to suggest that the girl move to New York and was relieved to hear that Suzanne's mother was already planning to do so.

Diana told Balanchine that in addition to her other qualities, the girl had something "special," but one of her feet had "virtually no instep." Farrell herself in later years gave the critic David Daniel an account of her strange "audition" with Balanchine. He asked her what she had prepared for him to see. She replied that she didn't know she was supposed to do a number; and her heart sank. He said it didn't matter. But instead of giving her a few steps and combinations to do, he asked her to take her shoe off the weak foot and make a pointe. He cupped his hand over the lower part of the instep and down over her toes, then pressed her foot backward so hard that it hurt. This made her angry. She stiffened her foot and toes and pushed them back against his hand to loosen his grip. He said, "Thank you." Two days later she got a letter telling her she had a full scholarship.

Soon after Suzanne entered the School, she met Balanchine in the elevator, and all she could think of to say was, "How is your cat, Mourka?" This period of shyness did not last long. Balanchine's interest in her grew rapidly. During the Russian tour they became friends, and soon after the company returned, she was promoted to soloist. In April 1963 she danced *Movements*; in December, *Meditation*—a pas de deux to Tchaikovsky music—created especially for her and Jacques d'Amboise. She was seventeen years old. The next year she danced the first ballerina's role in *Ballet Imperial* and Titania in *A Midsummer Night's Dream.* In the latter she was somewhat unsure of how to behave toward Bottom in his ass's head. "I hadn't a clue," she confessed later in a magazine article. "The boss said, 'Don't you have a cat or a dog you can talk to?' So I went out and got a cat and called him Bottom and talked his head off."

With her round cheeks and huge blue eyes, Suzanne herself as a young girl looked something like a cat, but in profile she already shone with the beauty of a Nefertiti. Her long legs and long neck made her appear even taller than she was. Silently and steadily she acquired knowledge and experience. She wanted to dance everything, and Balanchine was ready to give her everything. When Diana Adams commented to him later on the extraordinary variety of Suzanne's range, he nodded and said, "Well, you see, dear, Suzanne never resisted."

Balanchine and Nicolas Nabokov had for years discussed the possibility of staging a *Don Quixote* ballet, yet it is hard to see the work that was presented at the New York State Theater in 1965 as anything but the choreographer's homage to his "alabaster princess," Suzanne Farrell, who danced Dulcinea. Cervantes's hero was obsessed by the chivalric ideal of performing impossible deeds for the love of a beautiful lady; so was Balanchine. His ballet was a quixotic endeavor. Its many sets and costumes by Esteban Francés were handsome enough, but Nabokov's music was a strange patchwork. The justification for the ballet lay in the dances he arranged for Farrell.

Balanchine had performed in the Petipa-Minkus *Don Quixote* before the Russian Revolution. In this long work, the Don does not dance and is obliged to sit on one side of the stage for most of the evening, watching a series of divertissements to flashy music. Balanchine's Don did not dance either, but he was far from a lay figure. Balanchine called him "a secular saint," and Esteban Francés recognized him as "a Christ figure."

Within a few moments of the curtain rising on the Don in his library a maidservant, Farrell, comes in to open his curtains, wash his feet and dry them with her hair. She is thus first seen as a servant, then as the Magdalen. The Don falls asleep, and in his dream she appears to him as a damsel in distress. The walls of his room disappear, and he stands, sword in hand, to face the world. A religious procession passes: the maidservant is now the statue of the Virgin Mary.

As Balanchine taught the role of Don Quixote to Richard Rapp, he explained that the Don was "an old man, but . . . young in feeling and vigorous in movement." Balanchine himself was to play the part on several occasions, and one can imagine that he took a certain pleasure not only in sharing the ballet with Farrell, but in portraying himself as a kind of misunderstood outsider and idealist.

Act III, with its mysteriously beautiful moonlit forest, was the setting for Suzanne Farrell's great moment. Dulcinea and her two friends, supported by three knights, arrive just as Sancho has left his exhausted master sleeping. "Miraculous variations follow," wrote Denby. "Like a dream, these dances remind you of something recent. . . . The man's powerful variation . . . has arm gestures from the court dance. Dulcinea's variation—marvelous in the feet, in the novel and unorthodox épaulements—carries the hidden secret to its climax. Dancing faster and faster, more and more desperate, opposed by a woman in black like the Duchess, tortured by the enchanter Merlin, Dulcinea at last appeals to the sleeping Knight." "Fearless Farrell," someone dubbed her; the discovery that she could fall off pointe at an angle when dancing at speed was to lead to new inventions in Balanchine's choreography.

Don Quixote tilts at a giant, who turns into a windmill, is stampeded by swine, caged by courtiers and carried home. As he lies in bed, he imagines the burning of his books by the Inquisition. In a return to the opening of the ballet, he sees another vision of the Virgin and like a mystic levitating in ecstasy is raised high in the air; he collapses, sobbing, and dies. Finally the maidservant makes a cross from two sticks, walks slowly to the body of her master and places it on his breast.

Balanchine played the part of Don Quixote at the gala performance that preceded the premiere. Farrell later told a critic: "It was the most wonderful night of my life. Afterward we went to a champagne party, and then the two of us slipped away to have doughnuts and coffee. . . . He's so simple. I think I was a sort of relief to him. He doesn't expect a girl to be intellectual—and I found I could make him laugh. . . ."

Another member of the cast, Suki Schorer, who has for many years demonstrated the Balanchine style to students at the School, did not agree that *Don Quixote* was (as I suggested to her) "a crazy endeavor which didn't come off." But she thought that three hours of Nabokov's score was too much for most people.

Suzanne had no understudy, Schorer explained. "People would say, 'We have to have an understudy,' but he said, 'No, I don't want anybody else. If she can't do it, we won't do it.' She never missed a performance till she left."

I first saw *Don Quixote* nearly two years after its original production, by which time a gypsy solo for Farrell had been added. I went backstage after a Saturday matinee to congratulate first her, then Balanchine. I found him with Nabokov, tossing back glasses of brandy, and he praised the composer's versatility. "The score has music of all kinds—polyphonic, in the style of Vivaldi, a Passacaglia on the Gloria." In response to a word of praise for Farrell, he declared that she was incomparable. "I have seen every dancer, and there has never been one like her. She can do everything."

At this point, two shameless mothers with children burst into the room, exclaiming, "We want a ballerina." Balanchine's politeness was exemplary. The mothers had some idea of who he was, but they were not impressed; nor had the ballet been what they expected.

MOTHER   I don't like tragic things.

G. B.   What religion are you?

MOTHER   Jewish.

G. B.   Then you understand about sacrifice. *Don Quixote* is all true.

MOTHER   How old are you?

G. B. *(lying)*   Forty-five.

MOTHER   How long did it take you to get where you are?

G. B.   I started at eight years old. [He then explained why his company was called what it was, how many seasons it had every year, etc.]

MOTHER   How do you pronounce your name?

G. B. *(thoughtfully)*   Well, in French they say *"Bal en Chine"*—that means "a dance in China." In England they say "Bal*un*shun," to rhyme with "luncheon." In American, it's "Ball and chain."

Nabokov was laughing. Balanchine kissed both mothers and sent them off in search of someone more interesting. Then he walked me to the elevator.

.   .   .

WHATEVER Balanchine might say, Farrell could not "do everything" equally well. She herself complained that she had "lousy bourrées": Balanchine gave her continual pas de bourrées in *Don*

Quixote to force her to work at them. She was also not an allegro dancer and had not much of a jump. Balanchine tried to strengthen her feet, but he gave a minimum of jumping in class during "The Farrell Years." Yet, though he could see Suzanne's defects very clearly, he would not admit to anyone else that she had any. She had a strong musical sense, an incredible extension in développé and the kind of inexplicable glamour that amounts to genius.

Balanchine called her "Pussycat-fish." "Not just any cat and any fish," she explained. He meant she was a mixture of a cheetah (speed) and a dolphin (intelligence).

. . .

IN 1964 Richard Leach, director of programs at Lincoln Center, had the idea of building at Saratoga Springs in upstate New York a summer theater where the New York City Ballet and one of the big orchestras could have successive seasons in July and August. Kirstein was enthusiastic, but the New York Philharmonic had made other arrangements, so Leach at once telephoned the Philadelphia Orchestra, which fell in with the plan.

Eugene Ormandy, the orchestra's celebrated conductor, was the first to be consulted about the exact site of the Saratoga Performing Arts Center. In the early spring of 1964, Dick Leach showed him where Geyser Creek had hollowed out a natural amphitheater. At this time of year the waterfall was swollen by melting snow and roared like Niagara. Looking down through the trees, about a thousand of which would have to be felled, Ormandy said, "Dick, the waterfall must go. It will interfere with the pianissimi in *L'Après-midi d'un faune.*" Three costly dams were therefore constructed upstream. When the theater was built, it became possible, by flipping a switch, to turn off the waterfall for two hours every night.

For several months Balanchine, Kirstein and Leach held weekly meetings with the appointed architect, John MacFadyen. The roofed theater, seating 5,201, was to be open at the sides, so that at least another 5,000 could watch the dancing or listen to the music from the grassy slopes beyond. The proportions of the stage and the planning of the sight lines were to be based on those of the New York State Theater.

On April 22, 1966, Edward Bigelow drove Tanaquil LeClercq to Saratoga to inspect houses that she and George might rent; she fell in love with a ramshackle guesthouse in the Leaches' garden which no one had previously considered. Kay Leach had it painted and redecorated, and it became Balanchine's July home for sixteen years.

Balanchine had his first sight of the theater on May 6. Sitting on the windowsill of the dressing room that had been built for him and Eugene Ormandy to occupy in turn—but Balanchine relinquished it to Robert Irving—he surveyed the scene for a few moments in silence, then asked, "That is the waterfall Ormandy will turn off?" When Leach nodded, Balanchine gave his considered opinion. "Dick, much better, much cheaper—turn off Ormandy."

He never expressed any enthusiasm for the site or the theater, but the Leaches knew that he loved both. (It was the same, they noticed, when he was given a present.) His chief preoccupation, as ever, was with the stage. He and Bates had further perfected their method of construction. By June 25 the floor had been laid, and Balanchine came to test it. In silence he began to dance up and down and around, while Leach held his breath. "Better than stage in State Theater—springier" was the verdict.

On July 9, 1966, the New York City Ballet opened its first season at Saratoga Springs with *A Midsummer Night's Dream*.

. . .

THE LEACHES became and remained close friends of the choreographer. In addition to the animals on their farm, they kept dogs and cats, several of whom also made friends with Balanchine. Dick related:

We had a mongrel called Moka who became inseparable from George. Every summer she would leave us and move in with him on the instant of his arrival. George brought her bones from the store, and Moka knew the sound of his car. She was so devoted she could tell when he was about to leave. Several hours before his departure she would come and lie down under one of our bushes.

Then a tiny kitten appeared from the deep woods behind George's house and went straight to him. When he brought her over to us she *seemed* to have been there before, because she went up to all our dogs— we had six—as if she knew them; then she made straight for the back laundry, where the dogs' food was kept. George said she was "a second comer" and named her *"Bis"* [French for "encore"].

In 1966 the American Dressage Institution, whose instructors were riders from Vienna's famous Spanish Riding School, came to Saratoga and gave exhibitions to the music of Handel, Haydn, Mozart and Lanner concurrently with NYCB's performances. Balanchine spent two weeks learning to ride a retired Lippizaner stallion, getting to know the dance movements of a different creature.

．　．　．

THE URGE to make big ballets for the big theater at Lincoln Center doubtless prompted both the *Brahms-Schoenberg Quartet* of 1966— a ballet to Schoenberg's 1937 orchestration of Brahms's Piano Quartet No. 1 in G minor, Op. 25—and the concoction of *Jewels* the next year. The latter, alleged to be the first "abstract" ballet in three acts, used music by three very different composers, each with choreography in a different style. Actually, it was not a three-act ballet at all but three ballets called "Emeralds, "Rubies" and "Diamonds." Balanchine made vague and contradictory statements to explain it: "The whole thing was—I like jewels. I'm an Oriental—from Georgia in the Caucasus, and a Russian. I would cover myself with jewels." "The ballet has nothing to do with jewels. The dancers are just dressed like jewels."

In *Palais de cristal,* the original Paris version of Bizet's Symphony in C, Balanchine had dressed the dancers of the four movements in red, blue, green and white costumes, and the adornments of the different sets matched. For *Jewels* there was one chandelier that turned green, red and white during the different acts. It took me nearly twenty years to accept the hybrid nature of this work; then one night the critic George Dorris pointed out to me that *Jewels* was a perfect example of American "packaging": presented as a trinity, with an expensive-sounding title, the ballet's saleability was enormously increased. Once I had connived at the deception—if such it is—I found it easier to enjoy the individual merits of the parts. In any case, *Jewels* was a smash hit from its first performance.

In "Emeralds," a group of Fauré excerpts put together by Balanchine, the ballerina's waving arms conjure up a distant, medieval dreamworld; and although there are no period steps or trappings, the horn calls in Fauré's music enhance the impression that we are *"au fond du bois"* or witnessing the animation of a *"verdure"* tapestry. The ballet is in fact an incarnation of a "tipped ballroom" behind a scrim with "a projection of the sea on the scrim, which pulsates" imagined by Balanchine in 1958. The music of Fauré, which had seduced him then, had not lost its hold on him in the intervening years.

If "Emeralds" is "French," "Rubies" is "American." Set to Stravinsky's *Capriccio* for piano and orchestra (1929), it has deformed classical movements in the style of *The Four Temperaments* or *Episodes,* but because of its music, its two principals are called upon to be more deliberately witty than dancers in those earlier works. Villella, who was in the first cast, found the steps difficult to learn, though once learned, they seemed inevitable:

We had to find our way through Stravinsky, then through Balanchine's hearing of the score and the structure of his choreography. Once you got there it was obvious—so simple. He was so logical, you'd say "Oh, of course! It's just like geometry." In the last movement when these four boys are chasing me, I got a feeling that he was looking at me as this street kid from Queens and interpolating that into the ballet, still keeping a certain sense of elegance and of the wit and jazz quality of the thirties. With Balanchine there was always layer upon layer. You could go back time and time again and see something new. That's the major difference between a Balanchine ballet and a pedestrian ballet.

Patricia Neary, who was also in "Rubies," remembered how excited Balanchine became while arranging it: yet when it brought down the house, he was jealous for Farrell's success in "Diamonds," which followed, and asked Patricia, "Was that your mother applauding?"

For "Diamonds" Balanchine used the last three movements of Tchaikovsky's Symphony No. 3 in D major. It was a spectacular work with which to close the evening, an essay in the grand style of Imperial Russia. After the subtle "Emeralds" and the unpredictable "Rubies," an audience watching "Diamonds" felt safe and happy to applaud a kind of coronation for Farrell, supported by Jacques d'Amboise and a corps of thirty-four in noble alignments.

Farrell has said: " 'Diamonds' is hard because you're out there in white and there's no hiding. 'Diamonds' you can't sell. It's too dignified to sell. And you can't cover anything up." Balanchine himself in later years said, " 'Diamonds' is so boring. Only pas de deux is good."

■   .   ■

IN 1967, Balanchine escorted twenty-five dancers with a repertory of "small" ballets to dance for a week at the Edinburgh Festival. Jacques d'Amboise had to cancel at the last moment, which caused havoc with the casting. Villella was dancing almost the whole repertory, but not always with the partners best suited to him. Balanchine even tried to make him dance the *Tchaikovsky Pas de deux* with Farrell. He protested, "Mr. B., I really don't think I'm tall enough." "Don't worry, dear, we'll change. You know where you have the—we'll change. Don't worry." But after a couple of rehearsals the adaptable choreographer had to admit that even though the strong Villella could lift Farrell onto his shoulder and catch her in a fish dive, he would need a stepladder to reach above her head and support her in a finger-turn on pointe.

As for *Apollo,* Villella had danced it several times, but with Patricia McBride. Since the outing to Edinburgh was clearly to show off Farrell, Balanchine wanted her to dance Terpsichore. Where was her Apollo to come from? Balanchine tracked down Taras in his Paris apartment and asked him to go to Copenhagen and invite Henning Kronstam. Taras flew to Denmark, but Kronstam was unable to get away. However, Vera Volkova took Taras to the Royal Theater to watch a young dancer, Peter Martins, who had been taught *Apollo* by Kronstam and had danced it in Copenhagen.

On the Saturday night before the Edinburgh opening, Martins was having supper in Copenhagen with Stanley Williams, who had by now joined the staff of the School of American Ballet on a permanent basis. By coincidence, Martins was trying to find out what chance Stanley thought he had of a job in America at the very moment Volkova got through to him at the restaurant. Would he come at once for an audition? The young man, recently promoted to principal dancer, thought it was "too late in the evening" and that he was "beyond auditioning." He agreed to meet Volkova and Taras in the morning.

On Sunday morning, Taras arranged for Martins's air fare to Edinburgh and sent the young Dane off. Martins had stipulated that Stanley Williams go with him. The two men arrived in Edinburgh that afternoon and went for a walk. Balanchine, too, was out walking, showing Suzanne the extraordinary beauties of the Scottish capital, and they met the Danes. In his memoirs, Martins recalls, "Balanchine turned to Suzanne and said: 'This is your Apollo.' She tilted her head, and gave me a slow once-over. . . . 'Well, at least he's tall.' "

At rehearsal the next morning, Balanchine offered few comments on the way Martins danced *Apollo,* although he made some minor adjustments in the pas de deux. At Tuesday's rehearsal, however, he told him, "Before we begin, . . . you know, you do it all wrong." "I had been trying to make everything beautiful and grand," wrote Martins, "and he demanded shapes that looked grotesque but were packed with energy. . . . I fell in love with this man. . . . He was so wonderfully natural. . . . He radiated knowledge and authority." Still, Martins thought the New York City Ballet was unlike any company he had ever seen. "The dancers neglected or didn't bother with precision. The emphasis was on the energy and on movement itself, on timing and quickness."

Two months later Martins received a telegram inviting him to be a guest artist with the New York City Ballet during the *Nutcracker* season in December.

But if the trip to Edinburgh gained Balanchine a dancer, it also cost him one. Patricia Neary was already fed up with Balanchine's never giving jumping in class and leaving the theater after the first ballet when Suzanne was not in the second or third. Suzanne always wore white toe shoes in *Apollo* instead of pink, so the other Muses had to conform. In Edinburgh, Neary and Gloria Govrin, who were dancing Calliope and Polyhymnia, found to their consternation that Suzanne intended to wear pink shoes after all. Furious, they rushed out to Woolworth's for some dye. Patricia was devoted to Balanchine, but this was the last straw. When she returned to New York in September she told him, "I'm leaving. You've gone too far." Balanchine protested, "I have a right to love." "You should love all eighty of us," said Patricia; and she left.

· · ·

IN 1965, the year in which the Race Relations Act was passed, Lincoln Kirstein joined the protest marches in Alabama. When, in 1968, Martin Luther King, Jr., was murdered, Kirstein organized the first and only performance of Stravinsky's *Requiem Canticles,* arranged and staged by Balanchine at the New York State Theater, in his memory. This was given on May 2, 1968. I happened to be present, and wrote a review:

IN the Prelude a body of angels in transparent white gowns are seen in twilight. In the Exaudi they light their candelabra one by one. In the Dies Irae they surge about, potential Lucifers. In Tuba Mirum the hero appears—and this is Arthur Mitchell, a Negro—robed in purple and gold. During the orchestral meditation called "Interlude," the angels move lights like chessmen on the floor, and, stooping, illumine the hero's path to heaven. In Rex Tremendae he is led through diagonal avenues. In Lacrimosa, arches are formed, and a weeping girl, Suzanne Farrell, passes beneath them. In Libera Me, the angels move in circles. Then, on the first chord of the Postlude, Mitchell is raised aloft, and Farrell, like a timid soul in Purgatory, threads her way through a Stonehenge of blessed beings.

That same year, Balanchine and Kirstein helped Arthur Mitchell lay the foundation for his Dance Theatre of Harlem. A school was established on Morningside Avenue (it moved later to West 152nd Street)—Tanaquil Le Clercq became one of the teachers—and within three years the company opened its first season.

Tanaquil had developed a remarkable ability to manage by herself in her wheelchair, and with this increased independence she acquired a new group of young friends. She was, after all, only in her thirties. When Balanchine came home from work, he simply wanted to watch television. Apart from Westerns, he loved the detective series *Ironside, Barnaby Jones* and *Wonder Woman,* and he considered *The Muppet Show* the greatest American invention since the refrigerator. This was rather a strain for his wife. He was also making himself conspicuous with Suzanne Farrell. Eventually Tanaquil and he agreed to separate, with a view to divorce, but some old friends believed that she never ceased to love him.

When they parted, an awful decision had to be made: Who would have Mourka? Balanchine ceded him to Tanaquil. That summer in Connecticut, Mourka disappeared. Tanaquil frantically telephoned Balanchine, who was in Saratoga. He at once drove the two hundred miles to Weston and remained there until he had found the cat.

. . .

THERE was a young man in the New York City Ballet named Paul Mejia, of whom Balanchine had great hopes, both as a dancer and as a choreographer. Mejia, born in Lima, Peru, was the son of a South American father and a Russian mother, who had been a student at the School. Paul won a scholarship to the School when he was ten, and his progress, both there and in the company later, was swift. During 1968, Balanchine, Farrell and Mejia were often seen dining together in restaurants. In the autumn, Balanchine flew to Mexico to get a divorce. If the idea of marrying Suzanne was in his mind—and there is good reason to believe it was—the lady had other plans. In September 1968, the *New York Post* published in its column "Secret Stuff" a note that "the ballet world is excited about ballerina Suzanne Farrell's reported romane [*sic*] with a man of her own age." Balanchine's divorce came through on February 5, 1969, but before the winter season ended on February 16, he left for Germany to stage Glinka's *Ruslan and Lyudmila* for Rolf Liebermann's Hamburg State Opera. On February 21, Paul Mejia and Suzanne Farrell were married at the Church of St. Paul the Apostle, four blocks south of the State Theater on Ninth Avenue. Lincoln Kirstein was best man, and many members of the company were present. The next night Balanchine telephoned Barbara Horgan from Germany. He was very angry. When he heard that Barbara had been at the wedding, he implied that she had betrayed him. Her feeling had been that the sooner all the "nonsense" stopped the better; she welcomed the marriage because she thought it would give Balanchine no alternative but to see reason and "come back as a human being." Instead, he asked her if she would join him in Hamburg. She said she would, without seriously expecting to be sent for.

When she arrived at her office the next Monday, her first call was from Lufthansa, which had a prepaid ticket for her to leave the following day. Balanchine met her at the airport early on Wednesday morning, and they drove to the Vierjahreszeiten Hotel.

Their breakfast together was, for her, "a horrible experience." Balanchine swore that he would never go back to America. For ten days he and Barbara followed the same routine: they went to rehearsal every morning, lunched together and got drunk. She let him reiterate his complaints, but she felt all along that he knew he would eventually have to return to America and to his company.

Kirstein flew to the opening performance of *Ruslan* on March 30, taking Edward Bigelow with him. Next day he left for London, and Balanchine went with Bigelow to Berlin, where he came to an agreement with the West Berlin Ballet Ensemble about giving them certain works and sending dancers from New York to perform in them. He did not confide his private feelings to Kirstein but presented him with a series of absurd projects: to print no dancers' names on future programs; to commission a Georgian ballet from Khachaturian; to go to Persia in October; to go to Moscow and "give them 20 ballets." These were surely symptoms of desperation.

The spring season was due to start on April 22. On April 10, Balanchine returned to New York. His sense of humor was coming back. When Paul Mejia had been a new student at the School, one of the principal male dancers in the company had found him attractive. Balanchine noticed this and thought it a pity that the boy should be steered into a homosexual groove before he knew where his natural inclinations lay. He told Natalie Molostwoff that she should speak to Paul's mother about it. Natalie did, and the attentions ceased. Remembering this in the spring of 1969, Balanchine remarked, "No good deed goes unpunished." Meanwhile, however awkward he may have felt to be working with Farrell and Mejia under the circumstances, he took no action against them.

It was announced that at the spring gala on May 8, 1969, the closing ballet would be *Symphony in C,* in which Farrell always danced the second movement. Villella, because he was now appearing in a new Jerome Robbins work, asked to be left out of the third movement. Mejia, who had danced it several times, considered himself next in line, but he was not cast. He and Suzanne told Betty

Cage that if he did not dance in *Symphony in C* at the gala, they would both resign. There were several panicky program changes at the last minute to try to save Mejia's face and keep Farrell in the company. First, *La Sonnambula* was to be substituted for the Bizet, then the Bizet was to be given without the third movement. Finally the management settled for John Clifford's new ballet *Fantasies,* Robbins's new *Dances at a Gathering* and *Stars and Stripes.* There were no roles for either Suzanne or Paul in any of these.

On Monday, May 12, the Mejias told the press that they had resigned from the New York City Ballet. The reason proffered by Suzanne was that her husband was not given enough roles. Balanchine immediately telephoned Patricia Neary, who was appearing in Kansas: "Come back at once and do *Prodigal!*" She broke her contract and returned to the fold. Nevertheless, a certain "apathy"—to use Barbara Horgan's word—descended upon the choreographer. His only new ballet for the company in 1969 was the *Valse fantaisie* of Glinka, and it was merely a single movement from the four-movement *Glinkiana* he had staged in 1967.

Yet because of many extramural activities that year, the catalogue of Balanchine's projects in 1969, as listed in the Eakins Press *Choreography,* is longer than that of any other year in his life. Since he had agreed to allow the West Berlin Ballet Ensemble to stage his ballets, he went to work with young choreographers there, encouraging exchanges between Berlin and his own company. Between the New York and Saratoga seasons, he flew with NYCB to Monte Carlo to take part in a Diaghilev festival.

Dr. Herbert Graff, director of the Grand Théâtre de Genève, had asked him to suggest a ballet master for his opera house, and Balanchine interviewed one of his former dancers, Alfonso Catá, for the post. He then recommended Patricia Neary as ballet mistress, and after dancing with NYCB in Monte Carlo she went to Geneva to start work. In September, Balanchine staged a four-act

Swan Lake at Geneva's Grand Théâtre, with Neary as Odette. In West Berlin, he rehearsed the Berlin Opera Ballet in *Episodes*, *Symphony in C* and *Apollo* for its first all-Balanchine evening. Another Balanchine evening was presented at Geneva's Grand Théâtre, and the choreographer was given the title of artistic advisor.

To cheer him up, Nabokov and his new wife, Dominique, took Balanchine to spend Christmas with Baron and Baronne Philippe de Rothschild in Château Mouton in southwestern France. Although the château among the vines was a nineteenth-century Gothic building, inside the luxury was dazzling. The food and wine were perfect, but Balanchine, seated beside his hostess at dinner, was speechless. He begged the Nabokovs to cut short their visit: "Let's go to Bordeaux and have a little sausage with Beaujolais." In the train to Paris, he declared the restaurant's dinner the best meal he had ever eaten.

Barbara thought that at some time during the next few months he came to terms with himself. He was sixty-five and had been ripped apart. There were certain consummations he could no longer hope for; and he was never going to allow himself to be so miserable again.

In other directions, things were looking up. The Juilliard School had moved from its old home near Columbia University to Lincoln Center. In 1969, the School of American Ballet, which had leased part of Juilliard's third floor, transferred itself there. The four studios, nine offices, locker rooms and showers had been carefully planned. There was a handsome theater for workshop performances, in which the students would dance to the Juilliard orchestra. The new arrangement was what Balanchine had always hoped for: something like the Imperial School on Theater Street, St. Petersburg, where he had received his own training. Both training and performance could now take place on the same site. Moreover, the students chosen to dance in *Nutcracker* or *A Midsummer Night's Dream* could carry their practice tights and shoes to the State

Theater without even crossing a road; there was a bridge over Sixty-fifth Street.

•   •   •

FOR SOME TIME after his first guest appearances with the New York City Ballet, Peter Martins had been flying back and forth between the United States and Copenhagen, where he was expected to fulfill his duties with the Royal Danish Ballet. Presented by the latter with an ultimatum—"Either stay or go"—Martins chose Balanchine. He soon regretted this, for he began to feel that his new master was irritated by the "neatness" and "cool perfection" that were the results of his Bournonville training. He also found Balanchine's classes peculiar, and he began to study instead with his friend and compatriot Stanley Williams. He had, after all, been engaged in the first place because he was tall enough to partner Suzanne Farrell; after she left the company he felt less necessary.

The news that Martins was unhappy reached Ballet Theatre, and Lucia Chase made him an offer. Erik Bruhn advised him to accept. Martins met Lucia Chase for lunch in a restaurant to sign a contract. Suddenly it struck him that if he did, he could never go back to the New York City Ballet, for which he had left Denmark and renounced the state pension due to him on retirement. "I couldn't risk the loss of working with Balanchine," he wrote later. He did not sign.

At last he "cornered Balanchine."

I told him that . . . my ambition now was to dance his ballets . . . and I would do anything to make this possible. . . . He answered me, bluntly and directly. "You see, dear, you don't seem to be interested. I never see you anywhere, not in class, maybe in O'Neal's restaurant. When people show interest, I use them. If they don't, I leave them alone.

Martins told Balanchine that although people thought him "cool, self-possessed, distant," he knew he was full of energy and passion. He might be angry or impatient—but never bored. Balanchine said that it was up to him to prove his good intentions. If he succeeded, he could have any role he wanted. Martins later considered this conversation a turning point in his career.

Three years after she joined the company, Karin von Aroldingen, the German dancer Balanchine had met through Lotte Lenya, married Morton Gewirtz, a real estate broker, and in 1966 they had a daughter. Balanchine was much struck by the way Karin kept dancing and attending classes during her pregnancy, and he thanked her for her persistence. She had told Morton, "First I'm a dancer, then a wife, then a mother," and Morton understood this. In the plane to Monte Carlo in June 1969, Balanchine and Karin had a long heart-to-heart talk, and from that time on they were close friends. Karin, who had never known her own father, looked upon Balanchine not only as a father but as almost a god. In return, she and Morton gave him a warm family feeling, and he took a grandfatherly interest in their daughter, Margo, who was his godchild.

Meanwhile, other dancers, notably Kay Mazzo, had taken over most of Suzanne Farrell's roles. Balanchine's first ballet after Suzanne left was a jazzy piece to the music of George Gershwin songs. It was called *Who Cares?*

Chapter 13

....

HOMAGE TO STRAVINSKY:

SPRING 1972

O N APRIL 6, 1971, shortly before his eighty-ninth birthday, Stravinsky died after a long illness. Balanchine was not one of those who consider that old people's sufferings should be prolonged, that any kind of half life is better than death. Nor did he believe that death could take Stravinsky away from him. Although he must have decided at once that he would commemorate his most-admired friend, he said nothing about his intentions for over two months. He was rehearsing two works: Rolf Liebermann's *Concerto for Jazz Band and Symphony Orchestra,* in which twenty-one dancers of the New York City Ballet and twenty-three of Arthur Mitchell's Dance Theatre of Harlem took part, with Mitchell sharing the choreography; and an airport fantasia called

PAMTGG ("Pan Am Makes the Going Great"), to music taken from a television commercial.

On June 17, just before the curtain rose on the first performance of *PAMTGG*, Barbara Horgan had reason to go backstage. She found Balanchine, as usual at a premiere, standing calm and collected in the downstage right wing. He turned and said to her, "Next year, a Stravinsky festival." That was all.

The ineptness of *PAMTGG* and the indifference with which certain recent ballets by the company's other choreographers had been received prompted hints in the press that Balanchine, as choreographer and as artistic director, was losing his touch. His critics would discover in good time that he was, rather, planning his greatest endeavor.

It soon transpired, to the consternation of his colleagues, that Balanchine intended the Stravinsky Festival to last a week, with a different program every night—a far cry from the two-day, one-program Stravinsky "festival" of April 1937. He at once embarked on discussions with Robert Irving and Robert Craft, who would share the conducting. In Saratoga in July, he started work on a piano reduction of Stravinsky's very early Symphony in E flat. When the dancers went on vacation, Balanchine dined with Vera Stravinsky and Robert Craft, and Craft began to make a list of possibilities for the festival. He and Balanchine agreed that it should be a retrospective exhibition of Stravinsky's metamorphoses; and from what he wrote later, he apparently took for granted the inclusion of *Petrushka*, *The Rite of Spring*, *Les Noces* and *Jeu de cartes*. None of these, however, was to be staged.

Early in September, Balanchine and Barbara Horgan went to Rome to talk to Eugene Berman, because Balanchine had decided he was the obvious choice to design *Pulcinella*. It was probably during these discussions that the choreographer worked out a new story for the ballet he had found so "long and boring" when he saw the Massine version in the 1920s. There followed talks with Léon Leonidoff in Montecatini-Terme, where the agent took the waters every September; with Rolf Liebermann at the Paris Opéra; and with Nicolas Nabokov in Berlin. The possibility of making the Stravinsky celebration a worldwide event was clearly at the back of Balanchine's mind.

In New York in October, he had to face the question of fundraising. Everything depended on Richard Clurman, chairman of the board of the New York City Ballet. Balanchine told him that the week-long festival *must* open on the composer's ninetieth birthday, June 18, in the middle of the spring season; that to make final rehearsals possible the theater would have to be closed for the previous week, necessitating a considerable loss of income (about $130,000, in fact); and that he estimated the cost of the festival itself at a quarter of a million dollars. There seem to have been some protests against the proposal, but Balanchine would not be deflected.

Not only would NYCB's regular ballet masters, Balanchine, Robbins and Taras, participate; they would be joined by their old colleague Todd Bolender. There were also to be works by three young choreographers in the company, John Clifford, Lorca Massine (son of Léonide) and Richard Tanner. *Orpheus,* which had not been revived for seven years, was pieced together with the aid of Magallanes, Moncion and Le Clercq, members of the original cast.

Balanchine liked to turn a press conference into a party. The announcement of the Stravinsky Festival was made at one of his favorite restaurants near the theater. Mme. Stravinsky was there, and so was Goddard Lieberson, Vera Zorina's husband and chairman of Columbia Records (Stravinsky's recording company), who was to be chairman of the festival. A literal translation of Balanchine's words to the press could read as inconsequential and baffling, with their improvised expressions and unfinished sentences; but those who were present to see as well as to hear him, to note his gestures, watch his face and experience his charm, understood very well what he was getting at. It was only when they were obliged to organize for their readers the words they had taken down that they ran into difficulties.

Introduced as "artistic director" of the New York City Ballet, Balanchine said, "Don't call me artistic director—it's terrible. . . . all right in French maybe, but better I am just ballet master. That was enough for Petipa, enough for me." There followed some sweeping statements to be taken with a glass of vodka: "Stravinsky is who is responsible for anything we are using in music . . . everything we have in music he did first. . . . He was like Einstein—nobody like him. He made *musique dansante.* There have only been three who could do it. Delibes, Tchaikovsky, and Stravinsky. They made music for the body to dance to. They invented the floor for the dancer to walk on. . . . There are men who say there is no time, no space. But Stravinsky made time—not big grand time—but time that works with the small parts of how our bodies are made. According to our bodies they made our floor."

Nancy Goldner, who had been commissioned to put together a commemorative book, records Balanchine as saying:

In Russia we don't cry when a person dies. We are very happy. We throw rice with nice sweet things in it—vanilla and natural things—into the grave. Then we go home and have an enormous table of food and drink and we drink to the health of the guy who dies. The body is gone—we don't need—but we drink to his spirit. . . . [Like Shakespeare, Balanchine often harped on food.]

To show what *really* is Stravinsky you have to start with beginning, with *Sonata for Piano,* then do *Symphony Number One,* which Stravinsky did in the memory of Rimsky-Korsakov, then Opus 2, 3, 4, and for program one finish in 1910 with *Firebird.* In program two we go to 1914, and so on. Seven programs, thirty-six works, some old, some new, to show how his sound traveled through his life. So then the whole thing is interesting—a fantastic thing he went through. He was not accepted. . . . But who cares? We do. . . .

We dancers are like sailboats, not like engine boats. We go up and down with the waves, right? We don't cut through. So we know how great Stravinsky is to us. Probably dance would stop if we didn't have Stravinsky. Music is the main thing. And good food.

This time it doesn't matter how the ballets look—maybe lousy, so fast [rehearsed in such a hurry], maybe not enough money. But the music will be beautiful. We have a wonderful orchestra—will be good. We will show Stravinsky's life through sound and then you will see the whole thing in front of you.

Questions were encouraged, and to the first Balanchine replied: "Yes, it will be a retrospective. We finish with *Symphony of Psalms*—no dancers but enormous chorus. The last night we have as much as you like cold vodka, cold vodka and something else. No, not caviar, but something."

Where else might the festival be repeated? "We're already invited to do this all again in Munich and in Paris. They cannot do it there. Why? I tell you in private why."

Which choreographers will arrange which ballets? "Everybody will choreograph what they want. What they don't want, I will use."

"How did I meet Stravinsky? Lenin died. I was so depressed I left Russia. I was twenty. Diaghilev asked me to be ballet master. I accepted. The first ballet was *Chant du rossignol.* . . . Stravinsky played the music on the piano. The tempi was absolutely right. . . . Diaghilev comes—with cane, with monocle [a bit of miming]— he sits, he listens. He wants everything faster, faster, faster. I change everything for him. Then Stravinsky comes and says, 'didn't I tell you slower, slower.' That is how we met, in 1925. So you are all invited to come to see our festival, our party."

The New York Times printed the scheduled programs, in which drastic changes were later made. In fact, only the two final programs, Saturday's and the second Sunday's, would be performed as they had been announced to the press. Chronological order was obviously not going to work, because, for example, the dull Symphony in E flat of 1905–1907 would lower the temperature of the opening program, and the *Symphony of Psalms,* with which Balanchine wanted to end the festival, had been composed in 1930, before Stravinsky even settled in America. Also the box office required that there be at least one Balanchine ballet on every program.

The vacation between the end of the winter season and the rehearsal period for the spring season was cut from the usual four weeks to two. Although during March and April nine ballets by four different choreographers were rehearsed—two of them revivals—there were still ten more works to be begun in May and two in June. When the spring season opened on May 2, the dancers were rehearsing Stravinsky ballets as well as works in the current repertory, and performing in the evening.

Robert Irving began orchestra rehearsals on May 22, and for four weeks held three rehearsals, from two and a half to three hours long, every week. In the fifth and final week, when the theater was dark, there were rehearsals during the day and every night, when each ballet had a dress rehearsal.

Most of the new works, like a number of the old ones, would be given in practice clothes or plain leotards against a cyclorama. Nevertheless, there would be some new sets and costumes, and because the latter always arrived from Karinska's workshop at the last minute, Ronald Bates decided to wait until the final week to plot the lighting of all the new ballets. He had to light twenty-one that week alone, and he worked with his crew every day from eight in the morning till midnight.

No one had ever seen Balanchine in a hurry; he did not appear in a hurry now. Tamara Geva once compared him to a general. Anyone who has seen active service in the armed forces will confirm that a commander who never gets flustered in an emergency inspires the utmost confidence. Some of the organizers in the background, with whom the dancers did not concern themselves, must have had nightmares nonetheless.

Rosemary Dunleavy, who was now in charge of arranging the daily rehearsal schedule, only once saw Balanchine annoyed. She had taken the stage for two hours to rehearse the current repertory, and he arrived expecting to finish *Symphony in Three Movements.* The final fugue was not yet arranged, and it had to be done that very moment. Thirty-two dancers were rapidly assembled. Then Balanchine, who had worked out in his head exactly what he wanted, finished the ballet in forty minutes.

Balanchine even allowed journalists to watch some of the rehearsals, and took time to talk to them. Shirley Fleming of *Musical America* found him in a tight blue-denim shirt and nondescript gray trousers, wearing his celebrated turquoise bracelet. She quoted to him words that had been attributed to him in the Stravinsky number of *Dance Index,* twenty-five years before. It was a sentence about *Apollon Musagète* being "the turning point" in his life, which taught him that he too could "eliminate." "I didn't say that," he replied promptly. "I mean somebody else said I said it." Walter Monfried of the *Milwaukee Journal* asked him, after a two-hour rehearsal, "How do you relax after such hard work?" "It's not hard work and I don't relax—why should anyone want to relax?" "You should have hobbies and recreations." "Well, I do have a hobby. I'm a collector." "Of what?" "Wine bottles . . . but I'm not like a stamp collector—I use up what's inside the bottles before I add them to my collection. I have another recreation. After dealing with physical problems and solutions, I like to go beyond the physical into meta-physical speculation." "Such as Kant?" "Yes, yes, Kant is very important. . . ."

One week before the opening of the Stravinsky Festival, Balanchine told Bob Micklin, the music critic of *Newsday,* "I know what Stravinsky wanted, just as I know what Mozart and Tchaikovsky wanted. If the music is German, Russian, English, modern, I make dance that looks like it. I was born for that reason. . . . When you are choreographing . . . you have to make it interesting enough so the public will not go to sleep! . . . There is certain music that doesn't need anything added to it. I have never choreographed *Rite of Spring.* Bach's *St. Matthew Passion* doesn't need any performance beside the music. . . . You have to be very careful not to kill the music when you make dance."

36

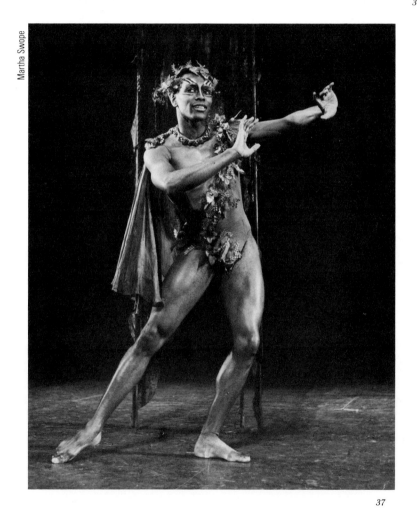

37

A Midsummer Night's Dream (1962): 36. Edward Villella as Oberon;
37. Arthur Mitchell as Puck.

38

39

40

41

38, 39. Suzanne Farrell and Jacques d'Amboise in Movements *(1965).*
EPISODES *(1959): 40. Allegra Kent and Nicholas Magallanes in "Concerto";*
41. Paul Taylor in "Variations."

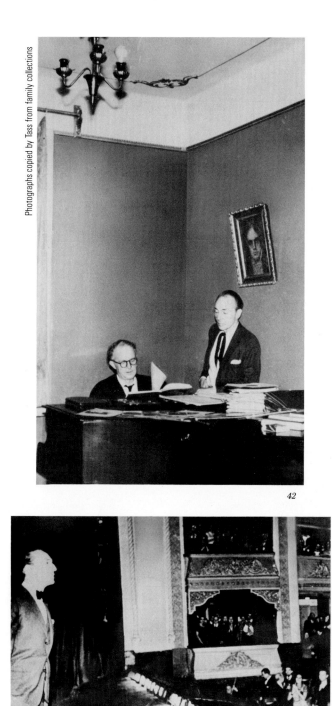

42

43

RETURN TO RUSSIA *(1962): 42. Balanchine with his brother in the latter's home in Tbilisi; 43. Balanchine acclaimed at the Tbilisi Opera House.*

44

45

46

DON QUIXOTE *(1965): 44. Suzanne Farrell in one of her variations;*
45. Richard Rapp and Deni Lamont as the Don and Sancho Panza;
46. Balanchine and Farrell as Don Quixote and Dulcinea.

66

67

66. Le Tombeau de Couperin *(1975)*. 67. *Karin von Aroldingen and Adam Lüders*
in Robert Schumann's "Davidsbündlertänze" *(1980)*.

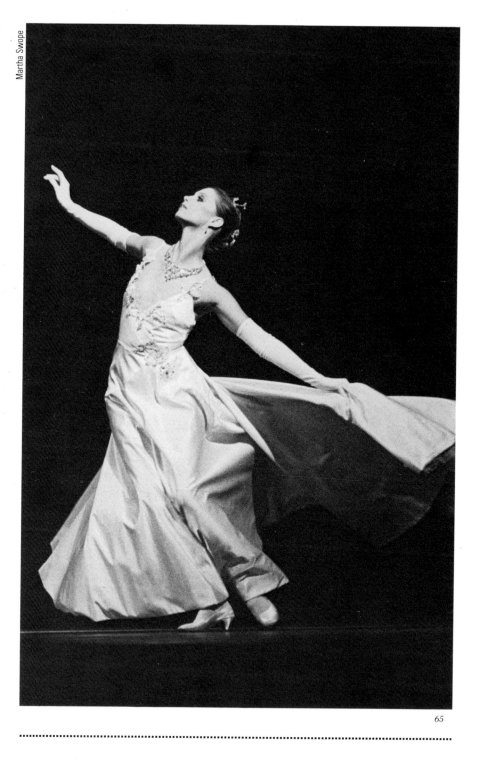

65. Suzanne Farrell in Vienna Waltzes *(1977).*

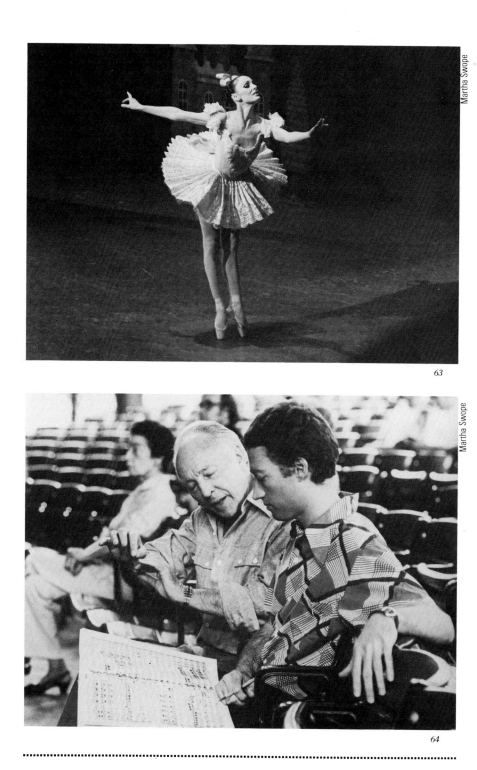

Martha Swope

63

Martha Swope

64

63. *Patricia McBride in* The Steadfast Tin Soldier *(1975).*
64. *Lucia Davidova, Balanchine and Gordon Boelzner at Saratoga (1977).*

61

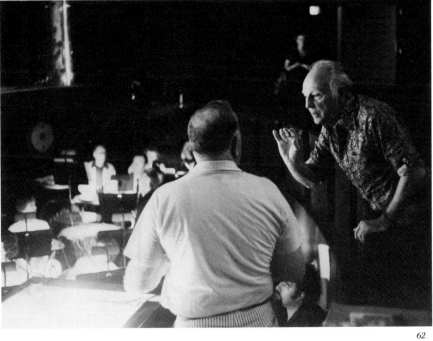

62

61. Balanchine rehearsing Merrill Ashley and Robert Weiss
in Ballo della Regina *(1978). 62. Balanchine with Robert Irving.*

58

59

60

58. *Helgi Tomasson in* Divertissement from "Le Baiser de la fée" *(1972).*
59. *Mikhail Baryshnikov in* The Four Temperaments *(1978).*
60. *Balanchine instructing Kay Mazzo (c. 1972).*

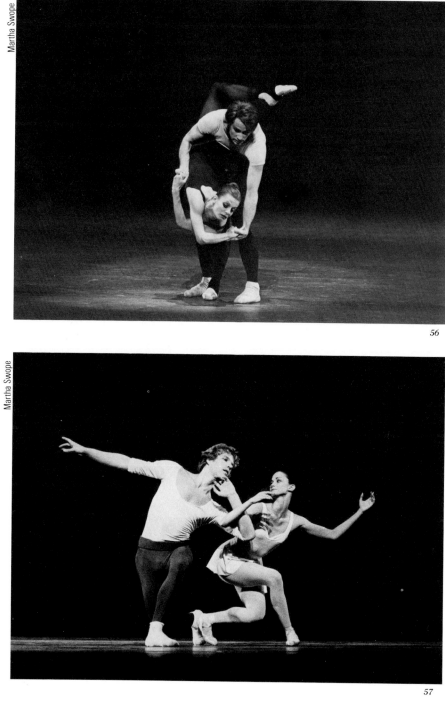

56

57

56. *Karin von Aroldingen and Jean-Pierre Bonnefous in* Violin Concerto *(1972).*
57. *Kay Mazzo and Peter Martins in* Duo Concertant *(1972).*

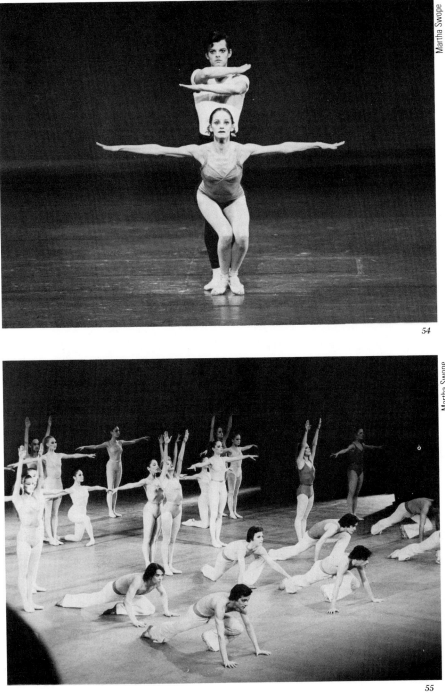

Martha Swope

54

Martha Swope

55

SYMPHONY IN THREE MOVEMENTS *(1972): 54. Sara Leland and John Clifford;
55. The final group.*

Martha Swope

51

52

53

JEWELS *(1967): 51. Violette Verdy in "Emeralds"; 52. Edward Villella in "Rubies"; 53. Suzanne Farrell and Peter Martins in "Diamonds."*

50

50. *Balanchine's Easter supper, 1964.*

Martha Swope

Martha Swope

Nancy Lassalle

47

48

49

47. *Balanchine and Farrell at a rehearsal with Anthony Blum and Richard Rapp (1965). 48. Balanchine, Ronald Bates and Lincoln Kirstein (c. 1965). 49. Balanchine at the School of American Ballet on Upper Broadway (c. 1965).*

68

69

68. *Darci Kistler and Sean Lavery in* Swan Lake *(1981). 69. Suzanne Farrell and Ib Andersen in the pas de deux from* Mozartiana *(1981).*

70

70. Balanchine taking a curtain call after the premiere of
Robert Schumann's "Davidsbündlertänze," *with Suzanne Farrell and*
Karin von Aroldingen, June 19, 1980.

. . .

CRITICS poured in from Washington, Chicago and Toronto; from Bonn, Berlin, Cologne, Vienna, Geneva, Copenhagen and London. On June 16, two days before the opening of the festival, *The New York Times* had a headline: "The World of Balanchine Still Awhirl in Creativity." Next day, the *New York Post*'s "Woman in the News" was Vera Stravinsky.

I was at that time ballet critic for the London *Sunday Times,* which sent me to New York for the Stravinsky Festival. I attended a few rehearsals and was amazed by the atmosphere of calm.

So many things happened before the first actual ballet that I was to write:

The opening night's program couldn't stop opening. First we had Stravinsky's Fanfare [written for the opening of the State Theater and dedicated to Kirstein and Balanchine]. Then Lincoln Kirstein welcomed us. Then Balanchine explained that he was interpolating a little unannounced *pas de deux* to the scherzo of a piano sonata composed in 1902 and recently found in a Russian book by Mme. André Malraux [who had been unable to copy it, but had memorized it]. She played it while Sara Leland and John Clifford performed a springlike childish dance. Then Robert Irving's fine orchestra gave us the "Greeting Prelude" ("Happy Birthday to You"), for Stravinsky, who would have been ninety that day. Next we had flashing "Fireworks," not danced—*then* the opening ballet.

This "opening ballet" was Robbins's arrangement of the *Scherzo fantastique.* Two of Balanchine's most important creations followed. In retrospect it seems odd—even mad—to have juxtaposed *Symphony in Three Movements* and *Violin Concerto,* either of which would have been the big hit of a normal season. (These works will be considered later.) Last came *Firebird.* In this revival, Balanchine made a disastrous attempt to abolish the ballerina's rapid dances in order to have her merge with the nightmare world of Chagall's décor: the unlucky Karin von Aroldingen was laden with a train, huge wings and a bird mask on top of her head, so that she would resemble the firebird painted on the front curtain.

"City Ballet Triumphs in Stravinsky Fete" ran the headline on the front page of *The New York Times* the next morning. Each of the first five programs was of a mixed character. The sixth had more unity, being devoted to *Apollo, Orpheus* and *Agon,* the historic trilogy. The seventh had a solemn tone, as planned.

As was to be expected, the bombardment of new works, night after night, was almost too much, even for persistent balletgoers. Halfway through the week, Clive Barnes remarked to me that he was so confused he could not remember what he *had* seen. Balanchine had showered his public with gifts, flinging real jewels and false indiscriminately.

In *Divertimento from "Le Baiser de la fée,"* Balanchine used most of Stravinsky's 1950 condensation of the ballet score written for Ida Rubinstein in 1928, and created a most subtle and ingenious work. When Stravinsky shrank his ballet music to a mere divertimento, the story of the boy snatched away by a fairy had to be discarded, but the pages were indelibly stained by his original metaphor (derived partly from Hans Christian Andersen's tale "The Ice Maiden"), which equated the kiss with the blessing and the curse of genius, so the choreographer was able to shed the trivial elements of narrative without relinquishing the essence of the composer's first idea.

Pulcinella, choreographed jointly by Balanchine and Robbins, had so many ideas, so many scene changes, such a large cast and such a plethora of mime, jokes and gambols, that there was no way to get it in shape in time for its Friday-night performance. Balanchine and Robbins, befeathered beggars, appeared briefly toward the end to belabor each other with sticks. Villella mimed furiously throughout—this time (as opposed to *Harlequinade*) in what he called a "down low, gross" genuine *Italian* comedy style. Even though much of the work that had gone into *Pulcinella* was lost onstage, Violette Verdy remembered her joy at the sight of Balanchine demonstrating passages of broad mime to Villella at rehearsal: "I was there watching with Lincoln Kirstein. We turned to each other, practically with tears in our eyes because it was so touching. I said 'It's incredible—it's everything that one knows about the theater.'"

Some of the ballets that bloomed for the festival were destined to fade after one exposure, leaving no trace behind. A few survived for a season or two. In 1974, Balanchine added a new pas de deux and a new ending to *Divertimento from "Le Baiser de la fée,"* which made it more complete. It was universally agreed that, apart from this *Divertimento,* he had created for the festival three works of outstanding merit—*Violin Concerto, Symphony in Three Movements* and *Duo Concertant*—and they have not grown less wonderful with the years.

In his score for the Concerto in D for violin, Stravinsky had placed two Arias between an opening Toccata and a Capriccio finale. The first Aria was danced by Karin von Aroldingen and Jean-Pierre Bonnefous, the second by Kay Mazzo and Peter Martins.

Kay Mazzo had been in the company for ten years before stepping into most of Farrell's roles; she was promoted to principal in 1969. To have danced Terpsichore, *Agon,* Titania, *Movements* and *Episodes* had been an education for her, but in the Stravinsky Festival she helped to model new works and break into unexplored territory. She was dark and fine-boned, with the figure of an adolescent girl. By contrast, Karin von Aroldingen, who had also spent ten years in the company, was tall and fair, square-shouldered and athletic. She felt that in *Violin Concerto* "Balanchine used everything I had for the first time." Peter Martins had been a full-time member of the company only since 1970. He thought that *"Violin Concerto* was my chance to show that I could dance 'Balanchine.' . . . He would demonstrate a passage and I would dive into it with enthusiasm, . . . extending its implications, playing with its accents . . . salt-and-peppering the steps. . . . Once he saw that he had captured my intensity and interest . . . he gave still more, and the experience gave me an incredible high. . . ."

In the first Aria, although Karin excelled in steps of elevation she was not allowed any. She knew, though, that she was a "realistic dancer, not a Giselle." So she was to be "earthbound," and Balanchine told her she was a snake—"You know, a bit sneaky." The opening chord on the strings warns that the relationship between this man and woman will not be a placid one. Her dance with her partner contains strange confrontations, tangles, stalking, catching, trapping; but she somersaults away from his last embrace, and he suddenly lies flat, as if he has had enough.

The mood of the second Aria, with its singing melody, is more tender. The passages Martins and Mazzo found so difficult to learn in rehearsal passed unnoticed in performance because, as Mazzo remarked, they were not there to make people gasp but because the choreographer found them visual equivalents of the music and suited to his dancers. She had to be raised from a near split on pointe, then to end in attitude with an arm over her leg on Martins's shoulder. To match the music, which was alternately sharp and fluid, taut poses melted into collapses. She had to crumple while standing on pointe, and if he failed to catch her by the knees she would fall. ("Don't go before she goes," Balanchine told him.) For one moment Kay became a violin, lying in arabesque across Martins's body, resting her head on his left shoulder, back to the audience. Finally, as she leaned against him, he made a sweeping gesture, enfolded her neck and stretched out his hand. "Make it look like an elephant trunk," Balanchine told him, and "then move out your hand as if you're asking for money." They both bowed over his extended arm, as if to the violinist. They were supposed to be saying, Balanchine explained, "*Bonjour,* Monsieur Stravinsky."

At the end of the busy Capriccio, the twenty dancers, stationary at last, make a gesture to the audience with both hands that seems to say, "Well, that's it!"

. . .

MUSICALLY, Stravinsky's *Symphony in Three Movements* is freakish; the first movement started life as a piano concerto or concerto for orchestra, while in the second, written as part of a commission but rejected, the *concertante* instrument is a harp. Piano and harp have to be brought together somehow, and they begin the fugue in the third movement. Yet from these odd sketches what a masterpiece emerged! First published in 1946, the score contained passages of the most Dionysiac music Stravinsky had written since the 1913 *Rite of Spring.*

Imagine a world ruled by implacable women. Must they not be under the orders of one particular woman, never seen, never spoken of, even in whispers? She holds sway over all the banks, all the mineral resources, all the airlines and railroads, all the munitions factories and all the funeral parlors in the world. Through her international army of women, she controls the men who think they decide the destiny of nations. But it is Madam who gives the signal for peace or war: the first for sowing the seed, the second for gathering her harvest. In their secret rituals, her female storm troopers are drilled like a high-kicking chorus of lethal drum majorettes. To men they show a sweeter side, to obtain marriage dowries, alimony and widows' pensions. Madam transports them from one country to another according to her need for reinforcements. In the first and third movements of the symphony we hear their sealed trains passing, steam trains—for we are in the forties—which shriek when they are about to enter a tunnel.

Behind the battlefront, in no matter what war she has instigated, Madam has her girls waiting. Now, in the second movement, we are in the fifties or sixties, and Westerners are increasingly being sent to battle in Asia; Stravinsky's music for this is Oriental. It is the soldier's weekend out of battle, and he looks for solace in a woman's arms; though she may be trained in every kind of unfamiliar artifice—as an Indian nautch girl, Japanese geisha or Siamese temple dancer—when he lays his head on her neck she becomes for a moment a symbol of all he loves best—mother, sister, sweetheart, the girl next door. She is expert in gilding his

moment of oblivion, a lovely interlude, well worth the money—
from which Madam will exact sixty percent.

In the third movement the trains are heard again, the women
celebrate their domination, and the surviving men are encouraged
to retain their illusions. Life of a kind must go on—for business
reasons. The sexes get together to pose for a victory photograph.
And we know what victories lead to.

That is all very well, someone who has seen the ballet may
protest, but what about the gay scudding dances of the six principals—of the man who, with jerky jumps, is the first to confront
the diagonal of threatening girls, and the man who leads the others
in the last movement? What about the jitterbugging? Even if the
diagonals and lineups of white-clad girls with ponytails, standing
with one foot advanced, stabbing the floor while they rotate their
right arms as if pitching a ball, are alarming, don't the three
principal girls smile and look charming in their conspicuous rose
pink? What about the lovers in the pas de deux? (Incidentally, the
strange nature of their movements was originally dictated by Balanchine's consideration for injuries Sara Leland and Edward Villella had sustained. One had a bad leg, the other a strained back.)
Don't they behave less as if they were in a brothel than as if they
were watching the sun rise from the window of a temple? So my
imagined scenario about the terrible women can easily be dismissed as nonsense.

And yet the impression has been shared, in part at least, by
others. In Nancy Reynolds's compendium of critical writings on
the company, *Repertory in Review,* there is, among other vivid
phrases by Paul Gellen, the following sentence: "The corps of
white-clad women suddenly leave the stage to line up from the edge
of the black sidecloths back into the wings, and you knew there
must be thousands of them stretching all around the globe." Turning to read again Stravinsky's account of how certain musical ideas
came to him, I found further evidence not incompatible with my
personal fantasy. The first movement (partly composed in 1942
with either a piano concerto or a concerto for orchestra in mind)

was inspired by "a war film . . . a documentary of scorched-earth tactics in China." "The third movement," said Stravinsky, "actually contains the genesis of a war plot. . . . The beginning . . . is partly, and in some—to me wholly inexplicable—way, a musical reaction to the newsreels and documentaries that I had seen of goose-stepping soldiers. . . . The exposition of the fugue and the end of the Symphony are associated in my plot with the rise of the Allies, and perhaps the final, albeit rather too commercial, D-flat sixth chord—instead of the expected C—tokens my extra exuberance in the Allied triumph." The slow movement in the middle was written (in 1943)—but never used—for the film version of Franz Werfel's *Song of Bernadette* and was intended to accompany the appearance of the Virgin Mary to the French peasant girl. Does it seem incongruous that the religious revelation the composer tried to convey should be transposed in my mind into so profane a context? For that matter, what would Stravinsky have thought of *Balanchine's* transformation of his goose-slepping storm troopers into women? Does not the brazen symmetry of Balanchine's final group, in which a phalanx of these women, kneeling or standing at attention, some with parallel arms upstretched in a double Hitler salute, others with arms extended sideways like flag-waggling signalers, and in which the men in the foreground are crouched like sprinters eager for the next race, bear out what Stravinsky called the "albeit rather too commercial" nature of his final chord, the celebration of a boastful "peace"?

. . .

ALTHOUGH *Duo Concertant* went into rehearsal on April 11, and according to Goldner was allotted about fourteen hours, Kay Mazzo remembers feeling that it was left very much to the last moment. Its first performance was on Thursday, June 22.

Balanchine decided to set up a reaction between his two dancers, Martins and Mazzo, comparable to Stravinsky's argument between—and marriage of—the strings of violin and piano. Throughout the initial Cantilena, however, the dancers simply stand listening to the music. Mazzo did not find it embarrassing to play this passive role, because she had been told by Balanchine, "Now we're going to have them listen," and she knew that listening to music was what the festival was about.

At the beginning of the first Eclogue, the two walk away from the musicians and stand facing the audience, a few feet apart. She raises an arm to one side, drops it; raises it again; drops it; she extends a foot, draws it in; repeats this. He takes up the challenge, plays the game. It is as simple as the opening of *Serenade.*

The two dancers experiment. He makes her try out some angular arm movements. For a moment it is as if they are conducting—rather than following—the music. They experiment with sculptural poses. They begin turning; he lifts her, and they use more of the stage. When she runs to the piano, he carries her backward in a great arc. After some beautiful port de bras, they slip into everyday slang, link arms and walk across to stare at the violin, as if seeking new ideas.

The two dancers are standing behind the piano when the second Eclogue begins. He leads her into a pas de deux, and to the singing violin she swoons in his arms. They make a révérence to the violinist, then, leaning together, face the music.

In the Gigue, they dance both alone and together. There is a bit of everything—tightrope walking, big classical movements, and as the violin plays pizzicato, ballroom dancing. They are allowed a rest on the floor, for this is a long number.

Before the final Dithyramb, there is a blackout. Balanchine had not told his dancers at rehearsals about the effect he planned, and it came as a surprise at the dress rehearsal on the morning of the performance. Mazzo had been astonished that the ballet should end with the emotional scene he had arranged: "It was quite unusual for him in his Stravinsky ballets." But she and Martins were transfigured by the lighting.

Stravinsky's short Dithyramb is not Dionysiac in character, as the dictionary says a dithyramb should be; it sings with a kind of serene ecstasy—if that is not a contradiction in terms—such as might be achieved by the success of a relationship, or the "bringing off" of a work of art. We may dare to guess, in passing, that Balanchine's moments of perfect fulfillment took place on a stage, for the world to witness, not in the privacy of a home. The little ballet he devised to Stravinsky's *Duo* could therefore be read as dual in significance, as well as in music and choreography.

Out of darkness, first the woman's head, then her torso, are revealed in a bright halo. She steps out, to leave her hand alone in the light. Then the hand is seen to touch her head before she vanishes again. In the pool of light both dancers' hands are seen stretching toward each other and meeting. The man appears in the light to mold her hand; then he kisses the back of it. Throughout this, her face has been invisible. He kneels in homage to the woman, ballerina, muse. She is disclosed, standing like Venus in a pose of classic simplicity. Suddenly the couple separate, and there are two pools of light. But he runs to her, and the lights merge as he kneels again. She takes first one, then the other of his hands and places them on her chest. When she runs off into the dark, he searches and then stands dejected. Her shoulders appear, then her head, looking down. She stretches out her arm and lays her hand against her cheek. His hand comes to take hers. Again he molds and kisses it and kneels, but this time sinking into the dark. Only the raised arm of Venus remains visible.

"After the premiere," wrote Peter Martins, "Balanchine embraced Kay and me and told us the ballet was ours." Indeed, Balanchine gave it to Kay.

.   .   .

THE FINAL Sunday night's program began with *Choral Variations on Bach's "Vom Himmel Hoch,"* an elaborate and beautiful work that, since it required an expensive choir and a crowd of children, was never repeated. The evening—and the festival—ended, as Balanchine had always intended, with the *Symphony of Psalms.* The singers were onstage and the dancers sat around at the back or on the sides. Rosemary Dunleavy went out front to watch. She saw Balanchine standing downstage: "He had finally paid homage to somebody he loved and admired. I swear you could see him communicate with Stravinsky."

Then everyone in the audience was given a free glass of vodka with which to toast the immortal composer.

When the sums were added up, it was found that the Stravinsky Festival had cost about $348,000 (including the loss of ticket sales during the preceding week, when the theater was closed). That was nearly $100,000 more than Balanchine had estimated, and there was no money for new productions during the winter season. But it had been worth it.

"It has been a wonderful week," Vera Stravinsky told the *Washington Post*. "This audience is such a pleasure—I never saw such a good one." The reviews were without exception ecstatic. A more general comment came from Richard Poirier in the *Atlantic Monthly* for September: "In the history of ballet, Balanchine at New York's State Theater is equivalent to Shakespeare at London's Globe."

"Wasn't it extraordinary," commented Gordon Boelzner, years after, "that the energy, enthusiasm and reverence which went to create this monument to Stravinsky should have come not from a symphony orchestra in a concert hall, but from a ballet company?"

Chapter 14

••

THE SPREADING EMPIRE:

FIRST LAST BALLETS,

1972 - 1981

B ALANCHINE enjoyed his Julys in Saratoga. In the morning, after he had made his tea, he took it out on the veranda. There was always a fresh croissant from Mrs. London's bake-shop and often a coffee cake of incredible richness. In summer, the usually deserted road that divided the Leaches' flower garden from their vegetable garden was busy with farm traffic, but nobody took any notice of Balanchine as he sat breakfasting in his tattered green bathrobe. Lincoln Kirstein sometimes appeared with an armful of newspapers. Balanchine's favorite newspaper reading was "Dear Abbie." He was convinced that the author wrote the letters in the column as well as the answers.

It was a matter of pride for Kay Leach to see the guesthouse kitchen was so well stocked that Balanchine had nothing to shop for. He crossed the road to pick his own herbs and vegetables and always arrived from New York with cases of wine and champagne. He gave frequent dinner parties. Karin von Aroldingen, Taras and Gordon Boelzner were often invited; from 1972 onward, Kay Mazzo, of whom Balanchine had become very fond, came too. Balanchine called Kay Leach, Kay Mazzo and Karin von Aroldingen his "Three K's."

In Saratoga or in New York, Balanchine could always produce a good meal at short notice. He often made soup or a pot roast on Mondays, when there was no performance. The refinements of his cooking were exquisite. He was an expert on herbs, and he laced his vanilla ice cream with vodka. He even made his own mustard with seeds brought from Russia, pounding them himself, mixing in herbs and sugar, adding a little tea at the end. "It was the best mustard ever," according to Kay Leach. "We use it still." He would bake the beets for borscht for almost an hour before adding the other ingredients, and his sauerkraut was prepared in Oriental style, using tiny dried mushrooms. He would then spread it over a leg of lamb. He was also very fond of potatoes. When, at the age of seventy-two, he told Dr. William Hamilton, the company's new orthopedist, that he had just bought a condominium on the end of Long Island with a thirty-year mortgage, he stressed his pleasure in the fact that it overlooked a potato field.

■ ■ ■

IN NEW YORK, Balanchine's apartment on Sixty-seventh Street, near the theater, was really two apartments made into one. He valued space and light above possessions. His white living room had two enormous windows facing north, from which he could see over the roofs of the brownstones on Sixty-eighth Street. There were smaller windows to the west and east, and Central Park was visible from the latter. The two small bedrooms on either side of the front door, one of which was used as a storeroom, looked out into a well.

Balanchine always woke when the sun rose. He made tea, read

or played solitaire; then, as Barbara Horgan was also an early riser, he called her between 7:30 and 8:00 to discuss the day's appointments. Since most of his time was spent giving class, rehearsing and attending performances, and since all these were printed on the daily call sheet, his engagement books recorded little except meetings with journalists and the directors of European theaters or the dates of his flights to Washington, Los Angeles, Paris or Geneva.

It took him no more than five minutes to walk to the theater. As he went up in the elevator he could often tell who had preceded him, for he carefully chose for each of his ballerinas a perfume he considered appropriate. On the fourth floor he passed on the left a door inscribed "Ducky," where Leslie Copeland, the English wardrobe master, got ready the men's costumes. His own corner room, with windows looking south and west, had a piano, a sofa, books and three large photographs of Mourka on the walls. He did not use it often, unless he wanted to read a score. At 11:00 it was time to teach class, but for reasons of his own (possibly to allow the dancers to warm up before he arrived, possibly because it is an old theatrical tradition) he always walked in ten minutes late.

Balanchine said that when young people joined the company their feet were clumsy, like teddy bears'. So he made them work on their tendus, repeating them again and again, starting slowly and building up gradually to an almost impossible speed. Strength in the feet was the last quality a dancer acquired and the first to go. He seriously advised his girls to do tendus at home when they were cooking. Once, after he had stood beside a boy counting, "Sixty-two, sixty-three, sixty-four," he remarked, *"Last one should be better than first."*

In jumping, a Balanchine dancer had to go up from a deep demi-plié with ferocity but land softly, through the toe, through the foot, unfolding at last with the heel barely touching the ground. He wanted a landing so soft that it wouldn't "break eggs." It did not matter how high you jumped so long as you landed "like a bird" or "like a pussycat." One day he was searching for a verb to describe the way a dancer could give the illusion of defying the force of gravity in order to land lightly. "To resist," the dancer Daniel Duell suggested; and Balanchine exclaimed, "That's it! To resist." He loved the word and from then on used it often in class.

The problem with hands, according to Balanchine, was to make them look both correctly placed and natural. They should be free at the wrists, yet solid as sculpture. "Hands must grow like leaves. . . . Not like that, it looks like dead chicken." When a dancer held her fingers together, he called it "chicken hands." He believed you should be able to see daylight between all the fingers, which were to be used as if "picking flowers or gathering in a bundle—the wash," or opening a French window onto a beautiful garden. "Then you step through to look at the garden." In arabesque you should reach farther, farther, as if stretching out for the thing you liked best—"candy, ice cream."

He told the boys that they didn't have to be sissies to have beautiful hands. He was very particular about how a boy took a girl's hand when partnering her—the fingers should be held gently over the top—and he always cited Fred Astaire as one who held his partner's fingertips delicately. So long as the ballerina was made to look right, he did not mind if her partner was not completely turned-out. The man could lounge, provided he looked strong; but he must not take the weight on both feet.

A favorite expression of despair Balanchine used with slow learners was, "I should have been a dentist. Teaching you is like pulling teeth." He once took hours to tell the story of a mule that would not move. Its rider pushed, pulled, then gave up. The man gathered sticks, piled them up underneath the mule, found two stones, rubbed them together and made a fire. Finally the mule moved two steps. One of his most repeated sayings was, "Dancers are like racehorses. They need a jockey on their backs."

If he was pleased, he said, "That's RIGHT"; and sometimes he would add, "But now, dear, make it beautiful." "Good," he remarked on one occasion. "If we go on like that, one day we'll get what we want. Not today. Because today it won't happen. Not tomorrow. Tomorrow it won't happen. Maybe next month. Maybe next year." He paused, looked round the room and concluded, "Maybe never."

During the season, Balanchine ate only a snack at lunchtime. He would say to Karin or Barbara, "Let's go to the Greek's," meaning the unpretentious diner of the Empire Hotel across the street. The Greeks in the restaurant always greeted him warmly, so that he felt at home, and after a Scotch he would order a sandwich—never the regular club sandwich on the menu but one improvised by himself, perhaps feta cheese with tomatoes. Then it was time for rehearsal.

In 1973 Melissa Hayden retired, and Balanchine made her a special ballet as a farewell present. *Cortège hongrois,* part classical, part character, was arranged to music from Glazunov's *Raymonda,* which he had used before. Melissa and Jacques d'Amboise were to lead the classical team, Karin and Jean-Pierre Bonnefous, the Hungarian character numbers. Although not one of Balanchine's masterpieces, it turned out to be a good "closing ballet."

That was the year Joseph Mazo, the dance critic of *Women's Wear Daily,* took time off to live with the company and record in detail its activities, including the staging of *Cortège;* in his book, *Dance Is a Contact Sport,* he has provided us with a good description of how the ballet was prepared. When Balanchine demonstrated the csárdás, a dance that begins with slow, dragging steps and ends in a stamping, whirling climax, he was, as Mazo pointed out, showing something he had learned at the Imperial Theater School sixty years before; the style of such a dance was second nature to him. "His knees are bent, his body seems light enough to float. His heels stamp out the rhythm, delicately but with great precision. . . ."

Another day, he rehearsed four boys in a strenuous number, which ended with tours en l'air. "That is pure Petipa," he said. "It is marvelous. So I used it. The rest of the ballet is me, but that is Petipa." Melissa Hayden had trouble with some swift backward pas de bourrée to a fast passage of music. Balanchine told her to ignore the music and do the steps to the counts. "*You* do it,"

Melissa told him. So Balanchine did it; she did it; and it proved to be just possible.

. . .

IN JANUARY 1974, Balanchine was seventy. In February, as if to show that he was still young at heart, he staged *Variations pour une porte et un soupir* (Variations for a Door and a Sigh) to *musique concrète* "sonorities" by Pierre Henry. This was an amazing twenty-minute invention for two dancers, a variation on the theme of man as victim of the cruel love goddess. For the most part, the two move alternately. The man, gray and miserable, crawls, clutches and crashes around, reduced to a subhuman state like a character in Samuel Beckett. The woman, almost a Cretan version of Berg's Lulu, with shiny black bobbed hair, has an immense train that covers the entire stage; it is later manipulated by stagehands to rise and billow in the air like a dark, poisonous cloud. Her music is that of a creaking door. The man's music resembles not so much a sigh as a bronchial wheeze. Balanchine thus compared love's anguish to a fight for breath. It was, in a way, his *Petrushka,* and it was booed at its first performance. When it was revived twelve years later, after his death, there were still scattered boos on the first night, but many people acclaimed it as a masterpiece.

No such uncertain fate awaited his next production, which was given its first performance at Saratoga that summer. With Hayden gone, Patricia McBride was NYCB's prima ballerina—not that Balanchine ever encouraged the use of such classifications. It was therefore for her—with help from the earliest of all his ballerinas, Danilova, who had an exceptional memory—that he staged *Coppélia,* in the Petipa version he had known in his youth. He had always cherished the Delibes music and once told Edwin Denby—exaggerating somewhat—that the dances in the first act to the "Variations on a Slav Theme" had been the inspiration for all his choreography.

It was another full-length ballet, good for a young audience, in which he could use children from the School and in the summer from Saratoga. He had his own ideas about how to fill the house: "If all the children in the ballet brought their brothers and sisters and parents—already we would have an audience."

In July 1974, Suzanne Farrell and Paul Mejia, who had been dancing for the past four years with Béjart's company in Brussels, but who spent the summers at their house on an island near Saratoga, came to watch performances at the Saratoga Performing Arts Center. At once, the speculation began: Would she be accepted back if she wanted to return? From New York, Suzanne wrote to Balanchine; he saw her privately, and she rejoined NYCB during the winter season of 1974–75. Mejia went to Chicago, where Maria Tallchief was director of the Chicago City Ballet, and became co-artistic director.

The company was curious to see how Balanchine would receive Suzanne. On the first day she came to class, the big hall was more crowded than it had ever been. She walked up to Balanchine and kissed him, then she took her old place at the barre. Her first, unannounced, appearance was in *Symphony in C.* When the audience recognized her, there was an ovation. McBride and Mazzo soon found that they had to give back most of the parts they had inherited.

For 1975, Balanchine decreed a Ravel Festival. This produced a bizarre crop of ballets. The choreographer staged his third version of *L'Enfant et les sortilèges,* and his other contributions ranged from the pseudo-Oriental posturings of *Schéhérazade* to the psuedo-Spanish excesses of *Rapsodie espagnole.* How different were *Sonatine,* "a stroll for two," delicately danced by Verdy and Bonnefous to a piano solo; *Tzigane,* spectacularly danced by Farrell (once more a gypsy) to a violin solo—"a new height in contemporary performance," wrote Arlene Croce in *The New Yorker*—and the *Pavane,* to more familiar music, performed by McBride alone with a scarf. Balanchine's most outrageous essay was his translation of the virtuoso suite for solo piano *Gaspard de la nuit* into dance, while his most unpredictable piece, *Le Tombeau de Couperin,* surprised by its simplicity. A beautiful invention, it outlasted

the festival and is likely to remain popular, but it was almost lost
before the festival took place. Balanchine worked it out in its
entirety at the very beginning of the rehearsal period, which for
him was unusual. Then he turned his attention to other ballets.
Time passed, and Rosemary Dunleavy began to fear *Le Tombeau*
would be forgotten, so she called the sixteen dancers and "got it
back together again." She had difficulty persuading Balanchine to
come and look at it: "Later, later," he kept saying. When at last
he sat and watched the whole ballet, which he had never seen from
beginning to end, Rosemary was worried by his silence. At last he
spoke. "You know, dear, I like it."

It is a work without soloists. In the Prélude, Forlane, Menuet
and Rigaudon, two quadrilles of eight dance separately, imitate
each other, merge and part. The mood is both pastoral and elegiac.
It is an amazingly varied web of pretty formations, and there had
never been a ballet quite like it before. In retrospect it is tempting
to regard it as the first of Balanchine's "last ballets"—something
for his company to dance by his grave after he was dead.

·   ·   ·

ERIK BRUHN, who arrived in 1960, had been the first Danish
dancer to appear, albeit briefly, with the New York City Ballet.
Peter Martins, who came to stay, was the second. Then Helgi
Tomasson, an Icelander but a former member of the Royal Danish
Ballet, arrived. Peter Schaufuss, son of two distinguished dancers
at Copenhagen's Royal Theater and already admired in England
for his spectacular technique, came in 1975.

Schaufuss stayed only two years, with a gap of eight months in
the middle owing to injuries. He was aware that certain dancers
accused him of putting in a lot of "tricks" not called for in the
choreography, but he maintained that Balanchine, whose works he
admired above all others, demanded a display of virtuosity and
wanted a replacement for the much-injured Villella. The real problem appears to have been that Schaufuss and Balanchine were both
attracted to the same woman.

Although his tenure was brief, Schaufuss bequeathed an important legacy to the company: his Danish colleague Adam Lüders, who had also left Copenhagen to join London's Festival Ballet. Lüders came to Saratoga during his summer break and took class. Like Peter Martins, he was tall and fair, but his small head on a long neck and his long legs gave him unusual proportions. Knowing that Balanchine liked male dancers to be solid rather than willowy, Schaufuss made Lüders wear three sweaters to class. Ignoring the sweaters, Balanchine saw a special quality in Lüders that appealed to him, and he invited him to join the company as a principal dancer.

Everyone, not only Danes, wanted to dance for Balanchine. Sean Lavery, an American who had appeared with the San Francisco Ballet and danced for two years in the Frankfurt company, both headed by Balanchine students, joined NYCB in 1977. Balanchine tried him out in the Élégie of the *Tchaikovsky Suite No. 3*, with which Martins had had trouble. At the end, when the drifting girls left him alone kneeling in a spotlight, Lavery felt, as he explained later, that he ought somehow to "project," so he began to "reach for the heavens." Balanchine said, "What are you reaching for? They are all looking for you. All you have to do is just look up and think. Then it's over." Lavery found it "scary" that Balanchine stood in the wings "two feet away," but "if he just gave you a nod, it was worth a thousand words. . . . The first time he told me 'That was very good work,' I was ready to retire and open the old ballet school right then."

. . .

IF BALANCHINE's contributions to his Ravel Festival were mostly on a miniature scale, 1976 and 1977 were to bring one important work of art and two blockbusters: *Chaconne, Union Jack* and *Vienna Waltzes*.

Balanchine had staged dances for the final scene of Gluck's *Orfeo* at the Hamburg State Opera as early as 1963; in 1975 he made a version for the Chicago Lyric Opera. On January 22, 1976, he presented his own company in *Chaconne,* which took its final form the following spring when he added an opening ensemble before the first duet. A dance for twelve girls with loose hair and drifting chiffon dresses was followed by a pas de deux for Farrell, also with hair flowing, and Martins. As he lifted her swimming against the blue cyclorama, the two seemed to be moving above the clouds. Then the ballet became more formal. Among other dances were a stately pas de deux for Farrell—her hair up now—and Martins, several glittering variations for each; and at last the grand promenade for the whole cast in the Chaconne that gave the ballet its name.

Union Jack, a tribute to Great Britain in America's bicentennial year, grew from Balanchine's memories of Cockney tunes and music-hall routines, his admiration for the swing of Scottish kilts at the Edinburgh Tattoo and Kirstein's heartfelt desire to demonstrate to the United States that a corner of the American consciousness remained "forever England." In the opening scene, a kilted "cast of thousands" parades and dances to traditional tunes such as "The Keel Row" and "Dance wi' My Daddy." This is followed by a pas de deux for a costermonger Pearly King and Queen. The Royal Navy, both male and female, dance hornpipes and finally, to the sound of "Rule, Britannia," spell out the message "God Save the Queen" with waggling flag signals, while an enormous Union Jack assembles itself in the background.

Balanchine had had a clear idea of the framework for *Vienna Waltzes,* his tribute to Austria, for more than a year before he began to work on it: he had discussed the ballet with members of the company and told stage designer Rouben Ter-Arutunian from the start that "there must be five trees." Three of these "trees from the Vienna woods," where the first two waltzes and the comic "Explosions Polka" are danced to the music of Johann Strauss, are magically transformed into the glittering Art-Nouveau curlicues of a restaurant resembling Maxim's—the background for Lehár's "Gold and Silver" waltz often interpolated in *The Merry Widow.* At the ballet's close, a ballroom with chandeliers formed from the trees' roots, now risen into the air, is the setting for Richard Strauss's *Rosenkavalier* waltzes.

The newcomer Sean Lavery was amazed at the speed of Balanchine's invention. Even so, at six o'clock on the evening of the gala preview the choreographer had still not found time to finish the couples' last big circle round the stage. The dancers stood waiting while Balanchine did what was necessary; what he arranged then he never had reason to change later. He was less happy with the "Gold and Silver" waltz and kept tinkering with it.

At the premiere the enchantment began when Sean Lavery, strolling with others in the Wienerwald, took Karin von Aroldingen's hand, bowed over it and kissed it. Their waltz was followed by a sylvan interlude with Patricia McBride and Helgi Tomasson, next came the "Explosions Polka," led by Sara Leland and Bart Cook. After Ter-Arutunian's dazzling transformation scene, Kay Mazzo, all in black, wearing a Merry Widow hat, chose Peter Martins in his white-and-scarlet Austrian uniform from a group of bowing admirers. The *Rosenkavalier* waltzes had Suzanne Farrell in a white satin ball gown dancing by herself. She was joined briefly by an elusive Adam Lüders, who came and went. Then the chandeliers lit up, and the stage was suddenly filled with a crowd of swirling couples, the women in identical white gowns holding up their trains with gloved hands, the men in black evening dress; the tall mirrors seemed to duplicate their number.

■   ■   ■

MEANWHILE, the School was flourishing. From 1975 on, Balanchine had sent selected dancers to visit scores of cities in search of talented children: those with promise were sponsored by local corporations, often with additional funds from private sources. The New York City Ballet could, however, absorb at most eight graduates from the School a year, more often four or six. All received superb training, so those who were not accepted were much in demand elsewhere. Former dancers of the New York City Ballet were running companies or the schools attached to them in many states (as well as in Europe), and these onetime "Balanchine dancers" were beginning to feed pupils they had trained in the master's methods back into the School of American Ballet. Thus the choreographer's network spread throughout the United States. In the last years of his life, Balanchine was in the position of an emperor with many proconsuls: Maria Tallchief and Paul Mejia in Chicago; Patricia Wilde in Pittsburgh; Todd Bolender, Diana Adams and Una Kai in Kansas City; Lew Christensen in San Francisco; John Clifford in Los Angeles; Barbara Weissberger and Robert Weiss in Philadelphia; Robert Barnett in Atlanta; Kent Stowell and Francia Russell in Seattle; William Dollar in New Jersey; Frank Ohman, Carol Sumner and Edward Villella on Long Island; Mimi Paul in North Carolina; Patricia Neary in Switzerland; Roy Tobias in Japan.

The increased scale and prosperity of the company brought new problems. In the old days, Balanchine's word had been law. In the summer of 1973, when the question arose as to whether or not dancers would go to film his ballets in Berlin, a vote was actually taken.

The dancers had been told they would dance five hours a day in Berlin, but Villella warned them that in film studios you worked twelve hours. With the growing popularity of video cassettes, the producers might in the future make a fortune out of these films, and the dancers would get nothing. Many of the younger dancers wanted to see Berlin, or to go just because Balanchine wanted them to. Edward Bigelow called Berlin but failed to get a five-hours-a-day clause inserted in the contract. A ballot was taken, and the votes in favor of acceptance won, fifty-three to seventeen. Eighty-one dancers went with Balanchine to Berlin in September and danced twelve hours a day for six weeks on a bad floor.

Then the musicians threatened to strike for higher pay. Although they did not call a strike before the fall season, they would not guarantee not to strike during it. Balanchine, who was proud of his orchestra, asked associate conductor Hugo Fiorato why the musicians wanted more money. Fiorato replied that they had families to support and were entitled to a decent living. "Why," he asked, "should a garbageman get more than a musician?" Balanchine thought the answer was obvious: "Because garbage stinks." The dancers, always resentful of the musicians' higher pay and shorter hours, asked the management to ensure that they would be paid in full for the fourteen-week season, whether or not there was a musicians' strike. This guarantee was not forthcoming. The dancers voted sixty-five to eleven for a strike, seven abstaining. On November 13, 1973, the night the season did not open, there was an "opening-night party" to celebrate the publication of Lincoln Kirstein's *The New York City Ballet.* He had been telling Balanchine's dancers for twenty-five years that "there is no justice"; now democracy had raised its head. Villella said, "It's history. Dancers for years have been subsidizing their art."

Balanchine, who thought life was too short to warrant strikes, remarked that if there was no early settlement, "We'll close the theater, and everyone will go home. The girls will marry; the boys will go and drive taxicabs."

The dancers went on unemployment and took class with Balanchine. The management came to an agreement with the musicians, whose salaries were raised; and the season began a month late.

Three years later, in the middle of the *Nutcracker* season, the orchestra went on strike and no settlement was reached for several weeks. According to Kirstein, Balanchine considered leaving for Europe; and although dancing was resumed before the season ended, the loss of revenue was nearly a million dollars.

∙   ∙   ∙

FOR SOME YEARS Balanchine had been conscious that Merrill Ashley, who had joined the company from the School in 1967, was going to be an outstanding dancer. Her legs were perfect, and her jump was big. In 1977 she became a principal, and in 1978 he made a ballet for her. This was *Ballo della Regina,* to music for dancing that Verdi had reluctantly inserted into *Don Carlos* to satisfy the requirements of the Paris Opéra. In her account of how she worked with Balanchine on this virtuoso ballet, Ashley described his adaptability, his tactful way of urging her partner Robert Weiss to adopt a nobler carriage by telling him, "This is a Nureyev entrance," his allowing her to insert a "big jeté with a backbend" which she had seen Plisetskaya do in the Bolshoi production of *Don Quixote,* and the pride he took in demonstrating all the partnering himself. *Ballo,* choreographed in a week, was shown at the gala preceding the opening of the winter season.

Balanchine had made his own piano reduction of *Ballo* for Gordon Boelzner to play at rehearsals, because none existed. Although the music was exactly suited to its purpose, he guessed that his sophisticated orchestra might scorn Verdi's tuneful numbers, so he took the trouble to tell them that he had something more interesting for them coming up; this was Hindemith's Kammermusik No. 2, for solo piano and twelve solo instruments.

It was prepared almost in secret. The musicians' strike had already prevented a production of *The Seven Deadly Sins;* Balanchine had got as far as the fifth sin when the orchestra walked out. It was on Karin von Aroldingen's return from Vienna, where she had been producing *Liebeslieder Walzer,* that Balanchine spoke to her about the Hindemith, which he perhaps intended as a consolation prize. In it he employed two couples, with—an unusual feature—a corps of eight boys. It was referred to as an inverted or neo-*Concerto Barocco* and was extremely difficult to dance. Karin called it *"Kammer-* computer." "It's so speedy," she explained, "that even a pianist can't play the notes. It took us forever to learn it. The movement is very angular, very fast. If you lose concentration for one second, you ruin it all." Sean Lavery felt that Balanchine "knew exactly what the corps were doing when the principals were doing something else. He was so fast, so in tune with the music, so ahead of himself, that we couldn't keep up with him. . . . He wanted it a bit spooky at times." Indeed, it is amazing that such inventions, such ominous images, should have sprung from the mind of a man in his seventies. Kirstein, who had not watched rehearsals, thought it one of Balanchine's greatest works.

．　．　．

THE GREAT holiday of the Russian Church is Easter, and Balanchine always served a traditional Easter feast. Days in advance he prepared pashka, kulitch, piroshki and sturgeon in aspic. In his later years the guests, apart from the hard core of Russians—Lucia Davidova, Natalie Molostwoff, John Taras, Rouben Ter-Arutunian and Eugenia Doll (one of Massine's widows)—included Edward Bigelow, Gordon Boelzner, Karin and her husband, Morton, Barbara Horgan, Kay Mazzo, the company orthopedist William Hamilton, and Balanchine's other doctor, Edith Langner.

On March 15, 1978, less than a month before Russian Easter, Balanchine had a heart attack. It was not a bad one, but he stayed away from work for a few weeks to rest—and cook. During this time Jerome Robbins, who had made a short ballet to Chopin for the celebrated Russian defector Mikhail Baryshnikov, came to see Balanchine to tell him that the young star, who was currently dancing with American Ballet Theatre, might be interested in joining the New York City Ballet. After thinking about it overnight—NYCB had never operated on the star system, and Balanchine was not certain how Baryshnikov would fit into the company—he called him at eight the next morning and asked him to come around.

The two men had met in Leningrad in 1972 during NYCB's second Russian tour. Baryshnikov had at first been taken aback by the idea of a company in which the choreographer was the star, but shortly afterward he danced in the third movement of *Symphony in C,* when Taras produced it at a benefit performance in honor of Natalia Dudinskaya. In the West he rapidly came to appreciate the range of Balanchine's invention. Although Ballet Theatre paid him well because he always filled the house, and he could command large fees for guest appearances, he aspired to dance for Balanchine. Baryshnikov and Balanchine liked each other, and Baryshnikov agreed to work for the usual NYCB rate. He made the most inconspicuous début possible the next summer, dancing, unannounced, in *Coppélia* in Saratoga. While they were rehearsing it, Balanchine constantly questioned him about Russian versions of the ballet, wanting to compare them with his own.

That July, Balanchine also taught him Villella's part in "Rubies," in which he was to make his début at the New York State Theater. In New York, he learned *Harlequinade;* the Pearly King in *Union Jack,* which he performed in traditional Russian mime style; *The Steadfast Tin Soldier; Orpheus;* the Cavalier in *Nutcracker;* the Poet in *La Sonnambula* and more than a dozen other roles. While he was learning *The Prodigal Son,* he felt that although Balanchine gave him the most meticulous instructions, especially about the penitent Prodigal's return home on his knees, the choreographer did not enjoy rehearsing the ballet.

Baryshnikov thought Balanchine, like Noverre, one of the earliest choreographers, tended to divide male dancers into two distinct types. There was the staccato, bravura dancer like Villella and the tall, imposing *danseur noble* like Martins. Baryshnikov himself did not fall neatly into either category (but then, neither did Nijinsky). He adjusted to the master's requirements but always "felt comfortable on his own scale"—meaning, perhaps, that, like Nijinsky, his genius entitled him to do things his own way. When the critics were hard on his interpretations of Balanchine's work, as he thought they usually were, Balanchine would tell him, "You're doing fine. People always misinterpret." "Balanchine was shy," Baryshnikov said, "but he was like a father to me. He was always asking, 'Are you having fun?'"

For Balanchine, however, no male dancer could ever be more important than the female. Baryshnikov noticed that he used to look scornful when a male star's fan started raving about his or her idol. "What do you mean, you're going to see Nureyev in *The Sleeping Beauty*? What do you mean, you saw Bruhn in *Giselle*?"

Balanchine often woke Baryshnikov early in the morning, telephoning to talk about the past, and the latter has given an interesting account of these conversations. "He didn't want to talk about

Diaghilev, he wanted to talk about the old days in St. Petersburg. He would speak of his character-dancing teacher, Monakhov, who taught him how to act—and he liked to act. He liked the *early* Nijinska. He knew the Russian theater very well, and he not only recited Pushkin's poems, he could say by heart Pushkin's long letter to his wife beginning *'Dusha maya'* [my soul]. This took about twenty minutes. He knew The Hermitage very well—the architecture more than the paintings." Baryshnikov believes that the fact that Balanchine was a mediocre dancer is what made him a choreographer. "The *premier danseur* is always in the wings, watching to see which rival may take his place. As a choreographer, Balanchine was more in control, more the center of attention than he would have been as a dancer. It was a question of ego. And, of course, he liked to make ballets for the women he loved." This is, perhaps, a star dancer's explanation.

. . .

In 1978, Balanchine traveled to Copenhagen with the company, but he suffered increasingly from fatigue, and in the autumn he began to have attacks of angina. In December, he went to Washington to receive an award from President Carter and had a seizure while waiting for the train back to New York. He gave class infrequently. Yet when the company set off on a tour of upstate New York in March 1979, he went to Switzerland to work with Patricia Neary, who had moved from Geneva to Zurich. Karin von Aroldingen was now teaching *Liebeslieder* to the Royal Ballet in London, and he subsequently joined her there.

Although he made *Le Bourgeois Gentilhomme* for Nureyev at the New York City Opera in April, since his heart attack he was working at half strength. Robbins, Martins and Susan Hendl had to help out with certain passages of choreography; both Anna Kisselgoff of *The New York Times* and Arlene Croce of *The New Yorker* found the result disappointing.

During NYCB's Chicago season later in April, Balanchine rehearsed Baryshnikov in the role of Apollo, and Taras thought he had never seen him take such pains in teaching the role before. He even changed the ballet. Just as Stravinsky had made condensed versions of some of his early successes, so Balanchine felt himself entitled to cut the dead wood out of his own works—even if it meant losing a little Stravinsky too. The first scene in *Apollo*, in which Leto gives birth to the god, was scrapped, along with the attendant goddesses, Apollo's first solo (which was restored in 1980 for Peter Martins and subsequent Apollos) and the staircase that had long ago replaced the mountain of Diaghilev's day.

Since there was no longer a staircase up which Apollo and the Muses could climb in solemn procession, Balanchine had to make a new ending; he repeated the famous "sunburst" group and had the three Muses, in arabesque, clinging to Apollo upstage center. Unfortunately, the effect—with the spotlight making a kind of setting sun behind them—looked to me like an advertisement for orange juice.

When Baryshnikov made his first appearance in the role on May 1, his stay with NYCB was already drawing to a close. Lucia Chase had decided to retire from the artistic directorship of Ballet Theatre, which she had founded, and Baryshnikov was invited to take her place. He asked Balanchine's advice, and Balanchine told him to accept, which he did. Baryshnikov's last performance as a member of the company was in *La Sonnambula* in Washington. He remained friends with Balanchine, however, and was at his Easter supper the following year.

On June 17, after a long postponement, Balanchine had a heart bypass operation. The night before, reflecting on the possibility of his not surviving the surgery, he remarked to Dr. Hamilton, "You know, I wasn't meant to marry Suzanne. It was God's decision." He had always told Lucia Davidova that he could not envisage God as "an essence": God to him was an old man with a white beard, as portrayed by Michelangelo, a father with whom he discussed matters face-to-face.

. . .

DR. HAMILTON, who also lived on West Sixty-seventh Street, had a habit of dropping in on Balanchine every morning on his way to work, to make sure he was all right. He usually found him at his favorite occupation of ironing, dressed only in his jockey shorts. One day early in 1980 Hamilton sensed a different atmosphere; he felt he was intruding. Sheet music was spread over the tables and chairs. It was Robert Schumann's *Davidsbündlertänze.*

When Schumann edited the *Neue Zeitschrift für Musik,* he invented an imaginary society of young enthusiasts, sworn to fight for their ideals against the forces of reaction and philistinism. This he called the *Davidsbund,* a band of Davids challenging Goliath. Two of its members were Florestan and Eusebius, who represented contrasting aspects of Schumann's own character—the active, optimistic side and the reflective, melancholy one. In his series of piano pieces entitled *Davidsbündlertänze* (literally, the David's Club Dances), the two friends are supposed to be reliving various love affairs, happy or sad, at a ball. Balanchine identified the Eusebius music with Robert Schumann himself and his partner with Schumann's wife, the pianist and composer Clara Wieck, but the other three couples remained unidentified—unless, as some believe, the role danced by Suzanne Farrell stands for the evasive beloved who always moves out of reach. Balanchine made the "Philistines," whom Fokine (and Bakst) had brought on rather absurdly at the end of *Carnaval,* with umbrellas and old-fashioned bonnets, into more sinister characters, as if seen in the light of Schumann's unbalanced imaginings. And he insisted on the cumbersome title *Robert Schumann's "Davidsbündlertänze."*

Adam Lüders, known for his arched instep and fine partnering, who danced Schumann, had a sensitive, visionary side rare among dancers of any nationality, which must have attracted Balanchine to him from the beginning. Karin, who danced Clara, thought his engagement of Lüders was an outstanding example of his insight, but Taras had often noticed that Balanchine was drawn to the unusual.

Although Balanchine told Lüders, "You are Schumann," when Karin first read about Schumann and Clara, she could not see that she in any way resembled the latter, and yet eventually she came to recognize something of herself in the role Balanchine made for her.

Both Kirstein and Karin had given Balanchine reproductions of the work of Kaspar David Friedrich, with which, it turned out, he was already familiar, and he told Ter-Arutunian, who was to design the ballet, that he would like something of that painter's quality in the set. The painted backcloth is of a cold, still lake—or else it is the Rhine, in which Schumann once tried to drown himself. From its waters rises the ghost of a cathedral. This distant view is framed by bare trees with branches like antlers, and by lengths of gauze that billow as the dancers come and go.

At the first performance, Gordon Boelzner was seated onstage at the piano, which became part of the décor, and it could be said that he, like Lüders, represented Robert Schumann. The four pairs of dancers appeared in turn, led by the elusive Farrell, with the older Jacques d'Amboise in pursuit. Then came the melancholy Lüders, with von Aroldingen as his tender muse, followed by Heather Watts and Peter Martins, tripping and charging. Last of all, Kay Mazzo and Ib Andersen, a brilliant new recruit from Denmark, entered with an impetuous surge. Throughout the ballet, the first, third and fourth couples seemed to form a frame around the dialogues of the second in their moments of intimacy. In the latter half, all combined in what might be called "social" scenes— hunting, toasting, praying—or in a formal dance passage. Later, madness threatened the hero; black, Goyaesque enemies (the Philistine critics) appeared briefly. His wife attempted to guide, soothe and heal him, but, with outstretched valedictory arm and tragic eyes, he backed away from her toward the Rhine.

Most critics admired the Schumann ballet while expressing surprise at its quite untypical emotional character. Most also recognized something autobiographical about the work, as well as in its casting. Balanchine had remarked to an interviewer in 1972, "Mozart never put his miserable life into his beautiful, gay music." Perhaps this was as near as the objective choreographer could come—except in *Don Quixote*—to exposing his private feelings. Martha Duffy of *Time* wrote:

Balanchine may have been putting a distance between himself and this outpouring of emotion by including Schumann's name in the full title. But on opening night he seemed positively merry, pleased enough with the ballet to take four curtain calls (in the past fans have clapped blisters onto their hands trying to get him to appear once). If the old master, now 76, is thinking about death, he is thinking about it creatively and at the highest level.

At Saratoga that summer, Karin came daily to help Balanchine cook and drive him wherever he wanted to go. In the fall, he traveled with the company to Copenhagen, Berlin and Paris. In the last two cities there were celebrations of the hundredth anniversary of Stravinsky's birth.

Back at home he discovered the girl who was to be the last of his ballerinas. During rehearsals for *Le Bourgeois Gentilhomme* in 1979, a fourteen-year-old student who was "marking" as an understudy fell on her behind with such a crash that Balanchine, Nureyev, Bonnefous and Martins stared at her in amazement. Covered with embarrassment, Darci Kistler nearly went straight home to California, where Taras had found her. But the next time Balanchine saw her, she made quite a different impression. Chosen to dance the lead in *Swan Lake* in the 1980 School Workshop, she turned in a performance that became the talk of the company—and of the audiences who attended. It was an extraordinary feat for a girl of any age, and almost unbelievable in a fifteen-year-old. Darci was taken into the company in the fall of 1980, became a soloist in 1981 and was made a principal (the youngest in the company's history) in 1982. By then she had already danced the second movement in *Symphony in C* and been singled out by Balanchine for special attention. There is a revealing picture of the two of them in the dancer Toni Bentley's journal of the 1980–81 winter season:

Balanchine is working on Darci. She is blond, thin, tiny and so young. He is old, gray; he squints and arches his head upward to make her analyze herself. He rises and jumps around, showing her where to go, how to do it. "Where did you learn that? Did you go somewhere?"

He is already fearful and suspicious that she will desert him and go to another for help. She assures him that no one taught her, she just did it alone. . . . He will change it.

All eyes focus on the two, moving from Darci to Balanchine, from Balanchine to Darci. Everyone wants to know what he thinks of her every step. The eyes flit back and forth, back and forth, trying to correlate and imagine their two minds. It is romantic, Darci at [not quite] sixteen, Balanchine at seventy-six, coaching. It is beautiful to see.

Darci did not at first realize that Balanchine's interest in her work was anything out of the ordinary, and when, in class, he slapped her on the rear "like your dad would do," she thought it was "a liberty." She remembers: "He once asked me: 'Where did you learn to do an awful second position like that?' and I said, 'At your School.' " But more and more she began to see that he was offering her invaluable help and advice: "One day I'm not going to be here," he said, "so you've got to remember. Be yourself. Don't act, don't emote, trust yourself." She realized that "if you did remember all you were taught, you'd had a whole lifetime."

•   •   •

DURING the run of *Nutcracker* that winter, the dancers of NYCB threatened to strike unless they were given a raise. Balanchine announced that he would speak to the whole company after class. As a result, the class was so crowded that it was difficult to squeeze into a place at the barre. When it was over, Balanchine came in very calmly and called the company around him. Most of them sat on the floor. He said the management's offer was final. If seventy out of one hundred and five voted for a strike—"Fine, okay, I will be happy. We will go elsewhere and make a new company in a day. This is the fifth company, and we will make the sixth. . . . I want a vote for myself, and I don't give a damn if it's illegal. Yes or no from a hundred and five!"

If he had asked them to raise their hands, Toni Bentley thought, no one would have dared not to. But he did not. After telling them how, when he was their age and working for Diaghilev, he had sold his pants at the flea market, he said there would be a box in which to drop their votes. A week later the company accepted the management's latest offer.

．　．　．

BALANCHINE was having trouble with his left eye. He had never liked to be seen wearing glasses, but now, when he watched a ballet from the wings, he was obliged to wear them; a dark lens covered the bad eye. Darci Kistler thought that even with a patch over one eye, Balanchine saw more than most people:

A lot Mr. B. told me was about myself. Sometimes he talked to me in a corner of the stage; once in a while he'd call me into his room. He talked to me about music. (I used to go to concerts alone; I'd rather have been an opera singer.) He said, "Dance should not exceed music. Never 'interpret' music. You can't choreograph Beethoven."

At the Théâtre des Champs-Elysées during the 1980 European tour, she was about to watch from the wings a ballet she had never seen before. Balanchine took her to a dark corner of the stage and said, "Just listen to the music."

Balanchine was at this time complaining more and more that the lighting was too dim; Ronald Bates was reluctantly forced to strengthen it until the stage became, as Dominique Nabokov put it, "like a gymnasium." The choreographer was also suffering from a bad back and tired easily. Despite these ailments, a two-week

Tchaikovsky Festival was scheduled for June 1981 and announced to the press at the Russian Tea Room on February 9.

Five days later, outside a butcher shop on Broadway, Balanchine was accosted by Solomon Volkov, the musicologist who had smuggled Shostakovich's autobiography out of Russia. Volkov knew Balanchine by sight only, but he had read of the forthcoming festival, and he spoke about Tchaikovsky. The choreographer invited him to write a piece for the festival program, and the two men began to meet and discuss Tchaikovsky and St. Petersburg. The valuable reminiscences that emerged from their conversations, which Volkov later published, have been quoted frequently in these pages.

· · ·

BOTH KIRSTEIN (who never owned a television set) and Balanchine (who did) had been dissatisfied with attempts to film ballets in the 1960s, but in the 1970s Merrill Brockway and Emile Ardolino of the Public Broadcasting System won the choreographer over. Once converted, he took endless trouble exploring the possibilities of television technique and willingly altered his ballets to make them look better on the small screen. Several programs were filmed for the *Dance in America* and *Live from Lincoln Center* series. Ardolino found that Balanchine understood very well that "television succeeds best in closeup" and that a wide shot of a big group reduced the dancers to ants, or, as Balanchine put it, "[on television] dancers don't go away and come back, they just get smaller or bigger."

He began by disliking panning shots, but later changed his mind. "It's so boring to stay on that long, wide shot—go to the panning one," he would say. He took an interest in every detail of lighting and makeup. In 1981 he persuaded Ardolino that television would be the perfect medium for Ravel's *The Spellbound Child*, which he had always staged with difficulty. The film was rehearsed in New York, shot in eleven days in Nashville, Tennessee, edited in New York and shown on May 25, 1981. This time,

Ardolino thought, the choreographer was moderately satisfied with the result.

. . .

WHEN BALANCHINE decided to make a new version of Tchaikovsky's *Mozartiana,* which he had first arranged in 1933, then for the American Ballet in 1935 and for the Ballet Russe in 1945, he explained to Suzanne Farrell and Ib Andersen at their first rehearsal, "It is Mozart. Nobody in Russia knew much of Mozart, so Tchaikovsky, who adored him, wanted his countrymen to hear his music. This suite was like an introduction for them."

Mozartiana was Balanchine's last great ballet. Former company member Robert Maiorano, who had abandoned dancing for writing, obtained permission from the choreographer to record the shaping of *Mozartiana* day by day, from its beginning in May to its first performance on June 4. His descriptions of how Balanchine devised the most taxing steps constitute an invaluable document. One does not have to be a specialist to enjoy Maiorano's detailed account of Balanchine's patience, endurance of physical handicaps and kindness to the four little girls who formed a frame for Farrell in her Preghiera (Prayer) solo.

Farrell had nearly always been dressed in white for Balanchine ballets, but in *Mozartiana* all eleven dancers wore black. The endless trouble Balanchine took to ensure the exact line, weight and trimmings of Farrell's black *point d'esprit* skirt, worn over lighter underskirts, was a small epic in itself. In Balanchine's earlier versions of *Mozartiana,* the Gigue had been performed first, as Tchaikovsky wrote it; but to make it possible for Farrell to dance the Preghiera as well as the Theme and ten Variations—the ninth of which was her pas de deux with Andersen—the order was changed to Preghiera, Gigue, Menuet, Theme and Variations, Finale.

The season was running its course throughout the rehearsals of *Mozartiana;* the three other ballet masters were rehearsing new ballets for the festival. Balanchine himself was planning to stage part of the Sixth Symphony and, because he wanted to show something of Tchaikovsky's lighter side, "Hungarian Gypsy Airs." "Why does all music have to be the best?" he exclaimed to Robert Irving. "Let's have some cheap restaurant music." But this music seemed to get on his nerves, and he lost his temper with a photographer who was present at a rehearsal.

Everyone was relieved when *Mozartiana* was "finished," even though it had not yet been rehearsed on the stage. But Balanchine's mind had already turned to a new project. "You know, maybe . . . I think I will do a waltz for Tchaikovsky." "When?" "Tomorrow." The program of the festival (due to open in two weeks) was therefore enlarged by the inclusion of the Garland Dance from Act I of *The Sleeping Beauty,* for twenty-five women, sixteen men and sixteen little girls from the School. It was one of the loveliest dances he ever made.

Victor Castelli, who was to dance the Gigue in *Mozartiana,* injured himself during one of the last rehearsals and had to be replaced by Christopher d'Amboise, son of Jacques, who had recently been taken into the company after years at the School. Suzanne Farrell dislocated a bone in her foot during the first performance, which she still managed to finish and which was an enormous success—though *Mozartiana* was not repeated during the festival. Ib Andersen partnered her for the first time, and Balanchine thought him so subtle and so musical a dancer that he exclaimed, "Ib *is* Mozart!" In later seasons, *Mozartiana* became one of Farrell's most popular roles, and a ballet constantly reevaluated by the critics.

The Tchaikovsky Festival served to remind Balanchine's audience that he had made ballets to Tchaikovsky's music throughout the five decades he had been in America. The last work of his last Tchaikovsky program was the Sixth *(Pathétique)* Symphony. The first movement was omitted; Robbins arranged a ballet to the second; the curtain was lowered while the orchestra played the third; and the fourth was staged by Balanchine in a ceremonial manner. It took its name from the musical direction for the movement: *Adagio Lamentoso.* Karin von Aroldingen had developed tendinitis after dancing in the only performance of *Hungarian Gypsy Airs,* but Balanchine asked her if she would take part in the *Pathétique.* "It's not much dancing—it's walking, barefoot." She and other dancers were "mourners"; there were twelve angels with immense wings, hooded figures in purple and monks who prostrated themselves in the shape of a cross. A child entered with a candle and, on the final chord of the symphony, blew it out, plunging the theater into darkness. The audience, stunned and moved, did not applaud. Many people interpreted the ballet as a valedictory gesture from the aging choreographer, especially since at the end of a Russian Orthodox funeral the candles held by the congregation are blown out. Karin found it "macabre, chilling," and was shaken when Balanchine told her, "You were wonderful. You know how to mourn."

That July, Karin stayed with the Leaches in order to be nearer to Balanchine and keep an eye on him. When her husband came for weekends, he shared Eddie Bigelow's apartment at the guesthouse. Karin produced *Liebeslieder,* for the third time, for Patricia Neary's company in Zurich that August. Balanchine and Barbara Horgan flew over for the premiere and went on to Monte Carlo with Karin. Every summer Princess Grace of Monaco, who was fond of Balanchine and persistently wanted him to form a ballet company in her husband's principality, held a *"bal de la rose."* This year it was the turn of the Yellow Rose of Texas. When the band played a waltz, Balanchine led Karin onto the floor. A spotlight was turned on them; no one else danced. "He barely got through the waltz," said Karin, "but it was unforgettable."

▪ ▪ ▪

WHEN he was not on one of his European trips, or filming in Nashville, Balanchine's life was passed in a very small area of the West Side of New York between his apartment on Sixty-seventh Street, the School and the theater. Many of his dancers lived in the same neighborhood; if they asked him to supper he had not far to go. For the most part he dined at one of the many restaurants that had sprung up in the now quite fashionable quarter.

Did it ever occur to him, as he sat dining and gossiping with Karin and Morton—or with Suzanne, for their friendship had been resumed—that his fame was greater than that of any choreographer who had ever lived? At any given moment of the day, the chances were that one of his ballets was being rehearsed or danced or written about somewhere in the world. Between 1978 and 1982 there had been productions of twenty-four of his ballets in seventeen countries on four continents. That is, of course, without reckoning performances by the New York City Ballet. Between 1960 and 1982 there had been twenty-eight different productions of *Apollo* in countries as far apart as Norway and Uruguay, Hungary and the United States. There had been thirty-nine productions of *Serenade* over the same period, as far north as Toronto, as far south as Australia, as far west as Seattle, as far east as Iran.

Balanchine was not interested in fame, nor did he covet honors. He refused many doctorates. A few may have been accepted for idiosyncratic reasons: from Brandeis University because the first School Workshop performances had taken place there; from the University of Cincinnati to please Suzanne. These and the doctorate of Fine Arts from Northwestern University date from 1967. In 1973 he received one from Columbia University. In 1970, Mayor John Lindsay gave him New York City's highest cultural award, the Handel Medallion; it was presented to him onstage after the premiere of *Who Cares?* In 1972, at the Whitney Museum, he received the New York State Award from Governor Rockefeller; and in 1975 the National Society of Arts and Letters presented him with its Distinguished Service Award. During his final illness, the Presidential Medal of Freedom, the highest American honor for civilians, was accepted on his behalf by Suzanne Farrell. The citation read: "The genius of George Balanchine has enriched the lives of all Americans who love the dance." In 1975 he became an Officer of the French Legion of Honor; in 1978 the king of Denmark made him a Knight of the Order of Dannebrog, First

Class; in 1980 the president of Austria awarded him the Austrian Medal for Learning and Art.

But Balanchine's real reward lay in the knowledge that he had improved the quality of dancing not only in America but in Europe and other parts of the world. In an interview with a Swiss reporter taped by Patricia Neary in Zurich in 1980, he humorously summed up one aspect of his achievement:

> They say classical ballet is rejuvenated. It's not rejuvenated. It's new. I was brought up in old ballet: small men, small women with big heads, short necks, little mouths like Pola Negri in silent movie. Corps de ballet never danced. They were graded—nearer the public were better. . . . Classical ballet is not rejuvenated. It's new. Now the sound is better, technique is better. Like football, swimmers, boxing are better. We taught people. I have a lot of young people. Technique won't die.

Most of the new race of slim, swift, beautiful girls had, of course, learned their craft at Balanchine's own School of American Ballet.

One day in the seventies Suki Schorer's father, the writer Mark Schorer, remarked on a fine performance of *Symphony in C,* and Balanchine said, "Yes, it's the best that's ever been." Relating this to me, Suki added, "Of course, it got better afterwards." I asked her, "Do you think it made him happy to have achieved all that he set out to do?" "Oh, yes, I think so," she answered. "I remember once he came to the School a year before he was sick. I was teaching this variation from the *Minkus Pas de Trois.* He said, 'It's amazing. When I made this variation, only *one* person could do that turning step, and now the *whole class* is doing it.' "

Interviewed by McNeil Lowry in 1979, Balanchine had boasted, "The dancing is good now; I don't have to tell them anything. . . . I tell Rosemary when she says, 'Shall I put this girl there? What would you like to do?' 'No,' I say, 'just put anybody, because they're so good—anybody.' "

Chapter 15

....

BALLET MASTER EMERITUS:

DECEMBER 1981-

APRIL 30, 1983

O NCE, when Balanchine was teaching *Apollo* to Suki Schorer, he explained to her, "It's like Greek frieze. Go and look at the vases in the Metropolitan." (Years later, she reminded him of this: "You used to tell me to go and look at the Greek vases. What good did it do me?" Balanchine answered, "But you married a Greek, dear"—which was true, if irrelevant.)

It would be fascinating to know more about Balanchine's reactions to painting and sculpture. A choreographer is a kind of sculptor and draftsman—even, because of his complex floor patterns, an architect—but he carves in perishable human bodies and draws on air. Nancy Lassalle remembers Balanchine taking her and Maria Tallchief to the Louvre in 1947, and John Taras is sure that a famous pose in *Serenade* was borrowed from Canova's *Cupid and Psyche.*

On the other hand, Boris Kochno, who was with Balanchine on his sightseeing excursions in Italy in the twenties, believed that, unlike Massine, Balanchine never derived ideas from the visual arts. Indeed, music was all he needed to start up the engine of his imagination. But at least one supreme work of art made its mark on him. Talking to me in 1977, he spoke of and mimed "the pointing fingers" of Michelangelo's Jehovah and Adam, "as big as this room—so great!"; and this symbol of God-given life is certainly echoed in *Apollo.* In later life, however, whenever Karin von Aroldingen asked him to go with her to a museum, he said, "I've seen all that."

■   ■   ■

WHEN, in December 1981, Britain's Royal Society of Arts awarded Lincoln Kirstein the Benjamin Franklin Gold Medal for his services to the arts, Balanchine insisted on accompanying him to the ceremony. The presentation took place at a dinner at the Royal Society's house, a block away from the Savoy Theatre where Kirstein had first made Balanchine's acquaintance in 1933. After this—as it turned out, last—visit to London, Balanchine flew to Zurich to see Patricia Neary's company, then spent Christmas with Karin and her family.

He was back in New York for New Year's Eve, and gave a little supper party at home. Barbara Horgan, who knew how his state of health could vary—he would be gray and almost speechless one day and sprightly the next—thought he looked extremely well. Yet as the days went on he was always tired and kept blaming it on jet lag. When the winter season ended on February 12, Barbara left for a week's vacation in Florida. Balanchine called her on the fifth day, and she was suddenly convinced that he was dying. He said, "When you get back, we are really going to find out what is the matter with me." Dr. Langner lined up ear and eye specialists, and on March 23, tests were made.

But there was still to be one more grand endeavor: the Stravinsky Centennial Celebration of 1982. Of the fifty-five works performed during the week of June 10–18, eleven were new; however, Balanchine needed help with his two big productions.

Noah and the Flood had been commissioned for television in 1962 and telecast by CBS with Balanchine's choreography and sets by Ter-Arutunian. It was possible to reconstruct the dances from the existing film. Even so, Balanchine was obliged to call in Jacques d'Amboise to help work on the choreography. Robert Craft, who had selected and arranged the text, conducted *Noah* on the second night of the festival.

Kermit Love designed *Perséphone,* and Balanchine conferred with him regularly during the first half of 1982. The Greek myth used by André Gide as a scenario for Stravinsky's melodrama, with its narrator, singers and dancers, was a parable of winter and spring. Balanchine told Love that he considered it a ceremony, which should be performed in a church. "I'd like to do it Russian, but we can't." The singers would be ranged on either side of the stage. Vera Zorina was not only to work with Balanchine on the production but to speak the words of Perséphone, while Karin von Aroldingen danced the role.

Alas, when it came to rehearsals, the choreographer was no longer in a condition to handle the complex task. It was known that his eyesight and balance were bad, but he now appeared to lack concentration, energy and even enthusiasm. As Zorina later pointed out, few people realized how ill he was. He could not hear the tenor, and the music hurt his ears. He was unable to finish the job, and Taras did his best to pull the ballet together. For Zorina, who had been so happy to work with Balanchine again, *Perséphone* was "a searing experience."

Balanchine had also devised a *Tango,* which was danced by Karin and Christopher d'Amboise at the gala first night of the festival. A new version of the last movement of *Variations for Orchestra*, danced solo, as before, by Suzanne Farrell, was not ready until two weeks after the festival ended, and it was clear to some members of the company that Farrell, who knew so well the workings of Balanchine's mind, was responsible for certain passages of dancing. Nevertheless, *Variations* was to be officially recorded as Balanchine's last ballet.

In Saratoga in July, Balanchine's giddiness was so bad that he could not go to the theater. Karin was again staying with the Leaches, so she and Kay Leach between them managed to look after him. Kay had her ankle in a cast, but when Karin went to the Performing Arts Center to rehearse or teach, Kay used to hobble over to the guesthouse and sit enchanted while Balanchine spoke of Russian history, Peter the Great, his own early life, and his wives. "I never left them," he invariably insisted. "They always left me."

Earlier in the year he had written the music for a popular song, "The World Is Turning Fast," with lyrics by Arthur Schwartz, and sold it to the music publisher Schirmer for $1,000. (It was dedicated to Karin.) That summer he sat for hours under the trees, writing more music and lyrics, then trying them out on the Leaches' piano. He told Kay, "I'm having such trouble with my balance and can't see well, so I think I'm going to change my career." Dick Leach guessed that Balanchine composed about forty minutes of music. He did not want to be useless. When he left Saratoga for the last time on July 25, he gave Kay the manuscript of one of his songs, written in pencil.

On August 16 he went into the hospital for three nights. A cataract was removed from his left eye and a soft lens inserted. He rested at home for a few weeks but soon grew bored. Throughout September he was seeing doctors. When he went with the company to Washington for their season at the Kennedy Center in October, he was taken ill and spent ten days in the hospital, where neurological tests were made. Back in New York he had an appointment with his dentist on October 25. After that day Barbara Horgan ceased to write in his engagement book.

With a nurse living in, it was hard to achieve any privacy in the Sixty-seventh Street apartment, and Balanchine resented this. Although Barbara, Eddie Bigelow, Karin and her husband were constantly in and out, cooking for him and taking care of him, there were days when he tried to do without the nurse and was left alone. This was dangerous, because he kept falling. Once he fell as he was going to answer the telephone; another time he blacked out and called Barbara, saying he did not know where he was. As she lived on West Fifty-sixth Street, she was at the apartment with Dr. Hamilton in a few minutes.

He had Karin and Morton to dinner one night and was proud to have cooked it himself. Suddenly Morton noticed a smell of burning coming from the bedroom. A candle on the altar in front of the icons had set fire to its plastic holder, and there was a blaze. Balanchine got up, fell and struck his head against a table. Karin and Morton put out the fire.

In Zurich Patricia Neary had a premonition and flew over to see him. Balanchine cooked roast beef for her and Barbara. At 7:30 he said, "I'm so tired. I think I'll go to bed." While the two women were cleaning up, Barbara told Patricia that this was usual. Next day, when Barbara and the nurse were both present, Balanchine fell again and cracked his ribs. Patricia found him terribly changed. He asked, "Was I like this yesterday?" She told him no. "Then," said Barbara, "he was very sweet. He said, 'You've done all you can and tried everything, but I shouldn't be here. My home is not a hospital.' I was very relieved." Dr. Hamilton admitted Balanchine to Roosevelt Hospital on November 4.

·   ·   ·

UNTIL his first heart attack, Balanchine had not made a will—perhaps, Barbara Horgan thought, because he suffered from the primitive superstition that to do so would hasten his death. Then, in 1978, he asked Barbara to find him a lawyer. She first consulted her own. She wanted someone who "would not scare George to death," yet she also knew his respect for men in authority such as priests or policemen; a bright young man would not do. She was introduced to Theodore Sysol, a quiet, pleasant, elderly gentleman who knew nothing about ballet, and brought him to see the convalescent Balanchine.

"What would happen if I died without making a will?" he asked.

"Have you any relations?"

"Yes, my brother Andrei, in Georgia."

"Then all you have would go to him."

Balanchine was fond of his brother but immediately had a vision of the Russian state seizing everything. He became—to use Barbara's expression—"apoplectic" and settled down to take the whole business seriously. He said, "I don't really have anything."

"You own this apartment?"

"Yes."

"You have a car?"

"Yes, a Mercedes." This with a touch of pride.

"A house in the country?"

"Yes."

Barbara made a list: two insurance policies; money in the bank; his share in Francis Mason's book. Then there were the ballets.

Balanchine pondered for a few weeks, telephoned Sysol and saw him alone. He bequeathed his apartment on Sixty-seventh Street to Karin, his Southampton condominium to Barbara and the money in the bank to Tanaquil Le Clercq. He left his brother two gold watches Kirstein had given him.

After he had struck a great many ballets off the list because he considered them uninteresting or impossible to revive, there were about a hundred left.

He had already made presents of a few works. He had given all rights of *Symphony in C* to Betty Cage, *A Midsummer Night's Dream* to Diana Adams, *Meditation* to Suzanne Farrell and *Duo Concertant* to Kay Mazzo. Now he bequeathed to Tanaquil Le Clercq the American rights of approximately eighty ballets, the remaining rights, media and foreign, to be divided between Karin and Barbara. All American and media rights to *Concerto Barocco* were to go to Lincoln Kirstein, for whose South American tour it had been made, as well as those of *Orpheus,* which Kirstein had asked Stravinsky to write. To Edward Bigelow he left the American and media rights of *The Four Temperaments* and *Ivesiana.*

Patricia McBride was to receive world rights to *Tarantella,* the Ravel *Pavane* and the Scriabin *Etude for Piano;* Suzanne Farrell to *Don Quixote* and *Tzigane;* Rosemary Dunleavy to *Le Tombeau de Couperin,* which she had remembered so well; Merrill Ashley to *Ballo della Regina;* Barbara Horgan to *Brahms-Schoenberg Quartet;* Karin von Aroldingen to *Serenade, Liebeslieder Walzer, Stravinsky Violin Concerto, Une Porte et un soupir, Vienna Waltzes* and *Kammermusik No. 2.*

. . .

ALTHOUGH Balanchine's malady was not diagnosed until after his death, when an autopsy revealed that he had suffered from the rare Creutzfeldt-Jakob Disease, it was clear that he was becoming increasingly feeble, and that his mind was deteriorating. During his first weeks in the hospital he sometimes telephoned the theater, even getting through to Kevin Tyler at his habitual post, downstage right, during a performance. Then, as his grip on the concerns of everyday life weakened, he asked only for Karin. Naturally, his friends in the company came often to see him. "What wonderful flowers!" Bill Hamilton exclaimed one day. "Yes," said Balanchine, "but flowers don't make you laugh." Hamilton thought he might be missing music and bought him a Sony Walkman. "What tapes shall I get you?" "Debussy perhaps, Poulenc . . ." "Would you like some Chopin?" "No, no, *no!*" Because of Balanchine's distorted hearing, music through earphones pained him, and the experiment was a disaster. One day Hamilton found him asleep. Then he opened his eyes and appeared to be looking into the distance. He said, "You know, I still hear pretty music, and I see people doing things. But you can't tell them, you have to show them."

Since the death of Felia Doubrovska in 1980, Balanchine had made friends with Father Adrian of the Cathedral of Our Lady of the Sign, who had conducted her funeral service. This Canadian-born priest had learned Russian and been converted to the Orthodox Church. He began to visit Balanchine in the hospital.

Russian-speaking visitors were, of course, particularly welcome, as Balanchine was always most at ease speaking his original tongue. Solomon Volkov came with his tape recorder to continue his talks about Tchaikovsky and St. Petersburg. Barbara Horgan wondered if these might not be troublesome to Balanchine, as he had known Volkov for so short a time; but when she put her head around the door one day while Volkov was in the room, she saw such an expression of happiness on Balanchine's face that she withdrew silently. Balanchine did not like the music of Shostakovich, whose pupil and friend Volkov had been, so he never referred to him at all. Volkov thought this showed tact and good manners.

For four years Leslie George Katz, Nancy Lassalle and Harvey Simmonds had been working to produce their monumental book, *Choreography by George Balanchine: A Catalogue of Works,* which many researchers had labored to perfect, and which was not only a hoard of information—some of it provided by Balanchine himself and his earliest collaborators—but also one of the most beautiful books of our day. On December 24, when Nancy brought Balanchine the first copy, which he was hardly able to read, he pointed to the lyre, based on Tchelitchev's design for *Orpheus and Eurydice,* which had been used as a decoration, and which was later carved on his tombstone.

.   .   .

I WAS in New York during January 1983. I had never considered myself a close friend of Balanchine's, and I could not make up my mind whether to visit him in the hospital or not. On January 15 I finally did go with John Taras, who told Balanchine, "I've brought Dicky Buckle to see you." I wondered if I would have been recognized without this cue. As it was, Balanchine opened his arms and exclaimed, "Dicky!" Never having embraced Balanchine in my life, I was taken aback, shook hands and regretted it later. I had with me a clipping from the sports page of a London newspaper about a horse named Balanchine winning a race. The choreographer pronounced his own name, perhaps reading the headline, folded the slip of paper and stuck it into the strap of his wristwatch. That afternoon at the State Theater I watched the Mozart *Divertimento No. 15* and thought no ballet could be more exquisite or better danced. (I had said the same of *Caracole*, arranged to the same music, in 1952.)

Indeed, Balanchine appeared to have worked with Mozart, as with other dead composers, like a twin who could read his brother's thoughts. I was particularly struck by one small instance of the close "collaboration." Although I could see there were more marvelous passages of choreography in the six Variations—and I thought how delightful it was that they succeeded one another so swiftly, almost overlapping—and in the Minuet, the moment that thrilled me most came with the appearance of a singularly beautiful melody in the finale. Here Balanchine's handling of Mozart was an illustration of "the marriage of true minds." In this Allegro Molto, Mozart flirts with his audience like a brilliant woman holding her lover in suspense. When the impatient jigging begins, we think, "This is it!" but we are wrong. Yet the moment of bliss is being heralded, for the horns respond to chords on the first violins like sentinels scanning the horizon and calling from tower to tower. Then, against a pulsating accompaniment, the A-flat major theme takes off for the stratosphere, and ecstasy is upon us. How does Balanchine convey the entry of this theme in visual terms? In the most elementary way. Three dancers—a boy between two girls, their crossed hands clasped—appear suddenly upstage. With a swinging step, they advance in a diagonal, smiling. It is like a rainbow.

That night, Rudolf Nureyev, recently appointed *maître de ballet* of the Paris Opéra, was seated beside me, and he, too, admired *Divertimento*. He asked after Balanchine. The next day or soon after, Dr. Hamilton opened the door of Balanchine's room to find Nureyev kneeling beside the bed, tears pouring down his face.

Baryshnikov thought Balanchine still retained his sense of smell, and he guessed that spicy Georgian cooking might tempt him. He knew of a Georgian restaurant in Brooklyn and more than once ordered a special meal from it—even including Georgian wine and an imported Georgian mineral water. He sent his limousine for it, then served it in the hospital room himself and shared it with Balanchine.

From all over the United States old friends and colleagues came to spend a few minutes with the master of all ballet masters. Ruthanna Boris called him: "I hear you're not very well." "I can't see properly, I can't work. There's nothing . . ." "Aren't there any pretty nurses?" "Oh that, maybe yes . . ." "I think I'll have to make a little journey."

She was in Seattle. When she arrived at the hospital, Balanchine had Karin with him. Ruthanna was wearing a gold Star of David on a chain around her neck, and he fingered it. She explained its significance, then, as he would not let it alone, she took it off and, with Karin, hung it round his neck. Karin left them together, and Balanchine went to sleep holding Ruthanna's hand.

Dr. Hamilton later admitted that his idea for a seventy-ninth birthday party for Balanchine on January 22 was a mistake. Anyway, as Karin pointed out, Balanchine had always cared less about his birthday than his name day. There were only twenty or so friends in the room, but for the sick man this was a crowd. Tables, plates and glasses were brought in. Karin had made seventy-nine *kotletki*, the way Balanchine had taught her, with a sauce of mushrooms and cream. Barbara Horgan, Edward Bigelow, Suzanne Farrell, Kay Mazzo, John Taras, Jacques d'Amboise and Lucia Davidova all came, bringing gifts, but the levity was strained, and the party did not last very long. Karin and Morton remained behind to clear up.

. . .

BECAUSE the New York City Ballet had become so huge an operation, the members of its board decided it must be given a new director. The pretense that Balanchine was "convalescing" could not be kept up indefinitely, and few believed that he would ever return to work. Orville Schell, the chairman, had visited him in Saratoga during July in the hope of asking him to appoint an heir, but Balanchine evaded the question, and Schell had been too shy to press the point. Peter Martins had also hoped, when he went to see Balanchine, that a successor might be named, but he, too, was disappointed. While the board probably considered that it would be better to have one man in charge, it was hard to pass over sixty-four-year-old Jerome Robbins, whose fame was widespread and whose ballets were needed by the company, in favor of thirty-six-year-old Peter Martins. But Robbins was unwilling to undertake administration. At a meeting on Tuesday, March 15, it was decided to appoint Martins and Robbins jointly as ballet masters in chief. Gillian Attfield, president of the board of directors, read a statement to the company, adding that Balanchine had been voted the new title of Ballet Master Emeritus, "to leave no doubt as to our love and respect."

"His place at the head of the greatest dance company in the world . . . has been taken over . . ." wrote Clive Barnes in the *Post*. "It is all but unthinkable," wrote *The New Yorker*'s "Talk of the Town," "that there will be no new Balanchine ballets." "End of the Balanchine Era" announced *Newsweek:* "It seems inconceivable."

Balanchine, however, was beyond knowing or caring. He listened for Karin's footsteps, which he could distinguish from those of all others. She sat with him, holding his hand, day after day. But his memory was so bad that he often called her soon after she left to ask, "When are you coming to see me?"

The last words Karin and Balanchine exchanged were on Sunday, April 24. She had brought her daughter Margo to visit him. As she left, Karin said, "I'll come and see you tomorrow. May I?" "Any time." Margo lingered behind and came out crying. The nurse ran after them to say that Balanchine had spoken Margo's name.

Darci Kistler was another of Balanchine's last visitors. "No one was allowed in," she told me. "And I threw such a fit. I said, 'It's unfair that the nurses should be allowed in and I'm not.' I threw such a fit that I did get in. And Mr. B. recognized me, and he listened to me." I was sure that this girl would have known exactly what to say to the dying choreographer, and I asked no further questions.

Balanchine died at about 4:00 A.M. on Saturday, April 30, 1983. Roosevelt Hospital informed Barbara Horgan, who telephoned Lincoln Kirstein, Karin, Peter Martins, John Taras, Rosemary Dunleavy and others. Peter called Karin to ask her if she could still dance in *Kammermusik* that afternoon, saying he was sure Balanchine would have wished her to. She agreed, but she was in such a state of shock that she later could remember nothing about the performance. The funeral was to be on Tuesday, May 3, at the Cathedral of Our Lady of the Sign, where Balanchine had attended Easter services, but according to the custom of the Russian Orthodox Church a *panikhida* (memorial service) was held daily until then.

Not only was the New York City Ballet performing at the State Theater, Ballet Theatre's season at the Metropolitan was to open on Sunday and Taras was rehearsing Balanchine's *Symphonie concertante* for them. Members of Nancy Lassalle's Advisory Council had also assembled from all over the United States for the annual Workshop performances of the School of American Ballet, the first of which was held on the day of Balanchine's death. Before the curtain rose on the matinee at the State Theater, before the School's performance at the Juilliard Theater in the evening, and again before the company's evening performance, Lincoln Kirstein, Peter Martins, Jerome Robbins and John Taras came out in front of the curtain, and Kirstein spoke a few words: "I don't have to tell you that Mr. B. is with Mozart and Tchaikovsky and Stravinsky. . . ." The first ballet at the evening performance was Mozart's *Divertimento No. 15.* The last was Bizet's *Symphony in C,* in which Peter Martins replaced Sean Lavery to dance the second movement with Suzanne Farrell.

Sunday's memorial service was to be at eight in the evening. Balanchine's body lay in an open coffin in the cathedral, with a ribbon across his forehead. Taras wrote:

I went at four and pinned the President's medal on his lapel and inserted the Legion of Honor rosette. Bigelow and Barbara had decided that the coffin should be as simple as possible. The one they chose was an Orthodox Jewish one, no metal. I ran out to get flowers for the top of the coffin. On a Sunday it was difficult, but I did find a florist and brought a spray of flowers before the evening service . . .

On the second [Monday] I arranged to have the body photographed. I had brought an antique cross to put in Balanchine's hands, and a crucifix that Doubrovska wanted to be buried with, but that was found only after her funeral. I put that in Balanchine's breast pocket and hoped he would pass it on. The service that day was at two and better attended, with television cameras and the press as well. . . . To the School performance at seven, where again we appeared before the curtain. Then I ran over to the opening night of Ballet Theatre at the Met. Misha came in front of the curtain in his Harlequin make-up to say a few words, and the orchestra played a short bit of *Symphonie concertante.* The moment they started, I stood up and was followed by the entire audience. On the third I was at the church at eight to rearrange the flowers. At last a blanket of white flowers [gardenias] arrived. . . . The service at eleven was very crowded and emotional.

When the mortal remains of Balanchine were borne down into the crowded courtyard of the cathedral, the actor Tom Lacy was standing near Lincoln Kirstein, whom he had never met, and he noticed:

As the coffin was carried out of the front door at the top of the high flight of stairs, it was jostled by the pallbearers. Suddenly that Mount Rushmore figure of Kirstein's began to quake. He sobbed mightily. It was moving to be near him, not knowing him, but aware of the fifty years that tied him and Balanchine together.

It was decided to bury Balanchine in Sag Harbor, a town he had admired, which was near his Southampton condominium. Tamara Geva, Alexandra Danilova, Maria Tallchief, Tanaquil Le Clercq, Allegra Kent, Suzanne Farrell, Karin von Aroldingen and Natalie Molostwoff were present to throw white roses into the grave.

Dr. Hamilton arrived late, and earth was already being shoveled. He found Suzanne Farrell alone beside the grave and saw her throw in a rose.

The duo-pianists Robert Fizdale and Arthur Gold, close friends of Balanchine who lived nearby, had, in true Balanchine tradition, prepared lunch for the mourners. "The food was delicious," wrote Taras. "Caviar, vodka, roast ham . . ."

Balanchine's death was announced in Sunday's *New York Times,* with a long summary of his career; in the *Washington Post,* London *Observer* and London *Sunday Times.* On Monday, May 2, the tributes began to appear throughout the United States and Europe. Edward I. Koch, mayor of New York, issued a statement: "New York City mourns the passing of George Balanchine, one of the greatest artists who has ever chosen to work and live in our city. Mr. Balanchine is the acknowledged master of ballet of the 20th century; his ballets are more widely performed throughout the world than those of any other choreographer. Mr. Balanchine loved our city. He lived in New York for 50 years and gave his company the city's name. In 1980, he devoted the proceeds of the New York City Ballet's opening night to the city to purchase bulletproof vests for police officers." There was more, and Kirstein was given due credit; but in five sentences the mayor had stated seven indisputable facts.

The headlines were international: "An Immortal Legacy"; "Mentor and Master: Dance World Mourns Balanchine"; "The Joy of Pure Movement"; *"La mort de 'Mister B' "; "Avec Balanchine disparait le chorégraphe du siècle"; "Balanchine: le plus grand."* In *Newsweek,* Hubert Saal began his "Farewell to Ballet's Mr. B." on a light note: "George Balanchine deplored inflated reputations. 'Why must everyone be great?' he used to ask. 'Isn't "good" good enough? Everyone's overrated. Picasso's overrated. I'm overrated, even Jack Benny's overrated.' " But Saal ended his appreciation with a just summing-up of what the ballet master had achieved:

Balanchine's ballets can be seen as a paradigm of 20th century art. . . . Their speed and economy reflect the style and pace of the century. . . . By liberating dance from story, by restlessly experimenting, by combining old and new, Balanchine stands beside Picasso and Stravinsky. But while they worked in accepted and respected mediums, Balanchine practiced what was still a second-class art. His most awesome achievement was that he elevated ballet almost single-handedly from a place below the salt to a seat at the head of the table.

In *Commonweal,* Don McDonagh celebrated the freeing of ballet from drama. He too repeated a typical self-deprecatory saying of the master who liked to "move people to music": "He compared himself to a cook or a carpenter and eschewed the word 'create' in relation to his ballets. 'Only God creates, I assemble.' "

To another interviewer, Balanchine had said:

People say, "Oh, my God, what will happen when you go?" But everybody goes. . . . It wouldn't be any good fifty years from now to do what we do now. . . . Maybe we won't even need the technique. People will look different, they will move differently. You will ask how to preserve for posterity. I say, "Preserve what?" . . . Look at the old movies. Look at Pavlova . . . it's ridiculous.

And to yet another:

I don't want my ballets preserved as museum pieces for people to go and laugh at what used to be. *Absolutely not.* I'm staging ballets for today's bodies. Ballet is NOW.

Balanchine was to the dance in the twentieth century what Michelangelo had been to sculpture in the sixteenth, and it could be argued that in one short ballet by the greatest of choreographers there were more ingenious "sculptures" than the Florentine master carved in the course of his long life. Balanchine enriched the lives of many million Americans by showing them, in a way that not even baseball could show them, the divine possibilities of the human body. He raised their standard of living.

BIBLIOGRAPHY

ALLEN, W. E. D. *A History of the Georgian People.* London: Routledge & Kegan Paul, 1932.

D'AMBOISE, CHRISTOPHER. *Leap Year: A Year in the Life of a Dancer.* Garden City, New York: Doubleday, 1982.

ANDERSON, JACK. *The One and Only: The Ballet Russe de Monte Carlo.* Brooklyn, New York: Dance Horizons, 1981.

ASHLEY, MERRILL. *Dancing for Balanchine.* New York: Dutton, 1984.

BALANCHINE, GEORGE. *Balanchine's New Complete Stories of the Great Ballets.* Edited by Francis Mason. Garden City, New York: Doubleday, 1968.

BENTLEY, TONI. *Winter Season: A Dancer's Journal.* New York: Random House, 1982.

BUCKLE, RICHARD. *Diaghilev.* New York: Atheneum, 1979.

Choreography by Balanchine: A Catalogue of Works. New York: Eakins Press/ Viking. Revised edition, 1984.

CHUJOY, ANATOLE. *The Dance Encyclopedia.* New York: Barnes, 1949.

——. *The New York City Ballet.* New York: Knopf, 1953.

CRAFT, ROBERT, ed. *Dearest Bubushkin: Selected Letters and Diaries of Vera and Igor Stravinsky.* (The correspondence of Vera and Igor Stravinsky, 1921–1954, with excerpts from Vera Stravinsky's diaries, 1922–1971. Translated by Lucia Davidova.) London: Thames & Hudson, 1985.

CROCE, ARLENE. *Going to the Dance.* New York: Knopf, 1982.

CRICHTON, RONALD. *Manuel de Falla: Descriptive Catalogue of His Works.* London: Chester/Wilhelm Hansen, 1976.

DANILOVA, ALEXANDRA. *Choura.* New York: Knopf, 1986.

DENBY, EDWIN. *Dancers, Buildings and People in the Streets.* New York: Horizon Press, 1965.

——. *Looking at the Dance.* New York: Horizon Press, 1949.

——. *Dance Writings.* Edited by Robert Cornfield and William Mackay. New York: Knopf, 1987.

DE VALOIS, NINETTE. *Invitation to the Ballet.* London: Bodley Head, 1937.

————. *Come Dance with Me: A Memoir, 1898–1956.* London: H. Hamilton, 1957.

DOLIN, ANTON. *Autobiography.* London: Oldbourne, 1960.

————. *Divertissement.* London: S. Low, Marston, 1931.

DUNNING, JENNIFER. *"But First a School": The First Fifty Years of the School of American Ballet.* New York: Elisabeth Sifton Books/Viking, 1985.

FOKINE, M. *Memoirs of a Ballet Master.* Edited by Anatole Chujoy, translated by Vitale Fokine. Boston: Little, Brown, 1960.

GEVA, TAMARA. *Split Seconds.* New York: Harper & Row, 1972.

GOLDNER, NANCY. *The Stravinsky Festival of the New York City Ballet.* New York: Eakins Press/Viking, 1973.

GRIGORIEV, S. L. *The Diaghilev Ballet, 1909–1929.* Translated and edited by Vera Bowen. London: Constable, 1973.

HASTINGS, BAIRD. *Choreographer and Composer.* Boston: Twayne, 1983.

HUCKENPAHLER, VICTORIA. *Ballerina: A Biography of Violette Verdy.* New York: Marcel Dekker, 1978.

JAMES, EDWARD. *Swans Reflecting Elephants: My Early Years.* Edited by George Melly. London: Weidenfeld, 1982.

KANIN, GARSON. *Hollywood.* New York: Viking, 1974.

KIRSTEIN, LINCOLN. *The New York City Ballet.* New York: Knopf, 1973.

————. *Thirty Years: Lincoln Kirstein's The New York City Ballet.* New York: Knopf, 1978.

————. *Ballet: Bias and Belief.* Brooklyn, New York: Dance Horizons, 1983.

Kobbé's Complete Opera Book. Revised and edited by the Earl of Harewood. London: Putnam, 1976.

KOCHNO, BORIS. *Diaghilev and the Ballets Russes.* Translated by Adrienne Foulke. New York: Harper & Row, 1970.

LE CLERCQ, TANAQUIL. *Mourka: The Autobiography of a Cat.* With photographs by Martha Swope. New York: Stein & Day, 1964.

LIFAR, SERGE. *Serge Diaghilev: His Life, His Work, His Legend. An Intimate Biography.* New York: Putnam, 1940.

————. *Ma Vie: From Kiev to Kiev.* Translated by James Holman Mason. London: Hutchinson, 1970. (The original French edition of *Ma Vie* was published in Paris in 1965.)

MCDONAGH, DON. *George Balanchine.* Boston: Twayne, 1983.

MAIORANO, ROBERT. *Worlds Apart.* New York: Coward, McCann & Geoghegan, 1980.

————, and VALERIE BROOKS. *Balanchine's* Mozartiana: *The Making of a Masterpiece.* New York: Freundlich Books, 1985.

MARKOVA, ALICIA. *Markova Remembers.* London: H. Hamilton, 1986.

MARSHALL, DAVID. *A Modern History of Georgia.* London: Weidenfeld, 1962.

MARTIN, RALPH G. *Lincoln Center for the Performing Arts.* Englewood Cliffs, New Jersey: Prentice-Hall, 1971.

MARTINS, PETER, with ROBERT CORNFIELD. *Far from Denmark*. Boston: Little, Brown, 1982.

MAZO, JOSEPH H. *Dance Is a Contact Sport: A Season with the New York City Ballet*. New York: Saturday Review Press/Dutton, 1974.

MOORE, LILLIAN. *Echoes of American Ballet*. Edited and with an introduction by Ivor Guest. Brooklyn, New York: Dance Horizons, 1976.

NABOKOV, NICOLAS. *Old Friends and New Music*. Boston: Little, Brown, 1951.

———. *Bagazh: Memoirs of a Cosmopolitan*. New York: Atheneum, 1975.

NEWMAN, BARBARA. *Striking a Balance: Dancers Talk about Dancing*. Boston: Houghton Mifflin, 1982.

NIKITINA, ALICE. *Nikitina by Herself*. Translated by Baroness Budberg. London: Allen Wingate, 1959.

PAYNE, CHARLES. *American Ballet Theatre*. New York: Knopf, 1978.

Portrait of Mr. B. Photographs of George Balanchine, with an Essay by Lincoln Kirstein. New York: Ballet Society/Viking, 1984.

REYNOLDS, NANCY. *Repertory in Review: Forty Years of the New York City Ballet*. New York: Dial, 1977.

ROSLAVLEVA, NATALIA. *Era of the Russian Ballet, 1770–1965*. New York: Dutton, 1966.

SEROV, VICTOR. *Serge Prokofiev*. New York: Reader's Digest, 1968.

SIMMONDS, HARVEY, and LOUIS H. SILVERSTEIN, compilers; NANCY LASSALLE, ed. *Lincoln Kirstein: The Published Writings, 1922–1977*. New Haven: Yale University Library, 1978.

SLONIMSKY, YURI. "Balanchine: The Early Years," translated by John Andrews, edited by Francis Mason. *Ballet Review*, Vol. 5, No. 3 (Winter 1975–76).

SOKOLOVA, LYDIA. *Dancing for Diaghilev*. Edited by Richard Buckle. New York: Macmillan, 1961.

STRAVINSKY, IGOR. *Selected Correspondence, Volume I*. Edited and with commentaries by Robert Craft. New York: Knopf, 1982.

———. *Selected Correspondence, Volume II*. Edited and with commentaries by Robert Craft. New York: Knopf, 1984.

———, and ROBERT CRAFT. *Conversations with Igor Stravinsky*. Garden City, New York: Doubleday, 1959.

———. *Memories and Commentaries*. Garden City, New York: Doubleday, 1960.

———. *Expositions and Developments*. Garden City, New York: Doubelday, 1962.

———. *Dialogues and a Diary*. Garden City, New York: Doubleday, 1963.

STRAVINSKY, VERA, and ROBERT CRAFT. *Stravinsky in Pictures and Documents*. New York: Simon and Schuster, 1978.

TANSMAN, ALEXANDRE. *Igor Stravinsky*. Paris: Amiot-Dumont, 1948.

TAPER, BERNARD. *Balanchine*. New York: Times Books. Revised edition, 1984.

TRACY, ROBERT, with SHARON DELANO. *Balanchine's Ballerinas: Conversations with the Muses.* New York: Linden Press/Simon and Schuster, 1983.

TWYSDEN, A. E. *Alexandra Danilova.* London: Beaumont, 1945.

VOLKOV, SOLOMON. *Balanchine's Tchaikovsky.* Translated by Antonina W. Bouis. New York: Simon and Schuster, 1985.

WALKER, KATHRINE SORLEY. *De Basil's Ballets Russes.* London: Hutchinson, 1982.

WARBURG, EDWARD M. M. *As I Recall.* Clifton, New Jersey: Cameo Printing Co., n.d. (Privately printed edition limited to two hundred copies.)

WHITE, ERIC WALTER. *Stravinsky: The Composer and His Works.* Berkeley and Los Angeles: University of California Press. Second edition, 1979.

WILSON, G. B. L. *A Dictionary of Ballet.* London: Black. Third edition, 1974.

ZORINA, VERA. *Zorina.* New York: Farrar, Straus & Giroux, 1986.

SOURCE NOTES

A distinction has been made between interviews, which were taped, and conversations, which were not. The date or approximate date of each is included in the list below. Unless otherwise stated, it took place in New York City.

ADAMS, DIANA. Interview with J. Taras, July 17 (Saratoga, N.Y.), 1984.

AROLDINGEN, KARIN VON. Interviews with R. B., June 2 and December 9, 1985.

ASHLEY, MERRILL. Interview with R. B., November 29, 1985.

BALANCHIVADZE, ANDREI M. Interviews with Kyril Fitzlyon and R. B., October 19 and 20 (Tbilisi), 1986.

BARYSHNIKOV, MIKHAIL. Conversation with R. B., December 27 (London), 1986.

BIGELOW, EDWARD. Conversation with R. B., December 7, 1983.

BOELZNER, GORDON. Interview with J. Taras and R. B., June 11, 1984; conversations with R. B., December 4, 1984; May 15 and December 2, 1985.

BOLENDER, TODD. Interview with J. Taras and R. B., June 14, 1984; conversation with R. B., May 31, 1985.

BORIS, RUTHANNA. Interview with R. B., December 3, 1985.

BROWN, VIDA. Interview with J. Taras, March 5 (Washington, D. C.), 1984.

CACCIALANZA, GISELLA. *See* CHRISTENSEN.

CAGE, BETTY. Many conversations with J. Taras and R. B., and with R. B. alone, 1983–1987.

CHRISTENSEN, LEW, and GISELLA CACCIALANZA. Interviews with J. Taras, August 6 (San Francisco), 1984.

DANILOVA, ALEXANDRA. Many conversations with J. Taras and R. B., and with R. B. alone, 1977 and 1983–1987.

DAVIDOVA, LUCIA. Interview with J. Taras and R. B., December 9, 1983; several conversations with J. Taras and R. B., and with R. B. alone, 1984–1986.

DONALDSON, VIRGINIA. Conversation with R. B., November 26, 1985.

DUELL, DANIEL. Interview with W. Lawson, July 17 (Saratoga, N. Y.), 1985.

DUNLEAVY, ROSEMARY. Interviews with R. B., June 1 and 8 and November 30, 1985.

FARRELL, SUZANNE. Conversation with R. B., August 29 (London), 1983.

FRANKLIN, FREDERIC. Interview with R. B., May 31, 1985.

GEVA, TAMARA. Many conversations with R. B., 1977 and 1983–1985.

GOLDNER, NANCY. Conversation with R. B., November 27, 1985.

HAMILTON, DR. WILLIAM. Conversation with R. B., December 12, 1985.

HIDEN, GEORGIA. Conversations with J. Taras and R. B., May 31 and June 6, 1984.

HORGAN, BARBARA. Conversations with R. B., August 26 (London), 1983, and New York, May 16, 1985. Interviews with R. B., December 2 and 12, 1985.

IRVING, ROBERT. Conversations with R. B., 1983–1986. Interview with William Lawson, July 16 (Saratoga, N.Y.), 1986.

JASINSKY, ROMAN. Interview with J. Taras and R. B., May 15, 1984.

KAI, UNA. Interview with J. Taras, June 24, 1984.

KISTLER, DARCI. Interview with R. B., November 24, 1986.

KOCHNO, BORIS. Interviews with J. Taras and R. B., September 29 and 30 (Paris), 1983. Conversations with R. B., October 16 and 18 (Paris), 1984.

KRONSTAM, HENNING. Interview with J. Taras, April 13 (Copenhagen), 1984.

LASSALLE, NANCY. Interview with R. B., December 4, 1985. Many conversations with R. B., 1983–1987.

LAVERY, SEAN. Interview with W. Lawson, July 16 (Saratoga, N.Y.), 1985. Interview with R. B., December 1, 1985. Interview with T. Lacy, April 17, 1986.

LEACH, RICHARD and KAY. Interview with R. B., December 8, 1985.

LOVE, KERMIT. Conversation with R. B., December 12, 1985.

LÜDERS, ADAM. Interview with R. B., December 11, 1985.

MCBRIDE, PAT. Interview and conversation with R. B., November 23, 1986.

MCBRIDE, PATRICIA. Interview with R. B., June 9, 1985.

MARKOVA, ALICIA. Interview with J. Taras, September 3 (London), 1983. Telephone conversation with R. B., October 9, 1983.

MAZZO, KAY. Interviews with R. B., June 6 and December 6, 1985.

MOLOSTWOFF, NATALIE. Interview with J. Taras and R. B., October 12, 1983; interview with R. B., June 3, 1985. Many conversations with J. Taras and R. B., 1983–1987.

MONCION, FRANCISCO. Interview with J. Taras, July 11 (Saratoga, N.Y.), 1984.

NABOKOFF, NATALIE (*i.e.,* NATALIE NABOKOV). Interview with J. Taras and R. B., June 13, 1984.

NABOKOV, DOMINIQUE. Conversation with J. Taras and R. B., June 5, 1984.

NEARY, PATRICIA. Interview with Balanchine and a Swiss journalist, April 14 (Zurich), 1980. Telephone conversations with R. B., February 19 (England), 1986; April 15 (Milan–England), 1986.

NUREYEV, RUDOLF. Conversations with R. B., January 15 (New York) and September 30 (Paris), 1983.

O'BRIEN, SHAUN. Interview with W. Lawson, July 17 (Saratoga), 1985.

REED, JANET. Interview with J. Taras, October 10, 1983.

REIMAN, ELISE. Interview with J. Taras and R. B., December 19, 1983. Many conversations with R. B., 1983–1987.

RIETI, VITTORIO. Interviews with J. Taras and R. B., November 26, 1983.

SANDBACH, ROBERT. Conversation with J. Taras and R. B., December 9, 1983.

SCHAUFUSS, PETER. Conversation with R. B., November 15 (London), 1986.

SCHORER, SUKI. Interview with R. B., December 10, 1985.

SOTO, JOCK. Interview with W. Lawson, July 17 (Saratoga, N.Y.), 1985.

STRAVINSKY, VERA. Conversation with R. B., May 11, 1977.

TALLCHIEF, MARIA. Interviews with J. Taras and R. B., June 7 and 8 (Chicago), 1984.

TER-ARUTUNIAN, ROUBEN. Interview with R. B., November 30, 1985; many conversations with R. B., 1983–1986.

TOBIAS, ROY. Interview with J. Taras, November (Tokyo), 1984.

TOUMANOVA, TAMARA. Interviews with J. Taras, August 1, 2, 3 (Hollywood), 1983.

TYLER, KEVIN. Interview with R. B., June 9, 1985.

VAZQUEZ, ROLAND. Interview with W. Lawson, July 15 (Saratoga, N.Y.), 1985.

VERDY, VIOLETTE. Interview with W. Lawson, July 29, 1985.

VILLELLA, EDWARD. Interview with R. B., November 30, 1985.

VOLKOV, SOLOMON. Conversation with R. B., December 3, 1986.

ZORINA, VERA. Conversation with J. Taras and R. B., May 22, 1984; conversations with R. B., November 30 and December 6, 1984.

1. A GEORGIAN IN ST. PETERSBURG: 1904–1924

p. 5: *bishop of Kutaisi.:* A. M. Balanchivadze interview.

p. 5: *in 1897.: New Grove Encyclopedia of Music,* p. 57; *Great Soviet Encyclopedia,* p. 577.

p. 5: *one quarter German.:* A. M. Balanchivadze interview.

p. 5: *Kirochnaya Street: Ibid.*

p. 6: *Glinka's letters.:* The edition was published to celebrate the fiftieth anniversary of Glinka's death. The editor, Nicolai Findeizen, wrote in his preface that the book was due to "the initiative of the well-known Georgian musical figure, M. A. Balanchivadze . . ."; and added that "the esteemed M. A. Balanchivadze made publication possible." (Information kindly provided by Dr. David Brown, University of Southampton [England].)

p. 6: *allowed to keep his house . . . :* A. M. Balanchivadze interview.

p. 6: *angel-like delicacy.:* Solomon Volkov, *Balanchine's Tchaikovsky,* p. 46.

p. 6: *wonderful cook . . . :* S. Volkov, p. 91.

p. 7: *tears to his eyes.:* Bernard Taper, *Balanchine,* p. 31. I repeated this story to A. M. Balanchivadze, who said, "It's possible."

p. 7: *would see him crying.:* A. M. Balanchivadze interview.

p. 7: *Andrei a composer.: Ibid.*

p. 7: *on the piano.: Ibid.*

p. 8: *sister and brother were accepted . . . :* B. Taper, p. 37.

p. 8: *he was discovered.:* A. M. Balanchivadze interview.

p. 9: *". . . play the piano.":* S. Volkov, p. 42.

p. 9: *. . . and Pinkerton.: Ibid.,* pp. 42, 43.

p. 10: *Hop o' My Thumb.:* A. Danilova, letter to R. B., February 24, 1985. She wrote that the boys from the school appeared "in the entourage of Carabos [*sic*]" and also in "the seven brothers."

p. 10: *was determined.:* B. Taper, pp. 38, 39.

p. 10: *Marius followed him.:* Lillian Moore, *Echoes of American Ballet.*

p. 11: *of consumption.:* S. Volkov, p. 64.

p. 11: *". . . in* The Nutcracker.": *Ibid.,* p. 56.

p. 11: *". . . the Maryinsky.": Ibid.,* p. 64.

p. 11: *". . . miss a thing.":* B. Taper, p. 40.

p. 11: *Alexandra Danilova:* A. Danilova, *Choura,* p. 43.

p. 12: *"Liszt's* Préludes.": S. Volkov, p. 162.

p. 12: *occupied by the army.:* B. Taper, p. 47.

p. 12: *in Petrograd:* A. M. Balanchivadze interview.

p. 13: *loving Georgi and Andrei:* Letter in the possession of A. M. Balanchivadze, translated by Kyril Fitzlyon.

p. 13: *finally a priest.:* A. M. Balanchivadze interview.

p. 13: *on the Neva.:* B. Taper, p. 47.

p. 13: *skinned them, . . . :* A. M. Balanchivadze interview.

p. 14: *". . . one after the other.":* S. Volkov, p. 68.

p. 14: *boys' quarters. . . . :* B. Taper, p. 50. He quotes the letter Vera Kostrovitskaya wrote him.

p. 14: *". . . serious for his years.":* A. Danilova, p. 42.

p. 15: *lent him books.: Ibid.,* p. 43.

p. 15: *at the Conservatory.: Ibid.*

p. 15: *something else. . . . : Ibid.,* p. 44.

p. 16: *". . . take it seriously.": Ibid.,* p. 49.

p. 16: *". . . for ballet rehearsal.":* S. Volkov, p. 57.

p. 16: *Saint-Saëns.:* Mikhail Mikhailov, "My Classmate: George Balanchivadze." Extracts from *Life in Ballet,* ed. D. I. Zolotinsky: Leningrad & Moscow: Iskusstvo, 1966, published in *Dance News,* March and April 1967.

p. 16: *spit blood:* A. M. Balanchivadze interview.

p. 17: *pas de deux from* Swan Lake.: M. Mikhailov, *op. cit.*

p. 17: *Danilova, among others:* A. Danilova, letter to R. B.

p. 17: *demi-caractère performer.:* A. Danilova, letter to R. B., February 24, 1985.

p. 18: *his horizons.:* A. Danilova, p. 58.

p. 18: *State Theater disapproved . . . :* T. Geva's comment written to R. B. on an early draft of this chapter.

p. 18: *velvet gowns and earrings.:* Told to Lincoln Kirstein by Kyra Blanc, who had a school in Moscow. From Kirstein's unpublished diary, July 8, 1934.

p. 18: *"plastic.":* G. B. conversations with R. B.

p. 18: *180 degrees.:* The information about Goleizovsky's influence on Balanchine is from J. Taras.

p. 18: *in 1922:* Yuri Slonimsky, "Balanchine: The Early Years," p. 42.

p. 18: *kneeling or recumbent.:* Illustration reproduced in N. Roslavleva, facing p. 192.

p. 19: *"hissing and applause":* Ibid., p. 202.

p. 19: *never repeated.:* Ibid.

p. 19: *hair long.:* Photograph in B. Taper, p. 63. Balanchivadze is clearly wearing black eye make-up.

p. 19: *black shirt.:* Aileen Elizabeth Twysden, *Alexandra Danilova*, pp. 46, 47. Also Danilova conversation with J. Taras and R. B.

p. 19: *Diaghilev Ballet.:* A. Danilova, letter to R. B., March 25, 1985.

p. 20: *". . . poet and general.":* Tamara Geva, *Split Seconds,* p. 272.

p. 20: *became friends.:* Ibid., pp. 270, 272, 277–79.

p. 20: *he was ill.:* T. Geva's comment, written on an early draft of this chapter.

p. 20: *never stood up for her.:* T. Geva, p. 285.

p. 20: *never saw her again.:* A. M. Balanchivadze interview.

p. 20: Marche funèbre.: *Choreography* quotes Balanchine's recollection.

p. 21: *". . . arms extended . . .":* Kostrovitskaya quoted in Y. Slonimsky, p. 50.

p. 21: *Vsevolod Meyerhold.:* Y. Slonimsky, p. 52.

p. 21: *played by Meyerhold.:* M. Fokine, *Memoirs of a Ballet Master,* p. 136 and fn.

p. 21: *music alone:* S. Volkov, p. 163.

p. 22: *friend of Georgi's father . . . :* T. Geva, p. 247.

p. 22: *from Kutaisi.:* A. M. Balanchivadze interview.

p. 22: *held out his arms.:* T. Geva, pp. 287–89.

p. 22: *". . . on our own.":* S. Volkov, p. 59.

p. 22: *black eyeshadow.:* T. Geva, pp. 295–96.

p. 22: *"I was.":* A. Danilova, letter to R. B., March 25, 1985.

p. 23: *"completely impassive.":* T. Geva, pp. 295–96.

p. 23: *". . . much about it.":* Ibid., p. 305.

p. 23: *last act . . . :* First performed September 15, 1923. The Mikhailovsky Theater was later called the Maly Opera Theater, and the Eakins Press *Choreography* refers to it by that name.

p. 24: *to the audience.:* Y. Slonimsky, p. 59.

p. 24: *at the Theater School.*: A. Danilova, p. 63.

p. 24: *in Western Europe.*: S. Volkov, pp. 214, 215.

p. 24: *in 1922 . . .* : A. Danilova, conversation with R. B., 1983. She said that she and G. B. had known Dmitriev a year or two before they left Russia.

p. 25: *"sawn-off fingers."*: N. Molostwoff conversations.

p. 25: *nature of the agreement.*: A copy of the contract was preserved by G. B. Translation by Nathalie Gleboff.

p. 26: *fake an accident.*: S. Volkov, pp. 146, 147.

p. 26: *rammed her.*: T. Geva, pp. 310–19.

p. 26: *". . . as Tamara described."*: A. Danilova letter, to R.B.

p. 26: *commissar of the State Theater.*: A. Danilova, p. 61.

2. IN WESTERN EUROPE: SUMMER 1924–WINTER 1932

p. 27: *a recital.*: Information supplied by Tamara Geva after reading an early draft of this chapter.

p. 28: *November 1.*: A copy of this document was preserved by Balanchine.

p. 28: *"Lousy music."*: A. Danilova, pp. 64, 65.

p. 28: *four weeks:* Programs in the Theatre Museum, London.

p. 28: *Fyodor Lopoukhov.*: A.E. Twysden, p. 53.

p. 28: *April 3, 1925.*: A copy was preserved by Balanchine.

p. 28: *rue du Pont-Neuf:* G.B. conversations with R.B.

p. 29: *taught her:* A.E. Twysden, p. 55.

p. 29: *of the group or none.*: G.B. conversations with R.B.

p. 29: *funds for all of them.*: A. Danilova, p. 67.

p. 30: *' Letter follows . . . '*: Telegram in Stravinsky-Diaghilev Foundation, New York.

p. 30: *to leave Russia.*: G.B. conversations with R.B.

p. 31: Children's Tales: Programs in the Theatre Museum, London.

p. 32: *less than indifferent . . .*: Ninette de Valois, *Come Dance with Me*, p. 68. (In "A Conversation with Alexandra Danilova," *Ballet Review*, Vol. 4, No. 4, p. 40, Danilova said, "He was excellent dancer, very able. I was always amused that Ninette de Valois never want to give him credit.")

p. 32: *new choreographer . . .*: Ibid., p. 68.

p. 32: *George Balanchin.*: Program in the Theatre Museum, London.

p. 33: *"imaginative facility. . . ."*: De Valois, p. 68.

p. 33: *for the rehearsals.*: Although the Addenda to the Eakins Press *Choreography* states that *L'Enfant* was not choreographed by Balanchine, both Danilova and Markova distinctly remember working on it and being rehearsed by him.

p. 33: *watch his rehearsals.*: G.B. conversations with R.B.

p. 33: *by trifles.*: B. Kochno interview.

p. 34: *". . . sure of yourself!"*: G.B. conversations with R.B.

p. 34: *from Marks to Markova.*: A. Markova interview with John Taras and subsequent telephone conversations with R.B.

p. 34: *soprano voice.*: G.B. conversations with R.B.

p. 34: *a rabbit: Ibid.*

p. 34: *come out right.*: A. Markova interview.

p. 35: *nothing to do with him.*: B. Kochno, "Balanchine: "L'Apesanteur et la grâce," interview in *Le Nouvel Observateur,* September 23–29, 1983.

p. 35: *leggings in class.*: A. Danilova, p. 73.

p. 35: *back again.*: G.B. conversations with R.B.

p. 35: *first night of* Rossignol: The first performance of Balanchine's version of *Le Chant du rossignol* is always recorded by historians as taking place in Paris on June 17, 1925, but see B. Kochno, pp. 141–144.

p. 36: *". . . understood orchestration."*: *Ibid.*

p. 36: *a Spanish marquis.*: T. Geva, pp. 344 *et seq.* Tamara Geva confuses the story slightly by having the Diaghilev Ballet go to Barcelona in 1926 instead of 1925.

p. 36: *her address . . .*: G. B., letter from Paris to Diaghilev in Italy, September 15, 1925. Dance Collection, Library and Museum of the Performing Arts, Lincoln Center, New York.

p. 37: *". . . aloud and throughout."*: Remark by T. Geva during a symposium on June 11, 1983. Transcript in *Ballet Review,* Vol. 11, No. 4.

p. 38: *likely backer.*: Richard Buckle, *Diaghilev,* p. 463.

p. 38: *support her properly.*: Lydia Sokolova, ed. R.B., *Dancing for Diaghilev,* p. 244.

p. 38: *". . . were everything."*: G.B. conversations with R.B.

p. 38: *"messy" libretto: Ibid.*

p. 38: *until 1929.*: Beecham's opinion is given in a letter of Lady Cunard's to Diaghilev, now in the Dance Collection, Library and Museum of the Performing Arts, Lincoln Center, New York. Newman's review was in the *Sunday Times* (London), September 4, 1926.

p. 39: *". . . throw it away."*: G.B. conversations with R.B.

p. 39: *". . . great and complete."*: *Ibid.*

p. 39: *Italian art?*: B. Kochno interview.

p. 39: *on September 14 . . .*: Telegram in Stravinsky-Diaghilev Foundation, New York.

p. 40: *". . . blustering confidence."*: Cyril Beaumont, *Bookseller at the Ballet* (London: C. W. Beaumont, 1975), pp. 351, 352.

p. 40: *". . . white dress . . ."*: A. Danilova, p. 82.

p. 40: *would not tell her.*: *Ibid.*

p. 41: *"It suits you."*: *Ibid.,* pp. 84, 85.

p. 41: *passage of dancing . . .* : G.B. conversations with R.B.

p. 41: *several companies.:* J. Taras's comment.

p. 42: *". . . time to rest.":* Dale Harris, "Balanchine on Stravinsky," *Keynote,* June 1982, p. 19.

p. 42: *a new work.:* B. Kochno conversations with R.B.

p. 42: *"Congratulations!":* G.B. conversations with R.B.

p. 42: *". . . turn very well.":* *Ibid.*

p. 42: *". . . don't think.":* *Ibid.*

p. 42: *including herself.:* A. Danilova conversation with R.B.

p. 43: *"clap her hands.":* G.B. letter to Diaghilev, September 28, 1927. Dance Collection, Library and Museum of the Performing Arts, Lincoln Center, New York.

p. 43: *". . . easy at first.":* G.B. letter to Diaghilev, undated. Dance Collection.

p. 43: *first time:* Stravinsky, telegram to Diaghilev, January 22, 1928. Stravinsky-Diaghilev Foundation, New York.

p. 43: *on Danilova.:* A. Danilova conversation with R.B.

p. 44: *"almost a joke.":* G. B. conversations with R.B.

p. 44: *"undanceable.":* *Ibid.*

p. 44: *discuss projects:* A. Danilova, p. 83.

p. 45: *classical ballet step.:* The account of *Apollon* is an extract from a much longer one by John Taras. Gordon Boelzner also contributed.

p. 45: *Piccadilly Circus.:* Told by Balanchine to J. Taras.

p. 46: *". . . father calling.":* G. Boelzner's recollection.

p. 46: *immediately after it):* The *Mask,* Vol. XV, No. 2, reprinted *Rood, Dance Horizons,* 1977.

p. 47: *"not much with him.":* The *Times* (London), June 26, 1928.

p. 47: *to cut it.:* A. Danilova, p. 98.

p. 47: *" '. . . no good.' ":* G.B. conversations with R.B.

p. 47: *turned out for the best.:* A. Danilova, p. 98.

p. 47: *to Monte Carlo.:* Beecham telegraphed from London to Diaghilev in Monte Carlo, April 30, 1928: "Handel music dispatched today." Stravinsky-Diaghilev Foundation, New York.

p. 47: *". . . pastoral allegories.":* B. Kochno, *Serge Diaghilev,* p. 268.

p. 47: *". . . bread and butter.":* A. Danilova conversation with R.B.

p. 48: *divorced Kniaseff.:* Kochno archives. This and other letters to Boris Kochno were translated from Russian into French by M. Kochno on October 15, 1984, and later from French into English by R.B.

p. 48: *"4,000 [francs].":* Telegram from Diaghilev in Berlin to Grigoriev in Paris, October 10, 1928. Stravinsky-Diaghilev Foundation, New York.

p. 48: *was unsuccessful.:* A. Danilova, p. 85.

p. 48: *". . . names on poster.":* Telegram, dated October 12, 1928, in Stravinsky-Diaghilev Foundation, New York.

p. 48: *Le Bal.:* B. Kochno conversations with R.B.

p. 49: *". . . such a fool.":* G.B. conversations with R.B.

p. 49: *". . . last few years.":* *Morning Post* (London), July 9, 1929.

p. 49: *dramatize it.:* S. Lifar, *Diaghilev,* p. 498.

p. 50: *". . . a thing about ballet . . .":* S. Volkov, p. 210.

p. 50: *was his.:* G.B. interview with Nancy Reynolds, reported by her in *Repertory in Review,* p. 106 fn.

p. 51: *"hang onto that.":* A. Danilova, p. 89.

p. 51: *". . . were crying.":* S. Lifar, *Serge Diaghilev,* p. 582.

p. 52: *generous Balanchine.:* G.B. conversations with R.B.

p. 52: *went away.:* John Gruen, "An Olympian Apollo," *Dance Magazine,* April 1981, p. 86.

p. 52: Aurora's Wedding . . .: The *Times* (London), July 13, 1929.

p. 52: *London season:* A. Danilova, p. 106, places Diaghilev's farewell in Vichy, but this is surely wrong. See R. Buckle, *Diaghilev,* pp. 533–35.

p. 52: *in his life.:* G.B. conversations with R.B.

p. 53: *Dolin and himself.:* *Dark Red Roses* was thought to be lost, but in 1984, during research for *Balanchine,* the two-part WNET/"Dance in America" program, Merrill Brockway, Judy Kinberg and Holly Brubach heard that a nitrate print of the old movie had been found in a farmhouse in Ireland. See Holly Brubach, "In Search of Balanchine," *Ballet News,* June 1984, p. 45.

p. 53: *front page.:* Anton Dolin, *Divertissement,* p. 214.

p. 53: *". . . took me to Florence . . .":* G.B. interview with W. McNeil Lowry, 1979, published after G.B.'s death in *The New Yorker,* September 12, 1983, p. 53.

p. 53: *"Ummm.":* *Ibid.,* p. 52.

p. 54: *returned to Paris.:* A. Danilova conversation with R.B.

p. 55: *never forget it.:* A. Danilova conversation with R.B.

p. 56: *Duke of Kent).:* G.B. conversations with R.B.

p. 56: *visa extended.:* *Ibid.*

p. 57: *wishes to Bébé [Bérard].:* B. Kochno archives. "Bébé" was Christian Bérard, the stage designer.

p. 57: *". . . doesn't love me.":* A. Danilova, p. 110.

p. 58: *Yours, G.B.:* B. Kochno archives. The Alhambra was not, in fact, to close down as soon as Balanchine believed.

p. 60: *G. Balanchivadze:* B. Kochno archives.

3. HOW KIRSTEIN BROUGHT BALANCHINE TO AMERICA:
JUNE–DECEMBER 1933

p. 61: *his troubled republic.:* When no source is given for the notes in this chapter, it can be assumed that information or reported conversations are taken from Lincoln Kirstein's unpublished diary for 1933, which he offered to R. B.

p. 62: *the Civil War.:* Facts supplied to R. B. by Lincoln Kirstein in a letter of July 30, 1983.

p. 62: *undertakings were begun.:* Information given by E. M. M. Warburg.

p. 62: *"audience for dancers":* Hound & Horn, Vol. IV, No. 4, 1931.

p. 63: *be its director.:* E. M. M. Warburg information.

p. 63: *and ungrateful.:* L. Kirstein, *Thirty Years,* p. 14.

p. 66: *". . . Igor Schwezoff":* (1904–82). Dancer, choreographer, teacher. Author of the autobiography *Borzoi* (published in England in 1935, issued in the U.S. [Harper, 1936] under the title *Russian Somersault*).

p. 66: *landed like a cat.:* R. Jasinsky interview.

p. 66: *Kirk Askew:* A partner in the firm of Durlacher. Askew was Tchelitchev's dealer in America.

p. 68: *he was homosexual.:* E. James, pp. 145, 154.

p. 69: *". . . 3 years time. . . .":* Letter in the Wadsworth Atheneum Museum archives, Hartford, Connecticut.

p. 70: *there were none.:* B. Kochno conversation.

p. 71: *back and forth:* These cables were preserved in the School of American Ballet.

p. 74: NOVEMBER FIFTEENTH.: In fact, they opened in New York on December 21.

p. 75: *. . . "a stone in my heart.":* T. Toumanova interview.

p. 75: *two months later.):* R. Jasinsky interview.

p. 79: *". . . ruins here already!":* E. M. M. Warburg letter, August 11, 1987.

4. THE SCHOOL ESTABLISHED—FIRST SKETCH FOR A COMPANY: JANUARY 1934–APRIL 1937

p. 84: *School of American Ballet.:* Unless otherwise stated, material in this chapter comes from Lincoln Kirstein's diary for 1934.

p. 85: *properly conducted.:* N. Molostwoff interview.

p. 85: *tall dancers.:* E. Reiman interview.

p. 86: *"Isn't it perfect?":* E. M. M. Warburg conversation.

p. 86: *School of American Ballet.:* E. Reiman interview.

p. 87: *". . . bite your knees.":* R. Boris interview.

p. 87: Serenade *took shape:* See L. Kirstein, *Thirty Years,* pp. 38, 39.

p. 87: *to apologize.:* R. Boris interview.

p. 88: *". . . our family place.":* E. M. M. Warburg, p. 54.

p. 88: *". . . from the shock.":* Ibid.

p. 89: *understanding of the material.:* E. M. M. Warburg letter.

p. 90: *". . . same reason as you."*: R. Boris interview.

p. 90: *until his death.*: L. Davidova interview.

p. 90: *". . . of him as a man."*: N. Nabokoff interview.

p. 91: *her whole placement.*: E. Reiman interview.

p. 91: *lesson in choreography.*: R. Boris interview.

p. 91: Serenade.: Told to J. Taras by G. Hiden.

p. 92: *". . . put them together."*: L. Christensen and G. Caccialanza interview.

p. 92: *Salvador Dali: The Hartford Daily Times*, December 7, 1934.

p. 93: Mozartiana *was classical.*: *Mozartiana,* though announced, was not performed during the season.

p. 94: *". . . hit of the evening."*: *The New York Times,* March 2 and 10, 1935.

p. 94: *". . . understand anything."*: *New York Post,* March 4, 1935.

p. 94: *" '. . . join the company?' "*: L. Christensen and G. Caccialanza interview.

p. 95: *". . . looking at his girls."*: Paul Magriel and Don McDouagh, "A Conversation with Marie-Jeanne," *Ballet Review,* Vol. 12, No. 4, p. 80.

p. 95: *the better teacher.*: *Ibid.,* p. 60.

p. 95: *". . . an American Ballet* [sic]*."*: *The New York Times,* August 18, 1935.

p. 95: *in Philadelphia.*: A. Chujoy, *The New York City Ballet,* pp. 21, 52.

p. 96: *". . . what to do."*: R. Boris interview.

p. 96: *"He never got mad."*: R. Tracy, *Balanchine's Ballerinas,* p. 72.

p. 96: *Elise Reiman recalled.*: E. Reiman interview.

p. 97: *" '. . . into this place.' "*: E. M. M. Warburg letter, August 11, 1987.

p. 97: *and spit.*: E. Reiman interview.

p. 97: *explaining to do.*: L. Christensen and G. Caccialanza interview.

p. 97: *erotic vein.*: A. Chujoy, p. 64.

p. 97: *attention to itself.*: *Ibid.*

p. 98: *" '. . . God and everybody.' "*: L. Kirstein, *Thirty Years,* pp. 67–68.

p. 98: *". . . like prima donnas."*: *New York Evening Journal,* interview with Dorothy Kilgallen, August 1935.

p. 98: *extend their powers.*: E. Reiman interview.

p. 99: *appeared as beggars.*: Information supplied by Eugene R. Gaddis.

p. 99: *kiss him, too.*: K. Love conversation.

p. 99: *". . . artist on holiday."*: *The New York Times,* April 12, 1936.

p. 99: *". . . before the orchestra . . ."*: T. Geva in a taped interview with Nancy Reynolds, Library and Museum of the Performing Arts, Lincoln Center, New York, October 19, 1972.

p. 100: *". . . things like this . . ."*: *Ibid.*

p. 100: *". . . it was very nice."*: V. Zorina, *Zorina,* p. 119.

p. 101: *". . . PROVES TRAVESTY"*: *The New York World Telegram,* May 23, 1936.

p. 101: *". . . are a part."*: *The New York Times,* May 31, 1936.

p. 101: *". . . very hard time."*: Barbara Newman, *Striking a Balance,* p. 32.

p. 101: *brought his own.*: L. Davidova interview.

p. 102: *". . . on his shoulder."*: R. Craft letter.

p. 102: *a poker game.:* V. Stravinsky and R. Craft, *Stravinsky in Pictures and Documents,* pp. 331–33.

p. 102: *Rossini's* Barber of Seville: L. Kirstein, *Thirty Years,* p. 58.

p. 102: *the Metropolitan's orchestra.: Ibid.,* p. 62.

p. 102: *Broadway musical: Choreography,* p. 136.

p. 103: *". . . false start.":* E. M. M. Warburg letter, August 11, 1987.

p. 103: *". . . in the choreography.":* L. Kirstein, "Working with Stravinsky," *Modern Music,* Vol. 14, No. 3, reprinted in *Bias and Belief,* p. 34.

p. 103: *in his ears.: Ibid.,* p. 69.

p. 104: *". . . your way out of it.":* B. Newman, pp. 36, 37.

p. 104: *". . . going to Heaven.": Ibid.,* pp. 34, 35.

p. 105: *by the hour.:* L. Christensen and G. Caccialanza interview.

p. 105: *difficult variation.:* E. Reiman conversation.

p. 105: *". . . height of his powers.":* I. Stravinsky, *Expositions and Developments,* p. 73.

p. 105: *". . . Les Noces.":* The New York Times, April 28, 1937.

p. 106: *". . . itself splendidly.":* New York Evening Post, April 28, 1937.

5. DIVERGING PATHS: APRIL 1937–MAY 1941

p. 108: *". . . refused to choreograph for us.":* Allen Ulrich with L. Christensen, *San Francisco Sunday Examiner,* May 6, 1984

p. 108: *". . . cowboy movies.":* L. Christensen and G. Caccialanza interview.

p. 108: *". . . Only one person.":* B. Taper, p. 185.

p. 108: *manage it for them.:* N. Nabokoff interview.

p. 109: *including Samuel Goldwyn.:* G. Kanin, *Hollywood,* pp. 90, 91.

p. 109: *her small son.:* N. Nabokoff interview.

p. 110: *"belch so nicely.": Ibid.*

p. 110: *treated her abominably.:* V. Zorina, pp. 97, 98.

p. 111: *working on* Goldwyn Follies.: V. Zorina conversation; see also V. Zorina, pp. 158, 159.

p. 111: *"have much fun.": Ibid.;* see also V. Zorina, p. 159.

p. 111: *on July 10:* V. Zorina, pp. 162–64.

p. 111: *ask her to dinner.: Ibid.,* pp. 164–66.

p. 111: *". . . marvelous host.": Ibid.,* pp. 166, 167.

p. 112: *process of selection.: Ibid.,* pp. 170–71.

p. 112: *four weeks of work.: Ibid.,* pp. 172, 173.

p. 113: *of the missing choreographer.:* N. Nabokoff interview.

p. 113: *". . . starlit sky.":* V. Zorina, p. 173.

p. 113: *California.:* V. Zorina conversation.

p. 113: *". . . would take time."*: V. Zorina, pp. 176, 177.

p. 114: *touch of Balanchine's):* Ibid., pp. 177, 178.

p. 114: *". . . disappearing in ocean."*: Ibid., p. 178.

p. 114: *"very sexy"*: Ibid.

p. 114: *dancers look taller.*: Ibid., pp. 188, 189.

p. 115: *". . . the real ending."*: Ibid., p. 191.

p. 115: *a few days longer.*: Ibid., p. 185.

p. 115: *"I love you" in Norwegian.*: *"Jeg elsker Dig."* Ibid., pp. 191–93.

p. 115: *by Rodgers and Hart?*: Ibid., pp. 187, 188, 194, 195.

p. 116: *dig at Balanchine.*: *The New Yorker,* June 11, 1938, pp. 27–30.

p. 117: *". . . love him to this day."*: V. Zorina interview with Nancy Reynolds, October 19, 1972. Transcript in the Library and Museum of the Performing Arts, Lincoln Center, New York.

p. 117: *"match" his love.*: V. Zorina, pp. 193, 201, 202.

p. 117: *she had ever seen.*: Ibid., p. 200.

p. 117: *". . . hands trembling."*: Ibid., p. 206.

p. 117: *of the fact.*: A. Chujoy, *The New York City Ballet,* p. 104.

p. 118: *". . . together in threes . . ."*: Article by H. Howard Taubman in unidentified newspaper, April 13, 1938.

p. 118: *into this dance:* V. Zorina conversation.

p. 118: *" '. . . in St. Moritz.' "*: V. Zorina, pp. 211, 212.

p. 118: *cut him out.*: Ibid., p. 214.

p. 118: *as a surprise.*: Ibid., pp. 219, 220, 221.

p. 118: *talked nonsense.*: N. Nabokoff interview.

p. 118: *". . . for some time"*: *The New York Times,* May 12, 1938.

p. 119: *". . . first choreographer of Broadway."*: Ibid.

p. 119: *"freshness."*: John Martin, *The New York Times,* September 8, 1940.

p. 119: *Christmas Eve supper:* N. Nabokoff interview. It was, however, Zorina who pointed out that Volodine was present.

p. 120: *no explanation was given.*: N. Nabokoff interview.

p. 120: *every skin.*: V. Zorina told R. B. that she still has the ermine coat.

p. 120: *different direction.*: N. Nabokoff interview.

p. 121: *your loving Georgi:* Undated letter in the possession of Andrei Balanchivadze, copied by Kyril Fitzlyon in Tbilisi on October 20, 1986, and later translated by him.

p. 121: *January 1939.*: *The New York Times,* January 16, 1939.

p. 121: *"Angel on Earth."*: *New York Daily News,* February 20, 1939.

p. 121: *to Mrs. Hartwig.*: V. Zorina, p. 227.

p. 121: *". . . put out the blaze."*: *New York Daily News,* February 24, 1939.

p. 122: *before his arrival.*: V. Zorina, pp. 230, 231.

p. 122: *". . . worked perfectly."*: Ibid., p. 233.

p. 122: *at the opera house.*: J. Anderson, *The One and Only,* p. 39.

p. 122: *but refused.*: Charles Payne, *American Ballet Theatre,* pp. 33, 36, 37.

p. 123: *". . . in Ballet History":* Poster of American Ballet Theatre's first season, reproduced in C. Payne, p. 46.

p. 123: *$200,000.):* C. Payne, p. 102.

p. 123: *". . . American organization . . .":* New York Herald Tribune, January 30, 1940.

p. 123: *". . . twelve times a day. . . .":* L. Kirstein, *Thirty Years,* p. 80.

p. 124: *never noticed.:* This is an extract from a detailed account by John Taras.

p. 124: *illustrous Russians.:* Numerous newspapers throughout the U.S. told the same story and used the same pictures.

p. 125: *Long Island:* Sunken Meadow Park occupies the site today. V. Zorina conversation.

p. 125: *never used it.:* V. Zorina, p. 246.

p. 125: *after the performance:* Ibid.

p. 125: *". . . uglier," she said.:* N. Nabokoff interview.

p. 125: *". . . a diamond necklace.":* T. Toumanova interview.

p. 125: *"Will people understand?":* Ibid.

p. 125: *old and rather bad photographs:* Such as those reproduced in *Dance Index,* Vol. 6, Nos. 10, 11, 12, p. 251.

p. 126: *reduced to the minimum.:* V. Zorina, pp. 249, 250.

p. 126: *American artists.:* V. Zorina, p. 249.

p. 126: *" '. . . in New York?' ":* Ibid.

p. 126: *until his death:* N. Molostwoff interview.

p. 126: *upper story of the School.:* New York Herald Tribune, April 1, 1941.

p. 127: *". . . destroyed me.":* N. Molostwoff interview.

6. SOUTH AMERICAN ADVENTURE: MAY–DECEMBER 1941

p. 129: *vocabulary of Petipa.:* J. Taras's comment.

p. 130: *for a corps de ballet.:* Ibid.

p. 130: *Peter and Paul.:* This account of *Ballet Imperial* is taken from a much longer description written by J. Taras.

p. 131: *"You'll never learn!":* G. Hiden conversation.

p. 131: *skip a meal:* John Taras diary.

p. 131: *never recurred.:* Quoted from J. Taras's specially written account, but see also Paul Magriel and Don McDonagh, "A Conversation with Marie-Jeanne," *Ballet Review,* Vol. 12, No. 4, pp. 40–42.

p. 131: *hurt her feet.:* L. Christensen and G. Caccialanza interview.

p. 131: *Lew Christensen said.:* Ibid.

p. 132: *pose to another.:* J. Taras's indication.

p. 132: *ever made on her.:* P. Magriel and D. McDonagh, *op. cit.,* p. 63.

p. 133: *fell apart with laughter.:* L. Christensen and G. Caccialanza interview.

p. 133: *took pictures.:* L. Kirstein, *Bias and Belief,* p. 83.

p. 133: *". . . 'organized chaos.' ":* G. Hiden conversation.

p. 133: *fell flat.: Ibid.*

p. 134: *asking for Dollar.:* J. Taras's recollection.

p. 134: *Argentinean winter.:* T. Bolender interview.

p. 135: *in the car.:* G. Hiden conversation.

p. 135: *on the stage.: Ibid.*

p. 135: *". . . shelf of green. ":* T. Bolender interview.

p. 136: *in North America.:* L. Kirstein, *Bias and Belief,* p. 90.

p. 136: *represented Rockefeller.:* L. Kirstein, *Thirty Years,* pp. 86, 87.

p. 136: *and sugar.:* J. Taras diary.

p. 136: *speak to the driver.:* G. Hiden conversation.

p. 137: *". . . damn near died. ":* L. Christensen and G. Caccialanza interview.

p. 137: *took photographs.:* L. Kirstein, *Bias and Belief,* p. 93.

p. 137: *return to the Colón.: Ibid.,* p. 90.

7. GETTING THROUGH THE WAR: DECEMBER 1941–OCTOBER 1945

p. 139: *for twenty-two years.:* L. Kirstein, "Stardom: Slav and Native," *Dance Magazine,* Vol. 4, No. 3, pp. 14–15. Reprinted in Kirstein, *Bias and Belief,* p. 44.

p. 140: *war charity.:* V. Zorina, pp. 258–61.

p. 140: *in the sawdust: Ibid.,* p. 260.

p. 140: *". . . Mozart ever wrote!":* G. Hiden conversation.

p. 141: *saw her again.:* V. Zorina, pp. 264–70.

p. 141: *". . . artistic genius.":* R. Tracy, p. 81.

p. 141: *putting on weight.:* N. Molostwoff conversation.

p. 142: *". . . in New York City. ":* R. Tracy, pp. 86, 87.

p. 142: *". . . a real crush. ":* F. Moncion interview.

p. 142: *". . . in* This Is the Army." A copy was kept among Balanchine's papers at the School.

p. 142: *salary was doubled.:* R. Tracy, p. 87.

p. 143: *a* "soubrette.": *Time,* May 17, 1943.

p. 144: *Sincerely yours, George Balanchine:* A copy of the letter is preserved among Balanchine's papers at the School.

p. 144: *were printed.:* Poster reproduced in C. Payne, p. 129.

p. 145: *". . . I'd yell at Hurok.":* G. Hiden conversation.

p. 145: *the whole Ballet Russe.:* J. Anderson, p. 90.

p. 145: *and they agreed.: Ibid.*

p. 145: *Goddard Lieberson.:* V. Zorina conversation.

p. 146: *". . . dear to me indeed.":* F. Franklin interview.

p. 147: *eyes lit up.: Ibid.*

p. 147: *at City Center.:* J. Anderson, p. 91.

p. 147: *more brightly still.:* Edwin Denby, *New York Herald Tribune,* September 17, 1944.

p. 148: *studying with Balanchine.:* M. Tallchief interview.

p. 149: *devoid of dancing.: The New York Times,* September 11, 1944.

p. 149: *Henry James: New York Herald Tribune,* September 17, 1944.

p. 149: *seventeenth century.: The New York Times,* February 22, 1945.

p. 149: *not the choreographer. . . .: The New York Times,* September 15, 1944.

p. 149: *". . . a million years.":* Claudia Cassidy, *Chicago Tribune,* October 8, 1944.

p. 149: *". . . for* Ballet Imperial.": R. Boris interview.

p. 150: *"That old ballet!":* V. Rieti interview.

p. 150: *in Houston.:* J. Anderson, p. 100.

p. 150: *". . . fun, glory and drinks.": Ibid.,* p. 99. Letter from S. J. Denham to "Dear Marion" (unidentified), dated December 21, 1944.

p. 150: *to bed with her.:* R. Boris interview.

p. 151: *gold cigarette case.: The New York Times,* March 18, 1945.

p. 151: *share his sorrow.:* R. Boris interview.

p. 151: *Then he walked away.: Ibid.*

p. 152: *need assistance.:* The wording of this letter, as well as its typing, was undoubtedly the work of Natalie Molostwoff. A copy of the letter is preserved among Balanchine's papers.

p. 152: *him and Brigitta:* G. Hiden conversation.

p. 152: *". . . getting a divorce.":* V. Zorina conversation.

p. 153: WAS FYODOR.: V. Stravinsky and R. Craft, p. 467. Retrospective caption to illustration of Stravinsky with G. B. on the composer's eightieth birthday.

p. 153: Comedia Balletica.: T. Bolender interview.

p. 154: *". . . he just loves it . . .": Ibid.*

p. 154: *got together:* J. Taras's recollection.

p. 154: *of his troubles.: Ibid.* Also T. Bolender interview.

p. 154: *". . . a lot from Petipa.": Ibid.* T. Bolender interview.

p. 155: *only solution.:* N. Nabokoff interview.

p. 155: *"George who?":* Conversation reported to J. Taras by Vida Brown.

8. NEW BEGINNINGS: NOVEMBER 1945–APRIL 1948

p. 156: *line would improve.:* M. Tallchief interview.

p. 157: *in his hands.: Ibid.*

p. 158: *he follows her.:* This account of the pas de deux is by J. Taras.

p. 158: *". . . pathos and beauty"*: Kobbé's *Complete Opera Book*, p. 505.

p. 158: *". . . a heaving floor."*: *Dance Magazine*, November 1946.

p. 159: *with the composer.*: *Dearest Bubushkin*, p. 136. Entry in Mrs. Stravinsky's diary for April 4, 1946.

p. 159: *scenario of* Orpheus: *Ibid.*

p. 159: *string ties.*: M. Tallchief interview.

p. 160: *unheard of:* A. Chujoy, *The New York City Ballet*, p. 158.

p. 161: *". . . magic on the stage."*: *Ibid.*, p. 159.

p. 161: *new to New York: L'Enfant et les sortilèges* had, however, been performed in San Francisco in 1930.

p. 162: *". . . you can do with it!"*: T. Bolender interview.

p. 162: *". . . for $250."*: Letter from Ernest Voigt, representing Hindemith, September 27, 1940.

p. 162: *was set aside.*: L. Kirstein, *Thirty Years*, p. 92.

p. 163: *". . . plan caught on."*: A. Chujoy, *The New York City Ballet*, p. 162.

p. 163: *". . . dancer who was no good. . . ."*: A copy of the typed letter was kept by Balanchine, September 11, 1946.

p. 163: *the secret.*: M. Tallchief interview.

p. 164: *drank wine.*: *Ibid.*

p. 164: *for Sérénade. . . .*: Mina Curtiss, *Other People's Letters*, pp. 74, 75.

p. 165: *scared to death.*: M. Tallchief interview.

p. 165: *much praised.*: A. Chujoy, *The New York City Ballet*, p. 176.

p. 165: *Palace of Diamonds:* Typescript in the Dance Collection of the Library and Museum of the Performing Arts, Lincoln Center, New York.

p. 166: *made on her.*: M. Tallchief interview.

p. 166: *New York at last.*: *Ibid.*

p. 167: *". . . do it first."*: *Ibid.*

p. 167: *"how much he suffered."*: *Dearest Bubushkin*, p. 142.

p. 167: *November 11, 1947.*: A. Chujoy, *The New York City Ballet*, p. 177.

p. 168: *work of genius.*: C. Payne, p. 154.

p. 169: *She was hired:* B. Cage conversations.

p. 169: *same program.*: I. Stravinsky, *Selected Correspondence, Vol. 1*, p. 265.

p. 169: *thirty-six strings.*: *Ibid.*, p. 266.

p. 169: *orchestrating the ballet.*: Eric Walter White, *Stravinsky*, p. 440.

p. 169: *received copies:* I. Stravinsky, *Selected Correspondence, Vol. I*, p. 268.

p. 169: *to play it.*: M. I. Tallchief interview.

p. 169: *into the score.*: *Ibid.*

p. 169: *was adopted.*: I. Stravinsky and R. Craft, *Dialogues and a Diary*, p. 78 fn.

p. 170: *". . . Russian direction . . ."*: Nicholas Nabokov, *Old Friends and New Music*, pp. 221–222.

p. 170: *they were shown.*: *Dearest Bubushkin*, p. 144.

p. 170: *a chef's hat.*: Note from G.B. to M. Tallchief.

p. 170: *word he said.:* M. Tallchief interview.

p. 171: *". . . kind of thing.":* N. Reynolds, p. 83.

p. 171: *of her career.: Ibid.*

p. 171: *". . . chalk on blackboard!":* F. Moncion interview.

p. 171: *". . . his* Symphony in C.": A. Chujoy, *Dance News,* April 1948. Quoted in Reynolds, p. 86.

p. 171: *". . . familiar tricks . . .":* The New York Times, March 23, 1948, quoted in *ibid.*

p. 172: *". . . you boys together.":* F. Moncion interview.

p. 172: *a great venture.: Ibid.*

p. 172: *went on diets.: Ibid.*

p. 173: *to take class.: Ibid.*

p. 173: *"great days": Ibid.*

p. 173: *". . . no less.":* L. Kirstein, *Thirty Years,* p. 99.

p. 173: *robbed a bank.: Ibid.,* pp. 100, 101.

p. 174: *subsequent revivals.:* J. Taras's account, written November 25, 1984.

p. 174: *". . . very happy.":* A. Chujoy, *The New York City Ballet,* p. 201.

p. 174: *"Too good to be true":* L. Kirstein, *Thirty Years,* p. 102.

p. 174: *"short and irritable.": Ibid.*

p. 175: *an American ballet.:* A. Chujoy, *The New York City Ballet,* pp. 202–3.

p. 175: *than before.: Ibid.,* pp. 204, 205.

p. 175: *to tell Balanchine.: Ibid.,* p. 203.

9. IN SEARCH OF A FORMULA: 1948–1957

p. 176: *New York City Ballet.:* U. Kai interview.

p. 178: *to applaud him.:* The New York Times, November 9, 1948, quoted in A. Chujoy, *The New York City Ballet,* p. 209.

p. 178: *company had increased.: Ibid.,* p. 211.

p. 178: *as a choreographer.:* N. Reynolds, p. 86.

p. 179: *". . . Well . . . perhaps.":* M. Tallchief interview.

p. 179: *for $2,500,:* B. Cage conversation. Hurok later tried to maintain that this sum was only for the rental of the properties.

p. 180: *new version . . . would take.:* M. Tallchief interview.

p. 180: *in New York.:* Copy of cable from David Webster, June 10, 1949, retained in the archives of the Royal Opera House, Covent Garden.

p. 180: *". . . Orpheus for them?":* B. Cage, letter to G.B., June 13, 1949.

p. 180: *discuss matters then.:* Copy of cable sent by B. Cage, June 20, 1949, on behalf of G.B.

p. 180: *debut of Sadler's Wells:* Copy of letter to L. Kirstein, August 29, 1949.

p. 181: *". . . from our school.":* L. Kirstein letter to R.B., September 10, 1949.

p. 181: *There was no time.:* N. Reynolds, p. 98.

p. 181: *". . . a football stadium.":* Ibid.

p. 182: *". . . from the audience.":* Time, December 12, 1949, quoted in *ibid.*, p. 96.

p. 182: *a firebird on it.:* M. Tallchief interview.

p. 182: *price of the materials.:* A. Chujoy, *The New York City Ballet*, p. 223.

p. 182: *good as Robbins.:* V. Stravinsky conversation.

p. 182: *". . . at double speed!":* M. Somes letter to R.B., May 21, 1984.

p. 182: *second movement:* M. Somes conversation during the 1960s.

p. 182: *all the pantomime.:* J. Taras's observation.

p. 183: *". . . to extract it.":* B. Grey, letter to R.B., May 20, 1984.

p. 183: *"Kitty, kittteee . . .":* Washington Star, June 19, 1972.

p. 183: *Ballet Imperial.:* L. Kirstein, *Thirty Years*, p. 112.

p. 183: *". . . almost like New York.":* G.B. letter to M. Tallchief, handwritten; undated, but clearly April 7, 1950.

p. 184: *tour was also planned.:* B. Cage conversation.

p. 184: *"Beaumont, Beaumont!":* P. Schaufuss conversation.

p. 184: *". . . undramatic or mild.":* Manchester Guardian, July 10, 1950.

p. 184: *and Croydon.:* B. Cage conversation.

p. 185: *"plain bad.":* A. Chujoy, *The New York City Ballet*, pp. 242, 243.

p. 185: *thirty-three years later.:* In 1952, 1964 and 1979.

p. 185: *for them:* For the Royal Ballet: *Serenade*, 1950; *Apollo*, 1964; *The Four Temperaments, Prodigal Son, Agon, Allegro Brillante*, 1973; *Concerto Barocco, Liebeslieder Walzer*, 1977. For Festival Ballet: *Bourrée fantasque*, 1960; *Night Shadow*, 1967; *Tchaikovsky Pas de deux*, 1972; *Symphony in C*, 1986.

p. 185: *fanned by eunuchs.:* This phrase is the author's, but it summarizes opinions expressed to him by L. Davidova.

p. 186: *walk on newspaper.:* L. Davidova conversation.

p. 186: *a game with her.:* E. Reiman conversation.

p. 186: *". . . liked Lew.":* M. Tallchief interview.

p. 186: *never forgave him.:* Ravel refused even to shake hands with Diaghilev, and turned away without speaking when they ran into each other in Monte Carlo at the time of the rehearsals of *L'Enfant* in 1924. Boris Kochno, who was present, told R.B. this.

p. 188: *"like going to a party.":* N. Reynolds, pp. 118, 119.

p. 188: *out of the steps.:* Ibid., p. 119.

p. 188: *". . . to destruction.":* Ibid.

p. 188: *heedless whirling.:* Doris Hering in *Dance Magazine*, April 1951, quoted in N. Reynolds, p.118.

p. 189: *avant-garde tradition.:* U. Kai interview.

p. 190: *recorded in 1947,:* R. Sandbach conversation.

p. 190: *". . . knows it immediately.":* Ballet, Vol. 12, No. 9, September 1952.

p. 190: *the man.:* B. Cage conversation.

p. 190: *every day.: Ibid.*

p. 190: *from Morton Baum.:* B. Cage letter from New York to G.B. in Milan, March 10, 1952.

p. 190: *". . . that's definite.:":* G.B. handwritten letter from Milan to B. Cage in New York, undated, but about March 13, 1952.

p. 191: *impressed him enormously.:* B. Cage conversation.

p. 191: *first intermission.:* J. Taras's recollection.

p. 191: *doves was released.:* A. Chujoy, *The New York Ballet,* pp. 340, 341.

p. 191: *during performances.:* B. Cage conversation.

p. 191: *Edinburgh Festival.:* L. Kirstein letter from New York to B. Cage in Paris, May 9, 1952.

p. 191: *". . . I am talking . . .":* L. Kirstein letter from New York to B. Cage in Florence, May 14, 1952.

p. 192: *". . . a third arabesque.":* E. Bigelow conversation.

p. 192: *". . . carnivorous lizards, etc.":* G.B. letter to B. Cage.

p. 192: *". . . screwing a steak.":* K. Tyler's recollection.

p. 192: *". . . something sacred.":* R. Tobias interview.

p. 194: *love George.:* G.B. in London to L. Kirstein in New York, letter dated August 4, 1952, undoubtedly typed by B. Cage.

p. 194: *". . . calling a meeting.":* L. Kirstein in New York to B. Cage in London, August 7, 1952.

p. 194: *tartan kilts:* U. Kai interview.

p. 194: *principals of his company:* M. Tallchief interview.

p. 195: *on the worse.:* B. Cage conversation.

p. 195: *fell on his head.:* M. Tallchief interview.

p. 195: *exhausted by the tour.:* A. Chujoy, *The New York Ballet,* p. 357.

p. 195: *Paris Opéra.: Ibid.,* p. 344.

p. 195: *sold out.: Ibid.,* p. 350.

p. 195: *". . . from New York.": Ibid.,* p. 351.

p. 195: *for a week.: Ibid.,* p. 355.

p. 195: *to see them.: Ibid.,* pp. 361, 362.

p. 195: *in Berlin.: Ibid.,* p. 362.

p. 195: *permanent base.: Ibid.,* p. 351.

p. 195: *so had Balanchine.:* B. Cage letter to L. Kirstein in New York; date indecipherable, but sometime in June 1952.

p. 196: *by comparison.:* E. Bigelow conversation

p. 197: *"not too pleased.":* M. Tallchief interview.

p. 197: *hung mirrors.:* V. Brown interview.

p. 197: *"It's O.K.":* M. Tallchief interview.

p. 198: *"to wait a little.":* V. Zorina conversation.

p. 198: *". . . gentle radiance":* P. W. Manchester in *Dance News,* December 1952.

p. 198: *impossible task:* He told Tanaquil Le Clercq: "I'd like to pose myself a puzzle." N. Reynolds, p. 143.

p. 199: *". . . but repulsed.":* T. Bolender conversation.

p. 199: *" '. . . Myself IN FOR?' ":* L. Kirstein letter to R.B., January 2, 1953.

p. 199: *whole business.:* G. Boelzner conversation.

p. 199: *to resign.:* B. Cage letter to L. Kirstein, October 3, 1953.

p. 200: *four New York seasons a year.:* Ibid., October 3, 1953.

p. 200: *Karinska for costumes.:* L. Kirstein letter to B. Cage, October 9, 1953.

p. 200: *". . . to junk it. . . .":* L. Kirstein letter to B. Cage, October 26, 1953.

p. 201: *afraid to tell Baum.:* L. Kirstein, *Thirty Years*, p. 132.

p. 201: *". . . and he will be happy.":* B. Cage conversation.

p. 201: *tragic character.:* Alexandre Benois, *Reminiscences of the Russian Ballet*, (London: Putnam, 1941), pp. 138, 139.

p. 202: *" '. . . Nutcracker: food.' ":* *Time*, January 25, 1954, pp. 30–34.

p. 202: *". . . or story-telling.":* *The New York Times*, March 28, 1954.

p. 202: *". . . drawings I made for him.":* G.B. letter to R.B., February 1954.

p. 202: *". . . from Francis Mason. . . ."* *George Balanchine's Complete Stories of the Great Ballets* contains much valuable evidence from Balanchine himself, as well as notes by Mason on ballets by other choreographers that Balanchine could not possibly have considered great. It has gone into many editions, been continually revised and sold more copies than any ballet book ever published. Francis Mason, who had contributed to *Ballet* magazine, became cultural attaché at the American Embassy in London and later curator of the Morgan Library and editor of *Ballet Review*.

p. 203: *George:* G.B. letter to R.B., typewritten, March 9, 1954.

p. 203: *Diaghilev in Venice.:* These drawings are in Boris Kochno's collection.

p. 203: *for £3,000.:* Illustrated in Sotheby's catalogue *Ballet Material and Manuscripts from the Serge Lifar Collection*, No. 64.

p. 203: *four-movement symphony.:* N. Reynolds, p. 161.

p. 204: *to Russia?:* L. Kirstein to B. Cage, September 14, 1956.

p. 204: *dollars in debt.:* L. Kirstein to B. Cage, September 28, 1956.

p. 204: *". . . no longer IF.":* L. Kirstein letter to B. Cage, October 2, 1956.

p. 204: *". . . they'd understand":* R. Tobias interview.

p. 205: *grew feverish.:* B. Cage letter to L. Kirstein, October 31, 1956.

p. 205: *you can think of. . . .:* L. Kirstein letter to B. Cage, November 3, 1956.

p. 205: *". . . painful for him.":* B. Cage letter to L. Kirstein, November 6, 1956.

p. 206: *Then he went off.:* H. Kronstam interview.

p. 207: *"You're very funny!":* D. Adams interview.

p. 207: *hotel bedroom.:* N. Molostwoff conversation.

p. 207: *about it:* B. Cage letter to G. B., January 18, 1957.

p. 208: *to his dancers.:* B. Cage conversation.

10. NEW BALLETS FOR NEW DANCERS: 1957–1964

p. 210: *". . . an inferior* Barocco.":: L. Kirstein letter to B. Cage, May 14, 1958.

p. 210: *"the applause machine. ":* "A Word from George Balanchine," introduction to NYCB's 1957 winter season in a *Playbill* program, November 19, 1957.

p. 211: *composer's hand.:* Reproduced in the souvenir program of NYCB's Stravinsky centennial celebration, June 1982.

p. 211: *was Stravinsky's.:* G.B. interview with Dale Harris, *Keynote,* Vol. VI, No. 4, June 1982.

p. 211: *". . . I was there. ":* D. Adams interview.

p. 212: *" '. . . on right foot.' ":* Ibid.

p. 212: *to a rehearsal.:* L. Davidova interview.

p. 212: *Balanchine's future biographer.:* B. Taper's comments on the rehearsal are given in his captions to Martha Swope's photographs, pp. 264–70.

p. 213: *". . . understand them either!":* R. Tobias interview.

p. 213: *"Wonderful!":* B. Taper, p. 269.

p. 213: *extra performances.:* I. Stravinsky, *Selected Correspondence, Vol. 1,* p. 291.

p. 214: *ten years of work.:* L. Kirstein letter to B. Cage, July 11, 1958.

p. 214: *". . . after we get home. ":* B. Cage letter to L. Kirstein, July 16, 1958.

p. 214: *Robert Irving:* L. Kirstein letter to B. Cage, August 6, 1958.

p. 214: *first job:* G. Boelzner conversation.

p. 215: *". . . myself to write. ":* L. Davidova interview.

p. 215: *notably Bartók.:* G.B. interview with Dale Harris, *Keynote,* Vol. VI, No. 4, June 1982.

p. 215: *in the Austrian composer.:* Craft wrote: "In the years between 1952 and 1955 no composer can have lived in closer contact with the music of Webern." Robert Craft, "A Personal Preface," *The Score,* June 1957.

p. 215: *soon discarded.:* Don McDonagh, *Martha Graham* (New York: Praeger, 1973), p. 257.

p. 216: *the music to her.:* Ibid.

p. 216: *". . . in sound. ":* G.B. interview with Jonathan Cott, reprinted in L. Kirstein, et al., *Portrait of Mr. B.,* p. 133.

p. 216: *found this funny.:* In G. Balanchine, p. 205, Balanchine is recorded as saying, "I sometimes think Americans feel obliged to laugh too much when there is not any reason to."

p. 217: *tried to do.: Ibid.,* p. 206.

p. 217: *". . . starve with the rest of us?":* J. Taras's recollection. He returned to New York in December 1959, and was appointed ballet master in 1960.

p. 218: *accepted in New York.:* Various degrees of admiration are registered in quotations from the press, given in Reynolds, pp. 199, 200.

p. 218: *. . . realize the role.:* E. Villella interview.

p. 220: *might be lost.:* R. Dunleavy interview.

p. 220: *reproduce his ballets:* N. Molostwoff told this to R.B. in 1985.

p. 220 *". . . on her hands and knees.":* S. Schorer interview.

p. 220: *put together the score:* G. Boelzner described how this was done in a letter to R.B. dated April 4, 1985.

p. 223: *". . . of clairvoyance.":* R. Vazquez interview with W. Lawson.

p. 224: *"do something for the boys.":* V. Verdy interview with W. Lawson.

p. 225: *on the mime.:* E. Villella interview.

p. 225: *extraordinary moment.: Ibid.*

p. 226: *"more interesting":* D. Adams interview.

p. 226: *sometimes implacable.: Ibid.*

p. 227: *". . . like someone else.": Ibid.*

p. 227: *"odd but interesting.": Ibid.*

p. 227: *asked for more.:* Nancy Lassalle, then secretary of Ballet Society, raised $5,000 to pay for this.

p. 229: *performed together.:* In 1963, *Monumentum* was coupled in performance with *Movements,* and this pairing stuck. The principal couple are always the same in both works, but the other women in *Monumentum* are always taller than the six in *Movements.*

p. 229: *Gesualdo's madrigals.:* In 1954, Stravinsky had concluded that Gesualdo's music was "uniquely vocal in character," but in 1960 he found three pieces he "could at least conceive of in instrumental form." I. Stravinsky and R. Craft, *Expositions and Developments,* p. 118. The three madrigals were Nos. 14 and 18 of Book V and No. 2 of Book VI.

p. 230: *". . . exciting work.":* Hugo Fiorato in "A Symposium on the Balanchine Style," chaired by Francis Mason, held at the Milford Plaza Hotel, June 11, 1983, and reprinted in *Ballet Review,* Winter 1984, p. 12.

p. 230: *". . . explored the result.":* I. Stravinsky and R. Craft, *Themes and Episodes,* p. 24.

p. 230: *". . . past me.":* D. Adams interview.

p. 230: *the only reply.:* J. Taras's recollection.

p. 230: *recumbent dancer.:* David Daniel, "Diana Adams on Suzanne Farrell," *Ballet Review,* Winter 1982, p. 16.

11. TO RUSSIA: OCTOBER—NOVEMBER 1962

p. 231: *". . . solo but regular.":* Letter from G.B. to B. Cage, dated Sunday 11 [February 1962].

p. 232: *"Don't tell him . . .":* Letter from G.B. to B. Cage, undated but evidently mid-February 1962.

p. 232: *set in time.:* K. Tyler interview.

p. 232: *". . . State Department delegates. ":* R. Maiorano, p. 163.

p. 232: *before the Revolution.:* L. Kirstein, *Thirty Years,* p. 170.

p. 233: *". . . romantic ballet. ":* R. Maiorano, p. 163.

p. 233: *". . . floodlights.":* The New York Times, October 7, 1962.

p. 233: *cameras disappeared.:* P. Neary conversation.

p. 233: *Maria Yudina:* A. M. Balanchivadze interview.

p. 234: *greatest ovation. . . .: The New York Times,* October 10, 1962.

p. 234: *on October 11:* I. Stravinsky and R. Craft, *Dialogues and a Diary,* pp. 273–85.

p. 234: *restaurants and stores.:* J. Taras's recollection.

p. 235: *". . . Meet-shell!":* R. Dunleavy interview.

p. 235: *John Martin.: The New York Times,* October 31, 1962.

p. 235: *all there was.:* B. Cage conversation.

p. 235: *to be the case.:* N. Molostwoff interview.

p. 235: *a hot potato.:* B. Cage conversation.

p. 236: *possibility of war.:* Ibid.

p. 236: *". . . your government. ":* N. Molostwoff interview.

p. 236: *". . . be cut off.":* B. Cage conversation.

p. 236: *even if there was war.:* B. Cage conversation with W. Lawson.

p. 236: *to drive on.:* B. Cage conversation.

p. 236: *was postponed.:* L. Kirstein, *Thirty Years,* p. 176.

p. 236: *". . . then cheered. ":* R. Maiorano, p. 176.

p. 236: *all the tables:* N. Molostwoff interview.

p. 237: *president's demands:* Details of the Cuban crisis were derived from Robert F. Kennedy, *13 Days,* and David L. Larson, ed., *The "Cuban Crisis" of 1962: Selected Documents and Chronology.*

p. 237: *" 'Bal-an-chin!' ":* L. Kirstein, *Thirty Years,* p. 175.

p. 237: *worried more.:* V. Verdy interview with W. Lawson.

p. 237: *regulations were.:* N. Molostwoff interview.

p. 238: *Balanchine refused.:* B. Cage interview.

p. 238: *company a class.:* V. Verdy interview with W. Lawson.

p. 238: *had never acquired.:* P. Neary conversation.

p. 238: *to his crotch.:* A. M. Balanchivadze interview.

p. 238: *". . . a story line.":* Quoted in *The New York Times,* October 31, 1962.

p. 239: *". . . Come back!": Ibid.*

p. 239: *very emotional.:* N. Molostwoff interview.

p. 240: *". . . many flowers.":* The New York Times, November 1, 1962.

p. 240: *". . . send them home . . .":* L. Kirstein postcard from Leningrad to R.B. in London, November 4, 1962.

p. 241: *" '. . . you are tonight.' ":* L. Kirstein, *Thirty Years,* pp. 177, 178.

p. 241: *". . . theater itself.":* The New York Times, November 9, 1962.

p. 242: *the female sex.:* V. Verdy interview with W. Lawson.

p. 242: *"the camel":* N. Molostwoff interview.

p. 243: *"Where are your pants?":* S. O'Brien interview with W. Lawson.

12. PROBLEMS IN PARADISE: 1964–1972

p. 245: *New York City Opera. . . . :* L. Kirstein, *Thirty Years.*

p. 245: *"to minimize injury.":* Facts derived from Don McDonagh article in NYCB winter season, 1982–83, *Playbill.*

p. 245: *ballet in America: The New York Times,* December 15, 1963.

p. 246: *"You'll be back.":* B. Horgan interview.

p. 246: *for ten years.: Ibid.*

p. 247: *point of departure.:* E. Villella interview.

p. 247: *on a book.:* Tanaquil Le Clercq, *Mourka: The Autobiography of a Cat,* with photographs by Martha Swope.

p. 247: *". . . no instep.":* David Daniel, "Diana Adams on Suzanne Farrell," *Ballet Review,* Winter 1982, p. 11.

p. 248: *full scholarship.: Ibid.*

p. 248: *". . . your cat, Mourka?":* Suzanne Farrell interview with Hubert Saal, *Newsweek,* January 13, 1969.

p. 248: *". . . and talked his head off.": Ibid.* The white cat Bottom, with his black mask, was one of the characters photographed by Martha Swope for *Mourka.*

p. 248: *". . . Suzanne never resisted.":* D. Daniel, *op. cit.,* p. 16.

p. 249: *"alabaster princess.":* The phrase is used in N. Reynolds, p. 238.

p. 249: *"a secular saint.": Ibid.,* p. 236.

p. 249: *"a Christ figure.": Ibid.,* p. 238.

p. 249: *". . . vigorous in movement.": Ibid.,* Richard Rapp quoted.

p. 250: *". . . the sleeping Knight.":* Edwin Denby, *Dance Magazine,* July 1965.

p. 250: *"Fearless Farrell":* N. Reynolds, p. 238.

p. 250: *Balanchine's choreography.:* In a public interview with Francis Mason, given at New York University on October 22, 1985, Suzanne Farrell described how Balanchine asked her to repeat a dangerous off-balance step, and then incorporated it into his choreography.

p. 250: *a mystic levitating:* A comparison of Denby's.

p. 250: *". . . make him laugh. . . .":* Suzanne Farrell interview with Hubert Saal, *Newsweek,* January 13, 1969.

p. 250: *". . . till she left.":* S. Schorer interview.

p. 251: *to the elevator.:* From notes taken by R. B., February 5, 1967.

p. 252: *to work at them.*: Suzanne Farrell in a public interview with Francis Mason, cited above.

p. 252: *dolphin (intelligence).*: *Ibid.*

p. 252: *at Saratoga Springs:* R. and K. Leach interview.

p. 252: *every night.*: *Ibid.*

p. 253: *". . . turn off Ormandy."*: *Ibid.*

p. 253: *was the verdict.*: *Ibid.*

p. 254: *[French for "encore"].*: *Ibid.*

p. 254: *retired Lippizaner:* L. Kirstein, *Thirty Years,* p. 191.

p. 254: *". . . dressed like jewels."*: N. Reynolds, p. 247.

p. 256: *a pedestrian ballet.*: E. Villella interview.

p. 256: *". . . your mother applauding?"*: P. Neary conversation.

p. 256: *". . . cover anything up."*: N. Reynolds, p. 250.

p. 256: *"Only pas de deux is good."*: P. Neary conversation.

p. 257: *finger-turn on pointe.*: E. Villella interview.

p. 257: *show off Farrell.*: P. Neary conversation.

p. 257: *sent the young Dane off.*: J. Taras letter to R. B., February 4, 1986.

p. 257: *". . . he's tall."*: Peter Martins, p. 37.

p. 258: *". . . timing and quickness."*: *Ibid.,* pp. 37–38.

p. 258: *season in December.*: *Ibid.,* p. 39.

p. 258: *some dye.*: P. Neary conversation.

p. 258: *she left.*: *Ibid.*

p. 259: *blessed beings.*: *Sunday Times* (London), May 12, 1968.

p. 259: *with Suzanne Farrell.*: N. Molostwoff conversation.

p. 259: *found the cat.*: R. and K. Leach interview.

p. 260: *together in restaurants.*: P. Neary conversation.

p. 260: *believe it was:* See Chapter 14, second note for p. 300 *(". . . God's decision.")*

p. 260: *". . . of her own age . . ."*: *New York Post,* September 12, 1968.

p. 260: *was best man:* *Ibid.,* February 27, 1969.

p. 260: *be sent for.*: B. Horgan interview.

p. 261: *to his company.*: *Ibid.*

p. 261: *to Kirstein:* L. Kirstein letter to B. Cage, April 1, 1969.

p. 261: *"give them 20 ballets."*: *Ibid.*

p. 261: *". . . goes unpunished."*: N. Molostwoff conversation.

p. 262: *Stars and Stripes.*: *The New York Times,* May 13, 1966.

p. 262: *returned to the fold.*: P. Neary conversation.

p. 262: *descended upon the choreographer:* B. Horgan interview.

p. 262: *and his own company.*: *Choreography,* p. 38.

p. 262: *Alfonso Catá:* B. Horgan interview.

p. 262: *to start work.*: P. Neary conversation.

p. 263: *ever eaten.*: D. Nabokov conversation.

p. 263: *so miserable again.*: B. Horgan interview.

p. 265: *in his career.:* P. Martins, pp. 56, 60.

p. 265: *his godchild.:* K. von Aroldingen interview.

13. HOMAGE TO STRAVINSKY: SPRING 1972

p. 267: *list of possibilities:* Nancy Goldner, *The Stravinsky Festival of The New York City Ballet,* p. 229.

p. 268: *into a party.:* V. Donaldson conversation.

p. 268: *chairman of the festival.:* *The New York Times,* March 7, 1972.

p. 269: *". . . made our floor.":* N. Goldner, *Stravinsky,* pp. 13, 14.

p. 270: *in front of you.:* *Ibid.,* pp. 14–15.

p. 270: *". . . our party.":* *Ibid.,* pp. 15–16.

p. 270: *to the press.:* *The New York Times,* March 7, 1972. All seven proposed programs are printed.

p. 271: *in the evening.:* N. Goldner, pp. 234, 235.

p. 271: *till midnight.:* *Ibid.,* p. 237.

p. 272: *in forty minutes.:* R. Dunleavy interview.

p. 272: *". . . said I said it.":* *High Fidelity/Musical America,* June 1972. G. B. interviewed by Shirley Fleming. She was referring to "Stravinsky in the Theatre," in *Dance Index,* edited by Minna Lederman, Vol. VI, Nos. 10, 11, 12, 1947.

p. 272: *". . . Kant is very important . . .":* *Milwaukee Journal,* June 4, 1972. G. B. interviewed by Walter Monfried.

p. 272: *". . . when you make dance.":* *Newsday,* June 11, 1972. G. B. interviewed by Bob Micklin.

p. 273: *Vera Stravinsky.:* *New York Post,* June 17, 1972.

p. 273: *the opening ballet.:* *Sunday Times,* (London), June 18, 1972.

p. 274: Italian *comedy style.:* E. Villella interview.

p. 275: *" '. . . about the theater.' ":* N. Reynolds, p. 304.

p. 275: *". . . everything I had . . .":* K. von Aroldingen interview.

p. 275: *". . . incredible high. . . .":* P. Martins, p. 61.

p. 276: *Balanchine told him.):* K. Mazzo interview.

p. 276: *". . . asking for money.":* P. Martins, p. 61.

p. 276: *". . . Monsieur Stravinsky.":* R. Dunleavy interview. See also Jonathan Cott's interview with G. B. for *Rolling Stone,* quoted in *Portrait of Mr. B.,* p. 135. G. B. states, "I made a little bow to Stravinsky."

p. 278: *a strained back.):* R. Dunleavy interview.

p. 278: *". . . around the globe.":* *Ballet Review,* Vol. IV, No. 3, p. 72.

p. 278: *concerto for orchestra in mind):* Alexandre Tansman recorded his impression that Stravinsky's early version of what became the first movement was to have been a *concertante* part for the piano. Stravinsky told Craft

(*Expositions and Developments,* p. 77) that he thought of it as a "concerto for orchestra."

p. 279: *". . . tactics in China.":* I. Stravinsky and R. Craft, *Dialogues and a Diary,* pp. 83–85.

p. 279: *". . . Allied triumph.": Ibid.,* pp. 51, 52.

p. 279: *Virgin Mary:* I. Stravinsky and R. Craft, *Expositions and Developments,* pp. 65–66.

p. 279: *last moment.:* K. Mazzo interview.

p. 280: *festival was about.: Ibid.*

p. 280: *". . . Stravinsky ballets.": Ibid.*

p. 281: *". . . ballet was ours.":* P. Martins, p. 69.

p. 282: *". . . communicate with Stravinsky.":* R. Dunleavy interview.

p. 282: *winter season.:* N. Goldner, p. 244.

p. 282: *". . . such a good one.":* V. Stravinsky interview with Jean Battey Louis, *Washington Post,* June 26, 1972.

p. 282: *". . . from a ballet company?":* G. Boelzner conversation.

14. THE SPREADING EMPIRE: FIRST LAST BALLETS, 1972–1981

p. 284: *his "Three K's.":* R. and K. Leach interview.

p. 284: *leg of lamb.:* K. von Aroldingen interview.

p. 284: *a potato field.:* Dr. W. Hamilton conversation.

p. 284: *into a well.:* B. Horgan interview.

p. 285: *day's appointments.: Ibid.*

p. 285: *Paris or Geneva.:* B. Horgan allowed R. B. to go through G. B.'s engagement books, held by Ballet Society.

p. 285: *considered appropriate.:* K. von Aroldingen interview.

p. 285: *ten minutes late.:* Joseph H. Mazo, *Dance Is a Contact Sport,* p. 30.

p. 285: *when they were cooking:* S. Schorer interview.

p. 285: *". . . be better than first.":* D. Duell interview.

p. 285: *touching the ground.:* R. Dunleavy interview.

p. 285: *"break eggs.":* M. Ashley, p. 62.

p. 286: *often in class.:* K. von Aroldingen interview.

p. 286: *solid as sculpture.:* J. H. Mazo, p. 38.

p. 286: *". . . like dead chicken.": Ibid.*

p. 286: *". . . look at the garden.":* R. Dunleavy interview.

p. 286: *". . . ice cream.": Ibid.*

p. 286: *beautiful hands.:* K. von Aroldingen interview.

p. 286: *both feet.:* R. Dunleavy interview.

p. 286: *moved two steps.:* Told by Suki Schorer to J. Taras, December 12, 1983.

p. 286: *". . . a jockey on their backs."*: M. Ashley, p. 188.

p. 286: *". . . make it beautiful."*: *Ibid.*, p. 233.

p. 287: *"Maybe never."*: J. H. Mazo, p. 39.

p. 287: *cheese with tomatoes.*: B. Horgan interview.

p. 287: *used before.*: He had produced *Raymonda* for the Ballet Russe in 1946; in 1955 he staged *Pas de dix;* in 1961, *Valse et variations.*

p. 287: *". . . great precision. . . ."*: J. H. Mazo, p. 120.

p. 288: *just possible.*: *Ibid.*, p. 128.

p. 288: *all his choreography:* Repeated by Edwin Denby to R.B. in the 1940s.

p. 289: *kissed him:* S. Farrell conversation.

p. 289: *"a stroll for two"*: N. Goldner, *The Nation,* June 7, 1975, quoted N. Reynolds, p. 320.

p. 290: *". . . I like it."*: R. Dunleavy interview.

p. 291: *sweaters to class.*: P. Schaufuss conversation.

p. 291: *"Then it's over."*: S. Lavery interview with W. Lawson.

p. 291: *". . . school right then."*: S. Lavery interview with Tom Lacy.

p. 292: *began to work on it:* R. Dunleavy interview.

p. 292: *Three of these:* Rouben Ter-Arutunian, lecture to the Friends of New York City Ballet, June 8, 1984.

p. 293: *tinkering with it.*: S. Lavery interview with W. Lawson.

p. 294: *School of American Ballet.*: N. Lassalle interview.

p. 294: *a bad floor.*: J. H. Mazo, p. 297.

p. 295: *". . . garbage stinks."*: B. Taper, p. 345.

p. 296: *partnering himself.*: M. Ashley, p. 158 *et seq.*

p. 296: *for them coming up:* The New York Times, May 6, 1984. Leon Goldstein, the author of the article in which this incident is recorded, had been a member of NYCB's orchestra for more than thirty years.

p. 296: *". . . keep up with him. . . ."*: S. Lavery interview with W. Lawson.

p. 296: *". . . spooky at times."*: S. Lavery interview with T. Lacy.

p. 296: *greatest works.*: L. Kirstein, *Thirty Years,* p. 299.

p. 297: *Natalia Dudinskaya.*: M. Baryshnikov conversation.

p. 297: *usual NYCB rate.*: L. Kirstein, *Thirty Years,* p. 315.

p. 298: *with his own.*: M. Baryshnikov conversation.

p. 299: *". . . the women he loved."*: *Ibid.*

p. 299: *result disappointing.*: Anna Kisselgoff, *The New York Times,* April 10, 1979. Arlene Croce, *The New Yorker,* May 7, 1979.

p. 300: *which he did.*: M. Baryshnikov conversation.

p. 300: *". . . God's decision."*: Dr. W. Hamilton conversation.

p. 300: *face-to-face.*: L. Davidova interview.

p. 301: *Davidsbündlertänze.*: Dr. W. Hamilton conversation.

p. 301: *his insight:* K. von Aroldingen interview.

p. 302: *Both Kirstein and Karin: Ibid.;* also Kirstein letter to R.B., July 30, 1983.

p. 303: *". . . gay music."*: G. B. interviewed by Louis Bolto, *Intellectual Digest,* June 1972.

p. 303: *highest level.: Time,* June 30, 1980.

p. 304: *beautiful to see.:* Toni Bentley, *Winter Season,* p. 124.

p. 304: *". . . a whole lifetime."*: D. Kistler interview.

p. 305: *drop their votes.:* T. Bentley, pp. 89–91.

p. 305: *". . . listen to the music."*: D. Kistler interview.

p. 305: *"like a gymnasium."*: D. Nabokov conversation.

p. 306: *for the festival program:* S. Volkov, pp. 11, 12.

p. 307: *moderately satisfied:* Emile Ardolino, "Balanchine and Television," an essay in the brochure "A Celebration of George Balanchine: The Television Work," annotating a series of screenings held at the Museum of Broadcasting, New York, September–November 1984.

p. 307: *". . . an introduction for them."*: R. Maiorano and V. Brooks, p. xix.

p. 308: *"When?" "Tomorrow."*: Ibid., p. 134.

p. 308: *"Ib is Mozart!"*: E. Bigelow conversation.

p. 308: *been in America.: Serenade,* 1934; *Ballet Imperial,* 1941, revived as *Tchaikovsky Piano Concerto No. 2,* 1973; *Swan Lake,* 1951; *The Nutcracker,* 1954; *Allegro Brillante,* 1956; *Tchaikovsky Pas de deux,* 1960; *Meditation,* 1963; "Diamonds" from *Jewels,* 1967; *Tchaikovsky Suite No. 3,* 1970.

p. 309: *". . . how to mourn."*: K. von Aroldingen interview.

p. 310: *east as Iran.:* These statistics are derived from the Eakins Press *Choreography.*

p. 311: *" '. . . the whole class is doing it.' "*: S. Schorer interview.

p. 311: *" '. . . anybody.' "*: G. B. interview with W. McNeil Lowry, *The New Yorker,* September 12, 1983, p. 53.

15. BALLET MASTER EMERITUS: DECEMBER 1981–APRIL 30, 1983

p. 312: *". . . a Greek, dear"*: S. Schorer interview.

p. 312: *in 1947:* N. Lassalle conversation.

p. 313: *visual arts.:* B. Kochno interview.

p. 314: *". . . but we can't."* K. Love conversation.

p. 314: *"a searing experience."*: V. Zorina conversation.

p. 315: *passages of dancing.:* M. Ashley interview.

p. 315: *"They always left me."*: K. Leach letter to R. B., January 1, 1986.

p. 315: *for $1,000.:* G.B. interview with John Corry, *The New York Times,* May 16, 1982.

p. 318: Kammermusik No. 2: B. Horgan conversation.

p. 318: *during a performance.:* K. Love conversation.

p. 319: *withdrew silently.:* B. Horgan interview.

p. 319: *good manners.:* S. Volkov conversation.

p. 319: *as a decoration:* N. Lassalle conversation.

p. 321: *down his face.:* Dr. W. Hamilton conversation.

p. 321: *Ruthanna's hand.:* R. Boris interview.

p. 321: *a mistake.:* Dr. W. Hamilton conversation.

p. 322: *press the point.:* B. Taper, pp. 385, 386.

p. 322: *was disappointed.: Ibid.,* pp. 391, 392.

p. 322: *". . . Balanchine ballets.":* The New Yorker, March 28, 1983.

p. 322: *"It seems inconceivable.":* Abigail Kuflik, *Newsweek,* March 28, 1983.

p. 322: *those of all others.:* Dr. W. Hamilton conversation.

p. 322: *". . . coming to see me?":* J. Taras's recollection.

p. 323: *Margo's name.:* K. von Aroldingen interview.

p. 323: *no further questions.:* D. Kistler interview.

p. 323: *about the performance.:* K. von Aroldingen interview.

p. 324: *". . . and Stravinsky . . .":* Jennifer Dunning, *The New York Times,* May 1, 1983.

p. 324: *Suzanne Farrell.:* Mindy Aloff, *Nation,* June 4, 1983.

p. 325: *him and Balanchine together . . .:* T. Lacy letter, February 24, 1986.

p. 325: *a rose.:* Dr. W. Hamilton conversation.

p. 325: *indisputable facts.:* Statement by Mayor Edward I. Koch, for release Monday, May 2, 1983.

p. 326: *". . . Immortal Legacy":* Sheryl Platow, *Washington Post,* May 2, 1983.

p. 326: *". . . Mourns Balanchine":* Amy Pagnozzi, *New York Post,* May 2, 1983.

p. 326: *". . . Pure Movement":* Michael Walsh, *Time,* May 9, 1983.

p. 326: *". . . 'Mister B.' ":* Le Matin, May 2, 1983. Article signed R. S. (René Servin).

p. 326: *". . . le plus grand.":* Les Nouvelles Littéraires, April 5–May 1, 1983.

p. 326: *head of the table.:* Hubert Saal, *Newsweek,* May 9, 1983.

p. 326: *" '. . . I assemble.' ":* Don McDonagh, *Commonweal,* June 3, 1983.

p. 326: *. . . it's ridiculous.:* G. B. interview with W. McNeil Lowry, *The New Yorker,* September 12, 1983.

p. 327: *Ballet is NOW.:* G. B. interview with Louis Bolto, *Intellectual Digest,* June 1972.

INDEX

RICHARD BUCKLE founded the magazine *Ballet* in England in 1939, and edited it, with a six-year gap during World War II, until 1953. From 1948 to 1955 he was ballet critic of the *Observer* and from 1959 to 1975 of the London *Sunday Times*. He has written many books, including the biographies of Diaghilev and Nijinsky and two volumes of autobiography. He designed The Diaghilev Exhibition (Edinburgh Festival and London, 1954–1955), and as his methods of display were considered novel, he was asked to design twenty others. In the late 1960s he conceived the idea of a theater museum for London; this was officially opened in the former flower market in Covent Garden on Shakespeare's birthday, 1987. Buckle admired Balanchine in the 1930s, met him in 1948, praised him on the first visit of the New York City Ballet to London in 1950, when most of the English critics were apathetic, and never doubted that he had raised the art of ballet to new heights.

JOHN TARAS, dancer and choreographer, was on the South American tour with Balanchine in 1941. He has been a ballet master of the Markova-Dolin Ballet, the de Basil, the Grand Ballet du Marquis de Cuevas, the New York City Ballet, the Paris Opéra and the Berlin Deutsche Oper. In 1970 he rejoined Balanchine, with whom he remained until 1983, and whose ballets he mounted throughout the world. In 1984 he became associate director of American Ballet Theatre.